Praise for Jill Shalvis and Her Novels

"Count on Jill Shalvis for a witty, steamy, unputdownable love story."
—Robyn Carr, *New York Times* bestselling author of *Harvest Moon*

"Shalvis writes with humor, heart, and sizzling heat!"
—Carly Phillips, *New York Times* bestselling author

"Jill Shalvis is a total original! It doesn't get any better."
—Suzanne Forster, *New York Times* bestselling author

"A Jill Shalvis hero is the stuff naughty dreams are made of."
—Vicki Lewis Thompson, *New York Times* bestselling author of *Chick with a Charm*

Lucky in Love

"Shalvis pens a tale rife with the three 'H's of romance: heat, heart, and humor. *Lucky in Love* is a down-to-the-toes charmer...It doesn't matter if you're chuckling or reaching for an iced drink to cool down the heat her characters generate—Shalvis doesn't disappoint."

—*RT Book Reviews*

"I always enjoy reading a Jill Shalvis book. She's a consistently elegant, bold, clever writer...Very witty—I laughed out loud countless times reading *Lucky in Love*...[It] is also one of the hottest books I've read by Ms. Shalvis. Mallory and Ty burn up the sheets (and the pages) with regularity and these scenes are sizzling."

—All About Romance (LikesBooks.com)

"Whenever I'm looking for a romance to chase away the worries of life, all I have to do is pick up a Jill Shalvis book. Once again she has worked her magic with the totally entertaining *Lucky in Love*."

—RomRevToday.com

At Last

"Full of laughter, snark, and a super-hot attraction between the main characters. Shalvis has painted a wonderful world, full of entertaining supporting characters and beautiful scenery."

—*RT Book Reviews*

"A sexy, romantic read...What I love about Jill Shalvis's books is that she writes sexy, adorable heroes...the sexual tension is out of this world. And of course, in true Shalvis fashion, she expertly mixes in humor that has you laughing out loud."

—HeroesandHeartbreakers.com

"A sexy, fun tale from the creative mind of Jill Shalvis...*At Last* will have you laughing, smiling, and sniffling...Another stellar read I highly recommend."

—RomRevToday.com

Forever and a Day

"4½ stars! Top Pick! Shalvis once again racks up a hit...laughter is served in doses as generous as the chocolate the heroine relies on to get through the day. Readers will treasure each turn of the page and be sorry when this one is over."

—*RT Book Reviews*

"[Shalvis] has quickly become one of my go-to authors of contemporary romance. Her writing is smart, fun, and sexy, and her books never fail to leave a smile on my face long after I've closed the last page...Jill Shalvis is an author not to be missed!"

—TheRomanceDish.com

"Jill Shalvis is such a talented author that she brings to life characters who make you laugh, cry, and are a joy to read."

—RomRevToday.com

Lucky Harbor

Also by Jill Shalvis

The Lucky Harbor Series

Simply Irresistible
The Sweetest Thing
Heating Up the Kitchen (cookbook)
Christmas in Lucky Harbor (omnibus)
Small Town Christmas (anthology)
Head Over Heels
Lucky in Love
At Last
Forever and a Day
"Under the Mistletoe" (short story)
It Had to Be You
Always on My Mind
Once in a Lifetime

Other Novels

Blue Flame
White Heat
Seeing Red
Her Sexiest Mistake

Lucky Harbor

JILL SHALVIS

NEW YORK BOSTON

Grand Central Publishing
Hachette Book Group
237 Park Avenue
New York, NY 10017

www.HachetteBookGroup.com

Printed in the United States of America

RRD-C

First trade omnibus edition: May 2014
10 9 8 7 6 5 4 3 2 1

Grand Central Publishing is a division of Hachette Book Group, Inc.
The Grand Central Publishing name and logo is a trademark of Hachette Book Group, Inc.

The Hachette Speakers Bureau provides a wide range of authors for speaking events. To find out more, go to www.hachettespeakersbureau.com or call (866) 376-6591.

The publisher is not responsible for websites (or their content) that are not owned by the publisher.

Library of Congress Control Number: 2013951308

ISBN 978-1-4555-5503-1 (pbk.)

Contents

Lucky in Love

Prologue

All you need is love. But a little chocolate now and then doesn't hurt.

Lightning sent a jagged bolt across Ty Garrison's closed lids. Thunder boomed and the earth shuddered, and he jerked straight up in bed, gasping as if he'd just run a marathon.

A dream, just the same goddamn four-year-old dream.

Sweating and trembling like a leaf, he scrubbed his hands over his face. Why couldn't he dream about something good, like sex with triplets?

Shoving free of the covers, he limped naked to the window and yanked it open. The cool mist of the spring storm brushed his heated skin, and he fought the urge to close his eyes. If he did, he'd be back there.

But the memories came anyway.

"Landing in ten," the pilot announced as the plane skimmed just beneath the storm raging through the night.

In eight, the plane began to vibrate.

In six, lightning cracked.

And then an explosion, one so violent it nearly blew out his eardrums.

Ty dropped his head back, letting the rain slash at his body through the open window. He could hear the Pacific Ocean pounding the surf below the cliffs. Scented with fragrant pines, the air smelled like Christmas in April, and he forced himself to draw a deep, shaky breath.

He was no longer a SEAL medic dragging his sorry ass out of a burning plane, choking on the knowledge that he was the only one still breathing, that he hadn't been able to save a single soul. He was in Washington State, in the small beach town of Lucky Harbor. The ocean was in front of him, the Olympic Mountains at his back.

Safe.

But hell if at the next bolt of lightning, he didn't try to jump out of his own skin. Pissed at the weakness, Ty shut the window. He was never inhaling an entire pepperoni pizza before bed again.

Except he knew it wasn't something as simple as pizza that made him dream badly. It was the edginess that came from being idle. His work was still special ops, but he hadn't gone back to being a first responder trauma paramedic. Instead, he'd signed up as a private contractor to the government, which was a decent enough adrenaline rush. Plus it suited him—or it had until six months ago, when on an assignment he'd had to jump out a second story window to avoid being shot, and had reinjured his leg.

Stretching that leg now, he winced. He wanted to get back to his job. *Needed* to get back. But he also needed clearance from his doctor first. Pulling on a pair of jeans, he snagged a shirt off the back of a chair and left the room as the storm railed around outside. He made his way through the big and nearly empty house he'd rented for the duration, heading to the garage. A fast drive in the middle of the night would have to do, and maybe a quick stop at the all-night diner.

But this first.

Flipping on the lights, Ty sucked in a deep, calming breath of air heavy with the smells of motor oil, well-greased tools, and rubber tires. On the left sat a '72 GMC Jimmy, a rebuild job he'd picked up on the fly. He didn't need the money. As it turned out, special ops talents were well-compensated these days, but the repair work was a welcome diversion from his problems.

The '68 Shelby Mustang on the right wasn't a side job. She was his baby, and she was calling to him. He kicked the mechanic's creeper from against the wall toward the classic muscle car. Lowering himself onto the cart with a grimace of pain, Ty rolled beneath the car, shoving down his problems, denying them, avoiding them.

Seeking his own calm in the storm.

Chapter 1

Put the chocolate in the bag, and no one gets hurt.

The lightning flashed bright, momentarily blinding Mallory Quinn as she ran through the dark rainy night from her car to the front door of the diner.

One Mississippi.

Two Mississippi.

On three Mississippi, thunder boomed and shook the ground. A vicious wind nearly blew her off her feet. She'd forgotten her umbrella that morning, which was just as well or she'd have taken off like Mary Poppins.

A second, brighter bolt of lightning sent jagged light across the sky, and Mallory gasped as everything momentarily lit up like day: the pier behind the diner, the churning ocean, the menacing sky.

All went dark again, and she burst breathlessly into the Eat Me Café feeling like the hounds of hell were on her very tired heels. Except she wasn't wearing heels; she was in fake Uggs.

Lucky Harbor tended to roll up its sidewalks after ten o'clock, and tonight was no exception. The place was deserted except for a lone customer at the counter, and the waitress behind it. The waitress was a friend of Mallory's. Smartass, cynical Amy Michaels, whose tall, leggy body was reminiscent of Xena, the warrior princess. This was convenient, since Amy had a kick-ass 'tude to life in general. Her dark hair was a little tousled as always, her even darker eyes showed amusement at Mallory's wild entrance.

"Hey," Mallory said, fighting the wind to close the door behind her.

"Looking a little spooked," Amy said, wiping down the counter. "You reading Stephen King on the slow shifts again, Nurse Nightingale?"

Mallory drew a deep, shuddery breath and shook off the icy rain the best she could. Her day had started a million years ago at the crack of dawn when she'd left her house in her usual perpetual rush, without a jacket. One incredibly long ER shift and seventeen hours later, she was still in her scrubs with only a thin sweater over the top, everything now sticking to her like a second skin. She did not resemble a warrior princess. Maybe a drowned lady-in-waiting. "No Stephen," she said. "I had to give him up. Last month's reread of *The Shining* wrecked me."

Amy nodded. "Emergency Dispatch tired of taking your 'there's a shadow outside my window' calls?"

"Hey, that was *one* time." Giving up squeezing the water out of her hair, Mallory ignored Amy's knowing snicker. "And for your information, there really was a man outside my window."

"Yeah. Seventy-year-old Mr. Wykowski, who'd gotten turned around on his walk around the block."

This was unfortunately true. And while Mallory knew that Mr. Wykowski was a very nice man, he really did look a lot like Jack Nicholson had in *The Shining*. "That could have been a *very* bad situation."

Amy shook her head as she filled napkin dispensers. "You live on Senior Drive. Your biggest 'situation' is if Dial-A-Ride doesn't show up in time to pick everyone up to take them to Bingo Night."

Also true. Mallory's tiny ranch house was indeed surrounded by other tiny ranch houses filled with mostly seniors. But it wasn't that bad. They were a sweet bunch and always had a coffee cake to share. Or a story about a various ailment or two. Or two hundred.

Mallory had inherited her house from her grandma, complete with a mortgage that she'd nearly had to give up her firstborn for. If she'd had a first born. But for that she'd like to be married, and to be married, she'd have to have a Mr. Right.

Except she'd been dumped by her last two Mr. Rights.

Wind and something heavy lashed at the windows of the diner. Mallory couldn't believe it. *Snow*. "Wow, the temp must have just dropped. That came on fast."

"It's spring," Amy said in disgust. "Why's it frigging snowing in spring? I changed my winter tires already."

The lone customer at the counter turned and eyed the view. "Crap. I don't have winter tires either." She looked to be in her mid-twenties and spoke with the clipped vowels that said northeast. If Amy was Xena, and Mallory the lady-in-waiting, then she was Blonde Barbie's younger, prettier, far more natural sister. "I'm in a 1972 VW Bug," she said.

As Mallory's own tires were threadbare, she gnawed on her lower lip and looked out the window. Maybe if she left immediately, she'd be okay.

"We should wait it out," Amy suggested. "It can't possibly last."

Mallory knew better, but it was her own fault. She'd been ignoring the forecast ever since last week, when the weather guy had promised ninety-degree temps and the day hadn't gotten above fifty, leaving her to spend a very long day frozen in the ER. Her nipples still hadn't forgiven her. "I don't have time to wait it out." She had a date with eight solid hours of sleep.

The VW driver was in a flimsy summer-weight skirt and two thin camisoles layered over each other. Mallory hadn't been the only one caught by surprise. Though the woman didn't look too concerned as she worked her way through a big, fat brownie that made Mallory's mouth water.

"Sorry," Amy said, reading her mind. "That was the last one."

"Just as well." Mallory wasn't here for herself anyway. Dead on her feet, she'd only stopped as a favor for her mother. "I just need to pick up Joe's cake."

Joe was her baby brother and turning twenty-four tomorrow. The last thing he wanted was a family party, but work was slow for him at the welding shop, and flying to Vegas with his friends hadn't panned out since he had no money.

So their mother had gotten involved and tasked Mallory with bringing a cake. Actually, Mallory had been tasked with *making* a cake, but she had a hard time not burning water so she was cheating. "Please tell me that no one from my crazy family has seen the cake so I can pretend I made it."

Amy *tsk*ed. "The good girl of Lucky Harbor, lying to her mother. Shame on you."

This was the ongoing town joke, "*good girl*" Mallory. Okay, fine, so in all fairness, she played the part. But she had her reasons—good ones—not that she wanted to go there now. Or ever. "Yeah, yeah. Hand it over. I have a date."

"You do not," Amy said. "I'd have heard about it if you did."

"It's a *secret* date."

Amy laughed because yeah, that *had* been a bit of a stretch. Lucky Harbor was a wonderful, small town where people cared about each other. You could leave a pot of gold in your backseat, and it wouldn't get stolen.

But there were no such things as secrets.

"I do have a date. With my own bed," Mallory admitted. "Happy?"

Amy wisely kept whatever smartass remark she had to herself and turned to the kitchen to go get the birthday cake. As she did, lightning flashed, followed immediately by a thundering boom. The wind howled, and the entire building shuddered, caught in the throes. It seemed to go on and on, and the three women scooted as close as they could to each other with Amy still on the other side of the counter.

"Suddenly I can't stop thinking about *The Shining*," the blonde murmured.

"No worries," Amy said. "The whole horror flick thing rarely happens here in Mayberry."

They all let out a weak laugh, which died when an ear-splitting crack sounded, followed immediately by shattering glass as both the front window and door blew in.

In the shocking silence, a fallen tree limb waved obscenely at them through the new opening.

Mallory grabbed the woman next to her and scurried behind the counter to join Amy. "Just in case more windows go," she managed. "We're safest right here, away from flying glass."

Amy swallowed audibly. "I'll never laugh at you about Mr. Wykowski again."

"I'd like that in writing." Mallory rose up on her knees, taking a peek over the counter at the tree now blocking the front door.

"I can't reach my brownie from here," Blondie said shakily. "I really need my brownie."

"What we need," Amy said, "is to blow this popsicle stand."

Mallory shook her head. "It's coming down too hard and fast now. It's not safe to leave. We should call someone about the downed tree though."

Blondie pulled out her cell phone and eyed her screen. "I forgot I'm in Podunk. No reception in half the town." She grimaced. "Sorry. I just got here today. I'm sure Lucky Harbor is a very nice Podunk."

"It's got its moments." Mallory slapped her pockets for her own cell before remembering. *Crap*. "My phone's in the car."

"Mine's dead," Amy said. "But we have a landline in the kitchen, as long as we still have electricity."

Just then the lights flickered and went out.

Mallory's stomach hit her toes. "You had to say it," she said to Amy.

Blondie rustled around for a moment, and then there came a blue glow. "It's a cigarette lighter app," she said, holding up her phone, and the faux flame flickered over the screen like a real Bic lighter. "Only problem, it drains my battery really fast so I'll keep it off until we have an emergency." She hit the home button and everything went really, really dark.

Another hard gust of wind sent more of the shattered window tinkling to the floor, and the Bic lighter immediately came back on.

"Emergency," Blondie said as the three of them huddled together.

"Stupid cake," Mallory said.

"Stupid storm," Amy said.

"Stupid life," Blondie said. Pale, she looked at them. "Now would be a great time for one of you to tell me that you have a big, strong guy who's going to come looking for you."

"Yeah, not likely," Amy said. "What's your name?"

"Grace Brooks."

"Well, Grace, you're new to Lucky Harbor so let me fill you in. There are lots of big, strong guys in town. But I do my own heavy lifting."

Grace and Mallory both took in Amy's short Army camo cargo skirt and her shit-kicking boots, topped with a snug tee that revealed tanned, toned arms. The entire sexy-tough ensemble was topped by an incongruous Eat Me pink apron. Amy had put her own spin on it by using red duct tape to fashion a circle around the Eat Me logo, complete with a line through it.

"I can believe that about you," Grace said to her.

"My name's Amy." Amy tossed her chin toward Mallory. "And that's Mallory, my polar opposite and the town's very own good girl."

"Stop," Mallory said, tired of hearing "good" and "girl" in the same sentence as it pertained to her.

But of course Amy didn't stop. "If there's an old lady to help across the street or a kid with a skinned knee needing a Band-Aid and a kiss," she said, "or a big, strong man looking for a sweet, warm damsel, it's Mallory to the rescue."

"So where is he then?" Grace asked. "Her big, strong man?"

Amy shrugged. "Ask her."

Mallory grimaced and admitted the truth. "As it turns out, I'm not so good at keeping any Mr. Rights."

"So date a Mr. Wrong," Amy said.

"Shh, you." Not wanting to discuss her love life—or lack thereof—Mallory rose up on her knees to take another peek over the counter and outside in the hopes the snow had lightened up.

It hadn't.

Gusts were blowing the heavy snow sideways, hitting the remaining windows and flying in through the ones that had broken. She craned her neck and looked behind her into the kitchen. If she went out the back door, she'd have to go around the whole building to get to her car and her phone.

In the dark.

But it was the best way. She got to her feet just as the two windows over the kitchen sink shattered with a suddenness that caused Mallory's heart to stop.

Grace's Bic lighter came back on. "Holy shit," she gasped, and holding on to each other, they all stared at the offending tree branch waving at them from the new opening.

"Jan's going to blow a gasket," Amy said.

Jan was the owner of the diner. She was fifty-something, grumpy on the best of days, and hated spending a single dime of her hard-earned money on anything other than her online poker habit.

The temperature in the kitchen dropped as cold wind and snow blew over them. "Did I hear someone say cake?" Grace asked in a wobbly voice.

They did Rock-Paper-Scissors. Amy lost, so she had to crawl

to the refrigerator to retrieve the cake. "You okay with this?" she asked Mallory, handing out forks.

Mallory looked at the cake. About a month ago, her scrubs had seemed to be getting tight so she'd given up chocolate. But sometimes there had to be exceptions. "This is a cake emergency. Joe will live."

So instead of trying to get outside, and then onto the bad roads, they all dug into the cake. And there in the pitch black night, unnerved by the storm but bolstered by sugar and chocolate, they talked.

Grace told them that when the economy had taken a nosedive, her hot career as an investment banker had vanished, along with her condo, her credit cards, and her stock portfolio. There'd been a glimmer of a job possibility in Seattle so she'd traveled across the country for it. But when she'd gotten there, she found out the job involved sleeping with the sleazeball company president. She'd told him to stuff it, and now she was thinking about maybe hitting Los Angeles. Tired, she'd stopped in Lucky Harbor earlier today. She'd found a coupon for the local B&B and was going to stay for a few days and regroup. "Or until I run out of money and end up on the street," she said, clearly trying to sound chipper about her limited options.

Mallory reached out for her hand and squeezed it. "You'll find something. I know it."

"I hope you're right." Grace let out a long, shaky breath. "Sorry to dump on you. Guess I'd been holding on to that all by myself for too long, it just burst out of me."

"Don't be sorry." Amy licked frosting off her finger. "That's what dark, stormy nights are for. Confessions."

"Well, I'd feel better if you guys had one as well."

Mallory wasn't big on confessions and glanced at Amy.

"Don't look at me," Amy said. "Mine isn't anything special."

Grace leaned in expectantly. "I'd love to hear it anyway."

Amy shrugged, looking as reluctant as Mallory felt. "It's just your average, run-of-the-mill riches-to-rags story."

"What?" Mallory asked, surprised, her fork going still. Amy had been in town for months now, and although she wasn't shy, she was extremely private. She'd never talked about her past.

"Well rags to riches *to rags* would be a better way of putting it," Amy corrected.

"Tell us," Grace said, reaching for another piece of cake.

"Okay, but it's one big bad cliché. Trailer trash girl's mother marries rich guy, trailer trash girl pisses new step-daddy off, gets rudely ousted out of her house at age sixteen, and disinherited from any trust fund. Broke, with no skills whatsoever, she hitches her way across the country, hooking up with the wrong people and then more wrong people, until it comes down to two choices. Straighten up or die. She decides straightening up is the better option and ends up in Lucky Harbor, because her grandma spent one summer here a million years ago and it changed her life."

Heart squeezing, Mallory reached for Amy's hand, too. "Oh, Amy."

"See?" Amy said to Grace. "The town sweetheart. She can't help herself."

"I can so," Mallory said. But that was a lie. She did like to help people—which made Amy right; she really couldn't help herself.

"And don't think we didn't notice that you avoided sharing any of *your* vulnerability with the class," Amy said.

"Maybe later," Mallory said, licking her fork. Or never. She shared just about every part of herself all the time. It was her work, and also her nature. So she held back because she had to have something that was hers alone. "I'm having another piece."

"Denial is her BFF," Amy told Grace as Mallory cut off a second hunk of cake. "I'd guess that it has something to do with her notoriously wild and crazy siblings and being the only sane one in the family. She doesn't think that she deserves to be happy, because that chocolate seems to be the substitute for something."

"Thanks, Dr. Phil." But it was uncomfortably close to the truth. Her family was wild and crazy, and she worked hard at keeping them together. And she did have a hard time with letting herself be totally happy and had ever since her sister Karen's death. She shivered. "Is there a lost-and-found box around somewhere with extra jackets or something?"

"Nope. Jan sells everything on eBay." Amy set her fork down and leaned back. "Look at us, sitting here stuffing ourselves with birthday cake because we have no better options on a Friday night."

"Hey, I have options," Grace said. "There's just a big, fat, mean storm blocking our exit strategies."

Amy gave her a droll look and Grace sagged. "Okay, I don't have shit."

They both looked at Mallory, and she sighed. "Fine. I'm stalled too. I'm more than stalled, okay? I've got the equivalent of a dead battery, punctured tires, no gas, and no roadside assistance service. How's *that* for a confession?"

Grace and Amy laughed softly, their exhales little clouds of condensation. They were huddled close, trying to share body heat.

"You know," Amy said. "If we live through this, I'm going to—"

"Hey." Mallory straightened up in concern. "Of course we're going to live. Soon as the snow lets up, we'll push some branches out of the way and head out to my car and call for help, and—"

"Jeez," Amy said, annoyed. "Way to ruin my dramatic moment."

"Sorry. Do continue."

"Thank you. If we live," Amy repeated with mock gravity, "I'm going to keep a cake just like this in the freezer just for us. And also..." She shifted and when she spoke this time, her voice was softer. "I'd like to make improvements to my life, like living it instead of letting it live me. Growing roots and making real friends. I suck at that."

Mallory squeezed her hand tight in hers. "I'm a real friend," she whispered. "*Especially* if you mean it about the cake."

Amy's mouth curved in a small smile.

"If we live," Grace said. "I'm going to find more than a job. I want to stop chasing my own tail and go after some happy for a change, instead of waiting for it to find me. I've waited long enough."

Once again, both Amy and Grace looked expectantly at Mallory, who blew out a sigh. She knew what she wanted for herself, but it was complicated. She wanted to let loose, do whatever she wanted, and stop worrying about being the glue at work, in her family, for everyone. Unable to say that, she wracked her brain and came up with something else. "There's this big charity event I'm organizing for the hospital next weekend, a formal dinner and auction. I'm the only nurse on my floor without a date. If we live, a date would be really great."

"Well, if you're wishing, wish big," Amy said. "Wish for a little nookie too."

Grace nodded her approval. "Nookie," she murmured fondly. "Oh how I miss nookie."

"Nookie," Mallory repeated.

"Hot sex," Grace translated.

Amy nodded. "And since you've already said Mr. Right never works out for you, you should get a Mr. Wrong."

"Sure," Mallory said, secure in the knowledge that one, there were no Mr. Wrongs anywhere close by, and two, even if there had been, he wouldn't be interested in her.

Amy pulled her order pad from her apron pocket. "You know what? I'm making you a list of some possible candidates. Since this is the only type of guy I know, it's right up my alley. Off the top of my head, I can think of two. Dr. Josh Scott from the hospital, and Anderson, the guy who runs the hardware store. I'm sure there's plenty of others. Promise me that if a Mr. Wrong crosses your path, you're going for him. As long as he isn't a felon," she added responsibly.

Good to know there were some boundaries. Amy thrust out her pinkie for what Mallory assumed was to be a solemn pinkie swear. With a sigh Mallory wrapped her littlest finger around Amy's. "I promise—" She broke off when a thump sounded on one of the walls out front. Each of them went stock still, staring at each other.

"That wasn't a branch," Mallory whispered. "That sounded like a fist."

"Could have been a rock," Grace, the eternal optimist, said.

They all nodded but not a one of them believed it was a rock. A bad feeling had come over Mallory. It was the same one she got sometimes in the ER right before they got an incoming. "May I?" she asked Grace, gesturing to the smart phone.

Grace handed it over and Mallory rose to her knees and used the lighter app to look over the edge of the counter.

It wasn't good.

The opened doorway had become blocked by a snow drift. It really was incredible for this late in the year, but big, fat, round snowflakes the size of dinner plates were falling from the sky, piling up quickly.

The thump came again, and through the vicious wind, she thought she also heard a moan. A pained moan. She stood. "Maybe someone's trying to get inside," she said. "Maybe they're hurt."

"Mallory," Amy said. "Don't."

Grace grabbed Mallory's hand. "It's too dangerous out there right now."

"Well, I can't just ignore it." Tugging free, Mallory wrapped her arms around herself and moved toward the opening. Someone was in trouble, and she was a sucker for that. It was the eternal middle child syndrome and the nurse's curse. Glass crunched beneath her feet, and she shivered as snow blasted her in the face. Amazingly, the aluminum frame of the front door had withstood the impact when the glass had shattered. Shoving aside the thick branch, Mallory once again held the phone out in front of her, using it to peer out into the dark.

Nothing but snow.

"Hello?" she called, taking a step outside, onto the concrete stoop. "Is anyone—"

A hand wrapped around her ankle, and Mallory broke off with a startled scream, falling into the night.

Chapter 2

If it's a toss up between men and chocolate,
bring on the chocolate!

Mallory scrambled backward, or tried to anyway, but a big hand on her ankle held firm. The hand appeared to be attached to an even bigger body. Fear and panic bubbled in her throat, and she simply reacted, chucking Grace's phone at her captor's hooded head.

It bounced off his cheek without much of a reaction other than a grunt. The guy was sprawled flat on his back, half covered in snow. Still holding her ankle in a vice-like grip, he shifted slightly and groaned. The sound didn't take her out of panic mode but it did push another emotion to the surface. Concern. Since he hadn't tried to hurt her, she leaned over him, brushing the snow away to get a better look—not easy with the wind pummeling her, bringing more icy snow that slapped at her bare face. "Are you hurt?" she asked.

He was non-responsive. His down parka was open, and he was wet and shivering. Pushing his dark brown hair from his forehead, she saw the first problem. He had a nasty gash over an eyebrow, which was bleeding profusely in a trickle down his temple and over his swollen eye. Not from where she'd hit him with the phone, thankfully, but from something much bigger and heavier, probably part of the fallen tree.

His eyes suddenly flew open, his gaze landing intense and unwavering on her.

"It's okay," she said, trying to sound like she believed it. "It looks like you were hit by a large branch. You're going to need stitches, but for now I can—"

Before she could finish the thought, she found herself rolled beneath what had to be two hundred pounds of solid muscle, the entire length of her pressed ruthlessly hard into the snow, her hands yanked high over her head and pinned by his. He wasn't crushing her, nor was he hurting her, but his hold was shockingly effective. In less than one second, he'd immobilized her, shrink-wrapping her between the ground and his body.

"Who the hell are you?" he asked, voice low and rough. It would have brought goose bumps to her flesh if she hadn't already been covered in them.

"Mallory Quinn," she said, struggling to free herself. She'd have had better luck trying to move a slab of cement.

Breathing hard, eyes dilated, clearly out of his mind, he leaned over her, the snow blowing around his head like some twisted paragon of a halo.

"You have a head injury," she told him, using the brisk, no-nonsense, I'm-In-Charge tone she saved for both the ER and her crazy siblings. "You're hypothermic." And he was getting a nice red spot on his cheek, which she suspected was courtesy of the phone she'd hurled at him. Best not to bother him with the reminder of that. "I can help you if you let me."

He just stared down at her, not so much as blinking while the storm railed and rallied in strength around them. He wasn't fully conscious, that much was clear.

Still, testosterone and dark edginess poured off him, emphasized by his brutal grip on her. Mallory was cataloguing her options when the next gust hit hard enough to knock his hood back, and with a jolt, she recognized him.

Mysterious Cute Guy.

At least that's how he was known around Lucky Harbor. He'd slipped into town six months ago without making a single effort to blend in.

As a whole, Lucky Harbor wasn't used to that. Residents tended to consider it a God-given right to gossip and nose into people's business, and no one was exempt. All that was known about the man was that he was staying in a big rental house up on the bluffs.

There'd been sightings of him at the Love Shack—the town's bar and grill—and also at the local gym, and filling up some classic muscle car at the gas station. But Mallory had only seen him once in the grocery store parking lot, with a bag in hand. Tall and broad shouldered, he'd been facing his car, the muscles of his back straining his shirt as he reached into his pocket to retrieve his keys. He'd slid his long legs into his car and accelerated out of the lot, as she caught a flash of dark Oakleys, a firm jaw, and grim mouth.

A little frisson of female awareness had skittered up her spine that day, and even wet and cold and uncomfortable beneath him, she got another now. He felt much colder than she, making her realize she had no idea how long he'd been out here. He was probably concussed, but the head injury would be the least of his problems if she didn't get him warmed up and call for help. "Let's get you inside," she said, ceasing to struggle beneath him, hoping that might calm him down.

No response, not even a twitch of a single muscle.

"You have to let me up," she said. "I can help you if you let me up."

At that, he seemed to come around a little bit. Slowly he drew back, pulling off her until he was on his knees, but he didn't let go of her, still manacling both of her wrists in one hand. His eyes were shadowed, and it was dark enough that she couldn't see their color. She couldn't see much of anything but she didn't need a light to catch the tension coming off of him in waves.

His brow furrowed. "Are you hurt?"

"It's you who's hurt."

"No, I'm not."

Such a typical guy response. He was bleeding and nearly unconscious, but he wasn't hurt. Good to know. "You're bleeding, and we need to get you warmed up, so—"

He interrupted this with an unintelligible denial, followed by another groan just before his eyes rolled up. In almost slow-motion, he began to topple over. She barely managed to grab onto his coat, breaking his fall with her own torso so he didn't hit his head again. But he was so heavy that they both fell.

"Oh my God," came Grace's quavering voice. "That's a lot of blood."

Mallory squeezed out from beneath him and looked up to see both Grace and Amy peeking out from between the fallen tree branches and the door frame.

"Holy shit," Amy said. "Is he okay?"

"He will be." Mallory scooped Grace's phone from the snow and tossed it to her. "I need help. I told him I'd get him inside but my car's better, I think. My phone's there, and I have reception. We can call for help. And I can turn on the engine and use the heater to warm him up."

Amy leaned over him, peering into his face. "Wait." She looked at Mallory. "You know who this is, right? It's Mysterious Cute Guy. He comes into the diner."

"You never told me," Mallory said.

Amy shrugged. "He never says a word. Tips good though."

"Who's Mysterious Cute Guy?" Grace wanted to know.

"When you get reception on your phone, pull up Lucky Harbor's

Facebook," Amy told her. "There's a list of Mysterious Cute Guy sightings on the wall there, along with the Bingo Night schedule and how many women managed to get pulled over by Sheriff Hot-stuff last weekend. Sawyer's engaged now so it's not as much fun to get pulled over by him anymore, but at least we have Mysterious Cute Guy so it doesn't matter as much."

Grace fell silent, probably trying to soak in the fact that she'd landed in Mayberry, U.S.A.

Or the Twilight Zone.

Mallory wrapped her arms around Mysterious Cute Guy from behind, lifting his head and shoulders out of the snow and into her lap. He didn't move. Not good. "Grace, get his feet," she said. "Amy, take his middle. Come on."

"It's karma, you know that, right?" Amy said, huffing and puffing as they barely managed to lift the man. Actually *dragged* was more like it. "Because you promised you'd go for the first Mr. All Wrong who landed at your feet. And here he is. Literally."

"Yes, well, I meant a conscious one."

"He's going on the list," Amy said.

"Careful!" Mallory admonished Grace, who'd dropped his feet. Too late. With the momentum, they all fell to their butts in the snow, Mysterious Cute Guy sprawled out over the top of them.

"Sorry," Grace gasped. "He weighs a ton."

"Solid muscle though," Amy noted, being in a good position to know since she had two handfuls of his hindquarters.

Somehow, squinting through the snow and pressing into the wind, they made it to Mallory's car. She hadn't locked it, had in fact left her keys in the ignition, which Grace shook her head about.

"It's Lucky Harbor," Mallory said in her defense.

"I don't care if it's Never Never Land," Grace told her. "You need to lock up your car."

They got Mysterious Cute Guy in the backseat, which wasn't big enough for him by any stretch. They bent his legs to accommodate his torso, then Mallory climbed in and again put his head in her lap. "Start the car," she told Amy. "And crank the heat. Get my phone from the passenger seat," she said to Grace. "Call 9-1-1. Tell them we've got a male, approximately thirty years of age, unconscious with a head injury and possible hypothermia. Give them our location so they can send an ambulance."

They both did her bidding, with Amy muttering "domineering little thing" beneath her breath. But she started the car and switched the heater to high before turning toward the back again. Her dark hair was dusted with snow, making her look like a pixie. "He still breathing?"

"Yes."

"Are you sure? Because maybe he needs mouth to mouth."

"Amy!"

"Just a suggestion, sheesh."

Grace ended her call to dispatch. "They said fifteen minutes. They said to try to get him warm and dry. Which means one of us needs to strip down with him to keep him warm, right? That's how it's done in the movies."

"Oh my God, you two," Mallory said.

Amy turned to Grace. "We're going to have to give her lessons on how to be a Bad Girl, you know that, right?"

Mallory ignored them and looked down at her patient. His brow was still furrowed tight, his mouth grim. Wherever he was in dreamland, it wasn't a happy place. Then suddenly the muscles in his shoulders and neck tensed, and he went rigid. She cupped both sides of his face to hold him still. "You're okay," she told him.

Shaking his head, he let out a low, rough sound of grief. "They're gone. They're all… gone."

The three women stared at each other for a beat, then Mallory bent lower over him. "Hey," she said gently, knowing better than to wake him up abruptly. "We've got you. You're in Lucky Harbor, and—"

He shoved her hand off of him and sat straight up so fast that he nearly hit his head on her chin, and then the roof of the car.

"We've called an ambulance," she said.

Twisting around, he stared at her, his eyes dark and filled with shadows.

"You okay?" she asked.

"Fine."

"Really? Because the last time you said that, you passed out."

He swiped at his temple and stared at the blood that came away on his forearm. "Goddammit."

"Yeah. See, you're not quite fine—"

He made a sound that managed to perfectly convey what he thought of her assessment, which turned into a groan of pain as he clutched his head.

Mallory forced him to lie back down. "Be still."

"Bossy," he muttered. "But hot."

Hot? Did he really just say that? Mallory looked down at herself. Wrinkled nurse's scrubs, fake Uggs, and she had no doubt her hair was a disaster of biblical proportions. She was just about the furthest she could get from *hot*, which meant that he was full of shit.

"Mr. Wrong," Amy whispered to her.

Uh huh, more like Mr. *All* Wrong. But unable to help herself, Mallory took in his very handsome, bloody face, and had to admit it was true. She couldn't have found a more Mr. All Wrong for herself if she'd tried.

Ty drifted half awake when a female voice penetrated his shaken-but-not-stirred brain.

"I'm keeping a list of Mr. Wrongs going for you. This one might not make it to the weekend's auction."

"Stop," said another woman.

"I'm just kidding."

"I still vote we strip him down." This was a third woman.

Wait. Three women? Had he died and gone to orgy heaven? Awake now, Ty took stock. He wasn't dead. And he had no idea who the fuck Mr. Wrong was, but he was very much "going to make it." He was stuffed in the back of a car, a *small* car, his bad leg cramping like a son-of-a-bitch. His head was pillowed on... he shifted to try to figure it out, and pain lanced straight through his eyeballs. He licked his dry lips and tried to focus. "I'm okay."

"Good," one of them repeated with humor. "He's fine, he's okay. He's also bleeding like a stuck pig. Men are ridiculous."

"Just stay still," someone close said to him, the same someone who'd earlier told him that he'd been hit by a branch. It felt more like a Mack Truck. Given where her voice was coming from, directly above him, it must be her very nice rack that he was pillowed against. Risking tossing his cookies, he tilted his head back to see her. This was tricky because one, it was dark, and two, he was seeing in duplicate. Her hair was piled into a ponytail on top of her head. Half of it had tumbled free, giving her—both of her—a mussed-up, just out-of-bed look. Looking a little bit rumpled, she wore what appeared to be standard issue hospital scrubs, hiding what he could feel was a very nice, soft, female form. She was pretty in an understated way, her features delicate but set with purpose.

A doctor, maybe. Except she didn't have the cockiness that most doctors held. A nurse, maybe.

"I know it looks like you've lost a bit of blood," she said, "but head injuries always bleed more, often making them appear more serious than they are."

Yeah. A nurse. He could have told her he'd seen more head injuries than she could possibly imagine. One time he'd even seen a head blown clear off a body, but she wouldn't want to hear that.

Her blessedly warm hand touched the side of his face. He turned into it and tried to think. Earlier when he'd woken up to the nightmare, he'd gone to work on the Shelby before taking it for a drive. He'd needed speed and the open road. Of course that had been before the snow hit, because even he wasn't that reckless. He remembered winding his way along the highway, the cliffs on his right, and far below on his left, the Pacific Ocean. The sea had been pitching and rolling as the storm moved in long, silvery fingers over the water. He remembered making it into town, remembered wanting pie and seeing the lights in the diner, so he'd parked.

That's when it'd started to snow like a mother.

He'd gotten nearly to the door when his memory abruptly ended. Damn. He hated that. He tried to sit up but six hands pushed him back down. Christ. That'd teach him to wish for a dream about triplets.

Someone's phone lit up, giving them some light, and Ty ordered himself to focus through the hammering in his skull. It wasn't easy, but he found that if he squinted he could see past the cobweb vision. Sort of.

Leaning over the back of the driver's seat was the waitress from the diner, though she was looking a little bit like a drowned rat at the moment. The woman riding shotgun next to her was a willowy blonde and unfamiliar to him.

As was the woman whose breasts were his pillow. "Thanks," he said to her. "For saving my ass."

"So...would you say you *owe* her?" the waitress asked.

"Amy," his nurse said in a warning tone. Then she shot Ty a weak smile. "You've had quite a night."

And so had she. She didn't say so—she didn't have to—it was all there in her doe-like brown eyes.

"The ambulance will be here soon," she said.

"Don't need one."

She didn't bother to point out that he was flat on his back and obviously pretty damn helpless. She kept her hands on him, her gaze now made of steel, signaling that in spite of those soft eyes, she was no pushover. "We'll get you patched up," she said. "And some meds for your pain."

"No." Fuck, no.

"Look, it's obvious you're hurting, so—"

"*No narcotics*," he growled, then had to grip his head to keep it on his shoulders, grinding his teeth as he rode out the latest wave of pain. Stars danced around in front of his eyes, shrinking to pin-points as the darkness took him again.

"They passed us up," Grace said worriedly, twisting to follow the flashing blue and red ambulance lights moving slowly through the lot and back out again.

"Did you tell them that we were inside my car, and to look for us here?" Mallory asked.

"No. Dammit." Grace grabbed Mallory's phone again. "Sorry. I'll call them back right now."

Mallory looked down at her patient. Dark, silky hair. Square scruffy jaw. An old scar along his temple, a new one forming right this very minute on his eyebrow. His eyes were still closed, his face white and clammy, but she could tell he was awake again. "Easy," she said, figuring she'd be lucky if he held off getting sick until they got him out of here.

"What happened?" he said, jaw tight, eyes still closed, his big body a solid weight against her.

It was not uncommon after a head trauma to keep forgetting what had happened, so she gave him the recap. "Tree on the head."

"And then Nurse Nightingale here came to your rescue," Amy told him. "And you said you owed her."

"Amy," Mallory said.

"She needs a date this weekend," Amy told him.

"Ignore her." Over his head, Mallory gave Amy the universal finger-slicing-at-the-throat signal for *Shut It*.

Amy ignored her. "If you go with her to the charity auction on

Saturday night at the Vets' Hall, you'd save her from merciless ridicule. She can't get her own date, you see."

Mallory sighed. "Thanks, Amy. Appreciate that. But I can so get my own—"

Unbelievably, her patient interrupted her with what sounded like a murmured ascent.

But Amy grinned and bumped fists with Grace. "Five bucks says Mr. Wrong will rock her world."

Grace looked down at the prone man in Mallory's lap with clear doubt. "You're on," she whispered back.

Mallory gave up trying to control Amy and eyed her patient. Even flat on his back, he was lethally gorgeous. She could only imagine what he'd be like dressed to the nines and on his feet.

"She'll meet you at the event, of course," Amy said to him. "Because even though this is Lucky Harbor, we're not giving you her address. You might be a serial killer. Or worse, just be a completely Mr. Right."

Another sound of ascent from Mysterious Cute Guy. Which, actually, might have been more of a moan of disbelief that he'd agreed to this craziness.

Right there with you, Mr. Wrong. Right there with you.

Chapter 3

By age thirty-five, women have only a few taste buds left:
one for alcohol, one for cheese,
and one for chocolate.

One week later, Mallory was walking around in a cloud of anticipation in spite of herself. The auction was tonight, and although she knew damn well Mysterious Cute Guy wasn't going to show up, she could admit a tiny part of her wanted to be proven wrong.

Not that she'd actually *choose* to date a man like him, with the guarded eyes and edgy 'tude. She didn't even know his name. Not to mention she'd chucked a phone at his face.

Mr. Wrong, aka Mysterious Cute Guy…

Truthfully, that whole stormy night at the diner was still pretty much a blur to her. The ambulance had eventually found them and loaded up her patient. The snow had stopped, and Mallory had been able to drive home, after a solemn pinky-swear vow with both Amy and Grace to meet weekly, at least for as long as Grace stayed in town.

Chocoholics—CA for short—was their name, chocolate cake was their game.

Mallory had then spent the rest of the week alternating between long shifts in the ER and working on the auction. A portion of the evening's take would go to her own pet project, the Health Services Clinic she planned to open in conjunction with the County Hospital Foundation. HSC would be a place for anyone in the county to get community recovery resources, teen services, crisis counseling, and a whole host of other programs she'd been trying to get going for several years. She still needed hospital board approval, and hopefully the money from the auction would ensure that. It's what should have been foremost in her mind.

Instead that honor went to one Mysterious Cute Guy. For the first time that day, Mallory walked by the nurses' station and eyed the computer. Thanks to HIPAA, a very strict privacy act, she couldn't access a patient's records unless she'd actually worked on the patient that day. This meant that if she wanted to know his name, she'd have to ask the nurse who'd seen him in the ER that night. Unfortunately, her own mother had been his nurse, so she decided against that option.

Luckily, she had six patients to keep her occupied. The problem was that her counterpart, Alyssa, was very busy flirting with the new resident, doing none of her duties. This made for a long morning, made even longer by the fact that one of Mallory's patients was Mrs. Louisa Burland. Mrs. Burland was suffering from arrhythmia complicated by vasovagal syncope, a condition that was a common cause of dizziness, light-headedness, and fainting in the elderly. She was also suffering from a condition called Meanness. "I brought you the juice you asked for," Mallory said, entering Mrs. B's room.

"I asked for that three hours ago. What's wrong with you? You're slower than molasses."

Mallory ignored this complaint because it'd been five minutes, not three hours. And because Mrs. B was so bitter that even the volunteer hospital visitors skipped her room. Before retiring, the woman had been a first grade teacher who had at one time or another terrorized most of town with a single bony finger that she liked to waggle in people's faces. She was so difficult that even her daughter, who lived up the road in Seattle, refused to call or visit.

"I remember you, you know," Mrs. Burland said. "You peed yourself in front of your entire class."

Mallory was surprised to find that she could still burn with shame at the memory. "Because you wouldn't let me go to the bathroom."

"Recess was only five minutes away."

"Well, obviously, I couldn't wait."

"And now you make me wait. You're a terrible nurse, letting your treatment of me be clouded by our past interactions."

Mallory ignored this too. She set the juice, complete with straw, on Mrs. Burland's bedside tray.

"I wanted *apple* juice," Mrs. B said.

"You asked for cranberry."

Mrs. Burland's hand lashed out and the juice went flying, spilling across the bedding, the floor, the IV pole, and Mallory as well. Juice dripping off her nose, Mallory sighed. Perfect. It took twenty minutes to clean up the mess. Ten more to get Mrs. Burland back into her now fresh bed, which had Mallory huffing a little with the effort.

Mrs. B *tsk*ed. "Out of shape, or just gaining some weight?"

Mallory sucked in her belly and tried not to feel guilty about the cinnamon roll she'd inhaled on a quick break two hours ago. She reminded herself that she helped save lives, not take them, and walked out of the room, purposely not glancing at herself in the small mirror over the sink as she went.

Paramedics were just bringing in a new patient, a two-year-old with a laceration requiring stitches. Mallory got him all cleaned up and prepped the area for the doctor. She drew the lidocaine, got a suture kit, 4x4s and some suture material, and then assisted in the closing of the wound.

And so it went.

At her first break, she made her way to the nurses' break room and grabbed her soft-sided lunch box out of the fridge. Her older sister Tammy was there and Mallory sidled up to her. Once upon a time, Tammy had been wild. For that matter, so had Mallory's younger brother Joe. And Tammy's twin, Karen. All three of them, as out of control as they came.

Not Mallory. She'd always been the good one, attempting to distract her parents from the stress of raising wild, out-of-control kids.

Then Karen had died.

Tammy and Joe had carried on for Karen in the same vein, but for Mallory, everything had pretty much skidded to a halt. Blaming herself, she'd fallen into a pit of desperate grief. She'd always walked the straight and narrow path, but she'd taken it to a new extreme, terrified to do anything wrong, to screw a single thing up and make things worse for her parents. Once during that terrible time, she'd accidentally forgotten to pay for a lip balm and had turned herself in as a thief. The clerk of the store had refused to press charges, instead calling Mallory's mother to come get her.

Mallory had felt as if she'd needed to be punished in some way for not paying enough attention to Karen, for being a bad sister, for something, *anything*. She'd put all of her energy into healing her family, but had not been even remotely successful. Her parents divorced and her father had left to go surf in Australia. He'd never come back, and Tammy and Joe...well, they'd gone even further off the deep end.

Joe was doing better these days, spending far less time at cop central and more time on the job. Tammy had improved, too. Sure, last year she'd headed to Vegas for a weekend and had come home with a husband. But to everyone's shock, the wedding hadn't been because of an unplanned pregnancy. It hadn't even been alcohol-related.

Well, it might have been a little bit alcohol-related, but unbelievably, Tammy and her hotel security guard-turned-shotgun husband were still married. She'd applied for and landed a housekeeping job at the hospital and—gasp—had actually held on to the job, the same as her marriage. And since their mother was a supervisory nurse, that meant there were *three* Quinns at the hospital working together. Or, more accurately, Tammy and Ella working as opposing magnets, with Mallory doing her best to hold on to them both.

Tammy had been on shift the night of the freak storm, and because she liked to know everything, in all likelihood she knew Mysterious Cute Guy's name.

Mallory knew that asking her would be better than asking her mom—or looking in the computer and losing her job, not to mention completely invading the guy's privacy—but not by much. Her best hope was for his name to come up in a conversation, all casual-like, maybe even "accidentally." The trick was to not let Tammy know what Mallory wanted, or it'd be Game Over.

The break room was crowded, as it usually was at this time of the day. Mostly it was filled with other nurses and aides. Today Lucille was sitting on the couch as well, sipping a cup of coffee in her volunteer's uniform.

No one knew exactly how old Lucille was, but she'd been running the art gallery in town since the dawn of time. She was also the hub of all things gossip in Lucky Harbor, and she gave one-hundred percent in life. This included her volunteering efforts, and since she knew *everyone*, she'd been hugely influential in helping Mallory gain interest in the Health Services Clinic. Fond of her, Mallory waved, then sat next to Tammy at the large round table in the center of the room.

Tammy smiled and put down her phone. "Heard about tonight."

Mallory stopped in the act of pulling out her sandwich. This might be easier than she thought. "What about tonight?"

"Rumor is that you have a hot blind date for the auction."

"No, I—" She went still. "Wait a minute. How did you hear that?"

"I'm psychic," Tammy said and stole Mallory's chips from her lunch bag.

Dammit, she *needed* those chips. Then she remembered what Mrs. Burland had said about gaining weight and sighed. "Just because you paid for an online course to learn to manage your Wiccan powers does not mean you actually *have* powers. How did you hear about the date?"

"Amy told me when I grabbed lunch at the diner yesterday."

Okay, she'd kill Amy later at their chocoholics meeting. For now, it was just the opening Mallory needed. "First of all, the date thing is just a silly rumor." Even if she was secretly hoping otherwise. "And second... did Amy happen to tell you *who* this silly rumor date might be with?"

"Yep." Tammy was munching her way through the chips and moaning with pleasure, damn her. Mallory hoped she gained five pounds.

"I can't believe you actually landed Mysterious Cute Guy," Tammy said, licking salt off her fingers.

"*Shh*!" Mallory took a quick, sweeping glance around them, extremely aware of Lucille only a few feet away, ears aquiver with the attempt to eavesdrop. "*Keep it down.*"

Unimpressed with the need for stealth, Tammy went on. "It's pretty damn impressive, really. Didn't know you had it in you. I mean, your last boyfriend was that stuffy accountant from Seattle, remember? The only mysterious thing about him was what you saw in him."

"You were here last weekend when he came in," Mallory said.

"The accountant?"

"My *date*."

Tammy smiled. She knew she was stepping on Mallory's last nerve. It was what she did. And this wasn't going well.

"So is it a silly rumor?" Tammy asked. "Or a real date?"

"Never mind!" Mallory paused. "But...did you hear anything about him?"

"Like...?"

Lucille was nearly falling off the couch now, trying to catch the conversation. Mallory turned her chair slightly, more fully facing her sister. "Like his name," she whispered.

This got Tammy's attention in a big way. "Wait a minute. You don't know his name?"

Shit.

"Wow, how absolutely naughty, Mal. You haven't done naughty since you were sixteen and turned yourself in for shoplifting. Now you may or may not have a date with a guy whose name you don't know. A fascinating cry for attention." Tammy turned her head. "You catching all of this, Lucille?"

"Oh, you know I am." Lucille pulled out a Smartphone and began tapping keys with her thumbs. Probably writing on the Facebook wall. "This is good; keep talking."

Mallory dropped her head to the table and thunked it but unfortunately she didn't lose consciousness and she still had to finish her shift.

After work, she drove home and watered her next door neighbor's flowers because Mrs. Tyler was wheelchair-bound and couldn't do it for herself. Then she watered her grandma's beloved flowers. She fed the ancient old black cat that had come with the house, the one who answered only to "Sweet Pea" and only when food was involved. And before she showered to get ready for the night's dinner and auction, she clicked through her e-mail.

Then wished she hadn't.

She'd been tagged on Facebook.

Make sure to buy tickets for tonight's elegant formal dinner and auction, folks! Supported by the hospital, organized by the nurses and spearheaded by Mallory Quinn, all proceeds will go into the Hospital Foundation's coffers toward the Health Services Clinic that Mallory's been working on shoving down our throats. (Just kidding, Mallory!).

And speaking of Ms. Quinn, rumor is that she'll 'maybe' have a date for the event after all, with Mysterious Cute Guy!

Go Mallory!

P.S. Anyone at the event with their cell phone, pictures are greatly appreciated!

Chapter 4

Chocolate will never fail you.

Ty's routine hadn't changed much in the six months he'd been in Lucky Harbor. He got up in the mornings and either swam in the ocean or went to the gym, usually with Matt Bowers, a local supervisory forest ranger and the guy who owned the '72 GMC Jimmy that Ty was fixing up.

Matt was ex-Chicago SWAT, but before that he'd been in the Navy. He and Ty had gone through basic together.

When Ty had injured his leg again, Matt had coaxed him out West to rehabilitate. They'd spent time hitting the gun range, but mostly they enjoyed beating the shit out of each other on the mats.

They had a routine. They'd lie panting side by side on their backs in the gym. "Another round?" Matt would ask.

"Absolutely," Ty would say.

Neither of them would move.

"You doing okay?" Matt would then ask.

"Don't want to talk about it," Ty would say.

Matt would let it go.

Ty would hit the beach, swimming until the exhaustion nearly pulled him under. Afterward, he'd force himself along the choppy, rough rocky beach just to prove he could stay upright. He'd started out slow—hell, he'd practically crawled—but he could walk it now. It was quite the feat. Or so his doctor kept telling him. He supposed this was true given that four years ago, he'd nearly lost his left leg in the plane crash thanks to a post-surgical infection.

Which was a hell of a lot less than Brad, Tommy, Kelly, and Trevor had lost.

At the thought of that time and the loss of his team, the familiar clutching seized his gut. He hadn't been able to save a single one of them. He'd been trained as a trauma paramedic, but their injuries, and his own, had proven too much. Later he'd been honorably discharged and he'd walked away from being a medic.

He hadn't given anyone so much as a Band-Aid since.

Working in the private sector had proven to be a good fit for him. In actuality, it wasn't all that different from being enlisted, except the pay was better and he got a say in his assignments. But six months out of work was making him think too much. He wasn't used to this down time. He wasn't used to being in one spot for so long. His entire life had been one base after another, one mission after another. He was ready to get back to that world.

He *needed* to get back to that world, because it was the only way he had of making sure that his team's death meant something.

But Dr. Josh Scott, the man in charge of his medical care until he was cleared, took a weekly look at Ty's scans and shook his head each time.

So here Ty was, holed up and recuperating in the big, empty house that Matt had leased for him, the one that was as far from his world as he could get. Far away from where he'd grown up, from anyone he'd known. Just as well, since they were all gone now anyway. His dad had been killed in Desert Storm. His mom had passed two years ago. With his closest friends resting beneath their marble tombstones in Arlington, there was no one else: no wife, no lover, no kids.

It made for a short contact list on his cell phone.

Instead of thinking about that, he spent his time fixing cars instead of people—Matt's 1972 Jimmy, his own Shelby—because cars didn't die on those they cared about.

On the day of the big hospital auction, after replacing the transmission on Matt's Jimmy, Ty degreased and showered, as always. Unlike always, he passed over his usual jeans for a suit, then stared at himself in the mirror, hardly recognizing the man looking back at him. He still had stitches over one eye and a bruise on his cheek from the storm incident. His hair was on the wrong side of a haircut, and he'd skipped shaving. He'd lost some weight over the past six months, making the angles of his face more stark. His eyes seemed…hollow. They matched how he felt inside. His body might be slowly getting back into lean, mean fighting shape, but he had some work yet to do on his soul. He shoved his hand in his pocket and pulled out the ever-present Vicodin bottle, rolling it between his fingers.

The bottle had been empty for two months now, and he'd still give his left nut for a refill. He had two refills available to him; it said so right on the bottle. But since Ty had started to need to be numb—with a terrifying desperation—he'd quit cold turkey.

This didn't help his leg. Rubbing it absently, he turned away from the mirror, having no idea why he was going to the auction.

Except he did. He was going because the entire town would be there, and in spite of himself, he was curious.

He wanted to see her again, his bossy, warm, sexy nurse.

Which was ridiculous. It'd been so dark the night of the storm that he honestly wasn't sure he even knew what she looked like. But he knew he'd recognize her voice—that soft, warm voice. It was pretty much all he remembered of the entire evening, the way it'd soothed and calmed him.

Shaking his head, he strode through the bedroom, slipping keys and cash into his pockets, skipping the gun for the night although he'd miss the comforting weight of it. His cell phone was up to fifty-five missed calls now, which was a record. Giving in, he called voice mail and waited for the inevitable.

"Ty," said a sexy female voice. "Call me."

Frances St. Claire was the hottest redhead he'd ever seen and also the most ruthless. The messages went back a month or so.

Delete.

"Ty," she said on one of them. "Seriously. Call me."

Delete.

"Ty, I'm not fucking around. I need to hear from you."

Delete.

"Ty, Goddammit! Call me, you bastard!"

Delete.

As the rest of the calls were all variations on the same theme, with slurs on Ty's heritage and questionable moral compass, he hit *delete, delete, delete...*

There was no need to call her back. He knew exactly what she wanted. Him, back at work.

Which made two of them.

Mallory paced the lobby of Vets' Hall in her little black dress and designer heels knock-offs, nodding to the occasional late straggler as they came in. From the large front gathering room, she could smell the delicious dinner that was being served and knew she should be in there. Eating. Smiling. Schmoozing. Getting people fired up for the auction and ready to spend their money.

But she was missing one thing. A date.

Her Mr. All Wrong hadn't showed, not a big surprise. She hadn't really expected him to come, but... hell. Amy had gotten her hopes up. And speaking of Amy, Mallory blinked in shock as the tall, poised, *gorgeous* woman stopped in front of her.

"Wow." She'd never seen Amy with makeup, or in a dress for that matter, but tonight she was in both, in a killer slinky dress and some serious kick-ass gladiator style heels, both of which emphasized endless legs.

Amy shrugged. "The hospital thrift store."

"*Wow*," Mallory repeated. "You look like you belong in a super hero movie."

"Yeah, yeah. Listen, I came out here to ask you if we need to review your mission tonight with Mr. Wrong."

"Nope. Mission cancelled."

"What? Where's your date?"

"We both know that I didn't really have a date." Mallory shook her head. "You look so *amazing*. I hardly even recognize you."

"Can't judge a book by its cover," Amy said casually. "Have you seen Grace? She didn't know any guys in town, and there's no one I'm interested in, so she's my date tonight."

In the time since Amy had shown up in Lucky Harbor, Mallory had never known her to go out on a date. Whenever Mallory asked about it, Amy shrugged and said the pickings were too slim. "Maybe I should be making you two a list of Mr. Rights," Mallory said.

Amy snorted. "Been there, done that."

Matt Bowers walked by and stopped to say hi to Mallory. She was used to seeing him in his ranger uniform, armed and in work mode. But tonight he was in an expensive dark suit, appearing just as comfortable in his own skin as always, and looking pretty damn fine while he was at it. He was six feet tall, built rangy and leanly muscled like the boxer he was on his off days. He had sun-kissed brown hair from long days on the mountain, light brown eyes, and an easy smile that he flashed at Mallory. "Hey," he said.

She smiled. "Hey, back."

Matt turned his attention politely to Amy, and then his eyes registered sudden surprise. "*Amy?*"

"Yeah, I know. I clean up okay." Her voice was emotionless, her smile gone as she turned to Mallory. "See you in there."

Matt's gaze tracked Amy as she strode across the lobby and vanished inside. Yeah, he looked very fine tonight—and also just the slightest bit bewildered.

Mallory knew him to be a laid-back, easygoing guy. Sharp, quick-witted, and tough as hell. He had to be, given that he was an ex-cop and now worked as a district forest ranger supervisor. Nothing much ever seemed to get beneath his skin.

But Amy had. Interesting. This was definitely going on the list of topics to be discussed during their next little chocoholics meeting. "You forget to tip her at the diner or something?" she asked him.

"Or something," Matt said. With a shake of his head, he walked off.

Mallory shrugged and took one more look around. At first, she'd been so busy setting up, and then greeting people, that she'd been far too nervous to think about what would happen if Mr. Wrong didn't show up.

But she was thinking about it now, and it wasn't going to be pleasant. She paced the length of the lobby again, stopping to look once more out the large windows into the parking lot. Argh. She strode back to the dining area and peeked in.

Also filled.

This was both good and bad news. Good, because there was lots of potential money in all those pockets.

Bad, because there was also a lot of potential humiliation in having to go in there alone after it'd been announced that she had a date.

Well, she'd survived worse, she assured herself. Far worse. Still, she managed to waste another five minutes going through the displays of the auction items for the umpteenth time, and as she had every single one of those times, she dawdled in front of one display in particular.

It was a small item, a silver charm bracelet. Each of its charms were unique to Lucky Harbor in some way: a tiny Victorian B&B, a miniature pier, and a gold pan from the gold rush days. So pretty.

Normally, the only jewelry Mallory wore was a small, delicate gold chain with an infinity charm that had been Karen's. It had been all she'd ever needed, but this bracelet kept drawing her in, urging her to spend money she didn't have.

"Not exactly practical for an ER nurse."

Mallory turned and found Mrs. Burland standing behind her, leaning heavily on a cane, her features twisted into a smile, only named so because her teeth were bared. "Mrs. Burland. You're feeling better?"

"Hell, no. My ankles are swollen, my fingers are numb, and I'm plugged up beyond any roto-rooter help."

Mallory was well used to people telling her things that would never come up in normal conversations. "You need to stay hydrated. You taking your meds?"

"There was a mix-up at the pharmacy."

"You need those meds," Mallory said.

"I tried calling my doctor. He's an idiot. And he's twelve."

Mrs. B's doctor was Dr. Josh Scott. Josh was thirty-two, and one of the best MDs on the West Coast.

"Trades on his cute looks," Mrs. Burland sniffed.

Mallory wouldn't have described Josh as cute. Handsome, yes. Definitely striking as well, and... serious, even when he smiled. So serious that he always looked like he'd been to hell and back. And had learned plenty along the way.

None of which had anything to do with his ability to do his job. Josh worked his ass off. "You're being very unfair to a man who's given you your life back. I'll check into the med issue for you first thing in the morning."

"Yes, well, see that you do. Where's your date?"

Mallory took a deep breath. "Well—"

"You've been stood up? A shame, since you're dressed to put out." Then the woman walked away.

Mallory went back to staring down at the bracelet. Mrs. B was right about one thing: it *was* totally impractical for anyone who had to be as practical as she did on a daily basis. The charms would snag on everything from patients' leads to the bed rails.

"Sweetheart, what are you doing out here?"

Perfect. Her mother. Ella was in her Sunday best, a pale blue dress that set off the tan she'd gotten on the hospital's upper deck during her breaks, where she sat reading romance novels and plotting her single daughter's happily-ever-after. "Pretty," Ella said of the bracelet, "but—"

"Impractical," Mallory said. "I know."

"Actually, I was going to say it's the type of thing a boyfriend would buy you. You need a boyfriend, Mallory."

Yeah, she'd just pick one up at the boyfriend store later.

"Where's your date?"

Oh good, her favorite question.

"Oh, honey. Did you get stood up?"

Mallory made a show of looking very busy straightening out the description plaque with the bracelet display. "Maybe he's just running a little late is all."

"Well, that doesn't bode well for the relationship."

Yeah, and neither did the fact that they didn't *have* a relationship. "You should have a date too, Mom."

"Me?" Ella asked in obvious surprise. "Oh, no. I'm not ready for another man, you know that."

Mallory did know that. Ella had been saying so for the past decade, ever since The Divorce, which Mallory—however twisted—still one-hundred-percent blamed herself for.

"You look a little peaked, sweetheart. Maybe you're catching that nasty flu that's going around."

No, she was catching Stood-Up-Itis. "I'm good, Mom. No worries."

"Okay, then I'm going back inside. Dessert's up next." Ella kissed her on the cheek and left.

Mallory walked around the rest of the auction items. She checked the parking lot again for Mysterious No-Longer-So-Cute Guy. By then, dessert was just about over. When the lights dimmed and the PowerPoint slide show started—the one she'd put together to showcase the auction items—she sneaked in. Tip-toeing to one of the back tables, she grabbed the first empty seat she could find and let out a breath.

So far so good.

She took a surreptitious peek at the people at her table but it was too dark to see across from her. To her right was an empty chair. To her left was a man, sitting still in the shadows, his face turned to the slide show. She was squinting, trying to figure out why he seemed so vaguely familiar when someone came up behind her and put a hand on her shoulder. "Mallory, there you are."

Her boss. *Crap*. She craned her neck and smiled. "Hello, Jane."

"I've been looking everywhere for you. You're late." Jane Miller was the director of nurses, and probably in her previous life she'd been queen of her very own planet. She had a way of moving and speaking that demanded attention and subtly promised a beheading if she was disappointed in the slightest.

"Oh, I'm not just getting here," Mallory assured her. "I've been behind the scenes all night."

"Hmm," Jane said. "And...?"

"And everything's running smoothly," Mallory quickly assured her. "We have a full house. We're doing good."

"Okay, then." Rare approval entered Jane's voice. "That's terrific." She eyed the chair to the right of Mallory. The empty spot. "Your date didn't show up?"

And here's where Mallory made her mistake. She honestly had

no idea what came over her: simple exhaustion from a very long week, or it might have been that her heels were already pinching her feet. But most likely it was sheer, stubborn pride—which her grandmother had always told her would be the death of her. "My date is right here," she whispered. As discreetly as she could, she gestured with her chin to the man to her left, praying that his date didn't take that moment to come back from the restroom.

"Lovely." Jane smiled politely at the back of his head. "Aren't you going to introduce us?"

Oh for God's sake. Mallory glanced over at the man, grateful he was paying them no attention whatsoever. "He's very busy watching the slide show."

Jane's smile didn't falter. She also didn't budge. It was her patent alpha dog stance, the one that hospital administrators, politicians, and God himself bent over backward for.

Mallory gritted her teeth and again glanced at her "date," expecting him to still be watching the slide show.

He wasn't.

He was looking right at her, and naturally the slide show ended at that very moment and the lights went up.

He had a bandage above his eye, which she knew covered stitches, and there was a small bruise on his cheek, where she'd nailed him with Grace's cell phone.

Mysterious Cute Guy.

Chapter 5

Do Not Disturb: Chocolate fantasy in progress.

Mallory's first thought at the sight of Mysterious Cute Guy: *Holy smokes.* The night of the storm she hadn't gotten a good look at him, but she was getting one now. Edgy expression, dangerous eyes, long, hard physique clothed in the elegant, sophisticated packaging of a dark suit. He'd managed to pack a wallop while prone and bleeding but that had been nothing compared to what happened to her now when he was upright and conscious. Before she could speak, a spotlight hit the stage, revealing a microphone.

"That's you," Jane said, pulling Mallory out of the chair. "You're introducing the auction, yes?"

Saved by the bell. Or by the end of the slide show. "Yes, that's me."

"Well?" Jane said to Cute Guy. "You're her date, aren't you? Escort her up there."

The expression on his face never changed from that cool, assessing calm. And even though Mallory had no idea what he did for a living, or even his name, she'd bet the last three dollars in her wallet that few people, if anyone, *ever* barked an order at him. "Oh," she said in a rush to Jane. "It's okay, he doesn't have to—"

But he was already on his feet, setting his hand at the small of her back, gesturing for her to go ahead of him.

Craning her neck, she stared up at him.

He stared back, brow arched, mouth only very slightly curved.

Hot, he'd called her. Sure, he'd also called her "bossy," and he hadn't been in full possession of his faculties at the time, but even now, the memory gave her a tingle in some places that had no business tingling.

"Mallory," Jane said in that Displeased Queen voice again. "Get on with it."

"Yes, *Mallory*," her "date" said, his voice low and grainy, with just a touch of irony. "Let's get on with it."

She nearly let out a short, half-hysterical laugh but she slapped her hand over her mouth. Later. She'd die of embarrassment later. She forced a smile for anyone looking at them, and *everyone* was looking at them. Speaking out of the corner of her mouth for his ears alone, she whispered, "You don't have to do this, pretend to be on the date you didn't want in the first place."

For the briefest flash, something flickered in his eyes before he smoothed it out and went back to his impassive blank face. Confusion? She wasn't sure, and it no longer mattered. Sure, an apology for standing her up would be nice, but beggars couldn't be choosers. For whatever reason, he was willing to play along, and at the moment, with Jane staring holes in her back, Mallory was grateful.

She threaded her way through the tables to the stage, managing a smile at everyone who caught her eye. But she couldn't have come up with a single name to go with those faces. Not when she was so completely aware of that big, warm hand at the small of her back to go along with the big, strong, gorgeous guy escorting her. He was close enough for her to catch his scent.

Which, by the way, was still fantastic, damn him.

As they got to the stage stairs, she caught the fact that he was limping. She glanced down at his leg. What had happened? He hadn't injured his leg in the storm that she knew of. "Are you okay?"

"Later," he said, and nudged her up the stairs to the stage.

With five hundred sets of eyes on her, she let it go and took the mic. "Good evening, Lucky Harbor," she said.

The crowd hooted and hollered.

In spite of herself, she felt a genuine smile escape at their enthusiastic greeting. She'd grown up in this town, had found her life's passion working as a nurse in this town, and knew that even if she somehow ended up on the other side of the world some day for whatever reason, she'd always smile at the thought of Lucky Harbor. "Let's make some money for health care tonight, okay?"

More wild applause. Then someone yelled out, "Who's the hottie with you?"

This was from Tammy, of course, sitting at one of the front tables, her hands curled around her mouth so that her voice would carry to the stage.

Mallory ignored her sister's heckling as best she could and turned to the big screen behind her. "Okay, everyone, get your bidding paddles ready because we have some great stuff for you tonight. Our favorite auctioneer, Charles Tennessee, is going to come up here, and I expect to see lots of action. I want cat fights, people. Hair-pulling if necessary. Whatever it takes to keep the bidding going. So let the fun begin—"

"We want to meet your date!"

Mallory let out a breath and looked down at Lucille, sitting at another front table.

Lucille gave her a finger wave, which Mallory also ignored, but it was hard to ignore the "*Do it, do it, do it*" chanting now coming from Tammy's table. Her brother was there too, looking every bit the part of the mountain biking bum that he was, with the perpetual goggle tan, the streaked, long brown hair. Tall and lanky lean, Joe sat with an arm slung around the blonde he was dating this week. Mallory caught movement at her right and glanced over as her so-called date strode up the stairs to the stage. Oh God, this wasn't going to help anything, and she shook her head vehemently at him to stop, to go back.

Instead he joined her.

She shook her head again, and she'd have sworn he was laughing at her without his mouth so much as twitching. His eyes were sharp with intelligence, wit, and absolutely no hint of remorse or shame at standing her up. She should probably get over that—and quickly—because the entire audience was now fixated on both of them, the anticipation palpable. With no choice but to be as gracious as possible, Mallory shook her head at the crowd. "Bloodthirsty lot, all of you."

Everyone laughed.

"One of these days," she said. "You're all going to get a life."

Everyone laughed again, but she knew no one was going to move on to the auction until she did this, until she introduced Mysterious Cute Guy. "Fine," she said. "But don't try to tell me you don't know the man standing next to me. I've seen his FB stats."

More laughter, and what might have been slight bafflement from the man himself. "Everyone," she said. "Meet…" She trailed off with one thought. *Crap.* Hard to believe that she could possibly have yet another embarrassing moment in her tonight, but she shouldn't have underestimated herself. Drawing a deep breath, she had no choice. She turned to him and she knew damn well that he knew what she needed.

His name.

Again, the very hint of a smile touched the corner of his lips as he looked at her, brow quirked. He was going to make her *ask*, the big, sexy jerk. Well, that's what she got for wanting Mr. All Wrong. Mr. Bad Boy. Mr. Smoking Hot. He was going to burn her, for sure, and she would lay the blame at the chocoholics' feet. But she'd yell at Amy and Grace later. For now, she had to deal with this. The question was how? She hadn't a clue. *Uncle*, she finally mouthed to him.

Leaning in close so that his broad chest bumped her shoulder, he wrapped his fingers around hers on the mic. They were tanner than hers, and work-roughened. And the touch of them made her shiver.

"Mallory's just being shy," he said to the audience, then slid her a look that she couldn't begin to decipher. The man was most excellent at hiding his thoughts. "I'm Ty Garrison. The... date."

Shy her ass. And she knew damn well he hadn't known her name either, not until Jane had said it. And now he was giving her that bad boy smirk, and she wanted to smack him, but at least she finally knew his name.

Ty Garrison.

It suited him. She'd known a Ty once in first grade. He'd pulled her hair, torn up her homework, and told Mrs. Burland that she'd stolen his. It fueled her temper a little bit just thinking about it. "So there you have it," she said, commandeering the microphone. "Now let's get to the auction, and have a good time." She quickly introduced the auctioneer and gratefully stepped down off the stage, happy to be out of the spotlight.

She walked quickly through the crowd, even happier to note that no one was paying her any attention now; they were all glued to the auctioneer.

Except Lucille.

Lucille, in a silver ball gown that looked like a disco ball, snapped a photo of Mallory with her phone and then winked.

Mallory sighed and was bee-lining for her seat when she was waylaid by her mom, who pulled her down for a hug. Mallory had no idea where her supposed date had gone. Apparently he'd vanished when she'd left the stage, which worked for her. She did not want to subject him to her mother.

The auction had begun with her bracelet, and Mallory quickly grabbed an auction paddle from Ella's table, unable to help herself. No one else was bidding, so she told herself it was a sacrifice for the cause, and raised her paddle.

"Mallory," her mother admonished. "You can't afford that bracelet."

This was true. Annoying but true. "I'm thirty, mom. I get to make my own dumb decisions now, remember?"

"Like going out with a man whose name you didn't even know?" She sounded scandalized. "That's as bad as finding a man on..." She lowered her voice to a horrified whisper, as if she was imparting a state secret. "—the *Internet*!"

"I'm not looking for a man on the Internet. And it's just a one-night thing with Ty."

Someone behind them won the bracelet, and the auctioneer went on to the next item.

"Listen to me, honey," Ella said. "Ty Garrison is not the kind of man who's going to marry you and give me grandchildren."

Well, her mom was absolutely right on that one. "I'm not looking for that, either." At least not right this moment.

"What *are* you looking for?"

Good question. "I don't know exactly." She looked around at the social crowd, who were all far more into the party atmosphere than bidding. "I guess I'm...bored."

Her mother looked as if she'd just admitted to smoking a crack pipe.

"And I'm restless too," Mallory said. "And...sad, if you want to know the whole ugly truth." She hadn't even realized that was true until it popped out of her mouth without permission, but she couldn't take it back now.

"Oh, honey." Ella squeezed her hand, her eyes suspiciously damp. "Out of all you kids, you've always been my easy one." The crowd got louder and so Ella did too. "The good one, and sometimes I forget to check in and make sure you're okay. Especially after Karen—"

"I *am* okay." And if she wasn't, well then she could handle it. But dammit, she was tired. Tired of doing what was expected, tired of feeling like she was missing something.

"Mallory," Ella said softly, concerned. "You've also always been the smart one. I depend on that from you, honey." She paused. "You're not going to do anything stupid tonight that you'll regret later, right?"

Well, that depended on her mother's definition of *stupid*. As for regrets, she tried hard to live without them. "I hope so."

Her mother looked at something over Mallory's shoulder and made a funny little noise in her throat. Mallory froze, closing her eyes for a beat before turning to find—*of course*—Ty.

Looking bigger than life, he stood there holding two glasses of wine. He handed one over to her while she did her best to stay cool. Downing half the glass went a long way toward assuring that. *Please let him not have heard any of that....*

"Ty Garrison," Ella said as if testing out the name. "Is my daughter safe with you?"

"*Mom*," Mallory said quickly. "Jesus."

"Don't swear, honey." But Ella held up a hand in concession. "And fine. I'll reword." She looked at Ty. "Are you going to hurt my daughter?"

Ty looked at Mallory as he answered. "She's too smart to let that happen."

Okay, so he *had* heard every word. Terrific. God, she was so far out of her league she could no longer even *see* her league. Her mom had asked if she was going to do anything stupid. And Mallory was pretty sure that the answer was a resounding yes.

As if he could read her thoughts, Ty gave her a sardonic little half toast with his glass, then surprised her by moving away.

Which meant *he* was smart too. "Well," Mallory said. "This has been lots of fun."

"I'm going to assume that was sarcasm," her mom said.

"Always knew I got my smarts from somewhere." Mallory leaned in and kissed Ella's cheek, then went back to her own table where she'd left her purse. That's when she realized that her problems were bigger than her own stupidity issues. Although the room was filled with the sounds of happy, well-fed people, they really were doing far more socializing than bidding. When a "Boating at the Marina" package came up and no one lifted their paddle, Jane locked her unhappy gaze on Mallory's.

Mallory smiled reassuringly while quivering inside. *Someone bid, someone please bid*, she thought with desperation, trying to make it happen by sheer will.

Finally, someone did, but it didn't bring in the money she'd expected.

The next item was a big ticket one, an expensive night on the town in Seattle, which included a limo, a fancy dinner, and an orchestra concert. The bidding began at another low, modest rate, and Mallory's heart landed in her throat.

They were going to have to do better than this. Much better. Again her gaze locked in on Jane, and her unease grew. Someone sank into the chair next to her and since her nipples got hard, she knew it was Ty. "Go away," she said, not taking her gaze off the stage.

Ty said nothing, and she glanced over just as he raised his paddle, bidding two hundred dollars higher than she could have even *thought* about offering.

She stared at him. "What are you doing?"

He didn't even look at her, just eyed the crowd with interest and a smile she hadn't seen from him before. It was a killer smile, she admitted to herself, and when someone joined him in the bidding across the room, he flashed it again and raised his paddle to up the bid.

And then the oddest thing happened.

More people joined in. Unbelievably, the bidding for the "Night on the Town" continued for five more minutes, until the money offered was nothing short of dazzling.

Ty won.

Apparently satisfied, he set down his paddle and leaned back, long legs stretched out in front of him, perfectly at ease as he watched the proceedings. Mallory should have been watching too, but couldn't take her eyes off him, while around them the night kicked into full gear with a new excitement. Everyone in the whole place was now bidding on all the items, playfully trying to outdo each other, or in some cases, not so playfully. It was...wonderful. But she couldn't get her mind off the fact that Ty had spent hundreds of dollars to get it going. "What are you going to do with that package you just won?"

"Have a night on the town, apparently."

There was no way he was an orchestra kind of guy. "But—"

"Trouble at three o'clock," he said casually.

She turned to look and found Lucille and another biddy from her blue-haired posse bidding fiercely for the next auction item—a date with Anderson Moore, the cute owner of the hardware store in town.

"This Anderson guy," Ty said to Mallory, still watching the old ladies upping the bid with alarming acerbity, "he's ninety, right?"

The auctioneer jokingly suggested the two older women share the date, and the bidding ended peacefully.

Ty winced in clear sympathy for Anderson, who now had to date not one, but two old ladies.

"Don't feel sorry for him," Mallory said. "He's got it coming to him. He goes after anything with breasts."

Ty slid her a look. "You have a little bit of a mean streak."

She laughed. It was true, even if not a single soul in Lucky Harbor would believe it. She had no idea what it said about her that Ty, a perfect stranger, saw more of her than anyone who actually knew her.

At her smile, Ty leaned close, his gaze dropping from her eyes to her mouth. "I like a woman with a mean streak."

She stared into his eyes, nearly falling into him before letting out another low laugh, this time at herself. God, he was good. Really good. "Save the charm. I'm immune." And look at her displaying another shockingly bad girl characteristic—lying through her teeth.

"Explain something to me," he said.

"What?"

"Why does everyone think I was your date tonight?"

She stared at him. "Last weekend, when I pulled you out of that storm, Amy told you about the auction and how I needed a date, remember?"

"No, actually."

She gaped at him. "Seriously?"

"I remember the storm," he said slowly, as if wracking his brain. "I remember getting hit by the tree. I remember you."

She was wondering if that was good or bad when he added, "Sort of."

Sort of? He "sort of" remembered her? What did *that* mean? She reached for her wine, wishing it was something harder.

"I remember there being a list," he said. "A list of...Mr. Wrongs."

She choked on her wine.

"And I definitely remember waking up in the ambulance with a mother of a headache."

She was silent for a shocked beat while she digested this astonishing fact. He had absolutely no memory of the fact that he was supposed to be her date tonight. Well, that certainly explained a lot of things. Like being stood up. Damn, it was going to be hard to hold that against him, though she was willing to give it a try. "So I guess that the next time I make a date with a concussed guy, I should pin a note to his collar so he doesn't forget."

"Good plan." His hand was next to hers on the table. He let his thumb glide over her fingers, a small, almost casual touch that sent a shudder through her. "I'm sorry I forgot our date," he said. He was so close she could see every single hue of green in his eyes, and there were many. She could feel the warmth of his exhale at her temple. In the crowded Vets' Hall, their nearness was no different from any other couple in the room, discussing their next bid, or laughing over a joke. But Mallory wasn't bidding or laughing. Her heart was suddenly pounding in her throat and there were butterflies going crazy low in her belly.

"Am I on that list, Mallory?" he asked, low and husky. "Am I a Mr. Wrong?"

Oh God, she was in trouble now, because she liked the sound of her name on his lips. Too much. "Don't get too cocky. There are others on the list." She lifted her hand to touch the bruise on his cheek.

He caught her hand in his. "Not what I asked."

"Yes," she admitted. "You're on the list. You're at the top of the list."

Chapter 6

What came first, woman—or the chocolate bar?

Ty had no idea what the hell he thought he was doing, flirting with Mallory.

Scratch that.

He knew exactly what he was doing. He was feeling alive for the first time in six months. Possibly in four years.

She was looking at him, her sweet brown eyes lit, cheeks flushed. She was feeling alive too, he was guessing. But she probably wasn't wondering if he still had a condom in his wallet, trying to calculate how old it might be.

But if she had a list, so did he. A short list of one, and she was it. "Why does a woman like you need a list at all?"

"Like me?"

"Pretty. Smart. Funny."

She laughed, then shook her head. "I don't know. I guess I don't have a lot of time to date."

He could understand that. Hell, it'd been a long time since he'd dated. It'd been a long dry spell without a woman at all, and she was all woman. Her dress was a deceptively modest black number that had little straps criss-crossing across her back and fell to mid-thigh, molding her curves and whetting his appetite for more. Her heels were high and strappy, emphasizing world-class legs that had been hidden beneath her scrubs. She had her hair up in some loose twist with a few tendrils falling across one temple and at the nape of her neck. Her only jewelry was a little gold necklace—no earrings, nothing to stop his mouth from nipping her throat along his way to her ear where, if he was so inclined, he'd stop to whisper promises.

He shouldn't be inclined. Mallory Quinn was sweet, warm, and caring. She was a white picket fence and two-point-four kids. She was a diamond ring.

She was someone's keeper.

Not his. Never his. He didn't do keepers.

And yet in that beat, with her mouth close to his, a smile in her eyes, he...ached. He ached and yearned for something. Someone. He wanted to wrap his arms around a woman, *this* woman, and lose himself in her.

A woman tapped Mallory on the shoulder, the same woman from before; tall, thin, and coldly beautiful, with a tight pinch to her mouth that said she was greatly displeased about something. Or possibly constipated. She wore authority and bitchiness as easily as she wore the strand of diamonds around her neck.

Mallory glanced up and straightened, her expression going carefully blank. "Jane," she said, in a tone that told Ty that the woman was either her boss or her executioner.

"I need a moment," Jane said.

Boss, Ty thought.

"Absolutely." Mallory followed Jane out of the hall and into the foyer.

The auction was moving ahead at full steam now, and people were into it, jumping up and waving as they bid. Telling himself he had to stretch his aching leg, that he wasn't at all curious about what had come so briefly over Mallory's face, Ty left the hall.

In the entranceway, Mallory had her back to him, facing Cruella Deville. "Absolutely," she was saying. "I'll go upstairs and get it right now. Thank you for your addition, Jane."

And then Jane went one way and Mallory the other, her sweet little ass sashaying as fast as she could move in those sexy heels.

Let it go, man. Let her go, he told himself. He'd heard enough from her mother to know she was a good girl just looking for a walk on the wild side. Probably she'd grown up in Lucky Harbor, which was pretty much the same thing as being in bubble wrap all her life. She was not for him.

Except.

Except here she was, clearly doing her damnedest to meet some pretty tough expectations from family and work and whatever, all while looking to spread her wings. She had guts, and he admired that. She was sexy and adorable, but no matter what she did to spread her wings, she wasn't going to match him in life's experiences.

Not even close.

She was clean and untainted and *not* jaded. She was his opposite. She was too good for him. Far too good, even when she was out there risking it all. She deserved *way* more than he had to offer, and he needed to just walk away. After all, he was out of here, maybe as soon as one more week. Gone, baby, gone.

He told himself all this, repeated it, and then followed her down the hallway anyway.

Mallory walked up the stairs, cursing the heels that were pinching her toes. Jane had sent her up here on a wild goose chase for an antique vase that had been accidentally left off the auction chopping block.

Mallory knew Jane's family had built the Vets' Hall in the early 1940s. Apparently the missing vase had sat in the entry for years, until last spring when the building had been renovated. The vase had never been put back on display and now Jane wanted it gone.

All Mallory had to do was find it.

The second story ran the length of the building. On one side was a series of rooms used by the rec center and other various groups like the local Booster Club. The other side was one big closed-off storage room. Mallory let herself in and flipped on the lights. Far above her was an open-beam ceiling and a loft area where more crap had been haphazardly shoved away. Mallory hoped like hell she wouldn't have to climb up there in her dress and annoying heels to find the vase.

The place was warm, stuffy, and smelled like neglect. She took a good look around and felt a lick of panic at the idea of finding her way out of here, much less locating the missing vase. She moved past a huge shelving unit that was stuffed to the gills with long-lost play props and background sets, and various other miscellaneous items for which there was little use.

Not a single vase.

She walked past more shelves and around two huge, fake, potted Christmas trees before coming to a large stack of boxes leaning against the wall. Assuming the vase wouldn't be stuffed away, she walked farther, gaze searching. Near the center of the room, she came to another long set of shelves. Here were some more valuable items, such as office equipment and furnishings, and miraculously, sitting all by itself on a shelf, a tall vase, looking exactly like the one Jane had described. Mallory couldn't believe it. She picked it up and turned to go, and ran directly into a brick wall.

A brick wall that was a man's chest.

Ty.

He'd appeared out of thin air, scaring her half to death. The vase flew out of her hands and would have smashed to the floor except he caught it.

His sexy suit might have given him an air of sophistication, but it did nothing to hide his bad-boy air. His hair was a little mussed, like he'd run his fingers through it repeatedly. On another man, this would have softened his look but not Ty. She wasn't fooled. There was nothing soft about him. He was sheer trouble, and she knew it. "What are you doing?" she gasped, hand to her pounding heart.

"What are *you* doing?"

She snatched the vase from his hands. "Working."

"Well, I'm helping my date work then."

"You're not my real date. You didn't even know you had a date."

He looked amused. "So you're one of those women who holds a grudge?"

"No! I'm—"

From somewhere far behind them, the storage room door opened. "Hello? Mallory, dear?"

"*Shit*," Mallory whispered, horrified. "It's Lucille."

"Your mother told you not to swear."

She narrowed her eyes at him.

"Mallory?" Lucille called out.

Mallory slapped her hand over her own mouth.

"Yoo-hoo...I saw your hot date follow you in here. I just want to get a picture of you two for Facebook."

Oh no. No, no, no...Mallory turned in a quick circle in the warm, dusty, overstuffed storage room, desperate for a place to hide.

Ty must have seen her panic because he briefly held a finger to her lips to indicate he needed her silence, then took the vase in one hand and her wrist in his other and tugged her along, farther into the shadows.

She followed, walking on her tiptoes to avoid the clicking of her heels, when suddenly Ty pressed her against the wall. "Shh," he breathed in her ear.

Stealth. She got it. She was depending on it. She also got something else, an unexpected zing from the feel of his mouth on her ear and his body pressing into hers.

"*Mallory*?" Lucille called out.

Ty had gone into 007 mode. His eyes were searching their surroundings, his body ready and alert. He opened a panel she hadn't even noticed, then pulled something from his pocket and used it inside the panel. In the next second, the lights went out.

Startled, she nearly gasped but he slid a hand over her mouth. That, combined with the way he was holding her against the wall, caused a tsunami of inappropriate feelings to rush through her.

"Don't move." He remained still until she nodded, and then he was gone.

Only not completely gone.

She jumped when she felt his hands on her ankles. He was crouched before her, removing first one heel and then the other. Her hands went out for balance and smacked him in the head. She heard his soft laugh, then he had her hand again and they were on the move. She couldn't see a thing, but Ty didn't appear to have that problem. He was navigating them both with apparent ease, leading her through the maze of the vast storage unit as if he could see in the dark. They turned corners and squeezed into spots, his hands sliding to her hips, guiding her exactly where he wanted her to go, taking care that she didn't bump into anything. She had no idea how he could see, or even know where they were going, but she followed him.

Blindly.

It was better than the alternative.

Each time they stopped, she was pulled up against his big, warm body, until she began to anticipate it.

Crave it.

"Mallory?" Now, accompanying Lucille's voice came a small beam of light.

Good Lord. The woman was using the same Bic app that Grace had. "Oh for the love of—"

Warm lips covered hers. "*Shh.*"

Right. Shh. Her knees were still melting. Her one hand was in his, trapped between their bodies, but her other hand slid up his chest, around the back of his neck and into his hair. Because she needed a hand grip, she told herself.

"How bad do you want to keep out of her sight?" Ty wanted to know, each syllable rumbling from his chest and through hers. He'd set the vase down, freeing up both his hands. She felt herself rock into him and tighten her grip on his hair, and it took a long moment to process his words because her brain was no longer firing on all cylinders.

"Mallory."

God, she liked the sound of her name on his lips. And she liked the feeling that had come over her too, the languid yet throbbing beat of anticipation. She certainly wasn't bored or sad now. "Hmm?"

"How bad?"

How bad did she want him? *Bad.*

With a little huff against her jaw that might have been another low laugh, he tightened his grip on her and spun her away from him, setting her hands on something that felt like cold steel.

"Hold on tight," he whispered and nudged his big body up behind hers, his biceps on either side of her arms, his chest against her back.

Her mind went utterly blank, but her body didn't. Her body went damp at the wicked thought of doing it right here, like this. From behind.

"Up," he said, and the fantasy receded. No, he didn't want sex. He had her in front of a ladder and wanted her to climb it.

Good thing it was dark because it hid the heat of the blush she could feel on her face. She pulled herself up, *extremely* aware that her butt was in his face, and then she was directly above him.

He was still apparently able to see in the dark. Which meant that he could see right up her dress. She was wearing a brand new silky black thong, her very best, but still, it couldn't be a very good angle for her.

At the top of the ladder was the loft. Moonlight slanted in from the sole round window, revealing more stored items, a couch and a large table with chairs. The table was stacked with more stuff. There were also rows of framed pictures and empty planters, and a whole horde of other crap. Everywhere.

Mallory moved aside for Ty to join her but the standing space was so small she lost her balance and fell onto the couch.

Ty followed her down.

On the night of the storm, Mallory had been beneath him too, but it felt different this time. Sexy different, and she let out a small, half hysterical laugh.

Ty covered her mouth with his hand, shifting a little to get the bulk of his weight off of her. In the execution, one of his thighs pushed between hers and *oh sweet baby Jesus*. She promptly stopped laughing and moaned instead. A totally involuntary, accidental moan that sounded needy and wanton. And horrifyingly loud.

Ty's hands tightened on her and they both stilled, craning their necks, looking down into the dark storage area, following the little beam of light as Lucille weaved through the aisles below.

Ty pulled his hand from Mallory's mouth. "Unless she can climb a ladder, we're good here until she gives up and leaves."

Yes. Yes, they were good here. Or very bad, depending on how one looked at it.

Above her, Ty was still as stone, a solid heated package of testosterone and sinew holding her down on the couch. She wasn't sure what it said about her that she felt just a little bit powerless and helpless, and that she liked it.

A lot.

Another thing she liked? The fact that every time he breathed, his leg shifted up against her core, putting her body on an entirely different page than her brain.

On the *get-more-of-him* page.

"She won't give up," she whispered, more than a little breathless.

"Watch." Ty shifted again—oh God *his thigh*!—and pulled something from his pocket, which he threw.

Mallory heard the ping of the coin as it landed with deadly precision all the way across the huge room near the storage room entrance.

Holy shit he could throw.

"Oh!" they heard Lucille exclaim, whipping around toward the sound. "You're escaping, you smart girl. Darn it all!"

They watched as the little beam of light wobbled back through the room to the entrance, and then in the next moment, vanished completely.

Silence reigned.

Well, except for Mallory's thundering heartbeat. She was in an attic loft, flat beneath her Mr. Wrong. Her common sense was screaming *flee*! But her secret inner bad girl was screaming *oh please, can't we have him? Just once?*

"You okay?" Ty asked.

Loaded question. "You have some impressive skills," she said. "I feel like a Bond girl."

"You weren't so bad yourself," he said. "The way you shimmied up that ladder is going to fuel my fantasies for some time."

So he *could* see in the dark. And now that they were up here with moonlight coming in the window, she could see too. She bit her lower lip because she could feel, too. She could feel him, *all* of him. Her breasts were mashed up against his chest, plumping out of her dress suggestively. She wasn't sure he'd noticed, but then he very purposely dropped his head, his lips just barely brushing her exposed skin. She sucked in a breath and felt him stir against her.

Yeah. He'd noticed. "I have lots of ladder practice," she said inanely.

"Yeah?" he asked, sounding intrigued. "You climb a lot of ladders in the ER?"

"Uh, no." Nerves had her laughing. And babbling. "But I had to clear the gutters on my house last fall before the rains hit. I nearly fell when I found a fist-sized spider waiting for me but managed not to accidentally kill myself."

A low laugh escaped him.

"So why did you do it?" she asked.

"The ladder? Nowhere else to go but up."

"No, I mean why did you help me hide? And thanks, by the way. You pretty much saved my butt." *Again.*

He slid a hand down her arm, squeezing her hip before shocking the hell out of her when he slid that hand further, cupping said butt. "My pleasure."

At the words, at the touch, her body liquefied. Or maybe that was his fingers, tightening on her hindquarters, making her want to squirm and rock into him.

The brand new bad girl in her took over and did exactly that.

Ty went still. She wasn't sure what that meant exactly, but she was feeling things she hadn't in far too long, and she intended to go with those feelings. So she squirmed again.

"Mallory." There was a warning in that low, sexy tone of his, a very serious warning.

She'd wanted a kiss, but hearing him say her name like that was almost as good. And now she wanted more. She wanted things she didn't even have names for. So she wriggled some more, hoping like hell she was getting her message across because she wasn't all that practiced in the bad girl department. Amy had been right; she needed lessons. She made a mental note to address this as well at the next chocoholics meeting. For now, she'd wing it. "Yeah?"

"Are you coming on to me?"

"Well, technically, you're on top of me," she pointed out. "So I think that means that *you're* coming on to *me*."

With a groan, he pressed his forehead to hers and swore beneath his breath, and not the good kind of swear either. And though she should have seen this coming, she hadn't.

He didn't want her.

It was perfect, really. Perfect for the way the rest of the night had gone. Horrified, humiliated, she pushed at him. "Sorry. I got caught up in the moment. I'm not very good at this, obviously." He didn't budge so she shoved him again. "Excuse me."

He merely tightened his grip. "Not good at what, exactly?" he asked.

"Really? You need me to say it?"

When he just waited, she sighed. "Attracting men. I'm not good at attracting men. Now if you could please *get off*."

He lifted his head and cupped the back of hers in one big hand, his eyes glinting with heat. "You first," he said rough and gravelly, leaving no mistake to his meaning.

She gasped, and he took advantage of that to kiss her, his lips moving against hers until she gasped again, in sheer pleasure this time.

Things went a little crazy then. Ty's mouth was firm and hungry, his tongue sliding against hers, and God, she'd almost forgotten what it was like to be kissed like this, like there was nothing on earth more important than her. That long-forgotten thrill of feeling soft and feminine rushed over her.

Then Ty lifted his head, and she realized she was touching his face, the stubble on his jaw scraping against the pads of her fingers.

"To be clear," he said, "I'm *very* attracted to you." And she believed him because the proof of that statement was hard against her hip.

"I think it's your eyes," he said.

She was a little startled by the unexpected romance of that. And then she was drowning in *his* eyes, which were smoldering. But then they were kissing again, and she couldn't think because he happened to be the world's most amazing kisser. Ever. She lost herself in it for long moments, loving the fact that he didn't seem to be in a hurry at all, or using the kiss as a means to an end. Kissing her was an act all unto itself, and she was panting for air when he finally broke from it. He shifted to pull away and she reflexively clutched at him. "Wait—We're stopping?"

Dropping his head, he rubbed his jaw to hers. "Yeah."

"But...why?"

He let out a low, innately male groan. "Because you're not the fuck-a-stranger-in-a-storage-room-with-her-boss-waiting type of woman."

Well, when he put it like that...Damn. Her inner bad girl retreated a little. More than a little.

You don't think you deserve to be happy.

Amy's words floated in her head. No, she'd never been the type to let a stranger into her heart, much less her body.

But this wasn't about her heart.

And Ty was no longer a complete stranger. He was the man who'd good-naturedly stepped in tonight when she'd needed him. Multiple times. He was the man who'd just given her the most amazing kiss of her life.

She wanted him to also be the man to vanquish her restlessness and loneliness. "I am for tonight," she said, and wrapped herself around him.

"Mallory." He stared down at her, the moonlight casting his features in bold relief. "I'm not a long-term bet. Hell, I'm not even a short-term bet."

"I just want this," she said. "Here. Now. With you."

This won her another long look, interrupted by a very rough, very male groan when she undulated against him, trying to sway the game in her favor.

"Christ, your eyes," he said on a long breath. "Come here then." Before she could, he pressed her down farther into the couch, his mouth trailblazing a path over her throat and collarbone.

Apparently, he wasn't one to over-think or second-guess a decision. Good to know. And when he came up against the material of her dress, he wasn't deterred by that either. A quick tug of his fingers and her straps slid down her shoulders to her elbows, trapping her hands at her sides and baring her breasts all in one economical movement.

Apparently, Ty didn't waste energy unnecessarily. Also good to know.

"Mmm," he said, a growl of approval low in his throat. He made his way to her breasts, paying such careful homage to her nipples that she was writhing beneath him by the time he moved down her stomach.

"So soft," he murmured against her, his breath gently caressing her skin. But there was nothing gentle about him as his work-roughened fingers pushed the hem of the dress up to her waist. He looked down at her black thong, gave another low growl of approval, then slid the tiny swatch of black silk to one side. This bared all her secrets both to the night air and his hot gaze. Lowering his head, he put his mouth on her, using his lips and his tongue, making her arch up into him. She was crying out within minutes, her hands fisted in his hair as stars exploded behind her eyes.

Before she'd even stopped shuddering, he'd shoved off his jacket, then unbuckled, unzipped, and was rolling on a condom. The sight made her moan, and then he was pushing inside of her and she lost her breath. He gave her a moment to adjust to his size, then his mouth found hers again and she could taste herself on his tongue. It was wildly sensuous, and so far out of her realm of experience she could only dig her fingernails into his back and hold on.

He swallowed her cries as he thrust into her, running a hand beneath her knee, lifting her leg up to wrap around him so he could get even deeper.

Deeper worked. Oh, how it worked. He took her right out of herself, and she thrilled to it. He was powerful and primal, and if he hadn't taken such care to make sure she was right there with him, she might have doubted herself. Instead, she rose to meet him halfway, unable to do anything but feel as he pushed her over the edge again, his hard length pounding into her, his tongue mimicking his body's movement as he claimed her. And it was a claiming, a thorough one. She was deep in the throes when he joined her, shuddering in her arms, his hands digging hard into her hips as he lost himself in his pleasure.

In her.

The knowledge nearly sent her over again, as did the low, hoarse, very male sound he made when he came. Tearing his mouth from hers, he dropped his head into the crook of her neck, his broad shoulders rising and falling beneath her hands as he caught his breath.

He was still buried deep inside of her when he lifted his head to see her face.

"What?" she whispered.

"Wanted to make sure you're okay. You're smiling."

"Am not." But she was. God, she so was. It would probably take days to get rid of it. But apparently she'd taken the Chocoholics modus operandi to heart. She'd just had her Mr. Wrong.

In a storage room.

Which just proved exactly how wrong Mr. All Wrong was for her, because she'd never had sex without a commitment in her entire life. She braced herself for the guilt.

None came.

In fact, Mallory felt unexpectedly fantastic. "No regrets," she whispered.

He gave her a curious look, then that almost-smile. "I like the way you think."

She ran a finger over the Band-Aid on his forehead, and then along the bruise on his cheek. "I'm sorry about this," she said. "About throwing the phone at your head when I thought you were a bad guy."

He shook his head, but his almost-smile became a full smile. "I don't remember that part."

"Oops. Then never mind." She heard thunderous applause from below them and remembered. The auction! "Oh my God, we've got to go. You first. Hurry." She gave him a nudge but he didn't move.

"I'm not going to just leave you up here," he said.

"Yes, you are! We can't be seen leaving here together." Just the thought brought more panic, and she pushed him again. "Go. Hurry!"

Not hurrying at all, he looked at her for another long moment. Leaning forward, he pressed his lips to her damp temple and finally pulled away. He helped her straighten out her clothing before taking care of himself.

She was still lying there with no bones in her body when he disappeared over the edge of the loft, vanishing into the night, giving her exactly what she'd asked for. Just this, here, now.

And now was over.

Chapter 7

There is no kiss sweeter than a chocolate kiss.

Ty slept hard that night, and apparently lulled by post-orgasmic glow, he didn't dream. Sex was the cure for nightmares. Good to know. His morning went pretty much status quo. Matt met him on the beach, and they'd gone several miles when Matt got a cramp and went down.

Ty was too far away, and his heart nearly stopped before he got to Matt and dragged his ass out of the water.

Matt rolled around in agony on the sand while Ty dug his fingers into Matt's calf and rubbed the cramp out. When he had, he collapsed to the sand next to Matt. "No more."

Matt was gasping for breath. "You're right. You're a fucking animal in the water. No one should be able to swim that long and hard."

"No, I mean because you nearly drowned yourself."

"Well," Matt managed, sitting up with a smile. "Only half drowned, thanks to you."

"Fuck it, Matt, I'm not kidding. You're not swimming with me anymore."

Matt's smile faded as he studied Ty for a long moment. "You do realize that not everyone's going to die on you, right?"

"Shut up."

"What crawled up your ass today?" Matt asked. "You had a good time last night. I saw you actually crack a smile at Mallory."

Mallory. God, Mallory. Ty pushed upright and despite his trembling limbs, he started walking.

"Good talk," Matt called out after him.

Ty kept going, heading back to the house. He wanted to run but his leg didn't have the same want. Brooding about that, he pushed hard, forcing himself to stay at the tide line where the sand was the softest and choppiest because that made the going extra teeth-grindingly difficult.

Difficult worked. He wanted to feel the pain, to remind himself why the hell he was here. Which was *not* to dally with the sweet, warm, giving, sexy-as-hell Mallory Quinn.

Though God, she'd been all those things and more, and she'd revved his engine but good. Every time he thought about how hot she'd looked lying all spread out for him on that couch, he got hard.

Stupid. What he'd done last night had been *beyond* stupid and he knew it. It was also selfish, and he had no excuse other than she'd blindsided him with her open, honest sweetness. He should have ignored the attraction, had fully intended to, but that hadn't worked out so well for him.

And now he could add being an asshole to his list of infractions. Because taking advantage of Mallory last night had been a real dick move. But she was...well, everything he wasn't.

Still, she didn't deserve the likes of him, or what he'd done. Probably she already hated him for it. He told himself this was for the best and took a long, hot shower. He pulled on clothes while eyeballing the empty Vicodin bottle on the dresser. This was a ritual, the stare down. In the end, he shoved the bottle into his pocket as he always did, wanting the reminder close at hand. The reminder to keep his head on straight, keep his mind on the goal—getting back in the game.

With that in his head, he left for his doctor's appointment.

"Looking better," Josh said an hour later, eyeing the latest screen of Ty's leg.

"I feel all better," Ty said, lying through his teeth. After this morning's exercise, he hurt like hell.

Not fooled, Josh gave him a long look.

"I'm good for light duty."

"Uh huh." Josh leaned back in his chair and studied him. "Lighter duty than what, rappelling out of helicopters, rescuing dignitaries, etcetera?"

This was the problem with having your boss put you on leave until you were medically cleared. Thanks to Frances, Josh knew far too much about him. Ty blew out a breath. It wasn't Josh's fault. He was a good guy, and under different circumstances, would even be considered a friend.

If Ty had friends. He didn't. He'd let his friends die on a mountaintop four years ago.

So what was Matt, a pesky little voice asked. *Or Mallory*? Accidents, he decided.

"Look," Josh said, leaning forward, "you want out of here. I get that. You're getting closer. But let's give it another week, okay?"

Another fucking week. But reacting badly wasn't going to help him. He'd use the week to finish Matt's Jimmy. And the Shelby. He couldn't leave without the Shelby. "Fine. But *you* tell her."

"Frances?" Josh smiled grimly. "Gladly."

When Ty got back to the house, his phone was blinking missed calls. He deleted them without a glance, then went to work on Matt's Jimmy. Later he switched to his real love, the Shelby, stopping to look up some parts on the Internet. There he got distracted by an e-mail from Matt with a link.

He'd been tagged on Facebook. In fact, on the Lucky Harbor page there was an entire note on him, listing sightings and news. They called him *Mysterious Cute Guy*.

It was enough to give a guy nightmares.

Except he was already having nightmares...

He waited until hunger stopped him and drove into town. Lucky Harbor was nestled in a rocky cove, its architecture a quirky, eclectic mix of the old and new. The main drag was lined with Victorian buildings painted in bright colors, housing the requisite grocery store, post office, gas station, and hardware store. Then there was a turnoff to the beach itself, where a long pier jutted out into the water, lined with more shops, the arcade and Ferris wheel, and the diner.

Eat Me was like something from an out-of-time Mayberry, except in Mayberry he'd probably not have gotten laid at Vets' Hall, in a storage attic above the entire town.

Noticing the brand new front door, he entered the diner and took a seat at the counter. Amy silently poured him a mug of coffee. This was routine; they'd been doing the same dance for months, rarely speaking. He really appreciated that in a waitress, and he liked her infinitely more than the eternally grumpy diner owner. Jan scared him, just a little bit.

Then Amy dropped the local paper in front of him and cocked a hip counterside.

Ty slowly pushed his sunglasses to the top of his head and gave her a level look. Her return look had bad attitude all over it. She wore a black tee with some Chinese symbol on the front and the requisite frilly pink apron that looked incongruous with her short denim skirt, boots, and general kick-ass attitude. She gestured with a short jerk of her chin to the paper, and he took a look.

The headline read: COUNTY HOSPITAL'S AUCTION—A HUGE SUCCESS.

So far so good, he thought, then read the first paragraph, which credited the success of the auction to the nurses, specifically Mallory Quinn, who along with her new boyfriend had gotten the entire Vets' Hall on its feet by starting off the bidding with a bang.

Ty reread the article. New boyfriend? *Mysterious Cute Guy*? He graced Amy with his no-nonsense, don't-fuck-with-me look. It had cowed many.

But Amy didn't appear impressed or even particularly intimidated.

He set down the paper and pushed it away.

She pushed it back with a single finger.

"Do you have a point?" he asked.

"Several, actually. First, Mallory's my friend. And I recently encouraged her to make a change in her life. You were that change. Don't make me sorry."

Ty wasn't much used to threats, however sweetly uttered. Never had been. He'd been raised by two military parents who'd taken turns parenting him when one or the other had been on tour overseas. He'd been loved, but weaknesses had not been tolerated. Even his current job added up to a life lived by rules, discipline, sheer wits, and honor.

The honor part was troubling him now.

Somehow in spite of himself and his reclusiveness, he'd managed to find celebrity status in this crazy-ass, one-horse town, and even worse, there was Mallory, wanting him to take her for a walk on the wild side.

Bad idea.

The *baddest*.

He'd done it anyway, fallen captive to those melted chocolate eyes, even knowing he planned on being out of Lucky Harbor any minute now. "She's a big girl," he finally said.

Amy stared at him for a long moment, then shook her head and walked away, muttering something beneath her breath about the entire male race being genetically flawed.

Ty was inclined to agree with her. He paid for his coffee and received another long, careful look from Amy.

Message received.

As to whether he was going to heed the warning, the jury was still out. He went straight back to his big, empty house. Cranking the music to ear-splitting levels, he worked on the Shelby. He'd seen the car in the newspaper on his first day in Lucky Harbor had hadn't been able to resist her.

He'd never been able to resist a sweetheart of a car.

Or, apparently, a sweetheart of a woman…

Mallory sat in a hospital board meeting surrounded by a bunch of administrators that included her boss and her mother, in what should have been the meeting of her life. Instead, her mind was a million miles away. Or more accurately, in a certain storage room.

Memories of that storage room, and what Ty had done to her in it, were making her warm. *Very* warm.

She still couldn't believe how fast she'd gotten naked with him.

Well, not quite naked, she reminded herself. She'd been in such a hurry that she hadn't even lost her panties, not completely.

Ty had simply slipped them aside with his fingers.

Just remembering made her damp all over again. God. She'd never gone up in flames so hard and fast in her entire life.

Heaven.

He'd taken her to heaven in seven minutes. A record for her. And she'd do it again, in a heartbeat.

That is, if the man who'd taken her to heaven hadn't vanished from the auction without a word. That should teach her to have completely inappropriate sex with a man whose name she'd learned only twenty minutes earlier.

But all it'd really taught her was that she'd been missing out. Man, had she been missing out. Worse, she knew the magnitude of her attraction for him now, and she was afraid that the next time she saw him, she was going to shove him into the nearest closet for round two.

And round three.

Mallory took a moment to fantasize about that, about what she'd be wearing the next time. Maybe her little black dress again; he'd seemed to really like it. And maybe next time she'd leave the panties at home—

"Mallory?"

She blinked away the vision of Ty and her panties and came face to face with a *not amused* Jane.

"The amount?" Jane asked in a tone that said she'd repeated herself several times already.

"Eighteen thousand." Mallory looked down at the check in her hands, a check she was incredibly proud of—the total of the proceeds from the auction. "You said the board would donate twenty-five percent of it to the Health Services Clinic."

"There isn't an HSC," Jane said. "Not yet."

Mallory bit back her retort, knowing better than to show weakness. "There will be. We've proven need."

"Have we?" Jane asked.

"Yes." Mallory forced herself to look the other board members in the eyes as she spoke, no matter how resistant they were. Dr. Scott was there, rumpled and gorgeous as usual. His eyes warmed when he met her gaze. No one else made eye contact. She took a big gulp of air. "The need is obvious. There's nowhere else in the entire county providing drug programs, teen pregnancy counseling, women's services, or an abuse hotline. We all know that. The ER is losing money because we're taking on patients who'd be better served by a Health Clinic."

"You mean people who can't, or won't, pay." This from Bill Lawson, head of the board of directors. He was tall, lean, and fit, looking forty instead of his fifty-five. He had sharp eyes, a sharper mind, and was all about the bottom line. Always. He *was* listening though, and Mallory appreciated that. This was important to her, had been since Karen had died because she'd had no place to go and get the services she'd so desperately needed.

People rarely talked about Karen and what had happened to her. But Mallory hadn't forgotten a thing, and she intended to make sure that no other scared eighteen-year-old girl ever felt the helplessness and terror that Karen had.

"We've run the numbers," she said, talking directly to Bill now. The hospital, just outside of Lucky Harbor, serviced the entire county but was private, run by a board of directors who all tended to bow to Bill's wishes. She needed his support. "A Health Services Clinic is eligible for programs and funding that the ER isn't. I've written the grant requests. If you go with my proposed plan and allow use of the old west wing, then one hundred percent of the HSC revenue will go right back into the hospital's pockets."

"It would also mean that the full financial responsibility for the Health Services Clinic would be the hospital's," Bill pointed out.

He already knew this. He just didn't like it. "Yes," she agreed. "But with the grants and donations, HSC will run in the black, and in the long run, it'll save your ER losses. We've got most of the first year's funds already."

"You're short ten big ones."

"True, but I won't stop until we have the rest," she promised. "This makes sense for our community, Bill, and it's the right thing to do." She paused, then admitted the rest. "I'm going to be a pain in your ass over this."

"Going to be?" Bill shook his head wryly. "Listen, Mallory, I believe in what you're trying to do, and I want to be on your side. But let's face the truth here—your proposed programs will bring a certain...demographic to Lucky Harbor, a demographic we typically try to divert away to other parts of the county. The town isn't really behind this."

"The town can be persuaded. People are in need, and HSC can meet that need."

Bill was quiet a moment, and Mallory did her best not to fidget. She was only moderately successful.

"I'll make you a deal," Bill finally said. "At this week's town meeting, I'll give everyone a formal spiel, then ask for thoughts."

People went to town meetings like they went to the grocery store or got gas. It was simply what everyone did. If Bill asked for opinions, he'd get them, in droves.

"If we get a positive response, I'll consider a one-month trial run for HSC. One month, Mallory," he said when she smiled. "Then we'll reevaluate on the condition of the actual costs and the bottom line at that time. If you've got the budget for the rest of the year after that month, and if there've been no problems, you're on. If not, you drop this." He gave her a long look. "Is that acceptable to you?"

There was only one answer here. "Yes, sir," she said with carefully tempered excitement.

"Oh, and that budget of yours better not include paying you to go to the pharmacy and pick up meds for our patients and then delivering them."

He was referring to how she'd picked up Mrs. Burland's meds for her just that morning and brought them to the woman's home. How he'd found out wasn't too much of a mystery. Lucky Harbor had one pharmacy. It was located in the grocery store, and everyone in town was in and out of that store often. Anyone from the pharmacist, to the clerk, to any of the customers could have seen her, and she hadn't made a secret of what she was doing.

Nor had Mrs. Burland made a mystery out of how she'd felt about Mallory delivering her meds.

"*Do you expect a tip*?" she'd asked. "*Because here it is. Put on some makeup and do something with your hair or you'll never catch a man*."

At the memory, Mallory felt an eye twitch coming on but she

didn't let it dampen her relief. She was closer to opening the HSC than she'd ever been. "I did that on my own time."

Bill nodded. "And if by some miracle, the town meeting goes well, how long would you need to get up and running?"

She'd had volunteer professionals from all over the county on standby all year. "I would open immediately with limited services, adding more as quickly as I can get supplies and staff scheduled."

"See that 'immediately' is actually immediately," Bill said. "And I'll expect to see numbers weekly."

"Yes, sir."

An hour later, Mallory was on the ER floor, still doing the happy dance. Finally she had something other than sexy Ty to think about, because hoping for town approval and actually getting it were two very different things.

Not that she had time to think about that either, thanks to a crazy shift. She had a stroke victim, a diabetic in the midst of losing his toes, a gangbanger who'd been shot up in Seattle and made it all the way to Lucky Harbor before deciding he was dying, two drunks, a stomach-ache, and a partridge in a pear tree.

In between patients, she worked the phones like mad, preparing for a *very* tentative Health Clinic opening the following week.

The west wing in the hospital had once been the emergency department before the new wing had been built three years ago. It was perfectly set up for the clinic, easily accessible with its own parking lot. It needed to be cleaned and stocked. And she needed staff on standby. The list of what she needed and what she had to do went on and on.

When she yawned for the tenth time, Mallory went in search of coffee. As she stood there mainlining it, waiting for it to kick in—her mind danced off to revisit a certain storage room...*big, warm hands, both rough and gentle at the same time, stroking her—*

"Mallory, my goodness. Where are you at in that pretty little head, Disneyland?"

Mallory blinked and the daydream faded, replaced by the sight of her mother, who stood in front of her smiling with bafflement. "I called your name three times. And the same thing happened in the board meeting. Honey, what in the world are you thinking about today?"

She'd been thinking about the sound Ty had made when he'd come, a low, inherently male sound that gave her a tingle even now. "Dessert," she said faintly. "I'm thinking about dessert."

"Hmmm." Ella looked doubtful but didn't call her on it. "You've seen the paper."

"You mean the local gossip rag masquerading as legit news?" They'd labeled Ty her *boyfriend*. Who'd run the fact check for *that* tidbit? "Yeah, I saw it." Every person she'd come across had made sure of it.

"Honey, I just don't think it's a good idea to risk so much on a man you know nothing about."

"It's not about taking risks, mom." And it wasn't. Mallory had risked nothing, not really. Well, maybe she'd risked getting caught having wild sex in a public place, but she'd felt safe enough or she'd never have done it. No, for her it'd been about being selfish for the first time in recent memory, taking what she wanted. And yeah, maybe that was going to wreak some havoc on her personal life. But since when was worrying about what people thought a life requirement?

Since a long time ago. Since she'd got it in her head that she had to be good to be loved.

"Mallory, honestly," Ella murmured, her tone full of worry. "This is so unlike you, seeing a man you don't even know."

Yes, Mallory, the shock. The horror. The good girl actually wanting something for herself. How dare she? "We're not seeing each other," she said. At least not how Ella meant.

"But the newspaper said—"

"We're not," Mallory repeated. Ty hadn't said so in words, not a single one in fact, but he couldn't have been more clear as he'd vanished.

"So you're telling me that I'm worrying about nothing?" Ella asked.

"Unless you enjoy having to wash that gray out of your hair every three weeks, yes. You're worrying about nothing."

Her mother patted her brunette bob self-consciously. "Four weeks and counting. Do I need a touch-up?"

Just then, Camilla came running through, looking breathless. Camilla was a fellow nurse, twenty-two years old and so fresh out of nursing school she still squeaked when she walked. She was a trainee, and as such, got all the crap jobs. Such as signing in new patients. "He's here," she whispered dramatically, practically quivering with the news. "In the waiting room."

"He?" Mallory asked.

Camilla nodded vigorously. "*He*."

"Does 'he' have a name?" Ella asked dryly.

"Mysterious Cute Guy!"

Her mother slid Mallory a look. But Mallory was too busy having a coronary to respond. *Why was he here?* "Is he hurt or sick?"

"He asked for Dr. Scott," Camilla said in a rush. "But Dr. Scott's been called away."

Mallory moved around Camilla. "I'll take him."

"Are you sure?" Camilla asked. "Because I'd be happy to—"

"I'm sure." Heart pounding, Mallory headed down the hallway toward the ER waiting room, taking quick mental stock. She had nothing gross or unidentifiable on her scrubs, always a bonus. But she couldn't remember if she was wearing mascara. And she really wished she'd redone her hair at break.

Ty was indeed in the waiting room. There was no noticeable injury. He was seated, head back, eyes closed, one leg stretched out in front of him. He wore faded Levi's and a black T-shirt, and looked like the poster boy for Tall, Dark, and Dangerous. Pretty much anyone looking at him would assume he was relaxed, maybe even asleep, but Mallory sensed he was about as relaxed as a coiled rattler.

He opened his eyes and looked at her.

Inexplicably nervous, she glanced at the TV mounted high in a corner, which was tuned to a soap opera. On the screen was a beautiful, dark-haired woman getting it on with a guy half her age in a hot tub. She was panting and screaming out, "Oh, Brad. Oh, please, Brad!"

Oh, good. Because this wasn't awkward enough. She hastily looked around for the remote but it was MIA. Naturally.

Ty's brows went up but he said nothing; he didn't need to. The last time she'd seen him, he'd been pouring on the charm and getting into her panties with shocking ease.

Okay, maybe not so much on the charm. Nope, he'd drawn her in with something far more devastatingly effective—that piercing, fierce gaze, which had turned her on like she'd never been turned on before.

Apparently nothing much had changed in that regard. She'd just handled three emergencies in a row without an elevation in her heart rate, but her heart was pumping now, thudding in her chest and bouncing off her rib cage at stroke levels.

He'd walked away from her, she reminded herself, clearly not intending to further their relationship—if that's what one called a quickie these days.

The woman on the TV was still screaming like she was auditioning for a porno. "Oh God, oh Brad, *yes*!"

The air conditioning was on, which in no way explained why she was in the throes of a sudden hot flash. Whirling around, she continued to search in desperation for the remote, finally locating it sitting innocuously on a corner chair. It still took her a horrifyingly long time to find the mute button, but when she hit it, the ensuing silence seemed more deafening than the "Oh Brad, please!" had been.

She could feel Ty looking at her, and she bit her lower lip because all she could think about was that he'd made her cry out like that too.

But at least she hadn't begged.

"I'd offer a penny for your thoughts," he said. "But I have the feeling they're worth far more."

"I'm not thinking anything," she said far too quickly, then felt the heat of her blush rise up her face.

"Liar." He rose from the chair and shifted closer, and she stopped breathing. Just stopped breathing. Which wasn't good because she *really* needed some air.

And a grip.

Ty leaned into her a little bit, his lips brushing her ear. "You weren't quite as loud as she was."

She closed her eyes as the blush renewed itself. "A nice guy wouldn't even bring that up."

He shrugged, plainly saying he wasn't a nice guy. And in fact, he'd never claimed to be one.

Of course there was no one else the waiting room, but just across the hall at the sign-in desk were Camilla and her mother, neither of them bothering to pretend to be doing anything other than staring in open, rapt curiosity.

Mallory turned her back on them. "I wasn't loud," she whispered.

Oh good Lord. That hadn't been what she'd meant to say at all, but it made him smile. A genuine smile that crinkled the corners of his eyes and softened his face, making him even more heart-stoppingly handsome, if that was possible. "Yeah," he said. "You were."

Okay, maybe she had been. But she couldn't have helped it. "It'd been a while," she admitted grudgingly. And he'd *really* known what he was doing.

As Tammy had reminded her, Mallory's last boyfriend had been

Allen, the Seattle accountant, who'd decided Mallory wasn't worth the commute. That had been last year. A very long, dry year...

Ty's eyes softened, and she realized that they weren't clear green, not even close. Lurking just beneath the surface were layers of other shades, which in turn softened *her*. He'd held her like no other, whispered sweet, hot nothings in her ear as she'd indeed panted and cried out, and begged him just like the soap opera actress. Damn, but she could still get aroused at just the memory of the strength of his arms as he'd held her through it, that intoxicating mix of absolute security and wild abandon.

"It'd been a long time for me too," he said, surprising her. How did a guy who looked as good as he did and exuded pheromones and testosterone like they were going out of style *not* have sex for a "long time"?

On the screen behind him, the woman was still going at it, and watching her without the sound made it seem even more X-rated. "I did *not* go on like that," she murmured, and though Ty wisely held his tongue, his expression said it all. "What, you think I *did*?" she asked in disbelief.

His gaze flicked to the screen, then back to her face. "If it helps, you looked way hotter and sounded much better while doing it."

Oh, God. She turned away from him and was at the door before his low, husky voice sounded again. "Where are you going?" he asked.

"Walking away. You should recognize it."

"I'm actually here as a patient."

At the only words in the English language that could have made her turn around, she did just that. "You are? Are you sick?"

He pointed to his head. "Josh told me to come back in ten days to get the stitches out."

Josh? He was on a first-name basis with Dr. Scott? "Dr. Scott got called to Seattle." She let out a long breath. "But if he left the order, I can remove the stitches for you."

Her mother and Camilla were still watching, of course, now joined by additional staff who apparently had nothing better to do than attempt to eavesdrop on Mallory and Mysterious Cute Guy. Mallory would lay odds that *this* Cute Guy sighting would go wide and be public by the end of her shift.

Nothing she could do about that. "Let's get this over with."

"Is it going to hurt?"

She looked at Ty, at his big, tough body, at the way he limped ever so slightly on his left leg, and then into his eyes. Which were amused.

He was teasing her.

Well, fine. She could give as good as she got. "Something tells me you can handle it."

Chapter 8

Eve left the Garden of Eden for chocolate.

Ty followed Mallory through the double doors to the ER and to a bed, where she then pulled a curtain around them for privacy.

In the military, Ty had learned defense tactics and ways to conceal information. He'd excelled at both. As a result, concealing emotion came all too easily to him. Not to mention, there wasn't much room for emotion in the underbelly of the Third World countries he'd worked in. So he'd long ago perfected the blank expression, honed it as a valuable tool. It was second nature now, or had been.

Until Mallory.

Because he was having a hell of a hard time pulling it off with her. Like now, for instance, when he was relieved to see her and yet struggling to hide that very fact. Clearly not so relieved to see him, she said "I'll be right back" and vanished.

Fair enough. As she'd pointed out, he'd vanished on her, and a part of him had figured he'd never see her again.

But another part had hoped he would.

He'd known that she worked here and imagined she was a great nurse. On the night of the storm, she'd been good in an emergency, extremely level-headed and composed.

Unlike at the auction, in his arms. Then she'd been hungry, and the very opposite of level-headed and composed. He'd loved that about her. Now she was back to the calm persona. She looked cute in her pale pink scrubs with the tiny red heart embroidered over the pocket on her left breast. He especially liked the air of authority she wore.

Hell.

He liked everything he knew about her so far, including how she'd tasted. Yeah, he'd really liked how she'd tasted. Which was the only explanation he had for being here, because he sure as hell could remove his own damn stitches.

From nearby, someone was moaning softly in both fear and pain. He stood, instinctively reacting to the sound as he hadn't in four years. Four years of ignoring the call to help or heal.

The moan came again, and Ty closed his eyes. Christ, how he suddenly wished he hadn't come. Unable to help himself, he stuck his head out the curtain of his cubicle. In the next bed over, a guy was hooked up to a monitor, fluids, and oxygen. He was in his early forties, smelled like a brewery, and either hadn't showered this month or he'd rolled in garbage. His hair was gray and standing straight up, missing in clumps. A transient, probably, looking small and weak and terrified.

"You okay?" Ty asked, staying where he was. "You need the nurse?"

The man shook his head but kept moaning, eyes wide, his free hand flailing. His eyes were dilated, and there was a look to him that said he was high on something.

Cursing himself, Ty moved to the side of his bed. He glanced at the IV. They were hydrating him, which was good. Catching the man's hand in his, Ty squeezed lightly. "What's going on?"

"Stomach. It hurts."

The guy's clothes were filthy and torn enough to reveal a Trident Tattoo on his arm, and Ty let out a slow breath. "Military," he said, feeling raw. Too raw.

"Army," the man said, slurring, clearly still heavily intoxicated, at the least.

Ty nodded and might have turned away but the guy was clinging to his hand like it was a lifeline, so Ty continued to hold on to him right back as he slowly sank onto the stool. "I was Navy," he heard himself say. He left out the Special Ops part; he always did. It had nothing to do with not being proud of his service and everything to do with not wanting to answer any questions. And there were *always* questions. "I'm out now."

Technically.

"You never get out," the man said.

Well, that was true enough.

"They should pay us for the long nights of bad dreams." The guy took a moment to gather his thoughts. This seemed to be a big effort. Ty wanted to tell him not to work too hard but before he could, the man spoke again. "They should give us extra combat pay for all the ways our lives are fucked up."

Ty could get behind that. They sat there in silence a moment, the man looking like he was half asleep now and Ty feeling a little bit sick. Sick in the gut. Sick to the depths of his soul. Yeah, definitely the hospital had been a stupid idea. This was absolutely the *last* time he let his dick think for him.

"I still think about them," the man said softly into the silence.

Ah, hell. Ty didn't have to ask who. He knew. All the dead. Ty swallowed hard and nodded.

The man stared at him, glassy-eyed but coherent. "How many for you?"

Ty closed his eyes. "Four." But there'd been others, too. *Way* too many others.

The man let out a shuddery sigh of sympathy. "Here." He lifted a shaky hand and slid it into his shirt, coming out with a flask. "This helps."

Mallory chose that very moment to pull back the curtain. "*There* you are," she said to Ty, then smiled kindly at the man in the bed. "Better yet, Ryan?"

Ryan, caught red-handed with the flask, didn't meet her gaze as he gave a jerky nod.

"Why don't I hold that for you, okay?" Gently, she pried the flask from Ryan's fingers, confiscating it without another word.

Ty didn't know what he'd expected from her. Maybe annoyance, or some sign that she resented the duty of caring for a guy who was in here for reasons that had clearly been self-inflicted. But she ran a hand down Ryan's arm in a comforting gesture, not shying away from touching him.

More than duty, Ty thought. Much more. This was the real deal, *she* was the real deal, and she cared, deeply.

"I've called your daughter," she told Ryan. "She'll be here in ten minutes. We're just going to let the bag do its thing, refilling you up with minerals, potassium, sodium, and other good stuff. You'll feel better soon." She patted his forearm as she checked his leads, making physical contact before she looked at Ty, gesturing with her head for him to follow her.

"Is he going to be okay?" Ty asked quietly on the other side of the curtain.

"Soon as he sobers up."

"He's on something besides alcohol."

"Yes."

"Does he have a place to stay?"

She gave him a long once-over. "Look at you with all the questions."

"Does he?"

She sighed. "I'm sorry, but you know I can't discuss his case with you. I can tell you that he's being taken care of. Does that help?"

Yeah. No. Ty had no idea what the fucking lump the size of a regulation football was doing stuck in his throat or why his heart was pounding. Or why he couldn't let this go. "He's a vet," he said. "He's having nightmares. He—"

"I know," she said softly, and reached out to touch him, soothing him as she had Ryan. "And like I said, he's being taken care of." She paused, studying him for a disturbingly long beat. "Not everyone would have done that, you know. Gone in there and held a vagrant's hand and comforted him."

"I'm not everyone."

"No kidding." The phone at her hip vibrated. She looked at the screen and let out a breath. "Wait for me," she said, pointing to his cubicle. "I'll be right there." And then she moved off in the direction of the front desk.

In front of Ty was yet another bed. This curtain was shut but it was suddenly whipped open by a nurse who was talking to the patient sitting on the bed. "Change into the robe," she was saying. "And I'll go page your doctor."

The patient had clearly walked in under his own steam, but he wasn't looking good. He was a big guy, mid-thirties, dressed in coveralls that had the Public Utilities Department logo on a pec. He was filthy from head to toe, clearly just off the job. As Ty watched, he went from looking bad to worse, and then he gasped, clutching at his chest.

Oh, Christ, Ty thought. Why the hell was he here? He should have left. Instead, he was hurtled back in time, back to the mountain, squinting against the brilliant fireball that had been a plane. He'd sat on the cliff holding Trevor in his arms, Trevor clutching at his crushed chest.

A million miles and four years later, the guy on the hospital bed groaned, dropping the gown he'd been holding. He slithered to the floor, his eyes rolling up in the back of his head.

Ty took a step back and came up against a rolling cart of supplies even as his instincts screamed at him to rush over there and help.

But the cart moved out from behind him, and he staggered on legs that felt like overcooked noodles.

Then suddenly people came out of the woodwork, including Mallory.

"He's coding," someone yelled.

And the dance to save the man's life began. Someone pulled Ty out of the way and back to his cubicle, where he waited for what might have been five minutes, or an hour.

Or a lifetime.

Mallory finally came in. When she found him still standing, she gave him a sharp look. "Sorry about that. You okay?"

"The guy. Is he…?"

"He's going to make it." She gestured to the bed. "Sit. You look like you could use it."

Like hell he did.

"Sit," she said again, soft steel.

Fine. He sat. On the stool, not the bed. The bed was for patients, and he wasn't a patient. He was a fucking idiot, but he wasn't a patient.

"Not a big hospital fan, huh?" she asked wryly.

"No."

She washed her hands thoroughly. "Personal experience?"

He didn't answer, wasn't ready to answer. Apparently okay with that, she pulled on a pair of latex gloves, then opened a couple of drawers. "Are you squeamish?"

He didn't answer that either. Mostly because only yesterday he'd have given her an emphatic *no*. Except what had just happened to him in the hallway said otherwise.

He'd changed.

Once upon a time, nothing had gotten to him, but that was no longer true. Case in point was Mallory herself. She got to him, big time.

She lifted a big, fat needle, and he blinked.

She smiled and put the needle down, and he realized she'd been fucking with him to lighten the mood. He heard the surprised laugh rumble out of him, rusty sounding. Muscles long gone unused stretched as he smiled and shook his head. "Guess you owed me that."

"Guess I did." After she'd loaded up a tray with what she wanted, she came at him. She set the tray on the bed and perched a hip there as well, letting out an exhale that spelled exhaustion. "If you don't want to sit here, I sure as hell do."

He found himself letting out another smile. "Tired?"

"I passed tired about three hours ago." She soaked a gauze in rubbing alcohol.

"So you're an RN."

"Yes," she said. "I bought my license online yesterday." She dabbed at the wound over his eyebrow and then opened a suture kit, which he was intimately familiar with. As a medic in the field, he'd gone through a lot of them patching guys up.

"Don't worry," she said, picking up a set of tweezers. "I've seen a guy do this once."

He wrapped his fingers around her wrist, stopping her movement.

"I'm kidding," she said.

"Oh I know. I just don't want you to be cracking yourself up when you put those things near my eye."

"Actually, I'm not all that amused right now," she said.

"What are you, then?"

She hesitated. "Embarrassed," she finally admitted.

This stopped him cold. That was the *last* thing he wanted her to be. "Don't be embarrassed," he said. "Pick something else, *anything* else."

"Like?"

"Mad. Mad would be better."

"You want me to be mad at you?" she asked, looking confused. "Why? I'm the one who said the 'here' and 'now,' remember?"

Yeah, he remembered. He'd loved it.

"And *I'm* the one who wanted a one-time thing," she said. "No strings attached."

"So why be embarrassed then?"

She sighed.

"Tell me."

"Because I'd never done that before." She lowered her voice to a soft whisper. "Sex without an emotional attachment," she clarified. "And now..." Her eyes slowly met his. "I'm thinking I should have requested a two-time thing."

This left him speechless.

She winced, shook her head, then laughed a little at herself. "Never mind." She leaned in close to look at the stitching. "Nice work. Dr. Scott's the best," she said. "But you'll probably still have a decent scar. Shouldn't be too much of a problem for you, women like that sort of thing. Apparently they'll fall all over themselves to sleep with you."

Still holding her wrist, he ran his thumb over her pulse. "You didn't fall all over yourself," he said quietly.

"Didn't I?"

"If you did, there were two of us doing the falling."

Again, her eyes met his, and he watched her struggle to accept that. "Well," she finally said, pulling her hand free, "as long as there were two of us." Some of the good humor was now restored in her voice. Which meant she was compassionate, funny, *and* resilient. His favorite qualities in a woman.

But he wasn't looking for a woman. He wasn't looking for anything except to get back to his world where he functioned best.

She leaned in close and used the tweezers to pull up a stitch, which she then snipped with scissors. "A little sting now," she warned, and pulled out the suture. "So what was it that you said you do?"

Oh, she was good, he thought. Very good. "I didn't say."

She pulled out another stitch and then gazed steadily at him.

She had the most amazing eyes. Mostly chocolate brown, but there were specks of gold in there as well. And a sharp wit that stirred him even more than her hot, curvy little bod.

A woman poked her head around the curtain, the same one who'd been at the front desk. Young. Eager. "Need help?" she asked Mallory, her eyes on Ty.

"Nope," Mallory said. "I've got this."

Her face fell, but she left without further comment.

Two seconds later another nurse appeared, and this one Ty recognized as Mallory's mother from the night of the auction.

"New arrival," she said to Mallory, eyeing Ty.

"It's your turn," Mallory told her.

Her mom frowned. "*Mal.*"

"*Mother.*"

The curtain yanked shut, and they were alone. "She hates when I call her 'mother.'"

"You work with your mom."

Mallory took a page from his book and went silent. It made him smile. *She* made him smile.

"She looked pissed," he said, fishing. Which was new for him. He never fished. He hated fishing.

"Oh, she is," Mallory said. She pulled another stitch, and he barely felt it. She had good hands, as he had reason to know.

"Because of me?" he asked.

"Now why would you think that?" she asked. "Because I left my own fundraiser to have sex in a storage room with a man whose name I barely knew?"

"Really great sex," he corrected. When she slid him a long look, he added, "Imagine what we could do with a bed."

She let out a short laugh, and he stared at her face, truly fascinated by her in a way that surprised him. She was supposed to be just a woman, a cute nurse in a small town that soon he'd forget the name of.

Except...he wasn't buying it.

"Hey, Mal." Yet another woman peeked into the cubicle, this one mid-thirties and wearing a housekeeping outfit. "Need anything?"

"*No!*"

"Jeez," she said, insulted. "Fine, you don't have to take my head off."

When she vanished, Mallory sighed. "My sister." She dumped the instruments she'd used into the sink, and still facing away from him, spoke. "What about your leg?"

"What about it?"

"Does it need to be looked at, too?" she asked.

"No."

She turned to look at him with an expectant air, saying nothing. It made him smile. "You can't use that silence thing against me. I invented it."

"What silence thing?" she asked innocently.

"You know what silence thing, where you go all quiet and I'm supposed to feel compelled to fill it in with all my secrets."

She smiled. "So you admit to having secrets."

"Many," he said flatly.

Her smile faded. "You're engaged. Or worse, you're married. You have ten kids. Oh my God, tell me you don't have kids."

"No. And I'm not engaged or married. I'm not...anything."

She just looked at him for a long moment. "Some secrets are toxic if you try to keep them inside. You know that, right? Some secrets are meant to be told, before they eat you up."

Maybe, but not his. In no time, he'd be long gone, back to a very fast-paced, dangerous life that would eventually, probably kill him. But not her. She'd find someone to share her life with, grow old with. "You watch too much *Oprah*."

She didn't take umbrage at this. She pulled off her gloves and tossed them into the trash.

"Does your whole family work here?" he asked, running a finger over the healing cut, now sans stitches. She'd done a good job.

"Just my mom, my sister, and me," she said. "And I also work at the Health Services Clinic."

"I didn't know there was one here."

"Well, there's not. Not yet. But if we get approval at the town meeting tomorrow night, it's a go for a tentative opening this weekend."

"Is there a need in a town this small?"

"This hospital services the entire county," she said. "Not just Lucky Harbor. And there's a huge need. We have a high teenage pregnancy rate, and drug abuse is on the rise as well. So is abuse and homelessness. We need counseling services and advocacy and educational programs. And there's going to be a weekly health clinic on Saturday for those who can't afford medical care."

God, she was so fierce she made his heart ache. They could use her at his work, he thought, but was doubly glad that she pretty much embodied Lucky Harbor. Hopefully she'd never live through some of the horrors out there, or lose her genuine compassion to jaded cynicism. "So what makes a woman like you take on such a thing?" he asked.

"What do you mean?"

"Usually this sort of thing is driven by a cause. What's yours?"

She turned away, busying herself with washing her hands again.

"Ah," he said. "So I'm not the only one with secrets."

She turned back to him at that, eyes narrowed. "Tell you what. I'll answer one question for every question you answer for me."

He knew better than to go there. He might have treated her like a one-night stand but he knew damn well she was different. By all appearances, she was pretty and sweet and innocent, but beneath that guileless smile, she held all the power, and he knew it. She'd have him confessing his sins with one warm touch.

She isn't for you...

"Yeah," she said dryly, hands on hips. "I figured that'd be too much for you."

It was. Far too much. He was leaving...and yet he opened his mouth anyway. "What time do you get off?"

This shocked her, he could tell. Fair enough. He'd shocked himself too.

"Seven," she said.

"I'll pick you up."

"No," she said. "You know the pier?"

"Sure."

"I'll meet you there. In front of the Ferris wheel."

She didn't trust him. Smart woman. "Okay," he said. "In front of the Ferris wheel."

"How do I know you're going to remember to show up for *this* date?"

A date. Christ, it was utter insanity. But he looked into her beautiful eyes and nearly drowned. "Because this time I'm in charge of all my faculties," he said.

Except, clearly, he wasn't.

Chapter 9

Stress wouldn't be so hard to take if it were chocolate covered.

As Mallory got into her car after her shift, her phone rang from an unfamiliar number.

"*He came to the hospital to see you?*" Amy asked.

Mallory didn't bother to ask how Amy knew Ty had been at the hospital earlier. It was probably put out as an all points bulletin. "Whose cell phone is this?"

"I just found it at the diner. Don't tell Jan; she likes to keep all the leftover phones for herself."

"Amy! You can't just use someone's phone."

"And that," Amy said dryly, "is why you need Bad Girl lessons. Okay, impromptu meeting of the Chocoholics commencing right here, right now, because you're in crisis."

"I am not."

"Lesson number one," Amy went on without listening. "*Always* use a situation to your benefit."

"*That's* lesson number one?" Mallory said. "What's lesson number two?"

"Lesson number two is *not* to get your exploits recounted on Facebook. Rookie mistake, Mal."

Mallory sighed. "Do you have any wisdom that might actually be helpful?"

"Yeah." There was some muffled talking, and she came back on. "Grace is here. She needed a big, warm brownie after pounding the sidewalk today looking for a job. She says lesson number three is to understand that guys are about the visuals, and she's right. Always wear Bad Girl shoes and Bad Girl panties. They create the mood."

The panties were self-explanatory. "Bad Girl shoes? *You* wear steel-toed boots."

More muffled talking as Grace and Amy conferred on this subject.

"Okay," Amy came back to say. "Grace thinks it's a frame of mind. I'm a shit-kicker, so the boots work. You're...softer. You need high heels. Strappy. Sexy."

The thought of high heels after being on her feet all day made Mallory want to cry. Then she remembered how it had felt when Ty had put his hands on her ankles and removed her heels for her. She'd liked that, a lot. "My only heels hurt my feet."

"Get another pair. Lesson number four," Amy said. "Get a hold of his phone and scan through the contacts."

"I'm not going to run through his contacts!" Mallory paused and considered. "And what would I be looking for, anyway?"

"Anyone listed as *My Drug Dealer*. That's when you'd run not walk."

Mallory blinked. "The guy who left his phone at the diner has a contact that says *My Drug Dealer*?"

"And also *Bitch Ex-Wife*. Oh, and *Mommy*." Amy sighed. "*Not* a keeper."

Grace got on the phone then, her mouth sounding quite full. "You're going to have to make the next meeting in person, Mallory. This brownie is orgasmic."

She could use an orgasmic brownie. "One of you take a turn now."

"Well, Grace here has been turned down for all the jobs she applied for from the Canadian border to San Diego," Amy said. "So I'm considering pouring her a shot of something to go with the brownie. In the meantime, I called Tara at the B&B, and they had no problem giving her the local discount to keep staying there for cheap, since she's a local now. As for me," Amy said, "I'm status quo. Waiting for warmer weather to make my move."

"Your move on what?" Mallory asked.

"Life. In the meantime, we'll concentrate on you," she said. "You're the most screwed up so it makes the most sense. Get some bad girl shoes."

Mallory hung up and drove to the pier. When she got out, she took a moment to inhale the salty ocean air as the sound of the waves hitting the shore soothed her antsy nerves. At the pier's entrance, flyers were posted, one for an upcoming high school play, another for a musical festival the following week. But it was the flyer for the town's monthly Interested Citizens Meeting that caught her interest.

This was where Bill Lawson would pitch her Health Services Clinic and get the town's collective reaction.

In the meantime, she had another meeting, one that, according to her heart rate, was imminent. She'd changed into a summer dress she'd borrowed from Tammy's work locker. Tammy had superior clothes. This was what happened when one was married to a mall cop. By way of her husband, Tammy got a hell of a discount.

Walking to the Ferris wheel, Mallory took quick stock of her appearance. Not too bad, she thought, although her walking sandals were definitely not up to Bad Girl code.

Next time.

The night was warm and moist, and the waves rocked gently against the pylons far below the pier. The power beneath her feet made the pier shudder faintly with the push and pull of the tide, which matched the push and pull of anticipation drumming through her.

You are not going to sleep with him again, she told herself firmly. *That was just a one-time thing. You're only here now because you're curious about him.*

And also because he'd looked hot today at the hospital. Damn, she had a problem. A big, attracted-to-him-like-a-moth-to-a-flame-type problem. How that was possible, she had no idea. Their goodbye on the night of the auction had been…abrupt. Although *nothing* about what had occurred before that had felt abrupt. Nope, everything had been…*amazing.*

She stopped at the entrance to the line for the Ferris wheel. When her inner drumming turned into a prickle at the base of her neck, she turned in a slow circle.

And found Ty watching her.

He was leaning back against the pier railing, legs casually crossed at the ankles, looking for all the world like a guy who made it a habit to be carefree enough to walk a beach pier.

They both knew that wasn't true.

And good God, just looking at him did something to her. His hair was tousled, like he'd been shoving his fingers through it. Stubble darkened his jaw, and his firm, sensuous mouth was unsmiling. The scar above his brow was new and shiny, and the mirrored sunglasses only added to the whole ruffian look he had going on.

It suited him, in a big way.

He was dressed in cargoes and a dark T-shirt snug across his broad chest and loose over his abs. He looked big, bad, built, and dangerous as hell.

And he was hers for the evening.

Hers.

Not one of her smartest moves. But stretching her wings wasn't about keeping her head. It was about…being. Living.

Feeling.

And the man definitely made her feel, a lot. Already in their short acquaintance, he'd made her feel curious, annoyed, frustrated, and the topper…

Aroused.

She was feeling that right now in fact, in spades. She wanted to shove up his shirt and lick him from Adam's Apple to belly button.

And beyond.

Slowly he pushed the sunglasses to the top of his head and his stark green eyes locked unwaveringly on hers. She knew he couldn't really read her mind, but she jumped and flushed a little guiltily anyway for where her thoughts had gone.

He pushed away from the railing and came toward her, all those muscles moving fluidly and utterly without thought. She had no idea what she'd expected, but it wasn't for him to take her hand in his and pull her around to the side of the Ferris wheel, out of view, between a storage shed and the pier railing.

"W-what are you doing?"

He didn't answer. He merely put his big hands on her, lifted her up to her tiptoes, and covered her mouth with his.

Her purse fell in a thud at her feet. Her fingers slid into his hair. And when his tongue slid over hers, all her bones melted away.

Then before she knew it, the kiss was over and she was weaving unsteadily on her feet, blinking him into focus. "What was *that*?"

He scooped up her purse and handed it to her. "I lost my head. You're distracting."

"And you're not?"

His eyes heated. "We could fix that."

"Oh no," she said. "You said you weren't a long-term bet. You said you weren't even a short one."

"But I'm on your list. Your list of Mr. Wrongs."

"Yeah, about that. I've rearranged the order of the list." This was a bold-faced lie. She'd not rearranged the list. He *was* the list.

He raised a brow. "Did what's-his-name from the hardware store get ahead of me? The one who sleeps with anyone with boobs?"

"Maybe."

"I was at the hardware store today," he said. "Anderson was there, flirting with some cute young thing." Leaning in, his mouth found its way to her ear. "You can take Anderson off your list."

Oh no he didn't. He didn't just tell her what to do. "I—"

He pressed her into the railing and kissed her again. Apparently he didn't want to hear it. That was okay, because she forgot her own name, much less who was on her list. She had her tongue in his mouth, her hands in his silky hair, and her breasts mashed up to his hard, warm chest. She'd have climbed inside him if she could.

You came here to ask him questions.

In an attempt to go back to that, she squeezed her thighs, thinking *keep them together*, but his knee nudged hers, and then he slid a muscled thigh between hers. Good. Lord. He felt so...*good.* Drawing on some reserve of strength she didn't know she had, she pushed on his chest. For a beat he didn't budge, then he stepped slowly back, his eyes heavy-lidded and sexy.

"Okay," she said shakily. "Let's try something that's *not* going to lead to round two of sex in a public place." His expression was giving nothing away. Not exactly open, but she was a woman of her word, and she wanted to know he was a man of his. "What do you do for a living? Are you...military?" she asked, letting loose of the one thing she couldn't seem to get out of her head. It was the way he carried himself: calm, steady, looking ready for anything, and that bone-deep stoicism. Not to mention how he'd looked while at Ryan's bedside—like he knew to the depths of his soul what Ryan was feeling.

A low, wry laugh rumbled out of him. "So we're going to ease into this then."

"Yeah." She was glad to see the smile. "You don't know this about me, but I tend to jump in with both feet."

"I noticed." He looked at her, his eyes reminding her that he knew other things about her as well, things that made her blush. "At the moment I'm rebuilding a few cars."

This didn't exactly answer her question, and in fact, only brought on *more* questions. "So you're a mechanic?" she asked.

"While I'm here in lucky Harbor."

"But—"

"My turn. The other night. Why me?"

She squirmed a little at this, although it was a fair enough question. He already knew that what they'd done that night at the auction had been a first for her, but what he didn't know, *couldn't* know, was that she'd only been able to do it at all because she'd felt something for him. Which was crazy; they'd been perfect strangers. "Like I said, it'd been a long time."

"So I was handy?"

"Well, Anderson already had a date, so..."

He growled, and she laughed. "I don't know exactly," she admitted. "Except..." *Just say it.* "I felt a connection to you."

He was looking very serious now, and he slowly shook his head. "You don't want to feel connected to me, Mallory."

"No, I don't want to. But I do. And there's more."

"The whole bored and restless thing?" he asked.

So he'd *also* overheard her entire conversation with her mother. The man had some serious listening skills.

"You used me to chase away your restlessness," he said quietly.

"Yes." She winced. "I'm sorry about that."

"Mallory, you can use me any time."

"But you said one-time only," she reminded him.

"Actually, *you* said that. And plans change. Apparently I left you needing more, which is the same thing as unsatisfied in my book." His gaze went hot and dark. "We'll have to fix that."

She felt her body respond as if he'd already touched her. He hadn't left her unsatisfied at all. In fact, she'd never been more satisfied in her life. "Ice cream," she whispered, her throat suddenly very dry. "I think I need ice cream."

He smiled knowingly but didn't challenge her. They walked to the ice cream stand. The server was small for a guy in his early twenties and painfully thin, but the warm smile he flashed at Mallory distracted from his ill appearance. "Hey, Mal," he said. "Looking good today."

Lance gave her this same line every time that he landed in the ER. He could be flat on his back, at death's door—which with his Cystic Fibrosis happened more than anyone liked—and he'd *still* flash Mallory those baby blues and flirt.

He was one of her very favorite patients. "Where's your pretty girlfriend?" she teased, knowing he'd been dating another nurse, Nancy, for months now.

An attractive brunette poked her head out from behind Lance and smiled. "She's right here. Hey, Mallory" Nancy's eyes locked onto Ty and turned speculative. "Seems like Lance isn't the only one with a pretty date."

Mallory laughed at the look on Ty's face. He actually didn't react outwardly, but it was all in his eyes as he slid her a glance. She decided to take mercy on him and wrap things up. "I'll need a double scooped vanilla."

"So the usual," Lance said. "You ever going to branch out? Add a twist of cookie dough, or go for a walk on the wild side and add sprinkles?"

Mallory very carefully didn't look at Ty. "Not this time." She'd already taken her walk on the wild side, and wild walk on the dark side was standing right next to her.

Lance served Mallory, then looked at Ty, who shook his head. No ice cream for him.

Which was probably how he kept his body in such incredible shape, Mallory thought as she reached into her pocket for cash. Ty beat her to it, paying for her ice cream.

"Watching your girlie figure?" Mallory asked him, licking at the ice cream as they walked.

His eyes never left her tongue. "Girlie figure?"

There was nothing girlie about him, not one thing. "Maybe you're dieting," she said. Another lick. "Fighting the bulge."

Ty Garrison didn't have an ounce of fat on him, and they both knew it. But he did have a very dark, hot look as he watched her continue to lick at her cone. Like maybe he was a hungry predator and she was his prey. The thought caused another of those secret tingles.

"You think I'm fighting the bulge?" he asked softly.

She reached out and patted his abs. Her hand practically bounced off the tight muscles there. "I wouldn't worry about it. It happens to all of us," she said lightly, taking another slow lick of her ice cream. "Does your break from work have anything to do with your leg?"

"Yes." His eyes never left her mouth. She was playing with fire, and she knew it.

"You know this whole man of mystery thing isn't as cute as you might think," she said. "Right?"

"I'm not cute."

"No kidding!"

A very small smile curved his mouth as he studied her for a moment, as if coming to a decision. "You asked if I'm military. I was."

Her gaze searched his. "And now?"

"Like I said, I'm working on cars."

"And when you're not working on cars?" she asked with mock patience. "What do you do then?"

Again he just looked at her for a long beat. "It's in the same vein as mechanics. I locate a problem and...rectify it."

"But...not on cars."

"No," he agreed. "Not on cars."

Huh. He was certainly *not* saying more than he was saying. Which wasn't working for her. "And the leg?" she asked.

"I was in a crash."

He hadn't hesitated to say it but she sensed a big inner hesitation to discuss it further. "I'm sorry," she said, not wanting to push. She knew exactly what it felt like to *not* want to discuss something painful, but she was definitely wishing he'd say more. And then he did.

"I'm in Lucky Harbor until I'm cleared," he said. "Matt and I go way back. He set me up in a house to recoup."

"Are you…recouping okay?" she asked softly.

"Working on it."

She nodded and fought the ridiculous urge to hug him. He wouldn't want her sympathy, she knew that much. "The leg is giving you pain. Are you taking anything for it?"

"No," he said, and with a hand on the small of her back, led her into the arcade. Conversation over, apparently. He handed some money over to the guy behind the first booth.

Shooting Duck Gallery.

"What are you doing?" she asked.

"I'm going to shoot some ducks. And so are you."

"I'm not good at shooting ducks," she said, watching him pick up the gun like he knew what he was doing. He sighted and shot.

And hit every duck, destroying the entire row.

"Show off," she said, and picked up her gun. She didn't know what she was doing. And she didn't hit a single duck. She set the gun down and sighed.

"That's pathetic." Ty handed over some more cash and stood behind her. "Pick up the gun again." He corrected her stance by nudging his foot between hers, kicking her legs farther apart. Then he steadied her arms with his.

This meant he was practically wrapped around her, surrounding her. If she turned her head, she could press her mouth to his bicep. His very rock-solid bicep. It was shocking how much she wanted to do just that. She'd bet he'd taste better than her ice cream.

He went still, then let out a low breath, his jaw brushing hers. "You're thinking so loud I'm already hard."

She choked out a laugh, and he pressed himself against her bottom, proving he wasn't kidding. "How do you know what I'm thinking?" she asked, embarrassingly breathless. "Maybe I'm thinking that I want another ice cream."

"That's not what you're thinking. Shoot the ducks, Mallory."

With him guiding her, she actually hit one, and her competitive nature kicked in. "Again," she demanded.

With a rare grin, Ty slapped some more money onto the counter. "Show me what you've got," he said to her, and to her disappointment, this time he remained back a few steps, leaving her to do it alone.

She hit one more out of the entire row, which was *hugely* annoying to her. "How do you make it look so easy?"

"Practice," he said in a voice that assured her he'd had lots. "Your concentration needs some work."

Actually, there was nothing wrong with her concentration. She was concentrating just fine. She was concentrating on how she felt in his arms, with his hard body at her back.

She liked it. Far too much. "Maybe I don't care about being able to shoot a duck."

"No problem." He tossed down another few bucks and obliterated another row of ducks himself.

"Dude," the guy behind the counter said, sounding impressed as he presented Ty with a huge teddy bear as a prize.

Ty handed it to Mallory. "My hero," she murmured with a laugh, and he grimaced, making her laugh again as she hugged the bear close, the silly gesture giving her a warm fuzzy. Which was ironic because nothing about the big, tough Ty Garrison should have given her a warm fuzzy.

She knew he didn't want to be her hero.

He dragged her to the squirt gun booth next, where he proceeded to soundly beat her three times in a row. Apparently he wasn't worried about her ego. He won a stuffed dog at that booth, and then laughed out loud at her as she attempted to carry both huge stuffed animals and navigate the aisles without bumping into anyone.

Ridiculously, the whole thing gave her another warm fuzzy, immediately followed by an inner head smack. Because no way was she going to be the woman who fell for a guy just because he gave her a silly stuffed animal that she didn't need. *You're not supposed to fall for him at all*, she reminded herself. "This is very teenager-y of us," she said.

"If we were teenagers," he said, "we'd be behind the arcade, and you'd be showing me your gratitude for the stuffed animals by letting me cop a feel."

"In your dreams," she quipped, but her nipples went hard.

They competed in a driving game next, the two of them side by side in the booth, fighting for first place. Ty was handling his steering wheel with easy concentration, paying her no mind whatsoever. Mallory couldn't find her easy concentration, she was too busy watching him out of the corner of her eye. When she fell back a few cars as a result, Ty grinned.

Ah, so he *was* paying attention to her. Just to make sure, she nudged up against him.

His grin widened, but he didn't take his eyes off the screen. "That's not going to work, Mallory. You're going down."

Not going to work, her ass. She nudged his body with hers again, lingering this time, letting her breast brush his arm.

"Playing dirty," he warned, voice low, both husky and amused.

But she absolutely had his attention. She did the breast-against-his-arm thing again, her eyes on the screen, so she missed when he turned his head. But she didn't miss when he sank his teeth lightly into her earlobe and tugged. When she hissed in a breath, he soothed the ache with his tongue, and her knees wobbled. Her foot slipped off the gas.

And her car crashed into the wall.

Ty's car sped across the finish line.

"That's cheating!" she complained. "You can't—"

He grabbed her, lifting her up so that her feet dangled, and then kissed her until she couldn't remember what she'd meant to say. When he set her back down, she would have fallen over if he hadn't kept his hands on her. "You started it," he said. He gave her one more smacking kiss and then bought them both hot dogs for dinner. They sat on the pier, she and Ty and the two huge stuffed animals, and ate.

"So what are you doing to recover from the crash?" she asked.

"Swimming. Beating the shit out of Matt." He took the last bite of his hot dog. "Who's Karen?"

If her life had been a DVD, in that moment it would have skipped and come to a sudden halt, complete with the sound effect.

"I heard your mother say her name," he said, watching her face carefully. "And you got an odd expression, just like now."

"Karen's my sister." She paused, because it never got easier to say. "She died when I was younger."

Concern flashed in his eyes, stirring feelings she didn't want to revisit. Thankfully he didn't offer empty platitudes, for which she was grateful. But he did take her hand in his. "How?"

"Overdose."

His hand was big and warm and callused. He had several healing cuts over his knuckles, like he'd had a fight with a car part or tool. "How old were you?" he asked.

"Sixteen."

He squeezed her hand, and she blew out a breath. "You ever lose anyone?" she asked.

He didn't answer right away. She turned her head and looked at him, and found him studying the little flickers of reflection on the water as the sun lowered in the sky. "I lost my four closest friends all at the same time," he finally said and met her gaze. "Four years now, and it still sucks."

Throat tight, she nodded. "In the Army?"

"Navy. We were a crazy bunch, but it shouldn't have happened."

"All three of my siblings are a crazy bunch," she said. "Not military, of course, just…crazy."

He smiled. "Not you though."

"I have my moments." She blew out a breath. "Well, moment."

"Us."

She nodded.

"So I really am your walk on the wild side." He paused, then shook his head. "I'm still not clear on why you chose me."

"I'm not clear on a lot of things about myself." She met his gaze. "But in hindsight, I think it's because you're safe."

He stared at her, then laughed and scrubbed a hand over his face. "Mallory, I'm about as unsafe as you can possibly get."

Yeah. But for some reason, she'd somehow trusted him that night. She still did. "If you're swimming," she said, "you must be healing up pretty good. When do you get cleared to go back to work?"

He looked into her eyes, his own unapologetic. "Soon."

"And it won't be in Lucky Harbor," she said quietly. She knew it wouldn't, but she needed to hear it, to remind herself that this wasn't anything but an…interlude.

"No," he agreed. "It won't be in Lucky Harbor."

The disappointment was undeniable, and shockingly painful. She'd really thought she could do this with him, have it be just about the sex, but it was turning out not to be the case at all. With a sigh, she stood. He did as well, gathering their garbage and taking it to a trash bin before coming back to stand next to where she was looking out at the water.

"I can't do this," she whispered.

He nodded. "I know."

"I want to but I—"

"It's okay." He brushed a kiss over her jaw and then was gone, proving for the second time now that he was, after all, her perfect Mr. All Wrong.

Chapter 10

Chocolate is cheaper than therapy, and you don't need an appointment.

Two days later, Mallory entered the Vets' Hall for the town meeting and felt the déjà vu hit her. Pointedly ignoring the stairs to the second floor storage room, she strode forward to the big central meeting room. It was full, as all the town meetings tended to be.

Heaven forbid anyone in Lucky Harbor miss anything.

With sweaty palms and an accelerated heart rate, she found a seat in the back. Two seconds later, her sister plopped down into the chair next to her.

"Whew," Tammy said. "My dogs are tired." She leaned back and wriggled her toes. "You medical professionals are slobs, you know that? Took me an hour to clean up the staff kitchen, and I was ten minutes late getting off shift. And I was scheduled to have a quickie with Zach on his twenty-minute break too. We had to really amp it up to get done in time."

"That's great. I really needed to know that, thank you." Mallory glanced over at the glowing Tammy. There was no denying that she seemed...well, not settled exactly, and certainly not tamed, but *content.*

"Why are you looking at me like that?" Tammy asked. "Do I look like I just had a screaming orgasm? Cuz I totally did."

Mallory grimaced. "Again, thanks. And I'm looking at you because you look happy. Really happy."

"I should hope so. Because Zach just—"

Mallory slapped her hands over her ears, and Tammy grinned. "Wow, Mal, you almost over-reacted there for a second. One would almost think you hadn't had sex in forever, which isn't true at all."

"How in the world did you know that?"

Tammy grinned. "Well, I didn't know for sure until now. Mysterious Cute Guy, right? When? The night of the auction when you vanished for an hour and then reappeared with that cat-in-cream smile? *I knew it.*"

Mallory choked. "I—"

"Don't try to deny it. Oh, and give me your phone for a sec."

Still embarrassed, Mallory handed over her phone, then watched as Tammy programmed something in. "What are you doing?"

"Making sure you can't forget your new boyfriend's name," Tammy said. "Here ya go."

Mallory stared down at the newest entry in her contact list. "Mysterious Cute Guy, aka Ty Garrison." She stared at Tammy. "Where did you get his number?"

"He left a message for Dr. Scott at the nurse's desk, including his cell phone number. I accidentally-on-purpose memorized it."

"You can't do that—"

"Oh relax, Miss Goodie Two-Shoes. No one saw me."

"*Tammy—*"

"Shh, it's starting." Tammy turned to face forward with a mock excited expression as the meeting was called to order.

Mallory bit her fingernails through the discussion of a new measure to put sports and arts back in the schools, getting parking meters along the sidewalks downtown, and whether or not the mayor, Jax Cullen, was going to run for another term.

Finally, the Health Services Clinic came up. Bill Lawson stood up and reiterated the bare bones plan and the facts, and then asked for opinions. Two attendees immediately stood up in the center aisle in front of the microphone set up there. The first was Mrs. Burland.

"I'm against this health clinic and always have been," she said, gripping her cane in one hand and pointing at the audience with a bony finger of her other. "It'll cost us—the hardworking taxpayers—money."

"Actually," Bill interrupted to say. "We've been given a large grant, plus the money raised at auction. There's also future fundraising events planned, including next week's car wash." He smiled. "Mallory Quinn talked everyone on the board into working the car wash, so I'm expecting each and every one of you to come out."

There was a collective gasp of glee. The hospital board was a virtual Who's Who of Lucky Harbor, including some very hot guys such as the mayor, Dr. Scott, and Matt Bowers, amongst others.

"Even you, Bill?" someone called out.

"Even me," Bill answered. "I can wash cars with the best of them."

Everyone *woo-hoo*'d at that, and Mallory relaxed marginally. Bill had just guaranteed them a huge showing at the car wash. People would come out in droves to see the town's best and finest out of their positions of honor and washing cars. They'd pay through the nose for it as they took pictures and laughed and pointed.

Lucky Harbor was sweet that way.

Still in the aisle, Mrs. Burland tapped on the microphone, her face pinched. "Hello! I'm still talking here! HSC will bring *undesirables* to our town. And we already have plenty of them." Her gaze sorted through the crowd with the speed and agility of an eagle after its prey, narrowing in on Mallory way in the back.

"Bitch," Tammy muttered.

Mallory just sank deeper into her seat.

"You all need to think about that," Mrs. Burland said and moved back to her seat.

Sandy, the town clerk and manager, stood up next. "I'm also against it," she said with what appeared to be genuine regret. "I just don't think we need to deplete our resources with a Health Services Clinic. Not when our library has no funds, our schools are short-staffed due to enforced layoffs, and our budget isn't close to being in balance. We could be allocating donations in better ways. I'm sorry, Mal, very sorry."

The audience murmured agreement, and two more people stood up to say they were also against the Health Services Clinic.

Then it was Lucille's turn. She stood up there in her bright pink tracksuit and brighter white tennis shoes, a matching pink headband holding back her steel grey/blue hair. She took a moment to glare at Mrs. Burland in the front row. The rumor was that they'd gone to high school together about two centuries back, and Mrs. Burland had stolen Lucille's beau. Lucille had retaliated by eloping with Mrs. B's brother, who'd died in the Korean War—not on the front lines but in a brothel from a heart attack.

Lucille was so short that the microphone was about a foot above her head. This didn't stop her. "A Health Services Clinic would be nice," she said, head tipped up toward the microphone, her blue bun all aquiver. "Because then, if I thought I had the clap, I'd have a place to go."

The audience erupted in laughter.

"What?" she said. "You think I'm not getting any?" She turned and winked at Mr. Murdock in the third row.

Mr. Murdock grinned at her, his freshly washed dentures so unnaturally bright white they appeared to be glowing.

Lucille winked back, then returned to the business at hand. "Also, we couldn't have an HSC in better hands than those of our very own Mallory Quinn. She's a wonderful nurse and has her degree in business as well. She's one smart cookie."

Tammy turned to Mallory. "Did you actually graduate with both of those degrees?" she asked, clearly impressed.

Mallory slid her a look. "You were at my graduation."

Tammy searched her brain and then shook her head. "I've got nothing. In my defense, I spent those years pretty toasted."

Lucille was still talking. "I know some of you might say that Mallory's too sweet to handle such a big responsibility as the HSC, and that her programs involving drug rehab and teenage pregnancies will be overrun by dealers and pimps. But we're not giving our girl enough credit. If she can't handle the riffraff that her clinic brings into town, well then her new boyfriend certainly can."

"Oh my God." Mallory covered her eyes. "I can't look."

Tammy snorted. "At least she didn't call him your lover. And that's not even your biggest problem. That honor goes to the fact that your only supporter so far is a crazy old bat."

"You know, *you* could get up there and support me," Mallory said.

"Not me," Tammy said. "I'm shy in front of a crowd."

Yeah, right.

Lucille took her seat. Four more people had their say, not a single one of them in favor of the HSC. Tammy had to practically sit on Mallory to keep her in her chair.

"Beating them up isn't going to help," Tammy said.

Mallory's phone was buzzing with incoming texts, like the one from her mother that said:

He's your boyfriend?

Finally, a tall, broad-shouldered guy in faded jeans and mirrored sunglasses stood at the microphone, which came up to his chest.

Ty Garrison.

By this time, Mallory was so low in her chair that she could hardly see him, but to make sure she couldn't, she once again covered her face with her hands.

"Gee, Mallory, that works like a charm," Tammy whispered. "I can't see you there at all."

Mallory smacked her.

Ty spoke, his voice unrushed and clear. "The Health Clinic will improve the quality of life for people who'd otherwise go without help."

The audience murmured amongst themselves for a beat. Then came from one of the naysayers, "There's other places in other towns for people to get that kind of help."

"Yeah," someone else called out. "People here don't need the HSC."

"You're wrong," Ty said bluntly. "There are people in Lucky Harbor who *do* need the sort of services that HSC will provide. Veterans, for instance."

No one said a word now, though it was unclear whether they were scared of Ty's quiet intensity or simply acknowledging the truth of what he said.

"You can keep sticking your heads in the sand," he went on. "But there are people who need help managing their addictions, people who don't have a way to find a place to go that's safe from violence, teens who can't get STD education or birth control. These problems are real and growing, and a Health Services Clinic would be an invaluable resource for the entire county." He paused. Could have heard a pin drop. "And Lucille's right," he said into the silence. "You couldn't have a better person running such a place than your own Mallory Quinn. Each of you should be trying to help. I'll start by donating enough money for a program for veterans, where they can get assistance in rehabilitation or job opportunities, or simply to re-acclimate to society."

Mallory's mouth fell open.

The entire place went stock still. A real feat when it came to the people of Lucky Harbor. No one even blinked.

"He is so hot," Tammy whispered to Mallory. "You really ought to keep him."

"Can't," Mallory said, staring at Ty in shock through the fingers she still had across her eyes. "We've agreed it was a one-time thing."

"Well, that was stupid. You can put your hands down now. It's safe. No one's going to dare cross him. He's pretty badass."

He *was* pretty badass standing up there, steady as a rock, speaking his mind. *Offering his help*...

"Hey, didn't he also save your ass at the auction too by getting the bidding going?" Tammy asked.

Yeah, he had, and here he was at it again. Saving her ass.

As if sensing her scrutiny, he met her gaze for one long charged beat across the entire audience before walking back up the aisle to leave.

He'd stood up in front of the entire town and defended her. Her, a one-night stand. *What did that mean?* It meant he cared, she decided. The knowledge washed over her, and she sat up a little straighter, craning her neck to watch him go.

"My boyfriend's ever so dreamy," Tammy whispered mockingly.

Mallory smacked her again.

In spite of Ty's rather commanding appearance, the next three people who stood up opposed the clinic. Then Ella Quinn had her turn. Still in her scrubs, she grabbed the microphone. "This is poppycock," she said. "Anyone against this clinic is selfish, ungiving, and should be ashamed of themselves. As for my daughter Mallory, you all know damn well that she can be trusted to handle the HSC and any problems that might arise. After all, she's handled her crazy family all her life without batting so much as an eyelash." She searched the audience, found Joe in the fourth row, and gave him a long look. "And call your mamas. No one's calling their mamas often enough. That is all."

Joe slunk in his seat, his shoulders up around his ears. The little blonde sitting next to him gave him a hit upside the back of his head.

The meeting ended shortly after that, and Mallory was rushed with people wanting their questions answered. Would she really be supplying drug dealers? Doling out abortions? It was an hour before she was free, and even knowing she wouldn't find him, she looked around for Ty.

But he was long gone.

That afternoon, a spring storm broke wild and violent over Lucky Harbor. Ty worked on the Shelby, and when he was done, he drove through the worst of the rain, flying through the steep, vivid green mountain canyons, his mind cleared of anything but the road. For once he wasn't thinking of the past, or work.

He was thinking of a certain warm, sexy nurse.

He'd shelved his emotions years ago at SEALs training camp, long before he'd ever met one Mallory Quinn. But no amount of training could have prepared him for her.

She was a one-woman wrecking crew when it came to the walls he'd built up inside, laying waste to all his defenses. Only a few weeks ago, there wasn't a person on earth who could have convinced him that she would have the power to bring him to his knees with a single look.

And yet she could. She had.

A few hours later, the storm was raging as he came back through Lucky Harbor. At a stop sign, he came up behind a stalled VW. Through the driving rain, he could see a woman fiddling beneath the opened hood, her clothes plastered to her. Well, hell. He pulled over, and as he walked toward her, she went still, then reached into the purse hanging off her shoulder.

Ty recognized the defensive movement and knew she had her hand on some sort of weapon. He stopped with a healthy distance between them and lifted his hands, hopefully signaling that he was harmless. "Need some help?"

"No." She paused. "Thank you, though. I'm fine."

He nodded and took in her sodden clothes and the wet hair dripping into her eyes. Then he looked into the opened engine compartment of the stalled car. "Wet distributor cap?"

Her eyes revealed surprise. "How did you know?"

"It's a '73 VW. Get the cap wet, and it won't run."

She nodded and relaxed her stance, taking her hand out of her purse. "I was going to dry the cap on my skirt but it's too wet." She shoved her hair back from her face and blinked at him. "Hey, I know you. You're Mysterious Cute Guy."

Christ how he hated that moniker. "Ty Garrison."

"I'm Grace Brooks. One of your three guardian angels in that freak snowstorm last week." She flashed a grin. "I'm the one who called 9-1-1."

"Then the least I can do is this." He came closer and took the distributor cap from her, wiping it on the hem of his shirt, which hadn't yet gotten drenched through. When he had the inside of the cap as dry as it was going to get, he replaced it and got her off and running.

Back in his own car, he ended up at the diner. Amy and Jan were there, Jan's gaze glued to the TV in the far corner. *American Idol* was on, and she was very busy yelling at the screen. "Okay, come on! That *sucked*. God, I miss Simon. He always told it like it was."

Amy rolled her eyes and met Ty at a table with a coffee pot. Guardian Angel Number Two, in a pair of low-slung cargoes and a snug, lacy tee. Normally she was alert as hell and on-guard but tonight her face was pale, her smile weak. "Pie?" she asked.

"Sure."

She came back two minutes later with a huge serving of strawberry pie. "You're in luck," she said. "It's Kick Ass Strawberry Pie from the B&B up the road. That means Tara made it," she explained to his blank look. "Best pie on the planet, trust me."

That was quite the claim but one bite proved it to be true. Ty watched Amy refill his cup, then gestured to the towel she had wrapped around the palm of her left hand. "You okay?"

"Fine."

Bullshit. Her other hand was shaking, and she looked miserable. But hell, if she wanted to pretend she was fine, it was none of his business. Especially since he was the master at being *fine.*

Problem was, there was blood seeping through her towel. "Do you need a doctor?"

"No."

He nodded and ate some more pie. Good. She was fine and didn't need a doctor. And God knew, he sure as hell didn't want to get involved. But when he was done, he cleared his own plate, bringing it to the kitchen himself.

"Hey," Jan yelled at him, not taking her gaze off the TV. "You can't go back there. It's against the rules."

"Your waitress is bleeding. That's against the rules too."

This got Jan's attention. Jan glanced into the back at Amy and frowned before turning back to Ty. "You going to patch her up? She has an hour left on her shift."

He had no idea what the hell he thought he was doing. He hadn't "patched" anyone up in a damn long time. Four years, to be exact. He waited for the sick feeling to settle in his gut, but all he felt was a need to help Amy. "Yeah. I can patch her up."

Amy was standing at the kitchen chopping block, hands flat on the cutting board, head bowed, her face a mask of pain. She jumped when she saw Ty and shook her head. "Guests aren't supposed to clear their own dishes."

"I'm going to ask you again. Do you need a doctor?"

"It was just a silly disagreement with a knife."

Not an answer. He unwrapped her hand himself and looked down at the cut. "That's more than a silly disagreement. You need stitches."

"It's just a cut."

"Uh-huh. And you need the ER."

"No, I don't."

There was something edgy in Amy's voice now, something Ty recognized all too well. For whatever reason, she had a fear or deep-rooted hatred of hospitals. He could sympathize. "You have a first-aid kit?"

"Yeah."

He drew a deep breath, knowing if he didn't help her, she'd go without it. "Get it."

The diner's first-aid box consisted of a few Band-Aids and a pair of tweezers, so Ty went to his car. He always kept a full first-aid kit in there, even though he hadn't ever cracked this one open. He returned to the kitchen and eyed Amy's wound again. He had Steri-strips but the cut was a little deep for that. "Trust me?" he asked her.

"Hell no."

Good girl, he thought. Smart. "Me or the hospital, Amy."

She blew out a breath. "All I need is a damn Band-Aid. And hurry. I have customers."

"They'll wait." She was looking a little greener now. He pushed her onto the lone stool in the kitchen. "Put your head down."

She dropped it to the counter with an audible thunk. He disinfected the wound, then opened a tube.

Head still down, she turned it to the side to eyeball what he was doing. "*Super glue?*" she squeaked.

"*Skin* glue. And hold on tight, it stings like hell." He started, and she sucked in a breath. "You okay?"

She nodded, and he worked in silence, finally covering the wound with a large waterproof bandage.

"Thanks." Amy let out a shuddery sigh. "Men are assholes. Present company excluded, of course."

With a shrug—men *were* assholes, himself included—he gestured to her hand. "How's that feel?"

She opened and closed her fist, testing. "Not bad. Thanks." She watched him put everything back into his kit. "Does Mallory know that you're as good with your hands as she is?"

"I don't answer trick questions."

She started to laugh, but choked it off at the man who suddenly appeared in the kitchen doorway.

It was Matt, still in uniform, brow furrowed. "Jan said you're all bloody and—" His eyes narrowed on the blood down Amy's white tee. "What the hell happened?"

"Nothing," she said.

"Jesus Christ, Amy." He picked up the bloody towel and jerked his gaze back to her, running it over her body, stepping close.

Amy turned her back on him, on the both of them, and Matt looked at Ty. "What happened to her?"

"She's declined to say."

"A knife," Amy said over her shoulder. "No big deal. Now go away. No big, bad alpha males allowed in the kitchen."

Not even a glimmer of a smile from Matt, which was unusual. Ty hadn't any idea that Matt had something going with the pretty, prickly waitress, which was telling in itself. Usually the affable, easygoing Matt was an open book, not the type to let much get to him. But there was a whole bunch of body language going on, all of it heating up the kitchen.

Then Amy made an annoyed sound and walked to the doorway. For emphasis, she jerked her head, making her wishes perfectly clear. She wanted them out.

Matt waited a beat, just long enough for Amy to give him a little shove. She wasn't tall by any means, though her platform sneakers gave her some extra inches. Still, Matt was six feet tall and outweighed her by a good eighty pounds. She could push him around only if he allowed it, but to Ty's shock, Matt acquiesced, and with a softly muttered "fuck it," he left.

Ty followed him out, telling himself that he wasn't here to get involved. If he had been, he'd have talked himself into Mallory's bed tonight—and he could have.

Easily.

That wasn't ego, just plain fact. She wanted him. He wanted her right back, more than he could have possibly imagined. Right this minute, he could be wrapped up in her sweet, warm limbs, buried deep. "Shit."

"Yeah," Matt muttered as they strode out to the parking lot side by side. "Shit."

"What was that back there?" Ty asked him.

"I don't want to talk about it."

"Why the fuck does that work for you and not me?"

Matt ignored this to stare in appreciation at the Shelby. "You get the suspension done?"

"Yeah, but there's still a lot left to do. I've been busy on your Jimmy. Almost done, by the way."

"Good. So how's this baby running?"

"Better than any other area of my life."

Matt laughed ruefully and slid into the passenger seat of the Shelby. Apparently Ty was getting company for his late night ride tonight. Silent, brooding company, but that suited him just fine.

Chapter 11

Eat a square meal a day—a box of chocolate.

On Saturday, the doors of the HSC opened to the public. The town hadn't exactly been on board, but enough tentative support had trickled in that Mallory had been able to talk Bill into giving her the one-month trial.

Mallory knew she had Ty to thank for starting that tentative support. After the town meeting, a handful of locals had pledged money for certain programs. Ford Walker and Jax Cullen, co-owners of the local bar, had donated money for a Drink Responsibly program. Lucille was donating supplies from her art gallery for an art program. Lance, Mallory's favorite CF patient, had donated time to help counsel the chronically ill. Every day someone else called. Bill decided it was too much money and goodwill to turn away and had given Mallory approval. But things had to go smoothly or it'd be over.

For now, they'd be open five days a week for services providing crisis counseling, and education and recovery programs. And on Saturdays, the HSC turned into a full-blown medical clinic.

They saw patients nonstop, thanks to their first attending physician, Dr. Scott. As Mallory began to close up at the end of the day, Josh came out from the back.

After a long day, Josh looked more badass ruffian than usual. His doctor's coat was wrinkled and he still had his stethoscope hanging around his neck. His dark hair was ruffled, his darker eyes lined with exhaustion. But there was a readiness to him that said he wasn't too tired to kick ass if needed. He'd worked a double shift to volunteer his time today, but Mallory knew his day wasn't over, not even close. He still had to go home to more responsibility—a young son, not to mention his own handicapped sister, both of whom he was solely responsible for.

"Nice job today," he said to Mallory.

"Thanks to you."

He lifted a shoulder, like it was no big deal. He was a big guy, over six feet and built like a bull in a china shop, which made his talent all the more impressive. He might be serious and just a little scary, but he was the most approachable doctor she'd ever met. He was also her favorite because he treated the nurses with respect. Such behavior should be automatic in doctors, but so often wasn't. This conduct also tended to land him on Lucille's *Most Wanted Single Male* list on Facebook far too often, which drove him nuts.

"I'm glad you got approval for this," he said. "You're doing something really good here."

She glowed over that as she locked up behind him. As the last staff member there, she walked each of the rooms, cleaning up a little as she went. They had two exam rooms, a very small staff kitchen, and the front reception area. There was a back walk-in closet being renovated for their drug lock-up, but for now the drugs and samples were kept in one exam room in a locked cabinet. The reception area was big enough to host groups, which was what they would likely have to do during the week.

Tomorrow night was their first scheduled AA meeting. Monday night would be Narcotics Anonymous—NA. Wednesday nights would host a series of guest speakers, all aimed at teen advocacy programs.

It was all finally happening, and it made Mallory feel useful. Helpful. Maybe she hadn't been able to help Karen, but she could reach others.

By the time she locked the front door and got to her car, yet another storm was rolling in. Night had fallen, and the lot wasn't as well-lit as she'd like. She was on the back side of the hospital, the entrance leading to a narrow side street. She made a note to get the lighting fixed tomorrow and slid into her car just as the sky started dumping rain. She inserted her key in the ignition and turned it.

Nothing, just a click. She tried again anyway and got nowhere. A dead battery, naturally. She peered out her windshield and sighed. Walking home would be a five-mile trek in the pouring rain, which she was far too tired for. Plus her feet hurt from being on them all day. With a grimace, she pulled out her phone and called Joe.

"Yo," her brother said. "Bad time."

"Bad time for me, too. I need you to come jump my car. I have a dead battery."

"You leave your lights on again?"

"No." *Maybe.* "You owe me, Joe." She had to put that one out there right away to start the negotiations. Joe was a deal maker and only dealt at all if the odds were in his favor. "I let you and your idiot friends borrow my car, remember?" she asked. "You needed more seats to get to that stupid trail party out at Peak's Landing. Maybe this is somehow your fault."

"No, the crack in the windshield is our fault. Not the battery."

She stared at the small crack in the windshield on the passenger's side and felt an eye twitch coming on. "Come on, Joe. I could really use your help tonight."

"Christ. Hang on." He covered the phone and murmured something to someone.

A muted female voice laughed, and then Joe was back. "Mal, if all you need is a jump, ask anyone around you." He lowered his voice. "I'm on a date. With *Ashley*."

She had no idea who Ashley was but she was assuming it *wasn't* his blonde. "What happened to whatshername?"

"That was so last week."

Mallory let out a disgusted sigh. "You're a man ho."

"Guilty," he said. And hung up.

Grinding her teeth, Mallory called him back.

He didn't pick up.

"Dammit." She scrolled through her contact list again. Her mother was out of the question. Ella wouldn't have a set of jumper cables, not to mention she'd want to talk about Mallory's social life. Maybe Tammy, she thought, and hit her sister's number. "Can Zach come give me a jump?"

"Honey," Tammy said. "He's a little busy jumping *me* right now."

Oh, for God's sake. Mallory hung up, her usually dormant temper beginning to steam. She would drop everything for any one of her family, and not a single one of them could help her. This depressing thought didn't change the fact that she was still wet, cold, and stranded in a dark parking lot. Again she thumbed her contacts and stopped at one in particular.

Mysterious Cute Guy, aka Ty Garrison.

She had the stuffed animals he'd won at the arcade sitting on her bed, like she was twelve and in middle school, going steady with the town bad boy.

Except would the bad boy really have stood up at a town meeting in front of everyone and defended her? Would he have stopped and helped a stranded woman on the side of the road? Grace had told her what he'd done. And so had Amy, saying that he'd patched her up with calm efficiency.

Yeah, Ty was far more than just some mechanic, though hell if she could figure him out.

She shouldn't call him for help. For one, they'd had inappropriate sex without involvement. To compound that mistake, she'd discovered she liked him. A lot. And to compound *that* mistake, she was dreaming about sleeping with him some more.

All really good reasons not to call him.

But then there was the one really good reason *to* call him.

He would actually come. She hit his number and held her breath. He picked up on the fourth ring, his voice low and calm as always. "Garrison," he said.

"Hi. It's Mallory."

He absorbed that information for a moment, probably wondering how she'd gotten his number, a conversation she absolutely didn't want to have so she rushed on. "I'm at the HSC," she said, "and my car won't start, and I'm the only one left here, and the stupid parking lot lights aren't working and—"

"Lock your doors. I'll be right there."

"Okay, thanks—" But he was already gone. She slipped her phone into her pocket and put her head down on the steering wheel. So tired...She thought about that and how her feet hurt. She could really use a foot rub. And a body rub. She'd gotten a massage once, last year for her birthday. It'd been a present from Tammy. Her masseuse had been Chloe Traeger, who worked at the Lucky Harbor B&B where there was a lovely day spa. The massage had been fantastic but Mallory wondered what it would be like to have a man rub his hands over her body.

And not just any man, either.

She knew exactly which one she wanted. Ty. She sighed again, picturing lying on her back on a deserted beach at sunset, Ty leaning over her in a pair of low-slung jeans and nothing else, his big hands all over her bikini-clad body.

No, scratch that.

No bikini. And Ty in board shorts. Yeah, board shorts that fell disturbingly low on his hips, his eyes creased in that way he had of showing his feelings without moving his mouth. Mmm, that was a much better image, and she sighed dreamily.

He was aroused. She could feel him when he leaned over her. Big. Hard. She smiled up at him.

Instead of smiling back, he flipped her over, face down on her towel, leaving her to gasp in shock, waiting breathlessly for him to touch her. When his lips brushed her shoulder, she wriggled for more.

"Lie still." His voice was a thrillingly rough command that she didn't obey, making him groan. He said her name in a warning whisper, running a finger down her spine, then between her legs until she was writhing with a moan of arousal.

He did it again.

And then again, until she was oscillating her hips in small, mindless circles, trying to get more of his fingers. He pushed a thigh between hers to spread her legs, and then pulled her up to her knees and entered her.

She came hard, her cries swallowed when she pressed her face to the forearm he had braced on the towel beneath her. He was right behind her, shuddering in pleasure as he collapsed on top of her—

A rap on her window had her jerking straight up and banging her head on her sun guard.

Mouth quirking, Ty waited patiently while she fumbled to roll down the window.

"Hi," she said breathlessly. "I was just..." God. *Dreaming about you making me come.*

"Sleeping?" he asked.

Or that. Which was far less embarrassing. She nodded and swiped at her sweaty temple with her arm. "Guess I'm tired."

"You look all flushed; you okay?"

She pressed her thighs together. She was more than flushed. "Yeah."

"Try starting it now."

She realized that not only had she slept through him parking next to her, he'd popped both their hoods and had hooked her car up to a set of cables.

Some nap. At least she hadn't screamed out his name. She turned the key, and her car started.

Ty turned and bent over her front end, his head buried beneath her hood. Absolutely *not* noticing how very fine his ass looked from that position, she pushed out of the car and stood next to him.

"You're going to need a new alternator sooner than later," he said.

She stared into the engine compartment, completely clueless about where the alternator might be. "Is that expensive?"

"Not for the part." He was still fiddling around. "The labor's expensive, but it shouldn't be. It's an easy thing to replace."

"So you *are* a mechanic."

He was still messing with…something. He pulled out her dip stick and checked the oil. "Always been pretty good with taking things apart and putting them back together again," he said.

She could vouch for that. A week ago, he'd certainly taken her apart and put her back together again. The ease with which she'd come for him in the storage attic still fueled her fantasies. She'd had sex before, even some pretty good sex, but she'd never gone off like *that.* "I don't think that was much of an answer," she said.

He looked at her. "You don't think so?"

"No."

His mouth curved. "Anyone ever tell you that you're a little—"

"Stubborn? Determined? Annoying?" She nodded. "Yep. Trust me, I've heard it all."

"You need oil. And I work for a government contractor doing the same sort of stuff I did in the military."

"Stuff?" Her inner slut drooled over the sleek back muscles bunching, stretching the material of his shirt taut as he replaced the dip stick. "Like I'd-tell-you-but-I'd-have-to-kill-you stuff?"

He actually turned his head her way and smiled, knocking off a few million of her brain cells. This wasn't good. She needed those brain cells.

"Something like that," he said.

Classified, she thought. Interesting. Disconcerting. But it certainly explained the always-ready air he had and the fact that he looked like a military recruitment poster, only better. She could see him in hot zones all over the world, working on machinery. Tanks. Subs. Missiles. Or maybe his mechanical talents were ship-oriented. He'd said Navy...Her stomach knotted at the thought of how dangerous his life must be. "You patched up Amy at the diner. That was nice of you."

This yielded her a shrug.

She waited for more information, anything, which of course was not forthcoming. "It's a good thing you look good in jeans."

Still beneath the hood, he turned his head and flashed her a quick smile.

"You're a conundrum, you know," she told him. "I mean you've got this whole hands-off thing going about you, and yet you have no problem putting your hands all over me."

"And mouth," he added helpfully. "I like my mouth on you."

Her entire body quivered. "What is it about me that you're attracted to?"

"For starters, the sexy underwear you put on beneath your clothes."

"You've only seen my underwear once."

"Twice," he said. "I looked down your top at the pier."

"You did not."

"Pink-and-white polka-dot bra."

"Oh my God."

"That's what I was thinking." He straightened out from beneath her hood. "And also, while we're on the subject, I like the noises you make when you—"

She covered his mouth with her hand.

He nipped at her fingers, and her knees wobbled. Stupid knees.

"I like your eyes," he said.

"What?"

"Yeah, I like the way they soften when you look at me."

She stared at him, wondering if he was just giving her a line, but he held her gaze evenly. "Keep going," she said slowly.

"I like the way you'd dive into a freak snowstorm to help a perfect stranger. I like how you treat everyone as if they're important, including a homeless drug addict. I like that you give one-hundred percent to every part of your life. You don't hold back, Mallory."

"You... you like all that about me?"

"And also that you like me." He smiled again. "I really like that."

"How about the fact that you're pretty cocky? Do you like that?"

"Mmm-hmm. And I especially like when you use the word *cock* in a sentence."

She pushed him, and he laughed, so she added another push, and of course, he didn't budge, the lout. Instead, he stepped into her, backing her to the car. "What do you like about me?" he asked.

"*Nothing.*"

He grinned. "That's not true. You like it when I—"

"Don't you say it."

"That's okay," he said. "I'm better with showing, not telling, anyway." And he covered her mouth with his. And then his hands got into the fray, and she heard a low, desperate moan.

Hers.

His big palm cupped the back of her head as he changed the kiss from sweet and friendly-like to demanding and firm and... God. *Hungry*. His hand fisted in her hair then, and he kissed her like he was starving for the connection.

Mallory was right there with him. By the time the kiss was over, neither of them were breathing steadily. "Wow," she said and shook her head to clear it. "You ought to be careful with those. A girl might forget herself."

Thoroughly challenged, he reached for her again, but she jumped back. "Oh, no," she said on a laugh. "You're lethal, you know that?"

"Am I still on your list?"

"Well, let's see. It is a list of Mr. Wrongs, and you're just biding your time until you're gone, which pretty much means you *define* Mr. Wrong." She narrowed her eyes and studied him. "But then you show up at the town meeting—after avoiding everyone for months, I might add—and stick up for me." She shook her head. "Who are you, Ty Garrison?"

Apparently he didn't have an answer for that because he was back beneath her hood. "When's the last time you had anyone look at this poor baby?"

"Uh…"

He shook his head and kept fiddling, muttering something about "the lack of respect for the vehicle, even if it *is* a piece of shit."

"Where did you learn respect for *your* vehicles?" she asked, teasing.

"My dad. He was a mechanic in the Navy."

"Ah. So it runs in the family."

"Yeah. And my mom was Air Force."

She smiled at that. "A military brat through and through, huh?"

"All I ever knew," he agreed, tightening some part or another.

"Which is why you're interested in a Vet program at the HSC," she guessed. And personal experience. And he'd made good on his promise too. She'd gotten a nice check, earmarked for what would be a damn good program by the time she was finished with it. Ty had asked her to make sure to get a good counselor involved, one who could help people like Ryan, and she would do just that. "What are they doing now, your parents?"

"My dad died in Desert Storm. My mom a couple of years ago from pneumonia."

Her heart stopped, and her smiled faded as she watched him

continue to inspect…whatever he was inspecting. "I'm sorry," she said quietly, knowing better than most how inadequate the words were.

"Everything else looks okay for now." He straightened. "I'll follow you home to make sure."

"There you go again," she said softly, still unbearably touched by his losses. "Wanting to be on my list of Mr. Wrongs but acting like…" *A Mr. Right.*

"Make no mistake," he said quietly. "I'm wrong for you. All wrong."

Of that, she had no doubt.

Chapter 12

It's not that chocolate is a substitute for love. Love is a substitute for chocolate. Chocolate is far more reliable than a man.

On Sunday, Mallory watched with satisfaction as the citizens of Lucky Harbor lined up in the hospital's back parking lot for the car wash. The schedule had been set in advance, and as heavily advertised, every board member had agreed to put in two hours.

They were charging twenty-five bucks a pop. Big price tag but people were paying for the joy of seeing their well-known town hotshots stripped out of their usual finery and working like regular joe-schmoes.

Mallory's shift was noon to two, and she was scheduled with Matt, Josh, and Jane. Matt was out of his ranger uniform. Josh was minus his stethoscope. Both of them wore board shorts. Matt was listening to the iPod he had tucked into his shorts pocket, his head banging lightly, an easy smile on his face as he worked his line.

Without a shirt.

Mallory knew he was a gym rat, and it was time well spent. He was solid sinew wrapped in testosterone.

His line was wrapped around the block.

Josh was wearing a pale blue t-shirt, but he'd gotten wet while washing a large truck, and the thin cotton clung to him like a second skin. He spent up to sixteen hours a day at the hospital, so Mallory had no idea where *his* amazing body came from.

His line was nearly as long as Matt's.

Jane was wearing long Capri-length pants and a man's button-down shirt. The forty-year-old was tall and statuesque, and in the ER, she could wield a cold expression like a weapon, laying waste to all in her path. She was no less ferocious today.

She had no line.

"I don't understand," she said to Mallory. "People hate me. You'd think they'd *want* to line up to see me washing their car, pointing out every spot for me to hand scrub."

"Yeah," Mallory said. "Um...can I make a suggestion?"

Jane slid her a long look. "I don't know. Can you?"

Mallory ignored the Ice Queen tone. "Push up your sleeves. Oh, and tie your shirt tails at your belly button, and undo three of the top buttons."

Jane choked out an offended laugh. "Excuse me? Are you asking me to pimp myself out?"

"Yes. And roll up your pants. You're not even showing knee."

"I have knobby knees."

Mallory stared at her. "Okay, you're my boss, so I'm not going to tell you how much I hate you if *that's* your biggest body issue. But I will tell you that if you undo a few buttons and tie up your shirt, no one's going to be looking at your knees. Oh, and bend over—a lot. Your line will appear in no time."

Jane put a hand on her hip. "I am *forty* years old, Mallory."

"Exactly. You're forty, not eighty. And you have a better body than I do. When was the last time you had a date?"

Jane thought about that and grimaced. "I don't remember."

Mallory reached out and undid Jane's buttons herself. It revealed only the barest hint of cleavage, but it was really great cleavage. Then she gestured for Jane to do the rest.

Jane rolled her eyes, but tied up her shirt.

"I knew it," Mallory said on a sigh. "Great abs. Your pants."

Jane bent over to roll up the hem of her pants, and three cars got in her line.

Mallory was grinning as Jane straightened, looking a whole hell of a lot less like the uptight Director Of Nurses and more like a tousled, sexy, confident woman with attitude.

Jane looked at her line and blinked.

"You see?"

"Hmm..." Jane headed for the first car. "They'd better tip well."

Mallory went back to her own decent line. Amy was first up in an old Toyota truck that had seen better days two decades back. "Are you kidding me?" Mallory asked her. "You could have either Matt or Josh slaving over this thing, and you're in *my* line? Maybe *I* should be giving the bad girl lessons."

Amy's eyes locked in on Matt. He was washing Natalia Decker's BMW. Natalia was a CPA who ran her own accounting firm, a cute little blonde who'd dated her way through the men in Lucky Harbor with exuberant glee. She hadn't gotten her nails into Matt yet, though by the way she was hanging out her window watching him, she was working on it.

Oblivious, Matt was bent low over her bumper, scrubbing, the muscles of his back flexing with each movement. He was tan and wet, and looking pretty damn hot.

"Go get in his line," Mallory told Amy. "One of us should get an upfront, close look at him."

Amy slid dark sunglasses over her eyes and muttered something beneath her breath.

"What?" Mallory asked.

"Nothing. I don't want to talk about it. Are you going to wash my car or what?"

"Yeah, but Amy...he looks at you—"

"I *don't* want to talk about it."

"Okay, but this is the *first* order of business at our next Chocoholics meeting. You hear me?"

"You have other things to worry about."

"Yeah? Like what?"

"Like the fact that your Mr. Wrong is behind me."

Mallory turned to look and went still at the sight of the classic muscle car there, complete with the sexy man behind the wheel in dark glasses, dark stubble, and a darker 'tude.

Ty had been awake since before the ass-crack of dawn. He'd gone for a punishing swim and found Matt waiting on the beach. Ty had given him a long look, but Matt didn't appear to care that he wasn't welcome. He'd simply swum alongside Ty—at least until he couldn't keep the pace, and ended up waiting on the shore.

"You're doing good," Matt said when Ty walked out of the water.

It was true; he was doing good. Feeling good. He was making real progress. After the swim, Ty ran, falling only once, and only because a crab had come out of nowhere and startled the shit out of him. Then he hit the gun range, needing to push all his skills. *This* was the week he was going to get cleared. He could feel it.

The range was about thirty miles outside of Lucky Harbor. He'd been coming back into town when he'd seen Mallory amongst the car washers. She was in a T-shirt and shorts, and was wet and soapy. She looked like the Girl-Next-Door meets *Maxim* photo shoot.

Drawn in like a magnet, he'd gotten in her line. When she caught sight of him, she squinted, furtively attempting to see through the bright sun and into his windshield. He felt something loosen deep within him and wasn't sure he could have explained the feeling to save his own life.

She'd piled her hair on top of her head, but it wasn't holding. Loose strands stuck damply to her temples and cheeks, and along the back of her neck.

She was soft there, and he knew that if he put his mouth on her neck, she'd make a little sound that'd go straight through him. Crazy, he told himself. He was crazy in lust with a woman he had no business wanting. Not that *that* seemed to deter him in the slightest.

"Hey, Mysterious Cute Guy!"

Ty nearly jumped out of his skin. He hadn't even heard Lucille come up to his passenger window. She smiled knowingly. "My neighbor's got a Charger. 1970, I think. Has a front end problem. Told him you might be interested. Are you?"

A Charger was a sweet old thing. Ty wouldn't mind getting his hands on one. "Yeah. I'm interested."

Lucille smiled. "That's right nice of you."

That was him, a right nice guy.

Mallory had finished Amy's car and came up to his driver's window. "Hey," she said. "Thanks for coming."

He let a slow, suggestive smile cross his mouth. Clearly realizing what she'd said, she went bright red. "Roll up your window," she warned. "Or you'll get wet." She paused, then blushed some more. "Dammit, now *everything* I say sounds dirty!"

He was laughing when he rolled up his windows.

She got to work, looking flustered, which he loved. And maybe a little annoyed, too.

Which he also loved.

She was doing a heck of a job washing, her arms surprisingly toned and buffed as she worked the sponge. Her shirt was dark blue, a modest cut knit tee, but she was wet and it was clinging to her. Her denim shorts were snug, and she had a streak of grease on her ass. She was backing away from his car, eyeing it with close scrutiny, clearly wanting to make sure she'd gotten all the soap off, when he rolled down his window. "Watch out," he said. "Or you'll trip over the—"

Soap bucket.

Too late. She tripped and, with a little squeal of surprise, went down.

He leapt out of his car just as she hit, her fingers reflexively gripping the hose nozzle as she landed on her ass in the soapy bucket.

A steady stream of water shot out of the hose and nailed him in the chest.

"Oh God," she said, dropping the hose and trying to get out of the bucket. "I'm sorry!"

Josh and Matt, washing cars on either side of her, rushed over, but Ty got to her first. "Are you all right?" he asked, pulling her out of the bucket.

She immediately took a step back from him, her hands going to her own butt, which was now drenched with soapy water. "No worries. I have lots of padding back there."

"You sure?" Josh asked her, reaching for her arm to brace her upright while she took stock. He was frowning at her ankle. "You didn't reinjure that ankle you broke last year, did you?"

"No." She laughed a little, clearly embarrassed but resigned. "Tell me no one got a picture of that."

"Everyone's too busy staring at Jane," Matt assured her, looking over at Mallory's boss himself. "Who's...not her usual self today."

They all looked at Jane then, who was indeed looking *very* unlike herself. She was smiling.

Someone from Josh's line honked a horn and yelled, "*Dr. Scootttt...*"

Josh swore beneath his breath, making Mallory laugh and gently pat him on the chest. "Your women are calling, Dr. Scott. Better get back to 'em. And don't forget to give them what they want."

"A clean car?"

"Lots of views of your ass when you bend over."

He grimaced and headed back to his line. Mallory turned to Ty, gasping with shock at how wet he was. "Did I do all that?"

"You going to try telling me that it wasn't on purpose?"

"No," she said on a laugh. "It wasn't on purpose, I swear! If it had been, I'd have skipped the embarrassing bucket part, trust me."

Matt had gone back to washing a car and was busy flirting with the pretty blonde owner of said car. But Ty was extremely aware that Josh was still watching them. Josh was a good man, one of the best that Ty had ever met. But he was also on Mallory's list, and Ty wasn't evolved enough to wish him the best with her. "Mallory."

"Yeah?"

He stepped closer to her. "You can take Josh off your list."

She choked out a laugh as he pulled his now-drenched shirt away from his skin. He was still wearing his gun in a shoulder harness from the range, and he removed the wet Glock, then realized the entire parking lot had gone silent. Everyone was staring at him. Actually, not him. His gun.

Christ. "It got wet," he said. "Guns don't like to get wet."

Matt stepped away from the car he was working on and came to Ty's side, a show of solidarity. Just the supervisory forest ranger and the crazy guy.

"It's okay," Matt said. "Ty's licensed to carry." He said this with his usual easygoing smile, putting a hand on Ty's shoulder, using his other to wave at someone who pulled into the lot.

And just like that, everyone went back to what they'd been doing, giving the two men some privacy.

Matt gave Ty a look. "I keep telling you this is Lucky Harbor, not the Middle East."

Ty returned the look and said nothing.

Matt sighed. "You know that Vet program you're funding at

HSC? The one you told Mallory to get a good counselor for? You ought to consider making use of it."

"I'm fine."

"Well, I'm glad to hear it. Maybe you could work on happy. You got any of that? Because you can get away with just about anything if you smile occasionally. Ought to try it sometime."

"Yeah, I'll keep that in mind," Ty said, but he didn't feel like smiling. He had no idea what he was still doing here. His leg was fine. And yet he'd stopped at the small town car wash because Mallory had been looking hot in shorts. He'd just agreed to fix someone's Charger. What the hell was he doing? He was gone, out of here, any day now, moving on as he'd done all his life.

So why the hell was he acting like he was sticking around? Why was he letting people in and making plans? It was not in the cards for him, this small town life. Ties and roots were not his thing. He paid for his car wash. He'd have said good-bye to Mallory but she was busy with another vehicle. He got into his car, but something had him looking back once more at Mallory. From across the lot she was watching him, her gaze long and thoughtful.

No regrets, she'd said.

But he thought that maybe this time, there would be at least one regret. A regret named Mallory Quinn.

That night, Mallory, Grace, and Amy sat in a corner booth at Eat Me, forks in hand, cake on a plate.

The Chocoholics were in session.

"So," Grace said, licking her fork. "The hardware store is hiring. The owner, Anderson, asked me out."

"Don't do it," both Amy and Mallory said at the same time.

Grace sighed. "He's cute. But I'd rather have the job. I filled out the application. I'm trying hard to find my happy."

"And you think counting nails is going to do it?" Amy asked.

"Is clearing dishes doing it for you?" Grace countered.

Amy shrugged. "It leaves me a lot of free time and brain cells to do what I like."

"Which is?" Mallory asked.

Amy shrugged again. "Drawing."

"You're supposed to be letting people in," Mallory reminded her. "It was your decree, remember? Drawing is a solo sport."

Amy stabbed her fork into the cake for a large bite. "I'm in training." She eyed Mallory. "You want to talk about today?"

"What about today?"

"Gee, I don't know—how about the fact that MCG is carrying?"

"MCG?"

"Mysterious Cute Guy. Ty Garrison. Hot stuff. The guy you smile dopily about every time he's mentioned."

"I do not smile dopily."

Amy looked at Grace. Grace pulled a small mirror from her purse and held it up in front of Mallory.

Mallory looked at her faint glow and—dammit—dopey smile, and did her best to wipe it off her face. "It's the chocolate cake."

Amy coughed and said "bullshit" at the same time.

Mallory sighed and set down her fork.

"Uh oh," Grace said.

"I like him," Mallory said.

"And that's a bad thing?" Grace asked. "You set out to stretch your wings, experience something new. It's happening."

"With a guy that could break her heart," Amy said softly. "Is that it, Mal? You're scared?"

"Like a little bunny rabbit," Mallory said. "Some bad girl I turned out to be."

Ty swam by moonlight, and then hit the beach for another run. He didn't fall this time, not once.

Progress.

When he was done torturing his body and his every muscle was quivering with exertion, he went to bed. Too tired for nightmares, he told himself.

Things started out good. He dreamed about the time his team had been assigned to rescue a diplomat's daughter out of Istanbul. Then the dream shifted to another mission, where they'd "commandeered" certain components from a godforsaken, forlorn corner of Iraq, components that had been waiting for another shipment, which when combined together would have been a huge terrorist threat. Then things transitioned again, to the time they'd managed to get to a bus loaded with U.S. and British journalists before their scheduled kidnapping...

All successful missions...

But then the dream changed, and everything went straight to hell in a handbasket.

He was thrown from the burning wreckage. When he opened his eyes, his ears were ringing, and although he could see the wild flames all around him, he couldn't hear a damn thing. It was a movie without sound.

His men. He belly-crawled to Kelly, but he was already gone. Ty found Tommy and Brad next and did what he could, then went after Trevor. Trevor was on the other side of the wreckage, gasping for air, his chest crushed, and all Ty could do was hold him as he faded away...

He woke up alone in bed, not on a godforsaken mountain. "Christ," he breathed and shoved his fingers through his sweat-dampened hair. "*Christ.*"

It was two in the morning but he rolled out of the bed, grabbed his jeans, and shoved his legs into them. His phone, blinking due to missed calls that were no doubt from Frances, was shoved into his pocket. Same with his empty Vicodin bottle.

He got into the Mustang and fired her up. With no idea what possessed him, he did a drive-by of Mallory's house. She wasn't the only one with recon skills, though he figured the only way she could have gotten his cell phone number was through the hospital records.

How very industrious of her.

And illegal.

He found it amusing, and in a world where nothing much amused him anymore, he was also intrigued. A deadly combination.

Distance. He needed a boatload of distance. He was working on that.

Mallory's ranch-style house was in an older neighborhood. Typical Suburbia, USA. The place was freshly painted, the yard clearly cared for, much more than the piece-of-shit car she drove.

Which was why he was here. Or so he told himself.

It took him all of six minutes to replace her alternator with the one he'd driven into Seattle to get for her.

Probably he needed to work harder on keeping his distance.

He really needed to get back to work. He needed to be fucking useful for *something* again. He put his tools back in his car and had started to get behind the wheel when he heard locks tumble. Her front door opened.

In the lit doorway, highlighted by both the porch light and a single light somewhere inside, stood Mallory. Her hair was a wild cloud around her face and shoulders, her bare feet sticking out the bottom of her robe. "Ty?"

So much for stealth.

"What are you doing?" she asked.

Funny thing about that. He had no fucking clue what he was doing. None. Not a single one. He shut his car door and walked up to her, crowding her in the open doorway.

"Ty?"

He didn't answer. If she backed up a step or told him he was crazy, or gave him the slightest sign that he wasn't welcome, he would turn on his heel and walk off.

He was good at that, and they both knew it.

And he definitely expected her to be unnerved. He'd seen her face at the car wash when he'd been holding his gun.

But she surprised him now by stepping into him, meeting

him halfway. Reaching for him, her body answered his touch with a slight trembling that made him feel pretty fucking useful, and wasn't that just what he'd wished for? To be useful again?

He kept telling himself that as curious and attracted as he was to her, if Mallory hadn't started things up between them at the auction, he'd have never initiated any sort of intimacy.

He was full of shit. She'd assured him that all she'd wanted was the one night, and he'd tried like hell to believe her, but somehow they kept getting in deeper.

She was like a drug. The most addicting kind, and he had a problem—he was pretty sure that she was developing feelings for him. He no idea what to do with that, or with his own feelings, which were definitely getting in his way. This whole "no emotional attachment" thing had gone straight to shit. Because Mallory Quinn was emotionally attached to every person she ever met, and she had a way of making that contagious. He craved contact with her in a way that he wasn't experienced with.

And he liked to be experienced.

But he couldn't think about that right now because her lips were parted, her cheeks flushed, her eyes telling him that his presence affected her every bit as much as hers did him. Helpless against the pull of her, he caught her up against him and stepped over the threshold, kicking the door closed behind him.

They staggered into the entryway together, mouths fused, bumping into her umbrella stand, knocking it over as she tripped on some shoes and slammed into a coatrack.

They were both laughing as he spun her away from danger, pressing her against a little cherrywood desk and mirror. He trapped her there, and all amusement faded as she gasped, the sound full of desire.

He wanted to hear it again, needed to hear it again. Lowering his head, he kissed the sweet spot beneath her ear, along her jaw, and then the column of her neck. He spent a long moment at the hollow of her throat because, oh yeah, that's where she made the sound again, her shaky hands clutching his shoulders.

"I was dreaming about you," she said softly.

He was glad, even more so since he'd been dreaming of pure hell. He'd had no idea how much he needed this, *her*, until this very minute. "Tell me."

"We were back at the auction." Her fingers wound their way into his hair, giving him a shiver. "Working our way through all the furniture," she murmured.

"Working our way through the furniture?"

"Yeah, you know..." She hesitated. "Doing it on each piece," she whispered.

He drew back far enough to see her eyes. When she blushed gorgeously, he laughed softly. "After what we did that night, you can still be embarrassed to say 'doing it'?"

She pushed at him but he didn't budge. "No," he said, pulling her in tight. "I like it." Hell, she had to be able to feel the proof of that. "What piece of furniture did we do it on first?"

She turned her head away. "I'm not going to say now."

He nibbled her ear. "Tell me," he coaxed, flicking his tongue on her lobe.

She gasped. "A table."

He grinned. "I did you on a table?"

She made a sound that was only *half* embarrassment now, the other half pure arousal.

"Tell me that I spread you out for my viewing pleasure and feasted on all your sweet spots," he said.

Glowing bright red, she stared at his Adam's Apple. "No. You, um, bent me over the table and then, you know, took me from behind."

Yeah, good luck with finding distance now. He was hard as a rock. Maybe distance wasn't the way to go. Maybe they needed this, needed to just go for it, to get each other out of their systems.

Yeah, that was the story he was going with. He turned them both so that she was facing the small foyer desk. "It was just a dream," she murmured into the mirror.

"Doesn't have to be."

She stared at his reflection, watching as his hands ran down her arms to take her hands in his, drawing them up, up around his neck where they'd be out of his way.

The air crackled with electricity. And need. So much need. "What are you wearing beneath the robe?" he asked.

She nibbled on her lower lip.

"Mallory."

"Nothing."

He groaned. Her body was so close to his that a sheet of paper couldn't fit between them. He reached for the tie on her robe. "Do you want this?"

"I—" She closed her mouth.

"Yes or no, Mallory."

"*Yes*."

One tug of the tie and the robe began to loosen.

"Wait," she gasped. "I—I'm..." She hesitated. "I can't watch."

And yet she didn't take her hands from his neck, or her hungry gaze off the mirror, eyes glued to his fingers as they gripped the edges of her robe.

"Full access this time," he said.

"Oh, God." She nodded. "Okay, but I—" She broke off when he slowly spread the robe open, eyes riveted to her own body.

Which he already knew was the body of his dreams. "Mallory," he breathed. "You're so beautiful." He stroked his hands up her stomach to cup her breasts, his thumbs brushing her velvety nipples, wringing another gasp out of her lips. He did it again, a light teasing touch before he took his hands off her.

She whimpered.

He pulled her hands from around his neck and pushed the robe off her shoulders to puddle at their feet. Taking her hands again, he pinned them out in front of her on the table, which forced her to bend over. He gently squeezed her fingers, signaling he wanted her to stay like that.

"Ty—" she choked out, holding the position with a trusting sweetness that nearly undid him, especially when it was combined with the sexy sway of her breasts and the almost helplessly uncontrolled undulation of her hips into his crotch.

He cupped those gorgeous full breasts, teasing her nipples before skimming one hand south, between her legs.

"H—here? We really shouldn't..."

"No?"

"No," she whispered and then spread her legs, giving him more room.

Dipping into her folds was pure heaven, and he groaned when he found her very wet. His fingers trailed her own moisture over her, exploring every dip and crevice, until she was undulating again, her fingers white-knuckling their grip on the table, her eyes closed, her head back against his chest.

"Watch," he reminded her.

Her eyes opened and locked on the sight of her own body, naked, bent over the table, his tanned hand on her pale breast, the other slowly, languidly moving between her legs. "Oh," she breathed. "We look..."

"Hot." He slid a wet finger deep inside her, and she gave an inarticulate little cry, straining against him.

"Ty—"

"Tell me."

"In me," she gasped, breathless. "Please, in me."

"Come first."

Giving her another slow circle with his thumb, he watched as she shuddered, still holding obediently onto the desk's edges for all she was worth. He could feel her tremble as the tension gripped her and added another finger and some pressure with his thumb, nibbling along the nape of her neck to her shoulder. Strung tight, she breathed in little pants, her spine and ass braced against him, her arms taut, her face a mask of pleasure.

"*Ty.*"

"Right here with you," he assured her, and sent her skittering over the edge. She cried out as she shattered, and would have dropped to her knees if he hadn't caught her.

"*Now*," she demanded breathlessly. "Right now."

Not one to argue with a lady, he stripped, grabbed a condom from his pocket and put it on before pushing inside her.

She cried out again. With one arm supporting her, his other hand found hers where it gripped the wood, and he linked their fingers. She was still shaking from her orgasm. Bending over her, pressing his torso to her back, brushing his mouth against her neck, he tried to give her a moment. But when she pressed her sweet ass into him, restless, he began to move, stringing them *both* up this time. She took each thrust, arching her back for more, insistent demand in her every movement.

Not so shy now, he thought with a surge of hunger and a rather shocking possessive protectiveness.

He couldn't tear his eyes from her, even as his every single nerve ending screamed at him to let go and come already. The fire she'd started in him was flashing bright, the ache for her tight and hard in his gut. He wasn't going to be able to hold on, but then it didn't matter because she went rigid and skittered over the edge again, her muscles clenching him in erotic, sensual waves.

It was not enough.

It was too much.

It was everything.

Gripping her hard, he growled out a heartfelt "oh fuck" and

buried his face in her hair as he followed her over, coming so hard his legs buckled.

He managed to gain enough control to make sure his knees hit the hard wood floor and not hers. He turned her to face him and pulled her tight, nuzzling her neck. After a minute, he pulled back to look at her.

Her smile tugged a helpless one from him as well. "Good?" he asked.

She traced a finger along his lower lip. "That's a pretty weak word for what that was. I bet you could come up with something better."

He nipped gently on her finger. "I'm more of a show-not-tell kind of guy."

"Yeah?"

"Yeah."

"So..." she said, softly. "Show me."

Chapter 13

Forget love—I'd rather fall in chocolate!

Mallory didn't know what had brought Ty to her in the middle of the night, or what he'd planned on doing, but sitting in her entryway naked was a pretty damn good start.

Or finish.

She blushed as he bent in to kiss her, and he laughed softly against her lips as if he could read her mind. To distract them both, she trailed a finger down his chest, over a hip, and found an unnatural ridge. She took a look at the jagged scar that ran the length of his body from groin to knee, and she stilled in horror for what he'd suffered.

She realized that she was all comfy cozy, cuddled up against his chest. The position couldn't possibly be comfortable for him. "Is your leg okay?"

"I can't feel my leg right now."

She laughed breathlessly, relieved at the lessening of the sudden tension in his big, battle-scarred, *perfect* body. "Good," she said. "I know it gives you pain from the car crash."

"The pain's faded." He paused, then grimaced. "And it wasn't a car crash. It was a plane crash."

She controlled her instinctive gasp of horror. "You survived a plane crash?"

"That wasn't as bad as the several days that went by before rescue."

"Oh, Ty," she breathed, feeling her throat tighten in pain for him, trying to imagine it and not being able to. "How bad was it?"

"Bad enough."

"Your injuries?"

"Cracked ribs, broken wrist, collarbone fracture. Some internal injuries and the leg. That was the worst of it for me. All survivable injuries." He paused again. "Unlike everyone else."

She couldn't even imagine the horrible pain he'd suffered. *For days.* And the others...*He'd been the only one to survive.* Aching for him, she ran her fingers lightly over his chest, feeling the fine tremor of his muscles. Aftershocks of great sex, maybe.

Or memories.

"Your friends," she said softly. "The ones you've mentioned before. That's where you lost them."

"Yeah. My team."

"Were you—"

"Mallory." He shook his head. "I *really* don't want to talk about this."

"I know." She clutched the infinity charm around her neck, knowing the pain. "No one ever wants to talk about Karen either. But she was really important to me. For a long time after she was gone—after I failed to save her—I couldn't bear to remember her, much less talk about her."

He sighed, a long, shuddery exhale of breath and drew her in closer, burying his face in her hair. "How did she die?"

"She took a bottle of pills." She felt him go still. "She was eighteen," Mallory said. "And pregnant. It was ruled an accidental OD but..." She closed her eyes and shook her head. "It wasn't. Accidental, I mean. She did it on purpose."

"Oh, Christ, Mallory." He tightened his grip on her. "Doesn't sound like you could have saved her."

"We were sisters. I knew she had a drug problem. I should have—"

"No," he said firmly, pulling back to look into her eyes. "There's nothing you can do, *nothing*, to help someone who doesn't want to be helped."

It was so regretfully true, she could barely speak. "How do you get past it?"

"You keep moving. You keep doing whatever keeps you going. You keep living." His hands were on the move again, tender and soothing…until her breath caught, and she murmured his name, hungry for him again.

His touch changed then, from tender and soothing to doggedly aggressive and doggedly determined, stealing her breath.

"Keep living," she repeated. "That's a good plan—Oh, God, Ty," she whispered when he sucked a nipple into his mouth, hard. "I thought we were talking."

"You go ahead and talk all you want," he said gently, then proceeded to not-so-gently once again take her right out of her mind, in slow, exquisite detail.

Much, much later, she lay flat on her back on the floor, completely boneless. "Good talk," she whispered hoarsely.

Ty woke up flat on his back, the wood floor stuck to his spine and ass, a warm, sated woman curled into him. He'd taken her on the floor and had the bruises on his knees to prove it. Somehow he staggered to his feet, then scooped up Mallory. He'd have to tell Josh that if his leg could hold out through marathon sex, it could hold out through anything, and see if *that* got him cleared.

"No," she muttered, the word a slur of exhaustion as she stirred in his arms. "Don't wanna get up yet."

He knew she'd been working around the clock, on her feet for twelve hours and more at a time. She worked damn hard. "Shh," he said. "Sleep."

Her muscles went taut as she woke. "Ty?"

Well, who the hell else?

"Where we going?" she asked groggily, slipping her arms around his neck.

"Bed." He was going to tuck her in and get the hell out, before he did something stupid like fall asleep with her. Sex was one thing. Sleeping together afterward turned it into something else entirely.

You idiot, it's already something else...

At her bed, he saw the two big stuffed animals he'd won for her leaning against her pillows. An odd feeling went through him, the kind of feeling that stupid, horny teenage boys got when they had a crush. This was immediately chased by wry amusement at the both of them.

He leaned over the bed to deposit Mallory into it, but she tugged and he fell in with her. "Cold," she murmured with a shiver and tried to climb up his body.

Pulling her close—just for a minute, he told himself—he reached down and grabbed the comforter, yanking it up over the top of them. He'd share some body heat with her until she stopped shivering. Once she was asleep, he'd head out.

"Mmm," she sighed blissfully, pressing her face into his throat, tucking her cold-ass toes behind his calves. "You feel good."

"I'm not staying," he warned, not knowing which one of them he was actually telling, the woman cuddled in his arms or his own libido. So he said it again.

It didn't matter. Two minutes later, Mallory was breathing slow and deep, the kind of sleep only the very exhausted could pull off. She was out for the count.

And all over him.

Her hair was in his face, her warm breath puffing gently against his jaw, her bare breasts flattened against his side and chest. She had one hand tucked between them, the other low on his stomach. In her sleep, her fingers twitched, and she mumbled something that sounded like "bite me, Jane."

Smiling, he ran his hand down her back. "Shh."

She immediately settled in with a deep sigh, trusting. Warm. Plastered to him like a second skin.

Christ. He didn't want to wake her, but he didn't do the sleepover thing. He never did the sleepover thing.

Ever.

But unequivocally lulled in by her soft, giving warmth, he closed his eyes. Just for a second, and fell asleep wrapped around her.

At some point, he felt the nightmare gathering, pulling him in. Luckily, he managed to wake himself up before he made a complete ass of himself. It was still dark. Too dark. Rolling off the bed, he grabbed up his jeans and was halfway out the door before he felt the hand on his arm. He nearly came out of his skin and whipped around to face Mallory.

Way to be aware of your surroundings, Soldier. Unable to help himself, he twitched free and took a step back, right into the doorknob, which jabbed him hard in the back. "Fuck, Mallory."

"I'm sorry. I didn't mean to startle you." Lit only by the slant of moonlight coming in through her bedroom blinds, she stayed where she was, a few feet away, concern pouring off her in the way that only hours before passion and need had. "You okay?"

And here was where he made his mistake. He should have lied and said yes. He could have done it, easily. If he'd added a small smile and a kiss, she'd have bought it for sure. She'd have bought anything he tried to sell her because she trusted him.

That was who she was.

But it wasn't him. He didn't want to do this, get this close. So he shoved his feet into his running shoes and grabbed up his wallet and keys.

"Ty?"

He headed down the hallway. She came after him; he heard the pad of her bare feet. *She's going to get cold again* was his only inane thought.

She caught him at the front door. It wasn't until he felt her fingers run down his bare back that he realized he'd forgotten his shirt.

"Did you have a bad dream?"

He went still. "No," came the instant denial.

She merely stroked his back again. "That night in the storm," she said quietly. "you had a nightmare. I thought maybe it happened again here."

He dropped his head to the door. "That's not it."

"Then what happened? Things get a little too real?"

He straightened. "I have to go, Mallory."

"Without your shirt?"

He turned to face her, and she smiled.

She was wearing his shirt. "Stay," she said with a terrifying gentleness. "Sleep with me. I won't tell."

He knew she was treading softly around the crazy guy, only wanting to help. But he didn't want her help. He didn't want anyone's help. He was fine. All he needed was to be able to get back to work. And maybe to be buried deep inside her again, because there he didn't hurt. There he felt amazing. But if he took her again, he'd never leave. "Can't."

"But—"

He pulled open the door and stepped into the chilly night sans shirt, leaving before she could finish the rest of her sentence.

Mallory plopped back onto her bed and stared up at the ceiling, haunted by the expression on Ty's face as he'd left. He'd been rude and abrupt, and she should be pissed.

She wasn't.

But she couldn't put a finger on exactly *what* she was.

This, with him, was supposed to have been about fun. Just a little walk on the wild side.

But it had become so much more. Unnerving, but it was the truth. She wanted even more.

And he was so Mr. Wrong it was terrifying.

She wanted him anyway. *How was it that she wanted him anyway*?

She was good at making people feel better, at helping them heal. Or at least she liked to think she was. But this, with him…She couldn't heal what ate at him, any more than she'd been able to heal herself.

The next morning she got up and went to work. A few hours in, she was paged to the nurses' station. "What's up?" she asked Camilla, who was sitting behind the desk when she got there.

Camilla jerked her head toward the hallway. Mallory turned and found a very familiar, tall, broad-shouldered man propping up the wall. His stance was casual, his body relaxed.

But she knew better.

"I'm on break," she said to Camilla and walked toward Ty. "Hey," she said.

"Hey." His eyes never wavered from hers. "Got a minute?"

"Maybe even two."

He didn't smile. Huh. That didn't bode well. All too aware of Camilla's eyes—and ears—on them, she gestured for him to follow her. They took the stairs down to the ground floor cafeteria, and Mallory led him to a corner table.

It was too early for the lunch crowd so they had the place to themselves, except for a janitor working his way across the floor with a mop.

"Smells like a mess hall," Ty said.

"I bet the food was better at mess hall."

"I bet not."

He was sitting close, his warm thigh against hers beneath the table. He wore jeans that were battered to a velvety softness and a midnight blue button-down with the sleeves shoved up to his elbows.

He looked edible.

And she was afraid he was here to tell her his time was up, that he was leaving. "You want anything?" she asked. "Coffee? Tea? Pancakes?" *Me*... "They have great pancakes—"

"Nothing. Mallory—"

"A sandwich," she said desperately. "How about a sandwich? Hell, I could use a sandwich myself." She hopped up, but he grabbed her wrist.

Fine. She could handle this, whatever *this* was, and slowly sat back down, braced for a good-bye. Dammit.

He was looking at her in that way he had, steady, calm. "You okay? You seem jumpy."

"Just say it," she said. "Say good-bye already. I can't imagine it's that hard for you."

His brows went up. "You think I'm here to say good-bye? And that it wouldn't be hard for me to do?"

"Would it?"

He stared at her, his eyes fathomless, giving nothing away. "I'm not here to say good-bye. Not yet anyway."

"Oh." She nodded, knowing she should be relieved, but she wasn't. Tension had gripped her in its hard fist, and she let out a slow, purposeful breath. "I think I need a favor from you, Ty. When it *is* time to go, I want you to just do it. Don't say good-bye. Just go."

"You want me to just leave without a word."

"Yes." Her throat was tight. Her heart was tight too. "That would be best, I think." She stood and started to walk away.

"I wanted to apologize for last night," he said, catching her hand. "I was an ass."

She softened, and with a gentle squeeze of his fingers, sank back into her chair. "Well, maybe *ass* is a bit harsh. I was thinking more along the lines of a scared-y cat."

He let out a rough laugh. "Yeah. That too."

"I understand, you know."

"You shouldn't," he said.

"Why? Because I've never faced anything that haunts me?"

His gaze never left hers. "I'm sorry about Karen," he said. "And you're right. You're stronger than anyone I know. But I meant you shouldn't understand, because you deserve better from me."

Before she could respond to that, the elevator music being piped into the dining area cut off and was replaced by an authoritative male voice. "Code Red."

Mallory jumped up. Code Red meant there was a fire, and personnel were to report in immediately. Today was a scheduled drill but she'd expected it later in the day. "You're either about to be evacuated," she told Ty, "or it's going to be a few minutes before you can leave." She slapped her employee card on the table. "When the drill's over, help yourself to something to eat."

"Code Red," the voice repeated. "All personnel respond immediately. Code Red. *Repeat, Code Red.*"

Her life had great timing.

Chapter 14

When the going gets tough, the tough eat chocolate.

With the hospital in temporary lockdown, Ty leaned back and waited. From where he sat, he could see out the cafeteria and across the reception area to the front door of the hospital. In less than four minutes, firefighters and other emergency personnel came pouring in.

A drill, he thought, since no one was being evacuated. Ten minutes later, the hospital employees reappeared, though Mallory didn't.

"You want something to eat?" the cook called out to Ty.

He realized he was starving. He stood and walked over to the cook's station and eyed all the various ingredients. A few more people came in behind him. Two women in scrubs took one look at him and began whispering between themselves.

"Quesadilla?" the cook asked. "Or maybe a grilled turkey and cheese? A burger? I have a hell of a Cobb salad today, but that's not going to fill up a big guy like you."

"Burger," Ty decided. If the plane crash hadn't killed him, or the second-story jump, then a little cholesterol couldn't touch him.

The women behind him were still murmuring. "In the Vets' Hall," one of them whispered, "where *anyone* could have seen them."

"How do you know that?" the other whispered back.

"Sheryl told Cissy who told Gail. It's really unlike her. I mean, you'd expect it of any of the other Quinns but not her..."

The cook slid Ty an apologetic glance as she flipped his burger. "Cheese?"

He nodded.

The whispers continued. "...thought she'd be more careful with her image, what with the HSC at stake and all. She's still short a lot of money and needs everyone's support."

"Do you think they did it in one of the closets *here*?"

Ty had never given a shit about image, and he didn't think Mallory did either, but this was really pissing him off. He turned to face the two nosy old bats.

They both gasped and immediately busied themselves with their trays. He stared at them long and hard, but neither of them spoke.

So he did. "Mind your own business."

They didn't make eye contact and he turned back to the cook, who handed him his plate. She gestured to the card he still held in his hand, the one Mallory had left him. "Just swipe it," she said, indicating the machine alongside the register. "Mallory's card will get you anything you want on her account. Should I add a drink? Chips?"

Mallory had given him her employee pass. She was still trying to take care of him. He wasn't used to that. Shaking his head, he pulled out cash.

"But—"

He gave the cook a look that had her quickly making his change. Extremely aware of the two women behind him boring holes in his back with their beady eyes, he took his burger and headed back to his table.

The two women bought their food and walked past him, giving him several long side glances that told him that all he'd done was make things worse.

And what the hell did he think he was doing anyway, messing around in Mallory's life? He was leaving soon but Lucky Harbor was her home, her world. He ate, feeling confused and uncertain, two entirely foreign emotions for him. He'd actually believed that *he* was the one giving here, that he was the experienced one imparting a little wildness and the dubious honor of his worldly ways. How fucking magnanimous of him.

Especially since the truth was that Mallory had done all the giving, completely schooling him in warmth, compassion, and strength. In the process, with nothing more than her soft voice and a backbone of steel, she'd wrapped him around her pinkie.

Christ, he really was such an asshole. He cleared his plate and headed out, slowing at the front entrance. There was a box there, similar to a mailbox where people could drop donations for the Health Services Clinic. He'd given money for the Vets' program, which wouldn't help if Mallory couldn't get the support for the HSC to remain open. He stared at the box and knew exactly what he was going to do to give back to the woman who'd given him so much.

On Mallory's drive home, she stopped at Eat Me. Grace had sent a text that said there was an emergency.

Mallory went running in and found Grace and Amy waiting for her with a box.

A shoe box.

"Bad girl shoes," Amy said, pushing the box toward her. "Happy birthday."

"My birthday was last month."

"Merry early Christmas."

"Oh no," Mallory said. "These meetings are always about me. It's one of you guys' turns."

"Nope," Grace said. "We can only concentrate on one of us at a time."

"Then let it be Amy," Mallory said.

"Yeah," Jan said from where she was watching TV at the other end of the counter. "She's screwed up. She's got that big, sexy, forest ranger sniffing around her, and all she does is give him dirty looks."

"Hey," Amy said. "That is none of your business."

Jan cackled.

"Not talking about it," Amy said firmly, and nudged the shoe box toward Mallory again.

Because they both looked so excited, Mallory relented and opened the box to find a beautiful pair of black, strappy, four-inch heels that were dainty and flirty and pretty much screamed sex. "Oh," she breathed and kicked off the athletic shoes she'd worked in all day, replacing them with the heels.

Two counter stools over, Mr. Wykowski put a hand to his chest and said "wow."

"Heart pains?" Mallory asked in concern, rushing over there in her scrubs and bad girl heels.

"No," he said. "Not heart pains."

"Where does it hurt?"

He was staring at her heels. "Considerably lower."

Amy snorted. Mallory went back to her stool.

Grace was grinning. "See? Use them wisely. They have the power."

"Power?"

"Bad girl power," Amy said. "Go forth and be bad."

The next day Ty brought Ryan dinner. Ryan was living in a halfway house outside of town, in a place that Mallory had arranged for him to stay in through HSC.

It was infinitely better, and safer, than living on the streets.

After they ate, Ryan asked Ty for a ride, directing him to HSC.

"What's up here tonight?" Ty asked.

"A meeting."

The sign on the front door explained what kind of meeting:

NA—NARCOTICS ANONYMOUS

Someone had attached a sticky note that said: *EMPHASIS ON THE* A, *PEOPLE!*

Ty didn't know whether to be amused that only in Lucky Harbor would the extra note be necessary, or appalled that the town was trusted with the *anonymous* at all.

But part of the process was trusting.

He'd always sucked at that. He turned to Ryan, who'd gone still, seeming frozen on the top step. "I'm too old for this shit," Ryan muttered.

"How old are you?" Ty asked.

"Two hundred and fifty."

"Then you're in luck," Ty said. "They don't cut you off until you're three hundred."

A ghost of a smile touched Ryan's mouth. "I'm forty-three."

Only ten years older than Ty. Ryan's body was trembling. Detoxing. Not good. Ty would have paid big bucks to be anywhere else right now but he figured if anyone was interested in him as a crutch, they had to be pretty bad off. "How long has it been since your last hit?"

Ryan swiped a shaking hand over his mouth. "I ran out of Oxycontin four days ago. Doctor says I don't need it anymore. Fucking doctors."

Ty slipped his hand into his pocket and fingered the ever-present empty bottle. Two months, two weeks, and counting. He thought about saying that he'd wait outside, but that felt a little chickenshit, so he went in.

He survived the meeting, and so did Ryan. An hour later they walked out side by side. Quiet. Ty didn't know about Ryan, but he was more than a little shaken by the stories he'd heard, at the utter destruction of lives that those people in there had been trying to reboot and repair. He knew he had to be grateful because he hadn't fucked up his life. At least not completely.

He was halfway back to Ryan's place when Ryan spoke. "So are you and Mallory a thing?"

Ty had been asked this many times in the past few weeks. By the clerk at the grocery store. By the guy who'd taken his money at the gas pump. By everyone who'd crossed his path. By the very same people who—until Mallory—had been content to just stare at him.

Mallory. Mallory was the heart and soul of this town, or at least she represented what its heart and soul would look like in human form. And while maybe he'd treated her like someone he could easily walk away from, he knew different. *She* was different. Still, there was no denying the fact that while *she* was grounded here, in this place, in this life, *he* was chomping at the bit to get back to his. "No," he finally said. "We're not a thing."

Ryan scratched his scruffy jaw. "She know that?"

It'd been Mallory's idea that this be just a one-time affair, though she'd accepted his latest visit as just an addendum to the original deal. And she'd let him off the hook for being an ass.

And then asked him to leave without a good-bye. "Yeah. She knows that."

The question was, did *he.*

"Because she's a real nice lady," Ryan said. "When I was living on a bench at the park, she'd bring me food at night. She ever tell you that?"

Ty shook his head, his chest a little tight at the thought of Mallory, after a long day in the ER, seeking Ryan out to make sure he was fed.

"Yeah, she can't cook worth shit," Ryan told him with a small smile. "But I ate whatever she brought anyway. Didn't want to hurt her feelings."

Ty heard himself choke out a laugh.

Ryan nodded. "If I was…" He lifted a hand to indicate himself and trailed off. "You know, *different*," he finally said. "I'd try for her. She's something special. Way too special for the likes of me, you know?"

Ty's chest tightened even more. Yeah. He knew. He knew *exactly*. "She'd be pissed off to hear you say that."

"She's pretty when she's pissed off," Ryan said wistfully. "One time she came to the park and some kids were trying to bean me with rocks. She chased them, yelling at them at the top of her lungs. I was in a bad way then, and still I think I looked better than she did. Her hair was all over the place, and she was in her scrubs. She looked like a patient from the place I'd stayed at after I got back from my third tour."

A mental facility. Ty pictured Mallory furious and chasing the kids off. He could see it: her scrubs wrinkled after a long day of work, those ridiculous fuzzy boots, her hair looking like it had rioted around her face.

Christ, she was so fucking beautiful.

"You've seen the stuff on Facebook, right?" Ryan asked.

Ty slid him a look. "How are you getting on Facebook?"

"There's a community computer at the house." Ryan shrugged. "Facebook's the homepage. There's a pic up of you two. You two seem pretty cozy for not being a thing."

Yeah. Cozy.

Except what he'd had with Mallory had been just about the opposite of cozy. It'd been hot. Bewildering.

Staggering.

And what the hell pic was up on Facebook?

He dropped Ryan off, then went home and worked on the Jimmy for Matt until late. He showered, then eyed his blinking phone. He glanced at the missed calls, getting a little rush at the thought that maybe Mallory had called him. The last time she'd been stuck. Maybe this time she just wanted to hear his voice. He sure as hell could use the sound of her voice right about now.

But the message wasn't from Mallory. It was from Josh. Ty was expected at the radiology department at seven for scans, and then at a doctor's appointment at eight.

Ty tried to read the tone of Josh's voice to ascertain whether the news was going to be good or bad, but Josh was as good as Ty at not giving anything away.

The next morning, Ty was led to Josh's office and told to wait. He'd perfected the art of hurrying up and waiting in the military, so when Josh strode in carrying a thick file that Ty knew contained his medical history, he didn't react.

Josh was in full doctor mode today. Dark blue scrubs, a white doctor coat, a stethoscope around his neck, and his hospital ID clipped to his hip pocket. Hair rumpled, eyes tired, he dropped Ty's file on his desk, sprawled out into his chair, and put his feet up. "*Christ.*"

"Long day already?"

"Is it still day?" Josh scrubbed his hands over his face. "Heard from Frances today. Or yesterday. Persistent, isn't she?"

"Among other things. What did you tell her?"

"That your prognosis was none of her goddamned business and to stop calling me."

This got a genuine smile out of Ty. "And she thanked you politely and went quietly into the night."

"Yeah," Josh said, heavy on the irony. "Or told me what she was going to do with my balls if she had to come out here to get news on you herself."

"Sounds about right." Ty looked at his closed file. "Verdict?"

"Scans show marked improvement. With another month of continued P.T., you could be back in the same lean, mean fighting shape you were. For now, I'd say you were probably up to where us normal humans are."

Another month off would fucking kill him. "So I'm good to go then."

Josh gave him a look. "Depends on your idea of go. You're not up to leaping out second-story windows."

"Yeah, but that hardly ever happens."

Josh put his feet down and leaned forward, studying Ty for a long, serious moment. "You're really going back."

"I was *always* going back."

"But you want to go back *now*."

"Hell, yeah," Ty said. "I wanted to go back the day I got here. Especially in the past few weeks, since I've been swimming and running again."

"So why didn't you? Go back?"

"I want to work," Ty said, gesturing to the file. "Need clearance."

"Yes, and that's going to come soon, but my point is that you haven't been exactly handcuffed to Lucky Harbor. You could have left."

A flash of Mallory's face came to Ty. Looking up at him while lying snuggled against him in her bed, wearing only a soft, sated smile and a slant of moonlight across her face.

It was no mystery what had kept him here.

"Mal know that you're just about out of here?" Josh asked quietly.

"This has nothing to do with her," Ty said flatly. "Sign the papers."

"You'd have to be on light duty."

"Fine. I'll push fucking papers around on a desk if I have to. Just clear me."

Josh shook his head, looking baffled. "You'd leave here for a desk job? Man, you're not a desk-job kind of guy and we both know it."

He'd deal. He needed to get close to the action, to get back to his world. He needed the adrenaline. He was wasting away here in Lucky Harbor.

"You know," Josh said with that infuriatingly calm voice, leaning on the desk, his elbows on the release papers. "Maybe we should get back to the real reason you're still here."

"Sign the papers, Josh."

Josh stared at him.

Ty stared back, holding the other man's gaze evenly. Steadily.

With a shake of his head, Josh signed the papers.

Ty spent two days *not* making any plans to get back to his life. First, he told himself he needed to finish up the Jimmy. Then he told himself he had to finish up the Charger for Lucille's neighbor, and the other two cars he'd taken on as well. And people kept calling him with new car issues. He couldn't just ignore them. Plus he needed to finish the Shelby, just for himself, but the truth there was that she was running like a dream.

After that, he ran out of excuses and decided he'd give himself a day off from thinking about it.

Which turned into yet another day...

Then he woke up to a message from Josh to stop by his office at ten. Ty got up and swam. He ran, hard. He played WWE with Matt at the gym for an hour until they fell apart gasping, sweating, and equally worked over. Then Ty dragged himself to the shower and drove to Josh's office.

Josh was in dress clothes today, a white doctor's coat over his clothing, the ever-present stethoscope acting as a tie. He looked up from the mountain of paperwork on his desk and scowled at Ty. "You call The Queen yet about being cleared?"

"No."

Josh gave him a long look, then stood and shut his office door. Back in his chair, he steepled his fingers, studying Ty like a bug on a slide. "Problem?"

"No. I've just got a little pain is all." He straightened his leg and winced.

"No doubt," Josh said dryly. "I was at the gym this morning; you never even noticed me. You were too busy wiping the floor with Matt. Who, by the way, is the best street fighter I've ever met. And you kicked his ass. How much pain can you be in?"

"I pulled something."

Josh's smile faded. "Yeah?"

"Yeah."

Josh was quiet a moment. "Then maybe you should give it another week," he finally said.

Ty nodded his agreement and left. He left the back way, which meant he stood in the bright sunshine in the hospital parking lot staring at Mallory's POS car. He wondered what the hell was wrong with him, but since that was probably way too big a problem to solve in this decade, he went home. He fiddled on the Shelby until he realized it'd gotten dark. He was just getting out of his second shower of the day when he heard the knock at his door.

He'd been off the job for more than six months, and still the instinct to grab his gun before answering was second nature. But this was Lucky Harbor. The only real danger was being killed by kindness.

And nosy-ass gossip.

Shaking his head, he grabbed his Levi's up off the floor and pulled them on, then opened the door to... Mallory.

She gave him a small smile, a sweet smile. Clearly she hadn't yet heard through the cafeteria grapevine that he was single-handedly ruining her life. "Hey," he said. A chronic idiot. That was him.

"Hey yourself." Her gaze ran over his bare torso. Something went hot in her eyes as she took in the fact that all he wore were

Levi's, which he hadn't yet buttoned up all the way. He did that now while she watched, and the temperature around them shot up even more.

She stepped over the threshold, and since he hadn't moved she bumped into him. He thought it was an accidental touch but then her hands came up and brushed over his chest and abs. No accident.

Nor was the fact that she was wearing a halter top, low-riding jeans and a pair of really hot heels that brought her up four point five inches and perfectly aligned their bodies. Her pulse was beating like a drum at the little dip in the base of her throat. Lifting a hand, he ran a finger over the beat, watching her pulse leap even more.

Her hand came up to join with his. "In the name of full disclosure," she murmured, "you should know that I talked to Ryan this afternoon."

Ty lifted his gaze.

"He landed in the ER," she said.

"What happened? Is he all right?"

"Someone on the highway caught sight of him wandering around and brought him in. He had a bottle of Jack and some dope he'd scored off some kids."

"*Shit.*"

"Yeah." She kept her hand on his, squeezing his fingers reassuringly. "He's fine. He's currently sleeping it off, but before that... he was talking."

"Was he?"

"You took him to NA."

That was a statement of fact so he let it sit between them.

"You... went into the meeting," she said. "You stayed."

Another statement of fact.

"Was he... unsteady?" she asked. "Did he need the assistance?"

Ah, and now he got it. She was on a fishing expedition. "He wasn't that bad off, no."

She nodded, and he waited for her expression to change but it didn't. There was no leaping to conclusions, no trial and jury, no pity, nothing.

Hell, he didn't know why that surprised him. She never did the expected. She was the warmest, most compassionate, understanding woman he'd ever met.

"Did you need something there?" she asked.

And she was also one of the most curious.

"Why don't you just ask me what you really want to know, Mallory?"

"Okay." She drew a deep breath. "Are you an addict, too?"

Unable to resist, he again stroked his thumb over that spot at the base of her neck before slipping his hand into his pocket to finger the ever-present Vicodin bottle. It was a light weight. Empty. And both those things reassured him. He'd fucked up plenty, but at least not with that. "Damn close," he said.

"Oh," she breathed, and nodded. "I see."

No, she didn't. But that was his fault. "After the plane crash, I wasn't exactly the best of patients. I was on heavy meds. A wreck, basically."

"You'd just lost your team," she said softly.

Something warm unfurled in him at that. She was defending him. To *himself.* "When I went back to work, I gave up the meds." He paused, remembering. "It sucked. Christ, it sucked bad. I liked the oblivion, too damn much."

Her eyes were on his, absorbing his words, taking it all in without judgment. So he gave her the rest. "Six months ago, I got hurt again. In the ER they got me all nice and drugged up before I could refuse the meds."

Something flickered in her eyes, and he knew she was remembering how he'd refused drugs the night of the storm.

"Then I was released," he said. "With a 'take as needed' prescription. I found myself doing exactly that and living for the clock, for the minute I could take more. That's when I stopped refilling."

"You went cold turkey?"

"I never understood that saying, cold turkey," he said with a grim smile. "It's more like *hot hell*, but yeah." He blew out a breath. "And I still crave it."

She was quiet a moment. "I think the craving part is normal. We all have our cravings. I gave up chocolate once. The cravings *sucked*."

He choked out a laugh. Christ, he liked her. A whole hell of a lot. What was he supposed to do with that? "I don't think it's exactly the same."

"True. I mean, I can't be arrested for hoarding chocolate cake," she said. "But it ruins my life. Costs money. And it makes my scrubs tight. You know how bad that is, when your drawstring pants are too tight? Pretty damn bad, Ty."

He was smiling now. He rocked back on his heels and studied her. "You're looking pretty damn good from where I'm standing."

"Because I only let myself have it once a week. Or whenever Amy calls. She's a very bad influence."

"Still crave, huh?" he asked with genuine sympathy.

"I'd give up my next breath for a piece of cake right now," she said with deep feeling. She sighed, as if with fond memories. "I think it helps to keep busy. Distracted. I know that much."

"I've been distracted plenty," he said, and her cheeks flamed. He loved that she could initiate sex in a storage room above about five hundred of her closest friends and family and *still* blush.

"Were you working on a car?" she asked. "I heard you're the new go-to mechanic guy."

"I was working before I showered."

"Show me?"

"The shower? Sure. I might have used all the hot water though."

She gave him a little laugh and a shove that took him back a step. He could have stood his ground but he liked the way she was letting her hands linger on his chest. He took one of those hands and guided her through to the kitchen and out the back door to the garage.

She looked around, taking in the cars and the slew of tools scattered across the work table. "What were you doing?"

"Brake line work on my Shelby."

"Show me," she said again.

"You want to learn how to put in new stainless steel brake lines," he said, heavy on the disbelief. "Mallory, those shoes aren't meant for working on a car."

"What are they meant for?"

"Messing with a man's head."

She smiled. "Are they working?"

"More than you can possibly imagine. Listen, this car shit, it's messy."

"So?" she asked, sounding amused, and he had to admit she had a point. She saw blood and guts and probably worse every single day. A little dirt wasn't going to bother her. Shaking his head at himself, he popped the hood. He grabbed a forgotten sweatshirt off the bench and handed it to her.

"I'm not cold."

His gaze slid to her breasts. Her nipples were poking at the material of her halter top. If she wasn't cold, then she was turned on. It would seem hard to believe since he hadn't touched her, but every time they got within five feet of each other he got a jolt to the dick, so who was he to say? "It's to keep your clothes from getting dirty." He pulled the sweatshirt over her head, unable to stop himself from touching as much of her as possible as he tugged it down her torso, only slightly mollified to hear her breathing hitch.

Yeah. They were on the same page.

The sweatshirt came to her thighs. She pushed back the hood. "It smells like you."

He felt that odd pain in his chest again, an ache that actually had nothing to do with wanting to get her naked. "And now it's going to smell like *you*," he said.

"Is that okay?"

It was so far beyond okay he didn't have words. Fucking sap. He kicked over the mechanic creeper, then his backup, and gestured her onto it. When they were both flat on their backs, she grinned at him. "Now what?"

"Under the car."

She slid herself beneath the car, and he joined her. Side by side, they looked up at the bottom of the chassis.

"What's first?" she asked.

He looked at her sweet profile. What was first? Reminding himself that he'd been cleared to leave Lucky Harbor. He handed her a roll of brake line. "You bend it to fit the contours of the frame as you go." He pointed out the route, and she began to work the brake line.

"It's peaceful," she said. "Under here."

He slid her a sideways look, and she laughed at him. No one ever laughed at him, he realized. Well, except for Matt, and Matt didn't look cute while doing it either.

"I'm serious," Mallory said, still smiling. "You don't think so?"

It was dirty, grimy, stuffy...and yeah. Peaceful. "I'm just surprised you think so."

"You don't think I can enjoy getting dirty once in awhile?" She bit her lower lip and laughed. "Okay, you know what I mean."

"Yeah. Here—" She wasn't able to put enough muscle into bending the line so he put his hands over hers and guided her. "Unravel another foot or so."

"'kay." She frowned, eyeing the space. "How long is that?"

"Like nine inches. I need twelve." He paused. "Twelve inches would be great."

He felt her gaze, and he did his best to look innocent, but she didn't buy it. "What the hell would you do with twelve inches?" she wanted to know.

He waggled a brow. "Plenty."

She shook her head. "Like you aren't lethal enough with what you have," she said, making him laugh.

They worked the brake line in companionable silence for a few moments, but Mallory didn't do silence all that well. "What do you think about under here?" she asked. "Besides your... inches?"

He smiled, but the truth was, he usually tried like hell not to think at all. "Sometimes I think about my dad."

"He was a Navy mechanic, too, right? He taught you all this stuff?"

Ty's dad had been a mechanic in the Navy, but not Ty. Yet correcting the misconception now, telling her that he'd once been a SEAL medic, wasn't something he wanted to get into. It was far easier to deny that part of himself rather than revisit it. "My dad didn't want me to learn mechanics, actually. He wanted more for me. I think he hoped that if he kept me away from anything mechanical, I'd become a lawyer or something like that."

"And...?"

"And when I was fourteen, he bought a Pontiac GTO." He smiled at the memory. "A '67. God, she was sweet."

"She?" Mallory teased, turning her face to his. She was so close he reached out and stroked a rogue strand of hair from her temple, tucking it behind her ear.

"Yeah, she," he said. "Cars are always a she. And do you want to hear this story or not?"

"Very much." She nudged her shoulder to his. "Every single detail."

"I took apart the engine."

"Oh my God," she said on a shocked laugh. "Was he mad?"

"It was a classic, and it was in mint condition. *Mad* doesn't even begin to cover what he was."

She stared at him, eyes wide. "Why did you do it?"

He shrugged. "I couldn't help myself. I liked to take things apart and then put them back together again. Only I couldn't. I had no idea what I was doing." Ty could still remember the look on his father's face: utter and complete shock at the empty engine compartment, horror that his baby had been breached and violated, and then sheer fury. "I can still feel the sweat trickling down the back of my spine," he said, shaking his head. "I hadn't meant to take it so far. I'd just kept undoing and undoing…"

"What happened?"

"I was pretty sure he'd kick my ass."

She gasped. "He beat you?"

"Nah, he never laid a hand on me." Ty felt a smile curve his mouth. "Didn't have to. He was one scary son of a bitch. He'd talk in this low, authoritative voice that dared you to defy him. No one ever did that I know of."

"Not you?"

"*Hell* no."

She was grinning wide, and he shook his head at her. "What's so funny?"

"You," she said. "You're so big and bad. It's hard to imagine you scared of anything." She touched his jaw, cupping it in her palm and lightly running her thumb over his skin.

He hadn't shaved that morning, and he could hear the rasp of his stubble against the pad of her thumb. As she touched him, he watched the flecks in her eyes heat like gold.

"I like being under a car with you," she said.

Working on cars was his escape. Beneath a hood or a chassis was familiar ground, no matter what part of the world he was in or where he lay his head at night. It was his constant. A buffer from the shit.

And Mallory was a single-woman destruction crew, outmaneuvering him, letting herself right into his safety zone, and then into his damn heart while she was at it. Because no matter what bullshit he fed himself, he liked being here with her, too.

"You ever going to tell me what you *are* scared of?" she asked.

He let out a short laugh. "Plenty," he assured her.

Her eyes softened, and she slid her hand into the hair at the back of his neck, fisting lightly, bringing him a full-body shiver of pure pleasure.

"Such as?" she asked.

You, he nearly said.

And it would be God's truth.

"Tell me."

"I'm afraid of not living," he said. He rolled out from beneath the Shelby, then crouched beside Mallory's creeper, putting his hands on her ankles to yank her out, too.

Sitting up, she pushed her hair back and met his gaze. "Don't worry, Ty. I know."

"You know what?"

"That this isn't your real life, that you're just killing time with me until—"

He put his finger over her lips. "Mal—"

"No, it's okay," she said around his finger, wrapping her hand around his wrist. "You're not the small-town type. I know it."

And yet here he was. Free to go, but still here.

"Are we done working on the car?" she asked.

"Yeah." Her legs seemed endless in those jeans and fuck-me heels. "We're done working on the car."

"So I can teach you something about *my* work now?"

He took in her small but sexy smile and felt himself go hard. "What did you have in mind?"

"Ever play doctor?"

Chapter 15

There is nothing better than a good friend, except maybe a good friend with chocolate.

The next morning, Mallory woke to a disgruntled *meow*. It was Sweet Pea, letting the world know it was past time for breakfast.

When Mallory ignored this, the cat batted her on the forehead with a paw.

"Shh," Mallory said.

"*Meow.*"

Mallory stretched, her body sore. She hadn't been to the gym since her membership had expired a year ago, which left only one thing to attribute the soreness to.

Ty, and his own special brand of workout.

She sighed blissfully and rolled over. She hadn't gotten home until late. Or early, depending on how you looked at it. She'd have liked to stay at Ty's all night but that would have been too much.

Not for her. For *him*.

She'd promised him that this was a simple fling. No use in telling him she'd broken that promise. Besides, she was pretty sure he was more than just physically attracted to her as well, but she wasn't sure if *he* knew it.

She loved being with him. That was the bottom line. The only line. There were no preconceived notions on how she should behave. It was freeing, exhilarating.

Amazing.

And also unsettling. She was in the big girls' sandbox when she played with Ty, and she was going to get hurt. There was nothing she could do about that so she showered. When she went to the closet for her white athletic shoes, she sniffed, then wrinkled her nose. "Oh no, you didn't," she said to Sweet Pea.

Sweet Pea was in the middle of the bed, daintily washing her face. She had no comment.

"You *poo'd in my shoe*?"

Sweet Pea gave her a look that said "see if you come home that late again" and continued with her grooming.

"Two words," Mallory told the cat. "*Glue. Factory*."

Sweet Pea didn't look worried, and with good reason. It was an empty threat, and they both knew it. Mallory cleaned up the mess, thankful Sweet Pea hadn't used her bad girl shoes. She flashed to Ty tossing her onto his bed in the shoes and nothing else... Yeah. She was going to bronze those suckers.

She grabbed her phone off her nightstand and headed out her front door to get to work.

Joe was in her driveway, head under her opened hood. "Hey," he said. "Who did your alternator?"

"No one. What are you doing? You said you were busy."

"And now I'm not. I picked up a new alternator for you this morning, but someone beat me to it."

"What?" She stepped off the front porch and took a peek at the thing he was pointing out, the one shiny, clean part in the whole car.

"See?" Joe said. "Brand new alternator. Maybe it was Garrison."

"Why would you think that?"

"Because he helped this guy...Ryan, I think...get a job at the welding shop. And Ryan told me you're seeing Garrison."

Ty had gotten Ryan a job. Everything in her softened at the thought of Ty caring that much, and she wondered if it was too soon to go back over there. She'd wear her heels again. And maybe a trench coat and nothing else...

"Hel*lo*," Joe said, irritated.

"What?"

"Are you seeing Garrison or not? Would he have done this for you?"

Mallory flashed back to finding Ty in her driveway in the middle of the night. She'd never questioned what he'd been doing here, figuring it had been about sex. She hadn't minded that; she'd wanted him, too, but she got a little warm fuzzy that it hadn't been about *just* sex.

She had no explanation for last night, which had been all her own doing. She'd have to tell Amy that she was right: bad girl shoes were awesome. Amy loved to be right.

She drove to work with the smile still on her face. She'd parked and was just getting out of the car when her phone vibrated. Odd, because she'd have sworn she'd set it to ring. Pulling it out of her pocket, she didn't even attempt to see the screen in the bright morning sun before she answered with a simple "Hello?"

There was a long beat of silence and then, "Who the hell are you and where the hell is Ty?"

Mallory blinked at the very sexy, snooty female voice sounding damn proprietary, then said, "Who is this?"

"I asked first. Oh, for fuck's sake. Just put him on the phone. *Now*."

Oh hell no, Mallory thought, feeling a proprietariness of her own, even though on some level she'd known that Ty had to have other women in his life. It made perfect sense, but that didn't mean she liked how it felt.

"Fine, have it your way," the woman snapped. "Tell him Frances called. Make sure you tell him that it's important, do you understand?"

"How did you get this number?"

"Cookie, you don't want to go there. Now listen to me. I don't care how good you suck him, I've known him longer, I know him better, and I'm the only one of us who will know him by this time next week. Give him the damn message."

Click.

Mallory stared at the phone, realizing that it wasn't her phone at all. It was an iPhone just like hers, but the background was of only the date and a clock, not the picture of the beach she'd taken last week.

She had Ty's phone.

Mallory tried calling *her* phone but it went directly to voicemail, signaling that Ty had either turned it off or she'd run out of battery. She chewed on the situation for a minute, then punched out Amy's number. "It's me," she said. "I'm using someone else's phone. Life is getting nuts."

"Nuts is all relative on the Bad Girl scale."

"Is that right?" Mallory asked. "So where on that scale would you put getting yelled at by the ex of the guy I'm sleeping with?"

Dead silence. Then, "So the bad girl shoes worked?"

Mallory blew out a breath. "Yes. Now concentrate." She told Amy all about the call. "And really," she said. "I have no one but myself to blame. *I* wanted this one-time thing. I mean I wanted the second time too, *and* the third, but now—"

"Now you're in this, and you're worried that maybe you're in it alone."

Mallory's throat tightened. "Yeah. I mean three times. To me that's..."

"I know." Suddenly Amy wasn't sounding amused. "It's a relationship."

"And I'm pretty sure Ty's allergic to relationships."

Amy paused again. "Mallory, are you sure you haven't bitten off more than you can chew?"

Mallory choked out a laugh. "*Now*? You think to ask me this now? *You* started this. You egged me on with the list of Mr. Wrongs! Hell, yes, I've bitten off more than I can chew!"

"Okay," Amy soothed. "We can fix this. You'll just downgrade to a *less* Mr. Wrong. Someone easier to drag around by his twig and berries, you know?"

Yeah, but she didn't want just anyone's twigs and berries. "Look, I'm at work. We'll have to obsess over this later. Have cake waiting. I'm going to need it."

"Will do, babe."

Mallory clicked off and went into the hospital.

Five minutes into her shift, Jane called her into her office. "Two things," her boss said cryptically, giving nothing away. "First up." She laid a piece of paper on her desk, facing Mallory. It was a receipt for a sizeable amount.

"Anonymous donation," Jane said. "For HSC."

"My God." Mallory sank to a spare chair. "Am I looking at all those zeroes correctly?"

"Yes," Jane said. "And they're all very pretty."

Mallory's eyes jerked up to Jane's. "Did you just make a joke?"

"Tell anyone, and I'll skin you." Jane let out a rare smile but it was fleeting. "Nicely done."

"How do you know I had anything to do with this?" Mallory asked, still astonished.

Jane gave an impressive eye roll. "Mallory, without you, there would be no HSC. Even *with* you, it's barely there, and it's on tentative footing. Someone you know or talked to donated this money."

Mallory absorbed that a moment. "Someone I know? I don't *know* anyone with a spare 10K."

"Don't you?"

"You're not talking about Ty," Mallory said, but Jane's eyes said that's exactly who she was talking about. "He already donated money for the Vets' program," Mallory protested. "Besides, he doesn't have this kind of money. But truthfully, she had no idea what Ty had or didn't have. *Ten thousand dollars*... "Why would he—"

"Don't ask me that," Jane said quietly. "Because honestly, Mallory? I don't want to know why he'd give you so much money for a Health Services Clinic in a town he has no ties to, a place he apparently plans on leaving very soon."

"Not me," Mallory said. "He didn't give the money to me. He gave it to HSC. If it was even him."

"Hmm," was all Jane said to this. She paused. "I really don't like to delve into my employees' private lives, but..."

Oh boy. "But...?"

"But since yours is being discussed over the water cooler, it's unavoidable. You're dating a man who no one knows anything about."

Well, technically, there was little "dating" involved. She was flat out boinking him. "No disrespect, Jane, but I really don't see how this affects my job."

"Whether he was the anonymous donor or not, he's been seen socializing with known drug addicts. And he yelled at two aides in the cafeteria."

Mallory's temper was usually non-existent but it flared to life at Jane's cavalier description of Ryan. "That's not quite how either of those two events went down," she said as evenly as she could. "Ty's involved in the Vets' program. He and Ryan connected because of their military backgrounds, and Ty's been helping him, giving him rides and bringing him food." Which she only knew because Lucille had told her, and thinking about it *still* melted her heart. She also knew about the hospital cafeteria incident, thanks to Lucille. "As for the radiation techs, they were just downright rude, so—"

"My point," Jane said, "is that you're not just an employee now. You're *running* the HSC. You're in a position that requires a certain public persona, and you have no one to blame but yourself for that one. You chose this, Mallory, so you have to understand that certain aspects of your life are now up for scrutiny. You have a moral and financial obligation to live up to that scrutiny."

Mallory was having a hard time swallowing this. "Are you saying I can't have a private life?"

"I'm saying that private life can't conflict with your public life. You can't date a man who might need the services HSC provides, wrong as that sounds. You just can't."

The words rang through Mallory's head for the next few hours as she dealt with her patients. She had a vomiter—oh joy—a teenager who'd let her new tattoo get infected, and an eight-months-pregnant woman who ate a jar of pickles and put herself into labor with gas pains.

Alyssa was little to no help. She was far too busy flirting with that cute new resident doctor, hoping to score a date for her night off. All of Alyssa's patients kept hailing Mallory down, until finally she physically yanked Alyssa away from the new resident and reminded her that she had actual work to do.

Mallory pretty much ran ragged until there was finally a lull. She used the rare quiet time to sit at the nurses' station and catch up on charting.

"Mallory!"

She looked up to find one of her patients, Jodi Larson, standing there beaming from ear to ear. Jodi was ten years old, a leukemia patient, and one of Mallory's all-time favorite people. She'd been in for her six-month check, and given the smile also on Jodi's mom's face behind her, the news had been good.

"Officially in remission," Jodi said proudly.

Jodi's mom's eyes were shining brilliantly as she nodded affirmation of the good news. Thrilled, Mallory hugged them both tight, and Jodi presented her with a plate of cookies. "Chocolate chip and walnut. I baked them just for you."

They hugged again, then Mallory got paged and had to go. It turned out the page was from her own mother.

"Mallory," Ella whispered, dragging her daughter into a far, quiet corner. "People are talking about how you were seen driving home at 3:20 in the morning. Why do I have a daughter coming home that late? Nothing good happens that late, Mallory. Nothing."

Oh, for the love of God. "Actually, it was only 2:30, so your source is dyslexic." And pretty damn annoying, but Mallory didn't bother to say so. Her mother had a point and she was winding up for it.

"You were with *that* man," Ella said.

Uh huh, and there it was. Mallory's left eye began to twitch. "That man has a name."

"Cute Guy."

"A *real* name."

Her mother's lips tightened. "Yes, I believe The Facebook is calling him *Mysterious* Cute Guy."

Mallory put a finger to her twitching eye. "Okay, for the last time, it's not *The* Facebook, it's just *Facebook*."

"Honey, please. It's time you came to your senses. You're going to end up as wild and crazy as Joe and Tammy, and that's not who you are."

"Mom, Joe is only twenty-four. He's not ready to settle down, so a little wild and crazy is okay. And Tammy is settled down in her own wild and crazy way. Maybe it's not what you wanted for her but she's adjusted and happy. What's wrong with being like them?"

Her mom's mouth tightened. "That's not what I mean, and you know it."

"No," Mallory agreed quietly, her chest tight. "That isn't what you mean, and I do know it. You're talking about Karen."

"No, we're not."

"Well, we should."

Her mother closed her eyes and turned away. "I have to go."

"She started dating a guy no one knew."

"I don't want to talk about this, Mallory!"

"He encouraged her to take a walk on the wild side, and—"

"*Don't*," Ella said stiffly. "Don't you—"

"And she changed. She stopped being who you thought she should be. And—"

Her mother whirled back, eyes blazing, finger pointed shakily in Mallory's face. "Don't you *dare* say it."

"Mom," Mallory said through a tight throat, suddenly *very* tired. "It's not the same this time. You know it's not the same for me. Karen was doing drugs."

"Your young man went to NA."

Mallory shook her head in disbelief. "That's *confidential*."

"It's Lucky Harbor," Ella said with a shrug that said Ty's privacy was nothing compared to her need to make sure her daughter was okay. "Remember that stormy night, when he ended up in the ER? He refused narcotics for pain. *Adamantly*."

"So?"

"Don't play dumb, Mallory. You know what I'm saying. He's an outsider, and I realize that sounds rude, but you've got to admit people are getting the wrong idea about you two."

Actually, given what she and Ty had been doing in the deep, dark of the night—and sometimes in the middle of the day—people had the exact *right* idea.

Ella took one look at Mallory's face and got a pinched look of tension. "See? It's happening. It's happening again, just like Karen with Tony."

"No," Mallory said firmly. God, no. "Tony got Karen both hooked and then pregnant, and she spiraled downward. I can't believe we're comparing my life to Karen's now, after all these years. Why not back then, when I *was* in danger of spiraling?"

Her mother looked as if Mallory had slapped her. "You...you weren't. You were our rock."

Mallory let out a breath and shook her head, feeling weary to the bone. And sad. Way too damn sad. "Forget it, Mom."

"I can't. Oh my God." She covered her face. "I thought—you were so sweet during that time. I never thought—Oh, Mallory. I'm so sorry. Are you...spiraling again?"

Mallory drew a shaky breath and stepped forward, putting her hands on her mom's arms. "No," she said gently. "I'm not spiraling again. I'm not going to kill myself, Mom." The big, fat elephant in the room. "I'm not Karen."

Ella nodded, and with tears in her eyes, hugged Mallory in tight. "I know," she whispered. Then, in the Quinn way of bucking up, she sniffed and pulled back to search her pockets, coming up with a tissue that she used to swipe her eyes. "You're really okay?"

"Really," Mallory promised.

"So can I have my sweet daughter back?"

A low laugh escaped Mallory. "I'm still sweet, Mom. I'm just not going to be amenable all the time, or compliant. And I'm not going to live my life exactly as you'd have me do."

"Are you going to keep seeing that man?"

Lucille walked by in her candy-striper uniform. "Well, I hope so," she said. "He's the hottest thing you've dated since...well, ever."

"Don't encourage her," Ella said. "This isn't just a silly thing. It's affecting her job."

"Phooey," Lucille said.

"Jane is concerned about it affecting the HSC as well."

"Phooey," Lucille said again. "And shame on you, Ella, for buying into that. It's about time our girl here stops paying for others' mistakes and regrets, don't you think?"

Ella turned and looked at Mallory for a long beat, seeming stricken by the thought of anyone thinking she wasn't fully supporting her own flesh and blood. "I never wanted you to pay for our mistakes and regrets."

"Well, she has," Lucille said, brutally honest as always, though her voice was very kind. She moved behind the nurses' desk, poured Ella some coffee, pulled a flask from her pocket, and added a dash of something that smelled 100 proof.

"Lucille!" Ella gasped. "I'm on the job!"

"You're clocking out, and it's time."

"Time for what?"

"Time for Mallory to not be the only one to stretch her wings. And speaking of wings," Lucille said to Mallory, "you're going to need wings for your next patient, and she's ready for you."

The new patient turned out to be Mrs. Burland.

"You," Mrs. B said when Mallory entered her room.

"Me," Mallory agreed and reached for the blood pressure cuff. "It says on your chart that you passed out after your bath again. Did you take your meds at the right time?"

"Well, of course I did. I'm not a complete idiot. They didn't work."

"Did you space the pills out with food, as explicitly instructed on the bottles?"

Mrs. Burland glared at her.

"I'll take that as a no," Mallory said. Mrs. B's color was off, and her blood pressure was far too low. "When was your last meal?"

"Hmph."

"Mrs. Burland." Mallory put her fingers on the woman's narrow, frail, paper-thin wrist to check her pulse. "Did you eat lunch today?"

Mrs. Burland straightened to her full four-foot-eight inches, quivering with indignity. "I know what I'm supposed to be doing."

Mallory looked into her rheumy, pissy eyes and felt her heart clench. *Dammit.* She had a feeling she knew the problem—Mrs. B didn't have any food. Probably she wasn't feeling good enough to take care of herself, and since she'd long ago scared off family and friends with her mean, petty, vicious ways, she had no one to help her. Mallory picked up the room phone and called the cafeteria. "Stella, it's Mallory. I need a full dinner tray for room three."

"Sure thing, Sweet Cheeks. Is your hunk-o-burning love going to be making any more visits my way?"

Mallory rubbed her still-twitching eye. "Not today."

When the tray came, Mallory stood over her grumpy patient. "Eat."

Mrs. Burland tried to push the tray away but Mallory was one step ahead of her, holding it still. "Oh no, you don't. You're not going to have a little tantrum and spill it, not this time."

Mrs. Burland's eyes burned bright with temper, which Mallory was happy to see because it meant her patient was already feeling better. Mallory leaned close. "I'm stronger and meaner, and *I've* eaten today."

"Well *that's* obvious." Mrs. Burland sniffed at the juice on the tray. "Hmph."

"It's apple."

"I have eyes in my head, don't I?" Mrs. Burland sipped the juice. In sixty seconds, her color was better. "You didn't used to be so mean."

"It's a newly acquired skill," Mallory said.

"I'm ready to go home now."

"You can't go home until I see you eat."

"You're making that up. This cafeteria food isn't fit for a dog," Mrs. Burland said.

Well, she had her there. Even Mallory, who'd eat just about anything, didn't like the cafeteria food, not that she'd ever say so to the cook. "Fine." Mallory went to the staff kitchen and pulled out her own lunch, which she brought back to Mrs. Burland's room. "Try my sandwich. Turkey and cheese with spinach." Which she'd only added because her mom kept asking if she was eating her vegetables. "There's a little bit of mustard and probably too much mayo but your cholesterol is the least of your problems." Mallory also tossed down a baggie of baby carrots and an apple.

Mrs. Burland took a bite of the sandwich first. "*Awful*," she said, but took another bite. And then another, until there was nothing left but a few crumbs.

"The carrot sticks and the apple too," Mallory said.

"Are they as horrid as the sandwich?"

"They're as horrid as your bad attitude. And I'll tell you this right now. You're going to eat it all if I have to shove it down your throat myself."

"*Mallory*," a voice breathed in disbelief from the doorway.

Jane. *Perfect.* Mallory turned to face her boss, but not before she saw triumph and evil glee come into Mrs. Burland's eyes.

"A moment," Jane said, face tight.

"Certainly." Mallory jabbed a finger at the carrots and apple. Mrs. Burland meekly picked up the apple.

In the hallway, Jane led Mallory just out of hearing range of Mrs. Burland. "New tactic?"

"Yes," Mallory said, refusing to defend herself. "She finish it all?"

Jane took a look over Mallory's shoulder at Mrs. B. "Every last bite. How did you do it?"

"By being a bigger bitch than she is."

"Nicely done."

By the time Mallory got in her car and left work, she was starving and exhausted. She solved the first problem by eating a handful of Jodi's cookies. Then she pulled her phone out and took a quick peek to see if she had any texts before remembering she had Ty's phone. She paused and eyed the remaining chocolate chip/walnut cookies. Fifteen minutes later, she pulled into Ty's driveway.

The garage door was open, and the man himself was flat on his back beneath his car, one long denim-clad leg straight out, the other bent. His black T-shirt had risen up. Or maybe it was his Levi's that had sunk almost indecently low on his hips. In either case, the revealed strip of his washboard abs had her mouth actually watering. She thought maybe she could stand here and just look at him all day long, but he seemed to enjoy looking at her right back and she'd had a hell of a long day and couldn't possibly be worth looking at right now.

Not that it appeared to make any difference. Ty's attraction to her was apparently based on some intangible thing she couldn't fathom. She knew she could think about that for a million years and not get used to it, to the fact that no matter what she did or what she looked like, he seemed to want her.

The feeling was far too mutual.

Chapter 16

Nothing chocolate, nothing gained.

Ty sat up on the mechanic's creeper and took in the sight of Mallory standing there. She was packing a plate of cookies, which he hoped to God were for him. He assumed she'd discovered the phone fiasco by now, but other than that, he wasn't sure what sort of mood to expect from her.

The last time he'd seen her, she'd been face down on his bed, boneless and sated right into a coma of bliss. He'd stroked a strand of damp hair from her face and she'd smiled in her sleep. His heart had constricted at the sight, his sole thought, *oh Christ, I am in trouble.* He'd been torn by the urge to tug her close, but then claustrophobia had reached up and grabbed him by the throat. Just as he'd chosen retreat, she'd awakened and gotten dressed to go.

That must have been when she'd grabbed the wrong phone, although he hadn't realized it then. He'd followed her home to make sure she got there safely, then driven back to his place and expected to crash. Instead he'd missed her.

Clearly he was losing it.

He had no idea what she was thinking, but he hadn't expected to see her smile at the sight of him, a smile that was filled with relief.

Relief, he realized, and surprise that he was still here in town.

Yeah, join my club. He was surprised, too.

She was in pale purple scrubs and white Nikes. She had two pens sticking out of her hip pocket, one red, one black. There were correlating ink marks on her scrubs. She followed his gaze and rubbed at the stains. "I'm a mess. Don't ask."

"Not a mess," he said. "Are those cookies?"

"Yes. And I had to fight the staff to keep them for you."

"Girl-on-girl fight?" he asked hopefully. "Did you get it on video?"

"You are such a guy." She came closer and crouched at his side, holding the plate out for him. He took a big bite of a cookie and moaned in deep appreciation.

"Did you give the HSC ten thousand dollars?"

Ah, there it was, he thought, swallowing. He'd been hoping she wouldn't find out, but he supposed that was unrealistic in a town like Lucky Harbor. Taking his time, he ate cookie number two, then reached for a third.

She held the plate out of his reach. "Did you?" she asked.

He eyed her for a long moment. "Which answer will get me the rest of the cookies?"

"Oh, Ty," she breathed, looking worried as she lowered the plate. Worried for him, he realized.

"Why?" she asked. "You already gave."

"HSC needed it."

"But it's *so* much money."

"If you're asking if I can afford it, I can."

She just stared at him, so he shrugged. "The job pays well." He paused. "Really well."

She let out a breath. She was already hunkered at his side so it took little effort to lean over toward him and press a kiss to his cheek. "Thank you," she whispered, and went to kiss the other cheek, but he turned his head and caught her mouth with his. They were both gratifyingly out of breath by the time he pulled back.

"You're welcome," he said, surprised when she rose and sat on the stool at his work bench.

"Don't let me keep you from what you were doing," she said. "I'll watch."

He arched a brow, feeling amused for the first time all day. "You want me to get back under the car?"

"I just don't want you to lose any time because of me."

"Is that right?"

"Absolutely."

Humoring the both of them, he lay back down onto the mechanic's creeper and lifted his hands above his head to the edge of the car.

She nibbled on her lower lip. Watching him work turned her on. The knowledge shouldn't have surprised him—she turned him on just breathing, but he laughed softly.

She blushed. "How did you know?"

"Your nipples are hard."

She made a sound in the back of her throat and covered her breasts, making him laugh.

"It's your jeans," she said. "They're faded at your, um." She waggled a finger in the direction of his crotch. "Stress spots. And your T-shirt, it's tight on your biceps and shoulders. And when you're flat on your back under the car, you look like you know what you're doing."

"That's because I do."

"It's the whole package," she agreed miserably.

He grinned. "If it helps, my *package* likes your package. A whole hell of a lot."

"Work!" she demanded, closing her eyes.

Obliging, he rolled back beneath the car. He heard her get to her feet and walk close, peering into the opened hood above him. "So how much wrenching do you do at your work?"

She was as see-through as glass. He knew that she'd put him back beneath the car because she'd gotten him to talk beneath a car before. But she was so goddamned cute trying to outthink him that he gave her what she wanted.

Which in hindsight made her a hell of lot more dangerous than he'd thought. "I hotwired a tank once," he said. "With my team. We stole it to disable rebel insurgents."

She squatted at his side. "You've led a very different life than mine." Her hand settled on his bad thigh. It'd been only recently that he'd even gotten feeling back in it, but he was having no trouble feeling anything now. It felt like her fingers had a direct line to his groin, and things stirred to life.

"Our phones got switched," she said.

There was a new quality to her voice now, one that had him setting down his wrench and pulling himself back out from beneath the car.

She was still crouched low, and from his vantage point flat on his back, he looked up into her face. As usual, she could hide nothing from him, and for once, he wished he couldn't see her every thought. They exchanged phones but her expression didn't change. "Problem?" he asked.

"A woman called. Frances? She wants you to call her."

"She always wants me to call her."

Mallory nodded, looked down at the ground and then back into his eyes. "Are you dating her?"

"I'm not much of a dater."

"You know what I mean."

Yeah, he did. And he didn't want to go there.

"I know," she said quickly. "We agreed that this thing with you and me was...casual."

He didn't like where this was going.

"A fling," she went on. "Right? Not a relationship." She rose and turned away from him. "But I was thinking that maybe that last part isn't true. I mean, we never actually said there *wasn't* a relationship."

"I'll say it," he said. "It's not a relationship."

She went still, turning back to stare at him with those eyes he'd never once been able to resist. "Why is that?" she asked. "Why can't there be an us, if there's a you and a someone else?"

He looked into her expressive face and felt a stab of pain right in the gut. He'd survived SEAL training. He'd lived through a plane crash. He'd kept on breathing when the rest of his team, his friends, his brothers, hadn't been able to do the same. But he didn't know how to do this. "There are some things I can't tell you," he said slowly. "Things that even if I wanted to, I couldn't."

"So the reason we can't be a *we* is classified?" she asked in disbelief. "Really, Ty?"

Well, hell. Yeah, that had been pretty fucking lame. Chalk it up to the panic now residing in his hollow gut. Whatever he did here, whatever he came up with, he needed her to want to keep her distance. Except Mallory Quinn was incapable of distance when her heart was involved. That was both painfully attractive and terrifying. "Don't fall for me, Mallory. That wouldn't be good for either of us. We're too different. You said so yourself."

She sucked in a breath like he'd slapped her. "And what, you and Frances are alike? Compatible?"

"Unfortunately, yes."

Hands on hips, she narrowed her eyes. "If you're sleeping with her, then why wouldn't she just roll over and talk to you? Why is she yelling about you not returning her phone calls?"

"Frances doesn't yell."

"*Strongly* suggested then," she said with mock politeness. She paused. "You're not sleeping with her."

Gig up. "I'm not sleeping with her. And as for the why she's pissed, there are a variety of reasons. I haven't seen her in six months, for one."

She stared at him, then turned away again.

Ty rose to his feet and walked around her to see her face. "Get the rest out," he said. "Let's finish this."

A wry smile twisted her mouth. "You aren't familiar with the Quinn pattern of holding onto a good mad, I see."

"Holding onto your mad only tortures *you*," he pointed out. "If you're mad at me, let me have it."

"Are you always so logical?" With a sigh, she shook her head. "Never mind. Don't answer that." She put a finger to her eye. "Damn twitch," she muttered to herself, then looked at him, chin up. "I snooped in your phone."

"I would expect nothing less from Walking-On-The-Wild-Side Mallory."

"I thought about not telling you. But stealth isn't one of my special talents."

"You have other special talents," he said, and made her laugh.

"Dammit," she said. "I don't want to laugh with you right now."

Lifting a hand, he wrapped it around the nape of her neck and drew her in. "You need some more time to be mad at me?"

"Yes."

"Let me know when you're about done." He knew he had no right to touch her, crave her like air, but he did both. And when he put his mouth on hers, he recognized the taste of her, like she'd been made just for him. Which made him far more screwed than he'd even imagined.

But suddenly she was pulling free, shaking her head. "Ty—I can't."

"You can't kiss and be mad at me at the same time?"

"Oh, I can do that. What I can't do is this. I can't do this and keep it…not real."

"It's real."

"Yes, but real for you means an erection. For me, it means..." She rubbed her chest as if it hurt and closed her eyes. "Never mind." She took a step back and then another. "I'm sorry, this really is my fault. I shouldn't have—"

"Mallory—"

"No, it's okay. Really. But I'm going now."

He watched her get into her car and drive off. Yeah, he thought, definitely time to go back to work. Past time.

Mallory parked behind her brother's truck in her mother's driveway.

Dinner with the Quinns.

It'd been a full day since she'd left Ty standing in his garage, hot and dirty and looking a little baffled, like maybe he'd lost his copy of the rule book for their little game.

But even though she'd started the game in the first place, she no longer wanted to play. Somewhere along the way, her heart had flipped on her. She could pretend to be a bad girl all she wanted. It was only an illusion. The truth was, she needed more than just sex. And that really pissed her off about herself.

And what pissed her off even more was how much she already missed him.

Her mother was in the kitchen pulling a roasted chicken out of the oven. It looked perfect. Mallory wouldn't even know where to begin to make food that looked like that and she sniffed appreciatively.

"Did you bring the dessert?" her mother asked. "That cake you brought to Joe's birthday party was amazing. I had no idea you were so talented. Tell me you made another of those."

Mallory held out the tray of cupcakes she'd gotten from the B&B this morning. Tara had promised they were absolutely to die for. Mallory knew this to be true because she'd already inhaled two of them.

"A woman who can bake like this," her mom said, "should have kids. I wouldn't mind some grandchildren."

"Mom."

"Just sayin'."

"Well, stop just sayin'."

Joe walked in and rumpled Mallory's hair. "Hey, think you can convince that cute new LN to go out with me?"

"No, Camilla's too good for you. And how do you know her?"

"I work with her brother at the welding shop. She brought him lunch."

"Stay away from Camilla," Mallory said.

Ella was shooing everyone to the table. "Joe, put your phone away. Oh, Mal, I almost forgot. Tammy wanted me to ask if you'd take Alyssa's shift this weekend so she and Tammy can have a girl's night out."

Mallory grabbed two rolls. "Can't."

Ella took one roll back. "You'll hate yourself in the morning. And why can't you take the shift?"

"I'm working at the HSC this weekend."

"Both days?"

"No, but I need a day off."

Ella blinked. "You never say no. You're always so good about helping everyone."

Oh how she hated that adjective applied to her—*good.*

Joe grinned and took two rolls without comment from Ella, the skinny rat-fink bastard. "I don't think Mallory likes being called *good*, Mom."

"Of course she does. Why wouldn't she?"

Right. Why wouldn't she…

She escaped as soon as dinner was over. Her family was…well, her family. She loved them but they had no idea how much their opinion of her wore her down, that she yearned for so much more, that she wanted to be seen. Seen for herself.

Ty saw her for herself.

Too bad he didn't see her as someone he wanted in his life.

She was halfway home when her phone rang. She pulled over and answered Amy's call.

"You see Facebook lately?"

Mallory's heart sank. "What now?"

"Someone caught a picture of you and Ty in what looks like the hospital parking lot. He was...under your hood."

Oh boy. "Tell me you really mean that. And not as some sort of euphemism."

"The picture is hot, Mal. No one can deny that you don't look good together."

"We're *not* together. And what the hell are we doing in the picture?"

"Kissing. And he's got a hand on your ass. They've relabeled him from Mysterious Cute Guy to Good-With-His-Hands Guy."

"Oh, God."

"And Mal?"

"Yeah?"

"I think you're ready to teach your own Bad Girl Lessons now."

Mallory thunked her head on the steering wheel.

"Oh, and chocoholics unite tomorrow. I'm getting a chocolate cake from Tara. It's got yours, Grace's, and my name on it. *You've* got a story to tell."

"So do you. I want to hear more about this thing with Matt—"

"There's no 'thing.'"

"Amy—"

"Sorry, bad connection. Must be going through a tunnel."

"You're at the diner!"

"Oh, well then it must be something I don't want to discuss." And she disconnected.

Mallory shook her head and got back on the road, hitting the gas hard. She wanted to see that Facebook pic. Two blocks from home, red and blue lights flashed in her rearview mirror.

Shit.

She pulled over, rolled down her window, and glared at Sheriff Sawyer Thompson as he ambled up to the side of her car. She and Sawyer had gone to high school together, though he'd been a couple of years ahead of her. She'd done his English papers, and he'd handled her math and science. Later, she'd patched him up several times when his wild, misspent youth had landed him on the injured list.

Then he'd settled down and become a sheriff of all things, now firmly entrenched on the right side of the law. There'd been a time when having the big, bad, sexy sheriff pull her over might have made her day. But that time wasn't now. "What?" she demanded a little crankily. "You don't have a bad guy to catch? You have to pull over people who are just trying to get home?"

"Give me a break, Mal. You were doing fifty-five in a thirty-five zone. I whooped my siren at you twice, and you never even noticed. What the hell's up with you?"

Crap. She sagged in her seat. "Nothing."

He shook his head and leaned against her car, apparently perfectly happy to take a break on her time. He sighed.

"Long day?" she asked sympathetically.

"Yeah." He slid her a look. "But clearly not as long as yours."

"I'm fine."

"Is that right?" He pulled out his iPhone and thumbed his way to a page, then turned it to her.

Facebook.

A picture had indeed been posted, just as Amy had said. It was small and grainy but it was her. In Ty's arms.

With his hand on her ass.

She stared at herself. She had a dazed, dreamy smile on her face. Not Ty. His expression was possessive as he stared down at her hungrily, and she felt herself getting aroused all over again in spite of herself. This was quickly followed by a surge of her supposedly rare temper. "Are you *kidding* me?"

Sawyer slipped the phone back into his pocket.

"That's an invasion of privacy!" she said. "Arrest someone!"

"You were in a public place."

"I didn't know someone was taking pictures!"

"Obviously," Sawyer drawled, still leaning back against her car as if he had all day.

"I'm going to kick someone's ass."

His brow shot up at that. "You don't kick ass, Mal. You *save* people's asses."

"I'm over it! Give me my damn speeding ticket and get out of my way before I run your foot over."

Sawyer flashed a genuine grin now. "Are you threatening an officer?"

"My ticket, Sawyer."

"I'm not going to give you a ticket, Mallory."

"You're not?"

"Hell, no. If I gave you a ticket now, I'd get skinned alive by...well, everyone."

This was thankfully true. "That's never bothered you before." If she wasn't so mad, she might have found humor in this. "It's Chloe. Having a girlfriend has softened you up."

He grimaced. "I'm tempted to ticket you just for saying that."

She found a smile after all.

He returned it and leaned in her window, tugging on a strand of her hair. "Want some advice?"

"I want to run your foot over."

"You're not going to run me over, because then you'd have to give me first aid and you're not in the mood." But he stepped back, proving he wasn't just all good looks. "Slow down," he warned her and tugged on her hair again. "*Everywhere.*"

"What does that mean?"

"It means that I don't want to see you hurt."

Well, it was too damn late for that, wasn't it. She already hurt, thank you very much.

She blew out a breath and eased out into traffic. She was careful not to speed again, even with her phone going off every two seconds. She ignored all calls, parked in her driveway, watered Mrs. Tyler's flowers, watered her grandma's flowers, and fed Sweet Pea.

Some habits were hard to break.

She bent down to scratch the cat behind the ears and got bit for her efforts. Yeah, definitely some habits were hard to break. She walked straight through the house and out the back door. In the backyard, she headed to the sole lounge chair. Plopping down, she hit speaker on her phone and finally accessed the messages, squinting as she did, as if that would help not hear them.

"Mallory," Jane said in her Displeased Voice. "Call me."

No thank you. Clearly her boss had seen the picture. Just as clearly, she assumed that Mallory had ignored her warning. Mallory supposed she should call in and let Jane know that the picture had been taken before their "talk." Or that she was no longer seeing Ty. But tired of being the peacemaker, she hit delete.

"Wow, Mal," came the next message. Tammy. "You're one serious badass lately. If you find yourself heading to Vegas, make sure you buy the wedding package *without* the photos. You don't need any pics; this one is perfect."

Delete.

Third message. "Mallory, this is Deena. From the grocery store? Yeah, listen, I play Bunko with a group every Wednesday night, and this week we had a drawing for who could go for Cute Guy and I won. So you're going to need to back off. He's mine."

He's all yours, Deena.

Delete.

Sweet Pea bumped her head into Mallory's shin. This wasn't a show of love but a demand for more food. "You have no idea how good you have it, cat," she said with a sigh. "All you have to do is sleep for, what, eighteen hours a day? No pressure, no expectations. No Mysterious Cute Guys messing with your head, giving you mixed signals."

Except the mixed signals had been all hers. He'd been honest with her from the get-go. Well, if not exactly honest, he'd at least been up front.

Don't fall for me, Mallory. That wouldn't be good for either of us.

Right. She'd just stand firm and not fall.

Except…

Except she already had.

Chapter 17

What is the meaning of life? All evidence to date points to chocolate.

After a sleepless night, Mallory worked a long shift, then took a detour home by Mrs. Burland's house. Last night the HSC had hosted a healthy living seminar given by Cece Martin, the local dietician, and Mrs. Burland had promised to go. Mallory had looked over the sign-in sheet from the event but Mrs. B hadn't shown up.

Mallory pulled into Mrs. B's driveway. The yard was neglected, as was the house. With a bad feeling, Mallory got out of her car, grabbed the bag of groceries she'd picked up, and knocked at the front door.

No one answered.

Mallory knocked again, knowing that Mrs. B probably wouldn't open the door to her, but something definitely felt off. She wriggled the handle, and the door opened. "Mrs. Burland?" she called out. "It's me, Mallory Quinn."

"Go away."

The voice sounded feeble and weak and somehow arrogant at

the same time. Ignoring the command, Mallory walked inside the dark house and flipped on a light.

Mrs. Burland lay on the scarred wood floor at the base of a set of stairs.

Mallory dropped everything in her hands and rushed to her, setting two fingers against Mrs. B's carotid artery to search out a pulse.

Strong.

Sagging back on her knees, she let out a breath of relief. "You got dizzy and fell down the stairs?"

"No, I like to nap here," Mrs. B snapped out. "I told you to go away. You have no right to be here."

Okay, so little Miss Merry Sunshine was stringing her words together just fine, with no obvious disorientation. It was her vasovagal syncope then. Mallory ran a hand down the older woman's limbs and found nothing obviously broken. "Can you stand?"

"Sure. I just chose to be the rug today," Mrs. B snapped. "Why the hell are you here? Don't you ever get tired of saving people? *Why do you do it*?"

"Well, in your case, I do it for your charming wit and sweet nature." And anyway, there weren't enough shrinks or enough time to cover why she really did it... "Can you sit up?"

Mrs. Burland slapped Mallory's hands away but didn't move.

Well, that answered that question. Mallory sat on the floor next to her and rifled through the bag of groceries she'd brought. "What's going to float your boat today? I've got soup, a sandwich, or—"

"Just go away! I'm old. I'm alone. I'm going to die any second now. Just *let me*."

"You're not old," Mallory said. "You're just mean. And FYI, *that's* why you're alone. You could have friends if you'd stop snapping at everyone. Lucille'd take you into her posse in an instant if you were even the slightest bit less evil. She *loves* snark."

"I'm *alone*."

"Hello," Mallory said. "I'm sitting right here! You're *not* alone. You have me." She pulled out a snack-sized box of apple juice. "Your favorite."

"Not thirsty."

"Then how about some chicken soup?"

Mrs. Burland showed another sign of life as a slight spark came into her eyes. "Is it from a can?"

"No," Mallory said. "I spent all day cooking it myself. After raising the chickens and growing the carrots and celery in my garden."

Mrs. Burland sniffed. "I don't eat soup out of a can."

"Fine." Mallory pulled out a bag of prunes.

Mrs. Burland snatched the bag and opened it with shaking fingers.

Mallory smiled.

"You're enjoying my misery?"

"I knew I'd get you with the prunes."

After a minute or two, with the sugar in her system, Mrs. B glared at Mallory. "I'd have been fine without you."

"Sure. You'd be even better if you took care of yourself."

"What do you know? You're not taking care of yourself either."

"What does that mean?"

"In a storage attic?" Mrs. Burland asked snidely, then snorted at Mallory's look of shock. "Yes, I heard about your little interlude. Someone caught your Mr. Garrison coming downstairs from the auction, and then you following him a few minutes later looking all telltale mussed up. Either you were practicing for a WWE tryout or you'd been having some hanky-panky. Don't think just because I'm old that I don't know these things. I remember hormones."

Oh good Lord.

"And what kind of a woman dates a man who takes her to a storage attic?" Mrs. B wanted to know.

A red-blooded one. Ty Garrison was *seriously* potent, and Mallory defied even the most stalwart of women to be able to deny herself a Ty-induced orgasm. Just thinking it made her ache, because in spite of herself, she missed him *way* too much. She hoped he missed her too, that he wasn't planning to fill the void with... *Frances*. "Actually," she said, "it's not really an attic, but more of a storage area. And we're not dating."

"So you're giving away the milk for free?"

"First of all, I'm not a cow," Mallory said. "And second of all, we're *not* discussing this."

"You're trying to save him, right? Like you try to save everyone? Surely even you realize that a man like that isn't interested in a small town nurse, not for the long term."

The jab hit a little close to home because it happened to be true. But Mallory wasn't trying to save Ty.

She wouldn't have minded keeping him, though... "Watch it," she said mildly. "Or the prunes come with me."

"Hmph."

They sat there on the floor for a few minutes longer while Mallory checked Mrs. Burland's vitals again, which were stronger now. Then she glanced up and nearly screamed.

Jack Nicholson from *The Shining* stood in the front doorway.

Or Mr. Wykowski. He stepped inside. "Louisa," he said quietly, eyes on Mrs. B. "You all right?"

The oddest thing happened. Right before Mallory's eyes, Mrs. Burland changed. She softened. She...*smiled.* Or at least that's what Mallory thought the baring of her teeth meant.

"Of course," Mrs. B said. "I'm fine."

"Liar," Mr. Wykowski said, squatting beside her. "You get dizzy again?"

"Of course not."

"*Louisa*."

Mrs. Burland's eyes darted away. "Maybe a little. But only for a minute."

Mr. Wykowski nodded to Mallory. "Good of you to stop by. She doesn't make it easy. She hasn't figured out that we take care of our own here in Lucky Harbor."

Mallory smiled at him, knowing she'd never be afraid of him again. "It's good to know she's not *alone.*" She shot Mrs. Burland a long look.

Mrs. Burland rolled her eyes, but shockingly not a single bitchy thing crossed her lips.

There were more footsteps on the front porch and then another neighbor appeared. Lucille. She was in a neon green track suit today, which wasn't exactly flattering on a body that gravity hadn't exactly been kind to. Her wrinkled lips were in pink. Her tennis shoes were black and yellow.

You needed a pair of sunglasses to look at her.

"There you are, Teddy," Lucille said, smiling at Mr. Wykowski. "Ready for that walk around the block?"

Mrs. Burland narrowed her gaze. "He was visiting with *me.*"

Lucille put her hands on her hips. "You don't even like visitors."

"Out of my house."

Lucille smiled. "Make me."

Mrs. Burland narrowed her eyes.

Lucille held out her hand. "Need help getting up first?"

Mrs. Burland struggled up by herself, glaring triumphantly at Lucille when she did it. "I could beat you around the block if I wanted."

"Yeah?" Lucille sized her up. "Prove it."

"I'll do that." Mrs. Burland moved toward the door, where Mr. Wykowski carefully drew her arm into the crook of his. Then Lucille flanked Mrs. Burland's other side.

And the three of them walked out the door and around the block.

Mallory went home. She parked, watered Mrs. Tyler's flowers, her grandma's flowers, and then unlocked her front door. She glanced at the little foyer desk—as she had every time since Ty had shown her a whole new use for it—and sighed. There was chocolate cake in her immediate future. If she wasn't going to have wild, high-calorie-burning sex, she was going to have to resort to some exercise.

"Meow."

"I hear you." She fed Sweet Pea and then changed, forcing herself to the pier for a run.

The quarter of a mile down to the end nearly killed her so she walked back, holding the stitch in her side. When she came up on the ice cream stand, she slowed even more. Lance wasn't working today but his older brother Tucker was.

"Hey Cutie," Tucker called out. "I've got a chocolate double with your name on it. Literally. We just created a new list of specials. Number one is The Good Girl Gone Bad."

She gave him a long, dark look and he laughed. "Come on," he said. "It's funny."

Maybe to someone whose name wasn't Mallory Quinn.

"Want one?"

More than her next breath. "No."

He leaned out the window, all lean, easy grace as he took in her sweaty appearance. "Wow, turning down ice cream. And you're running." His smile spread. "You're on a diet, aren't you?"

She blew out a breath. "Just trying to get some exercise and be healthy."

"You look good to me," he said.

Aw. That was nice. She was thinking maybe he'd be a nice addition to the Mr. Wrong list, but then he said, "And whatshisface should tell you that in every attic he gets you into."

"Okay, first of all, it's a *storage area*!" And dammit. She was going to have to move. She went back to running. Without her ice cream.

It was the hardest thing she'd ever done.

She went home and glared at her foyer desk. "Somehow," she told it, "this is your fault."

The table had nothing to say in its defense.

"Fine. It's not your fault. It's Ty's." Her body ached for him, but it was more than that. Her mind ached for him, too.

Shaking her head at herself, she showered, got caught up in a *Charmed* season six marathon, and then headed over to Eat Me at the appointed time for a meeting of the Chocoholics.

As she entered Eat Me, the comforting sounds of people talking and laughing washed over her, as did scents of foods that made her stomach growl.

She'd skipped dinner. Tonight was very different from their first impromptu meeting. For one, there was no storm. It was fifty degrees outside, clear, and the air was scented with late spring.

For another, it wasn't midnight so the place wasn't deserted. She slipped onto the stool next to Grace and eyed the empty spot in front of her. "You refraining tonight?"

"Waiting on you."

Amy appeared, holding a cake and three forks.

Mallory grabbed one and dug in, guilt free since she'd run.

"No less than five customers have already tried to buy this cake," Amy said. "So you are welcome." She had to come and go at first as the diner emptied out. Then she stood on her side of the counter inhaling her third of the small cake. "God," she said on a moan. "Heaven on earth."

"Amazing," Grace admitted.

Mallory couldn't speak. She was too busy stuffing her face.

Amy swallowed and licked chocolate off her lips. "I'm calling this meeting to order. Mallory, you're first up."

"Nope. Not my turn."

"We've told you, you're first until we fix you." Grace smiled. "So spill. Tell us all."

Mallory sighed. "I'd rather talk about Amy and Sexy Forest Ranger Matt."

Grace went brows up at this and looked at Amy. "You putting

out forest fires with that hot ranger who keeps coming in here for pie?"

"We have good pie," Amy said.

"There's all kinds of pie," Grace said.

Mallory nearly snorted cake out her nose, and Amy gave her a dirty look.

"This is *not* about me," she said haughtily and pointed her fork at Mallory.

Mallory stuffed in some cake.

"Uh oh," Grace said. "I'm sensing some slowdown in Mission: Bad Girl."

"I wore the shoes," Mallory said. "And it was fun."

"Um, honey, from all accounts, you had more than some fun," Grace said, licking her fork.

"Accounts?"

"FB." Grace turned to Amy. "And thanks for the Facebook tip, by the way. It's a little addictive."

"You can't believe everything you read on there." Mallory sank onto her stool a little bit. "It's only a small percentage of the truth."

"Is that right?" Grace asked. "So what percentage of that picture with you and Ty looking cozy would you say is the truth?"

Mallory blew out a sigh and stabbed into the cake for another big bite. "We weren't…cozy. Then."

Grace grinned. "He's got that look. That big, sexy, I-know-how-to-please-a-woman-in-bed look."

Mallory propped up her head with her hand. With her other, she shoveled in more cake. "I don't want to talk about it."

"Yeah, but see, we *do*," Amy said.

"I broke it off," Mallory said and sighed when they gasped. "I told you, I'm not hard-wired for this bad girl stuff. Every time we were together I would find myself…" She closed her eyes. "Falling."

Grace reached for her hand and squeezed it.

Amy pushed the cake closer to Mallory.

"Thanks." Mallory shook her head. "I couldn't keep things light. He's just…" She sighed. "Too yummy."

"He was swimming the other day," Grace said. "In the ocean. I was sitting on the beach pouting after spending gas money to get to Seattle for interviews that went nowhere. Anyway, he swam for like two hours straight. Didn't know anyone but a Navy SEAL could do that. Did you know a Navy SEAL can find or hunt down anyone or anything?"

"So?" Amy said.

"So, I bet a guy like that could locate a clit without any problems."

Both Amy and Grace looked at Mallory expectantly. Mallory choked on her cake, and was still choking when someone came up behind her and patted her on the back.

She knew that touch. Intimately. Whipping around, she came face to face with Ty. Her heart clutched at the sight of him. Traitorous heart. And she couldn't help but wonder, had he been a SEAL? It made perfect sense. He'd sure had absolutely no problem finding her clit…

His gaze met hers for an unfathomably long beat, and as always, just at the sight of him, she got a little thrill. And also as always, he looked bigger than life, and a whole lot more than she could handle. But there was something different about him tonight. Tonight he seemed weary and a little rough around the edges, and her heart clenched again.

God, she'd missed him.

She didn't understand it, but he'd never looked more appealing. Or real. She wanted to take his hand in hers and kiss away his problems. Hold him.

She wanted to hold a caged lion.

It made no sense but it was the truth. She knew he was leaving, and he'd be taking a big piece of her heart along with him when he did, but that was a done deal. She also knew something else—that she wanted whatever he had to give her in the meantime. Because with him, she wasn't a caretaker. She wasn't a sister. She wasn't thinking, planning, overseeing.

She was just Mallory. And she felt…alive. So damn alive.

His eyes smiled. He touched the corner of her upper lip, then sucked on his finger. "Mmm," he said. "Chocolate."

Amy's jaw dropped open. Grace fanned herself. Ty looked at them, and they suddenly got very busy. Though Amy did give Mallory a "see, meeting interrupted *again*" look before she went off to serve a customer, and Grace remembered something she had to go do.

Which didn't stop everyone else in the diner from staring at them. "Oh good Lord," Mallory said. "Come on." She took the caged lion's hand and led him outside.

The stars were out in force tonight, like scattered diamonds on the night sky. The waves crashed up against the shore. They walked along the pier, past the dark arcade and the closed ice cream shop. Past everything until there was nothing but empty pier ahead and the black ocean. There Mallory stopped and leaned over the railing. "I'm sorry about the other day," she said quietly, facing the water. "I mean, I started this thing between us. I laid out the rules. So I had no right to change them on you without saying so, and then hold it against you."

He didn't say anything, and she turned to him, searching his impassive face, hoping to see understanding. Forgiveness. Or at the very least, a sign that he understood.

She got none of that, and her heart sank.

After a minute, he mirrored her pose, leaning on the railing to stare out at the water. "I grew up with military parents," he said. "I went into the military. And when I got out, I went to work for a private contractor to the government, doing…more military-like work. It's my job, it's my life. It's who I am."

She nodded. "I know."

"It requires things of me," he said. "Being alone, being the protector, keeping myself protected." He lifted a shoulder. "I don't know how to be anyone else."

"I don't want you to be anyone else, Ty. Ever. I like who you are."

He was quiet, absorbing that. "Frances is my boss. She's… proprietary."

To say the least. But he wasn't giving her all of it. "You've been with her. Sexually."

"Yes," he said, bluntly honest as always. "Before I worked for her, a very long time ago. It's over."

"For you," she said. "It's over for you."

He acknowledged that with a shrug. Not his problem. So it wouldn't be Mallory's either, she decided.

Turning to her, Ty ran a finger over the dainty gold chain at her neck, then beneath the infinity charm, looking at it for a moment. "After I lost my team in the plane crash, I spent the first six months recovering alone, by choice." He let out a breath and dropped his hand from her. "I couldn't… I didn't want anyone close. I still don't want anyone close."

He'd lost his parents, his friends. Everyone. She couldn't imagine how alone he must have felt.

Or maybe she could. Hadn't she, even surrounded by all the people in her life, *still* felt alone? Mallory scooped her necklace in her palm and tightened her fist on it. "Karen gave this to me right before she—" She closed her eyes for a minute, and pictured Karen's own laughing eyes. "It's the infinity sign," she told him. "Forever connected. She wore it all the time, and I always bugged her to let me borrow it. I wanted to be just like her. It used to drive her nuts. Then one day, she took the necklace off and just put it around my neck. She kissed my cheek and told me to be good, that being good would keep me out of the trouble that she'd always found herself in. She made me promise. Then she said she'd be watching me, guiding my way, making sure I was okay. I thought—I thought how sweet, but then..." Her throat tightened almost beyond bearing. "It was the last time I saw her," she said softly. "The next day she..." She let out a shuddery breath and shook her head, unable to speak.

With a low sound of empathy, Ty slid his hand to the nape of her neck, drawing her in against him. It was her undoing, and she fisted her hands in his shirt as a few tears escaped.

"I know your losses hurt," she managed. "But you're not alone, Ty." She said this fiercely, choking out the words. "You're not. I mean the pain doesn't go away, it *never* goes away, but it gets easier to remember them. And then one day, you'll remember them with a smile. I can promise you that."

He tightened his grip on her and nodded. They stood like that, locked together, a light breeze blowing her hair around. A strand of it clung to the stubble on his jaw and he left it there, bound to her, liking it...

"I thought maybe you'd left," she said.

"Not yet."

But soon...Those words, unspoken, hovered between them. When he got medically cleared, he'd be gone.

"Maybe you can't walk away from me," she said, meaning to tease, to lighten the moment.

"I can always walk away," he said. "Discipline runs deep."

Okay, so he wasn't feeling playful. Shaken, she took a step back and came up against the railing, but he put his hands on her and reeled her back in. "I need to get back to what I do," he said.

"You aren't your work."

"I am." Maintaining eye contact, he tightened his grip on her. "But I'm not ready to go yet."

"It's the sex," she said.

"It's more than sex."

"Not if it's still something that can be walked away from," she said.

He held her gaze, his own steady. Calm. So sure. "It's the way it has to be, Mallory."

She already knew that, oh how she knew it. The question was the same as always—could she live with it?

Yes.

No.

For now... Because the alternative was losing him right now, right this very minute, and she'd tried that. It didn't work for her. She wasn't ready to let him go.

He pressed his forehead to hers. "Your call," he said quietly. "Tell me to fuck off. Walk away from me right now and avoid any more heartbreak, I'm not worth it. Or—"

"Or," she said with soft steel. "I choose the *or*."

"Mallory." His voice was gruff. "You deserve better."

She pulled him farther down the pier, past the yacht club entrance and around the side of the building where no one who happened by could see them. There she pushed him up against the wall and kissed him. She took full advantage of his surprise, opening her mouth over his, causing a rush of heat and the melting of all the bones in her legs.

He was a soldier and knew how to turn any situation to his own advantage, and this was no exception. In less than a single heartbeat, he'd taken complete control of the kiss, stealing her breath and her heart with one sweep of his finger.

"If the decision is mine to make," she said breathing hard, her voice utterly serious, "then I'm keeping you, for as long as I can have you."

Chapter 18

Falling in love is like eating a whole box of chocolates—it seems like a good idea at first...

The next day, Ty woke up in his bed with a gloriously naked woman sprawled out over the top of him. Not that he was opposed to such a phenomenon, but this gloriously naked woman was all up in his space, and he'd always valued his own space. He was a big guy and he didn't like to feel crowded. Mallory was half his size, and as it turned out, she was a bed hog. She was also a blanket hog and a pillow hog.

It's okay, he told himself. It was okay that they'd slept together because they both knew what this was and what it wasn't. They'd fallen asleep together, that's all. It didn't mean anything. Now if it happened again... well, *then* he'd panic. "Mallory."

She let out a soft snore, and he felt his heart squeeze. Fucking heart. "Mallory. Are you working today?" He already had one hand on her ass. Easy enough to add the other. When he squeezed, then went exploring, a low appreciative moan escaped her lips, and she obligingly spread her legs, giving him more room to work, murmuring something that sounded like "don't stop."

Then she froze and jerked upright. "*Whattimeisit?*"

"Seven," he said, nuzzling his face in her crazy hair.

"Seven? *Seven?* I have to be gone!" She leapt out of the bed, frantically searching for her various pieces of clothing.

Enjoying the Naked Mallory Show, he leaned back, hands behind his head.

"Where are my panties?" she demanded.

"Under the chair."

She dove under the chair, giving him a heart-stopping view that made him groan.

"They're not here!" she yelled, voice muffled from her head-down-ass-up position.

"No? Check under my jeans then," he said.

She straightened, and hair in her face—hell, hair everywhere—gave him a narrowed gaze.

He smiled.

She crawled to his jeans, another hot view, and snatched her panties. With her clothes in her arms, she vanished into his bathroom. Two minutes later she reappeared, dressed and looking thoroughly fucked. "Come here," he said, smiling.

"Oh hell no. If I come over there, you're going to kiss me."

"Yeah," he said. "I am."

"And then you'll...*you know*."

He laughed, feeling light-hearted and...happy. "I do know. I know exactly what I want to do to you. I want to put my mouth on your—"

"Oh, God." She shook her head and grabbed her keys. "*I have to go!*"

"Five minutes," he said, and thought he had her when she hesitated, biting her lower lip, looking tempted. "It'll be the best five minutes of your day," he promised.

"I usually need more like fifteen minutes."

"Not last night you didn't. Last night you only needed four before you—"

"*Bye*," she said, laughing, and shut his door.

Ty lay there smiling like an idiot for a few minutes. Then his phone beeped. Rolling out of bed, he accessed his messages. Once upon a not-so-long-ago time, there were only messages from Frances. That was no longer the case. The first message was from Ryan.

"Hey, man," the vet said. That was it, the full extent of the message. Pretty typical of Ryan, and it could mean anything from "let's have dinner" to "I'm jonesing and need someone to talk to."

Matt had called as well, looking for a sparring partner. Josh had called inquiring about his health—and Ty knew Josh meant his mental health, not his leg.

Ty stared at his phone in surprise. At some point, when he'd been busy resenting like hell this slow-paced, sleepy little town and everyone in it, something had happened.

He'd made ties, strings on the heart he wasn't even sure he had. His smile faded as he listened to his last message, which contained no words, just a seething silence.

Frances.

He should call her and check in. After all, he was cleared to go back. But he didn't call. Instead he checked up on Ryan, then he finished the last of the cars lined up for him—Matt's Jimmy.

Now he could go back.

Almost.

He showered and drove to the Health Services Clinic just as it was closing up for the day. It was Thursday, and he knew there were no activities or meetings scheduled there that night.

He'd checked.

The front room was empty, but he could hear voices so he followed them and found Mallory in one of the small rooms, door open. She was facing a woman in her sixties. The woman was sitting in a chair, her face pinched like she'd eaten a sour apple.

Mallory was wearing purple scrubs today, and it was a good color for her. Her hair had been tied back, probably hours ago, and as usual, strands had escaped.

She wasn't good at hiding her feelings, and right now she was on edge, tired, and frustrated.

A long day, no doubt, made longer since they'd spent most of the night tearing up his sheets. He knew exactly what he'd do to relax her, but he had to remind himself that she wasn't his to take care of.

His own choice.

He was leaving, and someday, maybe someday soon, she'd stay up all night with someone else. Someone who would take care of her, help her unwind at the end of the day. Maybe someone from her list.

But if it was Anderson, Ty was going to kick his ass, just on principle. And if it was Josh, Ty'd…Jesus. It'd be whoever Mallory chose, and Ty had nothing to say about it, not even if her new Mr. Wrong used the guise of showing her how to hold a tool to kiss her. Not even if that Mr. Wrong bent her over a piece of furniture, taking her in front of a mirror, forcing her to see how gorgeous and amazing she really was. It was none of his business.

But it sucked.

"Just trust me," Mallory said to her patient, moving to a cabinet. She pulled a set of keys from her pocket and eyed the medicine samples lined up there before grabbing a box. "Take these. One a day."

"What are you poisoning me with now?" the woman asked.

"Vitamins," Mallory said.

The woman set the samples down. "Vitamins are a sham. It's the drug companies' way of making money off all us unsuspecting idiots."

Mallory put the vitamins back into the woman's hands. "Your blood work shows you're anemic. These will help. Or you can keep passing out in the bathroom and waiting until EMS finds you on the floor with your pants at your ankles again. Your choice, Mrs. Burland."

There was a long silence during which the woman glared at Mallory. "You used to be afraid of me. You used to quail and tremble like a little girl."

"Things change," Mallory said in a mild voice. No judgment, no recriminations. "Take the vitamins. Don't make me come over every night and pinch your nose and shove them down your throat."

"Well fine, if you're going to out-mean me."

"I am," Mallory said firmly.

"See, you *have* changed. You've gotten a tough skin. You've learned to hold back and keep your emotions off your sleeve for the world to see. You are very welcome."

"Oh, it wasn't *all* you," Mallory said, and Ty felt an odd tightening in his chest, because he knew who'd changed her.

Him.

He was such an asshole.

Turning from the woman, Mallory caught sight of him standing there. Her surprised smile only added to the ache in Ty's chest but he nodded to her and stepped back, leaning against the wall in the hall to wait.

Mallory looked at her patient. "I have something else for you; hold on." She came out into the hall, shutting the door behind her. She flashed Ty another smile and vanished into the next room. When she returned, she handed her patient some flyers before guiding her from the exam room and out front.

A few minutes later Mallory was back. "Hey."

"Hey. You need a lock on the front door when you're here alone," he said.

"I wasn't alone until now, and this is Lucky Harbor. I'm as safe as it gets."

"You're not safe here with the drugs."

"The meds are locked."

"Flimsy lock," he said. "Especially for someone who's desperate."

"It's only temporary. We're getting a much better set-up next week." She smiled, still not taking her safety seriously enough for him. "So what's up? What brings you here?"

"You owe me a favor," he said. "And I'm collecting."

She sputtered, then laughed. "I owe *you* a favor? Since when?"

"Since the night I pretended to be your date at the auction."

"Pretended? You were supposed to be my date all along," she reminded him.

"But I was concussed and didn't remember making the date. Which means that you owe me for that, too, taking advantage of an injured guy." He *tsk*ed. "Shame on you, Mallory Quinn. Imagine what people would say if they knew you'd done such a thing."

She narrowed her eyes, clearly amused by his playfulness, but not fully trusting him.

Smart girl. He shouldn't be trusted. Not by a long shot.

"So what exactly is this favor?" she asked. "And don't tell me it involves any storage rooms." She paused. "Okay, so we both know I'd hop into another closet with you so fast it'd make your head spin."

With a laugh, he pushed off the wall and came toward her. "It's not that," he said. "I need the same thing you needed that night."

"An orgasm?" she asked cheekily.

"Only if you ask *very* nicely. But I meant a date."

Her expression went dubious. "A date? Now?"

"Yes."

She went from dubious to blank-faced. "A *last* date?"

Well, hell. What could he say to that? It was the truth. "Actually," he said. "I don't believe we ever had a first date." He took her hand and brought it to his mouth, brushing his lips against her palm as he watched her over their joined fingers. "Say yes, Mallory."

Staring at him, she turned her hand, cupping his face, her fingers gliding across his jaw. "Always."

He felt his heart roll, exposing its underbelly. Nothing he could do about that. He was equipped to eliminate threats, protect and serve.

Not to love.

Never to love.

Mallory didn't know what to expect. Ty wouldn't tell her where they were going, but they were on the highway, heading toward Seattle. Once there, he drove to a very swank block lined with designer shops and parked.

"Um," she said.

He pulled her out of the car and into a dress shop. "Something for the orchestra," he said to the pretty sales woman who came forward. He turned to Mallory. "Whatever you want."

She was confused. "What?"

"The auction. The night on the town package."

Again, she just gaped at him. "Was that supposed to be a full explanation?"

"It's tonight," he said. "Tonight's the last night of the orchestra."

"So you what, kidnapped me to take me to it?"

"Thought you could use a night off. And you said you never got to date much." He looked endearingly baffled. "And don't women like this surprise romantic shit?"

Aw. Dammit. "What, you mean romantic '*shit*'?"

He winced, for the first time since she'd known him, looking uncomfortable in his own skin. "You're right," he said. "This was a stupid idea. It's not too late to call this whole thing off and go get a pizza and beer. Whatever you want."

The guy had grown up on military bases and then given his adult years over to the same lifestyle. Mallory knew he was far more at ease in the role of big, bad tough guy than romance guy. Certainly he'd rather have a pizza and beer over the orchestra.

And yet he'd thought of her. He wanted to give her a night off.

He'd wanted to share that night off with her, and he'd brought her to a place filled with gorgeous, designer clothes to do it so that she wouldn't stress about the lack thereof in her own closet. It was a send off, a finale, a good-bye, and she knew it. But damn. Damn, she wanted this. With him. Stepping into him, she went up on tiptoe and kissed his smooth jaw. He'd shaved for her. "Thank you," she whispered.

He turned his head and claimed her mouth in one quick, hot kiss. "Take your time. I'll be waiting."

If only that was really true.

A limo pulled up front, and that's when she remembered: the package came with a limo. "Oh my God."

He leaned in close. "I'm hoping by the end of the night you'll be saying 'Oh, Ty'..." And with that, he walked out the front door toward the limo.

She stared after him. "That man is crazy."

"He's crazy *fine*," the sales clerk murmured. "And he did say whatever you wanted..." She gestured around her. "So what would you like?"

Thirty minutes later, Mallory was decked out in a silky, strappy siren-red dress that made her feel like a sex kitten. She kept trying to see the price tag but the clerk had been discreet, and firm. "He said you weren't allowed to look at the prices."

Good Lord.

By the time Mallory exited the shop, she felt like Cinderella. And her prince stepped out of the limo to greet her in a well-fitted, expensive suit that nearly made her trip over her new strappy high-heeled sandals. She'd seen him in a suit before. She'd seen him in jeans, in cargoes, and in nothing at all. He always looked mouth-wateringly gorgeous. But tonight, something felt different... "Wow."

Ignoring that, he took her hand and pulled her in. "You take my breath away," he said simply.

And that's when she realized. It was his eyes. He was looking at her differently. Heart-stoppingly differently.

Dinner was at a French restaurant and was so amazing she was starting to regret not going one size up on the dress. But the wine quickly reduced any lingering anxiety. The problem with that was, combined with a long day and almost no sleep the night before, by the time they got to the orchestra, her eyes were drooping. Still, she accepted another glass of white wine, and they found their seats. The curtain went up.

And that's the last thing Mallory remembered about the orchestra.

When she woke up, the theater was nearly empty, and Ty was leaning over her, an amused smile on his face.

"What?" she said, blinking, confused. "Where?"

His smile spread to a grin. "You snore."

"I do not!" She straightened, stared at the closed curtain on the stage and took in the fact that the few people left around them were leaving. "It's over? I missed the whole thing?"

He pulled her to her feet. "That's okay. You didn't miss the best part."

"What's the best part?"

"Wait for it." He led her back to the limo. He closed the partition between them and the driver, then pulled her onto his lap.

"Is this the best part?" she asked breathlessly when he slid his hands beneath her dress and palmed her butt cheeks, bared by her lacy thong.

"Wait for it," he whispered against her mouth, and spent the drive back to the Shelby creating a slow burn with nothing more than his mouth on hers and his hands caressing her curves.

"More," she demanded.

"*Wait for it.*"

"I'm growing very tired of those three words," she said.

He drove her home, then walked her in, slowly stripping her out of her beautiful new dress and bra and panties, groaning at the sight of her in just her heels.

"So help me, if you tell me to wait for it one more time," she warned, hands on her bare hips.

"Christ, you are the most beautiful woman I've ever seen," he said. He gave her a little push, and she fell to her bed. "I know how tired you are, so feel free to just lay there and relax."

"I'm not tired," she said. "I took a very nice nap at the orchestra."

With a soft laugh, he crawled up her body, taking little nips out of her as he went. "I'm offering to do all the work here."

"I'm more of an equal opportunity type of woman."

He smiled against her mouth. "Is that right? Well, however you want to be is fine with me. But you should know, I'm ready for the best part now."

"Me too. What is it?" she asked eagerly.

He gently bit her lower lip and tugged, then let it go, soothing the ache with his tongue, making every single nerve ending on her body stand up and beg for the same treatment. "You. You're the best part."

Her heart caught. "Me?"

"Definitely you," he breathed, and then set about proving it.

Chapter 19

I want it all. And I want it smothered in whipped cream and chocolate!

The next afternoon, Mallory was in the ER doing her damnedest not to dwell on the fact that Ty was probably leaving town at any moment. She kept busy and was checking in a patient that Sheriff Thompson had dragged in after breaking up a fight when she took a call from Camilla.

"I'm at the HSC, just closing after the teen advocacy meeting," the young LVN said. "And we have a problem."

Mallory raced over there, and Camilla showed her the medicine lock-up. "I think there's four boxes of Oxycontin missing."

Mallory's heart sank. "What?"

"A month's supply."

Mallory stared at the cabinet in complete and utter shock. "*What?*"

"Yeah. I called Jane," Camilla said. "I didn't want it to come out later and have anyone think it happened on my watch. I never got into the lock-up today at all."

Mallory nodded. That meant it had happened yesterday, when

she'd been in charge. She'd gone into the cabinet several times that she could remember off the top of her head. There'd been the birth control samples she'd given out to Deena and the smoker's patches she'd given Ryan. The vitamins for Mrs. Burland. Mallory recalled that one because Ty had been there. And she flashed back to him admitting he'd gotten too attached to his pain meds.

Cold turkey, he'd said with a harsh laugh. *More like hot hell.*

A tight feeling spread through her chest. Whoever had taken those samples had known what they were taking. There were only two reasons to take Oxycontin. To sell, or to use.

To use, she decided, remembering Ty's words. It was an act of desperation to steal them, and addicts were desperate.

Karen had been desperate, and Mallory had failed her. Badly.

Who else was she failing?

She went back to the ER heartsick. She was in the middle of teaching some brand new firefighter paramedics how to start IVs when she was summoned to Bill's office. She headed that way, expecting to get her hair blown back.

She didn't expect to face several board members, including Jane and her mother.

"Tell us how this could have happened," Bill said, tone stern.

Mallory drew a deep breath. "We received samples early yesterday for the weekend health clinic. I stocked the cabinet myself and locked it."

"Exactly how much is missing?"

He already knew this. He knew everything. He just wanted to hear her say it. "Four boxes," she told him. "Each was a week's supply."

"So a month. You've lost a month's supply of Oxycontin."

Mallory nodded. She was pissed, afraid, frustrated. She'd gone over the inventory a hundred times in her head, hoping she'd just miscalculated.

But she hadn't.

The meds were missing. Someone had stolen them from beneath her own nose. An anguished, distraught, frantic act, by someone she most likely knew by name.

"We'd like the list of everyone who came through the HSC yesterday," Bill said.

This was what she'd been dreading. She didn't know what she wished for the most, that Ty hadn't shown up at all, or that someone else she knew and cared about had. "Bill, we're supposed to be anonymous."

"And you were supposed to make sure something like this never happened. The list, Mallory. I want it by tomorrow morning."

"I can fix this," she said. "Let me—"

"The only way you can fix this is by trusting me to do my job," Bill told her. "And that job is the bottom line. I'm in charge of the bottom line. Do you understand?"

"Of course. But—"

"No buts, Mallory. Don't make this come down to your job being on the line as well as the HSC."

Mallory's heart lurched, and she ground her back teeth so hard she was surprised they didn't dissolve.

"And I'm sure this goes without saying," Bill said, "but until we solve this, the HSC stays closed."

A stab to the gut. "Understood." Somehow she managed to get out of there and through the rest of her shift. All she wanted was to be alone, but her mother caught up with her in the parking lot. "What aren't you telling us, Mallory?"

Mallory was good at hiding her devastation. She'd had lots of practice. "What do you mean?"

"Honey, it's me. The woman who spent thirty-six hours in labor with you. I *know* when you're hiding something."

"Mom, I have to go."

Ella looked deep into her eyes and shook her head. "Oh, no. Oh,

Mallory." She cupped Mallory's jaw. "Who are you trying to save this time?"

"Mom, please. Just go back to work."

"In a minute." Ella cupped Mallory's face and kissed each cheek and then her forehead. "You can't save them all. You know that, right?"

"Yes." Mallory closed her eyes. "I don't know what happened yesterday, but whoever it was, it was my fault. Someone I know is in trouble. And it's like Karen all over again." The sob reached up and choked her, shutting off her words, and she slapped a hand over her mouth to keep it in.

Her mother's eyes filled. "Oh, honey. Honey, no. What happened to Karen wasn't your fault."

Mallory closed her eyes. "She came to me that night."

Ella gasped. "What?"

"Karen. She came into my bedroom. She said she needed me." Mallory swallowed hard. "But I'd been…I'd been needing her and she hadn't been there for me. Not once. So I lashed out at her. I said terrible things to her. And you know what she did? She gave me her necklace. She told me she loved me. She pretty much said good-bye, Mom, and I missed it."

"Mallory, you listen to me," her mother said fiercely, giving her a little shake. "You were sixteen."

"She felt like she was alone, like she had no other options. But she *wasn't* alone. There were lots of options." Mallory let out a breath. "I failed her. I have to live with that. And now I'm just trying to make sure I don't fail anyone else. I need to make sure no one else falls through the cracks."

"But at what cost?" her mother asked softly. "You're the one who said it, Mallory. There are just some things that people have to do for themselves. They have to find their own will, their own happy. Their own path."

"Yes, and this is mine."

Ella sighed and hugged her. "Oh, honey. Are you sure? Because this one's going to cost you big. It's going to cost you your job and your reputation."

"It already has. And yes, I'm sure. I have to do this, Mom. I have to figure this out and fix it."

Ella nodded her reluctant understanding, and Mallory got into her car and drove straight to Ty's house. His house, not his home. Because this was just a stop on his life's path, a destination, not the finish line.

She'd admired that about him.

Now it scared her.

Lots of things scared her. Not too long ago, she'd asked him what he was frightened of, and he'd said he was afraid of not living.

They weren't so different after all, and God, she needed verification of that fact right now.

He didn't answer her knock. The place was quiet. Empty. She put a hand to her chest, knowing damn well that last night had been a good-bye. For all she knew, he was already gone. For a minute, she panicked. After all, she had asked him not to tell her when he left. A very stupid, rash decision on her part. But when she peeked into the garage window and saw the Shelby, she sagged in relief.

Her relief was short-lived, though, because she had no idea where he might go on a night like this. None. And that didn't sit so well.

She was falling in love with a guy that she was afraid she didn't know at all.

Talk about taking a walk on the dark side…

Frustrated and annoyed, she went home. She didn't bother with her usual routine. Screw the flowers. Screw everything, even the cat. She simply strode through her place, intending to get into bed and pull the covers over her head and pretend the day hadn't happened.

Denial. She was thy Queen.

She'd dropped her purse in the living room. Kicked off her shoes in the hallway. She walked into her bedroom struggling with the buttons on her sweater. Giving up, she yanked the thing over her head and got her hair tangled in the buttons. "Dammit!" She was standing there arms up, face covered by the sweater, when two strong arms enveloped her.

She let out a startled scream and was immediately gathered against a warm, hard form that her body knew better than her own. "Ty," she gasped.

He pressed her back against the bedroom door. "You expecting anyone else?"

"I wasn't expecting anyone at all. Help me, I'm caught."

Instead he slid a thigh between hers.

"*Ty*." She struggled with the sweater some more and succeeded in catching her hair on a sweater button. "*Ouch*! I can't get loose."

"Hmm." His hands molded her body, everywhere. "I like you a little helpless."

She fought anew. "That's sexist."

"Sexy," he corrected, untangling her, tossing the offending sweater over his head while still holding her captive against the door. "What were you trying to do?"

"Strip." Crash. Forget. "I went looking for you."

"You found me." He tugged, and then her scrub pants were gone.

She gasped. "What are you doing?"

"Helping you strip." He slid a hand into her panties, his eyes dark and heavy lidded with desire. "Tell me why you went looking for me."

There was something in his voice, something edgy, dark. "I wanted to see you." It was God's utter truth. She knew in her heart that he wouldn't have taken those meds. He wouldn't do anything to hurt her, ever. She knew that, just as she knew that her time with him was limited. Too limited.

She was going to be brave about that, later. "I want you," she whispered.

In the dark hallway, his eyes gleamed with heat and intent, and then his mouth was on hers, hard. She sucked his tongue into her mouth, swallowing his rough groan, savoring the taste of him. "My bed," she said. "I need you in my bed."

They staggered farther into the room and fell onto the mattress. "Hurry, Ty."

"Take everything off then," he demanded in that quiet voice that made her leap to obey. She pulled off her top and unhooked her bra. She was wriggling out of her panties when she got distracted by watching him strip. He tugged his shirt over his head, and then his hands went to his button fly, his movements quick and economical as he bared his gorgeous body. In two seconds he was naked, one hundred percent of his attention completely fixed on her. And apparently she was moving too slowly because he took over, wrapping his fingers around each of her ankles, giving a hard tug so that she fell flat on her back.

He was on her in a heartbeat. "I was working on a car, but all I could see was you, running your fingers over the brake line, holding onto the wrench. It made me hard."

She slid her hands down his sinewy, cut torso, planning on licking that same path as soon as she got a chance. "Me touching your tools makes you hard?"

"Yeah," he said silkily. "Your hands on my tool makes me *very* hard."

She laughed, and he nipped at her shoulder. "Your scent was there, too," he said almost accusingly. "In the garage, lingering like you were right there, pestering me with all your questions."

"Well—" She frowned. "*Hey.*"

His lips claimed hers in a hungry, demanding kiss. "I kept hearing your voice," he said between strokes of his tongue. "Pretending to be all sweet and warm, when really you had me pinned to the wall and were drilling me."

"Return the favor," she said breathlessly. "Pin me down and drill me, Ty."

He looked torn between laughter and determination to do just that. "You've had me in a fucking state all day, Mallory Quinn."

"How bad is this state?"

"*Bad*," he said, grinding his hips to hers to prove it. "So bad I couldn't function."

"Mmm," she moaned at the feel of him so hard for her. "So what did you do?"

"Jacked off."

She choked out a laugh. "You did not."

"Did."

The air crackled with electricity, and he kissed her again. His hands were just as demanding as his mouth, finding her breasts, teasing her nipples, sliding a hand between her legs. Finding her already hot and wet, he groaned.

"Please, Ty. I need you. I need you so much."

"Show me," he said.

"Show you?"

"*Show me.*"

Knowing what he meant, she bit her lower lip. He'd just admitted to touching himself while thinking about her; surely she could return the favor. In the end, he helped her, entwining their fingers and dragging their joined hands up her body, positioning them on her breasts, urging her to caress her own nipples. When she did, he pulled his fingers free and watched with a low groan. Then, apparently convinced she would continue on, he slid down her body, kissing his way between her thighs. Slowly, purposefully, he sucked her into his mouth, making her writhe so much that he had to hold her down. Her toes curled, her eyes closed, her fingers abandoned her breasts and slid into his hair to hold him to that spot because God, just one more stroke of that tongue—

But he stopped. Just pulled his mouth away until she looked at him.

"Keep your eyes open," he said, and when he lowered his mouth again, she did as he'd told her, watching as he took her right to the edge again. It was the hardest thing she'd done so far with him. But nothing about Ty was in her comfort zone, not his life's experiences, not the way he made her feel, and certainly not how he got her to behave in the bedroom. It felt so absolutely wicked to keep looking at him, to be a voyeur in her own bed, but try as she might to hold on, her vision faded when he pushed her over the edge with shocking ease.

When she could open her eyes again, he easily held himself just above her, making room for himself between her thighs as he cupped her face, his own now struggling with control.

She knew he'd never intended for things to go this far. She hadn't either. But as she tugged him close and kissed him, she felt their co-mingled best intentions go right out the window.

Taking control, he slid his big hands to her bottom and pushed inside her with one hard thrust. "Oh, fuck," he said. "You feel amazing."

It was just the passion of the moment, she tried to tell herself, but she felt him to the depths of her soul. And in her heart of hearts, she knew he felt far more for her than he let on. It was in his actions, and she wrapped her arms around his broad shoulders and melted into the hard planes of his body. Emotion welled up within her, and she had to clamp her mouth closed to hold in the words that wanted to escape.

"Mallory."

Opening her eyes, she stared up into his, her heart clenching hard. His hands slid up to her hips, positioning her exactly as he wanted, and when he thrust again, she gasped as pleasure swamped her. Wrapping her legs around his waist, she whispered his name, needing him to move.

Instead, he lowered his head and traced her nipple with his tongue, causing her to arch her back and shamelessly roll her hips into his. "*Ty*."

His fingers skimmed roughly up her spine, leaving a trail of heat that she felt all the way to her toes, until his hands gripped hers on either side of her head. "I'm right here," he promised, taking her exactly where she needed to go without words. And that was it, the beginning of the point of no return for her. He was exactly what she'd wanted, what she'd never had the nerve to reach out and grasp for herself before. Ironic, really. He didn't want her to depend on him, and yet he was the one who'd given her the security to be who she was. If only he'd keep looking at her the way he was right now.

For always.

It wasn't going to happen, she knew that. She had to settle for this, for the right now. Telling herself she was stronger than she knew, that she could do it, she cupped his face and let herself go, moving with him in the age-old dance of lovers. And her release, when it came, shattered her apart and yet somehow made her whole at the same time.

At some point in the night, Ty woke up wrapped in warm woman. And it wasn't her clinging to him. Nope, that was all him. He had one hand entangled in her crazy hair, the other on her bare ass, holding her possessively and protectively to him.

Jesus.

The night of the orchestra had been a mistake, and everyone was allowed one mistake. But if he slept with her tonight, it would be mistake number two.

He didn't make mistakes, much less the same one twice. It took some doing, but he managed to get out of the bed without waking her. He gathered his things and walked out of her bedroom, quietly shutting the door behind him. Dumping everything at his feet to sort, he hesitated. In his real life, hesitating was a good way to get dead. And yet he did just that, turning back to her bedroom door, his hands up on the frame above his head. He wanted to go back in there.

Bad.

Don't do it, man. He looked down at his shit. No shirt. One sock. From his pants pocket, his phone was blinking. Frances, he knew. Because she and Josh had finally connected. The gig was up; she knew he was cleared. His last message from her had been something along the lines of *get your sorry ass back to work.* This had been accompanied by a text with a confirmation number for a one-way, first-class airplane ticket back to D.C.

He stubbed his toe on his own shoes. Swearing softly, he kicked one down the hallway, then went still when the bedroom door opened and the light came on.

Mallory stood there blinking sleepily, tousled and rumpled and wearing nothing but his shirt. "Hey," she murmured. "You okay?"

"Yeah. Sorry. Didn't mean to wake you."

"Are you leaving?"

"Yeah, I... Yeah, I'm leaving." He needed to. Now. Because he was starting to wonder how he was going to leave Lucky Harbor at all.

Mallory made a soft noise in the back of her throat. She was looking at his jeans still on the floor, and the two things that had spilled out of his pockets. His keys.

And the empty Vicodin bottle.

She bent and picked up the bottle, staring at it for a long time. He saw her taking in the two-month-old date of the prescription, the fact that there were refills available to him which he clearly hadn't used. Finally she handed the bottle back to him with a gentle smile. "Stay, Ty. Stay with me for tonight. Just tonight."

He couldn't. Staying would be a mistake. "Mallory—"

She covered his mouth with her fingers, then took his hand in hers, drawing him back into her bedroom and into her bed, and into her warm, soft heart.

Chapter 20

Exercise is a dirty word. Every time I hear it
I wash my mouth out with chocolate.

The next day Ty and Matt spent time in the gym, then Matt went home with Ty to pick up the Jimmy. Matt took one look around the cleaned-up garage. "You're leaving."

"Always was." Ty held out the Jimmy's keys but Matt didn't take them.

"The lease on this place is paid up until summer," Ty said. "Use it if you want. And I want you to take the tools."

"I'll keep them for you. You'll be back."

Ty looked at him, and Matt shook his head. "Christ," he said on a disgusted sigh. "Tell me you're not just going to vanish on her and not come back at all. You're not that big a dick, right?"

"You want to test drive this thing or what?"

"So you *are* that big a dick."

"Look, she made me promise not to say good-bye."

"And you believed her?" Matt asked. "Shit, and I thought *I* was stupid with women."

"You are." Ty tossed him the keys at him, leaving Matt no choice but to catch them.

They took the Jimmy out on a test drive. Matt drove like a guy who knew the roads intimately, down-shifting into the hairpin turns, accelerating out of them. He took them along a two-lane, narrow, curvy highway that led almost straight up. On either side were steep, unforgiving, isolated peaks, so lush—thanks to a wet spring—that they resembled a South American rainforest.

When the road ended, Matt cranked the Jimmy into four-wheel drive and kept going, making his own trail.

"You know where you're headed, City Boy?" Ty asked.

Matt sent him a long look. "What, you think you can find your way around these mountains?"

"I could find my way around on Mars," Ty assured him. "Though if you get us dead out here, I'll follow you to the depths of hell and kill you again."

"Told you, not everyone's going to die on you. I'm sure as hell not."

"See that you don't."

Matt drove on, until eventually they came to a plateau. The three-hundred-and-sixty degree vista was staggering. The jagged mountain peaks were still tipped in white. The lower ranges were covered in a thick blanket of green. And to their immediate west, the Pacific shimmered brilliantly.

"Beaut Point," Matt said.

The plateau was about the size of a football field, giving a very decent view of the ocean smashing into a valley of rocks hundreds of feet below. "Good spot," Ty said.

"I chase a lot of stupid teenagers off this ledge. They come four-wheeling up here in daddy's truck to get laid. Then the geniuses get lost, and I end up having to save their miserable asses."

"Tough job."

"Beats scooping gangbangers off the streets of Chicago any day of the week," Matt agreed. "And I imagine it's also a hell of a lot more fun than Afghanistan or Iraq this time of year."

Ty looked over at him. "Don't forget South America. My favorite."

Matt smiled. "Nothing compares to Chicago in high summer in full tactical gear."

"Pussy."

"Sure. If being a pussy means staying in Paradise over leaving for a stupid adrenaline rush in some godforsaken Third World country."

Ty shook his head and stared out at "Paradise."

"Ever climb?" Matt asked.

"Only when I have to."

Matt gestured with his chin out to a sharp outcropping at least three miles across the way. "Widow's Peak. Climbed it last weekend. It's a get-your-head-on-straight kind of spot."

"Was your head crooked?" Ty asked.

"Yeah, actually. But today I figured that was you."

"My head's on perfectly straight, thanks."

"Yeah?"

"Yeah."

"Huh," Matt said.

Ty looked at him. "Okay, let's save some time here. Why don't you just tell me whatever it is that you're fishing for?"

"All right," Matt said. "Someone stole some samples out of the Health Services Clinic from right beneath Mallory's nose."

Ty's gut tightened. "Today? Was she hurt?"

Matt was watching him carefully. "Yesterday. And no."

"What was taken?"

"Pain meds. She doesn't know when it happened, actually. She says it could have been at a couple of different points during the day."

Ty went still, remembering last night, remembering the look on

Mallory's face when she'd seen the empty bottle fall out of his jeans pocket.

She'd known then, and she hadn't said a word. Had she thought he'd taken the pills? He tried to think of a reason that she wouldn't have mentioned the missing meds that didn't involve her thinking it was him. But with a grim, sinking feeling in his gut, he realized he couldn't. "Is she taking shit for it?"

"You could say that, yeah. As of right this minute, HSC is shut down, and if it gets out why, it's going to stay that way."

"She doesn't deserve the blame."

"She accepted the blame."

"How do you know all of this?"

"I'm on the hospital board. Look," he said at Ty's dark expression, "at this point only we board members know. They want her to turn in a list of who was at HSC during the hours that the meds went missing. She's objecting because it's supposed to be anonymous. That put her job in the ER at risk as well as at HSC."

Ty let out a breath and closed his eyes. "Oh, Christ."

"What?"

"I was in there yesterday afternoon." He opened his eyes and looked at Matt. "I was at HSC."

"Did you do it?" Matt asked mildly. "Did you lift the drugs?"

"Hell, no."

"Didn't figure you for being stupid," Matt said, watching as Ty pulled out his phone and hit a number. "And we don't get reception out here. No one does. Listen, this gets a little worse. Jane, her boss, rode her hard about this, and..."

"*And*?"

"Mallory walked off her job. She quit."

Ty held his hands out. "Keys."

"Excuse me?"

"I'm driving back." He needed to see Mallory. Now. *Yesterday*.

"Why are *you* driving back?" Matt wanted to know.

"Because we're in a hurry, and you drive like a girl."

Halfway back to town, Ty finally got phone reception and hit Mallory's number. While it rang in his ear, Matt *tsk*ed. "You need a blue tooth," he said. "Or you're going to get a ticket."

Ty ignored him, thinking *pick up, pick up*... but Mallory didn't. "She's probably at home, phone dead."

And he didn't have her house number.

Matt shook his head. "Nope, she's not at home."

Ty looked at him.

"Oh, did you want to know where she is?" When Ty just narrowed his eyes, Matt smiled. "Yeah, you want to know. She's at the diner. I was there earlier, heard Amy take a call from her. Something about a chocoholic meeting."

There was something in Matt's voice when he said Amy's name, and needing a distraction, Ty slid him a glance. "So what's with you and the pretty waitress?"

"Nothing."

"There's a whole lot of tension between you two for nothing."

Matt pleaded the Fifth.

"You screw something up?"

Matt's sunglasses were mirrored, giving nothing away. He was not answering, which was the same thing as saying yeah, he'd screwed something up. "What did you do?" Ty asked.

"Jack shit."

Yeah, right. They came into town and bypassed the road to Matt's house.

"Hey," Matt said.

"Hang on, coming in hot." Ty pulled up to the diner with a screech of tires.

Matt let go of the dash and looked at him.

Ty shrugged. "Maybe misery loves company."

"You mean maybe misery loves to watch other people fuck up."

"I'm not going to fuck anything up."

"Uh huh."

Ty shook his head and went into the diner, which had been decorated for spring. There were brightly colored papier-maché flowers and animals hanging from the ceiling tiles, and streamers around the windows. It didn't much match the 50s décor but it was definitely eye-popping.

The place was full with the dinner crowd, the noise level high. Ty recognized just about everyone there, which meant he'd been here far too long. He could see Jan hustling a large tray to a table. And there was Ryan in a far corner with two guys from NA. Blue-haired Lucille was there too, with a group of other blue-haired, nosy old bats. Ty shifted past the small group of people waiting to be seated because he could see Mallory at the counter. Grace was on one side of her, with Amy on the other side of the counter.

Ty came up behind Mallory, who was staring down at a cake that said "Happy Birthday Anderson" as Amy lit the candles.

All around them were the general, noisy sounds of a diner. Dishes clanking, voices raised in conversation, laughter—each table or group involved in their own world. This particular little world, of the three women, was exclusive, and not a one of them was paying their surroundings any attention.

Mallory, the woman who'd claimed to have given up chocolate, licked her lips. "We should skip the candles," she said to Amy. "You have a full house right now. You're too busy for this."

"Oh no," Amy said. "We agreed. When bad shit happens, we meet. We eat." She lit the last candle and handed each of them a fork. "I've already called Tara and told her that Anderson's cake met a tragic demise."

"She believe you?" Grace asked.

"She's smarter than that." Amy looked at Mallory. "But she

understood the emergency and is making another cake. The important thing is that we get Mallory through this situation."

Mallory sighed and thunked her forehead to the table.

Amy quickly slid the cake over a little bit, probably so Mallory's hair wouldn't catch fire. "So did you really tell Jane to stuff herself?"

"Yes." Mallory's voice was muffled, and Grace *tsk*ed sympathetically and stroked Mallory's hair.

"But that's not why I'm out of a job," Mallory said. "It's because I yelled it, and everyone heard. Bill said sometimes he wished Jane would stuff it, too, but we have to learn to not compound our errors. He was working up to firing me. He had no choice, really. And that's when I sort of lost it. I told him to stuff it, too, and left."

"Wow," Grace said. "When you decide to go bad, you go all the way."

Mallory let out a combination laugh/sob.

"What are your plans now?" Amy asked her. "Beg for your job back?"

"I'm thinking I'll end up working for some quiet little doctor's office somewhere and try to go back to behaving like myself." Mallory scooped up some cake and stuffed it into her mouth. "I don't want to talk about it."

"Tough," Ty said.

She jerked upright and whirled on her stool to face him. She had chocolate on her lips but she pointed her fork at him like she was a queen on her throne. "You need to stop doing that."

"You'd wither up and die of boredom in a quiet little doctor's office," he said.

She stared up at him, her eyes shining brilliantly. Everyone was looking at them, of course. Well, except Amy, who was looking at Matt. Matt had taken a seat at the counter to watch the circus.

Ty narrowed his eyes at everyone.

No one took the hint to give him and Mallory some privacy. Of course not. It used to be one gaze from him could terrorize people. But it hadn't worked for him in Lucky Harbor, not once. Giving up, he gestured to the candles as the little flames seemed to gather in strength. "You should blow those out," he said.

Amy blew out the candles. Grace feigned interest in a menu. Their ears were cocked.

Resigned at having an audience, Ty looked at Mallory. "Why didn't you tell me?"

"Which?" she asked.

Jesus. There was more than one thing? The candles flickered back to life on the cake, which he ignored. "Let's start with the missing drugs."

"Because I know that you didn't take them." Mallory eyed the cake. "You used trick candles?" she asked Amy.

"Yeah," she said. "They were from Lance's birthday party. His brother's idea. Tucker has a warped sense of humor. They're all I had."

"Excuse me," Lucille said, hopping off her stool and scooting close. "But I couldn't help but overhear. Missing drugs?"

"This isn't an open-to-the-public conversation, Lucille," Mallory said.

"But who would take drugs from the HSC?" the older woman asked. "A teenager? A drug dealer? One of your crazy siblings?"

Mallory pinched the bridge of her nose. "You're just as crazy as Tammy and Joe, and you know it."

Lucille blinked. "Are you sassing me?"

"Yes," Mallory said. "Apparently it's my new thing. Push me, and I'll even yell at you. Also a new thing. Now stay out of my business; I'm trying to have a private conversation here." She grimaced. "*Please*," she added politely.

Lucille blinked, then smiled. "Well, there it is. Been waiting a long time to see that."

"I *always* say please."

"Not that. Your backbone. You have one, and it looks great on you, my dear."

Mallory just stared at her, then at Ty. But he was still a little stunned at what she'd said before.

I know you didn't take them.

Somehow, in spite of his best efforts to hold back, Mallory knew him, she knew who he was, inside and out, and accepted him. As is.

And she'd believed in him, no questions asked.

This didn't help her now, he knew. Because someone *had* taken the meds under her watch. It could have been anyone. Only Mallory knew the truth, and Ty knew by just looking at her that she *did* know. She knew who it was, and she didn't want to say.

Even now she was trying to save someone.

It slayed him. *She* slayed him. "If you know I wasn't the one who took the pills," he said, "then why didn't you turn over the list of people who'd been inside the building?"

For some reason, this pissed her off. He watched as temper ignited in her eyes. Standing up, she stabbed him in the chest with her finger hard enough to make him wince. "Do you think you're the only one I care about?" she demanded.

"Uh..."

"No," she assured him. "You are not."

She was as mad as he'd ever seen her, in sky blue scrubs with a long-sleeved T-shirt beneath—*his* shirt, if he wasn't mistaken. There was a mysterious lump of things in her pockets and someone had drawn a red heart on one of her white tennis shoes. She still had chocolate on one corner of her mouth, her hair was completely out of control, and she was ready to take down anyone who got in her path.

She'd never looked more beautiful. "Mallory." He knew how much her job meant to her. How much the HSC meant. How much Lucky Harbor meant.

He was leaving, but she wasn't. Her life was here, and in that moment, he made his decision, knowing he could live with it. "I took advantage of you," he said, making sure to speak loud enough for all the eavesdroppers to hear. "Complete advantage."

Two stools over, Matt groaned. "Man, don't. Don't do it."

Mallory hadn't taken her eyes off Ty, and she was still pissed. "*What are you doing*?"

"Attempting to tell what happened," he said carefully.

"Now you all just hold it right there." Mrs. Burland was suddenly right there, pointing at Ty with her cane, almost sticking it up his nose. "Yeah, you little punk-ass," she said. "I'm talking to you."

Little punk ass? He was a foot and a half taller than her and outweighed her by at least a hundred pounds. He stared down at her in shock.

Everyone in the place sucked in a breath and did the same.

Except Matt. He grinned wide. "Little punk ass," he repeated slowly, rolling the words off his tongue in delight. "I like it."

Ty gave him a look that didn't appear to bother Matt at all. It'd been a hell of a long time since anyone had gotten in Ty's face, even longer since he'd been called a little punk ass, and by the looks of her, Mrs. Burland wasn't done with him yet.

"What the hell do you think you're doing?" she demanded.

"I'm trying to have a conversation," he said. "A *private* one."

Lucille leaned in. "There's no such thing in Lucky Harbor," she said helpfully.

Clearly tired of the interruptions, Mrs. Burland slammed her cane onto the floor three times in a row, until all eyes were back on her. She glared at Ty. "You have no right to confess to a crime you didn't commit."

Apparently, as well as being curmudgeonly and grumpy and mean as a snake, Mrs. Burland was also sharp as a tack. "Stay out of it," he said.

"You're trying to be the big hero," Mrs. Burland told him. "You think she's protecting someone, and you don't want her hurt."

Mallory turned to him. "Is that what you're doing?"

Ty opened his mouth but Mrs. Burland rose up to her full four feet eight inches and said, "It was me. *I* took the meds." She eyeballed the entire crowd. "Not a teenager. Not a drug dealer. Not any of the crazy Quinns. And not this—" She gestured toward Ty, and her mouth tightened disfavorably. "*Man*. He might be guilty of plenty, not the least of which is messing with *your* reputation, Mallory Quinn—not that you seem to mind—but he didn't take the pills. That was me."

"No." A young woman stood up from a table across the room. Ty recognized her as Deena, the clerk at the grocery store. "I was at the HSC yesterday," she said. "For birth control pills. *I* took the Oxycontin."

"That's a lie." This was from Ryan, at the far end of the counter. "We all know I have a problem. *I* took the pills."

Mallory's mouth fell open.

Nothing surprised Ty, but even he could admit to being shocked. The entire town was rallying around Mallory in the only way they knew how. He'd never seen anything like it.

Amy banged a wooden spoon on the counter to get everyone's attention. "Hey, I was there, too. I took the pills." Her eyes locked on Matt's, whose jaw bunched and ticked.

Mallory gaped at Amy. "You were not there—"

"Oh no you all don't!" Mrs. Burland yelled. "Listen you...you egocentric, self-absorbed, narcissistic group of *insane* people. Don't make me smack all of you!" And with that, she pulled a small box from her pocket.

A sample of Oxycontin.

"See?" she said triumphantly. "I have them. I have them all. I took them because I thought they were Probiotics for my constipation. They're the same color box. My insurance is crap, and even if it wasn't, I hate to wait in line at the pharmacy. I've spent the past decade waiting in stupid lines. A line to see the doctor. A line to wait for meds. Hell, I even had to wait in line to go to the bathroom a minute ago. I'm over it, and I'm over all of you."

"You don't need Probiotics," Lucille said. "All you need are prunes and a blender."

"*You* got Mallory fired?" Amy asked Mrs. Burland.

"No, Mallory's big mouth got her fired," Mrs. Burland said.

"I didn't get fired," Mallory said. "I quit."

Lucille tried to lean in again. "Excuse me, dear," she said to Mallory. "But—"

"*Not now*, Lucille. *Please*."

"Yes, but it's important."

"*What's more important than this*?"

"The candles."

They'd come back to life again, blazing good this time. The cake had been scooted back against the pile of menus, and several had fallen too close. The menus went up in flames just as Ty leaped toward them, grabbing Mallory's glass of water to dump it on the small fire.

The flames flickered and went out.

Except for the middle one, the largest candle. Which turned out to be not just a trick candle but some sort of bottle rocket, because it suddenly shot straight up and into the ceiling like...well, like a bottle rocket.

The fire alarm sounded, and then there was the *whoosh* of a huge pressure hose letting loose, and the sprinklers overhead came on.

And rained down on the entire diner and everyone in it.

Chapter 21

Strength is the ability to break up a solid piece of chocolate—and then eat just one of the pieces.

Mallory was shocked at how fast total chaos reigned. Instantaneously, really. As the overhead sprinklers showered down icy water, people began yelling and screaming. Everyone pushed and shoved at each other to get out.

Adding to the insanity, the decorations hanging from the ceiling soaked up the water and began to fall, pulling down ceiling tiles with them. A papier-maché elephant hit Mallory on the head, along with the attached ceiling tile. For a second she saw stars, then panicked. Someone was going to get seriously hurt. She tried to blink through the downpour to check the crowd for anyone who needed help. She could hardly see two feet in front of her but it appeared that *everyone* needed help. People were either running or down for the count. It was utter mayhem.

Mallory gulped some air and shoved her hair out of her face. Her hand came away bloody. Her cheek was bleeding, but before she could dwell on that someone grabbed her, tugged her up against his side, and began to steam-roll her toward the door.

Ty.

"Let me go," she said, banging on his chest, which was completely ineffective.

"No. I want you safe outside, *now*."

"Forget me, get Mrs. Burland and Lucille!"

"You first, goddammit." Then, still holding her tightly against him, Ty scooped up Mrs. Burland, too. Lucille was nowhere to be seen. Through the sprinklers, Mallory saw Matt grabbing Amy and Grace, shoving them out the door, and going back in for others. Ty dumped Mallory near them and went back inside.

Mallory went to leap in after him. Ty blocked her.

"I'm going in," she said. "People are hurt, Ty. I can help."

His jaw ticked but he stepped aside. The fire alarm was blaring, water from the sprinklers still pouring down. Mallory got several more people outside before she ran into Ty again. He had two of Lucille's posse by their hands but he dropped one and stopped to stroke the wet hair that wouldn't stay out of Mallory's face, ducking a little to look over her bloody cheek, then into her eyes. He was checking on her, making sure she was okay.

But he must know by now. She was always okay. Not that *that* stopped the warmth washing through her from knowing he cared. It was in every touch, every look.

And he was going to leave.

He had a job; she got that. She'd never want to hold him back from what fueled him, whatever that might be. But she'd sort of, maybe, just a little bit, wished that *she* could be what fueled him.

By the time the fire department came, they'd gotten everyone out. Several people were injured enough to require several ambulances, which arrived right behind the fire department. Mallory was helping those lined up on the sidewalk. Near her, Matt was assisting the paramedics. Ty, too, looked just as comfortable in a position of medical authority. He had Ryan, who'd somehow gotten a nasty-looking laceration down one arm, seated at the curb. Ty was crouched at the vet's side, applying pressure to the wound, looking quite capable.

Josh pulled up to the scene and hopped out of his car. Ryan was closest to him, so he stopped beside him first.

"He's in shock," Ty said quietly.

It was true. Ryan was shaking, glassy-eyed, disoriented. Definitely in shock. Josh went back to his car and returned with an emergency kit. Ty and Josh wrapped Ryan in an emergency blanket to get him warm, then made sure he was breathing evenly and that his pulse wasn't too fast. Mallory took over then, sitting at Ryan's side, holding his hand as she watched Josh and Ty work together in perfect sync on other victims.

When the paramedics were free, they took over Ryan's care and Mallory moved toward Ty and Josh.

"The least you can do," Josh was saying to Ty, "now that you're cleared and still sitting on your ass, is hire on. You know there's that flight paramedic opening out of Seattle General. That unit runs its ass off, no shortage of adrenaline there. And hell, look at how exciting Lucky Harbor can be."

Ty ignored him and crouched at Lucille's feet. "You okay?"

"Oh, sure, honey." She patted his arm. "You're a good boy."

Ty smiled, and Mallory didn't know if that was at the idea of him being a boy, or good. Then he straightened and turned to Mallory.

She wasn't surprised that he'd known she was standing behind him. He always seemed to know where she was. "Wow," she said with what she thought was remarkable calm. "Look at you."

His eyes locked in on her cheek, and he touched the wound. With a wince, she batted his hand away.

He pulled her away from all the prying eyes and ears. "You need that taken care of," he said. "Let me help—"

"No." She needed more help than he could possibly imagine. "It can wait." She didn't know where to start, but she gave it the old college try and started at the beginning. "How is it that a mechanic knows how to treat trauma victims?"

His gaze never left hers. "I was a medic in the SEALS."

"A medic. In the SEALs." She absorbed that and shook her head. "That's funny, because I could have sworn you told me you were a mechanic. A navy mechanic, who was doing similar work now."

"No," he said. "Well, yes. I work on cars. Sometimes. But that's for me, for fun."

"For fun." She paused, but it didn't compute. "I pictured you working on ships, maybe on helicopters and tanks. Not bodies. Why didn't you tell me?"

He responded with a question of his own. "Why does it matter what I was?"

"Because it's not what you were, Ty, it's who you *are*." How could he not see that? Or hear her heart as it quietly cracked down the center? "You're going back," she said. "You're only here waiting to be cleared..." She stared at him as Josh's words sank in. "Except you already *are* cleared." Oh, God. He could leave now. Any second. "How long have you known? And why would you hide so much from me?" But she already knew the answer to that. It was because they were just fooling around.

Nothing more.

And she had no one to blame but herself. Horrified at how close she was to breaking down, she took a step backward and bumped directly into Sheriff Sawyer Thompson. He'd strode up to the soggy group and now stood there, hands on hips. "What the hell happened here?"

Everyone was still there. No one wanted to miss anything. Every able body in the pathetic, ragtag-looking group immediately gathered ranks around Mrs. Burland, the mean old biddy who'd never done anything nice for a single one of them. In fact, she'd made their life a living hell in a hundred different ways. But they all started talking at once, each giving their story of the drug theft, and how they'd ended up being dumped on by the diner's sprinkler system.

Once again protecting one of their own.

Mrs. Burland still wasn't having any of it. She stood up, wobbled with her cane toward the sheriff and held out her wrists. "Arrest me, Copper. But don't even think about a strip search. I have rights, you know."

Sawyer assured her that he had no interest in arresting her, because then he'd have to arrest everyone else who'd confessed as well. Looking disgusted and frustrated, he started over, talking to one person at a time.

The crowd began to disperse.

Mallory sank to the curb and dropped her head to her knees, exhausted to the bone and far too close to losing it. Ty, holding so much back from her...How was that even possible? She'd given him everything she'd had.

He wasn't going to change now, and God help her, she was going to be okay with that if it killed her.

And it just might.

Two battered boots appeared in front of her, and she felt him crouch at her side.

Ty, of course. Her heart only leapt for Ty. He ran a big, warm hand down her back, made a sound of annoyance at finding her still drenched and shivering, and then she felt one of the emergency blankets from the firefighters come around her.

"I'm fine," she said.

"Yeah." He sat at her side and pulled her in against his warmth. "Extremely fine. But that's not what's in question here."

"What *is* in question?"

"You tell me."

"Fine," she said, and lifted her head. "I don't get the big secret about being a paramedic."

"It wasn't a secret."

"It feels like a secret," she said. "That day you came to the hospital to get your stitches out, you could have done that yourself."

"I wanted to see you."

Aw.

Dammit, *no* aw. "Okay, then what about what happened next?" she asked. "When that patient coded out? You got pale and shaky, almost shocky, as if you'd never seen anything like that before."

Ty was still balanced on the balls of his feet. He lowered his head and studied his shoes for a moment, then looked her right in the eyes. "Do you want to know the last thing I did as a SEAL trauma medic?" he asked, voice dangerously low. She wasn't the only one pissed off and frustrated.

"I dragged my teammates out of the burning plane," he told her. "Tommy was already dead, but the others, Brad, Kelly, and Trevor..." He closed his eyes. "I did everything I could, and they died anyway. Afterward, I couldn't do it. I tried, but I couldn't go back to being a first line trauma responder."

Her gut wrenched for him. "Oh, Ty."

"I was honorably discharged, and when I got work, it wasn't as a medic. I turned down anything like that for four years. Four years, Mallory, where I didn't so much as give out a Band-Aid."

Until he'd come to Lucky Harbor. "Amy's knife wound," she whispered.

He nodded grimly. "The first time I'd opened a first-aid kit in all that time."

And then today. Again, a situation that fell right on him, and he'd stepped into the responsibility as if into a pair of comfortable old shoes. She wondered if he realized that.

"My turn," he said. "Your job? You lost your job?"

"Not lost. *Quit.*" She took a moment to study her own shoes now, until he wrapped his fingers around her ponytail and tugged.

She lifted her head and met his gaze. "Mallory," he said softly. Pained. "Why?"

Why? A million reasons, none of which she wanted to say because suddenly, it was all too much. The job, the HSC, the diner, knowing how she felt about Ty and realizing he was going to leave anyway. Her head hurt, her cheek hurt. And her heart hurt, too. When her eyes filled, he made a low sound. Hard to tell if it was male horror or empathy. But then he wrapped his arms around her, and she planted her face in the crook of his neck.

She should have known he wouldn't be uncomfortable with tears. He didn't seem to be uncomfortable with much, when it came right down to it.

Except maybe his own emotions.

How had things gotten so out of control? All she'd wanted was to stretch her wings. Live for herself instead of for others. Try new things. She'd done that, and she'd loved it.

She loved him.

And therein lay her mistake. "The whole HSC drug fiasco is *my* fault," she said into his chest. "No one else's. I screwed up there." She sucked in a breath as once again her eyes filled. "As for everything else, I always wanted to go a little crazy, but as it turns out, I'm not all that good at it," she whispered.

He made a show of looking at the utter chaos of the diner. "I don't know," he said. "I think you're better at it than you give yourself credit for."

She choked out a laugh, realizing that no matter what she did, he had her back. He'd been there for her, one hundred percent. It was in his every look, touch, kiss. "I just wanted something for myself," she said softly.

"And you deserve that," he said with absolute conviction, warming her from the inside out. From the beginning, he'd treated her like someone special, from before they'd even known each other's names. He'd shared his courage, his sense of adventure, his inner strength.

Once, she'd been a woman terribly out of balance with herself and her hopes and dreams. That had changed.

Because of him.

She was in balance now but even that wasn't enough. Loving him wasn't enough. It wasn't going to get her what she wanted. Nothing was going to get her what she wanted—which was Ty. She really needed to cut her losses now before it got worse, but God. How could she? "Ty."

He pulled back to look into her eyes, his own going very serious at the look in hers.

She cupped his face. "I've screwed up. I'm falling for you." She gently kissed his gorgeous mouth so that he couldn't say anything. "Don't worry, I know you won't let yourself do the same." She kissed him again when he went to speak, because it was in his eyes. Sorrow. "I can't do this anymore," she whispered past a throat that felt like she'd swallowed cut glass. "I'm sorry."

"Are you dumping me, Mallory?"

Was she? The truth was that *he* was the one going, and yet he hadn't. She'd have to think about that later, but for now, for right now, what she had with him wasn't enough for her. "You were never mine to dump," she said.

Something crossed his normally stoic face, but he nodded and lifted a hand to her jaw, stroking his thumb over her lips in a gentle gesture that made her ache. She started to say something, she had no idea what, but someone tapped her on the shoulder. "*Mallory Michelle Quinn.*"

Only one person ever middle-named her. Her mom; just what she needed. She swiped at her eyes and turned, considering herself lucky to be so wet that no one could possibly tell if she was crying or not. "Mom, why are you here?"

"I heard about the diner. You're hurt?"

"Now's not a good time—" Mallory brushed her mom's hand away. "*Mom.*"

"Don't you 'mom' me! You have a cut on your cheek. And you let Jane *fire* you?"

"Okay, someone give me a microphone!" Mallory said as loud as she could. "Because I wasn't fired, I *quit.* There's a difference."

Her mother stared at her for a long beat, during which Mallory did her best not to look as utterly heartbroken as she felt. Finally Ella nodded. "Well, I hope to hell you took Jane down a peg or two while you were at it."

Shock had Mallory gaping. "You're not upset?"

"She's overworked you and taken advantage of your skills. The board's already banding together to try to get you back. I suggest turning down their first offer. According to what I overheard, their second offer will be a much better deal."

Mallory choked out a shocked breath. "Overheard?"

"Fine. I put a glass to the door of Bill's office and listened in. But I'm not proud of it." Ella hesitated. "What I am proud of is you. And Sawyer sent me over here to get you. He needs one last quick word from you for his report."

Sawyer was already headed for her.

He gave her a look of frustration. "You okay?"

No. "Yes."

"Good, because so far I've heard twenty different versions of what's going on. Tell me that you're going to come up with the *right* one."

She told him the entire story the best that she could, then turned to look for Ty and found her mom talking to him. Ella was animated, her hands moving, her mouth flapping, and Mallory's stomach sank. From the looks of things, she could be reading him the riot act, or...hell. She couldn't imagine. "I've got to go," she said to Sawyer.

Her mother saw her coming and met her halfway. "He has a way of looking at you, honey. Like you mean something to him."

Mallory shook her head. "What did you two talk about?"

"Are you asking if I accused him of destroying your reputation?" Ella looked over Mallory's shoulder and found Ty watching them. She sent him a little finger wave.

He didn't wave back but he did almost smile.

"You made it clear what you thought of my way of thinking," Ella said to Mallory. "And you were right. I've been holding the reins too tight, depending on you to be the calm in the storm of this crazy family. That was unfair, maybe even cruel, and I was wrong. I never should have done it. Just as I never should have allowed you to blame yourself for Karen. Or my divorce. Or the general insanity of our family."

"Mom—"

"Hush, honey. I told him I'd make him dinner," Ella said casually, almost as a throwaway remark, and stroked Mallory's wet hair back from her face.

"You *what*?"

"He's been good to you. I want to thank him. It's simple etiquette."

"You mean it's simple curiosity," Mallory said.

"Okay, that too."

"Mom, we're just..." God. Her heart hurt. "Friends."

"Oh, please," Ella said with a laugh. "I didn't fall for that with Tammy when she brought Zach home, and I'm not going to fall for it with you. He said yes."

"No, really," Mallory said. "We're not what you think we are. He said *yes*?"

"Sweetheart, you're drenched and still shivering. You're going to catch your death out here. Go home and take a hot shower, and put something on that cut on your cheek." Ella hugged her tight, then pushed her toward her car.

Mallory took a last look at the scene. Ty was back to helping. He was hauling things out of the wrecked diner with Matt. Two extremely fine examples of what a good use of gorgeous male muscle could do.

"Mallory." Josh gestured to Mrs. Burland, huddled on the sidewalk. "She's refusing to go to the hospital but mostly, she's just shaken up. If you're leaving, maybe you could drive her home."

Mallory ended up driving the entire senior posse home since Lucille was the only one of them still in possession of her license, and she was going into the hospital for X-rays. It took nearly an hour because each of them took forever to say their good-byes and get out of the car. When she'd finally gotten rid of them all, Mallory told herself to go home, but herself didn't listen. She drove to Ty's.

The garage was open, and he was beneath his precious Shelby.

She bet he'd never walked away from a car in his life.

Still working on adrenaline, frustration, and a pain so real it felt like maybe her heart had been split in two, she stormed up to the mechanic's creeper and nudged at his exposed calf.

Okay, maybe it was more of a kick. "You told my mother she could cook you dinner?"

He rolled out from beneath the car, and arms still braced on the chassis above him, looked up at her. He wisely didn't comment on what was surely a spectacularly bad hair day on her part. She'd been hit with the sprinklers, and then dust from the ceiling tiles, and the whole mess had dried naturally without any of her de-frizzing products that never really worked anyway.

"Problem?" he finally asked.

"Oh my God!" She tossed up her hands. "You did. You said yes. *Why*?"

"She said she'd make meatloaf. I don't think I've ever had home-cooked meatloaf. I thought it was a suburban myth."

She'd never wanted to both hug and strangle someone before. "*I'll* make you meatloaf!"

"You dumped me," he said reasonably. "And besides, you don't cook."

Dammit. Dammit, he was killing her. She pressed the heels of her hands to her eyes but she couldn't rub away the ache. Spinning on her heel, she walked out of the garage.

He caught her at her car, pulling her back against him. She felt the shaking of his chest and realized he was laughing at her.

At least until he caught sight of her face.

His smile faded then.

With a frustrated growl, she shoved him away and got into her car, but before she could shut the door, he squatted at her side, the muscles in his thighs flexing against the faded denim he wore. He blocked her escape with one hand on the door, the other on the back of her seat, his expression unreadable now. "This isn't about meatloaf," he said. "This isn't even about me. Tell me what the real problem is."

I'm in love with you…

"My problem," Mallory said, "is that you're blocking me from shutting the door."

"And you're shutting me out."

"That's pretty funny," she managed, throat inexplicably tight. "Coming from you. The King Of Shutting *Me* Out."

"I didn't shut you out intentionally."

"Ditto," she said, with no small amount of attitude.

He studied her for a long moment. "Tell me about the night Karen died."

She felt like he'd reached into her chest and closed his fist around her lungs. She couldn't breathe. "She's not a part of this."

"I think maybe she is. She took a walk on the dark side, and it didn't work out so well for her. She made you promise to be good, and you kept your word. Until me."

"Someone has a big mouth."

"*Many* someones," he agreed. "But then again, you love it here. You love all those someones. And they all love you."

Mallory dropped her head to the steering wheel. "Look, I'm mad at you, okay? This isn't about me. I know my painful memories are relative. My life is good. I'm lucky. This isn't about how poor little Mallory has had it so hard. I'm not falling apart or anything."

He stroked a hand down her back. "Of course you're not. You're just holding the steering wheel up with your head for a minute, that's all."

Choking out a laugh, she closed her eyes. "I'm okay."

"Yeah, you are. You're so much more okay than I've ever been. You're the strongest woman I've ever met, Mallory. Do you know that?"

"But that's just it. I'm not strong at all. I always thought I could save everyone. If I was good, I'd excel. If I was good, my family would stay together. If I was good, nothing bad could happen."

Ty's hand on her was calming. So was his voice, low and even, without judgment. And the dash of affection didn't hurt. "How did that work out for you?" he asked. "All that being good?"

Another laugh tore out of her, completely mirthless. "It didn't. All that work, all that time spent trying to please everyone, and it fell apart anyway. I failed."

"You know better than that."

"Do I?" She tightened her grip on the steering wheel. It was her only anchor in a spinning world. Nothing was working out for her. Not her job. Not the way she wanted people to see her. And not her non-relationship with Ty. "I don't want to talk about the past anymore. My sister made her choice. My family each made their own choices after that. My parents handled everything the best they could, including their divorce."

"Maybe," he said. "But it still chewed you up and spit you out."

"I'm okay."

"You don't always have to be okay."

"Well, I know that."

"Then say it. Free that sixteen-year old, Mallory. Say it wasn't her fault; not your parents' divorce, not Karen, none of it."

"Ty."

"Say it."

She gulped in some air and let it out. "It wasn't my fault."

He wrapped his hand around her hair and gently tugged until she'd lifted her head and was looking at him. "That's right," he said with terrifying gentleness. "It wasn't your fault. You did the best you could with what you had. You made the decision to progress beyond that little girl who lived to please. You stepped outside your comfort zone and went after what you wanted."

She felt the heat hit her cheeks. They both knew what she'd gone after.

Him.

Naked.

And she'd gotten him.

"Stop carrying all the responsibility for everyone," he said quietly. "Let it go, let it all go and be whoever the hell you want to be."

She gave him a little smile. "Are you going to take your own advice?"

"I'm working on it."

"You're pretty amazing, you know that?"

"Yeah." He flashed his own small smile. "Too bad you dumped my sorry ass."

She looked at him for a long beat. "I might have been too hasty on that," she whispered. "Twice now."

"Is that right?"

"Yeah. Because your ass is anything but sorry."

He gave her a smile. "Come here," he said, and then without waiting for her to move, rose to his feet and pulled her from the car.

She curled into him, wrapping her arms around his neck. "Where are we going?"

"To show you how much more amazing I can be when we're horizontal."

Chapter 22

A life without chocolate is no life at all.

Ty set Mallory down in his bathroom, and she looked around in confusion. "I'm not horizontal."

Leaning past her, he flipped on his shower and cranked the water to hot. Then he stripped. And oh good Lord, he looked so damn good without his clothes that it almost made her forget her problems, including the fact that *he* was her biggest problem. "What—"

"You're wet and frozen solid. Kick off your shoes."

While she was obeying that command, he peeled the wet clothes from her and let them hit the floor. And while she was distracted by his mouth-watering body, he checked the temperature of the shower, then pushed her in.

She sucked in a breath as the hot water hit her, and then another when he reached for the soap. He washed her with quick efficiency while she stared down at the erection brushing her stomach.

"Ignore it," he said.

She stared at it some more, and it got bigger.

He shook his head at her and washed her hair, his fingers heaven on her scalp, making her moan. Then he set her aside, soaped himself up with equally quick efficiency, which absolutely shouldn't have turned her on, but totally did.

It must have showed because his eyes went dark and hot. Turning off the water, he wrapped her up in a towel and sat her on the counter. With just a towel low on his hips, he crouched down, rooted in a drawer, and came up with a first-aid kit and a box of condoms. Both unopened. Saying nothing, he set the condoms on the counter at her hip.

She went hot looking at them.

Grabbing the first-aid kit, he straightened to his full height and pushed her wet hair from her face. He dipped his knees a little and eyed the cut over her cheek. "A few butterfly bandages will do you, I think." He disinfected the cut, and when she hissed out a pained breath, he leaned in and kissed her temple.

"Nice bedside manner," she murmured. "You patch up a lot of wet, naked women?"

"Almost never." He carefully peeled back the plastic packaging on the sterilized butterfly bandages and began to cover her wound.

"So what exactly happened that you're okay with handling this sort of thing again?" she asked.

"You happened."

"Come on."

He slid her a look. "You think you're the only one making changes in your life?" he asked. "You work your ass off, no matter how much shit you see, and you see plenty. You just want to help people, heal them. I used to be like that. I didn't realize I missed it, but I do."

"The job you're going back to," she said. "It's obviously very dangerous work."

"Not as dangerous as being a SEAL. That was about as bad as it can get."

"Like the plane crash," she said softly.

"Yeah. Like the plane crash."

"Do you have PTSD, Ty?"

"Maybe." He shrugged. "Probably, a little. Not debilitating though. Not anymore anyway."

He was still damp from the shower, his hair pushed back from his face. He concentrated on his task, leaving her free to stare at him. His mouth was somehow both stern and generous at the same time, his jaw square and rough with a day's worth of scruff that she knew would feel deliciously sensual against her skin. He had a scar along one side of his jaw and another on his temple. His chest was broad, his abs ridged with muscle.

He was beautiful.

"You really miss it," she said softly. "The action."

"Once an adrenaline junkie, always one, I guess." He finished with the cut on her face and lifted her hand, turning it over to gently probe her swollen and already bruised wrist. She had no idea how he'd noticed it.

"It's not broken," she said.

He nodded in agreement, then lifted it to his mouth and brushed a kiss to her skin.

While she melted, he expertly wrapped it in an Ace bandage, then looked at her shin.

Bleeding.

She hadn't even realized.

He dropped to his knees and attended to that with the same concentration and professionalism he'd given everything else. His head was level with the counter she was sitting on, and his hands were on her bare leg. And all she could think was if he shifted her leg an inch more to the left, her towel would gape, and he'd be eye level with her bare crotch.

It was a suggestive, erotic thought that led to others, and she squirmed, wondering how she could get her towel to drop without being obvious about it.

"You okay?" he asked.

"Why didn't you leave when you were cleared?"

He looked up into her face. "I think you know why."

"Me."

"You," he agreed.

There were some advantages to changing her life around, to living for herself instead of for others' expectations, she decided. For one thing, it had given her new confidence. So she accessed some of that and unwrapped the towel, letting it fall to the counter at her hips.

Ty went still, and a sensual thrill rushed through her.

He let out a breath and slid his hands up her legs, applying gentle pressure until she opened them for him. He groaned at his new-found view and pressed a kiss to first one inner thigh, and then the other.

And then in between.

His hands were on her, rough and strong but tender at the same time, and her body quivered, rejoicing in the rightness of his touch. He murmured something against her skin and though she couldn't hear him, she urged him on, clutching at his shoulders until her toes curled, until she cried out his name, until there were no more thoughts.

She opened her eyes and found him rising to his feet, eyes hot, mouth wet, as he helped her off the counter. Then she was staring at him as he turned and walked out of the bathroom. "What are you—"

Since he was gone, she followed him into his bedroom, watching as he quickly dropped his towel, but instead of finishing the horizontal lessons, he pulled on black knit boxers that barely fit over his massive erection. "What are you doing?"

"Someone's at the door." He slid his long legs into jeans and grimaced when he tried to button them up.

Still in her orgasmic glow, she was thinking that she'd like to trace the cords of every one of his muscles, starting with his chest and working her way down. It'd take a while but she thought it would be time well spent. Then what he'd said sank in. "Someone's at your door? I didn't hear anything."

A small smile escaped him. "That's because you were making more noise than the doorbell."

"I was not—" God. She covered her hot cheeks. "Who is it?"

"Your mother."

She squeaked. "*What*?"

"I caught sight of her walking up to the door from the bathroom window." He glanced down at his hard-on. "You're going to have to get it." He eyed her body from head to toe and groaned. "And probably you should get dressed."

"*Why is my mother here*?"

"Meatloaf."

She'd forgotten about the meatloaf. Panicked, she turned in a circle. "My scrubs are wet and in a pile on your bathroom floor!"

"Hydrogen, helium, lithium—"

She stared at him. "What are you doing now?"

"Listing the chemical elements so I can answer the door without a boner."

"And knowing my mother is on your porch isn't taking care of that?"

"Good point." He threw her a pair of sweats that had been lying on a chair and left the room.

In the end, she tossed dignity and wore his sweats instead of her wet scrubs, but by the time she got to the living room, it was empty.

She found Ty in the big kitchen setting down a large bag. "She didn't stay," he said. "She said she figured I had my hands full making sure you were okay. She said she'd water your flowers and feed the cat for you, that you were to just sit your tired patoot down and relax, and I was to make sure you did just that."

"My mother, the Master Manipulator."

"Is your patoot tired?" he asked, sounding amused though his eyes were very serious.

"No. Are you hungry?"

His eyes roamed hungrily over her features. "Yes, but not for food. You?"

"I'll have whatever you're having."

Ty had been wanting to get his hands on Mallory since he'd heard from Matt about the missing drugs. Hell, he'd been wanting to put his hands on her since...always. He *always* wanted to put his hands on her. His hands, his mouth. *Everything.*

He stood her by the bed, making short work of the sweats she'd pulled on. When he dropped to his knees before her, he found her still warm and wet, already making those noises he loved, and when he slid a finger inside her, she gasped and opened her legs even wider for him.

A woman who knew what she wanted.

He loved that about her.

Her fingers were in his hair, holding him to her as if she was afraid he'd stop too soon.

Not a chance.

He wanted to hear her cry out his name again, wanted to feel her fly apart for him, so he worked her slow and easy, driving her right to the edge before backing off. She'd tightened her hands in his hair, doing her best to make him bald. He smiled against her and finally took her to the end. She was still shuddering when he surged to his feet and tossed her to the bed. She lay back, arms stretched out at her sides and gave him a little smile.

Sweet.

Hot.

"Why are you still dressed?" she wanted to know.

It was a good question. He stripped, grabbed a condom and rolled it on. When he had, he pushed inside her, just one long, slick slide that had them both sucking in a harsh breath of sheer, unadulterated pleasure.

Nothing had ever felt so good as being buried deep inside her.

Nothing.

"Ty?"

He drowned in her eyes. "Yeah?"

"This is far more than I thought it would be."

He knew that. He knew it to the depths of his soul. With one hand in her hair, holding her for a hard, deep kiss, the other cupping her sweet ass, he began to move, thrusting into her slow and steady, and for the first time all day—hell, all damn *week*—his world started to make sense.

He'd been a military brat who'd never landed in one place for long, then a soldier himself. There'd been next to no softness in his life. He'd taken the time for the occasional relationship, although none of them were serious; none stuck long enough to affect him deeply. Certainly no previous relationship had managed to fit what his idea of love was.

Mallory was different.

In his heart of hearts, he knew that much. Hell, from that first stormy night, his tie to her had been undeniable. It'd happened in an instant and only strengthened with time, and he wanted to be with her. Talking, touching, kissing, fucking—whatever he could get, because she beat back the darkness inside him. But being with her was a double-edged sword, because every minute he spent with her absolutely changed his definitions of…*everything.*

She made him yearn for things he'd never yearned for before: home, family, love. And Christ if that didn't stump him. What did he know about any of those things?

All he did know was that this—her mouth open on his, her body warm and soft and welcoming, her hands sliding up his chest and around his neck—felt right. *Real.* "Careful," he murmured, kissing her swollen cheek, then her wrapped wrist. "Don't let me hurt you."

"You healed me," she murmured. "Now let me heal you." Her hands slid down his back and then up again, and that felt so good he nearly purred. She melted into him and he warned himself that she'd had a rough time of it, that he needed to go slowly, but then she wrapped her legs around his waist and he sank in even further. With a moan, she arched beneath him, head back, eyes closed, hunger and desire etched on her face. "Oh, Ty..."

He nuzzled her exposed throat, then sucked a patch of skin into his mouth, making her gasp and tighten her grip on him.

Everywhere.

It set him on fire.

She did it again, and he let it roll over him: the feel of her heat gripping him like a vise, her scent, the scent of them together, the sound of her ragged breathing combined with wordless entreaties. Yeah. This. *This* was what he'd needed, her body hot and trembling against his, everything connecting. She was rocking into each thrust, her cries echoing in his mouth as he drove deeper, then deeper still. She was saying his name over and over now, straining against him, and then she was coming, shuddering in his arms as she went straight over the edge, taking him right along with her.

It was so good. That was his only thought as he let himself go. So good, so damn good...

Her hair was in his face, but he didn't breathe because he didn't want to disturb her. Her body, still overheated and damp, was plastered to his. She had one leg thrown over him, her cheek stuck to his pec, her hand on his favorite body part as if she owned it.

She did own it. She owned his heart and soul as well.

Jesus. It had started out so innocuously. Innocent, even.

Okay, not innocent. They'd had sex that first night in an attic. Some pretty fan-fucking-tastic sex.

He'd not been in a good place then. He hadn't felt good enough for his own life, much less anyone else's.

Certainly not good enough for a woman like Mallory, who'd give a perfect stranger the very shirt off her back.

But watching her, being with her, made him feel good.

Worthy.

It was unbelievable to him that one little woman could do that, but she had.

And where did that leave him? He'd never intended to be anything to Mallory other than a good time, but best laid plans…

Maybe he should have run hard and fast that very first night, but there'd been something about her, something that had drawn him in.

Even when he'd cost her, with her job, with her relationships with her family, she'd never hesitated. She'd given him everything she had. And in return, she'd only asked one thing of him. Just one.

Don't say good-bye. Just go.

His arms involuntarily tightened on her, and although she gave a soft sigh and cuddled deeper into him, she didn't waken. Nor did she stir when he finally forced himself to let go of her and slip out of the bed.

Mallory came awake slowly, thinking about all that had happened the day before. The HSC being shut down, her quitting, the diner's destruction…Ty making it all okay. It was subtle, he was subtle, but last night he'd given her just what she'd needed. Responsive but not smothering, encouraging her to talk when she'd needed to, and letting her be quiet when it'd counted.

She stretched, feeling her muscles ache in a very delicious way. He'd worshipped her body until nearly dawn.

Not just sex.

In truth, it hadn't been just sex for her since their first time, but she hadn't been sure how Ty felt.

Until last night.

Last night, the way he'd touched her, how he'd looked while deep in the throes, shuddering against her, claiming her body and giving her his...that had been lovemaking at its finest. Smiling at the memory, she rolled over and reached for him, but he wasn't in the bed. His pillow was cold.

And something inside her went cold as well.

She grabbed her buzzing phone off the nightstand. She put it there before falling asleep, as was her habit. She thought it might be Ty, but it was a text from Jane:

Bill refused your resignation. Also, due to a new donation earmarked specifically for HSC, the place has been granted a stay of execution for the next six months. On top of that, you are no longer pro bono for your hours there. Your next shift is tomorrow at eight. Be there, Mallory.

A new donation... *What had Ty done now*? Wrapping herself in his sheet, she walked through his house, her glow quickly subsiding. There'd never been much of him anywhere in the place to begin with, but the few traces of his existence were gone. His clothes, his duffle bag on the chair, his iPhone.

Gone.

Running now, she got to the garage and flipped on the light. The Shelby was still there, pretty and shiny.

Finished.

Confused, she went back through the house and into the bedroom. There she found the note that must have been on his pillow but had slipped to the floor, weighted down by a single key. A car key. The note read:

Mallory,

It was far more than I thought it would be, too.

I left you the Shelby. Sell it, it's worth enough that you can take your time deciding on the job thing. Matt'll get what it's worth for you. If you keep it, don't park it on the street.

No regrets.

Love, Ty

She stared at the note for a good ten minutes. He'd left her his baby? Given her permission to sell it so she wouldn't have to worry about money?

And then signed the note *Love, Ty*?

She let out a laugh, then clapped her hand over her mouth when it was followed by a soft sob.

He loved her.

The fool.

Or maybe that was her. *She* was the fool, because she loved him, too. Oh, how she loved him. "No regrets," she whispered, and wrapped her fingers around the key.

Chapter 23

Life is like a box of chocolates—full of nuts.

Mallory sat in Bill's office staring at him in disbelief. "Wait," she said, shaking her head. "Tell me that last part again. Ty tried to give you another donation, and you turned him down?"

"Yes," Bill said. "He's done enough for HSC, and I mean that in the best possible way."

Mallory swallowed hard. It was true. He'd done a lot for her, too. And even as he'd gone back to his life, he'd tried to make sure she'd be taken care of. She wished he was still here so she could smack him.

And then hug him.

"You turned down money?" she asked. "You never turn down money."

"It's not always about the bottom line." He smiled briefly but warmly. "See, even an old dog can learn new tricks."

"But Jane told me there was a donation."

"Yes. Another donation did come in. Mrs. Burland donated one hundred thousand dollars and—"

Mallory gasped and Bill held up a hand. "And she wanted it to be clear that everyone know she was the donor. She said, and I quote, '*I want it yelled from the rooftops that I was the one to save HSC.*'"

Mallory just stared. "Mrs. Burland," she repeated. "The woman who hates all of us, especially me?"

"Yes," Bill said. "Although I don't think she hates you as much as the rest of us. I believe Jane told you, there's a special condition on her donation."

"Me."

"Yeah. Consider your new salary for HSC a raise since I don't have it in the budget to offer you one for your RN position in the ER."

"But I quit."

"So un-quit. Take the knowledge that HSC is now secure, and so is your job, and get out of my office and back to work."

She thought about that for all of two seconds. "Yes, sir." She got up and moved to the door.

"Oh, and Mallory?"

She turned back.

"Don't ever quit again. My voice mail and e-mail box is overloaded with just about everyone in town demanding I'd best not lose you. Your mother has been hounding my ass since you walked out. Hell, *my* mother is hounding me. Understand?"

For the first time since she'd woken alone that morning, Mallory managed a smile. "I understand."

One week later, Mallory's life looked good—on paper. She had her job back, the future of HSC was secured, and the town was behind her.

What she didn't have was Ty.

Get used to it, she told herself, but on Saturday she rolled out of bed with a decided lack of enthusiasm. She'd done as she'd wanted. She'd stepped out of her comfort zone. She'd been selfish and lived her life the way she wanted, and it'd been more exciting than she could have imagined.

But how did she go back to being herself?

You don't, she decided. She'd put her heart on the line for the first time in her life but she'd made the choice to do it.

No regrets.

That was the day she got the delivery—a plain padded envelope, the return address too blurry and smeared to make out. She opened it up and a carefully wrapped package fell out. Opening the tissue paper, she stared down at the beautiful charm bracelet she'd coveted from the charity auction all those weeks ago.

There was no note, but none was necessary. She knew who'd sent it, and she pressed her hand to her aching heart at what it meant.

Ty, of course. He'd understood her as no other man ever had. He got that she was vested in this town, maybe in the same way he'd yearned to be, that the bracelet meant something to her. He'd added a charm, a '68 Shelby. She had no idea where he could have gotten it from, or what it'd cost him.

What did it mean?

It meant he cared about her, she told herself. Deeply. It meant she was on his mind, maybe even that he missed her.

She missed him, too, so very much.

Throat tight, she put the bracelet on, swallowed her tears, and shored up her determination to continue stretching her wings.

Two weeks later, Ty was on a flight back to the U.S. after an assignment that had involved escorting diplomats to a Somalian peace treaty.

The team he'd been with were all well-trained, seasoned men with the exception of one, who was fresh out of the military. Their first night, there'd been a kidnapping attempt, but they'd shut it down with no problem.

There'd been no injuries on Ty's team unless he counted the newbie, who'd gotten so nervous when it was over that he'd thrown up and needed an IV fluid replacement. Ty had done the honors.

"Sorry," the kid muttered to Ty that night, embarrassed as he watched Ty pull the IV. "I lost it."

Ty shook his head. "Happens."

"But not to you, right?"

On Ty's first mission, and on every assignment up to the plane crash, he'd thrived on what he'd been doing. He'd believed in it with every fiber of his soul, understood that he'd belonged out there doing what he could to save lives.

After the crash, he hadn't just lost four friends. He'd also lost something of himself. His ability to connect. To get attached.

Until Lucky Harbor. Until the nosy, pestering people of Lucky Harbor, who cared about everyone and everything in their path. Including him.

And Mallory. God, Mallory. She'd been the last piece of his shattered soul fitting back into place. "Hell yeah, it happens to me."

The kid looked surprised to hear Ty admit such a thing but he nodded in appreciation. "I can do this," he told Ty. "I'm ready for whatever comes our way."

But nothing did.

They spent two entire weeks doing nothing more than cooling their heels in the African bush, where the most exciting thing to happen was watching through the long-range scope of a rifle as an elephant gave birth in the distance.

Ty had come back to this because he thought he'd needed the rush of the job to be happy.

So where in the holy hell was his happy?

He knew the answer to that. It was thousands and thousands of miles away, with a woman who'd decimated the carefully constructed wall around his heart. And that's when it hit him between the eyes: It wasn't the job that fueled him, that kept him sane.

It was Mallory.

She was his team. She and Lucky Harbor. When he was there with her, she filled him up. Made him whole.

Made him everything.

Christ, he was slow. Too slow. It was probably far too late for such realizations. He'd been a fool and walked away from the best thing to ever happen to him, and Mallory didn't suffer fools well.

He looked out the airplane window as they finally circled D.C. Normally, at this point he'd be thinking about his priorities: sleeping for two days, fueling up on good food, and maybe finding a warm, willing woman.

He could get behind the sleep and the food, but there was only one woman he could think of, only one woman he wanted.

He'd left Lucky Harbor certain this had been his future, the nomadic, dangerous work he'd given his life to. He'd told himself it was the right thing to do, that he had to do this to make his team's deaths mean something. Plus, he could never give Mallory the kind of life she wanted. It just wasn't for him.

He'd been wrong on all counts. He knew it now. Brad, Tommy, Kelly, and Trevor's deaths would *always* mean something. And *his* life meant something, too. Probably he'd always known that, but he hadn't had his head screwed on right for a long time. He had it on tight now.

Debriefing took far too long. Frances was waiting for him. A tall, stacked blonde, she had mile-long legs that looked so good in a power suit she was her boss' sole weapon for recruiting.

Once upon a time, she'd recruited the hell out of Ty.

Now there was nothing between them but an odd mix of hostility and affection. She looked him over from head to toe and then back again. "You look like shit."

"Aw. Thanks."

She didn't offer him a smile, just another long gaze, giving nothing away. "You're not staying," she guessed.

"I'm not staying." He tossed her his security pass and walked.

"Do you really think a place like Lucky Harbor has anything to offer you?" she called after him.

He knew it did. He had connections there, real ones.

"Dammit, Ty," she said to his back when he kept walking. "At some point, you have to stop running."

"That's exactly what I'm doing."

Ty caught a red-eye flight into Seattle, and as he landed he brought up Lucky Harbor's Facebook. He'd resisted until now, but as the page loaded, he felt a smile curve his mouth at the latest note posted on the wall:

By now, you've all heard about Mrs. Burland's $100,000 donation to HSC, and how she single-handedly saved the clinic, brought back Mallory Quinn, AND created peace on earth.

Okay, maybe not quite peace on earth, but we do worship the ground she walks on. (Did I get that right, Louisa?)

ANYWAY, last week's raffle raised an additional $5K for the hospital. Thanks to our own Mallory Quinn for her tireless efforts. The grand prize—a date with Hospital Administrator Bill Lawson—was won by Jane Miller, Director of Nurses. Rumor has it that there was a good-night kiss. Wonder if Bill put out? Sources say yes. Look for a summer wedding...

Dawn hit the eastern sky as Ty drove a rental car into Lucky Harbor. He wondered if Mallory was still asleep in her bed, warm and soft.

Alone.

Christ, he hoped so. It'd only been two weeks but he'd left abruptly. Cruelly. He had no right to be back, no right at all to ask her to forgive him.

But that's exactly what he was going to do.

The ocean was still an inky purple as he drove past the pier, then hit the brakes.

The Shelby was in the lot at the diner.

Heart pounding, he parked and entered. The place smelled like fresh paint. The floors looked new and yet seemed to be made of the same timeless linoleum as they'd been before the sprinkler situation. He found Amy, Grace, and Mallory seated at the counter eating chocolate chip pancakes.

Or they had been eating, until he entered.

Three forks went still in the air.

Grace's and Amy's gazes slid to Mallory, but she was paying them no attention whatsoever. She was staring at Ty, her fork halfway to her mouth.

He'd walked through fire fights with less nerves, but he took hope from the sight of the charm bracelet glinting on her wrist.

"This is a private meeting," Grace told him. "Locals only."

"Grace," Mallory said quietly, her eyes never leaving Ty, but for once not giving anything of herself away, either. Ty had absolutely no idea what she was thinking; her face was carefully blank.

A lesson she'd probably learned from him.

Chapter 24

In the cookies of life, friends and lovers
are the chocolate chips.

Mallory stared at Ty and got light-headed, which turned out to be because she wasn't breathing.

"I thought you chocoholics met over cake," Ty said.

Two weeks. It'd been two weeks since she'd seen him, and he wanted to discuss cake. She hungrily drank in the sight of him. He wore battered Levi's and a white button-down, looking as good as ever. But he'd lost some weight, and his eyes were guarded.

"We've been banned from cake," Grace said. "On account of the candles."

Amy pointed at Ty with her fork. "You planning on walking in and out of her life again?"

"Just in," he said, his gaze never leaving Mallory's. "We need to talk."

"So talk," Grace said.

Amy nodded.

Heart pounding, Mallory stood up and gave both of her friends a shake of her head. "You know what he's asking. Give us a minute."

"Okay, but this is his third time interrupting us," Amy pointed out. "And—"

"*Please*," Mallory said to her friends.

Amy looked at Ty, using her first two fingers to point at him, going back and forth between his eyes and hers, silently giving him notice that she was watching him and not to even *think* about misbehaving.

Grace dragged her away.

Mallory waited until they were out of earshot to look at Ty. Her entire being went warm as she drank him in. She had no idea why he was back but she hoped like hell she was part of the reason.

"You still trying to save me, Mallory?" Ty asked quietly.

Her heart was hammering so loud she couldn't hear herself talk. "I can't seem to help myself."

"I don't need saving."

No. No, he sure didn't. He was strong and capable, and more than able to take care of himself. "What *do* you need?"

"You," he said simply. "Only you."

"Oh," Grace breathed softly from behind them. "Oh, that's good."

Both Mallory and Ty turned to find that Amy and Grace had scooted close enough to eavesdrop. Grace winced and held up an apologetic hand. "Sorry. Continue."

Mallory turned back to Ty, who took her hand in his big, warm one to entwine their fingers, bringing them up to his chest. His heartbeat was a reassuring steady thump. "I know you've looked for Mr. Right," he said. "And then Mr. Wrong. I was thinking maybe you'd be interested in a Mr.... Regular."

Her throat went tight. "That'd be great," she managed. "But I don't see any regular guys standing in front of me."

The corner of his mouth tipped up and melted her but she wasn't going to be distracted by his hotness right now. "Your job," she said.

"Yeah, I thought that's what drove me, gave me what I needed. I was wrong, Mallory. It's you. *You* fulfill me, like no job or no person ever has. You make me whole."

There was a sniffle behind them. Two sniffles. Mallory ignored them, even as she felt like sniffling herself. "Won't you go crazy here?"

"There's an opening in Seattle for a trauma flight paramedic. Also, I was thinking I want to work with veterans at HSC. I think I could help. And if I get bored and need some real action, there's always the arcade."

Mallory was absorbing this with what felt like a huge bucket of hope sitting on her chest. "And me," she whispered. "I could show you some action. You know, once in a while."

"Mallory," he said, sounding raw and staggered and touched beyond words. "God, I was so stupid. So slow. I didn't know what to do with you. I tried to keep my distance but my world doesn't work without you in it."

She melted. Given the twin sighs behind her, she wasn't the only one. "But is a trauma paramedic job enough for you?"

"There's more important things to me than an adrenaline rush. There's more important things than *any* job. But there's nothing more important than you," he said. "Mallory, I lo—"

"*Wait*!" This was from Amy, and she looked at Mallory. "I'm sorry, but don't you think you should tell him about the car before he finishes that sentence?"

"*No*," Mallory said, giving Amy the evil eye. She wanted the rest of Ty's sentence, dammit!

Ty frowned. "What's wrong with the Shelby?"

"*Nothing*," Mallory said quickly.

"Nothing," Amy agreed. "Except for the dinged door where she parked too close to the mailbox."

"Oh my God," Mallory said to her. "What are you, the car police?"

"The *classic* car police," Amy said smugly.

"You parked the Shelby on the street?" Ty asked Mallory incredulously.

She went brows-up.

"Okay," he said, lifting his hands. "It's okay. Never mind about the car."

"I've got this one," Grace said, wrapping an arm around Amy, covering the waitress's mouth while she was at it. "Go on."

Mallory turned back to Ty, who pulled her off her stool and touched the small scar on her cheek before leaning in to kiss her. "I love you, Mallory," he said very quietly, very seriously. "So damn much."

Warmth and affection and need and so much more rushed her. "I know."

"You know?"

"Yes."

"Well, hell," he said with a small smile and a shake of his head. "You might have told me and saved me a lot of time."

"How about I tell you something else?" she said. "I love you, too."

The rest of the wariness he'd arrived with drained from him. "Tell me what you need from me for there to be an us," he said.

Hope blossomed, full and bright. "You want an us?"

"I want an us. Tell me, Mallory."

"I like what we had," she said. "Being together after a long day, maybe dinner out sometimes. That was nice. We could skip the orchestra, though."

"Mallory," he said on a short laugh. "Tell me you want more from me than that."

She bit her lower lip, but the naughty grin escaped anyway. "Well, maybe a little bit more."

He laughed softly, his eyes going dark. He pulled her in and kissed her hard, threading his hands in her hair. "How do you feel about sealing the deal with a ring?" he murmured against her lips.

All three women gasped.

"What?" Mallory squeaked. "You mean an engagement ring? To be *married*?"

"Yes," he said. "You're it for me, Mallory. You're everything."

He was serious. And suddenly, so was she. "I'd like that," she said softly.

"Good," he said. "Anything else we need to work out?"

Only a hundred things. Where was he going to live? *With her*, she thought possessively. She wanted him with her. Wait—Did that mean that she'd have to learn to cook? Because that might be a stretch. And she didn't have any room in her closet to share. And the cat. What if Sweet Pea pooped in his boots?

Ty cupped her face and made her look at him, deep into his eyes, and it was there she found the truth. All these worries were inconsequential. They didn't matter. Nothing mattered but this.

Him.

Besides, she had time to make room for him in her closet. The cat had time to get used to him. They had all the time they needed, because he'd told her he was hers, and he was a man of his word. "I've got all I need," she told him.

He leaned down and kissed her again, then stroked a finger over her temple, tucking a loose strand of hair behind her ear. "I want you to know," he said. "That you're the best choice I ever made."

"No regrets?"

"No regrets."

Heart full to bursting, she tugged him down and kissed the man she was going to spend the rest of her life with.

The Chocoholics' Wickedly Awesome Chocolate Cake

Cake

1 8-ounce bag of dark chocolate chips
½ cup and 3 extra tablespoons butter
1¼ cups cake flour
½ cup cocoa
1 box of instant chocolate pudding mix
½ teaspoon salt
½ teaspoon baking powder
¼ teaspoon baking soda
4 large eggs
¼ cup vegetable oil
½ cup white sugar
⅓ cup dark brown sugar
1½ teaspoon vanilla extract
⅔ cup milk

Preheat oven to 350° F.

Melt the chocolate chips in a microwave-safe bowl by combining the chocolate chips and 3 tablespoons of butter and microwaving on power level 3 for 2 minutes. Take the bowl out of the oven, stir, and put back in the microwave for 2 more minutes. Take it out, stir, and put back in the microwave for 2 final minutes. Stir until the melted chocolate is fully incorporated with the butter.

Mix the dry ingredients together in a medium bowl: cake flour, cocoa, pudding mix, salt, baking powder, and baking soda.

In a large bowl, using an electric mixer, beat the eggs, oil, and sugars together until it thickens, approximately five minutes. Reduce mixer to low speed then add in vanilla and milk. Gradually add in the dry ingredients and beat together.

After it's fully mixed, pour batter into a greased 8-inch square cake pan. Bake at 350 degrees until you can put a toothpick in the middle and it comes out clean, approximately 35 to 45 minutes.

Frosting

½ cup powdered sugar
¾ cup cocoa
2 tablespoons butter (softened)
1 8-ounce package of cream cheese (softened)
1 teaspoon vanilla
¼ cup milk

Mix the powdered sugar and cocoa together.

In a separate bowl, using an electric mixer, beat the butter and cream cheese together. Add vanilla and mix it in. Slowly start incorporating some of the sugar-cocoa mixture. When it starts to firm up, slowly mix in some of the milk. Alternate sugar-cocoa mix and milk until you have the right frosting consistency.

Frost the cooled cake and then... yum!

At Last

Chapter 1

Everything's better with chocolate.

I'm not lost," Amy Michaels said to the squirrel watching her from his perch on a tree branch. "Really, I'm not."

But she so was. And actually, it was a way of life. Not that Mr. Squirrel seemed to care. "I don't suppose you know which way?" she asked him. "I happen to be looking for hope."

His nose twitched, then he turned tail and vanished in the thick woods.

Well, that's what she got for asking a guy for directions. Or asking a guy for anything for that matter...She stood there another moment, with the high-altitude sun beating down on her head, a map in one hand and her Grandma Rose's journal in the other. The forest around her was a profusion of every hue of green and thick with tree moss and climbing plants. Even the ground was alive with growth and running creeks that she constantly had to leap over while birds and squirrels chattered at her. A city girl at heart, Amy was used to concrete, lights, and people flipping other people off. This noisy silence and lack of civilization was like being on another planet, but she kept going.

The old Amy wouldn't have. She'd have gone home by now. But the old Amy had made a lifelong habit out of running instead of taking a stand. She was done with that. It was the reason she was here in the wilds instead of on her couch. There was another reason, too, one she had a hard time putting into words. Nearly five decades ago now, her grandma had spent a summer in Lucky Harbor, the small Washington coastal town Amy could catch glimpses of from some of the switchbacks on the trail. Rose's summer adventure had been Amy's bedtime stories growing up, the only bright spot in an otherwise shitty childhood.

Now Amy was grown up—relatively speaking—and looking for what her grandma had claimed to find all those years ago—hope, peace, heart. It seemed silly and elusive, but the truth was sitting in her gut—Amy wanted those things, needed them so desperately it hurt.

It was harder than she expected. She'd been up since before dawn, had put in a ten-hour shift on her feet at the diner, and was now on a mountain trail. Still on her feet.

Unsure she was even going in the right direction, she flipped open her grandma's journal, which was really more of a spiral notepad, small enough that it fit in the palm of her hand. Amy had it practically memorized, but it was always a comfort to see the messy scrawl.

> *It's been a rough week. The roughest of the summer so far. A woman in town gave us directions for a day hike, promising it'd be fun. We started at the North District Ranger Station, turned right at Eagle Rock, left at Squaw Flats. And with the constant roar of the ocean as our northward guide, headed straight to the most gorgeous meadow I've ever seen, lined on the east side by thirty-foot-high prehistoric rocks pointing to the sky. The farthest one was the tallest, proudly planted into the ground, probably sitting there since the Ice Age.*

We sat, our backs to the rock, taking it all in. I spent some time drawing the meadow, and when I was done, the late afternoon sun hit the rock perfectly, lighting it up like a diamond from heaven, both blinding and inspiring. We carved our initials into the bottom of our diamond and stayed the night beneath a black velvety sky…

And by morning, I realized I had something I'd been sorely missing—hope for the future.

Amy could hear the words in her grandma's soft, trembling voice, though of course she would have been much younger when she'd actually written the journal. Grandpa Scott had died when Amy was five, so she couldn't remember much about him other than a stern face, and that he'd waggled his finger a lot. It was hard to picture the stoic man of her memories taking a whimsical journey to a diamond rock and finding hope, but what did she know?

She hiked for what felt like forever on the steep mountain trail, which sure had looked a whole lot flatter and straighter on the map. Neither the map nor Rose's journal had given any indication that Amy had been going straight up until her nose bled. Or that the single-track trail was pitted with obstacles like rocks, fast-running creeks, low-hanging growth, and in two cases, downed trees that were bigger than her entire apartment. But Amy had determination on her side. Hell, she'd been born determined. Sure, she'd taken a few detours through Down-On-Her-Luck and then past Bad-Decisionsville, but she was on the right path now.

She just needed that hope. And peace would be good, too. She didn't give much of a shit about heart. Heart had never really worked out for her. Heart could suck it, but she wanted that hope. So she kept moving, amongst skyscraper-high rock formations and trees that she couldn't even see the tops of, feeling small and insignificant.

And awed.

She'd roughed it before; but in the past, this had meant something entirely different, such as giving up meals on her extra lean weeks, not trudging through the damp, overgrown forest laden with bugs, spiders, and possibly killer birds. At least they sounded killer to Amy, what with all the manic hooting and carrying on.

When she needed a break, she opened her backpack and went directly to the emergency brownie she'd pilfered from work earlier. She sat on a large rock and sighed in pleasure at getting off her feet. At the first bite of chocolatey goodness, she moaned again, instantly relaxing.

See, she told herself, looking around at the overabundant nature, this wasn't so bad. She could totally do this. Hell, maybe she'd even sleep out here, like her grandparents had, beneath the velvet sky—

Then a bee dive-bombed her with the precision of a kamikaze pilot, and Amy screeched, flinging herself off the rock. "Dammit." Dusting herself off, she stood and eyed the fallen brownie, lying forlorn in the dirt. She gave herself a moment to mourn the loss before taking in her surroundings with wariness.

There were no more bees, but now she had a bigger problem. It suddenly occurred to her that it'd been a while since she'd caught sight of the rugged coastline, with its stone arches and rocky sea stacks. Nor could she hear the roar of the crashing waves from below as her northward guide.

That couldn't be good.

She consulted her map and her penciled route. Not that *that* helped. There'd been quite a few forks on the trail, not all of them clearly marked. She turned to her grandma's journal again. As directed, she'd started at the North District Ranger Station, gone right at Eagle Rock, left at Squaw Flats...but no ocean sounds. No meadow. No diamond rock.

And no hope.

Amy looked at her watch—six thirty. Was it getting darker already? Hard to tell. She figured she had another hour and a half before nightfall, but deep down, she knew that wasn't enough time. The meadow wasn't going to magically appear, at least not today. Turning in a slow circle to get her bearings, she heard an odd rustling. A human sort of rustling. Amy went utterly still except for the hair on the back of her neck, which stood straight up. "Hello?"

The rustling had stopped, but *there*, she caught a quick flash of something in the bush.

A face? She'd have sworn so. "Hello?" she called out. "Who's there?"

No one answered. Amy slid her backpack around to her front and reached in for her pocket knife.

Once a city rat, always a city rat.

Another slight rustle, and a glimpse of something blue—a sweat-shirt maybe. "Hey," she yelled, louder than she meant to but she *hated* being startled.

Again, no one answered her, and the sudden stillness told her that she was once again alone.

She was good at alone. Alone worked. Heart still racing, she turned back around. And then around again. Because she had a problem—everything looked the same, so much so that she wasn't sure which way she'd come.

Or which way she was going. She walked along the trail for a minute but it didn't seem familiar so she did a one-eighty and tried again.

Still not familiar.

Great. Feeling like she'd gone down the rabbit hole, she whipped out her cell phone and stared down at the screen.

One bar…

Okay, don't panic. Amy never panicked until her back was up against the wall. Eyeing the closest rock outcropping, she headed toward it. Her guidebook had said that the Olympics' rock formations were made up of shales, sandstone, soft basalts, and pillow lava. *She* would have said they were sharp and craggy, a fact attested to by the cuts on her hands and legs. But they were also a good place to get reception.

Hopefully.

Climbing out onto the rocks was fine. Looking down, not so much. She was oh-holy-shit high up.

Gulp.

But she had *two* bars now for her efforts. She took a moment to debate between calling her two closest friends, Grace or Mallory. Either of the Chocoholics were good in a tough situation, but Mallory was a Lucky Harbor native, so Amy called her first.

"How's it going?" Mallory asked.

"Taking a brownie break," Amy said casually, like she wasn't sitting on a rock outcropping a million feet above earth. "Thought you could join me."

"For chocolate?" Mallory asked. "Oh, yeah. Where are you?"

Well, wasn't that the question of the day. "I'm on the Sierra Meadows Trail…somewhere."

There was a beat of accusatory silence. "You lied about meeting you for a brownie?" Mallory asked, tone full of rebuke.

"Yeah, that's not exactly the part of my story I expected you to fixate on," Amy said. The rock was damp beneath her. Rain-soaked mosses adorned every tree trunk in sight, and she could hear a waterfall cascading into a natural pool somewhere nearby. Another bush rustled. Wind?

Or…?

"I can't believe you lied about chocolate," Mallory said. "Lying about chocolate is…*sacrilegious*. Do you remember all those bad girl lessons you gave me?"

Amy rubbed the spot between her eyes where a headache was starting. "You mean the lessons that landed you the sexy hunk you're currently sleeping with?"

"Well, yes. But my point is that maybe you need *good* girl

lessons. And good girl lesson number one is *never* tease when it comes to chocolate."

"Forget the chocolate." Amy drew a deep breath. "Okay, so you know I'm not all that big on needing help when I screw up, but..." She grimaced. "*Help.*"

"You're really lost?"

Amy sighed. "Yeah, I'm really lost. Alert the media. Text Lucille." Actually, in Lucky Harbor, Lucille *was* the media. Though she was seventy-something, her mind was sharp as a tack, and she used it to run Lucky Harbor's Facebook page like New York's *Page Six*.

Mallory had turned all business, using her bossy ER voice. "What trail did you start on and how long have you been moving?"

Amy did her best to recount her trek up to the point where she'd turned left at Squaw Flats. "I should have hit the meadow by now, right?"

"If you stayed on the correct trail," Mallory agreed. "Okay, listen to me very carefully. I want you to stay right where you are. Don't move."

Amy looked around her, wondering what sort of animals were nearby and how much of a meal she might look like to them. "Maybe I should—"

"No," Mallory said firmly. "I mean it, Amy. I want you to stay. People get lost up there and are never heard from again. *Don't move from that spot.* I've got a plan."

Amy nodded, but Mallory was already gone. Amy slipped her phone into her pocket, and though she wasn't much for following directions, she did as Mallory had commanded and didn't move from her spot. But she did resettle the comforting weight of her knife in her palm.

And wished for another brownie.

The forest noises started up again. Birds. Insects. Something with a howl that brought goose bumps to her entire body. She got whiplash from checking out each and every noise. But as she'd learned long ago, maintaining a high level of tension for an extended period of time was just exhausting. A good scream queen she would not make, so she pulled out her sketch pad and did her best to lose herself in drawing.

Thirty minutes later, she heard someone coming from the opposite direction she *thought* she'd come from. He wasn't making much noise, but Amy was a master at hearing someone approach. She could do it in her sleep—and had. Her heart kicked hard, but these were easy, steady footsteps on the trail. Not heavy, drunken footsteps heading down the hall to her bedroom…

In either case, it certainly wasn't Mallory. No, this was a man, light on his feet but not making any attempt to hide his approach. Amy squeezed her fingers around the comforting weight of her knife.

From around the blind curve of the trail, the man appeared. He was tall, built, and armed and dangerous, though not to her physical well-being. Nope, nothing about the tough, sinewy, gorgeous forest ranger was a threat to her body.

But Matt Bowers was *lethal* to her peace of mind.

She knew who he was from all the nights he'd come into the diner after a long shift, seeking food. Lucky Harbor residents fawned over him, especially the women. Amy attributed this to an electrifying mix of testosterone and the uniform. He was sipping a Big Gulp, which she'd bet her last dollar had Dr. Pepper in it. The man was a serious soda addict.

She understood his appeal, even felt the tug of it herself, but that was her body's response to him. Her brain was smarter than the rest of her and resisted.

He wore dark, wraparound Oakley sunglasses, but she happened to know that his eyes were light brown, sharp, and missed nothing. Those eyes were in complete contrast with his smile, which was all laid-back and easygoing, and said he was a pussy cat.

That smile lied.

Nothing about Matt Bowers was sweet and tame. Not one little hair on his sun-kissed head, not a single spectacular muscle, nothing. He was trouble with a capital *T*, and Amy had given up trouble a long time ago.

She was still sitting on the rock outcropping, nearly out of sight of the trail, but Matt's attention tracked straight to her with no effort at all. She sensed his wry amusement as he stopped and eyed her. "Someone send out an S.O.S.?"

She barely bit back her sigh. *Dammit, Mallory. Out of all the men in all the land, you had to send this one…*

When she didn't answer, he smiled. He knew damn well she'd called Mallory, and he wanted to hear her admit that she was lost.

But she didn't feel like it—childish and immature, she knew. The truth was, her reaction to him was just about the furthest thing from childish, and that scared her. She wasn't ready for the likes of him, for the likes of any man. The very last thing she needed was an entanglement, even if Matt did make her mouth water, even if he did look like he knew exactly how to get her off this mountain.

Or off in general…

And if *that* wasn't the most disconcerting thought she'd had in weeks…

Months.

"Mallory called the cavalry," he said. "Figured I was the best shot you had of getting found before dark."

Amy squared her shoulders, hoping she looked more capable than she felt. "Mallory shouldn't have bothered you."

He smiled. "So you *did* send out the S.O.S."

Damn him and his smug smile. "Forget about it," she said. "I'm fine. Go back to your job doing…" She waved her hand. "Whatever it is that forest rangers do, getting Yogi out of the trash, keeping the squirrels in line, et cetera."

"Yogi and the squirrels do take up a lot of my time," he agreed mildly. "But no worries. I can still fit you in."

His voice always seemed to do something funny to her stomach. And lower. "Lucky me."

"Yeah." He took another leisurely sip of his soda. "You might not know this, but on top of keeping Yogi in line and all the squirrel wrangling I do, rescuing fair maidens is also part of my job description."

"I'm no fair maiden—" She broke off when something screeched directly above her. Reacting instinctively, she flattened herself to the rock, completely ruining her tough-girl image.

"Just the cry of a loon," her very own forest ranger said. "Echoing across Four Lakes."

She straightened up just as another animal howled, and barely managed not to flinch. "That," she said shakily, "was more than a loon."

"A coyote," he agreed. "And the bugling of an elk. It's dusk. Everyone's on the prowl for dinner. The sound carries over the lakes, making everyone seem like they're closer than they are."

"There's elk around here?"

"Roosevelt Elk," he said. "And deer, bobcats, and cougars, too."

Amy shoved her sketch book into her backpack, ready to get the hell off the mountain.

"Whatcha got there?" he asked.

"Nothing." She didn't know him well enough to share her drawings, and then there was the fact that he was everything she didn't trust: easy smile, easy nature, easy ways—no matter how sexy the packaging.

Chapter 2

If God had meant for us to be thin, he wouldn't have created chocolate.

Matt loved his job. Having come from first the military, then Chicago SWAT, the current shortage of blood and guts and gangbangers in his workweek was a big bonus. But his day as supervisory forest ranger for the North District had started at the ass crack of dawn, when two of his rangers had called in sick, forcing him to give the sunrise rainforest tour—a chore he ranked right up there with having a root canal.

Without drugs.

Talking wasn't the problem. Matt liked talking just fine, and he loved the mountain. What he didn't love were the parents who didn't keep track of their own children, or the divorcees who were looking for a little vacay nookie with a forest ranger, or the hardcore outdoor enthusiasts who knew...everything.

After the morning's tour, he'd measured the snowmelt and then gone to the Eagle Rock campsites to relocate one royally pissed-off raccoon mama and her four babies from the bathroom showers. From there, he'd climbed up to Sawtooth Lake to check the east and west shorelines for reported erosion, taken steps to get that erosion under control, patrolled all the northern quadrant's trails for a supposed Bigfoot sighting, handled some dreaded paperwork, and then come back out to rescue a fair, sweet maiden.

Only maybe not so sweet...

She was still sitting on the rock outcropping, her mile-long legs bent, her arms wrapped around them, her dark eyes giving nothing away except her mistrust, and he felt the usual punch of awareness hit him in the solar plexus.

So fucking beautiful. And so full of 100 percent, hands-off-or-die bad attitude.

She wasn't his usual type. He preferred his women soft, warm, giving, with a nice dash of playful sexiness, so he had no idea what it was about Amy Michaels. But for the past six months, ever since she'd moved to Lucky Harbor, they'd been circling each other.

Or maybe it was just him doing the circling. Amy was doing a whole lot of ignoring, a real feat given that she'd been serving him at the diner just about every night. He could have asked her out, but he knew she wouldn't go. She turned down everyone who asked her.

So instead Matt had regularly parked himself at Eat Me, fueling himself up on diner food and her company when he could get it. Then he'd go home and fantasize about all the other ways she might keep him company, getting off on more than a few of them.

Today she wore low-riding jeans and a black tank top that hugged her curves, revealing slightly sunburned shoulders and toned arms. Her boots had both laces and zippers. City girl boots, meant to look hot.

They did.

"You going to tell me what's going on?" he asked.

"Nothing's going on."

"Uh huh." She was revealing a whole lot of nothing. Basically, she would admit to being lost over her own dead body.

Usually people were happy to see him, but not this woman. Never this woman, and it was a little baffling. He knew from watching her at the diner, serving everyone from the mayor to raunchy truckers with the same impassive efficiency, that she had a high bullshit meter and a low tolerance for anything that wasn't delivered straight up. "So Mallory's what, on crack?" he asked.

"She thinks she's funny."

"So... you're good?"

"Pretty much," she said.

He nodded agreeably. Fine by him if she didn't want to break down and admit to being lost. He enjoyed her fierceness, and the inner strength that came with it. But he still couldn't just walk away.

Or take his eyes off her. Her hair was a deep, rich, shiny brown, sometimes up, sometimes falling softly about her face, as it was today. She wore aviator sunglasses and lip gloss, and that tough-girl expression. She was a walking contradiction.

And a walking wet dream. "You know this trail closes at dusk, right?"

She tipped her head up and eyed the sky. Nearly dusk. Then she met his gaze. "Sure," she said with a tight smile.

Hmm. Not for the first time, he wondered how it'd be to see her smile with both her eyes and her mouth at the same time.

She retied her boots, those silly boots that didn't have a lick of common sense to them. He was picturing her in those boots and nothing else when she climbed off the rock and pulled on her cute little leather backpack, which was as impractical as her boots. "What are you doing all the way up here?"

"Just hiking," she said carefully. She was always careful with her words, careful to keep her thoughts hidden, and she was especially careful to keep herself distanced from *him*.

But Matt had his own bullshit meter, and it was deadly accurate. She was lying, which stirred his natural curiosity and suspicion—

good for the cop in him, dangerous for the man who was no longer interested in romantic relationships. "Hiking out here is big," he said. "But it can be dangerous."

She shrugged at this, as if the dangers of the forest were no match for her. It was either cocky, or simply the fact that she'd spent a hell of a lot of time in far more dangerous situations. He suspected the latter, which he didn't like to think about.

She moved back to the trail, clearly anxious to be rid of him. Not a surprise.

But along with Matt's BS meter came a honed ability to read people, and he was reading her loud and clear. She was exhausted, on edge, and his least favorite: scared, though she was doing her best to hide that part. Still, her nerves were shining through, and he knew it was because of him.

He wasn't sure what to do about that. Or her. He wasn't at all used to explaining himself, but he needed to explain a few things to her. Such as exactly how lost she was. "Amy—"

"Look, I appreciate you coming out. I did lose track of time, but I'll be going now, so..."

Knowing the value of a good, meaningful silence, Matt waited for her to finish her sentence.

She didn't.

Instead, she was clearly waiting for him to leave, and he suddenly got it—she wanted to follow him out. Pride sucked, as he knew all too well. "Okay, then," he said. "I'll see you at the diner real soon."

"Right." She nodded agreeably, the woman who was the singularly most disagreeable woman he'd ever met.

Having much more time than she, he leaned back against a tree, enjoying the flash of annoyance that crossed her face. "Right," he mirrored. It'd been a hell of a long day, and it was shaping up to be a longer night. He didn't have enough Dr. Pepper left to get him through it, but he was perfectly willing to try.

Amy sighed with barely concealed annoyance and stalked off down the path.

In the wrong direction.

Funny, Amy thought, how righteous indignation could renew one's energy level, not to mention make them stupid. And oh, how she hated being stupid. Even worse was being stupid in mixed company. She'd done it before, of course. Too many times to count. She'd thought she'd gotten past it but apparently not.

"Need help?"

With a grimace, she slowly turned to face Matt. Yeah, she needed help, and they both knew it.

He was still leaning against the tree, arms crossed over his chest, the gun on his hip catching the sun. He looked big and tough as hell, his shoulders broad enough to carry all her problems. His hair brushed his collar, a little shaggy, a lot tousled. Sexy. Damn him. He stood there as if he had all the time in the world and not a concern in his head.

And of course he didn't. *He* wasn't lost.

But there was something else, too. There was a sort of...crackling in the air between them, and it wasn't a bird or insect or frigging elk call either.

It was sexual tension. It'd been a long time, a real long time, since she'd allowed herself to acknowledge such a thing, and it surprised the hell out of her. She knew men, all of them. She'd been there, done that, bought *and* returned the T-shirt. She knew that beneath a guy's chosen veneer, whatever that may be—nice guy, funny guy, sexy guy, whatever—lay their true colors, just lying in wait.

But she'd been watching Matt for months now, and he was always...Matt. Amused, tense, tired, it didn't seem to matter, he remained his cool, calm, even-keeled self. Nothing got to him. She had to admit, that confused her. *He* confused her. "I'm actually okay," she said.

He expressed polite doubt with the arch of a single brow. Her pride was a huge regulation-sized football in her throat, and admitting defeat sucked. But there was ego, and there was being an idiot. "Fine," she said. "Just tell me which way is south."

He pointed south.

Nodding, she headed that way, only to be caught up short when he snagged her by the backpack and pulled her back against him.

She startled, jerking in his hands before forcing herself to relax. It was Matt, she reminded herself, and the thought was followed by a hot flash that she'd like to blame on the weather, but she knew better.

He turned her ninety degrees. "To get back to the ranger station and your car, you want to go southwest," he said.

Right. She knew that, and she stalked off in the correct direction.

"Watch out for bears," Matt called after her.

"Yeah, okay," she muttered, "and I'll also keep an eye out for the Tooth Fairy."

"Three o'clock."

Amy craned her neck and froze. Oh sweet baby Jesus, there really was a bear at three o'clock. Enjoying the last of the sun, he was big, brown, and shaggy, and *big*. He lay flat on his back, his huge paws in the air as he stretched, confident that he sat at the top of the food chain. "Holy shit," she whispered, every Discovery Channel bear mauling she'd ever seen flashing in her mind. She backed up a step, and then another, until she bumped into a brick wall and nearly screamed.

"Just a brown bear," said the brick wall that was Matt.

"Would you stop sneaking up on me?" she hissed over her shoulder. "I hate to be sneaked up on!"

Matt was kind enough not to point out that *she'd* bumped into him. Or that she was quaking in her boots. Instead, he set his drink down and very softly "shh'd" her, gently rubbing his big hands up and down her arms. "You're okay," he said.

She was okay? How was that possible? The bear was the size of a VW, and he was wriggling on the ground, letting out audible groans of ecstasy as he scratched his back on the fallen pine needles, latent power in his every move. Sort of like the man behind her. "Does he even see us?" she whispered.

As she spoke, the bear slowly tipped his big, furry head back, lazily studying Amy and Matt from his upside down perch.

Yeah, he saw them. Reacting instinctively, she turned and burrowed right into Matt. "If you laugh at me," she warned as his warm, strong arms closed around her, "I'll kill you."

He didn't laugh or mock her. For once, he was unsmiling, his jaw dark with stubble, eyes hidden behind his reflective Oakleys. "No worries, Tough Girl," he said, his warm, strong arms closing around her. "And anyway, I'm hard to kill."

Chapter 3

There's more to life than chocolate, but not right now.

As Matt drew Amy in close, he thought that laughing at her was just about the last thing on the list of what he felt like doing at the moment. Kissing her was on the list. Sliding his hands down her back to cup her sweet ass and rub up against her was also on the list.

But laughing? No. She'd nearly leapt out of her own skin a second ago, and it hadn't been all fear of the bear. Nope, a good portion of that had been when Matt had touched her unexpectedly. That bothered him, a whole hell of a lot. "I've got you."

"I've usually got myself," she murmured into his chest. "I'm just not much of a bear person." Her voice was soft and full of the reluctant gratitude he knew she'd never actually express. He liked this better than the wariness she usually showed him, but not even close to what he'd rather she be feeling.

He ran his hand up and down her back, trying to soothe the quivers he felt wracking her, trying *not* to notice how good she felt against him. Or how…fragile.

He'd never thought of her as fragile before, ever. He'd spent a lot of time watching her carry loaded trays at the diner and knew she was actually strong as hell. "You're not going to be bear bait," he promised, turning her so that she was behind him. "Not today anyway."

She grabbed a fistful of the back of his uniform shirt and pressed up against his back. "How do you know?"

"Well, you're behind me, for one thing. So if anyone's going to be bear bait, it'll be me. And brown bears are extremely passive. If we take a step toward him, he'll take off."

She let go of him, presumably so he could do just that, even giving him a little nudge that was actually more like a push. With a laugh, Matt obliged and stepped toward the bear, waving his arms. With a look of reproof, the bear lumbered to his feet and vanished into the bush.

Amy collected herself with admirable speed, which was just the slightest bit of a bummer because he'd been enjoying the contact. "A lot can happen this far out here on the mountain," he said. "You need to be ready for anything."

"Yeah, I'm getting that, thanks." In those ridiculous but sexy-as-hell boots, she moved unenthusiastically to the trail.

"Sure you don't want an escort out?" he asked. *Or some more comforting…*

"I've got it."

Just as well since he was out of the practice of comforting a woman. Several years out of practice, actually, since his ex had so thoroughly shredded him back in Chicago. He was still watching Amy hike off into the sunset when his radio squawked, and then Mary, his dispatcher, came on. "You find her?"

Mallory had called his office an hour ago, and Mary had reached him on the radio. Now Mallory was probably calling to check on Amy. "Yeah, she's on her way out now. I'm still up here near 06-04," he said, giving his coordinates.

"You might want to think about sticking overnight."

"Why?"

"One of the standing dead fell about twenty minutes ago, across the fire road at 06-02."

His route out.

"Can't get a saw up there until daybreak," she said.

This left him two choices—leave his truck and hike out like Amy or sleep up here. He wasn't going to leave his truck. Overnighting wasn't a hardship in the slightest since he had all his gear with him and had stayed out here many a night. "I'll stick. Take me off the board."

"Ten-four."

Matt turned and went in the opposite direction Amy had gone, stepping off the trail to take a considerable shortcut back to where he'd left his truck. He didn't hurry through the stands of spruce, hemlock, pine, and cedar. There was no need; he'd still beat her. And sure enough, when he'd gotten to his truck and four-wheeled farther down the narrow fire road to where it intersected with the Sawtooth trail, he came out just ahead of her. She came around a blind corner and kept moving, not seeing him.

"Amy."

She whipped around, feet planted wide, eyes alert, ready for a fight.

"Just me," he said easily.

"What the hell are you doing, besides trying to scare me to death?"

She'd been really moving. And, if he wasn't mistaken, she was also limping a little bit in her boots. "Just making sure you're still going in the right direction."

Breathing a little heavily, she tore off her sunglasses and narrowed her dark eyes at him, hands on hips. "You had your truck all along?"

"I offered you help. Think you're going to be okay for the three-mile hike back?"

"Three miles? What the hell happened to the '*moderate, two-*

mile round-trip hike that everyone can enjoy' that the guidebook promised?"

"If you'd have stayed on the Sierra Meadows Trail, that'd have been true," he said. "But you cut over to the Sawtooth Trail."

She blew a strand of hair out of her face. "You need better trail signs."

"Budget cuts," he said. "Next time stay on the easy-access trails down by the station. Those are clearly marked."

"Easy is for pansies."

"Maybe, but at least all the pansies are safe for the night. Because once it gets dark out here, it's best to stay still. And that's in about..." He tipped his head back and studied the sky. "Ten minutes. Ever been out here at night?"

She glanced upward uneasily. "No."

"It's a whole new kind of dark. No street lights, no city lights, nothing."

"Why aren't you in a hurry then?"

"I'm not going anywhere tonight," he said. "The fire road's blocked until morning by a fallen tree, and I don't want to leave my truck."

"So you're going to stay out here all night?" she asked. "Beneath the velvet sky?"

"Nice description."

"It's not mine." She pulled a small penlight flashlight from her backpack and flicked it on in the dusk, looking relieved that it actually worked. "You don't think I can get back before dark, do you?"

"No."

She sighed. "So if I stay out here, you going to ticket me for not having an overnight permit?"

"I think I can cut you some slack."

It wasn't often he didn't know what he wanted to do with a woman. In fact, this was a first. She was obviously unprepared. All she had was a flashlight. No water, no tent, no sleeping bag, no food that he could see.

Not that it was a problem, since he was prepared enough for the both of them. Plus, he'd be sticking to her like glue, and not because he'd been lusting after her for months, but because she was a statistic waiting to happen. "I have camping gear, if you want to share." Christ, listen to him. Such a sucker for melted-chocolate eyes.

"I'm fine."

Her mantra. And there was no doubt that she *was* extremely fine standing there, her long, lithe body throwing off attitude as she looked at him with that devastatingly powerful gaze, shadowed by things he didn't understand but wanted to. "Sleep near your fire," he advised, playing it her way. For now. "Keeps the coyotes back."

"Coyotes," she repeated faintly.

"And douse yourself in mosquito spray. It's getting to be that season. Keep your jean legs tucked into your boots when you lie down. You don't want any extra creepy crawlies getting up there."

She stared down at her skinny jeans, then at the boots that were most definitely *not* hiking sanctioned. "Creepy crawlies?"

"It's a little early for snakes, but you should keep a watch out for them, too," he said. "Just in case."

She nodded and took a long, uneasy look around them.

He had *no* idea what she thought she was doing, or why, but he wasn't *that* big an asshole to let her do it alone, no matter how brave she thought she was. "You know," he said quietly. "Sometimes, being alone isn't all it's cracked up to be."

She thought about that a moment. "You really have gear in your truck?"

"Standard operating procedure," he said, and it was true. But what wasn't SOP was to offer that gear to stranded hikers, no matter how sexy they were.

No fool, she slid him a long, steely-eyed look, and he did his best to look innocent.

"Listen," she finally said. "I might've given you the wrong impression when I... bumped into you with the bear thing."

"Bumped into me?" He couldn't help it, he laughed. "You tried to crawl up my body."

"Which is my point," she said stiffly. "My sleep-out adventure *isn't* going to include crawling up anyone's body."

"Will it include sleeping?"

She continued to study him, thinking so hard that he could smell something burning. He left her to it and turned to the surrounding woods, gathering dry kindling from the ground as the sky went from dusk to jet-black night in the blink of an eye. Moving to the center of the clearing, he quickly and efficiently built a fire, then grabbed the tent and sleeping bag. He raided his lockbox, pulling out—thank Christ—a can of Dr. Pepper, some beef jerky, a bag of marshmallows, and two bottles of water. "Honey, dinner's ready."

This earned him another long look across the fire.

"Tough crowd." Typical of mountain altitude, one moment it was a decent temperature, and the next, it was butt-ass cold. He moved closer to the fire, next to his camping partner, who was standing huddled-up as close as she could get without singeing her eyebrows. There was no moon yet, though a few stars began to glitter like diamonds in the huge, fathomless sky. Didn't get skies like this in Chicago, he thought, and took a moment to soak it in.

Amy was hands-out over the flames. He doubted her tank top was offering much, if any, protection against the evening breeze. This fact was confirmed by the way her nipples pressed against the thin knit material. Nice view. But he went back to his truck, grabbed his extra sweatshirt, and tossed it to her.

"What's this?"

"A way to get warm."

She stared down at it as if it were a spitting cobra.

"Works better if you put it on," he said.

"Wearing a guy's sweatshirt implies...*things*," she said.

"Yeah? What things?"

She didn't answer, and he dropped another log on the flames. By now she was visibly shivering. "It's just a sweatshirt, Amy, not a ring. It doesn't come with a commitment. Now my Dr. Pepper, *that* I'm not sharing."

She snorted and pulled on the sweatshirt without comment. It dropped past her hips to her thighs, swallowing her whole. She tugged the hood up over her hair, shading her face from him. "Thanks."

He should have just kept his mouth shut and let it go, but he couldn't. "Just out of morbid curiosity, what exactly did you think I'd expect in exchange?"

She slid him a long look that said it all, and once again he wondered what kind of assholes she'd come across in her life. "Come on," he said. "For a sweatshirt? I mean, *maybe*, if I'd given you the Dr. Pepper, that I could see. Or if I'd had to wrestle you from the bear..."

She actually smiled. It was a lovely smile that made her eyes shine, and he smiled back. "So who told you a guy gets sex for sharing his sweatshirt?" he asked.

"Guys only think about one thing."

He chewed on that for a few minutes, keeping his hands busy setting up the tent, tossing in his sleeping bag. "Sometimes we think about food, too," he finally said.

Amy laughed outright at this, and Matt felt like he'd won the lottery. He kicked a fallen log close to the fire and gestured for her to have a seat. When she did, he tossed her the beef jerky and marshmallows. "Dinner of champions. Which course do you want first?"

She eyed both, then opened the marshmallows. "Life's short," she said. "Dessert first."

"I like the way you think." He stoked the flames, then pushed aside the two burning logs to reveal the hot ashes—the sweet spot for roasting marshmallows. Moving to the edge of the clearing, he located two long sticks then handed one to Amy.

She in turn handed him a marshmallow for his stick. Look at them, all companionable and domestic. They roasted in silence for a few minutes, Amy staring speculatively into the fire. "Being out here makes me want to draw," she said quietly.

He looked at her. "Wait—Did you just offer a piece of personal information?"

She rolled her eyes. "I'm not a complete social moron. I can do the casual conversation thing."

"But your drawing isn't casual to you," he said.

She held his gaze. "No. It's not."

Forget her great laugh. *Now* he felt like he'd just won the lottery.

"Do you draw?" she asked him.

Was she looking for common ground? He'd like to give it to her, but this wasn't going to be it. "Stick figures," he said, blowing on his marshmallow before eating it. "I'm good at stick figures when I have to be for a report, but that's about it. Doesn't mean I can't get how inspiring it is out here though. What do you draw?"

"Landscapes, mostly." She glanced around at the dark night. "I'd love to do the trees silhouetted against the dark sky. Or the waterfalls that I saw on the way up here. I can still hear them."

"Yeah, there's more than sixty glaciers melting out here," he said. "Along with all the heavy rains we got this year. All that water's rushing 24-7 to the sea."

She handed him another marshmallow from the bag, and their fingers brushed. Her breath caught, and the sound went straight through him. She busied herself with her toasted marshmallow, popping it into her mouth, sucking some of it off her finger. He tried not to stare and thereby prove that she was right with *guys only think about one thing*, but Christ. She was *sucking* on her finger. A completely involuntary sound escaped him, and she stopped.

He met her gaze, and though he couldn't quite read her expression, she didn't look disgusted or pissed off. She nibbled on her lower lip for a beat, and suddenly it seemed like all the cool air got sucked out of the night, leaving only heat.

Lots of heat. But hell if he'd do one damn thing about it. Beautiful as she was sitting there by the fire's glow, he knew making a move on her would be fatal to any friendship they might have.

But she kept looking at him like she'd never really seen him before, and then suddenly they were a lot closer, their thighs touching. His hands itched to reach for her but he forced himself to stay perfectly still. Perfectly. Still. Which was how he knew that *she* leaned in first. Oh, yeah, but just as her mouth got to his, a coyote howled—a bone-chilling, hair-raising cry that was immediately answered by another, longer, louder howl that echoed off the mountain caverns.

Amy jerked, straightening up with a startled gasp.

"They're not as close as they sound," he said.

She nodded and leaned over to fiddle with her boot, using the ruse to scoot close again. He'd have teased her about it but he didn't want to scare her further off.

Another coyote howled, and then more joined in. Amy went rigid and set her hand on his thigh.

Matt silently willed the coyotes to come closer, but they didn't. Instead, when Amy realized where her hand was, she snatched it away. "Sorry."

"Don't be. You can hold on to me anytime." He threaded a row of marshmallows onto her stick for her, and then did the same for himself, watching Amy keep an eye on the shadows of the woods around them as though maybe, if only she concentrated hard enough, she'd be able to see through the dark.

"Not a big camper, huh?" he asked sympathetically.

"I'm more of a city girl."

"Which city?"

"New York. Miami. Dallas..."

"All of them?"

"Chicago, too," she said. "I moved around a lot."

He pulled his stick from the fire and wished he had chocolate and graham crackers to go with the perfectly toasted marshmallows. "I'm from Chicago," he said. "Born and bred in the rat race." Which he didn't miss. Not the weather, not the job, not the ex…Although he did miss his family. "When were you there?"

"Ten years ago." She shrugged. "Just for a little while."

He knew she was twenty-eight, so that meant she'd been eighteen when she'd been there. "You went to high school in Chicago?"

"No. I took the GED and got out early. Before Chicago."

"Ten years ago, I was just out of the Navy," he said. "Working as a cop. Maybe our paths crossed when you were in town."

"Yeah, not likely," she told him. "You were SWAT, not a beat cop running homeless teens off the corners."

He wasn't surprised that she knew he'd been SWAT. Everyone in Lucky Harbor knew everyone's business. He just wished he knew hers, but she'd been good at keeping a low profile. "You were a homeless teen?"

She let out a single syllable hum that could have been agreement or just a vague "don't want to talk about it."

Too bad that he did want to talk about it. "What happened to your parents?"

"I'm the product of what happens when teenagers don't listen in sex ed class. Nothing you haven't seen before on *16 and Pregnant*."

"That bad huh?"

She shrugged and stuffed the marshmallow into her mouth.

Conversation over, apparently. Which was okay. He'd get another chance. He enjoyed watching her savor each marshmallow like it was a special prize. He especially enjoyed how she licked the remnants off her fingers with a suction sound…

"You give good marshmallow," she said.

He gave good other things, too, but he kept that to himself.

When they were high on sugar, they balanced it out with the beef jerky. Amy unzipped her backpack, and he unabashedly peered inside, catching her drawing pad, colored pencils, a hiking guide, lip gloss, and a pocketknife before she pulled out an apple and zipped the pack closed.

She was a puzzle, he thought. All tough girl on the outside, girlie-girl on the inside, and a whole bunch of other things he couldn't quite put a finger on yet.

She handed him the apple. He took a bite, then handed it back. They shared it down to the core, drank their waters, and then Amy yawned wide.

"I'm sorry," she said, and yawned again. "I had the morning shift at the diner. I'm exhausted."

"Bedtime then." He stoked the fire, then rose and pulled her up as well, turning her toward the tent.

She stared inside at the still rolled-up sleeping bag. "This is yours. I can sleep in your truck."

"The bucket seats suck, and the truck bed's ridged and cold as hell. You've had a long day and need some sleep. Take the tent."

She bit her lower lip, her eyes suspicious again. "And you?"

"I'll be by the fire. I have an emergency blanket, I'll be fine."

"No," she said, shaking her head. "I can't let you do that. You'll get cold."

"Are you offering to share the tent?"

Her gaze dropped down to his chest, and she chewed on her lower lip again—which was driving him insane. *He* wanted to chew on that lower lip and then soothe the ache with his tongue.

"Sharing is a bad idea," she finally said. "A really, *really* bad idea." But she gave him another slow sweep. His chest, his abs, lower…Her pupils dilated, giving her away.

Either she had a head injury he didn't know about or looking him over had aroused her. "Sometimes," he said, "bad ideas become good ideas."

"No, they don't."

He didn't like to disagree with a woman, especially a pretty, sexy woman whom he'd been dreaming about getting naked and licking every inch of her body. But he absolutely disagreed on this.

Vehemently.

Instead of voicing that, he gave her a nudge into the tent. "Zip up behind you."

When she did, he let out a long breath and stood there in the dark between the fire and the tent for a long beat. *You're an idiot*, he told himself, and shaking his head, he moved closer to the flames. Leaning back, getting comfortable, or as comfortable as he could without a sweatshirt or his sleeping bag, he stared at the sky. Normally, this never failed to relax him, but tonight it took a long time.

A very long time.

It was his body's fault, he decided. He definitely had a few parts at odds with each other, but in the end, it was his brain that reminded him of the bottom line. He'd come here to Lucky Harbor for some peace and quiet, to be alone.

To forget the hell his life in Chicago had turned into.

And it *had* been complete hell, having to turn in his own partner for being on the take, then facing the censure of his fellow cops.

And then there'd been his marriage.

Shelly had never liked his hours or the danger he'd faced every day. In return, he'd never liked that she hadn't taken her own safety seriously enough. And when it had all gone bad and she'd gotten hurt…well, that had been another sort of hell entirely.

And his fault. He 100 percent blamed himself.

That had made two of them. Shelly had told him in her parting shot that he was better off alone, and he honestly believed that to be true. All this time he'd thought it…

At some point during this annoying inner reflection, he must have finally fallen asleep because he woke up instantly at the sound of Amy's scream.

Chapter 4

A day without chocolate is like a day without sunshine.

Breathless, heart pounding, Amy lay flat on her back in the pitch dark. *Shit.* Okay, so that was the *last* time she ever tiptoed into the woods by herself to find a nice, big tree to pee behind. Her downfall had been the walk back to camp. It'd been so dark, and her flashlight had given enough light for exactly nothing.

And she'd slipped on something and slid.

Down.

And down.

She'd lost her flashlight on the descent, and now she couldn't see much except the vague black outline of the canopy of trees far above her. Or at least she hoped those were trees. Claustrophobic from the all-encompassing blackness, and more than a little worried about creepy crawlies, she sat up and winced. Her left wrist was on fire. So was her butt. Great, she'd broken her butt. She could see the headline on Facebook now—*Amy Michaels cracks her crack during a potty break on the mountain.*

The worst part was that this was all her own fault. She was street smart and had been cocky enough to believe she could handle herself. Her mistake, because she should have known better—bad things could happen anywhere. They'd always happened to her, from back as far as when her grandma had died. Back then, a twelve-year-old Amy had gone to live with her mother for the first time, and oh how she'd hated that. Her mother had hated it, too, and Amy had grossly misbehaved, acting out in grief and teenage hatred. She'd sought attention, bad attention, in the form of inappropriate sex, using it as a way to manipulate boys. Then the game had been turned on her, and she hadn't liked it much. It'd taken her far too long to realize she was destroying herself, but eventually she'd given up dangerous sex. Hell, she'd pretty much given up men, no matter how gorgeous and sexy they were.

It'd been so long she felt like a virgin. At least an emotional virgin.

And now she was going to die as one.

A beam of light shined down on her from above. Not God. Not a fairy godmother. Just Matt, calling her name, concern clear in his voice.

"Down here," she said. *Where all the stupid girls end up on their broken butts.* "I'm coming."

"Don't move."

"But—"

"I mean it, Amy. Not a muscle."

"Well jeez, if you mean it…"

No response to that. Seemed the laid-back forest ranger wasn't feeling so laid-back right now.

He got to her quickly and without falling, she noted with more than a little bitterness. And unlike her, he could apparently see in the dark. Crouched before her, he was nothing but a big, built shadow holding her down when she'd have gotten to her feet. "Stay," he said, voice firm.

"Stay?" she repeated with a disbelieving laugh. "What am I, a dog?"

"Where are you hurt?"

"Nowhere."

He flicked the light over her, eyes narrowing in on the wrist she was hugging to herself. "Hold this," he said, and put the light in her good hand so he could probe at her other wrist.

She hissed in a breath, and he slid his gaze to hers. "Can you move your fingers?"

She showed him just how much her middle finger could move.

"Nice," he said. "So nature call, huh?"

She didn't answer, distracting herself by shining the light around them to make sure they weren't being circled by bears or mountain lions. What she *did* see stole her breath more than Matt's gentle maneuvering of her wrist.

They were at the base of a meadow. "Sierra Meadows?"

"Yeah, although this is the back way in." Matt glanced up at her face. "Why?"

"No reason."

"Why do you try to bullshit a bullshitter? You were looking for Sierra Meadows?"

"Yeah."

"It's not a very well-known place," Matt said. "Hard to get to—well, unless you fall into it."

"Ha ha." She wondered how hard it'd be to find this place again on her own.

"So why Sierra Meadows?"

"I read about the wall of diamond rocks. I wanted to see them."

"They're a couple of hundred yards across a very soggy meadow from here. But worth seeing—in the light of day." He took the flashlight back. "I don't think your wrist is broken but you've got a good sprain going. What else hurts?"

"Nothing."

He obviously didn't buy this since he gave her a rather impressive eye roll and began running a hand down her limbs with quick, impassive efficiency.

"Hey!" She pushed his hand away. "I already had my annual."

Finished with her arms, legs, and ribs, he merely tilted her head back and looked into her eyes. "How many fingers am I holding up?"

"One," she said. "But as I already showed you, it's much more effective when it's the middle finger."

He smiled. "You're fine."

"I keep telling you that."

"Come on." Rising to his feet, he pulled her to hers.

At the movement, pain shot up her tailbone, but she controlled her wince and let him help her back up the hill.

"I've seen just about everything there is to see out here," he said at the top. "But I've never seen anyone fall down that ravine before."

"So glad to give you a first."

"You should have woken me up."

For a pee escort? Hell no. They were at their campsite now, and he gave her a little nudge toward the tent. She crawled inside and back into the sleeping bag, pulling it over her head, hoping to pretend that she was at home, in a warm bed. But at home, she never had worries about bears and mountain lions, and for all she knew also the big bad wolf. She certainly never shivered like this at home either.

When had it gotten so cold?

Her butt suddenly vibrated, scaring her for a second until she realized it was the cell phone in her back pocket. With some maneuvering, she pulled it out and read the text from Mallory.

> *Good girl lesson #2: When your BFF sends you a gorgeous guy, you call her and thank her. That's good manners. Good girl lesson #3: Stop scowling. You'll scare away the aforementioned gorgeous guy.*

Amy was definitely scowling and didn't plan to stop anytime soon. She considered hitting reply and telling Mallory exactly what she thought of the good girl lessons so far, but just then the sleeping bag was yanked off her head, and it wasn't the big, bad wolf. Actually, if she squinted, there *were* some similarities.

"Your arm," Matt said, on his knees, head ducked low to accommodate the tent ceiling. He had a first-aid kit and had pulled out an ACE bandage, which he used to wrap her wrist. Then he slapped an ice pack against his thigh to activate it and set her wrapped wrist on it. He pulled out a second ice pack and eyed her.

She narrowed her eyes. "What?"

"You going to let me look at it?" he asked.

Her free hand slid to her own behind. "How did you know?"

"Wild guess," he said dryly. "Let me see it."

"Over my dead body."

He let out a breath and dropped his chin to his chest for a moment. Either he was praying for patience or trying not to laugh. When he had himself together, he moved with his usual calm efficiency and unzipped her sleeping bag, yanking it from her before she could so much as squeak.

Which she did.

He ignored that and held her down effortlessly with one hand on her waist and one on her thigh. "Be still," he said.

Be still? Was he kidding? "Listen, I'm going to *be still* with my foot up your ass—"

"You're bleeding."

"What?" She immediately stopped struggling and tried to see what he was seeing. "I am not. Where?"

"Your leg."

He was right, there was blood coming through her jeans on her thigh. She stared at it a little woozily. She hated blood, especially her own. "Um..."

Matt was rifling through the first aid kit again. "Lose your pants. We need to clean that up."

Well if that didn't make her un-woozy right-quick. She laughed at him, making him lift his gaze from the box. "Oh, hell, no," she said.

The only light in the tent came from his flashlight, so she couldn't see his exact expression, but she had no trouble sensing his surprise. Probably when he said "lose your pants" to women they generally tore themselves out of their clothes, in a hurry to get naked for him. "Over my dead body."

She sensed more than saw his smile. "I administer a lot of basic first aid," he said in that calm, reasonable tone that made her want to do something to rile him up.

Too bad she'd given up riling men a good long time ago. "Just give me a Band-Aid."

"We need to clean the cut." His voice was all reasonable friendliness, but laced with unmistakable steel. Authority. And yet...and this made no sense...it was also somehow the sexiest voice she'd ever heard. She didn't often let herself get curious about the people in her life, but this time she couldn't seem to help herself. "After all you've done," she said, "How the hell did you end up out here in the boonies saving the stupid chick?"

He laughed softly, the sound warming her a little bit. "Always did love the outdoors," he said. "I was twelve when I first spent a night outside."

"You ran away when you were twelve?"

"No." He slid her a look that said he found it interesting that her mind had taken her there. Interesting, and disturbing. "My older brother took me camping," he said. "He warned me not to go anywhere without him, not even to take a leak." He laughed a little at the memory. "I thought, well fuck that."

The smile in his voice was contagious, and she felt herself relax a little. "What happened?" she asked.

"Woke up in the middle of the night and had to take a leak. I was way too cool to need an escort..." He paused meaningfully, and she grimaced.

"Yeah, yeah."

"So I stumbled out of the tent and went looking for a tree. Walked straight into a wall of bushes and got all cut up. Nearly wet myself before I got free." He laughed again and shook his head. "My brother reamed me a new one when I got back. Man, he was pissed off that I was hurt. I told him to chill, that everything was fine. And the next morning, everything was still fine. But by that afternoon, I had a hundred-and-three temperature. My mom stripped me down to put me in a cool bath and found a nasty gash on my arm that had gotten infected."

His voice was magic, Amy thought, listening to him in the dark. Low and a little gruff. Listening to him was like listening to a really great book on tape. No regrets about his past, and then there was his obvious affection for both his brother and his mom...both things she had no experience with.

"I also had poison oak," he said. "*Everywhere.*"

She gasped. "Oh, God." Gentle interlude over, she sat up so fast she bashed her head on his chin. "Do you think I have—"

"No." He pressed her back down, rubbing his chin with his spare hand. "But you do have a cut that could get infected if we don't clean it out."

"By morning?"

"By midnight."

She stared up at him, looking for a single sign that he was being a perv about this. Because if he was, then he was also a dead perv. But there kneeling at her side, he looked at her evenly, steady as a rock.

This was also totally out of her realm of experience, a guy wanting in her pants for non-sexual reasons.

Maybe the scratch was already infected, and she'd lost her mind.

This was the only explanation she could accept for the teeny tiny smidgeon of disappointment. In which case, dropping trou was the least of her problems. So she blew out a sigh and unzipped her jeans. For a moment she panicked, unable to remember which underwear she'd put on that morning. She didn't know whether she hoped for laundry day granny panties, or something sexy. Laundry day granny panties...No, wait. Something sexy. *No!* Good Lord, she was losing it.

Shimmying the skinny jeans down to her knees wasn't easy or attractive, and Amy was also incredibly aware of Matt's big, solid presence at her side. And yep, he was right—there was a big gash on her thigh, curving around to the back. It was burning now, but she hardly noticed over the relief to find that she wasn't wearing granny panties. She was in the thin baby-blue, cheeky-cut panties that she'd gotten in a sale pack of three. Which is where the bad news came in, because they were a lot like wearing nothing. Worse, they said "booty-licious" across the butt, but luckily he couldn't see that.

There was a beat of complete silence.

And then another.

And then yet another.

Finally, she looked up. Matt was still as stone, his hands on his own thighs, eyes dilated nearly black.

"Matt?"

"Yeah?"

"You okay?"

"Working on it." His voice sounded unusually tight.

"I thought you said you did this a lot."

"Yeah. I do. But apparently not with anyone I'm wildly attracted to."

This caused certain reactions in her body that were best not experienced in mixed company. "It's just panties," she finally whispered.

"And they're really great panties," Matt agreed. "But it's not the panties, Amy. It's you."

She wasn't sure what to say to that, or even how to feel. She should feel weird; she knew this. Instead she felt...

Attractive. Sexy.

It'd been so long since she'd thought of herself in this way that it took her by surprise. So did the yearning running through her.

They were silent for another long minute. Then she heard Matt blow out a very long breath. In the next beat, he was cleaning her wound with a clean pad and antiseptic, which hurt like hell. She distracted herself by watching his long and callused fingers work on her. They felt decadent on her skin, like a long-denied treat. And it *was* long denied, being touched, being cared for.

Too long.

"Turn over," Matt said.

She hesitated, everything in her balking at his quiet command—just as at the same time, she was completely turned on by it.

"Amy."

She turned over. There was another long beat of silence as Matt took in the rear view, and she risked a glance over her shoulder. His face was more angles than curves, his silky hair brushing the collar of his shirt. He was so broad in the shoulders he blocked out any light the moon might have given them. This left only the meager glow from the flashlight, but she wasn't afraid of the dark.

Or him.

She was safe with him. She knew that. But at the same time, she was about as unsafe as she could get.

She knew that, too.

By the time he finished bandaging her up and she pulled her pants back up, they were both breathing a little unsteadily. He handed her the ice pack for her tailbone. She put it in place, and there was a long silence.

"You're still shivering," he said, and lay down beside her. "Come here, Tough Girl." He pulled her in close. The sleeping bag, still unzipped, was between them. He didn't try to get into it with her, simply wrapped her up in his warm arms and held her until she stopped shivering.

"Better?" he whispered against her hair.

He was rock solid against her, the muscles in his arms banded tight. Yeah, she was better. "Much, thank you."

He started to pull away but she slid her arms out of the sleeping bag and around his neck, pressing her face into his throat. It was a move that startled them both. It was also a really dumb thing to do. Normally she had so much more sense than this, but he was turning her on with every little thing he did. She didn't understand it but she understood this—holding on to him had nothing to do with being cold.

"Amy." He stroked a hand down her back. "You're safe, you know that, right?"

Safe from bears and coyotes and creepy crawlies, maybe. But she wasn't safe. Not from the yearning flowing through her and not from feeling things she didn't want to feel. Feeling things like this left her open to being hurt. "We're not the only ones out here," she said. "Right before you found me on the trail, someone was in the bushes, watching me. I saw just a face."

"There are a few people out here on this mountain tonight," he said, and rubbed his jaw to hers.

"But that's not what I meant."

"I know."

Again he stroked a hand down her back. "When I first took this job, it'd been a while since I'd gone camping. And then as it turned out, on my first night out here, I was stalked."

She tipped her head back and tried to see his face. "By…?"

"Every horror flick I'd ever seen."

She found herself smiling. "Was the big, bad forest ranger scared?"

"I started a fire," he said instead of answering, and the typical guy avoidance of admitting fear made her smile in the dark. "But even after I had a roaring fire, I still felt watched."

"What did you do?"

His hand was still gliding up and down her back, absently soothing, not-so-absently arousing her further. "I got up and searched the perimeter," he said. "Often. I finally fell asleep holding my gun, and at first light was startled awake by a curious teenage bear."

"Oh my God," she said on a horrified laugh. "What happened?"

Amusement came into his voice. "I shot the shit out of a tree and scared the hell out of us both. I fell backward off the log I'd fallen asleep on, and the bear did the same. Then we both scrambled to our feet, and he went running off to his mama. If my mama had been anywhere within two thousand miles, I'd have gone running off to her just the same as the bear."

She burst out laughing.

"What," he said, smiling at her, "you don't think I have a mama?"

"I think you wouldn't go running off to *anyone* if you were scared. You'd stand firm and fight."

He shrugged. "I've had my moments."

"So your mom…?"

"Lives in Chicago with my dad, tending to the three grandkids my brother's given them. We talk every week, and they ask me when I'm going to give them a few as well."

"When are you?"

He shook his head. "Not anytime soon."

"Why?" she asked, fascinated in a way she couldn't explain even to herself. "Kids not for you?"

He shrugged. "My ex seemed to think I don't do love, at least not the kind of love a family requires. Said I wasn't good with people."

"You were married?" She was surprised, though she shouldn't have been. Matthew Bowers was a catch.

"For about twenty minutes," he said. "Just after I got out of the military."

"When you were a cop," she said.

"Yeah."

"Is that why she thought you weren't family material?" she asked. "Because of your job?"

"Partly. And partly because I failed her. But mostly because she was pissed off at me."

Amy wanted to ask how he'd failed, but that felt too intimate, especially given that she was lying in his arms with his ice pack on her ass. But his ex's words didn't make sense. He wasn't the sort of guy to fail a stranger, much less someone he cared about. What he'd done for her today proved that. His job might have brought him here to check on her, but it hadn't been his job or responsibility to stay the night with her and keep her safe.

And yet he'd stuck.

She'd had people in her life who *had* been responsible for her and hadn't stuck. "Matt?"

His wordless response vibrated through his chest to hers, and he turned his head so that his face was in her hair, inhaling as he rubbed her back.

"I think you're pretty good with people," she said softly.

She could feel him smile against her. "Thanks," he murmured. "Now tell me about you."

"Nothing as interesting as you."

"Try me," he said.

That was the *last* thing she intended to do. "Well, I don't have an ex-husband..."

"How about a mom? Dad? Siblings?"

"A mom. We're not close." An understatement, of course. Her mom had gotten pregnant as a teen and hadn't been mom material.

"I was raised by my grandma, but she's gone now. She died when I was twelve."

"Any other family?"

No one she wanted to talk about. "No."

He tightened his arms around her, a small, protective, even slightly possessive gesture. It should have made her claustrophobic.

It didn't.

They fell quiet after that, and Amy wouldn't have imagined it possible since she was snuggled up against a very solid, very sexy man, but she actually fell asleep.

She woke up what must have been hours later, as dawn crept in, poking at the backs of her eyelids. For a moment, she stayed utterly still, struck by several things. One, she was no longer cold. In fact, she was quite warm, and the reason for that was because she'd wrapped herself like a pretzel around her heat source.

Matt.

She cracked open an eye and found him watching her from his own heavy-lidded gaze. He was looking pretty amused at the both of them. "Hey," he said, and to go along with that bedroom gaze he also had a raspy early morning voice. Both were extremely distracting. He wasn't looking like a forest ranger right now. He was looking sleepy, rumpled, and sexy as hell.

"Are you taking this anywhere?" he asked.

Not exactly a morning person, it took her brain a moment to process what he meant. And then she realized that by "this," he was referring to the fact that her hand had drifted disturbingly low on his abs. If she moved her fingers even a fraction of an inch south… "Sorry!" Face hot, she pulled back and closed her eyes. "This is all Mallory's fault."

"Actually," he said, looking down at his obvious erection. "It's not."

"No, I mean—" She broke off at his low, teasing laugh and felt her face flame again. "She sent you out here because she thinks something's going on with us."

"*Is* there something going on with us?"

She didn't want to touch that with a ten-foot pole. Or an eight-inch one. "It has nothing to do with us. It's payback for how I set her up with Ty at the auction a few weeks back."

"What if it's not?"

She met his warm gaze. "Not what?"

"Payback," he said.

Their legs were entwined. At some point in the night, the sleeping bag had fallen away so that there was no barrier between them. He was warm and hard.

Everywhere.

She felt herself soften as the heat of arousal built within her. Worse, her fingers itched with the need to touch him.

"Amy." Matt's voice was pure sin, not a warning so much as a statement, and her hands reacted without permission, migrating to his chest.

"Mm," rumbled from his chest as he slid a hand into her hair, tilting her head up to his. He searched her gaze. "You're all the way awake, right?"

"Yeah. Why?"

"Just making sure," he said, then rolled her beneath him.

Chapter 5

Other things are just food. But chocolate is chocolate.

Matt had given distance his best shot but it hadn't worked out. As he pressed Amy into the sleeping bag, her teeth bit into that plump curve of her lower lip again. Her breathing went erratic, and her pulse raced at the base of her throat. Her gaze darkened with the same thing turning him inside out.

She wanted him.

That was only fair since he'd wanted her for months. Ever since he'd first caught sight of her in the diner working her ass off, the tough, wounded, beautiful woman with the heartbreaking smile that didn't quite meet her amazing eyes.

At the moment, she looked softer than usual. Her long, side-swept bangs were sticking up a little in one spot, falling across her forehead in another. Her mascara had smudged. She'd been driving him bat-shit crazy all night, her and those mile-long legs, which were tangled up in his. He'd always been a confirmed ass man, but Amy seemed to be expanding his horizons.

She was still wearing his sweatshirt and now it smelled like her. He wanted to shove it up to her chin and nuzzle every inch of her.

And then kiss. And lick…All the erotic possibilities played in his mind, and he lowered his head until his mouth was only a breath from hers, giving her a moment to think about what was going to happen between them.

She stared up at him, her fingers in his hair. “Yes,” she breathed, barely audible.

He kissed her then, and the soft, little sound that escaped her went straight through him like fire. Her hands tightened on him as if to hold him to her. Not that he was going anywhere. Hell, no. For months, he’d wondered how she’d taste, if the reality would be as good as the dreams. They were.

She tasted like heaven.

This was made all the sweeter by having her amazing body shrink-wrapped up against his, a situation that was blowing brain cells left and right. Hoping he had enough to spare, he deepened the kiss, opening his mouth wider on hers.

She made the sound again, a small murmur deep in her throat that held as much surprise as arousal. He could feel her heart pounding. No, wait, that was his, because for the first time in all these months, she’d let him in. Not only had she let him in but she’d melted against him, completely surrendering, pressing her warm body to his. Sliding her fingers in his hair, she murmured his name against his mouth, squirming closer, then closer still.

And just like that, he was in deep, deeper than he’d been in some time. Warning bells clanged in his brain, but anticipation and erotic thrill overrode them. Slanting his mouth more fully over hers, he took everything she gave, wanting more still. So goddamn much more. He wanted all of her, panting his name, naked and writhing beneath him. Reaching for the hem of the sweatshirt, he went still when from outside the tent, he heard something—pine needles crunching. Someone was out there, walking around, and he lifted his head.

"What?" Amy whispered, hands still in his hair, her mouth wet from his. "A bear?"

He shook his head. Whatever was out there, it was definitely of the human variety. "Wait here." Rising off her in one fluid move, he adjusted himself as he left, not particularly wanting to meet an intruder with a boner in his pants the size of…well, the tent he'd just vacated.

The morning was so foggy he couldn't see much more than a few feet in front of himself but he carefully searched the clearing.

Empty of any mysterious intruders.

But someone had been here, he could see the footsteps in the morning dew. He checked out his truck, but everything seemed the same, with the exception of the flashlight he'd left on his rear fender. That was gone.

"Find anything?"

Matt turned to Amy. She stood with her back to the tent, a Swiss Army Knife in hand, ready for action. Her hair was wild, her wrist bandaged, her stance making it clear that she was ready to rumble. She was still in his sweatshirt, and he'd never seen anything so sexy. Probably she could wear a potato sack and he'd think she looked sexy. Probably he needed to also get a grip. "Nice job on the waiting thing," he said.

"I don't do the waiting thing."

Right. She could take care of herself. Message received loud and clear—except that it was his nature to do the taking care of, though really he should be over that by now. It'd been that exact characteristic that so completely detonated his life back in Chicago.

Which is why he was here. He needed to remember that. He was here for the quiet mountain life. It suited him. He liked being on his own, liked it a lot, and didn't plan to change that status anytime soon.

And yet here he was, wanting Amy. Unable to stop himself, he lifted a hand, cupping her face, running the pad of his thumb along her lower lip. She might look damn tough and on top of her world, but she sure was soft to the touch.

And he wanted to eat her up for breakfast. It'd be off the charts, he had no doubt.

But she took a step back. Okay, he'd expected that. Hell, he'd expected that last night, and he moved to his truck, grabbing his last Dr. Pepper—grateful their thief hadn't stolen that, too. He cracked it open and offered it to Amy first.

She went brows up. "Dr. Pepper for breakfast?"

"Breakfast of champions."

She took a sip, then studied him, looking amused. "What are you going to do if I drink it all?"

"Cry."

She laughed and lightened the tension considerably. Then he fell a little bit in love when she handed him back the rest of the soda.

"Not exactly what I'd have chosen for breakfast," she said.

Yeah. Him either.

They left shortly after that. Amy had to get to work, and she knew that Matt did, too. He would have taken her to the diamond rocks first but it was too foggy.

Plus then there was the real reason she'd passed on his offer. She wanted to be alone when she went and searched for her grandparents' initials.

And her hope…

An hour later, Matt had dropped her at her car, and she'd driven home. She took the longest shower known to man, not getting out until she ran out of hot water. When she'd dried off, she swiped the mist from the mirror and stared at herself. "You *kissed* him?"

Her reflection nodded, you 'ho.

Amy had no idea what she'd been thinking at all. Actually, she *hadn't* been thinking, that was the problem. She'd been *feeling*. Far too much.

At least there'd been no witnesses, she told herself. Well, except for their mysterious guest. With Amy's luck, that mysterious guest had been Lucille, and Amy and Matt would end up on Facebook as engaged, or something equally horrifying. Wouldn't that just make Mallory happy.

But would it make you happy?

The errant thought appalled her. She didn't need a man complicating her life, and she didn't need one to be happy either. Her life was complicated enough, thank you very much. She was very busy following her grandma's footsteps to find...well, she wasn't sure exactly, but hopefully she'd find herself.

Except, said a small voice, *if you really were interested in finding yourself, you'd have let Matt take you to the rocks.*

And really, what was she so afraid of? That she'd get to the end of Rose's journey and Amy's life would still be...meaningless? Because she didn't need a journey to feel that way. Her *life* made her feel that way, and had since her grandma had died.

Amy hadn't handled that scene too well. She was the first to admit it. By that time, her mom had pulled herself out of the gutter and had snagged a really great guy, the measurement of "great" being the size of his bank account, of course. Coming from the wrong side of the tracks to the only side that mattered, Amy had become the poster child for Poor Little Rich Girl, bumping up against a society she'd never been a part of and couldn't possibly understand. She'd chafed at the rules and had behaved textbook predictably, acting out with all sorts of mayhem. And she'd been good at it.

Until the day she'd run into real trouble. Bad trouble. Holy-shit trouble, and for once, it hadn't been her own doing. No, that honor had gone to her stepfather, who'd decided she needed to give him a little of what she was so freely giving to the boys her own age.

But he'd been no boy.

Amy had always been able to intimidate anyone who'd invaded

her space without permission, but not him. Scared for the first time in her life, she'd tried to get help. But no one had believed her.

She'd been on her own.

She'd been on her own ever since, and it'd worked out just fine for her. She didn't need anyone.

But once in a while, like now, she felt a little flicker of need. Just to be held. Touched.

Wanted.

Matt had amplified those feelings, in a big way. And if they hadn't been interrupted this morning, she'd have acted on them. She had no idea where that would have left them.

Well satisfied, no doubt, as Matt had a magic mouth and magic hands. Her reflection sighed in remembered pleasure. She wanted more. That wasn't a surprise. What *was* a surprise was how badly she also wanted to run her hands over Matt's tough, sexy body. She'd felt him vibrating with that same need, every single muscle, and he had a lot of delicious muscles.

Mutual pleasure. They needed it. She wasn't looking for more, and after what he'd told her about his ex and how he didn't do love, neither was he.

Could it be that simple? *No.* Nothing was ever that simple. Which meant she needed to steer clear of one sexy Matthew Bowers. Very clear.

Matt wasn't much for cooking. He could do it—his mom had made sure of it—he just preferred not to. But there were limited dining options in Lucky Harbor: the Love Shack, the only bar and grill in town, or Eat Me, the diner. The Love Shack had great beer on tap.

Eat Me had Amy.

The day after their overnight adventure, following a long ten hours on the job, Matt entered the diner. He sat at a booth, and Amy brought him a soda. He could have kissed her for that alone. She was wearing a black tee with a silver zipper running amuck in a zigzag between her breasts, the kind that could open from the top or the bottom. Her jeans were low riding and faded, with a hole on one thigh, the denim there held together by a few threads across her taut skin. She was wearing the Ace bandage on her wrist. "The usual?" she asked. "Burger, fries?"

"Yeah. How are the injuries?"

"Fine. The thigh's a little sore but my wrist's a lot better."

"And the other injury?"

She raised a brow. "You are *not* asking me about my ass."

He smiled.

"You aren't smiling at the thought of my ass either," she said.

"Not funny yet?"

She just looked at him.

"Okay," he said, letting a smile break loose. "Not funny yet."

Lucille walked by the booth and stopped, touching Amy's wrist. "What happened, honey?"

"I fell hiking. It's nothing." Amy slid a long look at Matt, daring him to say a word.

Matt wasn't a complete idiot. He wanted this woman, naked. So he held his silence.

Lucille hitched a thumb at him. "You fell in Ranger Hot Buns's forest?"

This had Amy flashing a rare *real* smile. "What did you just call him?"

"Ranger Hot Buns," Lucille said. "Are you telling me you haven't seen the side poll on Facebook to rank the town's current hotties?"

Christ. Matt slouched down into his seat.

"It's doubled our traffic," Lucille said. "Matt's out in front of Dr. Josh Scott, but just by a nose. You need to come by and vote."

"I'll do that." Amy's tone said that she'd be voting for Josh.

Lucille walked away, and Amy slid him a speculative look. "I'll go put in your order. Ranger *Hot Buns*."

He snagged her by her good wrist before she walked away. At the contact, he felt a current of electricity go straight through him.

She looked down at his hand on her. Apparently he wasn't the only one experiencing the shock of connection between them. She tugged free, stepping back, looking a little off her axis.

He knew the feeling. Their chemistry was off the charts.

She turned and disappeared into the kitchen. He wasn't all that surprised when a few minutes later it was Jan, Eat Me's owner, who served him his food. Jan was fifty-ish, with a perpetual frown on her face and a black cap of hair that made her resemble Lucy from the Peanuts comic strip. "Where did Amy go?" he asked.

"Break," she said in her been-smoking-three-decades voice. "She took her break."

That night, Amy was trying to lose herself in a *Friends* marathon on TV, complete with a huge bowl of popcorn and two Snickers bars, when her phone rang.

"Chocoholics meeting tomorrow night," Grace said when Amy answered. "Mallory wanted me to call you and let you know. She'd have called herself but she was about to go jump Ty's bones."

Yeah, or she was avoiding Amy after the whole sending-Matt-to-the-woods stunt… "I don't know," Amy said. "Jan says we can't meet at the diner over chocolate cake anymore." A couple weeks back, the Chocoholics had accidentally destroyed the interior of Eat Me when their chocolate cake had gone up in flames thanks to some trick candles.

"Brownies," Grace said without pause. "We'll meet over brownies."

Brownies worked.

"Mallory says to prepare yourself," Grace warned her. "Apparently now that her life is in order, we're moving on to yours. She says we're going to be giving you good girl lessons." She laughed. "I'm sorry."

"And this is funny why?"

"Well not funny *exactly*," Grace said, still sounding amused. "A challenge, maybe."

"Hey, I would make a good good girl." *If she wanted…*

Grace snorted. "Okay. See you tomorrow night, good girl."

"Maybe I'm busy."

"Are you?"

Amy hesitated. She wanted to be busy getting back up the mountain to Sierra Meadows, but she wasn't crazy enough to do it at night. She'd wait for her next day off.

"Amy?"

"I'm free. I just really think our time would be better spent fixing *your* life first. I can totally wait."

Grace had worked as a financial wizard back East until several months ago. Looking for some happiness, she'd stuck around town, but the employment opportunities here were pretty limited. "Nice try but you're up," Grace said. "Oh, and bee-tee-dub, Facebook says you were getting cozy on the mountain with Ranger Hot Buns."

"Bee-tee-*what*?"

"*B T W. By the way.* Jeez, don't you ever surf the 'net?"

Amy sighed. "Brownies. Tomorrow night."

"We'll expect the Ranger Hot Buns story."

Amy hung up and then got a text from Mallory: *Good girl lesson #4: Omitting juicy details to your BFFs is a sin. You slept with him????????*

Amy rolled her eyes and typed a response: *Haven't you heard—good girls don't tell all. Especially to nosy friends who sneakily set their supposed BFFs up when they don't want to be set up.* Amy sent the text off, knowing Mallory would stew over that all night. It was a small consolation, because half an hour later, there came a knock at her door. Amy's entire body went on high alert, especially her nipples, so she knew exactly who it was.

Matt Bowers.

Aka Ranger Hot Buns.

She'd known he'd show up sooner than later. The question was, did she want him to?

He knocked again, a sturdy, confident sort of knock. She looked through the peephole. Yep, one sexy-as-hell, uniformed forest ranger stood at her door, armed, locked, and loaded.

And hot.

Looking her right in the eye, he raised a brow.

Still silent, she bit her lip in rare indecision. Obey the hormones? Or ignore the need humming through her…

"All night," Matt said. "I can do this all night."

Blowing out a breath, she opened the door.

He rocked back on his heels, hands in his pockets, perfectly at ease as he took in her appearance. "Pretty," he said.

She was in her oldest T-shirt and a pair of cutoffs. She looked like a garage sale special, and the worst part was…he most definitely did not. He was looking waaaaay too good. "I'm a mess."

"Maybe. But you're a pretty one."

She narrowed her eyes, and he laughed. "You know, most women like it when a man calls them pretty."

"I'm not most women."

"Yeah, I'm getting that."

"Why are you here, Matt?"

"Get to it?" he asked. "Is that what you're saying?"

"Yes. Get to it."

"All right. Direct. I like that. But you might not. It's about the kiss."

Her stomach suddenly had butterflies. "What about it?"

"You've been acting weird ever since."

"No, I haven't."

"Liar." He leaned against the doorjamb, settling in, making himself comfortable. "So it's been making me wonder. "Did I have bad breath?"

Was he kidding? He'd tasted like heaven. "No."

"Did I kiss like a jackass? A Saint Bernard?"

She actually felt a smile threaten. How did he always do that, make her want to smile? Make her... *want* him, desperately. It was a conundrum, a big one. She really hadn't had a single intention of getting tangled up in a man, but this man had come from nowhere and blindsided her, and now she could think of little else. "No," she said. "You didn't kiss like a jackass or a Saint Bernard."

"Hmm." He stepped into her then, crowding her in the doorway.

"What are you doing?"

"Apparently I have something to prove." He pressed her up against the doorway. Fisting his hands in her hair, he kissed her. And just like that, with a single touch of his mouth to hers, her entire body disconnected from her brain. She kissed him back, too, hungrily pressing closer, as close as she could get.

The thing was, it'd been good the other night in the tent. Real good. But it was even better now—which made no sense. Neither was the way she could almost forget all her problems when he had his mouth on her. And what had begun as an irritating interruption quickly escalated into a heated frenzy, his body colliding with hers in all the right places. She was panting for air when he abruptly broke the kiss with a muttered oath and answered his radio.

She hadn't even heard the interruption.

"I have to go," he said, his breathing still a little ragged.

Nodding, she touched her wet mouth. "Yeah."

His gaze dropped to her lips, and his eyes heated again. He didn't want to go. He wanted her. Not that he'd ever made a secret of it, but the knowledge gave her a disturbingly warm glow.

"So we're good?" he asked.

Good covered way too much ground. "You've got to go, remember?"

"Amy—"

"Bye." Stepping backward into her apartment, she shut the door.

Then stared at it. He was still standing there on the other side, she could *feel* him.

"I'm going to take that as a yes," he said through the wood.

She let out a startled laugh, then clapped a hand over her mouth. Hell no, they weren't good. Not when he'd just proven what she'd already known—they were so far beyond good it was scary. They were *combustible.*

But she knew the power of it now, she assured herself. And it was okay because all she had to do was stay clear.

Which was going to be a little bit like trying to keep a moth from the flame.

Chapter 6

Chocolate is not a matter of life and death—it's more important than that.

Matt spent a few mornings a week in the gym, usually in the ring with Ty Garrison. This morning they were doing their usual beat-the-shit-out-of-each-other routine. He ducked Ty's left hook, feeling pretty damn smug for one solid beat—until Ty snuck a right uppercut to his gut.

Matt hit the floor with a wheeze, and then it was Ty's turn to be smug. "Gotcha."

Hell, no. They'd been at it for thirty minutes, and Matt was exhausted to the bone, but the last one down had to buy breakfast. Kicking out, he knocked Ty's feet from beneath him. Then it was Ty's turn to land with a satisfying thud.

"Jesus," Josh muttered from the weight bench.

Josh was also a good friend, but he didn't know much about having fun. He was a doctor, which left his taste for occasional recreational violence greatly diminished.

"You keep going at each other like that," Josh said, "and you'll end up in my ER."

Breathless, Matt rolled to his back. "Sorry, I only play doctor with the ladies."

Josh snorted and kept lifting. In Josh's opinion, weights were much more civilized.

Matt swiped the sweat off his forehead with his arm, keeping a close eye on Ty, a formidable opponent, as Matt knew all too well. They'd been in the Navy together. Matt had left after four years of service and gone to Chicago.

Ty had gone on to the SEALs. He wasn't someone to mess with lightly so Matt stayed back and gave him a careful nudge with his foot. Actually, it might have been more of a kick, but he knew better than to turn his back.

Josh stopped lifting. "At least check him for a pulse."

Matt poked Ty again. "Not falling for the dead possum shit, man."

"I've got an adrenaline pin I can stick him with," Josh said mildly. "Hurts like hell going in, but it should wake him right up."

"Come near me with a needle," Ty grumbled, "and you'll be the one who needs medical attention." He groaned and rolled over, eyeing Matt. "And that was a total pussy move."

"Yeah? Who's flat on his back?"

Ty swore and laid an arm over his eyes, still breathing heavily.

Matt collapsed back to the ground himself. He felt like he'd been hit by a bus, but at least his brain was too busy concentrating on the pain rather than on what his next move should be with Amy. If he didn't come up with something good soon, those few kisses would be all he'd ever get, and they hadn't been enough.

Not even close.

Ty staggered to his feet. "Another round."

Ty liked to push himself. Matt didn't mind doing the same, but he'd prefer to move onto something else—say a big plate of food. "I'm starving."

"Yeah," Ty said. "Because you skipped dinner last night. Loved getting stood up, by the way. I could have been with Mallory, and dinner with Mallory includes things you've never offered to do for me."

Matt laughed. He'd have pegged Ty as the *last* guy on the planet to hook up with the same woman more than once, much less commit to her, but that's exactly what Ty had done. He'd gotten serious with Mallory Quinn, Lucky Harbor's sweetheart. "Told you," Matt said. "Something came up."

"Like…?"

Like kissing Amy. "Had to see someone. About a work thing."

"A work thing? Since when do you work at night?"

"There was a lost hiker, and some follow-up." There. That was at least half the truth. Okay, maybe a quarter of the truth.

Ty flashed Matt a full-on smile. "You do remember I'm sleeping with the woman that Amy called first that day, right?"

Well, hell. "Fine, so I was visiting the lost hiker, who turned out to be Amy."

"Interesting," Ty said.

"What?"

"That you only go to the diner when Amy's working. And now you're finding excuses to 'visit' her."

Suddenly Matt was ready for round two after all. He pushed to his feet and gave Ty the "come here" gesture.

Ty, who'd never met a challenge he wasn't up for, grinned and came at him, but Josh whistled sharply through his fingers and stopped the action cold. He gestured to Matt's cell phone, which was buzzing on the floor.

"It's work," Josh said, tossing Matt the phone.

Ty sank back to the mat. "Handy, since I was going to hand you your own ass."

"Fuck if you were," Matt said, wisely stepping out of Ty's arm range before answering the phone.

* * *

Thirty minutes later, Matt was showered and on his way to Squaw Flats. A group of hikers had called in to report a theft from their day camp.

Matt parked at the trailhead and hiked up to the area. He took a report for the missing gear: a camera, an iPod touch, a smartphone, and a Swiss Army Knife. The campers hadn't bothered to lock up any of their stuff—a situation that Matt had seen a hundred times. He liked to call it the Mary Poppins Syndrome. People left the big, bad city for the mountains and figured they were safe because apparently the bad guys all stayed in the city.

The fact was that National Park Service Law Enforcement Rangers suffered the highest number of felonious assaults, as well as the highest number of homicides of *all* federal law enforcement officers. People never believed Matt when he spouted that fact, but it was true.

After taking the report, he spent a few hours in the area, a visible presence to deter any further felony mischief. He had four park rangers who worked beneath him, each assigned to a quadrant of the North District, and they patrolled daily, but the quadrants covered far too much area for them to be 100 percent effective.

Budget cuts sucked.

Since thieves rarely bothered to get a permit first, Matt detained everyone he came across to check them. At the south rim, he found two guys perched on a bluff, readying their ropes for a climb down into Martis Valley.

Lance and Tucker Larson were brothers, though you couldn't tell by looking at them. Tucker was tall and athletically built. Lance was much smaller and frail as hell thanks to the cystic fibrosis ravaging his twenty-something body. They ran the ice cream shop on the Lucky Harbor pier, and when the two of them weren't climbing, they were trouble seeking.

They both nodded at Matt, who gave them the once over, trying to decide if he needed to check their bags. The last time he'd found them up here, they'd been consuming Tucker's homemade brownies in celebration after a climb—brownies that had made their eyes red and put stupid-ass grins on their faces.

Not to mention, brownies that were also illegal as hell.

"Hey," Lance said with an easy smile.

Tucker, who was never friendly with anyone holding the authority to slow him down, didn't smile. Nor did he say anything.

"Any brownies today?" Matt asked.

"No, sir," Lance said. "No brownies on us today."

This made Tucker smile, so no doubt they'd already done their consuming. Great. "Careful on the rocks," Matt said. "You check our site for the latest conditions?"

"Mudslides," Lance said with a nod. "I'm hoping to see Tucker slide down the entire rim on his ass like he did last year in this very spot." He patted his pack. "Got my iPhone this time so I can get video for Lucille."

Matt shook his head and left them to it, intending to head back to the station, where a mountain of paperwork waited for him. But just outside the Squaw Flats campground, he found evidence of an off-site campfire. This was illegal, especially this time of year. The campfire was abandoned, but the ashes were warm, and as he stood there, he heard the footsteps of someone running away.

There was only one reason to do that: guilt. Someone had something to hide. Matt took off running, catching up to a figure dodging through the forest, off trail. A kid, maybe a teenager. "Stop," he said.

He didn't stop. They *never stopped.*

Matt sped up and caught the back of the kid's sweatshirt, yanking him to a halt. "Hold still," he said, when his arsonist fought to get free.

Of course he didn't, so Matt added a small shake to get his meaning across. The kid's hoodie fell back from his face, exposing dirty features, a snarling mouth, eyes spitting fury, and a surprise—he was a she. A scrawny she, who was lanky lean, as if three squares hadn't been a part of her recent program. "Let go of me!" she yelled, and kicked Matt in the shin. "Don't touch me!"

Christ. She was *maybe* sixteen. He let her loose, but before she could so much as lift another foot in his direction, he gave her a hard look. "Don't even think about it."

She lifted her chin in a show of bravado and crossed her arms tightly over herself. "I didn't do anything wrong."

Her voice was cultured and educated, but her clothes were dirty and torn and barely fit her. "Then why did you run?" he asked.

"Because you were chasing me." She didn't add the *duh*; she didn't have to—it was implied.

"Where're your parents?" Matt asked.

Her face was closed off and sullen. "I don't have to answer any of your stupid questions."

"You're a minor alone in the woods," he pointed out.

"I'm eighteen."

He gave her a long look, which she returned evenly. He held out his hand. "ID."

She produced an ID card from her ratty, old-looking backpack, careful to not let him see inside, which reminded him of yet another prickly female he'd come across, two nights ago now.

The girl's ID was issued by the Washington Department of Motor Vehicles for one Riley Taylor. The picture showed a cleaner version of the face in front of him, and the birth date did indeed proclaim her eighteen as of two weeks ago.

Handing the ID back, he nodded his chin toward the trail from which he'd come. "Was that your campfire back there?"

Her gaze darted away from his. "No."

Bullshit. "You need a permit or a paid campsite to overnight out here."

She just stared stonily at a spot somewhere over his shoulder. "I know that."

More bullshit. Matt eyed her backpack. "Some folks about a mile west of here were ripped off earlier today. You know anything about that?"

"Nope."

"What's in your backpack?"

She hugged it to her chest. "Stuff. *My* stuff."

His ass. The only thing that saved her was that when he'd grabbed her a minute ago, her backpack had seemed nearly empty. Far too empty to be carrying the stolen loot. She'd either fenced it already or she'd stashed it somewhere. "What are you doing out here?"

"Camping."

"With your family?"

A slight hesitation. "Yeah," she said.

More bullshit. "Where?"

"Brockway Springs." Again her gaze darted away.

She was racking up the lies now. Plus Brockway Springs was a campground about seven miles to the east. "That's a long way from here."

She shrugged.

"Look," he said. "You shouldn't be out here alone. You need to go back to your family. I'll give you a ride."

"No!" She took a breath and visibly calmed herself. "No," she said more quietly. "I don't take rides from strangers. I'm leaving now."

With no reason to detain her, there was little Matt could do to stop her. "Put your ID away so you don't lose it."

She once again opened her backpack, and he made no attempt to disguise the fact that he took a good look inside. A bottle of water, what looked like a spare shirt, and a flashlight. He put his hand on her arm. "Where did you get that flashlight?"

"I've had it forever."

It was the same model and make of flashlight that had gone missing off Matt's bumper the other night. It was also the most common flashlight sold in the area. More than half the people on this mountain had one just like it.

Riley zipped up her backpack, or tried to, but the ragged zipper caught. This didn't slow her down. She merely hugged the thing to her chest and took off, and in less than ten seconds, was swallowed up by the woods.

Matt shook his head and went back to the station, but he didn't sit more than thirty minutes behind his desk before he was called back out. Being supervisor of the district required him to wear many hats: firefighter, EMT, cop, S&R. Over the next several hours, he used the S&R hat to rescue two kayakers from the Shirley River, which at this time of year was gushing with snow melt. Finicky and dangerous, the river had been closed off to water play. But the kayakers had ignored the warning signs and had gone out anyway, then got stuck on the fast rushing water.

It took Matt, his rangers, and an additional crew from the south district to get the kayakers safely out of the water. Two rangers were injured in the rescue, but even after all that, the kayakers refused to leave, saying they had the right to do as they wanted on public land.

Matt ended up forcibly evicting them for violating park laws, and when they argued, he banned them for the rest of the season just because they were complete assholes.

Sometimes it was good to wear the badge.

Now down two rangers, he went on with his work. He assisted in the daily reporting on the condition of the trails, tracked the movement of various wildlife as required by one of the federal conservation agencies, then checked on the small forest fire that was burning on the far south end—which was thankfully 95 percent contained, which was good. By the end of his shift, he was hot, sweaty, tired, and starving. But before he left the area, he took the time to drive by the campsite where Riley had said her family was staying to check the registers. Easy enough to do, it was early in the season, and the snow had barely melted off in the past few weeks. He had four sites booked at this time, and only one of those sites had been booked by a family.

When he pulled up, that family was standing around their campfire roasting hot dogs and corn on the cob. His mouth watered. He'd had a sandwich hours and hours ago, before the river rescue.

The campers didn't have a teenage daughter.

Which meant that his dinner was going to have to wait. Turning his truck around, he headed back up the fire road to the site of the illegal campfire, where earlier he'd found the teen girl.

The fire was still out and still emitting residual warmth. Huddled up as close as she could get to it in the quickly cooling evening sat Riley.

She took one look at him and leapt to her feet.

He pointed at her as he got out of his truck. "Don't," he warned. "I'm not in the mood for another run through the woods." He was tired as shit and hungry, dammit.

"What are you doing here?" she asked, still as a deer caught in headlights, though not nearly as innocent as any Bambi.

"That's my question for you."

"I have rights," she said.

"You lied to me."

Her eyes flashed. "You weren't going to believe anything I told you!"

"Not true," he told her. "And for future reference, lying to law enforcement officers isn't a smart move. It makes them not trust you."

"Oh, please." Her stance was slouched, sullen. Defensive. "You didn't trust me before I even opened my mouth."

"Because you *ran* from me."

"Okay, well, now I know. You don't like running or lying. Jeez."

"I don't like attitude either," he said.

She tossed up her hands. "Well, what *do* you like?"

"Not much today. Where's your family, Riley?"

"Okay, fine, I'm not with my family. But you saw my ID. I'm eighteen now. I'm on my own."

"Where did you come from?"

"Town."

Well wasn't that nice and vague. "What are you doing in town?"

"Visiting friends."

He sighed. This conversation was like running in circles. "What friends?"

"I watch all the cop shows, you know." She crossed her arms. "I don't have to tell you anything."

Christ. "Fine." He gestured back to his truck. "Let's go."

"Wait—What?" Her eyes got huge, and she scrambled back a few feet. "You can't arrest me."

"Have you done something arrest worthy?" he asked.

"*No.*"

"Then you're not getting arrested. I'm driving you into town. To your *friends*." And then he planned to call his friend Sheriff Sawyer Thompson to run her ID to see if she was a person of interest or reported as missing.

She looked away. "I don't need a ride."

"You're not sleeping out here tonight. Get in the truck."

She threw her backpack into the truck bed with enough attitude to give him a starter headache. Then she climbed into the passenger seat and slammed the door.

Matt drew a deep breath and walked around to the driver's side. He drove her attitude-ridden ass into town, wondering what it was with him and stubborn females this week.

In the heavy silence of the truck cab, Riley's stomach grumbled. She ignored both it and Matt, keeping her face firmly turned toward the window. But by the time they drove down the main drag of Lucky Harbor, her stomach was louder than the venomous thoughts she was sending his way.

"Where to?" he asked.

"Here's fine."

Here was the corner where the pier met the beach. "Your friends live on the pier?" he asked dryly.

"I'll walk to their place." Her stomach cut her off with yet another loud rumble.

Matt sighed and pulled into the pier parking lot.

Riley immediately reached for the door handle but Matt gripped the back of her sweatshirt. "Not so fast."

She stiffened. "I'm not thanking you for the ride with anything that involves me losing my clothes."

Jesus, he thought, his gut squeezing hard. "I'm not looking for a thank-you at all, but I'm not dropping you off on the damn corner. I'm taking you into the diner to feed you."

She stared at him. "Why?"

"Because you're hungry. And no," he said before she could speak again. "I don't expect a thank-you for that either."

Like a cornered, injured, starving animal, she didn't so much as blink, and he felt the punch of her mistrust more forcibly than he'd felt Ty's right uppercut this morning.

"I don't have any money," she finally said.

"You're not going to need any."

This produced another long, unblinking stare.

In the silence, his own belly grumbled. "Let's go."

Her eyes swiveled to the diner on the pier's corner. "What kind of place is called Eat Me?" she asked, unwittingly cementing what he'd suspected all along.

If she hadn't known the name of the only diner in Lucky Harbor, she hadn't come from town. She didn't belong here any more than she'd belonged out on the mountain. And he knew what that likely meant, he'd seen it all too often in Chicago. Homeless teens, a rising phenomenon that no one had yet come up with a solution for. She was either a runaway, abandoned, or a juvenile delinquent dodging the authorities. "The food's good," he said. "And I'm starving. So are you."

The girl seemed to fold in on herself. "I'm not cleaned up good enough for a fancy place like that."

Eat Me was just about the furthest thing from fancy he'd ever seen, but he gave her a cursory once-over. "You look fine."

"But—"

"Now, Riley."

She slammed out of his truck and grabbed her backpack, hugging it tight to herself.

Matt almost told her to stop abusing his door but he thought back to all the times his dad had yelled at him for doing the same thing and kept his mouth shut. He refused to turn into his father. Not that there was anything wrong with his dad's parenting skills, but it was unnerving to hear himself become that guy.

As he opened the diner's door for her, he said, "The waitress is a friend of mine. Be nice."

"Friend or *friend*?"

Ignoring that, he nudged her to a booth, not happy that under the harsh fluorescent lighting, he could see a fist-sized bruise on her jaw.

Amy was several tables down, serving from a large tray and clearly babying her wrapped wrist. She was wearing a black sundress with her kick-ass boots, topped off by the ever-present pink Eat Me apron. Just looking at her short-circuited his brain.

She turned her head and met his gaze, revealing nothing. She was good at that, too good. But two minutes later, she came by their booth with two sodas, and Matt smiled at her.

Amy didn't return the smile but her gaze dropped to his mouth, and he knew she was thinking of their last kiss up against her door.

Worked for him, since he'd pretty much done nothing but.

Riley picked up the tension between them, Matt's smile and Amy's lack of, and cracked a small snarky smile. "Thought you said she was your girlfriend," she said to Matt. "She doesn't appear to like you much."

Amy gave Matt a long look.

Matt didn't bother to sigh. "Thanks," he said to Riley. "Thanks a lot."

The girl flashed her first real smile.

Not Amy. Her eyes narrowed in on Riley like a hawk. "Hey, you're the one who was watching me through the bushes on the mountain."

Chapter 7

Chocolate does a body good.

Amy couldn't believe it. She stared at the teenager who was still wearing the blue sweatshirt. Her face was dirtier than it'd been the other day, and her eyes were bright with false bravado and pride. Behind that lurked fear, plain and simple. There was a bruise on her jaw, too. Someone had hit her, and at that knowledge, Amy's gut squeezed.

"Amy, this is Riley. Riley, Amy." Matt met Amy's gaze. "Riley's hungry, and I'm my usual starving."

"No problem." Amy set a menu in front of the squirming, skinny Riley. She hadn't bothered to bring one to Matt. He knew everything they served.

Matt tapped on Riley's menu. "Whatever you want." Then he rose, and moving with his usual quick efficiency, took Amy's arm in a firm grip. "A minute?"

She opened her mouth to tell him she was swamped, but he met her gaze and she saw something in his—exhaustion. She let him direct her into the back hallway just outside the bathrooms. "You okay?" she asked.

There was a beat of surprise from him, then finally, he nodded. He was either fine or he didn't want to discuss it. "What is she doing here with you?"

He didn't answer the question, and by the way he was looking at her, she knew that wasn't what he'd brought her back here to discuss. She had no idea what that might be.

"I've been thinking about you," he said.

Not expecting that, or the punch of emotion the words brought, Amy stared into his light brown eyes. He hadn't even touched her, and that now familiar zing ran through her, from the very roots of her hair to her toes, and then straight back to every erogenous zone she owned—of which there appeared to be more than she remembered.

Not appearing to be bothered by the zing in the least, Matt put his hands on her hips and gently bumped her back a step, up against the wall.

Not only wasn't he bothered, she could feel that he liked the zing.

A lot.

There was nobody else in the hallway, so when he leaned in and kissed her, no one heard her soft murmur of surprise.

And arousal.

He gave her no tongue, nothing but his firm, warm lips, but the kiss wasn't sweet, not by a long shot. Nope, this kiss had purpose, and that purpose was to remind her exactly how explosive their chemistry was. In that moment, there was nowhere else she'd rather be, and she showed him by pressing close and deepening the kiss.

There wasn't much give to Supervisory Forest Ranger Matthew Bowers's body, not a single inch—except for his mouth, his very giving mouth. Not until her knees had dissolved and she was grasping his uniform shirt in her sweaty fists to keep herself upright did he break free, pulling back just enough to meet her gaze. He murmured something that sounded like "every fucking time," then gave a low laugh and shook his head, as if he couldn't quite believe it either. Once more he brushed his mouth across hers, a lighter caress this time, slowing the pumping blood slightly.

And then as if nothing had just happened, he spoke. "Found the girl in an illegal campsite. I think she's living out there. Has an ID that claims she's eighteen. I want to have Sawyer run the address and check her out, but first I want to feed her."

Aw. Aw, dammit. How the hell was she supposed to keep her distance when he kissed like that *and* had a soft spot for a teen in trouble? "She's not from around here?"

"I don't know. She lied to me about camping with her family, and now she's saying she's here in town visiting friends, but she's lying about that, too. I'd like to take her back to where she belongs, if I could figure out where exactly that is."

Amy grimaced.

"What?"

"Not everyone lives a fairy-tale home life," she said, painfully aware of what the girl might be trying to stay away from.

Matt's eyes and mouth were grim, suggesting that he understood that all too well, perhaps more than Amy gave him credit for. "Yeah," he said. "I know. I thought maybe you could help me figure her out a little."

Amy went still, staring up at him. He looked at her right back. Steadily.

He wasn't kidding. "Oh no," she said. "No, no, no."

"Why not?"

"Because what do I know about teenage girls?"

"You remember being one, right?"

Yes, far more than she wanted to admit. Like Riley, she'd ended up on her own at too young an age. Looking back, it was a miracle that she'd made it relatively unscathed, not to mention alive. "I really don't have time for—"

"Just soften her up a little," he said. "I want to help her but she's not overly fond of me, and I think she might be in some sort of trouble."

"What kind of trouble?"

"I don't know." He ran a hand over his face, as if he was bone-tired and barely keeping himself awake. And hell if that didn't soften her, too.

"Just get what you can out of her," he said, sensing her capitulation, not too tired to press his advantage. "That's all. A few minutes."

"And why me exactly?"

He ran a callused finger along her temple, making her shiver. "Because you have a way with people."

She choked out a laugh. Her way with people was usually to piss them off. "If I'm your best bet, you're the one in trouble."

He gave her a searing look that promised he was not only *in* trouble, he *was* trouble, and that he'd be worth every second of it. But his next words quickly doused any inner fire.

"I think she's been abused," he said quietly. "She doesn't like to be touched. And when I brought her here to feed her, she assumed I'd demand sex as payment."

Amy's gut clenched hard, but she nodded and then tried to move past him to go back to the dining area. Matt wrapped his fingers around her wrist, stopping her. "Hey." He dipped down a little to see directly into her eyes. "You okay?"

"Of course." Wasn't she always? She tugged, giving him a level look when he didn't immediately let go. Her patented "don't make me kick your ass" look. "I have to get back to work. Jan doesn't pay me to stand around and kiss her customers."

That alleviated some of the strain from his eyes, and he smiled. The kind of smile that made her want to kiss him some more. "You kiss a lot of customers?"

She gave him a push. He knew damn well he was the only one.

And despite what she'd said about needing to get back to work, she didn't go directly back to her tables. She took a moment and a deep breath. There was a lot going through her. She'd been serving a big table when that first prickle of awareness had raced up her spine, settling at the base of her neck, followed by a rush of warmth, and she'd known.

Matt had come into the diner.

Nothing unusual, really. He came in a lot. Tonight he'd been later than usual, which meant he'd had an especially long day. Shaking it off, she moved to the drink dispenser to get him another soda.

Jan was there, checking the ice machine. "Look at you jump for him," she murmured. "Never figured you for the kind to jump for a man."

"I'm not jumping for anyone."

Jan sent her a knowing smirk, which was both annoying and embarrassing. So she knew Matt would be thirsty after a long day and that he'd want a refill, so what? Matt was hugely popular in town. *Everyone* knew what he drank, and how much.

And yeah, okay, she'd followed him to the back when he'd wanted to talk. That had been business.

Sort of.

She shifted so that she could see him in the booth with the girl, soaking up the sight of him in his uniform, slightly dusty, a lot rumpled. Armed. Clearly weary, his long legs were sprawled out in front of him, his broad shoulders back against the booth. He'd probably been outside all day, his tanned features attested to that, but somehow he'd still smelled wonderful.

Which only annoyed and embarrassed her all the more, because she really needed to stop noticing how he smelled. Rolling her eyes at herself, she went to his table to take their order.

"I'll have the usual," Matt told her, and looked at the sullen teen across from him, who was meeting no one's eye. "Riley?"

"I don't care."

Matt sighed and turned to Amy. "Make it two of the usual."

"His usual," Amy informed Riley, "is a double bacon blue burger, fries, non-stop refills of Dr. Pepper, and a piece of pie. And by piece, I mean a quarter of an entire pie. You up for all that?"

Riley's mouth had fallen open, but she nodded.

Amy went back to the kitchen. Jan was there with Henry, their cook. Henry was ten years younger than Jan and born and bred in Lucky Harbor. He'd been a trucker for two decades before going to culinary school in Seattle. He claimed cooking had healed his soul. It certainly had healed Eat Me, which had been floundering since they'd lost their last cook, Tara Daniels, to the Lucky Harbor B&B.

Jan was at the pie case dividing the only remaining half of apple pie into three pieces. Amy stuck Matt's order into Henry's order wheel, then reached in past Jan and snagged the biggest piece of pie.

"Hey," Jan said. "I was going to serve that piece."

"There's still two left."

"Yeah, but you took the biggest one."

"It's for Matt," Amy said. She grabbed the second-to-last piece as well. "And this is for the girl who's with him."

"Why is Matt's piece the biggest one?"

"Because you cut it uneven."

"Yes, but why is *his* piece the biggest?"

"He tips the best," Amy said.

Jan stared at her, and then cackled, slapping her thigh in rare amusement. Henry joined her.

"Hey," Amy said, insulted, "it's true." Well, at least partially true. Matt did tip better than any of her customers. "He likes the pie."

"Girl," Jan said, "he likes you."

Amy ignored this, even as the words brought her a ridiculous shiver of pleasure. This was immediately followed by denial. Matt didn't know her, not really. Sure, he was attracted to her. She got that, loud and clear. And that was 100 percent reciprocated. But as for him *liking* her? She'd never really cared what anyone thought of her before, so it was disconcerting to suddenly realize she cared now. She set the pieces of pie aside, pointed at Jan to leave them alone, then made two dinner salads.

"There aren't any salads on his order," Jan said.

"What, you writing a book tonight?"

Jan cocked a brow.

"The girl's a runaway. She needs greens," Amy said.

"Hey, I don't care if she's the president of the United States. Somebody better be paying for those salads."

"You won't be shorted," Amy assured her and brought the salads to Matt's table.

The expression on his face was priceless as he stared down at the plate, looking as if maybe he'd swallowed something sour. "I don't like salads," he finally said.

"Why not?" Amy asked.

His brow furrowed. "Because they're green. I don't like anything green."

"Me either," Riley said, and pushed her plate away.

Amy put her hands on her hips and faced Matt. "Salads are healthy. And," she added with a meaningful look and a hitch of her chin towards Riley, "for people who aren't eating regular meals every day, they can be a critical addition to a diet."

Matt stared up at her, six feet plus of pure testosterone. She knew that, in general, he did as he wanted, and she figured he'd been doing so for a damn long time. But he'd asked for her help, and even if he hadn't, she wanted this girl to eat a frigging salad. The silent battle of wills lasted for about five seconds, and then Matt gave a sigh, picked up his fork, and stabbed at the lettuce with little enthusiasm.

Amy turned to Riley, who was staring open mouthed at Matt, clearly shocked that he'd caved, that he was going to eat the salad just because Amy had asked. Or *told*.

"You, too," Matt said to Riley, jabbing his fork in the direction of the girl's salad.

"But—"

"No buts," Matt said. "Amy's more stubborn than a mule. You're best off just doing what she asks or it's like beating your head against a brick wall."

Amy opened her mouth but decided to let that one go.

Riley sized her up for a beat and then blew out an exaggerated breath that spoke volumes on what she thought of being told what to do. Still, she began eating her salad.

Satisfied, Amy leaned against the outside of the booth, grateful to take some of the weight off her feet for a minute. For all Riley's bitching, she was inhaling the salad like she hadn't eaten in days. And hell, maybe she hadn't. "So where are you from?"

"Around," Riley said.

Well if that wasn't downright helpful. "You enjoy the mountains?"

"Yeah," Riley said around a big bite of lettuce. She was carefully avoiding the cucumbers as if they were poisonous snakes.

So was Matt.

"I'm going back up there to do some more exploring tomorrow morning, since I don't have to work until late afternoon," Amy said. "How long did you say you were camped out there?"

Riley went still, obviously shutting down. "I didn't say."

Amy nodded and met Matt's gaze, which was warm and fixed on her. She didn't want to think about why that made her feel warm in return, so she left them and went back to the kitchen. When the food was ready, she brought out the order, setting down Riley's plate first. "You might want to—"

Riley began inhaling the burger and fries with vigor.

"—Take it easy," Amy continued. "Too much on an empty stomach isn't good."

Riley didn't slow down.

Matt moved over and patted the place next to him, and Amy caught Jan's eye to let her know she was taking a quick break before sitting. "You been on your own for a while," Amy said.

Riley shrugged.

"When I was living on my own," Amy said, "it was a jar of peanut butter and raw ramen noodles for the week. Used to be able to get those for like nineteen cents each."

Riley was halfway through her burger already. "On grocery Tuesdays, you can get other stuff cheap, too."

"Grocery Tuesdays?" Matt asked.

Riley lowered her gaze and hunched over her food, like she'd accidentally imparted a state secret.

Amy's throat tightened and she looked at Matt. "It's when some of the grocery stores throw out their older stock to make room for the new stock."

Matt's gaze slid back to Riley, but he didn't say anything more.

From the kitchen, Henry dinged the bell, signaling that Amy had another order ready. She sent Matt a did-the-best-I-could look and walked away. It was what she did with problems. Walk. Teenage life sucked? She walked. Her mom's new husband giving her trouble? She walked. Her own guy trouble? She walked. It was her MO.

But this time, for the first time, she wasn't proud of it.

Matt watched Amy go, something new unfurling in his gut as certain things began to click for him. She didn't like being approached unexpectedly, or startled. She'd once survived on peanut butter and ramen. And she was slow to trust.

At some point in her life, things had been bad, possibly worse than he could imagine. It wasn't any of his business, and it certainly wasn't his job, but that didn't stop him from aching for her and Riley both. Amy didn't want his sympathy. He knew this. Riley didn't want his sympathy either, but she was in trouble. He knew it deep in his gut. He'd like to help but he held no delusions on his ability to do that for either of them.

He didn't have a great track record when it came to fixing people's problems. In fact, he had a downright shitty record when it came right down to it. He turned his attention to Riley. Clearly she was on the run, maybe from someone abusive, or at the very least, she'd been sorely neglected. She'd practically licked her plate clean, eating everything except for the cucumbers. Couldn't blame her there. "Better?"

She answered with a nod, though she did smile when Amy delivered the pie. The way to a woman's heart...dessert. Good to know.

Riley waited until Amy moved on to another booth. "Your piece is bigger," she said.

"So?" Matt said. "*I'm* bigger."

"Yeah, that's not why your piece is bigger."

Matt ignored this. When they'd finished, he paid the bill. The salads hadn't been on it, which meant that Amy intended to pay for them out of her own pocket, so he made sure his tip covered the cost plus, then led Riley back to the parking lot. He could feel her anxiety level rising. "You have two choices," he said. "You can tell me where your friends live so I can drop you off there, or I can run your ID and figure out your secrets."

He was going to do that anyway, but she didn't have to know it.

"I'm of age," she said. "I don't have to give you my friends' address."

"Don't have to...or can't, because there are no friends?" he asked.

She stared at him, the silence broken by the sound of someone clearing her throat.

Amy. She was standing in the parking lot, purse slung over her shoulder, keys in her hand. "I got off early," she said. "I have a spare bedroom, Riley. It's the size of a piece of toast, but it's all yours for the night if you'd like."

"No," Matt immediately said. It was one thing for *him* to get involved with a troubled teen they knew far too little about, another entirely for Amy to do it for him.

"No," Riley said, echoing Matt. "I couldn't do that. But thanks. I just want to go back to the woods."

"You're done with the woods," Matt said. "No more illegal camping. It's not safe, and I can't have you out there."

"And besides, you don't *have* to camp," Amy said to Riley. "Just come to my place. You'd get a hot shower and a roof."

Matt opened his mouth, but Amy gave him a small head shake. To Riley, she gestured toward her car, and to his surprise, Riley got into it.

Amy turned to him, her expression one of grim determination. He could see that Riley had stirred something inside of her. Protectiveness, certainly, but memories too, and it didn't take a genius to see that those memories made her sad.

His fault. "Amy—"

"I'm doing this," she said.

Clearly, whether he liked it or not. And for the record, he didn't. "When I asked for your help, I didn't mean for you to—"

"I know. But I can't leave her here, Matt. I just can't." There was something in her voice, something that twisted the knife deeper within him. "We'll be fine," she murmured, and slid behind the wheel of her car. He stepped between her and the driver's door before she could shut it, crouching at her side. "Be careful."

"Always am."

He paused, but he had no further reason to detain them so he stood and backed up, watching her drive off. He didn't feel good about this, about sending a possible juvenile delinquent home with the woman he had a thing for. He wasn't sure what kind of thing exactly, but it didn't matter at the moment. This was his doing, and if something went wrong, he wouldn't be able to live with himself.

So he followed them. He parked on the street outside of Amy's building and watched them go inside together. A minute later, the lights came on. While he watched from his truck, he called Sawyer, requesting a search for a missing persons report on one Riley Taylor.

If Riley Taylor was even her real name…

While he waited to hear back, Matt spent the time keeping an eye on the building, and maybe playing solitaire on his phone.

When Amy knocked on the driver's window, she nearly gave him a coronary.

"If you're not going home," she said through his window, "you might as well come in."

She'd showered and was wearing an oversized T-shirt and tiny booty shorts that revealed her mile-long legs. Her hair was wet, her long, side-swept bangs falling over one eye. She smelled like shampoo and soap—and warm, soft woman. He followed her up the stairs, watching her ass in those short shorts. She could've led him right off a cliff and he'd never have noticed.

Her place was a tiny two bedroom, emphasis on the tiny. The living room, kitchen, and dining room were all one room that was not much bigger than his truck. Small as it was, it was also cheerful. Sunshine yellow paint in the kitchen, bright blue and white in the living room. Clearly the place had come like this because he was quite certain that Amy wouldn't have picked such vibrant colors. Amy was a lot of things—smart, loyal, fiercely protective, beautiful, edgy—but not exactly cheerful.

Proving the point, she gave him a blanket, a pillow, the couch, and a long look that he didn't even try to interpret. "Thanks," he said.

She nodded and turned away.

Then turned back.

Their gazes caught and held for a long moment, and the air hummed with hunger and desire. Fuck it, he thought, tossing the blanket and pillow down, but just as he stepped toward her, she hightailed it into her bedroom.

Smart girl.

Two hours later, he was still tossing and turning on the couch that wasn't wide enough for his shoulders and about two feet too short. What the hell was he doing here? Thinking of sex, that's what he was doing. Sex with Amy, which he was no longer sure was a good idea.

In fact, he was pretty damn sure it was a *bad* idea now that he suspected Amy had an extremely rough past. A past he'd likely stirred up for her by bringing Riley into her life. He needed to stay the hell away from her, that's what he needed to do. She didn't need the complication.

Getting comfortable was impossible, so he sat up and put his feet on the small coffee table. Slightly better. Count sheep, he told himself, but when he closed his eyes, sheep wasn't what came to mind.

Amy came to mind. Amy, straddling him.

Naked.

Damn if that wasn't a hell of a lot better than sheep. But it wasn't exactly conducive to falling asleep, so he rose, thinking a kitchen raid might work. A rustle warned him that he wasn't the only one awake just as he collided into a willowy, warm body that his own instantly recognized. *Amy.* Catching her, he dropped backward to the couch, taking her with him.

She landed sprawled over the top of him, all soft, tousled woman, her breasts rising and falling against his chest with every breath. "You okay?"

Apparently she was, because she fisted both hands in his hair and kissed him, a really deep, wet, hot *holy shit* kiss. Yeah, this. *This* was what he'd needed all fucking day long. It was perfect.

She was perfect.

Instantly hard, he rolled to tuck her beneath him, spreading her legs with his to make room for himself, pressing into her so that he was cradled between her thighs. It was dark so he couldn't see much, but he sure could feel. And what he felt just about stopped his heart. She appeared to be wearing an oversized shirt, panties, and nothing else, as he discovered when his hands slid beneath the shirt to cup her bare breasts.

Amy gasped his name, and he went still, realizing he had her pinned beneath him, a perfect breast in each hand. And he wanted to keep kissing her, keep touching her until she was too hot to stop him. Even the thought revved him up. But Jesus, he'd forgotten the reason he was even here—Riley was in the next room. With a Herculean effort, he managed to let go of Amy and rise to his feet.

The distance didn't help. Nor did the sight of Amy still sprawled on the couch trying to catch her breath. Her shirt had risen up, her cute little panties looking very white in the dark of the room. He wanted in those little panties. Wanted that more than his next breath.

Not happening. Snatching up the pillow and blanket, he strode to the door. "I'm going to sleep in my truck."

A lie. He wasn't going to sleep at all.

"I thought the truck was uncomfortable," she said.

Yes, and so was a hard-on. He'd just have to live with it.

•

Chapter 8

The best things in life are chocolate.

Amy got up early. She had until four this afternoon to try to get up to Sierra Meadows and back. *Try* being the key word. She wasn't at all sure she had any confidence in her ability to do so, but she had to try.

She had some hope to get to.

She was deciding whether or not to leave Riley a note or wake her up when the teen staggered out of the spare bedroom. She was wearing the same ratty jeans as yesterday but a different shirt, this one strategically torn in some sort of misguided teenager sense of fashion.

"Sleep okay?" Amy asked her.

"Yeah." Riley looked out the kitchen window. "The cop's gone."

Yes, Matt was gone. She'd heard him leave before the crack of dawn. She'd been lying in her bed awake, hot, aching, remembering what his hands had felt like on her when she'd heard his truck start up and drive away. "And he's not a cop. He's a forest ranger."

"Same thing."

Pretty much, Amy agreed. And she recognized some of the authority issues in Riley's voice well enough since she'd always had her own to contend with. "Listen, I'm going up to Sierra Meadows. Feel free to stay and catch up on some sleep. There's food, hot water… TV."

Riley looked around, her wariness showing. "I don't know."

"No one will bother you here. Is that what you're worried about? Because if someone's bothering you, maybe I can help—"

"No," Riley said quickly. Too quickly. "I don't need help. I'm fine."

Amy's heart squeezed because she'd been there, right there where Riley was, terrified and alone with no one to turn to. Well, actually that wasn't quite correct. She'd had people to turn to, but she'd screwed that up, so when she'd needed help, no one had believed her.

"You're safe here," Amy said.

Riley nodded, and Amy felt relieved. Maybe she'd stay and be safe for the day, at least. "Is there someone I can call for you, to let them know where you are?"

"No."

Well, that had been a long shot.

"I left out some spare clothes if you're interested," Amy said. "There's some food in the fridge, but not much. If you walk down to the diner later, I'll make you something to eat, whatever you want."

"Why?"

Riley wasn't asking about the food, and Amy knew it. What she didn't know was how to answer, so she went with to-the-bone honesty. "Because I know how it sucks to not know where your next meal's going to come from. You don't need to feel that, not today anyway."

It took Amy two hours to get up to Sierra Meadows, made easier by the fact that now she knew where to go. Lungs screaming, huffing like a lunatic, she climbed to the same spot where only a few nights ago she'd teetered and then fallen, sliding down on her ass in the inky dark.

There was no fog now so she could see, and the view was breathtakingly gorgeous. The sun poked through the lush growth, dappling the trail. Far below, down in the meadow, the steam rose from the rocks as the sun hit the dew. Making her careful way down the steep incline to the meadow floor, she walked through shoulder-high grass and wildflowers to the wall of thirty-foot prehistoric rocks on the far side. The meadow was a lot longer than it appeared from above, and there was no path, so this took another half hour. Finally she stood before the towering rocks, feeling quite small and insignificant.

Heart pounding, she slowly walked the entire length of them. Names and dates had been carved into the lower stones by countless climbers before her. Not needing to read her grandma's journal, Amy followed the right curve as far as she could and found the last *huge* "diamond" rock. There were rows of initials, and she painstakingly read each and every one, looking for the RB and SB that was Rose Barrett and Scott Barrett. It took her another thirty minutes to decide they weren't there.

Frustrated, she sat in the wild grass and stared at the rock. To give herself some time to think, she pulled out her sketch pad and drew the rocks. She needed to start back soon but she was hesitant to leave without answers. She looked at the rocks again and let out a breath.

Then she reached for her phone and called the one person who could help her.

"Hello?"

Amy went still at the sound of her mom's voice.

"Amy?"

Amy cleared her throat, but the emotions couldn't be swallowed away. Guilt. Hurt. Regret. "How did you know?"

"You're the only one who ever calls and says nothing. Though it's been a few years." Her mom paused. "I suppose you need something."

Amy closed her eyes. "Yeah."

Now her mother was quiet.

"I'm in Lucky Harbor," Amy said. "In Washington State."

More silence.

"Following grandma's journal."

This got a reaction, a soft gasp. "Whatever for?" her mom asked.

For hope and peace, Amy nearly said. *To find myself…* But that was all far too revealing, and her mother wouldn't believe it anyway. "Her journal says they left their initials on the mountain, but there's no RB and SB for Rose and Scott Barrett anywhere that I can see."

Nothing.

"Mom?"

There was a sigh. "It was all a very long time ago, Amy."

"You know something."

"Yes."

Amy wasn't breathing. "Mom, please tell me."

"You're looking for the wrong initials. You should be looking for RS and JS. JS is for Jonathon Stone." Her mom paused. "Your grandma's first husband."

Amy felt her heart stutter. "What?"

"Rose ran away when she was seventeen, you knew that. She eloped."

She hadn't known *that*. "With Jonathon Stone."

"Yes. Their families didn't approve. Not that Mom ever cared about what people thought. You're a lot like her in that regard…" Amy's mother sighed again, and when she spoke this time, there was heavy irony in her voice. "The women in our family don't tend to listen to reason."

Amy ran back to the rock and searched again. It didn't take but a minute to find it, the small RS and JS together. She pressed a hand to the ache in her chest. "No," she agreed softly. "We don't tend to listen to reason."

There was another awkward pause, and Amy had this ridiculous wish that her mom might ask how she was. She didn't. Too much water under the bridge. But she hoped there was enough of a tie left to at least get the answers she wanted. Needed. "What happened to Jonathon?"

"It's a sad story," her mom said. "Jonathon was sick," her mom explained. "Lung cancer, and back then it was even more of a death sentence than it is now. Jonathon had a list of things he wanted to do while he could. Rock climb the Grand Canyon. Ski a glacier. See the Pacific Coast from a mountaintop..."

The Olympic Mountains. Where Amy currently sat. "Did he get to do those things in time?"

Her mom was quiet, not answering.

"Mom?"

"You haven't called me in two years. Two years, Amy."

She sighed. "Yeah."

"It'd have been nice to know you're alive."

The last time Amy had called, her mother had been having marital problems with husband number five—shock—and she'd wanted to play the place-the-blame game. Amy hadn't wanted to go there. So it'd been easier not to call. "What happened to Jonathon, Mom? And do you know where it was exactly that Grandma Rose ended her journey? Her journal is clear on the first two legs of their trek in the Olympic Mountains, but it's vague on the last stop." Where Rose had found heart... "Do you—"

"I'm fine, you know. Thanks for asking."

Amy grimaced. "Mom—"

"Is this your cell phone? This number you called me from?"

"Yes," Amy said.

"You have enough minutes in your phone plan to make a few extra calls?"

"Yes."

"Good. Call me again sometime, and you can ask me another question. I'll answer a question with each call. How's that sound?"

Amy blinked. "You *want* me to call you?"

"You always were a quick study."

"But—"

Click.

Amy stared at the phone. This was almost too much information for her brain to process. Her Grandma Rose had made this journey when she'd been seventeen years old. *Seventeen.* And she'd been a newlywed, in love with someone who'd died young and tragically.

How had that brought her hope? Or peace? Or her own heart...?

Amy pulled out the journal. She'd read it a hundred times. She knew that there was no mention of Jonathon.

Just the elusive and misleading "we."

It's been a rough week. The roughest of the summer so far.

Well, that made sense now. Jonathon had been sick. Dying. Amy flipped to the next entry.

Lucky Harbor's small and quirky, and the people are friendly. We've been here all week resting, but today was a good day so we went back up the mountain. To a place called Four Lakes this time. All around us the forest vibrated with life and energy, especially the water.

I never realized how much weight the water can remove from one's shoulders. Swimming in the water was joy. Sheer joy.

I could hear the call of gulls, and caught the occasional bald eagle in our peripheral. The sheer, vast beauty was staggering.

Afterward, we lay beneath a two-hundred-foot-tall old

spruce and stared up through the tangle of branches to the sky beyond. I'd always been a city girl through and through, but this... out here... it was magic. Healing.

I carved our initials on the tree trunk. It felt like a promise. I had my hope, but now I had something else, too, peace. Four Lakes had given me peace.

A little shocked to find her eyes stinging, her knees weak with emotion, Amy sank to the grass, emotion churning through her. As odd as it seemed, she'd found the teeniest, tiniest bit of hope for herself after all. Maybe her own peace was next...

"Phone's for you!" Jan yelled to Amy across the diner. "You need to let people know that I'm not you're damn answering service!"

Amy had gotten to work on time, and though she was still reeling from the afternoon and all she'd learned, she managed to set it aside for now. That was a particularly defined talent of hers. Setting things aside. Living in Denial City.

For now, she had to work; that's what kept a roof over her head and food in her belly. She had no idea who'd possibly be calling her here at the diner, but she finished serving a customer his dinner and then picked up the phone in the kitchen. "Hello?"

Nothing but a dial tone. She turned to Jan. "Who was it?"

"Some guy." Jan shrugged. "He wanted to talk to the waitress who'd been seen with the runaway teen."

Amy went still. "And you didn't think that was odd?"

Jan shrugged again. Not her problem.

Amy had a bad feeling about this, very bad. To save money, she'd never gotten a landline at her apartment. This meant she couldn't check on Riley, which she felt a sudden real need to do. "Going on break," she said.

Jan sputtered. "Oh, no. You just got here an hour ago."

Amy grabbed her keys. "I'll be back."

"I said *no*." Steam was coming out of Jan's ears. "You've got a room full of hungry people."

Amy understood, but there was a sinking feeling in her gut that Riley needed her more. "Sorry." She headed out the back door as Jan let out a furious oath.

There was no Riley waiting at home.

And no note.

No nothing, though the clothes Amy had set out for Riley were gone. Unhappy, Amy left Riley a sticky note in case she came back, then returned to work, eyeing the door every time someone came in.

But Riley never showed.

At the end of Amy's shift, Mallory and Grace arrived. Amy waved them to a booth, grabbed the plate of brownies she'd been saving as well as the charity jar from the counter, and joined them. She plopped down, put her feet up, head back, and sighed out a very long breath.

"Long day?" Mallory asked sympathetically.

Amy looked at Mallory. "*You*, I'm not talking to."

Mallory winced, guilt all over her face, clearly knowing Amy was referring to the Matt-to-the-rescue episode.

Amy popped the lid off the money jar and pulled out a wad of cash, 100 percent of which would go directly to the teen center at the local health services clinic that Mallory ran. "Two hundred and fifty bucks. Even if I am mad at you."

"Luckily you're not the type to hold a grudge," Mallory said sweetly, taking the money.

"I hope we're going to talk about guys," Grace said, picking out a brownie. "I'm in the middle of a man drought, and I need a thrill. I plan to live vicariously through you two."

"Ask Mallory here to set you up," Amy said dryly.

"Actually," Mallory said, ignoring the jab, "there're *plenty* of single guys around here. My brother's newly single. Again."

"Yes but he's a serial dater," Amy said. "Even I know to stay away from serial daters."

"Even you?" Mallory asked.

"I don't date." But she did, apparently, lust after sexy forest rangers who shared their tents and last Dr. Pepper.

"Why?"

Amy shrugged. "Not my thing."

"Again," Mallory said. "Why?"

"I don't know. I guess because I haven't had much time for that sort of thing."

"That sort of thing?" Mallory repeated. "Honey, *every* woman has enough time for love. It's what makes the world go round."

"No, that's chocolate. And of course you think love makes the world go round. You're getting lucky every night with Ty."

Mallory grinned. "True." Her smile faded. "Tell me the truth—how bad did I screw up by sending Matt to the forest?"

"Yes!" Grace whooped and pumped her fist. When Amy and Mallory stared at her, she winced. "Sorry. It's just that we're really going to dissect Amy's life instead of mine." Happy, she stuffed a brownie in her mouth.

Mallory was looking expectantly at Amy, who gave in with a sigh. "It's not your fault," she admitted, digging into her own very large brownie. "I'm the idiot who got lost on the mountain. Matt helped me out. And then, because of a stupid *tree*, we ended up camping out overnight."

They both gasped, Mallory in delight, Grace in horror. "*With no electricity?*"

Mallory laughed. "They spent the night together and *that's* what you want to know? About the lack of electricity?"

"Hey," Grace said, "a woman's morning routine is complicated enough *with* electricity."

"We didn't sleep together," Amy said, then grimaced. "Well, at least not until I fell down a ravine trying to find a place to pee in private, sprained my wrist, cut my leg, bruised my ass *and* my ego, and had to be rescued *again*." She waved her bandaged wrist for their viewing pleasure.

Mallory's eyes were wide. "You fell down a ravine going to pee, and he rescued you? Were your pants still around your ankles? Because that's not a good look for anyone."

"*No*," Amy said. "My pants were *not* around my ankles. But your concern is touching." She kicked Mallory, who was snorting with laughter. "And how would that have been funny?"

"Oh, trust me, it would have been. Come on, this is the stuff that chick flicks are made of—the classic meet-cute, you know? *And* a story for your kids someday."

"There will be no kids!"

Mallory licked a brownie crumb from her finger. "I'd suggest that good girl lesson number five should be to keep your pants *on* during a first date, but the truth is I can't really talk in that regard since I slept with Ty on our first date."

"Actually," Amy said, "technically, you slept with Ty *before* your first date. And fine, if you must know my pants weren't down when I fell but they might have come down shortly thereafter."

Grace and Mallory gasped in delighted tandem.

"Get your heads out of the gutter," Amy said. "I had a cut on my leg, and he had to doctor me up."

"Of course," Grace said dryly, and then leaned forward, brownie forgotten. "What kind of undies were you wearing, a thong or granny panties?"

"What does that matter?"

"Oh, it matters," Mallory said.

"I can't remember," Amy lied.

From the next booth over, a face popped up. It was Lucille, local art gallery owner and all-around gossip extraordinaire. She exited her booth and stood in front of the Chocoholics, a smile on her face. She wore eye-popping lime green sweats today with Skechers tennis shoes that gave her four-foot-nine-inch frame an extra few inches. Her steel-gray bun gave her a few more. She shoved a twenty into Amy's now empty charity jar while sliding her dentures around some. "What's this I hear about panties and Ranger Hot Buns?"

Both Mallory and Grace pointed at Amy like the Two Stooges.

Good friends.

Amy pulled the entire plate of brownies toward herself. "Good girl lesson number six—don't be traitors." She looked at Lucille. "I had a little trouble out on the trail and got some assistance. End of story. Nothing more to report."

"But he rescued you from the latrine," Lucille pressed. "I don't suppose you have a pic?"

"No!" She didn't need a picture. Everything that had happened, from being rescued to the feeling of lying in Matt's arms, was engrained in her brain.

"Well, jeez," Lucille said. "No need to get your panties in a twist." She paused. "But if you *did* get your panties in a twist, what kind of panties would they be? You know, for accuracy in reporting's sake?"

Amy narrowed her eyes at her, and Lucille backed away. "Oops, look at the time—I've gotta skedaddle."

When she was gone, Mallory eyed the brownie plate.

Amy tightened her grip on it. "Don't even think about it."

"Forget the brownies. What happened with Ranger Hot Buns?" Grace demanded to know.

"We shared his tent," Amy said. "Nothing happened." Well, nothing except for some pretty amazing kisses...

"Let me get this straight," Grace said in disbelief. "You slept with Matt Bowers, the hottest guy in town, and nothing happened? Are you kidding me? That's a crappy story."

"Matt's pretty hot," Mallory agreed. "But I wouldn't say he's the *hottest* guy in town. Because Ty's pretty damn hot. I mean think about them, side by side..."

There was a beat of silence as the three of them thought about the incredible hotness that was Ty and Matt, side by side. Amy let the image sink in and shivered, which she covered by stuffing another big bite of brownie into her mouth. There were certain things she knew for sure. When in doubt, eat chocolate. When stressed, eat chocolate. When in doubt *and* stressed, eat chocolate. *Especially* when that doubt and stress were related to a man and her feelings for said man.

"Did you at least dream about all the things you would do to him?" Grace asked. "Cuz that's what I'd have done."

Hell, yes, Amy had dreamed about all the things she'd like to do to Matt. Repeatedly. Not the point. "Yesterday he found a homeless teen up where we camped and brought her here to the diner. We fed her and then took her to my place so she could have a bed and a hot shower."

"We?" Mallory asked. "You took Matt home with you as well?"

"He showed up on his own. I found him outside my house keeping watch." She shook her head. "Not sure what that was about, to be honest."

"I bet he wanted to make sure you were okay," Mallory said.

Amy laughed, and Mallory and Grace exchanged a telling glance. "I'm *always* okay," Amy said. "Probably he didn't trust me not to screw it up."

"Honey." Mallory covered Amy's hand with her own. "Why wouldn't Matt trust you?"

Because no one ever had. But that was before, she reminded herself, before she'd worked so hard at growing up and separating herself from the past. She needed to remember that.

Mallory squeezed her hand. "Can I ask you something?"

"No, you can't have another brownie. They're all mine now."

Mallory smiled but shook her head. "Why would you give Riley a chance and not Matt?"

"What are you talking about? Matt's never wanted a chance with me."

"Oh, please." Mallory gave her a get-real look. "The guy comes into the diner only when you're working. He sits at *your* table, and he watches you the same way that Ty watches me."

"Yeah, and how's that?" Amy asked.

"Like you're lunch."

Amy squirmed a little bit because deep down she knew it was true. She'd caught him at it. It never failed to evoke a multitude of emotions, not the least of which was an undeniable lust in return, but also something deeper and far more complicated than sheer desire.

And that's what made it so uncomfortable. That's what scared her.

"So I'll ask you again," Mallory said quietly. "Why not give him a shot?"

It was a question for which Amy didn't have the answer.

Chapter 9

A balanced diet is a chocolate in each hand.

Matt knew he had a reputation for being laid-back and easygoing. He wasn't sure that either of those things was exactly true, but part of the appearance came from being prepared for anything at any time.

This ability had been honed in the military and then on the streets of Chicago. If a guy could survive warfare and SWAT, he could survive anything. Certainly one willowy, enigmatic, tough-nut-to-crack brunette named Amy Michaels.

He wanted to see her again. He'd resisted for two days now, but then he caught sight of her at the front counter of the ranger station. His office was down a hallway so she hadn't seen him, but he'd seen her just fine. After she left, his junior ranger manning the desk had said she'd asked for a map to Four Lakes.

Matt had known she'd gone back up to Sierra Meadows the other day. He'd seen her there, amongst the diamond rocks, sketching. It'd taken all he'd had to leave her to the privacy she'd obviously wanted.

But why was she suddenly out on the mountain on her days off, hiking alone? He didn't know, but he wanted to, so he made it a point to patrol today instead of trying to conquer the mountain of paperwork in his office. Just as well since he'd been taking a ribbing all morning for a certain Facebook post that had gone up the other day, something about how he'd added two new duties to his job description: rescuing maidens and playing doctor.

His staff had loved that. So had Josh and Ty, both of whom had called him with the news like two little girls, the fuckers. Matt could only imagine what Amy thought of it.

He found her just where he thought he would, up at Four Lakes. What he hadn't expected was that she'd be about fifteen feet up a huge five-hundred-year-old spruce at the base of the first of the four lakes, which were connected by little tributaries.

Amy was holding a sketch pad and was talking either to herself or to the tree.

"If you fall," she was saying, "you know who's going to come get you, right? And just your luck, you'll break your fat ass this time..."

"Your ass isn't fat," Matt said, staring up at the long, toned leg hanging down. "It's perfect. And what the hell are you doing up there?"

She went still, then leaned over a branch and peered down at him. "I'm not lost."

"Good. But that doesn't answer my question."

This was met by silence and a rainfall of pine needles as she began to climb down. Her backpack dropped to the ground and then the sketch pad. Then those long legs came within reach, so Matt grabbed her around the waist and pulled her out of the tree. "Hey there, Tough Girl."

"Hey." Her warm body slid down every inch of his, and there was a moment just before her feet touched the ground where he'd have sworn she even nestled into him.

Or maybe that was his imagination, because then she stepped free. She was wearing jeans shorts, emphasis on short, and a V-neck tee that was loose enough to be hanging off one shoulder, revealing a bright blue bra strap. She had a scratch on her jaw and a smudge of dirt across her forehead. "The tree's taller than I thought," she said.

"What were you looking for?"

"Nothing important."

Nothing important, his ass. She wasn't the type of woman to climb a tree just for the hell of it. But if he knew anything about her, it was that he couldn't push for answers. He needed a diversion for now, then he'd work his way back to the subject at hand. "How's Riley?" He'd heard back from Sawyer that the teen wasn't a missing person, or even a person of interest, so there'd been no legal reason to interfere in her life again. But he wanted to know that she was okay.

"I haven't seen her after the sleepover," Amy said. "I know you were worried about her, and also about me taking care of her, but she's gone. I'm sorry."

Unable to stop himself, Matt stroked a strand of hair out of her pretty eyes. "I was never worried about you taking care of her."

"Maybe you should have been."

"Why?" he asked, confused.

"Well, it's not like you know me, not really. I could be a horrible person, who's done horrible things."

"I know enough," he said firmly.

"But—"

He put a finger on her lips. She stared at him for a long beat, as if taking measure of his honesty. Or maybe she was deciding on a way to kick his ass for shushing her. Then her gaze dropped to his mouth, and he hoped she was remembering how good it felt on hers.

Because that's what he was remembering. Ducking a little, he cupped her jaw and eyed her newest injury—the scratch. It could use some antiseptic. He ran his other hand down her arm to her wrapped wrist. "How is this doing?"

"Better."

He shifted his hand to her leg, his fingers brushing bare skin thanks to the shorts, before landing on the bandage there. "And your thigh?"

She didn't answer as quickly, and when she did, her breathing wasn't as even as before. "Better."

"And your..." His hand slid around now and cupped her very sweet ass.

She choked out some reply and gave him a shove to the chest that made him grin. Turning, he scooped up her sketch pad for her. Before he could open it, she snatched it from him and shoved it into her backpack. "Thanks," she said.

He watched her fiddle with her stuff a moment. She was clearly waiting him out, assuming he'd move on.

She was wrong. "So are you going to tell me what you're doing out here?" he asked. "Or maybe you were hoping to find *me*."

She laughed. "Nice ego. But no. Not hoping to find you."

"Ouch."

"Yeah, I'm sure you're crushed." She zipped her backpack. "My grandma came here one summer, a long time ago. She used to tell me stories about the places she hiked to and the things she'd seen."

"It's a pretty unforgettable place," he said.

"Her stories were my fairy tales growing up. Her trip out here was important to her. It changed her life."

"Are you looking to change your life?" he asked quietly.

She shrugged. "Maybe. A little."

"Why now?" he asked.

"What do you mean?"

"Your grandma died when you were twelve, right?"

"Yes," she said, looking surprised that he remembered. "And then I went to live with my mom and her new husband. Until I was sixteen."

He waited but she didn't go on. "What happened when you were sixteen?"

Some of the light went out of her eyes, but then she turned her head from him pretty quickly. She looked out at the water.

Okay, so this wasn't up for discussion. He stood at her side and looked out at the first lake as well. There were wet prints on the rocky shore. She'd gone swimming. He'd have liked to see that. "So... where did you go at sixteen? Is that when you traveled around?"

"Yes."

"What did you do with yourself?"

"I grew up," she said flatly. "That took a while. And then, finally, I ended up out here in Lucky Harbor."

"To recreate your grandma's journey. To change your life."

"Yes." She paused, clearly weighing her words. "She wrote in her journal that out here she found... things."

"Things."

"Hope. Peace." She paused, grimacing as if she was embarrassed. "Her own heart. Whatever that means."

"In a tree?"

She gave a little laugh and told him about the initials at Sierra Meadows, about Jonathon, his illness, and how Rose had found hope there at the base of the diamond rocks.

"And what about you?" he asked. "Did *you* find hope?

She looked into his eyes, and the air seemed to crackle between them. "I found something," she said softly. She held his gaze for another beat and then turned back to the water. There was a light breeze now, rippling the surface of the lake, raising whitecaps.

"What did Rose find here at Four Lakes? Peace?"

"Apparently. Her initials are on the tree trunk, up about twenty feet. I think she saw Jonathon swimming and feeling stronger, and she realized that they could fight the illness. And before you ask, I don't know where she found her heart. The journal entries aren't as clear when it comes to the last leg of her trek, something about going around in a circle." She was quiet a moment. "Out here, it's unlike anything I've ever seen. No buildings, no people. People always say the city is a scary place, but to me, this is scary. It's big."

He nodded. He knew exactly what she meant. In the city, there was always something right in front of you. A car, a building, people. Out here there was nothing but space, wide open space. "It's just different from what you're used to."

"Very," she agreed on a low, throaty laugh. "And it takes my breath the way the mountains cut into the cliffs and valleys. Everything's so tough and rugged."

"Like the people who roam here." He got a smile out of her for that one. He wanted to ask her more about her past but knew she wasn't ready to tell him. And he didn't need to know, he reminded himself. This wasn't a relationship.

She picked up a smooth, round rock and tried to skim it across the water, but it plopped instead. "When you saw me on the trail that first time," she said, "I was having trouble locating Sierra Meadows and the wall of rocks there."

He picked up a rock, flatter than the one she'd used. "You could have told me." He skimmed the rock across the surface of the lake six times.

"Show-off," she said. "And I didn't want help. But then I fell down that ravine and found the meadows by accident. Four Lakes was *much* easier to find. The tree though..." She sent it a look. "Not so much."

He eyed the entire stand of trees around them, at least ten. "How many did you have to climb before you found the right one?"

She rubbed at the scratch on her jaw. "Five. Not bad odds for a city rat."

"Did you find peace?"

"No. I found sap, and the will to never climb another tree again."

He smiled. "I bet."

"But I enjoyed the day," she said with some surprise. "It made me want to have more days like this one."

He met her gaze. "Maybe *that's* peace."

"I don't know." Her expression was more open than he'd ever seen it, and he felt a surge of something swell in his chest.

Not good.

Not good at all.

She rubbed at her scratch again, and he brushed her hand away, then bent and kissed her jaw just above it.

She sucked in a breath and went still. Then she turned her head so that their mouths were lined up, a fraction of an inch apart. "What are you doing?"

"Kissing your owie and making it better. Consider it just another of the services I provide."

"Maybe I should see a list of these services," she said.

"For you, anything goes."

Her smile faded, and her eyes went very serious, though she didn't step back from him. Her warm breath commingled with his. It was an incredibly erotic feeling, alone on a mountaintop, surrounded by hundreds of thousands of acres of wild land, standing toe to toe.

Mouth to mouth.

Sharing air.

"Matt?"

"Yeah?"

A sigh escaped her lips. "I really want to sleep with you, but..."

"Damn," he said. "That was a great sentence right up to the 'but.' "

"But," she repeated firmly, then hesitated and blew out a breath, "I have...qualms."

"Tell me."

"Okay. The thing is, I think the sex would be good—"

"Good? Try off the charts."

She acknowledged that with a nod. "Yeah, probably."

Definitely.

"But..."

He sighed. The "but" again.

"*But*," she repeated, "if you want anything more than that, I'm not interested."

Wait—What? Had he heard her correctly, or just projected the words he'd want to hear?

She was waiting for a reaction, and it was just so unbelievable, and unbelievably perfect, that he laughed out loud.

Chapter 10

Flowers and champagne might set the stage, but it's chocolate that steals the show.

Amy stared at Matt as he started laughing and felt her eyes narrow. "I'm sorry, but how exactly is the idea of us having sex funny?"

He laughed some more, looking quite gone with amusement, and it pissed her off. He made a clear effort to control himself, but it was too late. She was over it, and over him. And embarrassed to boot. "You think because I'm a woman I'd automatically want more than just sex? Well guess what Ranger *Hot Buns*—" She took a beat to enjoy his wince. "Women want just-sex as much as any guy." *Some more than others. Some had suppressed their urges for far too long and were fire rockets just waiting to go off.* "So welcome to the twenty-first century," she said. "Where women *like* just-sex."

For some reason, this set him off again, and she pushed him. He didn't budge, though, so she pushed him again, or at least she meant to. But her brain scrambled the signal, and her hands fisted in his shirt. "I ought to shut you up."

This got his attention. "Yeah," he said, hands sliding to her hips, "shut me up."

"Fine." She shut him up with one hell of a kiss. By the time it ended, she was plastered up against his hard body, her own humming. The force of his personality came through every touch of his rough, callused hands, exuding heat and the promise of unbelievable ecstasy. "Not laughing now, are you?" she said.

"Hell, no." He came at *her* this time, and she found herself melting into him like suddenly there was no invisible line in the sand between them, nothing but this incredible pleasure, pleasure she couldn't remember ever getting out of a simple kiss before.

Problem was, nothing about Matt was simple. Not for her. His arms held her close, and the scent of clean, warm male was making her heart pound. Her head was overrun with wicked thoughts involving her tongue and every inch of his body. Unable to help herself, she nipped at his throat.

"Amy." His voice was thrillingly quiet and gruff as he ran his lips along her jaw. "Don't promise what you don't want to deliver."

Turning her head, she cupped his face and pulled it closer. He let out a sound and sucked hungrily on her bottom lip. And while his mouth and tongue were very busy, so were his hands, gripping her hips.

"I rarely make promises," she told him. "But when I do, I deliver." She nibbled at his ear next, then, when he groaned, did it again.

A phone vibrated, Matt's, but he ignored it. Whoever it was called back again immediately. Swearing quite creatively, Matt yanked the phone off his service belt. "Busy," he said and shoved it into his pocket.

"When do you get off?" Amy asked.

"If we're not careful, in less than ten seconds."

She looked down at the hard-on threatening the zipper of his uniform trousers. "I meant off work."

He once again pulled his cell phone and looked at the time. "Twenty minutes."

She bit her lip and looked around them. There was the lake and a lovely area of wild grass, but it might be full of the creepy crawlies he'd mentioned the other night.

Reading her mind, he smiled but shook his head. "Not here. Not the first time."

"There's only going to be one time." That was all she needed to take the edge off. The fact was, it'd been so long. Too long. She hadn't realized how much she missed the feel of a man's body against hers, how much she needed an orgasm that wasn't a self-serve. And she wanted that without the pomp and circumstance, without planning, without anticipation. She wanted it now, wanted the sweet oblivion, the little bang, and then she'd go back to her day. "You've never done it in the great outdoors?"

"That's not where *we're* doing it," he said firmly.

"Hmm." She ran her finger down his chest, hoping to infuse some of her urgency into him.

He caught her wandering hand in his. "*Hmm* what?"

"Didn't peg you for a prude."

His eyes narrowed dangerously at the implied insult to his manhood, and he tightened his grip on her. "You're going to take that back in a little bit."

She had no idea what it said about her that this ridiculous display of alpha-ness brought her a delicious shiver of anticipation. "Yeah?"

"Oh, yeah. Where's your car?"

"At the trailhead," she said. "Your truck?"

"On a fire road, a quarter of a mile from here."

Not too far...

He read her expression, and his own went dark, further quickening her pulse. "I live close." His hand slid into her hair, tipping her head up to his. "If we leave now, I'll be off the clock by the time we get to my cabin."

"Yes," she breathed. His gaze tracked to her mouth, which he gave one quick, hard kiss before leading her to his truck.

The drive took them up old Highway 20, then down a narrow, curvy road. Amy caught sight of the occasional cabin, but not much else. When the road ended, Matt kept going, on a dirt road now, which opened up to a small clearing, and then his house.

"Two minutes left," she said, staring at the rugged cabin in front of her. It was way off the beaten path, which suited him. So did the inside. The ceilings were open beamed, the floors scarred hardwood. Everything was wood accented, including the big, comfy looking furniture and the frames of the pictures on the walls of the Northwest Pacific landscape.

Amy felt a little ping deep in her chest. Not of jealousy, but envy. Matt had found his place in this crazy world. He knew who he was and what he wanted. And he'd gotten it for himself.

Someday soon, she promised herself. She was working on doing the same.

"Want a drink?" he asked. "Something to eat?"

The tension between them was so palpable she could taste it. "No." She was here for one thing, and it was nourishment of a different nature altogether. With any luck, they'd do this and get each other out of their system. Then maybe she could go back to concentrating on why she was in Lucky Harbor—following Grandma Rose's journey. She dropped her backpack to the floor.

He tossed his keys to the coffee table.

"No getting attached to me," she said, hands on hips. "Cuz I'm not going to get attached to you."

He gave her a smile. "Can you resist?"

"Yes," she said firmly. It was her specialty. She shrugged out of her shirt and let it fall on top of her backpack.

His eyes heated.

She bent to undo her boots, but he said, "I have fantasies about those boots," so she left them on.

His gaze drifted warmly over her, heating her in the places yearning for his hands and his mouth.

"You're lagging behind," she said.

He unholstered his gun and set it on the coffee table. Next to that went his utility belt. He kicked off his boots. Then before he got to anything good, he stepped toward her.

"More," she said.

"Oh, there's going to be a lot more." His voice was husky with the promise of it. "But I want you in my bed." He took her hand and tugged her into him. Then he slid his other hand up her back and into her hair, holding her for his kiss. It was slow and romantic. And not what she wanted. So she broke away and went for the button on his uniform cargo pants. She'd long ago learned that to get what she wanted from a man, all she had to do was get him naked.

Luckily this time what she wanted and what this man wanted were perfectly in sync. She got his button popped, his zipper down, and slid her hand inside, wrapping it around his glorious, hard length.

He made a sound that was pure male hunger before stopping her. "Bedroom," he said again firmly, and gave her a nudge to the hall.

She nudged back and pushed him up against the wall, just to the side of his fireplace. He'd asked if she wanted something to eat, and she did. "Dessert first," she said. "Always."

His mouth curved. She was amusing him. Turning him on, too, the proof was hard against her belly. Her body responded to that, and she kissed him, long and deep as she unbuttoned his shirt. God, his torso. Hard. Ripped. She wanted to lick him, and started in the dip at the hollow of his throat.

His groan reverberated in his chest, and in response, the blood pounded through her body. His hands were on her, everywhere. One glided down her back to her bottom, the other cupped a breast, his thumb teasing back and forth over her nipple. He murmured her name as his body shifted, and she knew he was about to take the control from her. So she dropped to her knees on the fireplace rug and took it first, slipping her hands back inside his open pants, freeing him so that she could run her tongue up his hot, silky erection.

With an inarticulate growl, his head thunked back against the wall and again his hands slid into her hair. She could feel the fine tremor in his legs, and that turned her on. He was the epitome of a strong and dominant male, and she had him weak at the knees at one touch of her tongue, so she gave him another. And another…

"Jesus," he gasped. "Jesus, Amy. We've got to slow down."

She didn't, and he lasted only a few minutes more before swearing roughly and creatively, his fingers tightening reflexively in her hair. "Keep that up, and I'm going to come."

She wanted him to. Making him lose control was really working for her, and when they were done with this, she was going to take him apart in a different way.

"Christ. Amy—"

She kept going, taking him through what sounded like a very happy ending. She was still enjoying the little aftershocks running through his big, powerful body when he dropped to his knees and pulled her into his lap. He unhooked her bra and bent her back over his arm, sucking a nipple into his mouth, hard.

With a gasp of pleasure, she gripped his head. Not to pull him away but to keep him there. God yes, right there. A minute later, she realized he'd somehow peeled her out of her shorts and panties as well. In only her boots, he adjusted her so that she was straddling him right there on the floor. His hand traveled down her torso, between her open thighs, his long fingers playing slip and slide.

Pleasure swamped her, making her cry out. She never cried out. Shocked at the hurry-up noises she was making, she bit his shoulder to shut herself up.

Matt hissed in a breath but kept stroking her with those talented fingers, in and out, in a rhythm that became her center of gravity.

He commandeered her mouth as well, kissing her hard and deep, reducing her to a gasping, panting, pleading mass until, unbelievably, he sent her flying. She came back to herself to find him still idly stroking her core, his mouth soft and gentle. "Round one," he said silkily, "is a tie." Then he laid her out on the rug, holding her still when she wriggled, trying to get on top.

She was always on top.

But he shook his head, a smile curving his mouth, a very wicked smile. Lowering his head, he kissed his way down her body, stopping to pay special homage to each breast, and then her stomach, playfully tugging her crystal belly button piercing with his teeth before moving lower.

"Matt. Matt, wait—"

He didn't listen to her any more than she'd listened to him a few minutes ago. With his broad shoulders holding her legs wedged open, he took all her power away with one perfectly placed stroke of his tongue. Reduced to a whimper, she slapped her hands down on the rug on either side of her hips as he sucked and nibbled and drove her straight out of her ever-loving mind.

It was a shockingly short drive, and this time she came back to herself, boggled. Normally she had to concentrate to climax at all, and yet he'd given her a twofer, so effortlessly she hadn't even known what hit her. She didn't know whether to thank him or be embarrassed. "Well." She rose up on her elbows and eyed the room for her clothes, which were scattered. Except for her boots. Those she was still wearing. "I'm going to need a ride."

He rose up, too, still between her legs. His smile deepened, turning positively wicked. And unbelievably, she felt her body react.

Again.

"Yes," he said. "I believe I can give you a ride." Stripping out of his remaining clothes with a few economical motions, he then turned his attention to her boots, pulling them off for her. When they were both bare-ass naked, he scooped her up and kissed her, his tongue sweeping and sucking and stroking in demand.

And damn. Damn, she couldn't hold back her breathless moan, because good Lord the man knew how to use his mouth, stirring up emotions during an act that should have been only a physical release, and he did it effortlessly. She tried to pull back to think about that, but he had a good hold on her, and next thing she knew, they were on the move to his bedroom.

He set her down on a huge bed, then before she could scramble away, he stretched his body over hers.

And let's face it, scrambling away would have been tricky without any bones left in her body.

He produced a condom, and in the next instant, thrust inside her, and oh, God, the pleasure, the panic... Because she knew. She knew it even as she cried out and clutched him closer to her that she was in the worst sort of trouble now.

Because this wasn't just a physical release at all.

Not even close.

"Look at me," he said.

With effort, her eyes fluttered open, and she focused in on his face, transfixed by the expression of pure ecstasy etched on his features. She had no idea what it was with her, whether it was the eroticism of what they'd already done to each other, or that she could still taste him on her tongue, or maybe it was just the incredible feel of him so hard, so deep within her, but she wanted him with a desperate need she hadn't even known she could feel. Bringing her legs up, she wrapped them around his waist, whimpering when he slowly withdrew only to push back inside her.

"Good?" he asked.

She didn't answer. *Couldn't*, she was drowning in the sensations. He ran his hands down her arms until their fingers were entwined, then drew them up above her head, securing them there.

That brought her out of herself a little. She arched into him, trying to tug free but he held her down as he nudged his hips, giving her a slow, glorious thrust. Another cry was torn from her lips, and she couldn't quite understand what was happening. He was claiming her completely—heart, body, and soul in the most primal, raw way she'd ever allowed. And as he did, his eyes held hers prisoner in the same way he held her body, watching as her body writhed under his ministrations.

Branding her as his.

It was too much, and she tugged hard. "No."

He immediately let her hands loose, a frown of concern forming, but before he could say a word she rolled him, knocking him flat to his back. Holding *him* down now, she mirrored his actions, running her hands up his arms until their fingers were linked over *his* head.

Ha.

His hooded eyes searched hers for a long beat before he gave her a sexy smile. "Better?"

"Much," she said, and the next sound out of either of them was two shuddering breaths of pleasure as she lifted up before sinking back down on him.

Matt's groan was rough and heartfelt, and he let her do as she wanted, as she needed, which was to ride him hard and fast, every thrust sending electric heat sparking and crackling along each nerve in her body. And in the end, when they'd both shattered and she'd sagged boneless to his chest, when he'd gathered her in and pressed a sweet, tender kiss to her damp temple, she realized the truth.

When it came to Matt Bowers, she had no control at all.

An hour later, Matt stood in the dusty staging area at the trailhead, watching Amy drive off. He'd taken her to her car as she'd asked, and she'd left him so quickly his head was still spinning.

Seemed what they'd shared had gotten a little too close for comfort back there in his cabin, and apparently, Amy wasn't all that fond of that.

Well she could join his damn club. He'd come here to Lucky Harbor to get away from everyone, *not* to get too close for comfort ever again.

Something else he'd failed at.

"Remember," she'd said back in his bed, bare-ass naked, tousled, and gorgeous. "That was just sex."

He'd nearly asked if she'd been reminding him—or her. But she'd had an emphatic look on her face, making it clear that *she* was in no danger of wanting more.

The drive to her car had been made in silence. Hard to tell if it'd been good or bad silence since his woman-radar had been broken ever since Shelly had packed her shit and walked right out of his life.

Actually, she'd run.

He shook his head but it was no good. His brain was still scrambled. Amy had scrambled it good with the best blow job he'd ever had. Then she'd ridden him like a bronco, detonating any brain capacity he might have managed to retain. She'd taken him her way, all the way, clearly not liking being vulnerable, just as clearly needing to be in charge.

Which had been new and…interesting.

It sure as hell would be hard to argue that he hadn't had a great time. It'd been the kind of sex that every guy dreamed about, down and dirty, mindless.

No strings attached.

And isn't that exactly what he'd wanted from her?

Chapter 11

So much chocolate, so little time.

The next day, Amy worked at the diner. It was a slow, uneventful shift, made even slower due to a daylong downpour. The pier was empty as the rain beat down on the entire Washington coast, and the diner remained empty, too. This left Amy with way too much time to think.

Not a good thing when she kept flashing to the memory of Matt in bed moving over her, his voice a sexy, erotic whisper in her ear, their bodies slick with sweat, their limbs entangled. Every time she replayed it, she felt a tingle in spots that had no business tingling while she was serving customers.

It'd been so long since she'd been with someone. That's what she told herself. Years long, in fact, since an ugly night in Miami years ago now, when she'd landed in yet another rough situation that she almost hadn't gotten out of. Just another case of a guy wanting more than she wanted to give. She'd forgone sex completely after that.

But it had been different with Matt, so different than anything she'd ever shared before. Sex with him had meant intimacy, and she hadn't been prepared.

Not even close.

To take her mind off Matt, she used her break to hole herself up in the tiny back office of the diner and pull out her cell phone. She wanted to plan the last leg of her grandma's journey, but she was at a bit of a loss.

Call me again sometime, and you can ask me another question. I'll answer a question with each call. How's that sound?

Her mom's words were echoing in her head. They'd had such a tempestuous relationship, always, from the day Amy had gone to live with her at age twelve, to the day Amy had walked away at age sixteen. But hindsight was twenty-twenty, and Amy could admit that she wasn't blameless, that she'd had a big hand in how things went down. Facts were facts, and Amy had been a liar. A petty thief. A girl who'd wielded her burgeoning sexuality like a magic wand.

A nightmare.

And she'd walked away without looking back, without even considering how her mom might feel. Not caring…

Amy let out a shaky breath and hit her mom's number. The phone was answered quickly, with a breathless, "Amy?"

"Yeah, Mom. It's me."

There was a silence, and Amy grimaced, feeling unwanted and stupid. And God how she really *hated* feeling stupid. She shouldn't have done this; she shouldn't have—

"I'm glad you called."

Amy sucked in another breath. "You are?"

"You surprised me last time. I didn't get a chance to ask you if you're okay."

Amy's chest physically hurt. She didn't do this, this emotional stuff. And yet it seemed like lately that was all she was doing. "I'm okay. You?"

"Good. I'm…single again. I just wanted you to know that."

Probably the closest thing to an apology she was going to get.

"You still in Lucky Harbor?" her mom asked. "Do you have a place? An address?"

"Yeah." Amy cleared her throat and gave her the apartment address. "You said I could ask you a question."

"Yes."

Amy drew a deep breath. "Do you know where Grandma Rose ended her journey exactly?"

"I'm sorry," her mom said with real regret. "I don't. All she ever told me was that in the end, she went full circle."

Full circle. Same thing the journal had said. Disappointment clogged Amy's throat, thick and unswallowable. "Oh. Okay, well, thanks. I've got to get back to work."

"Will you call again?"

Amy closed her eyes. It'd been a long time since she'd ached for someone's approval. A damn long time. Since her Grandma Rose's death probably. Amy had told herself a million times that she'd outgrown needing acceptance. Would she call again? Honestly, in that moment, she had no idea. "I have your number," she said carefully.

"Okay."

"And Mom?"

"Yes?"

"You have my number now, too."

At the end of her shift, Amy gathered the trash and left out the back door. She dropped it in the Dumpster on her way to her car and nearly tripped over Riley in the alley. "Hey," Amy said, surprised. "What are you doing?"

But the answer was clear. It'd been pouring steadily, relentlessly, all afternoon, and Riley had been rained out of wherever she'd been staying in the woods. She was wet through and through, huddled up against the wall on the stoop. "You okay?" Amy asked.

Looking miserable, Riley nodded.

"Come on, I'll give you a ride."

Riley didn't ask where, or even bother to argue, which told Amy exactly how wet and cold the teen was. Once they were inside Amy's piece-of-shit car, Riley sidled up against the heating vents, rubbing her arms over the long-sleeved tee that Amy had given her. "You know, if you'd stayed at my place, you'd be warm and dry right now."

"Didn't know how long I could stay."

Amy's heart squeezed. "How about until something better comes along?"

Riley was huddled into herself, shivering, and didn't answer. Amy understood that, too. When Amy had been that age, nothing better *ever* came along. Amy pulled out of the diner parking lot and drove home. They climbed the stairs in silence, and inside she nudged Riley toward the bathroom for a hot shower. By the time the water turned off, Amy had pulled out another spare outfit from her own meager stash for Riley.

They ate grilled cheese sandwiches at the small kitchen table—Amy's go-to comfort food. Riley inhaled every last crumb. "Thanks," she said when they were done. She was looking a whole lot less like a drowned rat now. Her hair was drying in soft, natural curls, and with her face clean, Amy realized just how pretty she was. "Got a call about you the other day," she said. "A hang-up, actually." She told Riley about the phantom phone call she'd received at the diner.

Riley didn't say a word but went pale.

Amy frowned at her. "What is it? You know who called?"

Riley shrugged.

"You want to talk about it?"

"No."

Well there was a surprise. "You know you don't have to live like this, on the run, right?" Amy asked. "You could get some help, make some roots. Stick around."

"I don't have any money."

"So get a job."

"I'm not good at anything."

"Well, that's not true. For instance," Amy said, "you're a great conversationalist. And such a sweet, sunny, friendly nature, too."

Riley had the good grace to grimace at the gentle teasing.

"Look," Amy said, "you could bus tables at the diner. You won't get rich or anything, but you could support yourself. There's a lot of freedom in that, Riley."

Riley remained quiet while staring at her empty plate.

"And as a bonus, you could eliminate the sitting in the rain bit entirely, fun as that probably was. And with all your spare time, you could get good at whatever you want to be good at. You could go to school, or whatever you want."

Riley looked at her. "What are you good at?"

"Drawing."

"I suck at drawing."

"So you'll find something you don't suck at," Amy said. "Something for you. It's all about choices and decisions."

"I usually choose to make really bad decisions."

Amy laughed softly in sympathy. "I hear you. I happened to major in bad decisions myself. But I'm working on it. Part of that comes from stopping the cycle, getting some good sleep and decent food in your system so you're not reacting off the cuff. Stay here tonight."

Riley shrugged.

"Yes or no."

Riley looked out the window, where the rain was still pouring down. She sighed. "Yes."

"Now see? There's a good decision."

The next day, Matt was hanging off the North Rim, forty feet above ground, holding on to the granite with only his fingers and toes.

Josh was at his right and a foot or so below him.

It was a race to the top, with the loser buying dinner. Josh had bought the past four meals in a row, which he'd bitched about like a little girl, claiming that the finishes had been far too close to call.

Bullshit. Matt had won fair and square, though granted he'd only done so by an inch or two. But a win was a win.

"Move your ladylike fingers," Josh groused when Matt reached out far to his right for a good fingerhold. "You're in my way."

Matt didn't move. The sun was beating down on his back, and he felt sweat drip down the side of his jaw. "Hey, Josh?"

"Yeah?"

"Which ladylike finger am I holding up now?"

Josh took in Matt's flipping him the bird and *tsk*ed. "Rude."

"You want rude? I'm having everything on the menu at Eat Me tonight, on *your* dime."

"Fuck you," Josh said. "I'm not buying you everything on the menu."

"Is that what you say to the ladies?"

"The *ladies*," Josh said with a grunt as he pulled himself up another few feet, "can have anything they want."

Matt eyeballed the ledge above him and tried to figure out the best way to get there. "Fine. If you don't want to buy dinner, you're going to have to beat me to the top."

Apparently getting a second wind at the thought, Josh pulled himself up another few feet. This put him in the lead. Matt wasn't too worried. There were still a few feet to go, and Josh was breathing hard. "You're sucking some serious wind, Doc. You need to get in the ring before you go soft like... like a doctor."

Josh snorted. There wasn't an ounce of fat on his large six-foot-four-inch frame, and they both knew it. People teased him that he was like a bull in a china shop, but the truth was, Dr. Josh Scott was so highly regarded as a doctor that he had to turn patients away.

And for all his big talk, Josh turned away the women, too.

"When's the last time you even got any?" Matt asked.

Josh slid him a look behind his dark sunglasses. "You want to swap stories?"

"Do you even have a story to swap?"

Josh let out what might have been a sigh. "Been busy."

"No one should be that busy, man."

"My practice is swamped. And Anna's been acting up. And Toby…he needs me at home."

Josh had sole custody of his five-year-old son, Toby. He'd also taken in his younger sister after their parents died six years ago. Anna was twenty-one now and hell on wheels, literally, having ended up in a wheelchair from the same car accident that had killed their parents. She'd spent her teen years dedicated to making Josh insane, and she'd nearly succeeded, too. It'd be a lot for any guy to handle, but with Josh's job, it'd been nearly impossible.

"So you and Amy finally did it, huh?" Josh said.

Matt nearly fell off the face of the mountain. "Who told you that?" he demanded, once he'd recovered his hold and had secured himself so that his own death wasn't imminent.

Josh dipped his head to eye Matt over the top of his sunglasses, mouth curving. "You. Just now."

"Shit." He had nothing else to say. Mostly because he didn't *know* what else to say. What'd happened between him and Amy had been…hot as hell. But it was also still bugging him, how much she'd hidden behind the act itself. How much she hid in general.

Pot, kettle. He knew this. He hated this. He'd called her earlier to check on her, just to see if she was okay. According to her, she'd been fine. She'd also steered clear of a real conversation, other than to tell him that Riley was back and staying with her.

"So you and Amy, huh? Funny."

"How's that funny?"

Josh shrugged. "She always acts like she hates you."

"Turns out there's a fine line between hate and lust," Matt muttered.

Josh slid him another look. "You've wanted her forever. You should be grinning like an idiot. It wasn't good?"

He'd done his share of grinning like an idiot. And it'd been good. Hell, if it'd been any better, they'd have gone up in flames. But—

"*Yes!*" Josh yelled in triumph, because while Matt had been thinking too much, Josh had used his gorilla arms to reach the ledge. With a whoop, Josh collapsed on the plateau like a limp noodle, lying there gasping. "I *finally* beat you."

Matt rolled over the ledge. "Fluke. Just a one-time fluke."

Josh came up on an elbow, sweaty and dirty and grinning. "*Everything* on the menu. I want everything on the menu."

"Fuck." Matt stared up at the sky, also gasping for breath. "Fine. But I'm not putting out afterward."

Amy would have liked to be studying a map and planning her next leg of Grandma Rose's journey. But nope. She was working. She was *always* working, it seemed.

And as a bonus, it was raining again. Or still. But Jan had put out a buy-one-entree-get-one-free Facebook post, and now, for the dinner rush, Eat Me was packed. The crowd was rowdy, but Amy had learned she could serve and daydream at the same time.

The call to her mom hadn't yielded much help, and Amy still had no idea what the third and last leg of Rose's trip had been. All she knew was that Rose had found her heart. Giving up a bathroom break, Amy pulled her grandma's journal from her purse, and in a back corner of the kitchen, flipped through it.

> *It's been three weeks since we'd last been on the mountain. A long three weeks during which I refused to give up my newfound hope and peace.*
>
> *Good thing, too, because I needed both of those things to get all the way around and back.*

But I managed.

And it was worth it. Looking out at a blanket of green, a sea of blue, and a world of possibilities, the whole world opened up. There on top of the world, I promised myself that no matter what happened, I would never settle. I would never stop growing. I would never give up.

And as the sun sank down over the horizon, I was suddenly at the beginning again.

Hope.

Peace.

And something new as well, something that had truly brought us full circle—heart.

All the way around and back…Not much in the way of directions, Amy thought. But she was beginning to wonder if maybe her grandma might have meant that they'd taken the Rim Trail all the way around from the north rim to the south rim. It was a good possibility, or at least the best one she had.

"Amy!" Jan yelled. "Another call for you!"

Amy put the journal away. This time when she picked up the kitchen phone and said "hello," there was a pause but not a hang-up. "*Hello?*" she repeated.

The voice was raspy and male. "Tell Riley that she can run, but she can't hide."

Adrenaline kicked in. "Who is this?"

Nothing.

"*Hello?*" Amy said. "Don't hang up—"

Click.

And then a dial tone.

Dammit. Amy served the food waiting for her and waved at Jan. "Taking five."

"The hell you are."

"Okay, two then." Without waiting for approval that she wasn't going to get, Amy grabbed the new backpack that she'd bought at the hardware store half a block down the street, then stepped out the back door on a hunch.

The hunch paid off.

Riley was sitting on the stoop, under the protection of the overhang, watching the rain come down. Amy sat next to her and set the backpack in the teen's lap.

"What's this?" Riley asked.

"Yours is all ripped up."

Riley ran her fingers over the tags still attached to the pack. "So you bought me a new one?"

"Yeah."

Riley started to shake her head and push the backpack away, but Amy put her hand on it, holding it in Riley's lap. "It was on sale, and Anderson—the shop owner—gave me a big discount, so it's no big deal. I want you to have it."

Riley stared down at the backpack and then unzipped it. Inside were the incidentals Amy had put in there: flashlight, water bottle, beef jerky…

Riley swallowed hard and said nothing.

Amy looked at her for a long moment, not sure how to proceed. When she'd been in Riley's situation, showing emotion had been the same as showing weakness, and there'd been no room for weakness and vulnerability in her life. None. Even if a person had meant well, Amy hadn't been able to let her guard down to show any vulnerability.

Riley couldn't either.

Amy got that, but damn, it was hard to watch, wanting so badly to reach out and help, knowing that Riley wouldn't easily let herself be helped. "There's a set of spare batteries in the inside pocket. Being unprepared sucks beans, and trust me, I know it all too well."

"You didn't have to do this."

"I know." Amy looked at her. "And you could have come inside. I've been hoping you'd show up. I've got a fully loaded club sandwich, fries, and a big fat glass of soda with your name on it."

Riley stared at her, clearly at war between her pride and her need for sustenance. "How did you know I'd be out here?"

"Guessed." Amy didn't have the heart to tell Riley that kids like her were creatures of hard-learned habits. Along with Amy's apartment, Riley had been fed here and taken care of here at the diner. Sheer need would drive her back to the same few places over and over until that changed. "Come on." Amy stood and gestured with a jerk of her chin to the back door. "I've got to get back in there before Jan blows a gasket. Believe me, no one wants to see that."

Amy sat Riley at the front counter and served her a big plate of food. Lucille and her cronies were at a table close by, cackling it up over something one of them had on her smartphone. Josh and Matt came in the front door. Both were wearing climbing clothes and looking like extremely fine male specimens. As they walked through the diner, every female in the place watched. Lucille even snapped a picture on her iPhone, which Amy figured would be on Facebook before she could serve their drinks.

Not that she was immune to the men, or their allure. Josh always looked good, and this evening, even dusty and slightly sweaty, he looked like he could walk right onto the cover of *Outside* magazine.

But Amy's eyes were on Matt. Because if Josh looked good, Matt looked amazing, and *way* too sexy.

Why was he still so sexy to her?

He pushed his dark sunglasses to the top of his head and searched her out. There was no other word for it. His eyes roamed over the diner until he found her. He looked her over, making her every nerve ending tingle with awareness, though his gaze was more inquisitive than sexual, as if making sure she was okay, though she had no idea why she wouldn't be.

Then he smiled, and oh, how her misbehaving nipples loved

that predatory smile. If his intense, concerned once-over had done things to her, his smile just about undid her from the inside out.

Then she realized Lucille had left her table and was talking to Riley, though the teen was backing away, shaking her head adamantly. Amy moved close enough in time to hear Lucille say "all the newcomers do it, honey. And putting you up on Facebook will help you make friends."

Riley looked horrified and not a little panic-stricken. Amy stepped between Lucille and the escaping Riley. "No Facebook pictures of her."

"She says she's eighteen," Lucille said. "And she looks lonely. I thought I could help—"

"You can help by *not* putting any information about her on Facebook at all," Amy said firmly.

At Amy's serious tone, Lucille went quiet for a moment, studying Riley's sullen face. "I understand," Lucille finally said, quite gently. "If you need anything..."

"I'm fine," Riley said, and turned and fled for the door.

Amy headed after her. "Riley—Hey, wait up."

"Thanks for the food, but I've got to go."

"Just a second." She grabbed Riley's wrist. "I wanted to tell you—that guy called here again."

Riley went still for a beat and then turned abruptly toward the door again, moving much faster now.

Amy followed her outside and stood still on the top step for a beat while her eyes adjusted from the bright diner to the dark, moonless night. "Riley?"

Footsteps. Amy ran after them, barely catching up with Riley just as she was leaving the lot. Backpack slung over her shoulder, she was on the street, thumb out.

"No way," Amy said. "No way am I letting you hitchhike."

"This is Lucky Harbor, right? Nothing bad ever happens in Lucky Harbor."

Amy shook her head. "Something bad is happening to you, and if you'd just tell me about it, I could help."

Riley turned away and waggled her thumb at the cars going by.

"Dammit, Riley. Don't do this."

"Sorry, but I can do whatever I want."

"Where are you going?" Amy asked. "Tell me that much, at least."

Riley waggled her thumb at a passing truck, which slowed.

Crap. Jan was going to kill Amy for walking out on a full diner, but Amy couldn't let Riley go, not like this. "Stay at my place again tonight," she said quickly, watching the truck's blinker come on.

Riley shook her head. Some of her color had come back but not much. She was clearly freaked out, and it didn't take a genius to figure out it had been the phone call. "It's time for me to move on."

She was going to leave Lucky Harbor. Afraid Riley would get into the truck and never be seen again, Amy shook her head. "No. Please stay."

The truck had pulled over, and the driver honked. Riley would have jumped right into it, but Amy grabbed her. "You don't have to do this, you know you don't. Stay. You've got a job here if you want it, and people who care."

The truck driver honked again, and Amy flipped him off. The driver rolled down his window and blasted them with a litany of foul oaths before hitting the gas, choking them with dust.

Riley looked impressed. "Wow, you flipped that guy off."

"*Stay.*"

Riley shook her head, baffled. "Why do you even care?"

Because once upon a time Amy had been in trouble, and there'd been *no one* to care. Because she recognized the helplessness in Riley's eyes. "Maybe I need to see something good happen to someone like us. Stay, Riley. Stay and say you'll think about the job."

Riley stared at her for a long beat. "I'll think about the job."

Relief filled Amy, and she relaxed a margin. "Come on. You can come back inside and wait for me to get off work."

The teen paused and then shook her head. "I still can't stay with you."

"Why?"

Riley's mouth tightened. Clearly, she had her reasons, good reasons, and just as clearly she wasn't going to say what those reasons were. Amy had a terrible suspicion that Riley was in some way trying to protect Amy by not staying—which didn't make her feel any better. "Where will you sleep?"

Riley hesitated.

"Riley."

"You have to promise not to tell."

Oh, boy. Nothing good ever started with that sentence. How could she make such a serious promise like that when Matt would want to know what was going on? "Listen—"

"*Promise.*"

Riley's desperation was palpable, and Amy looked into her eyes and saw fear mixed in with a desperate need to believe in *someone.* Damn. That someone was going to be her. "I promise," Amy said softly. "Riley, I promise you."

"Not a single soul."

Oh, how she hated to make such a promise, especially one she was already regretting, but the look on Riley's face made her do it. "Not a single soul. I promise."

And still Riley hesitated. "I'm going back to the forest."

"Riley." Amy shook her head. "You know Matt asked you not to camp illegally."

"He won't know."

"He'll ask," Amy said.

"Then tell him I'm still with you."

Oh, no. That was a very bad idea. "Riley—"

"You *promised.*"

Behind them, the door to the diner opened, and the man himself stepped out. How did he do that? Did he sense when she was thinking about him? Amy met his gaze and then turned back to Riley to tell her that they really needed another plan. But Riley was gone.

Matt strode across the lot. Amy had no idea what was on his mind, though she knew what was on hers. Worry for Riley. Anxiety that she'd just agreed to lie to the one man who'd made her feel something since...well, ever. And as always, that conflicting sense of free falling and yet being safe, simply because he was near.

"You okay?" he asked.

She nodded.

"And Riley?"

She nodded again and hoped that covered everything he wanted to know. But she should have known better. Matt wasn't the sort of man she could brush off or fool with a smile. He might be laid-back and easygoing, but he was sharp as a tack.

"Problem?" he asked.

She shook her head no while thinking *yes*. Big problem. Many problems. There was a secret between them, something that wouldn't have bothered her in the past but was bothering her greatly now. She had no idea what she was doing with him, but the anxiety ratcheted up a notch now. "I'm just really bad with morning-after discussions," she said. "Even though technically, this is an afternoon after. Or evening after. Or—"

"Maybe you'd be less bad at them if you didn't run off."

Yeah, maybe. Probably. But running off was what she did.

"Okay," he said with a shake of his head, as if he wasn't sure how they'd gotten on this track. "Let's start this conversation over. You really okay? And I mean that as a general how-are-you question."

"Yes," she said. "I'm really okay. You?"

"Better than okay."

She rolled her eyes, but felt a smile threaten. How he did that, coaxed the fun out of her when she'd been fresh out of fun, was a big mystery.

He nudged his chin toward where Riley had vanished. "Tell me about Riley."

Well if that didn't wipe her smile right off. He thought Riley was staying with her, and he thought that because she'd told him so. By not correcting that assumption and telling him that Riley now would be back in the woods was as good as lying to him.

But she'd promised. She'd promised a teen who desperately needed to be able to trust. "Nothing to tell, really. I was feeding her."

Matt studied her for a long moment, eyes sharp and assessing. She could feel the heat of his body, the easy strength of him, and felt the utterly inexplicable urge to reach for him. It confused her. She'd spent most of her teens and early twenties doing her best to ruin her own life. This had involved some pretty stupid and massively unsafe things, like hitchhiking across the country, accepting rides and places to stay with no concern for her own safety.

Not having family to call had only increased the sense of walking on a tightrope.

She'd gotten good at it.

She'd also gotten good at self-preservation. She'd managed to survive in spite of herself, and yet here she was at the ripe old age of twenty-eight, and all she wanted to do was turn and burrow her face in Matt's chest and let him be the strong one.

He'd do it, too. If she made the first move, he'd absolutely wrap her in his arms and hold her close. He'd murmur something in that low, calming voice, something she might not even catch, but it wouldn't matter. She'd know everything was going to be okay.

He'd given her that, a sense of security, and it terrified her.

Reaching for her hand, he turned her to face him. "Amy."

With a sigh, she let him tug her in against him, and when he kissed her, his mouth was warm and knowing, tasting both familiar and right. It was like coming home. That was her only excuse for letting him deepen the kiss, for wrapping her arms around his neck and kissing him back until she had no air left. Finally she broke it off because this wasn't like last time, when he'd been just getting off work and they could race to his house to get naked like two horny idiots. She had a long shift ahead of her. "I have to get back inside before Jan kills me," she whispered against his mouth.

He let her unravel from him, but when she would have walked away, he tightened his grip on her hand. "Amy."

"Yeah?"

His gaze held hers, and she did her best to keep her thoughts to herself.

"You'd tell me if there was trouble," he said.

Some of her glow diminished. "What kind of trouble?" she asked cautiously.

"*Any* kind of trouble."

Maybe she wasn't quite as good at lying as she thought. "I can take care of myself. You know that, right?"

"That's the thing, Amy. You don't have to. You have connections here. Friends. People who care. *I* care."

Hadn't she just had this conversation in reverse with Riley? And now Matt was the one trying to be there, for Amy. Hell if that didn't put a lump in her throat, which she ruthlessly swallowed. "There's no trouble." *Please don't ask me to promise.*

He didn't. Without another word, he nodded and let go of her hand, and without much of a choice, she went back inside the diner.

Chapter 12

God gave the angels wings and the humans chocolate.

Two days later, Matt found Amy at the ranger station, studying the big board of trails. She was wearing her hip-hugging skinny jeans tucked into her kick-ass boots and a snug, thin tee with some Chinese symbols on it that he figured he didn't want to know the meaning of. She was concentrating on the board, brow furrowed, lips moving as she read the names of the trails. Just the sight of her made him both smile and ache.

"Where to?" he asked.

She didn't take her attention off the board. "I'm thinking of walking from the north rim to the south rim."

"For…your heart?"

"For my *grandma's* heart."

He nodded agreeably. "You're going to want to take the eastern trail to the top," he said, nursing the Dr. Pepper he'd picked up at the convenience store on his way in. "It's the longest, but it's the only easy-to-moderate way to the top. There's a loop but don't take it. Come back the same way."

She turned her head and looked at him, and he felt the same

punch to the gut that he always felt when they were this close. He wanted to think she felt it too but it was hard to tell. She was damn good at keeping her thoughts inside. "You planning on overnighting again?"

Her mouth curved slightly. "No. I don't think overnighting in the wilds is for me."

He begged to disagree. He could remember, vividly, how she'd looked in his sweatshirt, in his sleeping bag, in his tent. *Hot.* "Then you want to make sure you turn around by three or four to get back before dark."

She saluted him, the smart-ass, and made him smile. "We could meet up after," he said.

Again, her brow furrowed. "For?"

"To go out."

"Out," she repeated, like the word didn't compute.

"On a date," he clarified.

"A *date*?"

"Yeah," he said, laughing ruefully at himself. At her. "Unless you're allergic to dates. Then we could call it something else."

She opened her mouth, then hesitated.

He cocked his head. "You're afraid to see what happens next."

"There aren't plans for what happens next, remember? *No* getting attached."

"Plans change."

She stared at him as if he wasn't speaking her language. "Why? Why would you want to go out with me? I'm grumpy, and irritable, and frankly, not all that nice a person."

"I'll give you the grumpy," he said. "But you're off on the nice thing. You're a better person than you give yourself credit for, Amy."

She was staring at him suspiciously, like maybe he had an ulterior motive for buttering her up. "Not reason enough to want to go out," she said. "Why, Matt?"

The easy answer was because he wanted her again. That was also the hard answer. "Because I feel good when I'm with you," he said simply.

She let out a breath. "Matt, I—"

"No. Don't say you can't, because I know you're not working tonight. And don't say you don't want to, because there were two of us in my bed the other night. I know what you felt, Amy. I saw it."

She just kept looking at him like he'd lost his mind. And hell, maybe he had.

"You're a hard guy to say no to," she finally said.

"So don't say it. Say yes."

She shook her head, clearly thinking this was a bad idea, but then gave him the word he'd wanted. "Yes."

For Amy, the Rim Trail was much more "moderate" than "easy." But at least it was clearly marked and easy to follow, even if it was a straight-up climb of 2,500 vertical feet.

She'd gotten lucky finding the first two legs of her grandma's journey. She was worried about this last leg.

In the end, she'd gone full circle. That's what the journal had said.

Amy sighed. She could only hope that when it came to the end, she'd figure it out.

Halfway, she took a break at a natural plateau, behind a sheer rock face that was staggering. In front of her was a narrow creek running from pure snow melt. And far below, she could see the Pacific Ocean churning under a sky dotted with white puffy clouds. It looked so perfect and beautiful that it could have been a painting.

Needing to catch her breath, she sat with the creek at her feet and pulled out her sketch pad, wanting to draw this place, wondering, hoping, her grandma and Jonathon had sat somewhere nearby enjoying the view, three decades earlier.

It took an hour to sketch in the basics enough that she could finish it up later. As she'd been doing for some time now, she thought about Riley, and hoped the girl was okay. Amy wasn't used to worrying about others, but she worried about Riley, big time.

Hungry, she grabbed the lunch she'd packed and ate the brownie first. Heaven, but even soft, gooey chocolate couldn't keep her brain from going back to her shocking problem.

She was going out with Matt tonight.

A date.

She went for her sandwich next and pulled out her phone to call Mallory, who didn't pick up. Probably working a shift at the ER or the health services clinic. She tried Grace next and got lucky. "I have a problem."

"Oh, thank God," Grace said with feeling. "I've filled out fifty job apps, and no one's hiring. No one wants me except you. I need to feel useful. Tell me your problem. Tell me *all* your problems. Need a good girl lesson? What number are we up to now, seven? *Always be available when your friend is feeling like a loser.*"

"I'm available," Amy promised. "And I've told you, if you're desperate enough, we need a bus person at the diner. I offered the job to Riley but I don't think she's going to take it."

"Nothing personal, but I'd rather take a shift running the Ferris Wheel at the pier than work for Jan. If I worked for Jan, I might have to do something drastic."

"Like kill yourself?"

"Like kill *Jan*," Grace said. "Now talk to me."

"I'm going out tonight."

"Out?"

Amy sighed. "On a date."

There was a complete beat of silence. "Hang on," Grace said, and there was a click.

Two minutes later, Grace was back. "Okay," she said. "I've got Mallory on the line too. I wasn't qualified to handle this problem alone."

"Hey," Mallory said, sounding breathless. "You just caught me. I'm on break. It's going to be a full moon tonight, and we've already had two women in premature labor and a fight victim from the arcade. Better make this quick. What's the emergency?"

"No emergency," Amy said. "I just—"

"It's a *complete* emergency," Grace interrupted. "Amy has a date with Ranger Hot Buns."

Mallory squealed with delight so loudly that Amy had to pull the phone away from her ear. "Jeez!" Amy said. "Warn a girl. And how did you know it would be with Matt?" she asked Grace. "I hadn't said."

Grace laughed. So did Mallory.

"What?"

"Well who else could it be?" Mallory asked. "Matt's the only guy you've ever looked at twice. And good Lord, the way he looks at you is contributing to global warming."

Amy flashed to the look on Matt's face when he'd been buried deep inside her and felt herself go damp. Yeah, the way he looked at her was pretty boggling. The way he did *everything* was boggling, especially the naked stuff. He was *exceptional* at the naked stuff, knowing when to be sweet and coaxing, knowing when to *not* be either of those things. And the things he'd whispered in her ear... He'd given her everything he had, until he'd been taut and quivering with his own need.

Damn. She wanted him again.

"So where's he taking you on this date?" Mallory asked.

"And what are you wearing on this date?" Grace wanted to know.

"Okay, why do we have to keep saying *date*?" Amy asked. "I mean you eat, you talk, you get naked... we don't have to *label* it."

"It's supposed to be labeled," Mallory said calmly, the voice of reason. "It's supposed to be a lovely time."

Amy rolled her eyes.

"I heard that," Mallory said. "Now tell me what's the problem with a gorgeous guy, a really *good* gorgeous guy, taking you out and calling it a date? He's got a job, a home, and the best abs I've ever seen. Besides, he's already charmed you out of your pants, right?"

"Okay," Amy said to Grace's unladylike snort. "First of all, the *only* reason I took off my pants was because I had a cut on my thigh."

"That wouldn't be my first guess," Grace said.

"And second of all," Amy went on as if Grace hadn't spoken, "it wasn't a big deal! I was on a hike, and I got lost and—"

"—And he rescued you," Mallory pointed out. "Another check in the pro column. The man is hot *and* he rescues fair maidens in distress."

"I wasn't in distress! I called *you* first, and you—"

"—Wouldn't have charmed you out of your pants," Mallory said.

Grace burst out laughing.

Amy thunked her head against her knees. "You aren't listening."

"Then say it again in English this time," Mallory said.

"Fine," Amy blew out a breath. "I've never been on a real date."

Utter silence. Amy checked the phone screen to see if she still had reception. "Hello? You guys still there?"

"How old are you?" Grace asked, sounding confused.

"Twenty-eight."

"And you're still a virgin?"

"I didn't say *that*," Amy said with a laugh. "And no, I'm not." She was just about as far from a virgin as one could get. "Look, it's not a big deal. I left home when I was sixteen, and after that, it was more about survival than dating." She'd done what she'd had to, and sometimes that had involved being with a guy because he had a place to stay or food—neither of which meant a "date" in any sense of the word.

"And then somehow I just never got to a place where dating was really an option," she said, staring at the creek at her feet. A butterfly had landed on the water and was floundering, trying not to drown. Amy knew the feeling. Leaning forward, she tried to rescue the thing but it was swept away in the current. She knew that feeling, too. "Listen, I've got to go so I don't get stuck up here again."

"No, wait," Mallory said. "Please wait. I'm sorry we laughed at you. I think it's lovely that Matt asked you out."

Amy sighed. Mallory was sounding like maybe she was feeling very emotional—which didn't really count because lots of things made Mallory emotional. Like the sun rising and setting. Last time they'd watched TV together, Mallory had sobbed openly at one of those save the puppy SPCA commercials.

"You should go with him, Amy," Mallory said. "Do the eat and talk thing. But not the naked thing, not yet."

Amy winced, keeping to herself the fact that she'd already done the naked thing.

"Just enjoy your first date," Mallory said. "And FYI, I have a good girl lesson for you. This one is serious, Amy. *Really* serious."

"I don't need—"

"You deserve good things," Mallory said anyway. "You deserve good people in your life, and Matt is both good *and* good people."

Dammit. Amy's throat felt tight, and there was no SPCA commercial in sight. "How can a man be both an adjective and a noun?"

"Trust me," Mallory said. "Ty's both. And so is Matt."

"I agree with Mallory," Grace said. "You should definitely go tonight with Matt. But I say *do* the naked thing."

"*Grace*," Mallory admonished.

"Hello," Grace said. "This is Matt Bowers we're talking about. You've seen him. Gorgeous, built, sexy-eyed Matt. And he wears a uniform. With a gun..." She sighed dreamily. "I'm sorry, but Amy has a duty to get naked with a guy like that and report back. With details."

Amy disconnected and resumed her hike. Grace was right, Matt *was* gorgeous and built, in just about every way a man could be, but she'd gotten him out of her system. There'd be no more getting naked.

At three o'clock, she stood at the top of a cliff looking down on the four small lakes she'd been at the other day. *Way* down. She could see a few otters playing along the shore of the first lake, and as she stood there in awe, a fish leapt out of the water, executing a perfect gainer before flopping back.

Her legs were wobbling from the climb. Or maybe it was from looking down from the dizzying height, but in either case, she could hear her grandma's voice in her head.

It felt like a promise. I had my hope, but now I had something else, too, peace. Four Lakes gave me peace.

Amy closed her eyes and inhaled deeply, then opened them again, feeling them burn with emotion. Jesus, what was with her today? But there was no denying the truth. She'd been feeling flickers of hope ever since Sierra Meadows. It was new and tenuous, but it was there. As for peace, she hadn't been quite sure. When she thought about her life, she knew she'd always lived it to survive. But she was beginning to see that there was more to life than mere survival, so much more. And maybe that was peace right there, just learning that.

Which left heart, something she'd never believed in for herself and had, in fact, openly mocked.

But she didn't feel like mocking it now, and she had no idea if maybe that was thanks to Lucky Harbor, to the friends she'd made here, or…a certain forest ranger that was filling up something deep inside her that she hadn't even known was empty.

Matt knocked at Amy's door. He was early for their date because… well, he didn't really have a reason, other than he wanted to see her. He had no idea what the night would bring, but if it went anything at all like their other encounters, it wouldn't be boring.

Her car was in her parking spot but she didn't answer. He

knocked again, and then when she still didn't answer, he tried the door. It opened, which didn't make him feel better—Amy wasn't a woman to leave her door unlocked. "Amy?"

Nothing, so he stepped inside. "Hello?"

Still nothing.

Her place was small enough that he could see from one end to the next. Her bedroom door was open, and he stepped closer. It looked like a bomb had gone off. A female bomb. Clothes spilled out of the dresser drawers and closet and were scattered across the bed, but no one was actually *in* any of the clothes.

The bathroom was damp and misty, as if she'd recently showered. There were girlie things on the counter, tubes and bottles, and the place smelled like sexy woman. A pair of black lace panties and matching bra lay on the floor. Nice. He turned back to the living room.

There was a small slider leading to a tiny deck area, and it was cracked open. He pushed it further. The thing squeaked like hell and was all but impossible to move, and yet the woman sitting with her back to him didn't budge.

This was because she had in earphones that led to the phone or iPod in her pocket and she was singing.

Off-key.

She was drawing, too, sketching something from memory, as she hunched over her pad, a pencil in her hand moving furiously over the paper, a bundle of additional colored pencils in her other hand.

He listened to her sing for a second and felt the grin split his face. Guns N' Roses, "Welcome to the Jungle." He cleared his throat, but she kept singing. "*Welcome to the jungle, feel my, my, serpentine, I, I wanna hear you scream…*"

Still grinning, Matt reached out and set a hand on her shoulder. Amy nearly came out of her skin. Her pad and pencils went flying, and whipping out the ear buds, she whirled around, leading with a roundhouse kick that would have leveled him flat if he hadn't ducked.

"Are you crazy?" she asked when he straightened. "I nearly took off your head."

"You had your music up and didn't hear me." He bent to pick up her pad and pencils, which she snatched out of his hands and hugged to her chest. She was staring at him, breathing fast. Too fast. She wore a strapless sundress with a colorful print that was sexy as hell. She wasn't in her usual kick-ass boots, but the heels in their place were still pretty damn kick-ass. If she'd connected with his head, he'd still be down for the count. "You're not wearing black."

She shifted, then shrugged. "It's Mallory's."

"You look beautiful," he said.

She wasn't impressed by the compliment. "You just let yourself into my place?"

"You didn't answer my knock. I thought something was wrong."

"Well it's not," she said. "And I don't like surprises."

"I'm sorry." He rubbed his jaw and considered her. "I scared you."

"I told you. I told you I don't like it when someone sneaks up on me."

She *had* told him that, last week on the trail, and his gut clenched hard over how she might have learned she didn't like to be surprised. Slowly he stepped closer, taking her iPod, setting it down on the chair she'd just vacated. Then he took her pad and pencils and did the same. "Breathe," he said softly, gently running his hands up her arms and then down.

She exhaled a shuddery breath.

He inhaled slowly and deeply, and she did the same, and this time when she exhaled, she relaxed marginally. "Sorry," she said. "Didn't mean to take your head off. I left my door unlocked for Riley and forgot."

"No apologies necessary."

She tipped her head up and looked at him. "You're being sweet."

"I'm not feeling sweet." Not even close. His hands dropped to her hips. The material of her skirt was silky smooth and thin. He could feel the warmth of her right through it. She smelled so good he couldn't stop himself from lowering his head and pressing his face to her neck.

She slapped a hand to his chest and leaned back. "Are you smelling me?"

"Yeah." He did it again, an exaggerated inhale that made her laugh. "You smell amazing," he said. "Reminds me of how amazing you taste."

She sucked in a breath and moved against him, just a little rock of her hot bod that finished off the job that the panties on the bathroom floor had started. His lips were at her throat. He sucked on her skin, and the sound she made, the soft, feminine sound of arousal, nearly did him in.

The next sound that she made came from her stomach as it rumbled. Laughing softly, he pulled back. "Time to go."

"Where?"

"Food. Wine. Maybe music." Taking her hand, he pulled her through her place. "Whatever you want."

"We were already doing what I wanted."

He stopped and glanced back at her with a smile. "Yeah?"

"Yeah."

His body revved. *Down, boy.* "I like that idea," he told her. "I like it a lot. *After* I take you out."

"You don't have to."

Okay, he was missing something here, and he stopped, dipping down a little to look into her eyes. "Did you change your mind?"

"No." She shifted and looked away. "I'm just saying, I don't need the pomp and circumstance before we…"

"Duly noted," he said slowly. Yeah, definitely missing something. Which meant they were in trouble because she clearly wasn't going to spell out the problem and he was clueless. "Maybe *I* need the pomp and circumstance."

She eyed him with a narrowed gaze. "*You* need to be romanced?"

"You think that's stupid?"

"No." But contradicting that, she laughed, then slapped her hand over her mouth and shook her head, eyes sparkling. "Really, I don't."

"Look at you, lying through your teeth…" Tugging her in, he kissed her, then let their gazes hold. "Such a beautiful liar."

Something flickered in her gaze, and he wondered. Guilt? Regret? But not wanting to ruin the night ahead, he shrugged it off and took her hand, leading her outside.

Chapter 13

The calories in chocolate don't count because chocolate comes from the cocoa bean, and everyone knows that beans are good for you.

Amy had no idea where they were going, but when they passed the pier and got onto the highway, she knew they weren't going to the diner, or anywhere in Lucky Harbor. "So," she said, pretending she wasn't nervous, "where to?"

"Thought we'd try a night out without worrying about showing up on Facebook. I was thinking Seattle."

That sounded good to her. There for a moment, back at her place, she'd thought maybe they'd be getting straight to the naked part of the date, but he'd said he wanted this first. She'd decided to take that in the sweet spirit he'd intended. But who'd have thought that the big, bad ranger truly had a sweet side?

You did... You knew it from that day on the mountain when he'd stayed with you all night.

They were halfway to Seattle when his phone buzzed. He glanced at the ID and let out a breath and a softly uttered "damn." He shook his head. "Sorry, but it's Sawyer. I have to take it."

Amy listened to him as he spoke to the sheriff. She could tell by Matt's quick, short replies that it was about work, and it wasn't good.

"I have to go to Crescent Canyon," he said when he'd clicked off. "Sawyer arrested a guy this morning, someone that law enforcement here has been looking for, in conjunction with a drug bust we made a while back. He's squealing something about his partners and some more stash in an old abandoned ranger station out at Crescent Canyon, in the north district—my territory. I need to meet Sawyer out there to check it out. I'm going to have to take you back."

"Aren't we closer to Crescent Canyon now than my place? Don't waste time, I'll just go with you."

"No. Hell, no."

This was not the first time that Amy had seen Matt's protective nature. After taking care of herself for so long, watching her own back, she still didn't know how she felt about him doing it for her. But she couldn't deny that it certainly wasn't a bad feeling. "You're not in your work vehicle," she said reasonably. "So it's not against the rules, right? I'll stay in your truck."

He slid her a look, and she held up her hand in a solemn vow, making him smile. "Were you a Girl Scout?" he asked.

"Not even a little bit," she said. "But I rarely make promises." She thought of the last one she'd made, to Riley, the one she was *still* conflicted about. "And I never make one I can't keep."

Or so she hoped…

His eyes held hers. "Never?"

She drew a deep breath. "Not yet anyway."

"Good to know." He left the highway and drove them up toward Crescent Canyon. The road turned into a dirt fire road that forked off a dozen times or more. Amy was completely lost in three minutes, but Matt seemed to know exactly where he was going. The road narrowed, and the going got so rough she ended up clinging to the sissy handle.

Matt glanced over at her. "You okay?"

"You tell me."

He flashed a grin. "No worries, I hardly ever drive off the edge by accident."

She steeled herself and took a peek over the "edge." A three-hundred-foot drop. "Good to know," she said dryly, repeating his earlier words back to him, making him laugh.

Twenty minutes later, they pulled into a clearing in front of a small building, just as Sawyer did the same from the other direction in a black-and-white official Bronco.

There was a car already parked, an older Ford truck of indeterminate color and rust. "Stay here," Matt said to Amy, eyes on the building, reaching into the back for a utility belt, gun, and cuffs. "Under no circumstances are you to get out of my truck. If it all goes to shit, I want you to slide over behind the wheel and drive out of here, do you understand?"

"What? No, I'm not going to leave you here," she said.

He spared her a quick look, mouth and eyes grim. "I can take care of myself. Promise me, Amy."

Goddammit. Thanks to her own big mouth, he now knew that she took her promises very seriously. "I promise."

He and Sawyer got out of their vehicles and drew their guns. Amy watched the two of them as they looked at each other, seeming to communicate without a word. Sawyer gave a quick hand gesture, then went toward the front of the building while Matt vanished around back.

Just as Sawyer reached the front door, it crashed open. Three huge guys flew out, tackling Sawyer to the ground. The dirt pack was dry, and dust flew up, making it impossible for Amy to see anything but a tangle of limbs. From inside the car, she gasped, horrified, sitting up straighter, desperately trying to keep her eyes on Sawyer at the bottom of the pile. Her first instinct was to do something to help, and she whirled around, looking for something, a weapon, *anything*. A baseball bat would have been her first choice but there was nothing. She carried a knife in her backpack, but all she had tonight was a small purse with a little cash and her phone. She hadn't planned on needing anything else except maybe a condom.

And then there was her promise to stay in the truck.

It was the worst feeling, the most helpless thing imaginable, sitting there watching Sawyer go down, unable to help.

From inside the building, another guy came stumbling out. His hands were cuffed behind him, and he was being pushed along by Matt. Matt caught sight of the scuffle and shoved his guy down to the ground. "*Stay*," he barked and broke into a run toward the mêlée.

One of the men broke away from the fight and staggered for his truck. Matt dove after him, taking him to the ground.

Amy gasped again and covered her mouth, as if by making any sound she might distract Matt and get him hurt. The two men rolled twice, and then Matt was on top, flipping the other man over, holding him there with a knee in the small of the guy's back. Matt reached behind himself for a set of flexi-cuffs from his utility belt and cuffed the guy. Without looking at him again, he turned back to Sawyer's fight and waded right in. He grabbed one of the two remaining guys by the back of the shirt and hauled him to his feet. No easy thing considering that the guy appeared to be six and a half feet tall and close to three hundred pounds. "Down," Matt said, and pointed to the ground, both his voice and actions cool and calm and utterly in control.

The big guy dropped to the ground.

Sawyer had the other one facedown in the dirt now and was cuffing him. Sawyer had a cut lip and torn clothes but otherwise appeared unharmed. The cuffed men were all moaning and groaning about their injuries, which both Sawyer and Matt ignored. There was a short conversation between Sawyer and Matt, then they both made calls.

Twenty minutes later, three more black-and-white SUVs appeared. Matt spoke to the officers, then to Sawyer. Then the cuffed men were loaded up and driven away.

Matt turned toward his truck and Amy. He was head-to-toe filthy. He had a tear in one knee and another on his elbow. He was sweaty.

And he looked like the best thing she'd ever seen.

He ambled back over and slid behind the wheel, pulling out of the clearing and back onto the fire road as if nothing had just happened. Like it was an everyday thing to drag bad guys off his mountain and engage in hand-to-hand combat.

And hell, maybe it was.

Clearly, he knew what he was doing. Protecting himself and Sawyer, and by extension her as well, had been as second nature as breathing. Not for the first time, she wondered about all he'd seen and done and how it'd molded him into the man he was, so laid-back and quick to smile and yet ready for battle at all times.

She also wondered why the hell she felt so on edge right now, like she was going to die if he didn't grab her and kiss her. Strip her. Take her.

"You okay?" he asked, making her jump. He swiveled his head to look over at her, and their eyes held. Suddenly there wasn't enough air in the vehicle, not even close, as the tension rose. It was a good kind of tension, the kind that had her squeezing her thighs together. Was she okay? She had no idea, but her insides were quivering, her hands itching with the need to lay them on him. "That was actually my question for you," she managed.

His gaze never left hers. "You're shaking."

Yeah, she was. Every part of her. "I was scared for you." She hugged herself. "Which is ridiculous, since like you said, you're good at taking care of yourself." Something they had in common.

They were on a deserted road, hidden from all sides by trees so thick she couldn't see beyond them. Still trembling, and greatly annoyed, she stared out the window, gasping in surprise when Matt pulled off the road. Turning to her, he slid a hand along the back of her seat, palming her neck. "It's okay, Amy. Everything's okay."

Feeling stupid for her shocked reaction, she nodded and drew in a shaky breath, but his touch had only accelerated her heart rate. She didn't know what to feel, or do. She wanted to jump over the console and personally search every inch of him for injury. She also wanted to rip off his clothes and climb on top of him. "Matt."

"Yeah?"

"I need—" Breaking off, she closed her eyes.

"What do you need, Amy?"

"*You.*"

A low sound escaped him, and then his other hand joined the fray, cupping her face, gliding down her arms, pulling her toward him.

She wasn't exactly sure what happened next, whether she'd done as she'd thought about and climbed over the console, or if he actually lifted her, but then she was straddling him, and nothing else mattered.

He was holding her above himself, trying to keep her from touching him. "Wait—I'm all dirty and sweaty."

"I don't care."

With a groan, he hauled her in close, kissing her long and deep.

He was right; he was hot and dirty. And he was real, more so than anyone she knew, and in turn he made *her* feel real. She forgot that they were stuffed together in his driver's seat, that the steering wheel was pressing into her back, or that anyone could come upon them. She only knew a need for this man so close against her, his scent, his taste, and she rocked into him.

Beeeeeep, went the horn when she knocked against it, startling her into jerking upright, where she banged her head on the visor.

Laughing softly, Matt cupped her head in one big palm, rubbing it. Then he sighed against her neck and dumped her back onto her side of the vehicle.

"Hey," she said.

"Not here."

"Why not? We're on a date."

With a rueful smile, he adjusted himself. "Is that what you think a date is about? Sex?"

"Well…yeah."

He shook his head. "Even if that was true, there's not enough room in this truck for what I want to do to you."

Her nipples tightened even more. "Now you're just teasing me."

"Sweetheart, when I start teasing you, you'll know it."

She shuddered in anticipation. She knew him now, knew the magic of his touch. She knew he could back up that cocky statement with shocking ease.

"I need to go change," Matt said.

"Are you going to tell me what happened back there?"

He looked at her, assessing, and she held his gaze, seeing the concern in it. Was he worried she was too fragile to hear about his work? Had his ex been that way? Because Amy was as far from fragile as she could get. "I *want* to hear about it," she said. "I'd really like to know."

"Not too long ago, we made that big drug bust I told you about," he said. "We found some of the principals and what we thought was all the drugs. Wrong on both accounts."

So casual. But what she'd seen had been anything but casual. It'd been like something right out of a movie. "You and Sawyer took on four guys," she said. "Four *huge* guys."

"We've faced worse."

That thought gave her a shiver as he pulled up to his cabin.

"I'm sorry I screwed up our date," he said.

She shook her head. "You didn't."

"I'll shower and change real quick," he promised, and left her in his living room while he vanished into his bedroom.

Through the open door, Amy heard the thunk of his shoes being kicked off one by one, and then the shower came on. She tried not to think about him stripping down to skin and failed. To distract herself, she looked around. The first time she'd been here, she hadn't had time to take it all in, what with the jumping of each other's bones and all.

He had running shoes half under the couch, a newspaper scattered on the coffee table. Next to the front door was a baseball bat and mitt. A laptop sat on the couch.

This wasn't just a place where Matt hung his hat at night. He *lived* here.

Had he loved here?

She was surprised at the yearning to know. His shower turned off. Next came the sound of a drawer opening and then some rustling.

"We missed our reservations," he called out to her. "But maybe they'll still take us anyway."

It would be at least a forty-five minute drive, and undoubtedly a wait, and while she imagined the food would be worth it, she didn't want the fancy dinner, the crowd, the candles and dancing thing. "We could just eat here," she said.

A beat of silence, and then he appeared in the doorway wearing low-slung Levi's.

And nothing else.

He held a shirt in his hands as his eyes met hers. "You want to stay here?"

His hair was wet and had been barely finger-combed, leaving it standing up and spiky. He smelled like soap and shampoo and himself. And he hadn't been all that efficient with a towel either because his chest was damp.

And so was she. "I'll cook," she said, thinking she was *already* cooking, from the inside out.

He followed her into his kitchen. "You don't like to cook."

Actually, she liked to cook just fine. She just wasn't all that good at it. But she did have one specialty. "If you have bread and cheese and a pan, we're in business."

He shrugged into his shirt, and she wished he hadn't. Eating grilled cheese with the spectacular view of his chest and abs would've been better than any dessert she could have whipped up.

He stepped close, his eyes dark and heated. "I like where your thoughts just went."

"Did I say them out loud?" she asked, startled.

"No, but you were thinking them clearly enough." He backed her to the kitchen counter and caged her in with a hand on either side of her hips. Ducking a little, he looked into her eyes. "You want me."

She blew out a breath. Seemed silly to try and deny it now, especially since she'd said so in his truck. His eyes were deep and dark and beautiful and filled with affection and a devastating heat. He looked so...alive, him and that megawatt smile as he wrapped his arms around her and lifted her to the counter.

"Um..."

With a polite cock of his head to let her know he was listening, he pushed between her legs, spreading them wide so that he was flush up against her. When she didn't finish her sentence—couldn't even remember what she'd wanted to say—he kissed her. He kissed her until she couldn't remember her own name and then backed away and went to his refrigerator.

She stared at his back and tried to access some brain cells. "So what made you decide to be a ranger? SWAT not exciting enough for you? You decided you'd rather rescue fair maidens and wrangle drug runners?"

He pulled butter and cheese from the fridge. He grabbed a loaf of thick sourdough bread from the counter and grabbed a knife. "It's complicated."

"Yeah?"

He set a pan on the stovetop and turned on a burner. He began to butter the bread slices, but she took the knife from him and took over the task.

"I promised to cook for you," she said. "You talk."

He met her gaze. "I didn't think talking was one of your favorite things to do."

He was throwing the ball back at her. She recognized the technique well. And he was right, she wasn't much of a talker. She'd never been all that curious about a man either. There were a whole bunch of firsts going on here tonight. "I want to know," she said simply. "I want to know more about you."

Chapter 14

There are two food groups: chocolate and fruit. And if it is fruit, it should be dipped in chocolate.

Matt turned to Amy, surprised. "You want to know more about me? Why?"

Looking both embarrassed and resigned, she bit her lower lip. "I know, I made a whole big deal about not getting involved..."

He laughed softly at the both of them. Because he knew that *neither* of them wanted to get involved—or attached—but it was happening anyway. "What do you want to know?"

"I suppose you learned to handle bad guys like that in SWAT and probably the military, too. Army?"

"Navy," he said. "Ty and I went through basic together and then spent some quality time in the Gulf."

"Ty...Mallory's boyfriend?"

He nodded.

"That's where your readiness comes from. The cool calm. The ability to take down four huge potheads single-handedly."

"It wasn't single-handedly tonight," he reminded her. "I had Sawyer."

"Still pretty impressive." She paused. "You've seen and done a lot in your life."

He held her gaze. "I have." More than she knew.

"So what made you come here and be a forest ranger?"

Turning in his partner for being on the take. Having his marriage fall apart after failing to keep Shelly safe from his job. Basically, his entire life had detonated in the span of a few months, and he'd needed out. But he wasn't about to spell out his failures to a woman he hoped to have naked and under him by the end of the evening. "I like the uncomplicated life here."

"So you wanted peace and quiet?"

He hadn't yet found the peace, but he *had* found the quiet, and he'd settled for that. "Yeah."

Studying him, she tilted her head to the side a little. "Do you ever miss it? The big city, the people? Your family?"

"I see my family. And no, I don't miss it."

"And your wife?" she asked softly. "Do you miss her?"

"*Ex*-wife," he reminded her. "And no."

"But..."

He really didn't want to have this conversation. He wasn't about to spill his guts and have her look at him differently. So instead of letting her lead him back to a past he didn't like to remember, he leaned in and kissed her. Lightly at first. Warm. Then not so lightly. He kissed her until she let out a low hum of arousal and slid her hands up his chest and into his hair to hold him to her.

Not that he was going to let go. Hell, no. And just like that, what had started out as a distraction technique quickly escalated into something else entirely, into that same unquenchable hunger he always felt for her, the one he'd had since she'd first shown up in Lucky Harbor.

It might have taken him six months to get here with her, but he was done wasting time. Luckily, she appeared to feel the same way because she turned off the stovetop burner, took his hand, and led him to his big sofa in the living room.

The last time they'd been here, right here, she'd commandeered the reins. He had no idea if he'd earned her trust enough yet for it to be his turn, but he hoped so. Either way, he was perfectly willing to give her whatever she needed, just as long as she was with him all the way.

Amy looked into his face, her expression one of reluctant affection and enough heat to steal his breath. He cupped her face for a kiss and she let him do it, even making a soft hum of pleasure before suddenly pushing him down to the couch.

Okay, so she still didn't trust him enough to let him lead. He allowed himself to fall but he made sure to take her with him, tugging so that she landed on his lap. Her short skirt slid up her gorgeous thighs to dangerous heights.

He'd been dying to get a peek beneath all night, but before he could, she nipped his bottom lip, hard, and then soothed the sting with one very sexy, slow swipe of her tongue. He went instantly hard even as he got the answer to the big question.

No, she wasn't ready to make love. This was still going to be sex. Sex was good, but he forced himself to slow down, to slow them *both* down. Stroking back her hair, he murmured her name as he kissed his way to her ear, because if nothing else, he was going to make damn sure that there'd at least be some tenderness to go with it.

Amy loved having Matt beneath her, warm, strong, and hard. She couldn't get enough of him. It was quite shocking.

He'd called one thing right—she wanted him. Bad.

She turned in his lap, straddling him now. His hands immediately slid beneath her skirt and palmed her butt. Gripping his biceps, she kissed him. Letting out a low growl of pleasure, he kissed her back, plundering her mouth without trying to break free of her hold or rush her. He didn't tear off her clothes or roll her beneath him either. He just took what she gave, all relaxed and at ease, willing to let her do as she wanted with him.

And there *was* something she desperately wanted. She ground herself against his erection and heard his breath hitch, making her realize that he needed her as badly as she needed him. Releasing his arms, she slid hers around his neck.

He broke the kiss and gave her a searching look before kissing her again, his hands shifting on the move. Clever fingers unhooked her bra so that he could cup her breasts, his thumbs brushing over her nipples.

Then it was *her* breath that hitched.

God, she really needed him inside her. She needed the big bang, the relief, and only he could give it to her. "Condom," she gasped against his mouth.

"Back pants pocket." They broke apart to undress in a frenzy, and then she was sliding onto him.

"Oh, fuck," he said reverently as he filled her.

It gave her such a rush, reducing this smart, sharp man to nothing more than single syllables. And she knew exactly how he felt because she could hardly think; he felt so good inside her. She moved on him, slowly at first. When she was ready for more, she tried to pick up their pace but he wrapped a hand in her hair, his other hand going to her hip to hold her still.

"No." His voice was serrated, thick, his grip preventing her from racing them both to the finish line. "Don't move. Not a single muscle—Oh, Christ," he grated out when she clenched on him. "Christ, you feel good." His fingers tightened, and she knew she'd have bruises.

She didn't care. His tongue was back in her mouth, moving in tune to the way his body moved within hers, and it was more than she could take. She broke loose and undulated her hips as she climbed higher, then higher still when he reached a hand between them to stroke his thumb over the current center of her entire universe.

Crying out, she clutched at him, out of control and unable to care. When she came, it was hard and fast. She heard Matt swear reverently as he rocked her through it, and then he was flying with her.

Finally, they stilled against each other. Sated, she laid her head against his shoulder as he pulled her in tight. When her breathing calmed, she sighed. "You make me lose myself."

"Good."

She met his gaze. "Yeah?"

"Everyone should lose themselves just like that, as often as possible." And then he flashed her a smile before dumping her off his lap. He smacked her lightly on the ass, rose to his feet, and then strode naked into the kitchen. "Starving," he said over his shoulder.

She gaped after him. "You going to eat like that?"

"Yeah. And so are you."

She hated being told what to do. Always. It made her run away.

But she didn't run. Instead, she followed him like a lovelorn puppy into the kitchen, where they consumed grilled cheese sandwiches while leaning against the counter. Naked.

He told her about his day, making her laugh at how he'd been followed around by a group of camping biologists who'd wanted him to discuss the bodily functions of the otters in the cold water streams that fed into the water supply. He spoke fondly about his family, about his warm but nosy mom, his take-no-shit dad, his brother who had three little girls of his own now—karma's idea of a joke since his brother had been crazy wild. He told her how he and Ty had beaten the shit out of each other just that morning in the gym, with Josh standing over them on the sidelines like a worried den mother…

And all she could do the whole time was soak up every word and marvel that he trusted her, that he enjoyed her company, and that he wanted to be with her. It softened her in a way she hadn't expected, and she found herself just staring at him.

"What?" he asked, with a small smile.

She shook her head, unable to explain how she felt when she was with him. Like she was on a tightrope without a net. An overdose of adrenaline, terror-filled, excited, and overwhelmed all at once.

"Tell me," he said.

It was that voice of his, the low, calm, utterly commanding voice that made her do just that. "This has been a really great first first date."

"First *first* date? As in your first date *ever*?"

She grimaced. "Yeah, sort of."

He looked at her for a long moment. "Explain."

She opened her mouth and then closed it again. She shrugged, embarrassed, and spent a moment getting a glass of water. It was hard to believe talking about herself made her feel more naked than actually being naked, but there it was.

"Were you a nun until recently?" he asked.

She laughed. "No."

"Sheltered?"

She laughed again, this time a little bitterly. "No. It's no big thing. I've obviously been with men. I've just never done this, the dressing up and going out thing."

"Which we never got to," he said with deep regret.

"It's okay. It was still really great."

He took the drink from her hand and drew her out of the kitchen. They dressed, and he drove them to Seattle after all, to a small intimate bar downtown that had a really great band. They danced, talked, and laughed, and then danced some more.

Amy had never once had a guy set an entire evening around her and her needs. It made her feel things, and for once she didn't mind. She felt special. Cherished. And hours later, when they pulled back up to his cabin, she turned to him and smiled. "Heck of a first date, Ranger Hot Buns." Leaning in, she kissed him softly.

"Thank you," she whispered against his mouth, which curved gently.

"You're welcome." He tucked a loose strand of hair behind her ear. "But it's not over yet."

"No?"

He led her inside and to his kitchen, where they shared a three a.m. plate of cookies and mugs of milk, dressed this time. She sat on his counter, and he stood at her side, smiling at her.

"What?" she asked.

"You have a crumb..." He licked the corner of her mouth, then used the excuse to kiss the daylights out of her.

"That was a ploy," she said when they broke apart for air.

"Uh huh." He started removing her clothes, until she sat bare assed on his counter, trying not to squeal at the feel of the cold tile beneath her cheeks. "Okay, this can't be sanitary."

He smiled and stripped, making her heart stutter in her chest because he was so beautiful. "Nice," she said.

He pushed her legs open and stepped between them, and she forgot all about being cold or sanitary.

Wrapping his hand in her hair, he gently tugged her head to the side and kissed her neck.

"Again?" she breathed, melting when he opened his mouth and sucked a little patch of skin.

"Oh, yeah, again," he said. "And then again."

"We won't be able to walk."

He nipped her collarbone and headed south toward her breast. "I'm going to be so good to you, you won't care."

Chapter 15

Researchers have discovered that chocolate produces some of the same reactions in the brain as marijuana. The researchers also discovered other similarities between the two but can't remember what they are.

That next morning, Matt's alarm went off. He was alone. Nothing unusual about that, he told himself, and rose.

Half an hour later, he and Josh were hanging off a cliff together. It was barely dawn, and Josh was tense and bitchy because he'd only gotten three hours of sleep thanks to a long ER shift.

Matt hadn't gotten even three hours of sleep but he wasn't tense and bitchy. Maybe a little freaked out. He had no idea what he was doing with Amy. At least not other than making her cry out his name whenever she was naked. *That*, he'd discovered, he was very good at.

"Shut up," Josh said.

"I didn't say anything."

"You didn't have to. Your just-got-laid smile is saying it all for you. Loudly. Have some sympathy on those of us not getting any."

Matt slid his longtime friend a look. "You could be getting some.

What happened to what's-her-name? That hot red-headed nurse you were talking about?"

"She told me how she'd been dreaming about marrying a doctor since she was eight."

Matt winced. "That'll do it. What about that cute brunette you met when you operated on her brother's mysterious head injury?"

"Turns out she's the one who gave him that injury."

"Ah. Okay, how about that new chick...Grace? The one who's friends with Amy and Mallory?"

"Hell, no."

"Why not? She's pretty."

"Yeah, but she's Mallory's and Amy's friend," Josh said.

"So?"

"*So*," Josh said in the tone that suggested Matt was a complete moron. "Ty fell for Mallory. It might be contagious."

Matt laughed. "You're a doctor. Whatever you catch, just give yourself a shot and get over it."

"Is that what you're going to do? After you finish falling for Amy, you're just going to get over it?"

This shut Matt up because he had no clue.

Josh shook his head. "I've given up dating for now. It's just too damn hard anyway, with Toby and Anna."

"Your son and sister wouldn't want you to give up your life for them."

Josh lifted a shoulder. "I'm working seventy-five hours a week. I don't have time to date."

"Man, that's just sad."

"Says the guy who works the same crazy hours I do. How are you fitting your relationship with Amy into that schedule? You prepared for the pissy girlfriend act when she finds out how you're always on the job?"

"She's not my girlfriend."

Josh snorted. "You haven't seen Facebook yet today, I take it."

"You don't have time for women, but you have time for Facebook?"

"My office manager has it as my homepage," Josh said. "Thinks she's amusing. But it was very amusing today. You went out with Amy, a date that ended with you being a fucking action hero."

Matt stared at him. "How the hell did *that* get out?"

"Lucille was at the station when Sawyer brought the guys in. She'd just bailed out Mrs. Burland for running over her neighbor's foot—twice." Josh raised a brow. "Nice start to a date, playing Superman. How did that work out for you?"

Pretty good. He could still remember every breathy pant, every soft moan, every hungry "oh, please, Matt" that Amy had whispered in his ear. Not wanting to go there with Josh, Matt ignored the question and kept moving.

"Wow, evading," Josh said. "Subtle."

"Why don't I climb with Ty?" Matt wondered out loud. "He doesn't ask stupid questions."

"Because he's too pussy to climb."

Matt laughed. Ty wasn't "pussy" about much. Except heights.

They were halfway down when something caught Matt's attention across the long, broad chasm at Widow's Peak, the cliff three hundred feet across the way. Climbers. They were at the midpoint plateau of Widow Peak's face, which he knew they'd had to have gotten to by way of a closed-off trail. He knew this because he'd closed off the trail himself.

The climbers were whooping and hollering it up, and Matt shook his head. "Shit."

"Kids?" Josh asked.

"Can't tell."

"Isn't that entire area closed off?"

"Yeah," Matt said grimly, scrambling down. "I closed it because of rock slide problems. It's not safe."

Josh hit the ground only three beats behind him, squinting

through the sun, shading his eyes with a hand. "Looks like a total of four idiots. Nope, five."

Matt pulled binoculars from his pack and took in the sight of the climbers passing something between them. Tension gathered in a ball at the base of his spine. "They're getting high first," he said, shoving the binoculars at Josh, then gathering his gear.

"We going to go scare them off?"

"Hell, yeah."

They moved to Matt's truck, where he replaced his climbing gear with a utility belt, including weapons.

"Do I get one of those?" Josh asked.

"No."

"But I get to look all scary and intimidating, right?"

Matt looked Josh over. Out of his scrubs, Josh didn't look much like a doctor. He looked like a six-foot-four NFL linebacker. "I don't know," Matt said, baiting him. "Can you do scary and intimidating?"

Josh narrowed his eyes. "If I hadn't taken an oath to *save* lives, not take them, I'd show *you* scary and intimidating right now."

"Save it for the idiots."

Fifteen minutes later, Matt parked at the trailhead to Widow's Peak. "Hell."

"What?" Josh asked.

"The gate's open." And he'd locked it personally. "The CLOSED sign is missing."

"That's not good."

"Nope." Matt drove through the gate, taking the fire road that would bring them to the same midpoint plateau that the climbers were on. They had to park about a quarter of a mile from the area, where they found another truck—the climbers' vehicle, no doubt. Matt and Josh hiked the rest of the way in, startling the guys just as they were getting ready to take a go at the peak.

"This area is closed," Matt told them.

The climbers were in their late teens. Three of the four of them took one look at Josh and Matt and just about shit their pants. Not their ringleader, whom Matt recognized as Trevor Wright, the teenage son of Allen Wright, a very successful builder who thought he was God's gift to the entire county. With a cocky grin, Trevor held his ground. "Who're you, the climbing police?"

"Yeah, I'm the climbing police." Matt badged him. "And you're not supposed to be here."

"Public property, dude."

Matt shook his head. This was the problem with the Wrights in general. They thought they owned Lucky Harbor, and everything around it. They also thought the laws didn't apply to them. All four boys smelled like weed. Hell, there was practically a cloud of it around Trevor's head. "The gate was shut and locked," Matt said mildly. "And there was a CLOSED sign."

"Sorry, man. That gate was wide open, and I didn't see no sign. And you're hassling us for no reason. We haven't done nothing wrong."

Trevor's friends weren't looking so comfortable anymore and had started to back up. "Come on, Trev," one of them said. "Let's hit it."

Trevor widened his tough-guy stance. "They can't do anything to us," he said, smiling right at Matt. "They're only rangers. They know the names of the flowers and how to start a fire."

"Luckily I know how to do a little more than that," Matt said. "And if you're carrying drugs, I'll arrest you."

Trevor shrugged out of his backpack and tossed it over the cliff, where it promptly vanished into thin air, careening off the rocks as it fell to the valley floor hundreds of feet below. "I'm not carrying anything."

"Jesus, Trevor," one of his friends said. "You're crazy."

"Yeah," another said. "We're outta here." He and the others took off.

Trevor stood there posturing for a long beat and then started after his friends, shoulder checking Matt hard as he did. "You see that?" the little dickwad said to Josh. "Your partner *pushed* me." He pointed at Matt. "Not cool, man."

Josh waited until Trevor vanished down the trail after the others. "Okay, so why didn't we crack some heads, specifically his?"

Matt slid him a look. "You have a contact high. You *save* lives, remember?"

"Yes, but the occasional head cracking would be fun."

Matt shook his head. "My job's to chase them out of here. They're chased. Let's go."

They closed the gate, and Matt radioed dispatch that he needed a new lock and sign brought out. Then he and Josh drove all the way around the canyon and hit the meadow floor, looking for that backpack.

They didn't find it.

An hour later, Josh, who'd called in to the hospital that he was going to be late so that he could help Matt search, rubbed his stomach. "I'm starving. You're buying."

"Why me?" Matt asked. "Your paycheck's a *lot* bigger than mine."

"You got laid last night."

"What does that have to do with who's buying breakfast?"

"Everything."

"How much farther?" Grace asked breathlessly.

"We've only gone a quarter of a mile," Amy said.

"But I'm ready for a chocolate break." This was from Mallory, who swiped an arm over her damp brow.

"You both walk farther for your morning coffee," Amy said. She'd been worrying about Riley, and was tired of waiting for the girl to come to her. Amy was going proactive. So they were heading toward the Squaw Flats campgrounds, though Amy had told the

Chocoholics only that it was a great day for a hike and had lured them up the mountain with the promise of brownies as a prize.

"Here's another good girl lesson," Mallory said. "Never refer to your friends' lack of fitness."

Grace looked around at the lush, thick growth and inhaled deeply. "It smells like Christmas out here."

"Tell me again why we're hiking instead of sitting in a nice booth at the diner?" Mallory asked.

"We're calorie burning," Amy said. "It means guilt-free brownies. Just another quarter of a mile or so."

"Seriously," Grace said, huffing and puffing as they moved along. "This taking the Chocoholics on the road experiment might be a bust. Are we almost there yet?"

Amy shook her head. "And I thought *I* was a city girl."

"I have to pee," Grace said.

"There's a bunch of trees," Amy said. "Pick one."

"Like I trust *your* judgment on pee spots."

"Maybe you should," Mallory said. "It caught her Ranger Hot Buns."

"True," Grace mused. "Do you ever call him that?" she asked Amy.

Amy laughed. "Not if I want to live."

They came across a small clearing. The sun was strong here, and it was beautiful. But they weren't the only ones enjoying it. Leaning with their backs to a fallen log sat Lance and Tucker. The two brothers were eating sandwiches and sucking down bottled water. Covered in dust from head to toe, their grins appeared all the whiter when they flashed them.

"Hey, ladies," Lance said in his low and husky voice, roughened from years of the lung-taxing coughing the CF caused him. "Looking good."

Tucker held up a baggie of brownies. "Anyone want to join us?"

"Oh my God, *yes*," Grace said with great feeling. "Amy's being a brownie Nazi."

Mallory put out a hand and halted her, serving the brothers a careful, narrow-eyed gaze. "Are those brownies *home*-made?"

Tucker grinned, slow, lazy and unabashed, and Amy burst out laughing. She hadn't thought about the *quality* of their brownies, but she should have when it came to Tucker.

Mallory shook her head at the guys. "What did I tell you about your brownies?"

"Uh..." Tucker said, trying to think. "That they kill brain cells?"

"Chocolate doesn't kill brain cells," Grace said, oblivious to what they were talking about. "Chocolate is God's gift."

"Not the way these two make it," Amy told her as Mallory gave them the bum's rush back onto the trail.

A few minutes later, they neared Squaw Flats. "You two rest here for a few," Amy said, and pulled out the lunch she'd packed from the diner, handing out sandwiches. "I'm going to just go up the road another half a mile to check out a vista I want to draw later. Wait here."

"Where're the brownies?" Grace asked.

Amy pulled out the stash. "Not as good as what Tucker had," she said dryly. "But they'll do. I'll be right back."

"Don't fall down any ravines," Mallory said, and took a big bite out of her brownie. Apparently she liked dessert first, too. "I've got the same first aid skills as Matt, but I doubt I've got the same bedside manner."

Grace snickered, and Amy rolled her eyes. But it was true. Matt had some seriously good bedside manner.

Amy found Riley about a third of a mile away, sunning on a rock, staring pensively out at a colorful meadow. The rains had been steady last season, leaving the meadow alive with head-high grass and wildflowers. All around them, the air pulsed with buzzing insects and butterflies.

Riley looked over, caught sight of Amy, and sighed.

Amy pulled a bag from her backpack and dropped it at Riley's feet.

"What's this?"

"Look inside," Amy said.

Riley paused for a long beat, making it clear that she would do only whatever she wanted to do and on her own schedule. But clearly her curiosity finally got the best of her and she opened the pack. Inside was more bottled water, a lunch like the one she'd packed the Chocoholics, and soap and shampoo.

"Thought you might be low on supplies," Amy said.

Riley nodded. "Thanks." While she looked over the goods, Amy looked *her* over. Riley had shadows in her eyes and dark circles under them. She wasn't getting enough sleep, that much was clear.

"There's a key to my place in the side pocket. It's yours." Amy paused. "Come back with me."

"I'm good here."

"You're not supposed to be here."

"You said you wouldn't tell."

Amy sighed and sat next to her. "I haven't. I won't. But it's not safe for you."

"Trust me," Riley said, pulling out a sandwich. "It's safer than anywhere else."

Amy's heart squeezed. God, she'd so been there. "I realize you think you have no one to trust, but it's not true."

Riley slowed down the inhaling of her sandwich. She didn't respond, but Amy knew she was listening.

"I ran away from home when I was sixteen," Amy said softly. "I never looked back. My goal was to get as far away as possible. I hitchhiked with strangers and slept in alleys. I trusted no one, and as a result, no one trusted me."

Riley hugged her knees to her chest. "How did you do it?"

"I lied about my age and took whatever jobs I could get. Except for hooking, I managed to avoid that one."

"I never hooked either," Riley said quickly.

"Good. Because you're worth far more than that. You know that, right?"

Riley hunched her shoulders. "I know I don't want any guy's hands on me."

Amy let out a shaky breath as her own memories hit her hard. This was as she suspected, and as she feared. "Who put his hands on you?"

Riley laid her head down on her knees, her face turned away from Amy.

"Someone at home?"

Still as a statue, Riley didn't respond.

"Your dad?"

"Don't have one. And I got taken away from my mom. She wasn't fit."

"So you were in foster care," Amy said.

A pause. Then a quiet, "yeah."

Where she'd probably been mistreated, possibly sexually abused, and had decided that the entire male species sucked golf balls.

Couldn't blame her, though Amy herself had gone the opposite route. Sex had become power, and for a long time, she'd really liked holding the power.

"I just want to be free to do what I want," Riley said. "Without anyone trying to force me to do something I don't want to do."

"Well, of course. *Everyone* wants that," Amy said. "Everyone deserves that. Riley, you aren't alone."

Riley turned her head and looked at Amy, seeming heartbreakingly young.

"You have me," Amy said. "And together we're a 'we.' "

"But you're already a 'we.' With the ranger."

Amy had never been a "we" with a man. At least not for more than a few hours, and that Riley thought Amy was with Matt startled her. But she sure as hell didn't want to explain to Riley that all she and Matt had was a mutual enjoyment of rubbing their favorite body parts together.

"Not exactly," she said. "Did you think about the job?" It would keep her in sight, and Amy could watch over her, make sure she was safe and eating. She waited for Riley to once again ask why Amy cared but she didn't.

Progress.

"I've thought about it," Riley said. "I'll do it."

Baby steps, but that was okay. Amy had discovered life was all about baby steps.

Chapter 16

One of life's little mysteries is how a two-pound box of chocolate can make a person gain five pounds.

Matt had a hell of a long day, which included noncompliant picnickers, a search-and-rescue mission for a beginning biker on an advanced trail, a small wildfire in the fourth quadrant, which had nearly gotten away from them, and the arrest of an idiot for illegal poaching. When he finally left his post, he went to the diner for a late meal.

Okay, he went to the diner to catch sight of Amy. He deserved it after the day he'd had. Amy happened to be on a break when he walked in, sitting at a small table in the far corner, bent over something.

Drawing, he realized when he got closer. She was sketching on her pad, oblivious to the room. Or at least she was until he got about halfway across the diner, then suddenly she went still, lifted her head, and met his gaze.

Lots of things flickered across her face, with heat leading the way. But what grabbed him by the throat and held on was the reluctant affection.

She wanted him. He'd proven that. Hell, he wanted her right back. But she also liked him. She didn't want to, but she did. Inexplicably buoyed by that, he slid into her side of the booth, pressing his thigh to hers. "Hey."

"Hey." As always, she closed her sketch book and slid it away from him. "I was just taking a break."

"You ever going to let me see your drawings?"

"I don't know. They're sort of personal."

He leaned in close. "You've shared your body with me. And that felt pretty personal."

She gave him a little shove and a laugh. "*Not* the same thing."

Enjoying the sound of her amusement and the fact that she looked so pretty smiling, he let one of his own escape. "One of these days, you're going to *want* to share with me."

"My drawings?"

"Those too."

She nudged him again, less of a shove this time. "Move. I'll get up and get your order going."

He didn't move, but he did enjoy her hands on him, one on his arm, the other on his chest, especially since they lingered as if she couldn't help herself. "I'm a patient man, Amy. I can wait."

"It's late, and you've got to be hungry," she said, purposely misinterpreting that sentence. "At least let me put your order in. The usual, right? Or a double-double?"

They'd shared a double-double just last night, and it hadn't been food. And actually, she'd gotten more than two orgasms. Maybe even a quadruple. He smiled at the memory, and she pointed at him.

"Stop that," she said.

"Stop what?"

"You know what. You're thinking *things*."

He laughed. "Okay, you caught me. I'm definitely thinking… *things*."

She looked around to see if anyone was paying them any attention. No one was. He'd come late enough tonight that the place was nearly emptied out. Only two customers were at the counter and one at a table on the far side of the diner. Leaning in, Matt put his mouth to the sweet spot just beneath Amy's ear. "Why don't you tell me what things you think I'm thinking?"

She actually blushed beet red, which was so adorably revealing that he laughed. She shoved him again, which made him laugh more.

"You're crazy," she said.

Yes. It was entirely possible that he was crazy. Crazy for her.

Riley walked by. She was wearing ratty jeans, battered sneakers, a sweatshirt he recognized as Amy's, and a bright pink Eat Me apron. She was carrying a tray of dirty glasses and dishes and a very large chip on her shoulder. Matt looked at Amy.

"I got her a job," she said, and when he smiled at her, she lifted a shoulder. "It was no big deal."

But it was. "You're helping her."

"Anyone would."

"That's the thing," he said. "They wouldn't. They don't."

She stared at him. "You seem to have this blind faith in me, like I'm a good person and some sort of decent influence."

"You are." He reached out and pushed a strand of hair back off her face, stroking it behind her ear. "You don't give yourself enough credit."

She was already shaking her head. "You don't know me."

"I know enough. It's all there in your eyes."

Those eyes met his now, filled with a warmth he didn't know if he'd ever get used to.

"Your life has been very different from mine," she said.

"Does it matter?"

"Depends."

"On what?"

She looked around the diner, then back at him. And then she put her hand on her sketchbook and pushed it across the table toward him.

Not one to squander an opportunity, Matt put his hand over hers on the book. "Yeah?"

She paused and then pulled her hand free. "Yeah."

He held her gaze, smiled at her, then opened the book and found himself completely speechless at the sheer mind-blowing talent leaping off the page. Each drawing was a rendering of the Pacific Northwest in some fashion or another. Squaw Flats, Eagle Rock, Four Lakes, Sierra Meadows, and Widow's Peak, she'd done them all, rendering them in colored pencil, so perfectly that he could almost smell the pines and feel the breeze. "Amy, Jesus. You're amazing."

"Thanks." Her cheeks were a little pink with the praise, making him wonder if she'd ever shown anyone her drawings before.

He flipped back to Sierra Meadows. "This is close to where I found you that night, when you were... not lost."

That earned him a small smile. "The night I fell down the ravine. The night you shared your tent."

"Which has been in heavy rotation in my fantasies ever since."

"You have some sort of a rescue fetish, Ranger Hot Buns?"

"No, I have a pale blue panty fetish."

She let out a low laugh. "It was dark."

"I have panty x-ray vision. God-given talent."

She laughed again, and the sound warmed him, but he couldn't take his eyes off her work. "You're so talented," he said, truly awed. "You should show these more often. You know Lucille runs an art gallery, right? She'd love these."

"They've always been just for me."

He met her gaze. "So what changed? Why show me now?"

She paused. "Well, I guess it's because you let me in. You told me about your childhood, your family. Your past. You've counted on me to help Riley." She shrugged. "You shared yourself with me, so I guess that somehow makes it okay for me to share with you."

At this, Matt felt his smile slowly fade, and guilt twisted in his gut. She thought he'd opened up, when in fact he'd purposely told her only the good things. What was even worse was that he'd let her think she could trust him, count on him. He liked the idea of her trusting him, a lot, but the last time he'd been down this road, he'd fucked up. Royally. His ex could attest to that. He'd promised not to get attached, but he was.

Deeply.

And suddenly, he wasn't in the least bit hungry. Suddenly his stomach was burning and churning. Suddenly, he had to go. Be alone. Now. Gently, he pushed her sketch pad back to her.

She cocked her head to the side, eyes on his, clearly sensing a change in him, but just as clearly not understanding what.

As he couldn't understand it either, there was no way to explain it to her. "Jan's trying to get your attention," he said.

She held his gaze a moment longer, eyes sharp. He hadn't fooled her. But in classic Amy fashion, she took the easy way out and let him distract her. She glanced up at Jan, who was indeed pointing to her watch.

Matt stood up and let her out of the booth. She brushed against him as she did and sucked in a breath at the contact.

He did, too, but he managed to keep his hands to himself, shoving them into his pockets to ensure it. *She's not for you...*

Amy hesitated for a moment, and Matt held his breath, though he shouldn't have bothered. She didn't press for answers. She wouldn't, because as he'd counted on, that's not how she operated. And then there was the bottom line—she didn't want this any more than he did.

That night Amy went home, running through the light rain to her apartment, hoping the damp had brought Riley back.

It hadn't.

She grabbed her mail and dropped it all on the kitchen table. Mostly junk, but there was a manila envelope from New York, and she recognized her mother's handwriting. She spent a moment staring at the package as if it were a striking cobra before she opened it.

Inside was a short note and a small notebook. The note said:

> *I've had this all these years, but it occurred to me after you called that maybe it's your turn to hold on to it. Mom*

The notebook was identical to her grandma's journal. She opened it and then realized it wasn't identical at all. The paper in this notebook wasn't lined. And someone had filled the pages with sketches. Not in colored pencil, like Amy did, just black charcoal, but the sketches were so eerily similar to her own that Amy sank to a chair, weak-kneed. Lucky Harbor, Sierra Meadows, Four Lakes, Squaw Flats... the images wavered as Amy found herself choked up.

She hadn't known her grandma could draw.

She flipped through, marveling, swiping her eyes on her sleeve. There was only one picture she didn't recognize, the very last one—a vista of rough-edged, craggy mountain peaks that was so wonderfully depicted she could almost smell the trees.

This drawing was different than the others. This drawing had a figure sketched in, a woman. Drawn in shadow, she stood in profile on the plateau, the wind blowing her hair and scarf out behind her as she held something above her head. A container. From it came a cloud of dust—

Oh, no. Amy's heart sank. Not dust. She thought back to the journal entry before, where her grandma had switched from the "we" to "I."

She'd not been with Jonathon on this journey, at least not a living, breathing Jonathon.

Amy turned to the journal and reread the last entry again.

...standing at the very tippy top, looking out at a blanket of green, a sea of blue...

Amy eyed the drawing. It certainly looked like the tippy top. She opened her map. The highest peak was Widow's Peak. Her grandma hadn't left her initials on that mountain.

She'd left Jonathon's ashes.

I would never settle. I would never stop growing. I would never give up...

Coming here had given her grandma the hope and peace she needed to go on with her life after losing Jonathon. She'd gotten the hope to go on. And the peace to live without him. Amy understood that. She'd followed her grandma's journey to make a change in her life, too, to learn about herself. To grow.

Baby steps, and like Riley, she was taking them.

She ran her fingers over her grandmother's drawing of Widow's Peak. Her grandma had never settled, and she wouldn't either. She'd never give up. She went through the pictures one last time, and when she finally closed the book, her resolve to finish this journey was renewed. She definitely had hope and peace now, and she wanted the rest. She wanted to find her heart.

Two days later, Amy had a day off and was mountain-bound, equipped with her grandma's drawings. She'd studied the map and had found a trail called Heart-Stopper. Was it possible that grandma's "heart" moment had been a play on words? The problem was that the Heart-Stopper Trail ran perpendicular along the Rim Trail, except higher up, along the top of the peaks, from the north rim all along to the south rim in a huge semicircle, connecting the two. The loop that Matt had insinuated was too hard for her. She'd have to break it up into a few separate trips.

Or she could show Matt the drawing and see if he could help.

And she would have—except she kept playing that night in the diner over and over in her head. He'd backed off, and she didn't know why.

But it was okay. She could figure this out, just like she'd figured all her other shit out.

She cheated by taking the fire roads up past Squaw Flats and Sierra Meadows, straight to the trailhead of Heart-Stopper. It was beautiful, but she felt…off.

That's because you miss Matt…

How ironic was that? She'd told him not to get attached, and then she'd done it. She'd gotten damn attached.

Not that it mattered, not that it would slow her down. Matt wasn't her journey. *This* was her journey.

But though she managed to hike half the Heart-Stopper Trail before she had to turn back, she never found anything specific. Unlike at Sierra Meadows or Four Lakes, there was nothing obvious, nothing in her notes to point out a direct item. And of course, there were a million trees. It was like looking for a needle in a haystack, and she'd had to admit defeat for the day. She got back to the North District Ranger Station just before dark. Matt's truck was in the lot, and seeing it put butterflies in her belly. She *never* got butterflies. Damn man. So they hadn't spoken in a few days, so what? It wasn't a big deal, and certainly not the reason why she entered the building. Nope, she just needed a new map is all.

And maybe, if she saw him, she'd tell him about her grandma's drawings. Not that she wanted to see him…

But she did. He was on the phone behind the reception area, his broad back to her. Amy picked out the new map and paid the young ranger-in-training behind the desk while simultaneously trying not to notice that Matt really earned the moniker of Ranger Hot Buns.

He turned and caught her staring. Still on the phone, he arched a single brow.

She waved her map at him and ran out. "You," she said to her reflection in the rearview mirror when she was in her car and on the road, "are an idiot."

At home, she showered then joined Mallory and Grace for a night out. They went to the Love Shack, Lucky Harbor's one and only bar and grill. The place was done up like an old Wild West saloon, complete with walls of deep bordello red, lined with old mining tools. Lanterns hung over the scarred bench-style tables. The bar itself was a series of old wood doors attached end to end. Run by former world sailing champion Ford Walker and Lucky Harbor's mayor Jax Cullen, the place was never wanting for customers.

The three women got a table and ordered a pitcher of margaritas, which was served by Jax himself. Tall, dark, and handsome, Jax poured them each an iced, salted glass with a smile that could charm the panties right off a nun. "Enjoy, ladies."

"He's hot," Grace said, watching his ass as he walked off.

"Yes," Mallory agreed. "And very taken by one sweet Maddie Moore, who runs the B&B down the road." She lifted her glass. "To leaving Chocolate-ville for Margarita-ville."

Grace lifted her glass. "To new chapters."

Amy clicked her glass to theirs. "To *no* good girls tonight."

They all drank to that, until Grace suddenly choked.

"What's the matter?" Amy asked, pounding her on the back.

Grace coughed and sputtered some more, then recovered, as in unison Amy and Mallory swiveled their heads to see what she'd been looking at.

Two tables over sat three guys. Three gorgeous guys. Ty Garrison, Dr. Josh Scott, and Forest Ranger Hot Buns, all focused in on the Chocoholics' table, smiling as if they saw something they liked.

Ty set down his drink and ambled over. He pulled a grinning

Mallory from her chair and into his arms, and without a word, planted a long, hot, deep kiss on her. Finally, when surely they had to be out of air, he pulled back. "See you later," he said with a naughty smile, then guided Mallory carefully back to her chair as if she were a precious commodity.

He was back at his table with the guys before Mallory recovered. "He's mine," she said, sounding shell shocked. "Can you believe it?"

Grace was fanning herself. "Does he always kiss you like that?"

"That?" Mallory asked, still looking dazed. "That was just the appetizer on the Ty menu of kisses."

"You are one lucky woman," Grace said.

Mallory grinned. "I am, aren't I?"

Amy's gaze was still locked in on Matt. He was as fixated on her.

The music was loud, the sounds in the bar joyous and rambunctious. There was dancing, and after a few minutes, Ty came back and stole Mallory away. Several other guys lined up to ask Grace to dance, and someone asked Amy as well.

But she didn't want to dance with a stranger.

She didn't want to dance at all.

What she wanted felt complicated and scary, but hell, baby steps, right? *Right.* So she got up and walked to where Matt and Josh were sitting. Both men smiled at her, but she had eyes only for Matt. He was still in his uniform, hair mussed, eyes shadowed and brooding. He'd gotten some sun today, but he looked weary to the bone.

Clearly it'd been a long day.

But there was something about this quiet, brooding Matt that got to her. He was so...real. Everything he was, everything down to the bone, was genuine.

And he'd come here instead of to the diner. To avoid her? Something settled in her gut. Disappointment. Regret. Worry. She tried to gauge his thoughts but couldn't. He wasn't drinking; the only thing in front of him was a soda, no doubt his beloved Dr. Pepper.

Maybe he was still working…

Josh stood up and took her hand. "You owe me a dance."

She laughed. "I do not."

"Okay, I owe you a dance. For all that great service you always give me at the diner, complete with such sweet smiles."

She gave him a long look. She wasn't known for her sweet smiles. They all knew that she wasn't known for her sweet *anything*.

But he flashed her a grin and smoothly pulled her onto the dance floor before she could protest. "Look at you," she said, surprised. "You can move."

"You know it," he said, dancing with the kind of abandon only a big white guy with absolutely no sense of shame could pull off.

She had to laugh, and then again when he moved in close and purposely bumped his very nice body up against hers, his hands on her hips. "Josh," she said, smiling up at him, "why are you flirting with me?"

He grinned. "Because it's pissing off Matt."

She glanced over at Matt, still at the table, still nursing his soda, staring at them with an unreadable look on his face. "Nothing pisses Matt off," she said. "He doesn't let anything get to him."

Josh chuckled and leaned in closer. "Don't let his cool exterior fool you. He lets plenty eat at him. He's just good at hiding it."

"Well, then you're mistaken about his feelings for me," Amy said. "He won't care that we're dancing."

"Hmm," Josh said, noncommittally. The music slowed, and he pulled her close so that she felt his chest rumble with his own amusement. "What's he doing now?" he asked.

Amy took a peek, and her heart skipped a beat at the sight of Matt, still slouched in his chair. "Just watching."

"Watching, and getting more and more irritated with me, I'd bet." Josh sounded quite pleased at the thought. "He cares, Amy, big time."

"And you're doing this why?"

"Because I'm banking on the fact that you care, too."

The song ended, and Josh gave her a hug, and then ambled off toward the bar. When she walked past Matt's table to get to hers, he stood up.

"Hey," she said, her heart taking a good hard leap just before she realized he wasn't looking at her. He was on his cell phone. "Sorry," she mouthed.

He shook his head, silently telling her it wasn't her fault, but he didn't stop. Instead, he headed straight for the door.

She stared after him. There was no denying it. She'd hoped to see him tonight, maybe talk. And if he hadn't looked so...well, distant, she might have also thought about stealing a kiss.

Or two.

Yeah, that's what she really wanted. She could admit it to herself. She wanted his arms around her. She wanted his warm eyes looking into hers, making her feel like the only woman on earth, like only he could do.

She wanted to taste him, have him taste her. She'd wanted to slide her fingers into his silky hair and feel his warm strength surround her, making her feel safe.

And instead, he'd walked away from her without looking back. And though she'd done just that too many times in her life to count, she hadn't realized how bad it sucked to be on the receiving end until now.

Chapter 17

Chocolate. It isn't just for breakfast anymore.

Matt moved out of The Love Shack and into the night. As he got behind the wheel of his truck, Josh opened the passenger door and took the shotgun position without a word.

"Hell no," Matt said. "You're walking."

Josh chuckled but locked his door and buckled in. "Man, you are so gone over her. You ran out of there like a scared little girl and nearly forgot your wing man."

"You suck as a wing man. And I was heading out because I got a call. Climber down."

Josh's smile faded. "Injuries?"

"Bad. That's all I know."

"Hit it."

"You had a beer," Matt said.

"Never got a chance to even take a sip, so I'm good."

Matt nodded and hit the gas, heading toward Widow's Peak while Josh pulled up a GPS of the area.

"I know exactly where we're going," Matt said grimly. "The

guys we chased off of the face last week went back tonight for a moonlight hike."

"Shit."

Matt turned off the highway and spared Josh a glance. "And since when are you Fred Astaire?"

Josh shrugged. "Pretty girl in my arms. What's not to like?"

Matt ground his teeth. Amy *was* a pretty girl. She was *his* pretty girl.

Except she wasn't.

He'd caught the look she'd given him tonight as he'd left. In spite of the fact that he'd been an asshole, she was concerned. Worried.

About him.

When she looked at him like that, all sweet eyed and tender-hearted, it did something to him. She'd looked at him like she wanted to take care of him, like she wanted to make it all better for him, and for a beat, he'd wanted her to do just that.

Which was not going to happen. He didn't need anyone to take care of him.

"And you told me to find a woman," Josh said. "Remember? You said—"

"Not *that* woman."

"Well you should have been more specific," Josh said in such a reasonable tone that Matt wanted to wipe the floor with his face.

Knowing it, Josh laughed softly, which Matt ignored because his phone was going crazy. First dispatch checking his ETA, then his boss wondering what the fuck a group of climbers were doing on Widow's Peak at ten o'clock at night, in an area supposedly closed off to the public.

Matt would like to know the same thing.

"Did you get an injury update?" Josh asked when he'd hung up.

"No one's on scene yet. S&R are en route, too." Matt took the fire road that would bring them to the same midpoint where they'd found the climbers before. Once again, they had to hike the last quarter mile in, this time in the dark.

At the cliff's edge, two guys were huddled, glancing anxiously down. A third had attempted to climb over to rescue the fourth and had gotten stuck, terrified, about ten feet down.

Much farther down, thirty feet or so, was the fourth, lying still on a ledge.

Trevor Wright.

Search and rescue arrived just as Matt and Josh did. Everyone mobilized quickly, and in ten minutes, they had the first climber up. He had no injuries. Ten minutes more and they had the still-unconscious Trevor on a stretcher belaying him up with ropes, where he was then immediately airlifted out with Josh on board, looking grim.

Matt headed back to his truck alone and drove to the station, where he wrote up his report before heading to the hospital. He was furious, at himself. He'd known those kids would be trouble and should have found a way to keep them off the mountain.

Unfortunately, the update on Trevor wasn't good. He was in critical care, and his very connected father was already making noises about suing the state, the county, the forest service, and Matt as well. Everyone and anyone over his son's injuries.

The North District station was going to have a battle on its hands, and for Matt, it felt like Chicago all over again.

He grabbed an hour of sleep and by dawn was heading out with Sawyer to talk to the three uninjured climbers. Each of them vehemently denied that drugs or booze had been involved in the previous night's climb.

Matt could only hope that the tests run on Trevor proved otherwise. He and Sawyer had just pulled away from the last climber's house when Matt's boss called, reaming him for the entire fiasco from start to finish.

"What?" Sawyer asked when Matt hung up and swore. "The kid take a turn for the worse?"

"No," Matt said. "In fact, he woke up long enough to claim that none of them touched the gate, that they honestly believed the trail was open."

"Bullshit."

"Gets worse," Matt said. "He also says that I put my hands on him that day I chased him off the peak. That I pushed him."

"Little dick syndrome," Sawyer said. "Fucking punks."

"Yes but he's also a punk with a lawyer, who's already all over it."

"Fine," Sawyer said. "You have Josh as a witness that you didn't touch any of them."

"There's still going to be a formal inquiry. I'm going to have to go in front of the board to explain how this happened on a closed trail, a trail I shut down myself."

Sawyer shook his head and spoke grimly. "They're going to blame you for minors vandalizing the gate locks and sign, then trespassing on a closed trail while possibly under the influence. Fuckers."

"They're going to do what they have to in order to resolve this without a lawsuit." Matt punched Josh's number into his cell. "Talk to me."

"He's lawyered up."

"Tell me something I *don't* know," Matt said. "There's going to be an inquiry. This is a great time to spill about Wright being under the influence of something."

"Shit, Matt." Josh let out a long breath. "You know I can't tell you that. He's a minor. He's got all sorts of rights." He paused. "But per protocol, tests have been sent to the labs."

Okay, Matt could read between the lines on that one. There was the hope that in case of a lawsuit, the results could be subpoenaed. But hope wasn't good enough. Hope wasn't going to save his ass. He disconnected and swore again.

Sawyer took a look at Matt's face and whipped his SUV around.

"What are you doing?"

"You're taking me to the site," Sawyer said. "We're going on a little evidence scavenger hunt."

For the second time in twenty-four hours, Matt climbed up to Widow's Peak and scoured the area. He and Sawyer also searched the meadow floor just beneath the cliffs, where they found five empty bottles of beer and a roach clip. Sawyer bagged them up for DNA evidence.

"Christ," Matt said, the situation hitting him. "This could actually go to trial."

"I don't think it'll get that far," Sawyer said. "These guys are all about the bragging. Trust me, someone will open his mouth about attempting Widow's Peak, and then we'll nail them for trespassing, underage drinking, and whatever else we can get them for."

Matt hoped he was right.

The next night, after a long shift, Amy drove toward home, then made an unexpected detour.

A big one.

She headed toward the mountain and parked in front of Matt's cabin. His truck wasn't there, and she didn't know if that was a good or bad thing. For the third night in a row, he hadn't come to the diner for food, and this time she knew why. All day long she'd heard the gossip about the fallen climber and Matt's supposed negligence. She glanced at the bag she'd packed up, the one sitting on the passenger seat, and called herself all kinds of a fool.

Matt didn't need her to look after him. He was a big boy. But she got out of the car and then found herself standing on his porch, trying to figure out if she should leave the food for him or if that would attract bears, when a truck drove up.

Matt, of course.

Their eyes met as he got out of his vehicle, and her tummy quivered. He was still in uniform, looking dusty, hot, exhausted, and like maybe he could use a good fight.

"Hey," she said softly when he hit the porch.

"Hey." He unlocked his door then turned to her. "I'm not much company tonight."

"You've had a bad day."

He let out a sound that didn't hold any mirth. "Yeah. A bad day." He stepped inside, leaving the front door open.

Not exactly an invite, and she paused, knowing damn well that he clearly wanted to be alone. She recognized the need, since it was how she felt most often.

Sometimes being alone isn't all it's cracked up to be...

He'd said that to her, all those nights ago on the mountain at Sierra Meadows. And he'd been right.

So she stepped inside and shut the door behind her.

He glanced over. Obviously he'd expected to find her gone because he raised a brow at the sight of her.

"Want to tell me about it?" she asked.

"What, the gossip train didn't come through the diner today?"

"Yeah, and I'm the type to get on that train," she said dryly. "How's the guy who fell?"

"In ICU, but it looks like he's going to make it." He shoved his fingers through his hair. "He shouldn't have been on the peak. I had the trail closed off. I chased him and his friends out of there less than a week ago, but they came back."

There was something in his tone that caught her attention. Self blame. "Matt, it's not your fault."

"Yeah, it is." He let out a long, jagged breath. "My district. My problem."

She'd never known anyone like him, so willing to be in charge, and just as willing to take the responsibility that went with that. "Come on, give yourself a break here. You couldn't have known those guys would go back on that climb."

"I knew."

She moved closer. "Well then you also know that you couldn't have stopped them. You're just one man. How are you supposed to keep the entire area patrolled?"

"It's my job to figure out a way."

She ran a hand down his tense back. "God complex much?" she teased.

He moved away from her touch, and while she tried to be okay with that, he spoke again. "I fucked up, Amy. And it's not the first time." He strode into the kitchen and opened the refrigerator. Yanking out a beer, he stared at it, then set it back in the fridge and grabbed a soda. He opened it and handed it to her, then took another for himself. "You asked why I came here from Chicago."

"Yes." She took a long drink because her throat felt suddenly dry.

"I came after everything went to shit. My job, my marriage... *Both* my fault, by the way."

"Matt," she said, setting down her soda, shaking her head. "You—"

"No, it's true. My partner was on the take. I knew it, and I was told to look the other way. I didn't. He tried to implicate me. He couldn't quite pull that off, but he caused enough doubt about me on the job that it hurt my career, and I—*Hell*." Again he shoved his fingers in his hair and turned away from her, staring out the window.

"You what?" she asked softly.

"People didn't like what I'd done, turning Ryan in. He maintained his innocence throughout his trial, and he was well liked. No one wanted to believe it of him."

So he'd taken the heat for turning on him. "You did the right thing," she said, aching for him. He always did the right thing, even when it wasn't the easy thing. "My God, would they have rather he continued?"

He shrugged. "People believe what they want to believe. And it was damn hard for them to believe that of Ryan, even after he went to jail. It was easier to..."

"Blame you?" She shook her head. "You did what you had to. You couldn't have lived with yourself if you'd done nothing."

"I ruined his life. And I ruined Shelly's, too."

"Your ex?"

"Yes. Our marriage failed because she hated being a cop's wife, hated the privacy restrictions my job imposed and the extra security it took to keep her safe when there were bad guys gunning for me. She never believed there was really a threat until she was stalked by someone I'd once put away."

"Oh my God. What happened?"

"He got out of jail and came after her and found her an easy mark. He jumped her in a grocery store parking lot. Pulled a gun on her, but she was able to get away without injury." He shook his head. "The marriage, not so much."

"She blamed you," Amy said quietly.

"She did."

"She knew who she was marrying, Matt," she said carefully. "She knew what she was getting. Telling you that you ruined her life doesn't seem anywhere in the vicinity of fair—"

"It had nothing to do with fair." His voice was grim. He'd obviously blamed himself for it, all of it.

"Oh, Matt." She had no idea how to console him, but he clearly had no desire to be consoled. "I'm sorry."

"You wanted to know," he said. "You wanted the story, and you've got it. You should stay as far from me as you can get, before I screw up your life, too."

"Okay, that's a little—" She broke off because he snatched his keys off the counter and headed out the door. "Matt—"

He turned back to her. "You told me not to get attached, that this was just sex. That still true?"

Shocked, she stared at him, unable to think.

He took in her expression and nodded as if she'd answered the question. "I have to go." He shut the front door behind himself, leaving her alone.

In his house.

She heard his truck start and take off, and she shook her head. *What had just happened?* Did she really let him go, thinking that what they had was just sex? And did he honestly believe that he didn't deserve happiness? He was the best man she'd ever known. If anything, *she* was the one *he* should run from. *She* was the one who'd been stupid and hurtful to the people in her life, not Matt. With every fiber of her being she wanted to help him, but she had no idea how or what to do. Nothing in her life had given her the experience required for this. Good girl lessons certainly hadn't covered this. She was way out of her depth and out of her league.

She drove back to town, still reeling. She glanced at the time. Riley was due to get off work from the diner. The other day, Amy had caught her hitchhiking back to the forest.

Hitchhiking was a good way to get around. Amy had done it herself for years. But it was also a good way to get dead.

She pulled into the diner's parking lot with the intention of driving Riley herself. Jan was closing up, locking the front door. "Girl's out back," Jan called through the glass. "Dumping the trash."

Amy walked around and found Riley standing on the back step tying up a trash bag. "Hey, I'll give you a ride."

Riley looked up. She actually almost smiled before she caught a good look at Amy's face. "What's wrong?"

"Nothing." Since when were her feelings that visible? How had that happened? Once upon a time, she'd been so good at hiding them that no one had ever been able to gauge her moods.

Riley wasn't fooled. "Something's wrong."

"Long day," Amy said. "Come on, I'm parked out front."

Riley shrugged and tossed the trash into the Dumpster, and a minute later, they'd walked around and gotten in Amy's car.

"You going to tell me now?" Riley asked.

"Tell you what?"

"Why you're pissed at me."

Amy blew out a breath and studied the pier ahead of them, shame filling her that she'd let Riley think she could be mad at her, even for a second. "It's not you. I'm sorry if I made you think that." It was late, and everything was quiet and dark. Even the Ferris wheel was still, as still as her heart. "I had a fight with someone."

"Yeah? You kick their ass?"

"Not that kind of fight."

"Oh." Riley sounded disappointed. "Was it with Matt?"

Without warning, Amy's throat tightened. Not wanting to speak, she simply nodded.

Riley sucked in a breath. "He hurt you?"

"No." She turned to Riley and saw the worry in her expression. "No, he'd never hurt me."

Riley relaxed slightly. "But he made you sad."

"Well…a little, yeah. Forget it. It's not your problem."

Riley rustled around in her ratty backpack and came up with two lollipops, clearly pilfered from the small can at the hostess station from the diner. She very sweetly offered out the stolen loot.

Reminded of just how young Riley was, Amy took one. Under normal circumstances, Riley would probably be having her first relationship with a boy about now, writing his name on her notebook, dreaming of proms and football games instead of figuring out where to find her next meal or who was going to try to hurt her next.

"You'll make up," Riley said. "Because he's totally into you. I can tell by the way he's always looking at you. Not like pervy looking," she said quickly, "but like…like he loves you."

Amy doubted that very much. She knew Matt loved being in bed with her, and as it turned out, she loved that, too. And maybe deep, *deep* down, she'd told herself she might have eventually let it turn into more, but she'd been fooling herself. He didn't know her well enough to even think about loving her.

And if he had, he'd have run from her even sooner. "Where's the sweatshirt I gave you?" she asked Riley. "It's cold tonight."

"Crap," Riley said, smacking her own forehead. "I forgot it in the kitchen. Wait here, I'll try to catch Jan before she locks the back." She dashed out of the car and vanished around the corner of the diner.

Amy sighed and set her head down on her steering wheel. Her mind was going too fast.

Or not fast enough.

She didn't understand how it had gone so badly with Matt. And if she was admitting not understanding that, she also didn't understand something else.

He'd walked away from her. Actually, not walked.

Run.

If it had truly been just physical chemistry between them, then why? There'd been no reason for him to go, though she understood the concept well enough. After all, she'd spent her life making sure she was always the one to go. Now it was second nature.

And yet somehow, this time, this one time with Matt, she'd felt different. Like maybe she'd thought that this time there'd be no walking away.

She'd been wrong.

She lifted her head, wondering what was taking Riley so long. *Too* long. She got out of the car and retraced her steps to the back door of the diner.

Riley was there, pinned up against the alley wall by a guy in a hoodie and homeboy jeans. "You owe me, you greedy little bitch," he was saying, hand at Riley's throat, the other one on her breast. "You know you do."

"*Hey!*" Amy yelled, white-hot fury taking over. And something else just as white-hot: Fear. And a terrible sense of déjà vu. "Let her go!"

Mistake number one. Because the guy dropped Riley and turned toward Amy.

Swamped with the memories of another time and place, of a different man who'd wanted Amy to pay what she'd owed, she took a step backward. She tripped over her own feet and went down. Mistake number two.

Because then the guy was on her.

Chapter 18

Man cannot live by chocolate alone,
but it sure is fun trying.

Panicked and driven by horror, Amy scooted back on her butt, but the guy was fast and already towering over her. She reacted with instinct, swinging out with her foot. He hit his knees on the cement steps, and she flung her keys as hard as she could into his face.

"Bitch," he snarled, and slapped a hand over his eyes. "Goddammit, bitch."

"No, Troy, *you're* the bitch," Riley yelled from behind him and clobbered him over the head with what looked like an empty beer bottle.

It shattered.

The guy's eyes went blank, then rolled up in his head, and he slowly fell over.

"Oh my God." Amy lunged over him and grabbed Riley's arms. "Are you okay?"

"F-fine," Riley said, clearly not fine, shaking like a leaf. Amy knew the feeling since she was shaking, too. She pulled Riley over the crumpled body, and they both tumbled inside the kitchen.

Jan, sitting alone at the island, counting receipts, looked up in surprise. "What—"

"Police," Amy managed, slamming and locking the door. "We need to call—"

"No," Riley gasped. "Please don't. I'm fine. He'll go."

Amy looked through the back door window, mouth gaping in surprise. The back stoop was empty. "You're right, he's gone."

"Told you," Riley whispered.

"Who's gone?" Jan asked.

Amy ripped open the back door and stared in shock at the spot where there'd been a body only a moment before. She whipped around and looked at Riley.

Riley lifted a shoulder.

"You knew him," Amy said, once again shutting and locking the door.

"He was just some guy."

"No, you *knew* him. You called him Troy. He said you owed him."

"Just a misunderstanding," Riley said, staring out the window into the night. She'd gathered her wits quickly.

Amy supposed she'd learned how to do that the hard way. "Riley—"

"Don't sweat it."

"Don't *sweat* it? He was attacking you."

"It's nothing I can't handle," Riley insisted, then paused. "He's my stepbrother."

"*What?*"

"Yeah, um, thanks for the help back there but I've gotta go."

"No. Riley—"

But Riley had unlocked and unbolted the door and hightailed it into the night. Amy swore and helped herself to Jan's purse hanging on a hook.

"Hey," Jan said.

Amy pulled out the pepper spray she'd known that Jan carried, waving it. "Borrowing this!" she said, then went outside after Riley, pepper spray at the ready in her hand in case Troy showed up again. She had a pounding headache and a nagging side ache to boot, which made no sense, but there was no Troy.

And no Riley either. She was gone.

Completely gone.

Hoping she'd show up at home, Amy went there first.

No Riley. Teeth gritted, she grabbed her flashlight and went back out into the night, heading to the forest.

No Riley there either.

Tired, hurting, terrified for Riley, Amy finally gave up and went back to her apartment, hoping against hope the girl had miraculously shown up.

But it wasn't Riley she found on her doorstep. When the unexpected shadow rose, tall and built, moving toward her, she gasped in terror.

"Just me," Matt said, stepping under the light. His gaze was steady and his expression solemn, not so much as a glimmer of a smile on his usually good-humored, affable face.

Amy drew a deep breath to deal, but suddenly her vision swam, then shrank to a pinpoint. From what seemed like a great distance, she heard Matt call her name. She opened her mouth to answer, but couldn't.

Odd.

Odder still was that her bones seemed to dissolve. Matt grabbed her just as she would have fallen. She blinked and then pushed at him, but he completely ignored her struggles and held on.

"I'm okay," she said.

"You just about passed out."

"I'm fine now." She shook her head to clear it. "It was nothing. Why are you here?"

"Because I'm an ass," he said. "And bullshit, it was nothing. Something scared you nearly into a faint."

"I don't faint. But you almost got a face full of pepper spray." She tugged free, and this time he let her go, reluctantly.

"Why are you wet?" he asked, looking at his hand before going utterly still. "Amy, you're bleeding."

"What? No, I'm—" She stared down at her sweater, which had a growing dark patch, making it cling to her side. "Huh." She gulped in a panicked breath and nearly passed out again, but Matt's hands were back on her, utter steel.

Her anchor.

"I've got you," he said, nudging her down to the step, lifting her sweater. They both looked at the two-inch-long gash on her side.

"Look at that," she said weakly. "He got me."

Matt yanked his own shirt over his head and turned it inside out before gently pressing it against her side. "He who?"

"Actually, I think it was the bottle," she said. "It broke, and I must have rolled on it."

"What bottle? Amy, stay with me."

She struggled to do just that, but the pain of the cut was hitting her now, stealing her breath. "Riley used a bottle to hit her step-brother over the head. It broke, and I rolled away from him but..." More old memories surfaced. Her stepfather's footsteps coming down the hallway toward her bedroom. *You owe me, Amy. You owe me big...* Yeah. She knew *exactly* what Troy had wanted from Riley. Amy had escaped her own nightmare before it'd come to fruition by being strong and mean. She hoped Riley had escaped as well, but she was having her doubts.

"Amy." Cupping her face, Matt made her look at him. "Keep your eyes open." He spoke evenly, his voice remarkably matter-of-fact, as if he might be inquiring about the weather. She found the simple tone incredibly steadying.

"Riley's brother," he said. "That's who attacked you?"

"No, he attacked Riley. I attacked him."

He drew a breath and squeezed her hand very gently. "Are you hurt anywhere else?"

"I don't think so."

He nodded, then ran his hands over her body himself, checking to make sure before lifting her in his arms and carrying her toward his truck.

"Where are we going?"

"The ER. You need a few stitches."

"What?" Adrenaline surged. So did panic. She hated doctors. Hated hospitals. "No. I want to try to find Riley."

He didn't slow down.

"Matt, no. No hospital."

"No would normally work on me," he said. "But not this time."

"I—"

"Nonnegotiable, Amy."

Matt carefully buckled Amy into his truck and jogged around to the driver's seat, simultaneously calling Josh. By luck, Josh was at the ER and promised to be waiting for them.

Matt had been on an untold number of search-and-rescue calls and highway patrol assists, not to mention all he'd seen and done as a SWAT cop in Chicago.

But Amy bleeding undid him.

She undid him. Completely. He hadn't wanted to get involved in a relationship with her, but given his current accelerated heart rate, he'd done exactly that. For so long he'd blamed himself for his failed marriage, which had allowed him to easily keep his distance from other women.

And then Amy had walked right past all his brick walls. What was it about her?

"I don't need stitches," she said for the tenth time.

He turned to glance at her as he pulled out of her parking lot, but the interior of the truck was too dark.

"I don't," she said firmly, but her voice trembled, giving her away.

"Did you know that Riley had a brother?" he asked, hoping to distract her because they *were* going to the ER.

"Stepbrother," she said. "And no, I didn't know."

"What did he want?"

"Riley," she said grimly. "He had her pinned to the wall. I yelled at him, trying to get his attention off of her and onto me instead."

Jesus. "And that's when he cut you."

"No. I was backing away from him and tripped. He was on me before I could blink, and that's when Riley came after him with a bottle. Knocked him out." She shook her head. "I dragged us into the diner to call the police, but then Troy vanished. And so did Riley. I ended up at home, and you were there. Why were you there again?"

Good question. He'd felt like such a complete dickwad about how he'd acted earlier. He had no excuse, none, and he'd come to her place to apologize. "Did he touch you? Did he—"

"I'm fine. I just want to go home."

"Soon." He pulled into the ER. Josh met them as promised. Mallory was there as well, in her scrubs, ready with a warm hug and a calm, steady smile as she got Amy settled into a cubicle and prepped for stitches.

Josh examined the wound. "Nicely done, Champ. What happened?"

Amy was shaking. The pain and shock had hit her. "Had a fight with a broken bottle," she said.

Josh *tsk*ed. "Hate that." He nudged Matt out of his way, then sat on the stool at Amy's side. "I have a few questions. Want me to kick out the brooding ranger first?"

Amy's eyes slid to Matt, who did his best to look like a piece of equipment. A very necessary piece of equipment. Amy shook her head. "No. He can stay."

Which was good, since he wasn't going anywhere.

Josh shooed him around to the opposite side of Amy's bed,

where he could take her hand and be the moral support team. Mallory stayed next to Josh, behind the instrument tray, ready to assist.

"So who was wielding the bottle?" Josh asked.

"Riley," Amy said, and rubbed her temples. "But it wasn't her fault. She was fighting off her stepbrother."

"He touch you? You hurt anywhere else?"

"No."

Josh ran a gentle finger over her cheek, where a small bruise was forming. "What's this from?"

"I don't know. Maybe from when I fell. I'm not sure."

Josh nodded, not taking his eyes off hers. "Sometimes a victim doesn't like to talk about what happened to them, but—"

"*Nothing* happened." Amy met first Mallory's concerned gaze, and then Matt's, before looking back at Josh. "Really. Riley knocked him out, and he vanished before I could call the police. The end."

"Did you call the police afterward?" Josh asked.

"I never got a chance to make the call. Troy vanished, and then I was with Riley..."

"That's okay," Josh said. "You've got a law enforcement officer right here." He gestured to Matt.

Amy turned her head and looked up at him. He nodded, stroking the hair back from her face. "We'll make a report," he said. "Then find Riley. Okay?"

She hesitated, her gaze searching his, then slowly, she nodded.

"Stitches first," Josh said.

"I'm not good at stitches," Amy said.

Josh smiled. "That's okay. I am."

"This is true," Mallory assured her. "He's the best."

Josh was examining the wound closely. "Looks like maybe five to six stitches total. Won't leave much of a scar."

"Can't you just glue it or something?" Amy asked.

"Not this time," Josh said. "But I'll be quick, and you'll be nice and numbed up, no worries." From out of Amy's range of sight, he reached for a fat needle and nodded to Matt.

Matt bent low and brushed his lips over Amy's temple, palming her jaw to keep her face turned to him and not at what Josh was doing. "Hey, Tough Girl."

"Hey back. This sucks," she said, wincing when Josh began to numb her. "This sucks golf balls."

"It'll be over before you know it," Josh promised. "That's how good I am."

Amy grimaced again but said nothing as he continued to work.

Matt did his part to keep her attention off the needle, stroking a finger over a small scar bisecting her eyebrow. "This one looks interesting. How did you get it?"

Amy let out a shaky breath. "When I was seventeen, I stole my boyfriend's brand-new bike to get to work, then crashed it."

Josh chuckled, his big fingers working quickly, efficiently. "If I'd been around back then, you wouldn't still have the scar."

"Cocky."

"Just very good," he said. "Keep looking at pretty boy there."

Matt slid Josh a look, which Josh ignored with a smirk.

"Check out his chin," Josh said to Amy. "Two years ago, Matt fell at the South Rim. It was a pussy climb, too. Luckily for him, I was right there. He dislocated his shoulder and cut up his face. I fixed him up so that he can still be a cover model any time he wants."

Amy laughed softly. "Cover model?"

Matt opened his mouth but Josh beat him to it. "He made the cover of *Northwest Forestry* last year. You probably missed that issue, but the nurses here have it hanging in their break room." Josh was smiling as he told this story, and if he hadn't been wielding the needle with smooth dexterity while he was at it, Matt might have been tempted to shut his mouth for him.

"You're doing great, Amy," Josh said. "Three stitches in, only a couple more to go."

When he'd finished, he helped her upright, gave her some prescriptions, and then was paged away.

"You okay?" Matt asked her.

She nodded. "I'm good to go."

Impressed with her toughness, he slid an arm around her. "I'll take you home. I want to talk to Riley."

Amy went still for a beat, then did a forced relax thing that had Matt taking a second look at her. "What's the matter?" he asked.

"Nothing."

He shouldn't care that she didn't trust him. It shouldn't matter. He hadn't wanted her to trust him, hadn't needed her to trust him, because this wasn't going to be a relationship. But apparently he'd finally gotten over himself and could face the fact that he was ready to move on from the past. Because for the first time in recent memory, he *wanted* to be trusted. By her.

Amy was definitely not on her A-game, which was the only explanation she had for walking right into a trap of her own making. Riley wasn't staying with her. Riley wasn't going to show up to sleep at her apartment tonight. Which Matt didn't know because Amy had lied to him. She'd known this would happen, that it would come back and bite her in the ass. She needed to think, but the problem with that was her brain wasn't in gear.

"Amy." Right there in the hospital hallway, Matt sat her in a chair, then crouched in front of her, weight balanced easily on the balls of his feet. "Where's Riley?"

Conflicting emotions battered her, but she let anger lead the pack. He'd walked away from her so he didn't get to look at her like he was right now, all warm, genuine concern. It hurt. It hurt more than her side did, which was really saying something.

"Amy."

Damn. Damn him. Because she wasn't angry at all. She was sad. She ached to tell him the truth—that Riley wasn't staying with her.

But how could she? The terrified teen was going through hell, and she'd *trusted* Amy.

Trust that hadn't been easily given.

If Amy told Matt the truth, he'd be forced by his job to act, and Riley would think she couldn't trust anyone.

But it was more than that. No one had ever really trusted Amy, not like Riley had. Not even Matt trusted her like that. There was no way in hell that Amy would betray her.

"Amy." Matt's voice was low and calm, and also laced with steel. He wanted answers.

"I don't know where she is exactly." She didn't owe him more, she reminded herself. "How can I? I'm here."

Matt didn't say anything to this, though he registered her defensive tone with an arched brow.

"I'd like to go home now," she said. "I'm tired." Tired of the both of them.

Matt rose to his feet, wrapped his jacket around her, then led her outside to his truck. They went to the pharmacy first for her antibiotics and pain killers, then Matt drove her home in silence, for which Amy was eternally grateful. She was hurting, both physically and mentally. She was also confused. Historically, she'd made her most craptastic decisions while hurt and confused, which meant that the best thing for her right now was to be alone.

Matt parked, and she made her move before he'd even turned off the engine. She opened the door to hop out, but was snagged by the back of the jacket he'd loaned her.

"I want to go with you and check things out," he said.

No. If he came inside, she'd forget to be upset with him. She'd also have to face her lie about Riley. "Not necessary."

"Maybe not, but I'm doing it anyway."

"No," she said.

He went still. "Excuse me?"

He probably wasn't told *no* very often. He looked as if the word didn't even compute. "I'm fine," she said.

His expression was carefully blank. She suspected that he thought she was being an unfathomable pain in his ass. "Look," she said. "You don't owe me anything. I can get inside my own place without help."

"Goddammit, Amy. I was wrong to walk out on you like that."

"No," she said flatly. "You weren't."

"I was. I had a shitastic day and took it out on you, and I'm sorry for that. So goddamn sorry."

Not used to apologies or people taking responsibility for their own mistakes, this set her back. "It's okay."

"No, it's not," he said.

Diversion, she thought desperately. "Is that kid, the climber, still going to be okay?"

A muscle in his jaw twitched, and for a moment she thought maybe he was going to call her out on the quick subject change, but he didn't. "Yeah," he finally answered. "But his family is gearing up to sue everyone, claiming negligence on the forestry's part."

He'd spoken calmly enough, but she sensed that the situation was causing him some heavy stress. She could see it in the fine lines around his eyes and the tightness to his mouth.

Or maybe that was *her* making him so unhappy. "It seems more like vandalism," she said. "If they took down the signs and broke the lock on the gate."

"We're working on it."

She nodded and slipped out of his truck, but almost before her feet touched the ground, he'd come around to help her.

"Don't brush it off," he said, and she instantly knew he wasn't talking about his work, but about how he'd left her before, at his place. "Don't give me a free pass." Gently he pressed her back to the truck and cupped her face, stroking her bruised cheek. He moved his head next to hers, and his lips traced over the line of her jaw. "I'm sorry," he said again, softly.

Her knees wobbled, and she locked them because he was right. She shouldn't give him a free pass. She never gave anyone a free pass. "I'm going in now."

He looked up at her place. Dark. "Riley say where she was going?"

"I'm not her keeper."

He said nothing to this, and short of telling him the entire truth, there was nothing more she could add.

"Wait here," Matt said at the top of the stairs and left her on the doorstep while he pulled his gun and entered her place.

He came back a moment later, gun holstered.

"Overkill much?" she asked.

"You were attacked tonight, and he could have tailed you home."

She let out a breath as the truth of that hit her. "I don't think I was followed."

He nodded and gestured her in. All the lights were on inside. Matt followed her through the living room, silently regarding her when she sank to her couch, leaned carefully back, and stared at the ceiling.

"Can I get you anything?" he asked.

"No, thank you."

He grimaced at her polite tone. "Amy—" He broke off when his phone buzzed, looking down to read his screen. "Fuck."

"You have to go," she guessed.

"Dispatch." His expression was grim when he came close and crouched at her side. "Someone shot and killed a bear tonight. I don't want to leave you alone but I have to get out there and—"

"I'm fine, Matt."

He looked at her for a long moment. "You'll call me if you have any problems."

"I won't have any problems."

"Amy." His voice was serious. His eyes were serious. Everything about him was terrifyingly serious.

"Okay," she said on a sigh and closed her eyes. "Okay. I'll call you if there are any problems."

She felt his weight shift, then the brush of his mouth against her temple. "Lock up behind me," he said, and then she heard the front door closing, leaving her just as she'd told him she'd wanted—alone.

It was three in the morning before Matt got done, and he made a drive-by past Amy's place.

It was dark.

He stared up at her window, hoping Riley was there now, and that both she and Amy were sleeping.

At home, he fell into bed exhausted and got two hours of sleep before his alarm went off. On his way to the station, he made another drive-by, this one at the hospital. He still hadn't gotten to talk to Trevor. Unfortunately, the kid was sleeping and not to be disturbed until visiting hours, when of course his attorney would be present.

Matt made his way to Josh's office and found him pacing in the hallway, looking down at his phone. Josh's five o'clock shadow had its own five o'clock shadow. His eyes were dark with exhaustion. He was either hungover as shit or hadn't slept either. Matt shook his head. "Let me guess. You fucked up at work, and a stupid kid got himself hurt, and now his rich daddy is trying to ruin your life."

Josh huffed out a mirthless laugh and dropped his head, rubbing a hand over the back of his neck. He was in scrubs and a white doctor's coat with a stethoscope hanging around his neck. "No. There was a gas leak in my house, had to evacuate Anna and Toby."

"Where are they?"

Josh grimaced. "In there," he said, gesturing to his office. "I gave Anna money to go to the cafeteria and get them breakfast, thinking they could sit quietly in my office and watch videos on my computer while I made morning rounds. Anna got donuts."

"Any left?" Matt asked hopefully.

"I don't know, but there's a sugar high going on in there that rivals Looney Tunes. They're both bouncing off the walls." Josh stared at his closed office door like it was a hissing cobra. "Toby's nanny is sick. I've called everyone in my contact list for a temp babysitter, but no one answered my calls."

Matt laughed softly. "That's because Thing One and Thing Two have worn out everyone in town."

Josh blew out a breath. "Mallory called Lucille for me. Lucille said she'd give me a couple of hours if I promised to pose for her Facebook photo album."

Matt found a laugh in what was proving to be a shit day. "With clothes, or without?"

"Fuck you."

"Not my type." Matt pulled open Josh's office door.

Anna was spinning in her wheelchair. Toby was in her lap, the both of them howling with laughter. At the sight of Matt, Anna grinned wide but didn't stop spinning. "Matty!" she yelled, knocking a stack of files off Josh's desk.

Matt caught and righted the stack, then stuck his foot into the spokes of one of the wheels of her chair, stopping her on a dime. Leaning down, he hugged them both, then smiled at Toby. Josh's mini-me was holding a donut in one hand and a lightsaber in the other, chocolate all over his face.

"What's with the lightsaber?" Matt asked, snagging a donut.

Toby slashed the lightsaber through the air. It lit up and made a *swoosh* sound.

Matt rumpled the kid's hair. "So you're a Jedi."

Toby nodded.

Matt looked at Anna. "You guys are driving your brother nuts. You know that, right?"

Anna grinned. "It's a short drive."

Matt laughed softly. "Try to take it easy on him."

"Why?" Anna asked.

Good question. Matt took a second donut because it was a second-donut kind of day and left to face it. Double fisting his breakfast jackpot, he went back into the hall just as Josh was shoving his cell phone in his pocket.

"Your climber's awake," Josh told him. "His lawyer's on his way. You might want to get a better breakfast than that," he said, nodding to the double donuts. "You look like you haven't slept in days."

Matt finished donut number one. "It's the job."

"Yeah?" Josh asked. "Thought maybe it was the sexy waitress."

"Bite me."

Josh grinned for the first time all morning. "Ah, man. You're so going down. Just like Ty. Give me half that donut."

"Hell no."

"I need it more than you."

Matt shoved it into his own mouth.

"You're an asshole," Josh said.

"Maybe." He chewed and swallowed. "But I don't have two people swinging from the chandeliers in my office."

Chapter 19

Sure, chocolate has more calories than love, but it's way more satisfying.

Amy woke up at dawn, groggy from the pain pill. Josh had put a waterproof bandage on her wound, so she was able to shower. After, she dressed and then walked out of her bedroom to start the coffee, stopping short on her way to the kitchen.

Riley was asleep on her couch.

"Hey," Amy said in surprise.

Snapping to immediate alertness, Riley jerked upright, her hand coming up with something glinting in her fist.

A knife.

"Whoa," Amy said, bending a little at the waist to ease the tightening on her stitches. "Just me."

Riley's hand vanished behind her. "Sorry. You startled me." Her eyes narrowed in on the way Amy was favoring her side. "What's wrong?"

"Nothing. I got cut on the broken glass last night, needed a few stitches."

Riley paled. "Oh, my God. *Oh, my God.*" She rushed off the couch and came toward Amy. "I'm so sorry. Are you all right?"

"Yes. Are you?"

"I'm fine—Forget me. How many stitches? *How did I not know this?*"

"Maybe because you vanished on me. Are you really okay?"

Riley blew out a breath and nodded shakily. "This shouldn't have happened to you."

Amy pushed a pale, shaky Riley back to the couch. She sat next to her and reached for her hand. "I'm okay, honest. And I'm glad I was there. If I hadn't shown up when I did..."

Riley closed her eyes. "I know." She opened her eyes, her expression fierce. "I didn't do anything wrong."

"I know."

"I mean, I've changed. I'm changing."

Amy leaned in and hugged her tight. "It wasn't your fault."

"But it was! He was after me, not you." Riley pulled free and stood. She picked up her backpack.

"Riley," she said softly. "Can't you tell me about it? I can help. I can—"

"No." Riley shook her head violently. "I've screwed everything up." Riley closed her eyes for a beat, then headed to the door.

"I know more than you think," Amy told her. "I was the queen of screwup when I was a kid, and I only got worse as a teen. I screwed up over and over again, and then, by the time I was in real trouble, no one cared. I'd made sure of it."

Riley turned to face her but said nothing, breaking Amy's heart with her doubt.

"You can tell me anything," Amy said. "*Anything.*"

Riley hesitated, then shook her head and reached for the door. "Sorry. I'm so sorry, but I gotta go."

And then there was nothing but the sound of the front door shutting hard.

Amy was still sitting on the couch when her cell rang.

"I'm giving you today off," Jan said.

"Not necessary."

"You were stabbed on my premises last night," Jan said. "I don't want Lucille getting the story or pics. The negative press will kill me. Take a damn day off."

"I wasn't stabbed!"

"Good. Go with that."

"But—"

But Jan was already gone.

Fine. Amy loaded her sketchpad and a few snacks into her backpack. If she couldn't work, she'd clear her head and draw. In fact, now that she thought about it, she needed that more than anything she could think of.

Well…other than the need to be near Matt, the guy she'd promised herself she wouldn't fall for. Except she'd broken that promise. How else could she explain parking at the North District Ranger Station? She could have gone out on her own patio to sketch, but she'd come here.

Fine. Maybe she wasn't up for a hike or figuring out her grandma's cryptic journey right now, but the grounds here were beautiful and peaceful, and she spent an hour sitting on a rock in front of a creek with her sketchpad, trying to clear her mind.

It refused to be cleared. Instead, it kept wandering to Matt. This distance between them was her own doing. Not a surprise, as she'd been sabotaging her own happiness for a long time. She'd known this thing with him would eventually fall apart, but she'd been secretly hoping it wouldn't.

And if that wasn't a terrifying thought. For the first time in her life, she wanted to ride the train to the end of the line instead of jumping off before it even stopped.

You lied to him…

Worse, she'd lied to herself. All her life she'd lived with something hanging over her head. But being in Lucky Harbor this year, staying in one place, making a life for herself…she'd lost her vigilant edge.

She didn't regret that.

She liked having a decent place to live, a job that paid the bills and allowed her the freedom to draw when she wanted. She liked making the kind of keeper friends she'd always dreamed of having.

That's what Mallory and Grace were to her, keepers.

Matt, too, if she was being honest. Yeah, she liked him, *way* too much. She was going to have to face that sooner or later. The truth was, she'd long ago given up believing or trusting in others.

And then she'd come here to Lucky Harbor.

Inhaling the damp forest air, she looked up and locked eyes on Matt. He stood a football field away, on the porch of the ranger station building, his back to her as he talked to two other uniformed officers. He looked big and tough as hell, with his shirt stretched taut over his broad shoulders, the gun on his hip gleaming in the sun.

Flustered to find herself aroused just looking at him, she glanced down at her sketch and then up again, insistently drawn to him.

He was gone.

She forced herself to sit there another few moments. He hadn't seen her, she told herself. Because if he had, he'd have come over. He wasn't a coward like her. She inhaled a deep breath, found her backbone, packed up her things, and headed to the building. "Is Matt Bowers busy?" she asked the ranger at the front desk.

The guy laughed. "Always. But his office is the last on the right, go on back."

She found him standing before his desk, hands on hips, jaw dark with stubble, looking down at a mountain of paperwork like he was facing a firing squad. He seemed impossibly imposing, and a little pissed off. His eyes tracked directly to her and though nothing in his tough-guy stance changed, his eyes warmed.

In response, *everything* within her warmed. She didn't really understand that, how it could still be this way, how it felt stronger each and every time she saw him. He'd hurt her. She'd hurt him—though he didn't even know it yet. And still, she wanted him. She wanted his hands on her, his mouth on her, *him* on her, making her forget everything in the way only he could. "Am I interrupting?" she asked.

"Not even a little bit."

Given the stacks on his desk, this was an obvious lie. His gaze roamed over her. "How are you?"

"Fine."

"Truth, Amy."

Truth... The truth was that his shoulders were so wide they practically blocked out the light, plenty wide enough for her to set her head down and lose herself in him for a few. Only a few.

Not that she would. "I'm managing."

"I drove by your place last night. Everything looked dark and quiet. You sleep okay?"

"Yeah."

"I came by again about an hour ago to talk to Riley. She wasn't there."

"She had things to do."

Their eyes met and held for a long beat.

"You're not okay," he finally said. "You're flushed."

"Sunburn. I forgot sunscreen."

He didn't say anything to that, and the silence just about did her in. "It's not just sex," she said. "Not to me."

He still didn't speak, but she knew by his absolute stillness that she had his undivided attention.

"I'm sorry I let you think it," she said. "And okay, maybe some of it *is* about the sex, but that's because it's the best sex that I've ever had. But it's not *all* about the sex."

Matt might be laid-back and easygoing but he wasn't slow. In three steps he closed the distance between them and pulled her in, right up against him. He felt so good she actually moaned, a sound he silenced with a kiss.

She had no idea how a man could be so terrifyingly gentle in the way he held her and yet at the same time plunder her mouth so roughly. But that's exactly what he was, both gentle and rough.

It was exactly what she needed.

"Don't let me hurt you," he said, lips on her jaw, making their way to her ear.

Too late, far too late. To share the pain, she turned her head and nipped his lower lip. Sucking in a breath, he laughed softly. "Tough girl," he murmured, and cupping her face, kissed her again. There was nothing controlled about him now as his tongue tangled with hers, his hands wandering madly from her face to her hips, ending up back in her hair to hold her head still. She pressed even closer, needing him in a way she couldn't even fathom. She wanted him, wanted him to pull off her clothes, wanted to pull off his, *now*. She glanced at his overloaded desk.

Matt followed her gaze, his own darkening. "I like the way you think," he said, and shoved all the stacks of paperwork to the floor. "Lock the door."

Her nipples tightened into two ball bearings. "Will anyone hear us?" she whispered.

His smile was lethal and filled with nefarious, bad boy intent. "Us?"

She flushed, and he laughed softly. "You're going to have to be quiet. *Very* quiet," he said.

She quivered and went damp. "I can do quiet."

"The door, Amy."

She turned to do just that, but it opened before she could and Ty strode in. He had a bag from Eat Me in one hand and two long-necked soda bottles dangling from the other. He wore dark, reflective sunglasses and the navy blue coverall of a paramedic with FLIGHT CARE across his back in white letters.

He dipped his head and eyeballed them over the top of his glasses, taking in Matt's hair standing up on end from Amy's fingers and then her disheveled appearance as well. His lips quirked. "I take it you forgot I was bringing lunch," he said. "Since it looks like you're already in the middle of yours."

"It's not what you think," Amy said.

"No?" Ty asked, amused. "What do I think?"

Amy opened her mouth, then sighed. It was *exactly* what he thought.

Matt came forward, grabbed the bag and both drinks from Ty, then pushed his friend backward over the threshold and shut the door in his face. "I'm going to pay for that in the gym in the morning," Matt said, handing Amy the sodas and food. "So we should probably enjoy this."

"What if he's hungry?"

"He's always hungry. And on second thought, so am I." Matt took the stuff back out of her hands and set them on a chair, then hauled her up against him. "Where were we?"

Amy slid her fingers back into his hair. "You had your tongue down my throat. And your hands up my shirt."

He nodded and slid his hands up her shirt again, fingertips resting just beneath her breasts, which were tingling from his touch.

"And you?" he asked, voice husky. His bedroom voice. "Where were you?"

She bit her lower lip. They both knew exactly where she'd been. Her fingers had been heading for his zipper.

He laughed softly at her, kissed her long and deep, then tore his mouth from hers. Grabbing her hand, he tugged her to the door. "Change of plans. I've got fifty-five minutes left on my lunch break."

"That's enough for lunch *and* dessert."

He smiled. "Yeah, and we're going to have dessert first. But not here. It's not nearly private enough for what I want to do to you."

Her knees wobbled as she followed him out, having no idea where they were going and not caring. She'd probably follow him anywhere.

And if that wasn't unsettling, he walked them down the hallway past several coworkers, moving with unconscious confidence that spoke of a man on a mission. And he *was* on a mission—to do her. At the thought, she cracked up, and he looked back questioningly.

"Nothing," she said.

As if he could read her naughty thoughts, he gave her a heated look. "We're doing this."

"Yes, please."

He smiled. "I like the 'please.' More of that."

And she laughed again. It wasn't often that she wanted to laugh and jump someone's bones in the space of a few seconds. But then again, it wasn't often that she wanted to both run like hell from someone and hold on tight to him either.

Normally Matt could make the drive from work to home in eleven minutes, allowing for the occasional deer crossing or traffic if he got behind someone not used to the narrow, two-lane, curvy highway.

Today, with Amy next to him practically vibrating with sexual tension, he made it in seven. He pulled up to his cabin with a screech of tires, then turned to her with some half-baked, Neanderthal idea of dragging her into his house. But she beat him to it, crawling over the console to straddle him before covering his mouth with hers.

His first response was a resounding *oh, hell yeah*. This was what he'd needed. Amy in his arms like a tempting, forbidden treat, her dark eyes full of wanting.

And then there was her mouth. God, that mouth, it could give a full-grown man a wet dream. He staggered out of his truck, pulling her out with him, careful to protect her injury.

At his front porch, they stopped to kiss. "Matt," she whispered, and God, how he loved the sound of his name on her lips. He pressed her against his door. *Take*, his body demanded. Instead, forcing himself to be gentle, he leaned in and nibbled at her throat.

With a moan, her head thunked back to give him access. Trusting...that was new, and tenderness swamped him as he kissed her softly now, a sweet brush of his lips over her skin.

She moaned again, and damn if all his good intentions didn't go up in smoke, the kiss quickly deepening into a hot, hungry intense tangle of tongues.

Tearing her mouth free, she rained kisses down his jaw, her small hands very busy at the buttons of his shirt, her expression one of such fierce intent that he groaned. "Amy—"

She gave up on his buttons and went for his belt and zipper, having some trouble working around his gun and utility belt. And then he was in her hands. Literally.

"Not here," he heard himself say roughly, though he was gentle as he lifted her up, still aware enough to be careful of her stitches. She wrapped her legs around him, and he cupped her ass in one palm, supporting her as he unlocked the door with his free hand. Kicking it closed, he strode with her through his house, ignoring the couch, the fireplace rug, everything except his big bed. By the time she'd begun working off her clothes, he'd stripped naked and was reaching for her.

She'd toed off her kick-ass boots but was still struggling out of her jeans. He tugged them off and the rest of her clothes as well. His arms glided up hers, taking her hands in his above her head. Palm to palm, chest to chest, thigh to thigh, he looked into her beautiful face and lost his breath. But as he knew she would, she tugged to free her hands. "Amy." He nuzzled at her throat but then made eye contact. "Let's try it my way this time."

She went still. In fact, she appeared to stop breathing. "What way is that?"

"The way where you trust me."

Her eyes met his, heartbreakingly wild. He steeled himself against the surge of unexpected emotion and held her gaze, willing her to look deep and see what he was finally starting to get about himself. He *could* be trusted. She could trust him.

"Matt—"

"I would never hurt you," he breathed, lowering his head to kiss her softly. "Trust me."

She closed her eyes, then opened them again, relaxing her body into his. "I do. I do trust you."

Chapter 20

Nine out of ten people love chocolate. The tenth person lies.

Hunger and desire pounded through Amy's veins, but there was unease now. And fear. Not that she believed Matt would ask anything of her that she wouldn't be willing to give, but that she'd give him everything. Willingly.

He lowered his head and whispered her name against her lips before kissing her slow and deep. He took his sweet-ass time about it, too, and her entire world came to a stop on its axis. "Matt—"

"Still right here," he murmured, spreading hot, wet kisses down her jaw, along her collarbone. Her breast. "Mmm, you smell like heaven, Amy."

"You have to hurry," she reminded him, rocking into him, trying to get him to pick up the pace. "You don't have much time left."

"I don't like to hurry."

No kidding! His tongue curled around her nipple, and he growled in approval when it beaded for him.

She bucked, and he did it again, reaching for the bedside drawer, grabbing a condom. *Thank God.* He'd come to his senses. They were going to get this show on the road. He protected them both, and then palmed her thighs, opening them. This wrenched a groan from his throat, and he took his time eyeing her all spread out for him. "Missed this," she heard him say, the softly uttered words making her heart kick crazily in her ribcage as he lowered his head and kissed her. Lapped at her. Sucked, until she climaxed with shocking ease.

She was still shuddering when he brushed a kiss over her bandaged side and looked up at her. "You okay?"

Her entire body was humming, and she couldn't feel her toes. Or access her brain cells. "I'll get back to you on that one."

"You do that," he said huskily, and slid into her.

She cried out and arched up. *Hard and fast*, her body demanded, every muscle straining with the need to feel him possess and take her.

But Matt didn't get the hard and fast memo. As if he had all the time in the world, he cupped her face, kissing her as he slowly began to move, grinding against her body in fluid, rhythmic motions, like the ebb and flow of the waves against the shore. Each movement sent a current through her body, making her arch into him, molding herself to him. "More, Matt. Please, more."

"Everything," he promised, then dipped his head to her breasts, taking his time with each before pressing a kiss between them, right against her heart.

Which leapt against his mouth. Never in her life had she felt more open, more... vulnerable. It shocked her. It overwhelmed her.

Because this *wasn't* just sex. He was making love to her, so thoroughly and completely that he'd sneaked in past her defenses, leaving her feeling cherished.

Loved.

He slid his hands to her hips and stilled them, making her realize that she'd been bucking against him. He moved against her, slowly, surely, even deeper now. Thinking became all but impossible as her fingers roamed, touching every part of him she could reach, his shoulders, his back. His face. Her heartbeat was different, faster yes, but beating just for him, it seemed.

Only for him, and she panicked at the barrage of emotions, freezing up.

"I've got you," he murmured, stroking her, holding her. It wasn't the first time he'd made this promise, but it was the first time she really heard him, believed him. He thrust into her, again and again, and her senses took over. The sight of his face, drawn in fierce concentration as he gave her pleasure, the delicious scent of him, the sound of her own heart thundering in her ears, and her panting echoing off the walls as she fought for air. Toes curling, her gaze locked on his, and she was hit with the one-two punch of his eyes. Her heart tightened along with the rest of her as she barreled toward the mother of all orgasms. When it hit, she called out his name in shock, in surprise, in sheer overwhelming passion. He stayed with her right into the waves of ecstasy, and then followed her there, coming with a rough, ragged groan as he pressed his hips to hers in one final, hard thrust. Seeing stars, she clutched at him, her only anchor in a spinning world.

She was still trembling from the aftermath when she felt him push the damp hair from her face. She kept her eyes closed because *oh, God.*

God, she'd really done it now.

She'd fallen for him.

She had no idea how he felt as he held her snug up against himself, stroking her slowly cooling skin, and that was for the best. Knowing she was desperately close to making a complete fool of herself, she turned over to crawl out of the bed, but found herself pinned flat.

"What?" she asked, not liking how her breath hitched, how her body wanted to rock into his, unable to get enough of him.

Matt flipped her over and looked into her face. He searched for something, probably for a hint that she was still on board with the whole trusting him thing. Whatever he found made him smile. "That's more like it," he said, all male smug and satisfied, the big, sexy jerk.

"Move," she said, trying to buck him off.

"Why? Going somewhere?"

"Yeah, and so are you. Back to the station."

"Not yet." He rolled to his side and pulled her in, kissing her slowly and leisurely until she curled right into him like she belonged there. "Your side hurt?" he asked.

"No."

"Good."

She waited for him to make a move for round two but though he pressed his mouth to her temple and ran a hand down her back, he just held her. "Last night shook you," he finally said quietly.

Her gut tightened. "Well, yeah."

"You were scared."

"I was terrified. For Riley."

"I know. But it was something else, too."

Her heart took another hard leap—into her throat.

"You don't scare easily," he said. "You waded right in to protect her. You were brave as hell."

She didn't like where this was going and tried to push him away. "You really have to get back to work."

"Soon." His grip was gentle but inexorable. "What got you, Amy? Something triggered some bad memories. What was it? That it was Riley's brother hurting her?"

"*Stepbrother.*"

He nodded. "You've told me about your grandma, about how after she died you went back to your mom's. You didn't last there long, leaving when you were sixteen, right?"

"Yeah. So?"

"So what happened to send you running from your only family?" His gaze was steady, calm, his body warm and strong around hers as he delivered his final, devastating question. "And what happened last night that reminded you of it?"

She opened her mouth to deny it but her breathing hitched, audibly. She closed her eyes, pressing her face into his throat, finding comfort in the scent of him. He smelled like the woods, like his soap, like Matt the man, and it had the most amazing calming effect on her.

But Matt pulled her face back and met her gaze before lowering his head, brushing his lips sweetly over hers, letting her know he was there, right there. She was safe with him, safer than she'd ever been. She could tell him.

But in his eyes, she was strong and fierce and could handle anything. She liked that he saw her like that and not as a victim. If she told him about her past, about who she'd once been, that would change, and it would break her.

Matt slid a hand up Amy's slim spine. So deceptively fragile. But in truth, she was a rock. And she was holding back. He slid a hand into her hair and tilted her face up to his.

She met his gaze. "I... I was a horrible teenager."

"Horrible *is* the definition of teenager."

"No, I mean *really* horrible. And it got worse after my grandma died."

"You were grieving."

"Yes, but I was awful about it," she said. "I acted like my grandma had left me on purpose. My mom had this new husband, and he was rich. I never realized how poor we'd been until I moved in with my mom. Suddenly we had things, and I was in a very different environment, with no experience on how to handle it. I really stuck out like a sore thumb. I think I did it on purpose."

"Probably for attention."

"Yeah." She lifted a shoulder, not meeting his gaze, and he knew there was more, a lot more, and that it was bad.

"My mom," she said. "She's not good at picking men. But this guy, he seemed different than her usual. He was on the board of some exclusive school, so they sent me there. I didn't fit in any more than I'd fit in anywhere else." She paused. "I stole stuff. I ditched. And if I wasn't ditching, I was cheating. I got in a lot of trouble, and every single time I had a ready lie about how it was never my fault."

"Seems about right for the age," he said.

"No." She shook her head, and her hair spilled silkily over his arm. "I was really rotten, Matt. To the core. The girls hated me and with good reason. The boys…they didn't hate me. I made sure of it. I led them around by their egos, which at that age is between their legs." She squeezed her eyes shut. "I was constantly looking for trouble and then weaseling and scrambling my way out of it and blaming someone else." She paused. "Until I couldn't."

It was her grim tone, more than the words themselves, that sent a chill up his spine. "What happened?"

"I finally ran up against someone bigger, older, and smarter than me, someone I couldn't control or manipulate. He wanted—He wanted something I didn't want to give him."

His gut clenched. "And what was that?"

"Me." Her heart kicked as she said it. He could feel it beat against his own.

"He—" She broke off and shook her head.

"Ah, Amy. No." He pulled her in a little closer, hugging her tight, wishing like hell he could fight this years-old battle for her. "Did he rape you?"

"No." She swallowed hard again, and he thought maybe she wasn't going to say anything more, but she forced the words out. "I was able to stop him."

"Good," he said fiercely.

"It wasn't out of the blue, what he wanted. I mean I'd been promiscuous at best and totally indiscriminate. Everyone knew that."

"I don't care if you were *selling* yourself," Matt said tightly. "No is no. And you were just a kid. Tell me you turned him in. That you told someone."

"I did. I told my mom."

Something in her voice told him he really wasn't going to like what came next.

"She thought it was another of my stupid lies."

Yeah, he'd been dead right on that one. He didn't like it, not one fucking bit. He opened his mouth, but she put her fingers over his lips. "I was the girl who'd cried wolf," she said quietly. "I'd lied for so long, *no one* would have believed me."

"Who was it?" he asked, knowing by what she'd said and everything that she *hadn't* said, that she'd known the fucker. "Who did this to you?"

She hesitated. "My stepfather."

He tensed, and Amy ran a hand down his arm. She was trying to soothe *him*. Jesus. Still holding her tight, he cupped the back of her head in his palm and pressed her face into the crook of his neck. He needed a moment, maybe two.

"It was a long time ago," she murmured.

"I know." Just as he knew it didn't matter how long, not if it still came back to her in an instant when she'd seen Riley with her stepbrother. "I'm glad you told me, Amy. I'm so sorry it happened to you."

"It's okay. I've got some perspective now. I was hardly blameless."

"You were fucking sixteen. You *were* blameless."

"I wasn't sixteen when I spent the next five years using sex to manipulate anyone in my orbit."

"You did what you had to."

"I was at least smart enough to always use protection," she said softly.

"You did good, Amy."

"No. I used sex as a weapon. As power, as a tool." She pressed her face into his throat. "At least at first. I stopped when I realized I was becoming immune to emotions, especially during..."

"Sex?"

"Yeah," she said softly, face still hidden.

"Until me."

She didn't say anything, and he pulled back to see her. "Until me," he repeated softly.

"Until you." She paused. "But maybe that's because it'd been so long."

"Bullshit." He'd been there, experienced just how explosive it'd been every time. How before, during, and after he'd been so into her he couldn't breathe, and hell if she hadn't been right there with him. He knew she had been. He'd lay everything on the line with that bet. The way she'd wrapped herself around him when he'd been buried so deep that there'd been no telling where he ended and she began. How she'd kissed him like she was going under for the count and he was the only thing that could save her. The look in her eyes as she clung to him, those unbelievably sexy little whimpers in her throat when he'd taken her where she'd needed to go.

Everything he'd ever dreamed of he'd found there in her arms with her mouth hot on his, her body moving against him, all warm, soft, desperate hunger and need, and she'd felt it back.

So fuck no, it hadn't been just because it'd been a long time for her. He met her gaze and shook his head. "You know it was more than that. Much more."

Chapter 21

Coffee, chocolate, men... some things are just better rich.

Amy didn't know how to respond to Matt, but her body didn't seem to have the same problem. It was responding to just his voice. It always had. She kept figuring it would stop, any minute now, but that hadn't happened yet. "It's nothing personal," she said, not wanting him to be angry. "I've just never been one to feel much."

He stared at her. "No," he said, to what exactly, she had no idea. He rolled her beneath himself, taking care to keep his weight off of her side by bracing himself up on his forearms. "*No*," he repeated. "You felt something different with me."

Her hands slid up his arms, his taut, ripped, gorgeous arms, because she couldn't help herself. She had to touch him. "You can't tell me how I feel, Matt. Nor can you make me tell you what you want to hear."

"Maybe not." But apparently she'd issued some sort of challenge to his manhood because he stripped the covers from them and looked down at her naked body with more than a little wicked, purposeful intent. "But I can make you show me," he said.

Her good parts rippled with anticipation. "Don't be silly. You have to get back to work."

"After."

"After what?"

"After I prove that you feel a whole hell of a lot when I touch you."

Which he did with slow, purposeful, shocking ease.

Much later, after Matt had brought Amy to her car, she headed back to town. Halfway there, she got a cryptic call from Jan to "get here, *fast*."

Having no clue what she could possibly want after she'd told Amy not to come in today, she drove straight to Eat Me.

"Good Lord, girl," Jan said at the sight of her.

"What?"

"What? You just got yourself some, that's what. You're glowing. That should be illegal, flaunting your good fortune around like that."

Henry was at the stove. He stopped stirring and stared at Amy, then let out a slow grin.

Amy clapped her hands to her cheeks. "You can't tell just by looking at me."

"Okay, and I suppose you still believe in Santa Claus," Jan said. "I'd ask if it was any good, but that's all over your face, too. You'd best get yourself together, Sawyer's gonna be here any second. We have a problem."

It had to be a big one if the sheriff was involved. Most problems Jan took care of herself—with sheer orneriness. "What's up?"

"Mallory's money jar went missing, that's what's up," Jan said. "She's on her way, too."

Amy's stomach hit her toes. "Her HSC money jar? The one for the teen center?"

"Yep. Luckily you emptied it out a few nights back. Still, I reckon we lost about a hundred bucks, and it pisses me off. That girl's ass is grass."

Amy had thought her stomach couldn't get any lower than her toes, but she was wrong. "What are you talking about? What girl?"

Jan looked at her like she was a dim bulb. "Riley."

"Wait—You can't think that Riley did this."

"Hell yeah, I can," Jan said. "She stole the money, sure as day."

"Did you catch her at it?" Amy asked.

"Well, no. But she was in earlier, and it's her day off. She was slinking around, and then she was gone. And so was the jar."

Amy's gaze slid to Henry, who gave her a slow nod. "Sorry, babe," he said. "But she was in here, just like Jan says, and she was looking guilty as hell."

"But you know how she is," Amy protested, feeling sick. How many times had she herself done something so stupid, something so desperate? But Riley wouldn't. She had no such need anymore, Amy assured herself. She'd been feeding and clothing her, not to mention the girl had been working at the diner, so there was no reason for this. "She's just sullen and defensive naturally. She *always* looks guilty."

"She's a loose cannon," Jan said. "An unknown."

"*All* teenagers are loose cannons," Amy said. "It doesn't mean she did it. How many customers have you had in here today? How many people at the counter? Hell, how many helped themselves behind the counter to pour their own coffee because you were too busy watching the cooking channel to be bothered?"

Jan shrugged, unwilling to be repentant about her own serving deficiencies. "She's an *unknown*," she stubbornly repeated.

"*I* was an unknown," Amy said. "And you took a chance on me."

Jan shrugged, again signaling that Amy might not quite have 100 percent proven herself yet either. Nice. "Look," Amy said, not nearly as calmly as she'd have liked, "it wasn't Riley, okay? She wouldn't do that. She's trying to get her life together."

Jan was shaking her head. "That girl is feral. She'd do whatever she needed to in order to survive, and you know it."

Yeah. She knew it all too well. Just as she also knew how shitty a person's life had to get in order to live that way. "Well, I refuse to believe it of her. And I can't believe *you* believe it. My God, Jan, just last night there was some guy out back attacking her. You saw that, both of you," she said, encompassing Henry. "You both saw us come in here right after the fight. She's *in* trouble. She's not *the* trouble."

"I saw you both afterward," Jan allowed. "But I didn't see anyone attack her."

"So I made it up?" Amy asked in disbelief. "Because *I* saw, Jan. I saw him." She lifted up her shirt to reveal the covered stitches. "I was there."

Jan sighed. "Look, I get that, and I'll be sure to tell Sawyer what I know. But the person who stole this jar was someone *inside* the diner. *Today.* Not the guy in the alley outside. This was someone who walked through here, familiar enough with our comings and goings, someone we recognize, someone we serve or talk to on a regular basis. Someone we know."

"Yes," Amy agreed. "So let's start talking to the customers."

"Oh, hell no." Jan was already shaking her head. "It was the girl. I know it."

Sawyer walked in the back door, immediately followed by Mallory.

And then Matt.

The sight of him both stopped Amy's heart and filled her with dread, because she knew right then and there that the promise she'd made to Riley was about to blow up in her face. She whipped back to face Jan, who met her gaze evenly and without apology.

Thirty minutes ago, Matt had sent her skittering over the edge into an orgasm with just the heat in his eyes. Now those eyes were filled with concern.

For her.

She shook her head as the dread doubled, heavy in her gut.

Jan pushed everyone out of the kitchen and into the dining room, where they all sat at one of the big corner booths. Jan gave the gist of what happened, including last night's alley fight.

All eyes turned to Amy, who then spent the next few minutes repeating the story from her point of view. When she was done, Jan jumped back in with her theory on Riley, making a damn tight case.

"Okay, so it looks bad," Amy agreed. "But it wasn't Riley. I really think we should question the customers—"

"No," Jan said, standing up. "No way. I can't have this getting out. I don't want people to think I don't trust them, or worse, that I hire thieves. I don't want anyone to be worried about coming here."

Amy opened her mouth, but Matt put a hand on her arm. She met his calm, quiet gaze, and got his silent message. He wanted her to know that this would be okay.

But she had no idea how.

"No one can know," Jan insisted to Sawyer. "No one!"

"Then you should stop yelling about it," Sawyer told her. "Sit down, Jan."

Jan's lips tightened, but she sat. "I'm not yelling."

"Yeah, you are." This from Lucille, who'd been eating two tables over with her entire blue-haired, bingo-loving, trouble-seeking posse. "And I couldn't help but overhear..."

Jan rolled her eyes.

"You hired the girl," Lucille reminded her, coming over. "Scoot," she said to Sawyer, who scooted. Lucille sat. "You knew Riley was trouble. So raising your voice at everyone else isn't doing you any good."

"Riley's *not* trouble," Amy said, and when Matt's hand tightened on her arm, she yanked it free. Screw being calm. "None of you know what you're talking about. There's no proof it was her. It could have been anyone."

"Honey," Mallory started.

Amy shook her head. "No. Riley's doing her damn best to make a life for herself. She's working hard at changing—" Horrifying herself, her breath hitched. She sucked in some air and met Matt's warm gaze.

They both knew she was talking about herself. Dammit. "Move," she said, shoving at him, needing the hell out of the booth.

He slid out in his usual unhurried manner, and she barely resisted shoving him again to make him move faster. When his big, stupid, *perfect* body was out of the way, she jerked to her feet and went to pull out her ordering pad because she needed something to do. She planned on insisting that everyone order a damn meal just to keep herself busy, except she pulled out her pocket sketchpad instead.

Before she could replace it, Lucille gasped in delight and yanked it from her hands, flipping through the small sketches, making little noises of approval as she went through. Finally, she looked up at Amy, eyes sharp. "You're not a waitress."

"Actually, I am."

"Girl, you're an artist."

"Well, I..."

"A damn *artist*," she repeated, almost accusingly. "And you've been right under my nose this whole time?" She looked around the group, thrusting the book at each of them in turn. "Seriously? I keep track of every single one of you and your needs, and no one bothers to tell me that I have the next hottest thing serving me coffee?" She snatched the book close and hugged it as she turned back to Amy. "I want to see all of it."

"Excuse me?"

"Your portfolio. Your drawings. Your pads. All of them. Bring them to me."

"I don't—"

"Whatever you have," Lucille said, waving a bony finger in her face. Then she sent Jan a calculating, shrewd look. "She won't be a waitress for long. You should know that right now. Look at this." She opened the pad to a colored-pencil sketch of Lucky Harbor at night, drawn from the end of the pier looking back at the town, with the brightly lit Ferris wheel in the foreground. "This one should be on all the town's marketing efforts and on the website, at the very least. It's a work of art and a pot of gold waiting to happen."

Amy stared down at it. "Is it?"

Lucille smacked Matt upside the back of the head. "How could you not have told her this already? How could you have kept such a secret?"

"Jesus, Lucille." Matt rubbed the back of his head. "And I *did* tell her they were amazing. But her head is even harder than mine."

Lucille turned back to Amy. "You listen to me. People *love* local art. Especially Pacific Northwest art." She waved a dramatic hand in the air. "I'm seeing a series of hand-drawn postcards, detailing all the popular trails." She smiled. "You're going to hit it out of the ballpark, honey. Out of the ballpark, I tell you."

Amy shook her head, her brain too full to deal with this right now. Sawyer stood up and gestured to Matt.

"Where are you going?" Jan asked. "I'm a crime victim here."

"We're going to talk to Riley." Sawyer looked at Amy. "She's at your place, right?"

"Uh..." Unexpectedly cornered, Amy went still. "Actually, no."

"No?" Matt asked.

"No." Suddenly uncomfortably aware of everyone's attention on her, she met Matt's gaze pleadingly, not even sure what she wanted from him. Here she'd thought her biggest problem today would be keeping her mind out of the gutter after what she and Matt had done back at his place. No such luck. "She's not staying with me."

"Since when?" Matt asked.

She managed to hold his gaze, knowing there was no way to keep this from him now. "Since that first night. Well, she was around this morning, but I think that was only to make sure her stepbrother didn't come after me for saving her."

There was a very heavy beat of silence at this. Sawyer looked at Matt, but Matt didn't take his eyes off Amy. "Where has she been staying?"

This wasn't the guy who'd cuddled her after she'd fallen down a ravine. Or the one who'd slid his body down hers and put his mouth on her until she'd come, crying out his name. This wasn't that easygoing, sexy guy at all. He was the law now, distant and cool.

"In the woods," she said quietly. "Camping."

More weighted silence. And a muscle ticked in Matt's jaw. "Illegally camping, you mean?"

She gave a mental cringe. "Yes."

Oh, he was good, an utter professional, not allowing his shock and anger to show, but Amy felt the blast of it just the same. And something else, too, something far more devastating.

Hurt.

"Riley's innocent," she said. And knowing she had no right, she turned and appealed directly to Matt. "Completely innocent."

His gaze roamed her features but didn't soften like they usually did, and she tried again. "She's been through hell..." Her throat tightened. He knew this, goddammit, he did. "And I know you might not understand it, but you have to believe me. She wouldn't do this. She's just a scared, lost runaway, and she needs us. She needs to be trusted, to believe someone cares."

"Honey." Lucille took her hand and gently squeezed, her rheumy eyes surprisingly shiny. "You know we all love and trust and care about *you*, right?"

Her own past was biting her in the ass, all those times she'd screwed up, lied, pushed people away... until no one had believed her. She'd hated that. She'd felt so helpless. Just like she felt now. "Then believe me about this."

Lucille squeezed her hand again. “Love and trust are earned, Amy.”

No one knew this better than she. Unfortunately, she’d just blown any hope of either of those things with Matt, which made her sick to her stomach. She knew that, in his eyes, she’d chosen Riley over him, and that sort of thing couldn’t be undone.

Sawyer turned to leave, and Matt was right on his heels. Amy excused herself and ran after them, stopping Matt just outside the diner with a hand on his arm.

Sawyer looked at them both, then met Matt’s gaze.

“Two minutes,” Matt said to him.

Sawyer nodded and gave Amy what might have been the briefest glance of sympathy. “I’ll be in the truck,” he said.

When they were alone, Matt just looked at her.

“I’m sorry,” she said in a low voice. “I couldn’t break my word to Riley.”

“But you could break your word to me.”

“I never gave you my word.”

“No,” he said in a voice that sounded terrifyingly final. “You sure as hell were careful not to do that.”

She felt like he’d slapped her. “What’s that supposed to mean?”

“Nothing.” He took a step back. “Nothing at all.”

“Look, I said I was sorry, but I had to do this for her. She needed me.”

“I understand,” he said. “After all, all you and I ever had was sex, right?” And with that, he turned and walked to Sawyer’s truck.

Chapter 22

Love's a fad. Chocolate's the real thing.

In the end, Matt drove up to Squaw Flats by himself. Sawyer had gotten an emergency call, leaving Matt alone to search for Riley.

That she'd been camping, alone, vulnerable—not to mention against the law—drove him nuts. And she'd been doing it with Amy's blessing, which really fried his ass. He understood that Amy's loyalty to Riley had a lot to do with Amy's own painful past and lack of adult guidance, but damn.

He parked at the campgrounds and headed into the forest where he'd first found Riley, all too happy to have something concrete to do rather than think about Amy and what had just happened.

She'd lied to him, and he was good and pissed off about that. Except it hadn't been an out-and-out lie, more like an omission. Even as furious as he was, he understood her thought process. He knew how badly she wanted, *needed* to believe in Riley.

Just as he knew that Riley had taken the damn money.

Amy wouldn't thank him for finding out one way or the other, but he made his way to what was most likely going to be the final nail in the coffin of...whatever the hell they had going. Which was fine. His life had been fine before Amy had been in it, and it would be fine without her.

Fucking fine.

As he walked, he couldn't help but remember how he'd found Amy up here not that long ago, and let out a reluctant smile. She'd been so out of her element.

And now he was out of his.

Ten minutes later, he found Riley at her illegal camp spot. She was packing, shoving things into the backpack that Amy had bought her. When he stepped closer, she spun around and jumped up, something glinting in her hand.

A knife.

The minute she registered him, the knife vanished, tossed behind her. She shoved her hands into her ratty pockets, shoulders hunched.

"Expecting someone else?" he asked.

"No."

"Where you going?"

She shrugged and didn't meet his eyes. "Nowhere."

"You're packing."

"Well, you told me I couldn't stay here."

"I told you that two weeks ago," he said. "And you've been staying out here anyway."

Nothing.

He blew out a breath and walked up to her backpack.

"That's mine," Riley said, but before she could snatch it, he pointed at her.

"Stay," he said, and crouched at the bag.

"Hey, you can't just look in there—" She broke off when he reached inside.

And pulled out the charity jar.

"Damn, Riley." She hadn't even tried to hide the thing. The

money was still in it. Furious, *sick*, he sat back on his heels and regarded her.

She was studying something fascinating on her battered sneakers.

"You have any idea what this is going to do to her?" he asked.

At that, Riley's head snapped up. She'd paled to a pasty white. "You can't tell her!"

Matt stood. "No?"

"No!" Riley's cry was fierce. She nearly deflated with it, her entire body sagging as if the only thing holding her up had been Amy's belief in her. "*Please don't.*"

"Okay."

Riley sagged in relief.

"I'm not going to tell her," Matt said quietly. "Because *you* are."

She went from pale to flushed in an instant, her eyes shimmering brilliantly. "I can't do that."

"If you can steal it, you sure as hell can give it back."

Riley's lip quivered, but she bucked up and shook her head. "No."

So she was going to be difficult. Shock. "Let's go."

"You going to arrest me?" she asked.

Matt would rather be just about anywhere other than here, facing this. Give him Afghanistan. Give him a crack house to bust. Anything other than this. But that's not how his day was going so far. "Your knife."

"Huh?"

"Give me your goddamn knife."

She bent and picked up the knife she'd tossed behind her and handed it over.

He took it and then held out his hand. "And the other one."

Riley stared at him.

He stared back, steadily.

She let out the sigh of a martyr and bent, pulling a Swiss Army Knife from her sock.

"What else do you have on you?" he asked.

"Nothing."

He picked up the backpack and shouldered it. "Get your other stuff."

She grabbed an ancient looking folded-up tent and sleeping bag. He had no idea where she'd gotten them and didn't want to ask, afraid he'd have to add to the list of things she'd stolen.

"I didn't take them," Riley said. "If that's what you're thinking. Some old guy out here gave them to me."

Great. "You got anything else?" he asked.

"You see anything else?"

He ignored the belligerent tone because he recognized false bravado when he saw it. For the moment, he was willing to let her have that. It beat the shit out of tears any day of the week.

But it killed him that those two things, along with the backpack on his shoulder, were her entire worldly possessions. "My truck's down the road."

"So?"

"So you're going to walk there with me and get in it."

"Why, so you can arrest me?"

"Just get moving, Riley."

"I want to hold my backpack."

"I've got it," he said, patience wearing thin.

"I want—"

"Now, Riley."

She hesitated, just long enough to make him wonder if he was going to have to force her. Finally she started walking—practically dragging her feet—but she was moving.

At his parking spot, she stared at his truck. "There's no backseat for prisoners."

"You're not a prisoner."

They tossed her tent and sleeping bag into the truck bed, and her gaze locked in on her backpack.

"No," he said, and put it behind his seat.

"I didn't ask anything."

"Just making a blanket statement. Get in. Buckle up."

"Where's the handcuffs?"

Jesus. "Just get in the damn truck, Riley."

Matt drove the sullen girl and her evidence back into town. Instead of heading to the sheriff's station, however, he drove to the diner. He parked, pulled out his cell phone, and called Amy.

"You find her?" she asked breathlessly, as if she'd been waiting on tenterhooks for his call.

His gut twisted again. He didn't want to give a shit. Not even a little bit.

But he did.

He was still angry, but he knew damn well how hard this was going to hit her. "Come out to the lot."

There was a very loaded pause. "Are you going to arrest me for something?" she finally asked.

What the hell? Were all the females in his life crazy? "No," he said with a calm he didn't feel. "Why would I arrest you?"

"I don't know. Why would you command me to the parking lot?"

He rubbed the ache between his eyes with a finger. "Just come out to the damn lot." He paused. "*Please.*"

"That still needs work," she said, "but I'll be right there."

Amy walked out to the lot, not at all sure what to expect. It sure as hell wasn't to find Riley in Matt's passenger seat. Amy had been sick with worry, but now a very bad feeling settled inside her to go with it. "You okay?" she asked the teen.

Riley nodded.

Matt had gotten out of the truck and gestured Amy to the back, where presumably he could speak without Riley overhearing. Amy knew whatever it was, she wasn't going to like it.

"Problem," Matt said.

Before Amy could respond, the passenger door opened, and Riley joined them, shoulders hunched, hands shoved in her front pockets. "It's me," she said, staring at her shoes. "I'm the problem."

Amy looked at Matt, then back at Riley, her heart pounding dully in her ears. "Tell me."

"He didn't already do that?" Riley asked. "Text you on the way over here and let you know what happened?"

"No," Amy said carefully. "Why would he do that?"

"Because you two are a thing."

"No, we're not," Amy said, not looking at Matt. "Tell me what's going on, Riley."

Riley blinked. "Wait—What do you mean you're not? You *were*." She divided a confused look between them, and when neither of them responded to her, she seemed to deflate even more. "Because of me?"

"No," Amy said, heart tight and heavy. "Now talk to me."

"I did it," Riley whispered. "I took the money."

Amy felt the words lance right through her. She made a low, involuntary sound of shock and denial, and Riley spoke quickly. "I was going to pay it back, I swear!"

Amy reached out and grabbed the side of the truck. "You took the money."

A big, silent presence at Amy's side, Matt opened the truck bed and gestured for her to sit on the tailgate, which she did, staring at Riley.

Riley sat next to her and focused straight ahead. "I only did it because I had to pay Troy back, or he wasn't ever going to leave me alone."

"Troy," Amy said quietly. "Your stepbrother?"

"Yes. Last year I had to change foster homes again. Troy was there. He said he'd be my brother."

"Being in the same foster home doesn't make him your brother in any sense of the word."

"I know," Riley said. "But he wanted to be related to someone. He called us brother and sister and said he'd take care of me. But then he…" She looked away. "He wanted payment. And not with money or anything."

Amy felt sick. She knew this story and knew the ending. "Oh, Riley." She hugged the girl, looking over her head to Matt.

He had his cop face on. No help there, which she could admit wasn't a surprise. She'd led him to believe she trusted him, and then she'd held back. Riley had held back. He had good reason to be quite over them both.

"What happened next?" Amy asked Riley.

"I turned eighteen and was released from the system." Her voice was muffled since she had her face down, pressed into Amy's shoulder. "I left the house, but I needed money. Troy loaned me some. He said I had to pay it back, but I couldn't get a job. No one was hiring. So I had to borrow some more from him."

"Where was he getting his money?" Matt asked.

Riley lifted her head. "I don't know. Finally I got work at a fast food place, but it didn't pay enough for me to live and pay him back. He kept showing up and…" She closed her eyes. "The manager told him to leave me alone, and they fought. Troy broke the manager's nose, and the next day I got fired."

"Is that when you came to Lucky Harbor?" Matt asked.

She nodded. "I camped out, hoping Troy would forget about me. But he didn't. He found me, and he wanted money."

"So you stole it to give it to him," Matt said. "Instead of coming to me or Amy and telling us the problem."

Riley stared at him as if he'd grown a third eye. "You wouldn't have believed me." A tear slipped down her cheek, and she angrily swiped it away. "You don't even like me."

"Actually, I do like you," Matt said. "I like you a lot. You've got grit and determination. You were picking yourself up, dusting yourself off, and trying to make a go out of the cards you were dealt. I liked that a whole hell of a lot, too. And for the record? I'd have believed you, Riley. Remember that for next time."

"But now...now you don't trust me."

"You've lied. And you're right, like you or not, I don't trust liars."

Amy flinched. Lost in her own misery, Riley crumpled. "I'm sorry," she said in a small, breathlessly rushed voice. "I thought I could do this and be free." She stared down at her shoes, but her words were directed at Amy. "I didn't mean to hurt you. You were the first person to ever believe in me, and if I could have, I'd have stayed forever. I'm really sorry."

"I know," Amy told her. "It's okay. I—"

"No, it's not okay." Riley swiped at her nose with her arm. "Because now I made you and Matt break up. I messed everything up. I always do."

"You are not responsible for me and Matt," Amy said fiercely, throat burning. "You're not taking the blame for that." That was all on her...

"But the money..." Riley whispered.

"That," Matt said, "you are going to take the blame for."

For Amy, it was a terrible, gut-wrenching déjà vu. *She'd* always been the one to mess up. She was supposedly an adult now, but at the moment, watching Riley suffer through her own mistakes was bringing back those awful memories. Hardly able to breathe, she glanced at Matt.

Sympathy was the last thing she expected to see, but that's what was on his face. He let out a breath, the kind a very frustrated man lets out when he's been put in a bad situation by a female he cares about. And Amy's heart hurt even worse.

Riley pulled her knees up and dropped her head to them, hunched into herself on the tailgate next to Amy, her face covered by her hair. "Why couldn't you just let me go? I could have kept running. I could have—"

"No." Matt crouched at her side, waiting until she lifted her tear-stained face and looked at him. "Listen to me," he said. "You can get through this. You can get through anything and still make your life something. You hear me? All you have to do is want it bad enough. I believe in you, Riley. I believe you can do this, make this all okay."

Amy's heart rolled over and exposed its tender underbelly. She'd never seen anything quite so fierce and amazing as Matt telling Riley, a girl who'd done nothing but give him trouble, that he believed in her.

It gave her a terrible ache and miraculous hope at the same time.

Riley stared up at Matt, solemn, red eyed. And slowly nodded.

He gave her a nod right back, then rose to his full height and turned to Amy. "We need to go see Sawyer. It'll be up to Mallory and Jan if they want to press charges. Whatever happens, we'll deal with it."

Amy nodded and again hugged a trembling Riley, then watched her get back into Matt's truck like she was going to the guillotine. She got one last unreadable look from Matt, and then they were gone.

Amy swiped her nose and stood there in the lot and called Mallory. "I'm sorry, Mal. I have no right, but I'm going to ask you for a favor."

"Yes," Mallory said.

"You don't even know what I'm going to ask."

"The answer's still yes."

Amy's throat burned. "That's like a blank check. Didn't anyone ever tell you to keep your guard up when someone's going to ask something of you?"

"That's the thing," Mallory said. "You're not supposed to have a guard with good friends."

Her heart swelled, feeling too big for her chest. "Dammit, Mallory."

"Part of the pact. Are you learning nothing from those good girl lessons?"

In spite of herself, Amy's eyes filled, and she sniffed. *Shit.*

"Are you crying?" Mallory asked.

"No, I have something in my eye."

Mallory laughed. "You're such a cute sap. Who knew? What's the favor? Like I said, anything. Well, unless you want Ty. I'm afraid I can't share him. Not even for you, babe. He's all mine."

Amy choked out a laugh. "Keep him, you deserve him."

"I do." Mallory let out a dreamy sigh, then got to business. "Okay, so spit it out. I have to get to the clinic. I'm running a thing tonight."

"Riley stole your money," Amy said.

"I know."

"What? How do you know?"

"I might have been born here in Lucky Harbor," Mallory said, "but I wasn't born yesterday. What can I do to help Little Sticky Fingers? I'm thinking she had a damn good reason for that level of desperation."

"She does," Amy said grimly. "Matt has the jar with the cash. He has Riley, too. They're heading to see Sawyer now."

"Oh, boy. Poor kid."

"I know…" Amy knew both Mallory and Jan had the right to press charges against Riley. Amy wouldn't interfere there, but she could try to soften Riley's way. "Do you think that if charges are pressed, you'd be willing to let her make restitution?"

"Absolutely," Mallory said. "And if you want it to be painful, I just opened a Parents' Night Out at the clinic. Starts tonight, in fact. Parents get to drop off their kids for a free night of babysitting. I'm short babysitters. Can't think of a more fitting punishment for a teenager to face than babysitting little kids, can you?"

Amy found a laugh in the day after all. "You're amazing, you know that?"

"I do know it," Mallory said. "But I'll be sure to put out a press release."

Amy barely made it through the rest of her shift. She played phone tag with both Matt and Sawyer, but didn't connect with either, until just as she was getting off work, Sawyer came by.

"Mallory didn't press charges," he told her. "Jan might have, but Matt managed to convince her that the girl would be paying restitution and making it right. I guess he called Mallory, who suggested Riley be forced to volunteer weekends at the health services clinic for the next three months."

Not for the first time that day, Amy felt swamped with love for Mallory. Restitution, *and* Riley would stay in Lucky Harbor for a while longer. "So where is Riley now?"

"Working her first shift," he said. "I dropped her off with Mallory." He laughed ruefully. "I don't know who I feel more sorry for, Riley or the kids."

When he'd left, Amy looked down at her phone. No message from Matt. She supposed she hadn't expected one.

But she'd wanted one.

She drove to the HSC. Mallory met her in the foyer of the building, holding a Nerf bow-and-arrow set. "I'd hoped you'd show up—" She broke off to whirl around and shoot a soft Nerf at a boy tiptoeing up behind her. He had his own Nerf bow-and-arrow set slung over his shoulder, but Mallory was faster, and her arrow nailed him in the chest.

With a wide grin, he spun in dramatic, action-adventure fashion before throwing himself to the ground. He spasmed once, twice, and then a third time, drawing out his "death scene" by finally plopping back and lying still.

"Nice," Mallory told him. She looked at Amy. "You look like you need a brownie, bad."

"Or a hammer upside the head."

Mallory's eyes filled with sympathy. "Aw, look at you, showing all your feelings. No more good girl lessons for you. You've graduated. I'm so proud."

Grace popped her head out of one of the rooms. "The babies," she declared with exhaustion, "are asleep. They all zonked out like a charm."

"Maybe you should get a job as a nanny," Mallory suggested, loading another arrow as she eyed the hallway with a narrowed eye.

But the boy who'd come around the corner was already locked and loaded and got her in the arm. She sighed. "Hit," she said, and lay down on the floor.

"You're supposed to fall," the boy complained, looking greatly disappointed.

Grace continued the conversation through this chaos as if Mallory wasn't prone on the floor. "There's not enough money in the world for me to take a nanny job. Are you kidding? Me and kids do not mix." She grabbed Mallory's bow and arrows and shot a second kid busily sneaking into the foyer. "Hey, Amy," she said as three more boys appeared. "You going to pitch in or what?"

"She came to check on Riley," Mallory said, sitting up.

"Hey," the first boy said. "You're supposed to stay dead."

"If I stay dead, who'll hand out snacks?"

The boy thought about this for a moment and nodded. "Plus, now I can shoot you again."

"Not if I shoot you first," Mallory said, making him laugh and run off. She stood and brushed herself off. "Riley's doing okay," she said to Amy. "She's quiet, reflective I think, but okay."

Relief filled Amy. "I'm so sorry about the money."

"We did this already. *You* didn't take it."

"No, but—"

"Hush," Mallory said, and when she told people to hush, they generally hushed.

Amy tried, she really did, and for about five seconds she managed. But in the end, she wasn't much for remaining quiet when she had something to say. "I brought Riley into the diner. I'm the one who got her the job."

"Yes," Mallory said. "And Matt's the one who brought her to you. Is he here saying he's sorry for that? Is *he* apologizing for what Riley did?"

Matt wasn't doing much talking, period. Amy was painfully aware of her silent phone in her pocket. "It wasn't his fault."

"And...?"

Amy let out a breath. "Fine, I get it. It's not my fault either."

Mallory smiled and hugged her. "I love you, Aimes, but you sure do like to carry that chip on your shoulder, don't ya?"

"I do not." But she did. She so did.

"Riley said she made you and Matt break up," Grace said.

"No," Mallory said. "That wasn't her fault."

"Was it yours?" Grace asked Amy.

Amy sighed. "Very possibly."

"Honey, do you remember when I was so stubborn about falling in love with Ty?"

"You mean do I remember when you wore those five-inch stilettos to get his attention and then ended up giving Mr. Wykowski a heart attack?"

Mallory grimaced. "Heartburn."

"*And* a boner," Grace added with a shudder.

"Hello," Mallory said. "I have a point here. It hurts to love."

"Well that's no newsflash," Grace said.

"It is if you let me finish my damn sentence," Mallory said. "It hurts even more if you love someone and don't let that person know how you feel." She gave Amy a long, meaningful look.

"Okay, wait a minute," Amy said. "I never said I love Matt." Her heart raced just from saying the words out loud. "In fact, that's ridiculous. Totally ridiculous. *One hundred percent* totally ridiculous."

Grace shook her head. "Party foul. *Two* too many uses of ridiculous." She looked at Mallory. "She's in love all right."

"You know what? You've both taken a few too many Nerf arrows to the heart," Amy said, backing to the door. "I just came to check on Riley, that's it. I wanted to make sure she was okay, that *you* were okay," she said, pointing at Mallory. "And that everything was—"

"Okay," Mallory finished for her. "It is." She snagged Amy's hand and tugged her down the hall, cracking open a door.

Riley sat on a rug in the middle of a room, surrounded by toys and four little kids. Two were climbing on her, one was playing with her hair, and the last one was attempting to tie her shoelaces together.

They were all laughing, including Riley.

Amy looked at her and felt a clutch in her heart. She was still so furious at her for taking that money. Furious and sad and...messed up. Why had she so blindly trusted her? Had she so immersed herself in Lucky Harbor that she'd let her guard down? Apparently so. She'd let Riley in. She'd let Matt in.

And gotten her heart stomped but good.

Mallory touched her shoulder to Amy's. "She's going to stay at the new women's shelter until Sawyer finds the guy who's been harassing her and puts an end to it. Just like you wanted."

No, what Amy had wanted was for everything to go back to how it'd been before.

Too late for that.

"And Sawyer *will* find the guy," Mallory said. "You can lay money down on that, you know you can. Matt's helping him. Together they'll handle it."

Amy nodded. Sawyer was a good man. Matt was a good man.

The best.

Riley had support. She could make it through this.

The question was, would Amy?

Chapter 23

Chocolate cures adversity.

Matt spent the next long hours dealing with bureaucratic bullshit. His superiors were taking heat from Trevor Wright's parents, who were filing civil lawsuits all the way to hell and back. Matt's own interdepartmental inquiry was in two days. He had no idea how it would go, but given the meetings he'd had so far, things weren't good.

It was late, but he made yet another stop at the hospital. Trevor was still too doped up to talk. Matt was just leaving the hospital when someone whispered for him.

"*Psst.* Ranger Hot Buns. Over here."

He turned and found Lucille standing in the doorway to the staff's break room. She was wearing sunshine-yellow sweats that made him wish for his sunglasses. "You did *not* just call me that."

She grinned unrepentantly. "Sorry, you don't like it?"

Before he could strangle her, she laughed again. "Guess you haven't been checking Facebook, huh? The poll there is two-to-one in favor of making a Ranger Hot Buns calendar. In your honor, of course."

He shook his head, trying to rid his brain of that image. "What are you doing here?"

"I volunteer here." She gestured to her badge. "I bring patients magazines and read to them, that sort of thing."

"In the middle of the night?"

Lucille smiled. "It's bingo night, and it went late on account of Mr. Swanson falling over in the middle of calling out the numbers. He wasn't our first choice—Mr. Murdock was—but he lost his dentures, so Mr. Swanson filled in. Anyway, he was calling out the numbers and then he started clenching his chest, saying he was dying of a heart attack. I followed the ambulance here because I greet all the new patients and also because I was his date. Normally he's quite the live wire."

"Is he okay?" Matt asked.

"Oh, sure. He's made of hardy stuff, that Mr. Swanson. Peasant stock, he always says. Turns out, he ate fettuccini and sausage for dinner and had heartburn but they're keeping him overnight for a few more tests. I was just sitting with him for a while until he fell asleep."

Matt felt dizzy. It was a common condition when he was in Lucille's presence. "I've got to go."

"I know. You're probably still looking for evidence that those punk-asses were doing something you can nail them for, right? Like, say, underage drinking and smoking?"

"I can't discuss the case with you, Lucille."

"Well of course not. But I can discuss it with you." She whipped out her phone. The screen was a picture of her art gallery, which reminded Matt of Amy—as if he needed a reminder. She was a hole in his chest at the moment, and now he felt a headache coming on. He pinched the bridge of his nose. "Lucille, I don't really have time for—"

"You're handsome," Lucille said. "I'll give you that. Probably in the top five here in Lucky Harbor, though Mr. Swanson himself could give you a run for his money. But looks aren't everything. Brains are, and the thing is, I figured you for having some."

He narrowed his eyes at her, then took another look at her screen. Facebook, of course. "Now," she said, "*you* wouldn't be able to see this picture because you're not his friend. But I automatically friend everyone in Lucky Harbor. I do that because I'm nosy as hell, and it keeps me up-to-date on the goings on."

"Lucille." He needed Advil. An entire bottle. "I don't—"

She thumbed to a different page. Caleb Morrison's Facebook page. Caleb was Trevor Wright's best friend and had been one of the uninjured climbers the other night. Caleb's latest Facebook post said: *Check out our latest climb!* This was accompanied by a photo of four guys in climbing gear sitting on a group of rocks with Widow's Peak behind them, *all* of them smoking what appeared to be weed.

Lucille smiled at the look on Matt's face. "Who do you love?" she asked.

"*You*," he said with great feeling.

"Aw." She beamed. "Honey, you're just the sweetest, and very good-looking, as I've mentioned. But I'm trying to land Swanson right now, so you'll have to be satisfied with being just friends."

Amy lay awake staring at the ceiling. She'd really thought she'd been onto something good, that her life here in Lucky Harbor was going to be the life she'd always secretly wanted.

But she'd been too afraid to really go after it.

After all she'd been through in her life, was she really going to let her own fears of trust and love hold her back?

Her mind wandered to her grandma's journey. Hope. Peace. Heart. Her grandma had found the courage to come out here to find her heart—

Whoa. Wait a minute. Amy sat straight up in bed and opened the journal, skimming to the part she wanted.

It's been three weeks since we'd last been on the mountain. A long three weeks during which I refused to give up my newfound hope and peace.

Good thing, too, because we needed both to get all the way around and back.

Full circle.

It was worth it. Standing at the very tippy top, looking out at a blanket of green, a sea of blue, and a world of possibilities, the whole world opened up. I would never settle. I would never stop growing. I would never give up.

And as the sun sank down over the horizon, we were suddenly at the beginning again.

Hope.

Peace.

And something new as well, something that brought us full circle. Heart.

Full circle. Without thinking, she picked up her cell phone and called her mom.

"Amy?"

Amy winced at the husky tone of her mother's voice. "I woke you, I'm sorry."

"Are you okay?"

Amy couldn't speak for a minute, stunned that her mom would ask.

"Amy? You still there?"

"Yes," she managed. "I'm sorry, I didn't think about the time. I'm fine. I just wanted to thank you for sending grandma's drawings. They're beautiful. I had no idea…"

"Her drawings were personal to her. She kept them hidden. I think they reminded her of Jonathon."

Amy nodded, which was stupid, her mom couldn't see her. "He died before their trip."

"Yes, of course. I thought you knew from the journal."

"No."

"I guess it was too painful to write about. Jonathon lived longer than was expected, and she always said that the trip, taking his ashes to his favorite spots on earth, gave her the tools to go on."

Tools. Hope. Peace. Heart. In her own heart, Amy knew that was it. "I was just wondering if you could remember anything about grandma's journey at all. In the end, she went full circle but—"

"I told you, she never discussed the trip details with me. I'm sorry."

"It's okay." But it wasn't. The disappointment was a bitter pill.

"I don't mean about that. I... I don't know how to say this, Amy," her mom said. "I made a lot of mistakes with you."

Amy opened her mouth, shocked to discover that hearing those words actually meant something to her. "Well, I made mistakes, too."

"No," her mom said. "Well, yes, but not like mine. I'm the mom. I'm supposed to believe in you, every time. Nothing can undo what happened, I know that, but I wanted you to know, I think about you. I think about you all the time."

Amy had spent so much of her life mistrusting everyone, especially her mom, but the fact was the woman was as human as Amy. No, nothing could undo the past, but if Amy held on to that past, she would turn out like her mother. Full of regrets. She didn't want that. For either of them. "I think about you, too."

"Take care, Amy. And maybe you'll call."

"Yes. And maybe you will as well."

When she'd set her phone down, Amy sat there in the dark, the ache in her chest just a little bit less intense. She and her mom had come full circle, it seems.

Full circle...

She blinked. Maybe Rose and Jonathon had gone full circle, back to where she'd started, at Sierra Meadows. It seemed *exactly* like something her grandma would do. And Amy would bet that it'd been an *accidental* full circle, which meant her grandma had come at Sierra Meadows from another way, possibly stumbling into it again by sheer luck. There was no way of knowing for sure, but Amy was willing to give it a shot.

Hell, she needed to give *something* a shot.

Before dawn, she was packed. No mistakes this time, no more being unprepared or getting lost. She had a journey to finish, and there was nothing to stop her.

Not a runaway.

Not a man.

Not her own hang-ups or history. After all, she'd just lectured Riley on not letting her past rule her life, so it was time to live what she preached.

She sent texts to both Grace and Mallory with her hiking itinerary. Just in case of…well, anything. She started at the North District Ranger Station and purposely didn't allow herself to look for Matt's truck. She'd checked out the map and had planned her route. She managed to move along the trail at a good clip. Apparently she couldn't get her life in order, but she'd accidentally gotten in shape.

Good to know.

She adjusted her backpack and kept going.

And going.

She was going to figure out this last leg of her grandma's journey if it killed her. Which she knew it wouldn't. She'd experienced much worse and was still breathing.

By late afternoon, she was approaching Sierra Meadows from the opposite direction as last time. She was exhausted, but forced herself to keep going, and just when she thought she couldn't take another step, she turned a particularly tight switchback corner and…came out at the top of a ravine that looked down at Sierra Meadows.

But this time, because she was on the opposite side of where she'd fallen down, she was looking down at the diamond rocks. She dropped her pack and sat on a rock, staring at the most incredible, awe-inspiring, 360-degree vista she'd ever seen.

She pulled out a bottle of water and her sketchpad. She flipped through the drawings, each as familiar as her own face. All her life they'd given her comfort, like a security blanket. That had always vaguely embarrassed her, but Lucille's reaction had given her something new.

Hope.

Peace.

She had her grandma's drawings, too, and she looked at the last one, with the vista of rough-edged, craggy mountain peaks—

It was Widow's Peak.

And even more important, it was the exact same view Amy had from this very spot. Heart pounding, she pulled out her grandma's journal. *Standing at the very tippy top, looking out at a blanket of green, a sea of blue…*

Here. Right here was where her grandma had come full circle, staring at Widow's Peak as she'd sprinkled Jonathon's ashes. The late afternoon sun slanted over the precipices, right into her eyes. Amy shaded them with her hand and looked at the beautiful mountains. It was unbelievable to her that by following her grandma's adventure, she'd somehow stumbled into her own as well.

She loved this place. She loved that she had real friends. She loved the sense of community here. Lucky Harbor had become home in a way that no other place had.

But there was more. She'd found herself here. She'd salvaged a crappy life and carved out a little niche for herself.

She'd also fallen in love. How was that for making changes and facing fears? She'd been looking for her grandma's heart, and she'd lost her own.

The sun set a little lower, and its rays burst through the sharply defined rock and trees in such a way that it lit up Widow's Peak like it was on fire. Quickly she grabbed her pencils, wanting to capture it on paper. It took her less than a minute to stare down at her drawing and realize what she was seeing, and she squinted through the bright sun to look at the view again.

With her eyes squinted in protection, the outline of the peaks took on the shape of two interlocking hearts. And within those hearts, the tree lines seemed to form letters. RS. And there was a J, too. And if she squinted really, *really* hard, she could just make out an S…

Amy stared in disbelief at the mountains, then down at her drawing, and let out a low laugh. Just her imagination? Wishful thinking? Probably. But it was also fate.

I left my heart on the mountain, her grandma had told her. And it was right there for Amy to see. It'd been there all these years, waiting for her.

Eventually she walked across the meadow and climbed up to the site of her first overnight camping trip. The sun began to sink, but Amy had prepared for it this time, planned to sleep out here. Alone. She'd faced so many of her fears lately that she'd wanted to look her last one in the eye and prove she could do this.

Leaning back, she could almost feel her grandma smiling down at her.

In the morning, she would finish her drawing and hike out in time to get to work for her afternoon shift. She texted Mallory and Grace again with her whereabouts for the night so that no one called out search and rescue.

Or Matt. Not that he'd be looking for her.

Don't go there…

She started a fire and pitched the tent that she'd borrowed from Ty. Then she sketched until the light was gone.

Once that happened, it was dark. Very dark. But she'd gotten good at facing her fears: letting people in, loving people, trusting people...*camping*! Yep, she could check off the entire list. She crawled into her borrowed sleeping bag and lay still, listening to the forest noises, wishing she had her sexy forest ranger to warm her up.

Matt pulled up to Amy's place and stared at her dark windows.

She wasn't home.

His formal inquiry was at eight a.m. sharp. He would present his findings and hopefully prove that there'd been no negligence on his part or on the part of the forest service. Thanks to Lucille, he had his ducks in a row—at least all the ducks he had—but that didn't necessarily mean anything in the land of bureaucracy. He knew it could go either way, and at the moment, he didn't give a shit. The only person he gave a shit about wasn't home, and he had no idea where she might be.

Trust.

That's what it was all about for her, being able to trust. Not that she'd extended the courtesy to him. He stared up at her dark windows and had to admit he hadn't given her a whole lot to go on in that regard either.

He was such a fucking idiot.

He called her cell but it went straight to voicemail. He'd already checked the diner, but she wasn't working. So he called Mallory. "Where is she?"

Mallory gave him nothing but an angsty silence.

"Mallory."

"I can't tell you."

"Tell me anyway."

More angsty silence.

"Mallory," he said tightly.

"I pinky-swore, Matt! I'm sorry but us Chocoholics have to stick together. It's the Good Girl Code of Honor."

Jesus. "Since when does a good girl hold out on her boyfriend's best friend?"

"Okay, that's not fair," she said. "Asking me to pick loyalties between Ty's BFF and mine."

"Nothing's fair in love or war."

"And is this love or war?" she asked very seriously.

"I need to see her. Now. Tonight."

She went quiet, and Matt knew he had to get this right if he wanted her help. "Is there an emergency clause in that Good Girl Code?" he asked. "Say, for guys who are a little slow on the uptake and need to prove themselves trustworthy?"

"Maybe," she said slowly. "Maybe if, say, I didn't actually *tell* you where she was because you *guessed*."

"Give me a hint."

"Okay…Oh! Remember when I called you and said my friend needed a rescue because she'd gotten lost on the trail?"

Jesus Christ. "Tell me she did not go back up the Sierra Meadows Trail by herself."

"Exactly. I'm not telling you." She hesitated. "You're going after her, yes?"

Matt could hear Ty in the background saying, "Of course he's going after her. He's *whipped*."

Matt ground his back teeth into powder. "Tell him I'm going to wipe that smile off his face the next time we're in the gym together."

"You will not," Mallory said. "I love his smile."

In the background, Ty laughed, and given the sounds that came over the line next, he also thoroughly kissed Mallory, then he came on the line himself. "You're going down, man," Ty said. "Hard."

Matt wasn't sure if Ty meant in the gym or over how Matt felt about Amy. Both, probably. He disconnected and started his truck. Amy had gone to finish her grandma's quest.

Alone.

At night.

He whipped the truck around and headed to the station, telling himself he was wrong. She wouldn't be crazy enough to do this, but sure enough, he found her car was parked in the lot. Engine cold.

Okay, so she'd probably left much earlier in the day, which brought a whole new set of problems. Why wasn't she back? Was she hurt? He thumbed through his contacts and called Candy, the ranger-in-training who'd been running the front desk today.

"Yep," she said cheerfully. "That car was there when I locked up for the night."

Damn. He called Mallory again, but this time Ty picked up.

"Man, you're *really* starting to ruin my sex life."

"Overshare. Ask Mallory when she last heard from Amy."

There was a muffled conversation, and Mallory took the phone. "I got a text from her half an hour ago. She was fine and settled in for the night."

"She's staying the night up there? Alone?"

Silence.

"Cone of silence, Good Girl. We're in the cone of silence. Just tell me."

"Overnight camping without a permit isn't allowed," she said primly.

Shit. He hung up and glanced at the sky. Dark-ass black, which sucked. He pounded out Josh's number next. "Problem."

"Are you bleeding?" Josh asked. "And by bleeding, I mean an aorta nick because I'm in the middle of something here. And by something, I mean sleeping. For the first time in thirty-six hours."

"I'm going to miss my inquiry in the morning."

"Ah," Josh said agreeably. "So not an aortic bleed, but a brain leak. *Have you lost your fucking mind?*"

"Amy went up to Sierra Meadows. Alone. I'm going after her."

"This is your job on the line," Josh reminded him. "Job before chicks, man."

"That's *bros before 'hos*. And irrelevant. I let her think I didn't believe in her, that I didn't trust her. I have to prove her wrong."

"By throwing away your livelihood?"

"If Toby needed you, you'd do the same."

"I love Toby."

Matt blew out a breath. "Yeah."

There was a loaded beat of silence, but it didn't last long. "Jesus," Josh breathed. "You're as bad off as Ty. Go. Go do what you have to. If you lose your job, I'll hire you as my nanny."

Matt hung up, grabbed his emergency pack out of the back of his truck, and hit the trail. Ten minutes later, at midnight, his flashlight died. He pulled out his backup. He was halfway there and had downed his five-hour energy drink stash, and now his eyes were flashing and his heart was pounding from the caffeine. He hadn't slept last night thinking about Amy and Riley. He hadn't slept the night before because he'd spent the hours tearing up the sheets and expending some high-quality passion with Amy. And the night before that, he'd never hit the sheets at all because of the injured hiker.

If anyone else had come out here in the forest in his condition, he'd think they needed a psych eval. Hell, he *did* need a psych eval.

It was twelve thirty a.m. when his backup flashlight died. So much for the Energizer Bunny. He pulled out his iPhone. He had no reception but he did have a flashlight app. Apple was his new best friend.

It was 1 a.m. when he got close. It was 1:05 when his cell phone died.

Apple was relegated to below the Energizer Bunny on his shit list, a fact that was drummed home when he took a step off the trail to take a leak and fell.

And fell.

Amy had fallen asleep by her fire, but at some point she sat straight up, startled, heart pounding. She'd heard something. A loud something, a crash…

Her fire had died down. She tossed more wood in, then grabbed her flashlight, surveying the forest around her.

Nothing.

Had she imagined it? She stood up and walked to the edge of the clearing, shining her light all around her. "Hello?"

No one answered. That was good, she decided. Unless it was a hungry bear...She glanced around nervously at the thicket of trees in front of the ravine and was vividly reminded of what had happened last time she'd been here at night.

A smile curved her mouth in spite of herself, and she moved closer, shining the light down, remembering how she'd fallen and been rescued by Matt, and—

Oh, God. There was rustling down there, *big* rustling, and she immediately thought of that bear. But a bear wouldn't be swearing the air blue.

In Matt's voice.

Chapter 24

Love is like swallowing hot chocolate before it's cooled off. It takes you by surprise at first, but then keeps you warm for a long time.

Matt?" Amy stared into the dark ravine with utter shock. "Is that you?"

"No, it's fucking Tinker Bell."

This irritated statement was followed by more rustling and more swearing.

"What are you doing down there?" she asked, flicking her light in the direction of his voice, but not seeing much. "You told me not to go down that way, remember?"

"Yes, Amy, I remember, thank you." He paused. "I fell."

"Oh, my God. Are you okay?"

He didn't answer right away, and she panicked. "*Matt?*"

"Yeah. I just jacked up my shoulder a little bit."

Fear joined the panic as she stared down into the inky black abyss. "I'm coming down right now." *Soon as she figured out exactly how to do that in the dark.*

"Don't," he called up to her. "I'm fine."

Ignoring that line, which was her own personal favorite bullshit line, she began to make her careful way down.

"Go back, Amy. I'm coming up right now."

That'd be great, if it were true, but she couldn't hear him moving so she kept going. This proved tricky as it was harder going down than it had been coming up. It was steep, and she needed both hands. She also needed her flashlight, so she stuck it down her top and into her bra. This mostly highlighted her own face but gave her enough of a glow that she could see.

Sort of.

"Amy, *stop*."

"I'm not leaving you here—" She broke off with a startled scream as her feet slid out from beneath her on the damp, slippery slope. She fell the last few feet and hit her butt.

"You okay?" Matt demanded.

"Sure. Lots of padding." She rushed to his side.

"You don't listen," he said. He was sitting up, his back to a stump, jaw tight. "Are you sure you're not hurt?"

"Yes."

"Is that your flashlight down your top?"

"Yes again. Is your shoulder broken?"

"Just dislocated, I think. Lean a little closer."

"Why?"

"So I can see down your top."

Okay, so he wasn't on his deathbed. "I'll flash you when we get you back to my camp," she promised, realizing he was breathing through clenched teeth. Pulling out her flashlight, she used it to take a good long look at him. Despite the chilly night, a drop of sweat ran down his temple, and he seemed a little green. "What can I do, Matt?"

"You could flash me now as incentive."

"I'm serious."

He sighed. "I'm okay, just give me a minute."

Well isn't that just like a man. "You shouldn't have come."

"No shit," he said. "And neither should you."

"I meant because you have your inquiry in the morning. In a few hours! Your job—" It all hit her, and she sank back on her heels to stare at him, waving her hand aimlessly. "God, Matt, you're going to miss it. Why would you do this?"

He took her hand, caressing her wrist with his thumb right over her pulse point. Bringing her hand to his mouth, his lips pressed against her palm. "I wanted to be here with you. Did you find what you were looking for?"

"Well, yes, actually."

"I knew you would. That was your goal, and you're not a quitter. You finish what you start. And I came to finish what *we* started."

Her heart caught. "We already finished. And for the record, I *am* a quitter. I quit everything and everyone. That's who I've always been."

"Don't bring Amy-the-teenager into this," he said. "She quit a bad life and got herself a new one. She—" He shifted and broke off with a grimace of pain.

"Oh, God, Matt. We need to—"

"Here—Hold this," he said, and using his good hand, lifted his arm to a certain angle. "Hold tight and don't let go."

She wrapped her hands around his arm. His muscles were quivering. "But—"

Matt jerked, and she heard a pop, and then he sucked in a harsh breath and sagged away from her.

She followed his movement, practically straddling him to see into his face. He was sweating good now, but his color was coming back, and he offered her a weak smile. "Got it in one," he said, and then closed his eyes.

"Matt!"

"Shh," he said, not moving. "I'm not quite up to chasing off any curious bears at the moment. And I don't think the ones in China heard us yet. Help me out of my shirt."

She leaned over him and unbuttoned his shirt, then spread it open to gingerly pull it away from his bad shoulder.

"I like it when you take off my clothes," he said.

"I thought you liked it when I took off *my* clothes."

"That, too." His voice was soft and silky. "I *really* like that. Tear the shirt in half for me."

She tried but she didn't have enough strength so he took it back from her, and holding it between his good arm and his teeth, easily tore the shirt in half.

This caused her to get a hot flash, which she ignored. Matt showed her how to fold the torn shirt into a makeshift sling for his arm.

"Better?" she asked when they'd finished.

He let out a careful breath and rolled his shoulder. "Yeah."

"We need to get you to the ER."

"Nah, I'm good now."

"And you say *I* don't listen." She slid her arm around him to pull him upright, muttering to herself. "No one ever listens to me. Not that I can blame them. I believed in Riley and look how that turned out."

Matt slid a hand to the nape of her neck and tilted her face up, his own solemn. "I'm listening to you," he said. "I'll always listen. I might not agree, but I swear to you, I'll always listen. I didn't mean to hurt you, Amy."

Just like that, her throat clogged. Her eyes burned. "Matt—"

"I never wanted you to give up on Riley," he went on quietly. "The kid made a mistake, that doesn't mean she *is* a mistake." He stroked her hair out of her face. "She's making restitution. She's finding out how to make things right when she screws up. That's because of you, Amy. You set her up to succeed. Don't you see? The *best* thing that could ever have happened to her is having you in her corner." He paused, eyes warm as they roamed over her features. "Now more than ever, don't give up on her."

She stared into his eyes and shook her head, incredibly aware of the heat of his body under her hands. "I won't. I…can't."

"Good," he said. "Because I can't give up either. Not on her. Not on you. And not on us."

Her heart stopped, and he smiled, which kick-started her heart again, painfully. Then he rose to his feet, slipping his good arm around her shoulders, leaning on her as he caught his breath. He turned toward the rocks.

"Matt—"

But he was already climbing back up.

"Matt—"

"I'm fine."

Great, he was fine. But she was so *not* fine. She was worried sick. She stayed right behind him, though what she was going to do if he fell, she had no idea. At least she had a really great view, since he was stripped to just his pants and boots.

"We could see better if you shined the light out in front of us instead of at my ass," he said mildly.

Crap. She redirected the light and ignored his soft laugh.

Finally they made it back to her campsite.

They sat on the log in front of her fire, Matt holding his arm tight to his chest.

"You're not okay," she accused.

"Might have torn something," he admitted.

"How are we going to get you back?"

"I'll be fine by morning."

"It *is* morning. And you have to be back!"

"Amy." Using his good arm, he pulled her in against him. "It's just a job."

She couldn't believe it, couldn't believe what he'd done for her. She burrowed through her backpack and came up with the

Dr. Pepper she'd packed. At the time, it'd felt a little pathetic, carrying one of Matt's sodas simply to be reminded of him. But she was so glad she'd done it. She opened it and handed it over to him.

He looked as if she'd handed him the moon. She waited until he'd downed it. "Matt," she said quietly, "you love your job."

"I do. But I loved my last job, too, and I put that job ahead of everything else, including my own instincts and my marriage. I'm not doing that ever again."

"Ever is a long time."

"*Ever*," he repeated firmly. "And something else I'm not doing ever again..."

"What?

"Taking off my shirt unless you take off yours." He knocked her backward off the log and followed her down.

"Careful of your shoulder!" she squeaked, flat on her back, held to the ground by two-hundred-and-twenty pounds of sexy forest ranger.

"It's not my shoulder you should be worried about," he said, then covered her mouth with his. She cupped the curve of his jaw, feeling his stubble scrape against the pads of her fingers. His lips moved against hers, and though she meant to stop this craziness before he got hurt any further, she found herself kissing him back hungrily, not able to get enough of him.

How could she have forgotten how she felt when he kissed her like this? She was panting for air when he rolled to his back. "Are you okay?" she managed.

"No. Come here."

She moved over him. His fingers were surprisingly dexterous given that he had limited motion and had to be hurting like hell. Dexterous and gentle and tender as he got her out of her clothes in record time. He urged her up, then up some more, until she was sitting on his chest. "Matt, what—"

"More," he said, pulling at her until her knees were on either side of his ears. "There," he said with deep satisfaction.

There was nothing gentle or tender about him now, not when he nipped her inner thigh, or spread her legs even farther and buried his face between them. With one stroke of his tongue, he had her in a heated frenzy, crying out as she climaxed. Before she'd stopped shuddering, he'd guided her down onto his body and shoved his pants down enough to push inside her as his mouth found hers again.

She could taste herself on his tongue. She was trying to be careful with his shoulder but her nails dug into his back. He swallowed her cries as he thrust up into her, powerful and primal. She couldn't think, all she could do was feel, and what she felt so overwhelmed her that she felt her eyes fill.

His eyes were dark and heated as he looked up at her. "Again," he said. "Let go for me again."

That was all it took to send her flying. He was right with her, shuddering in her arms, his good hand gripping her hip as he pulled her down and tucked his face into the crook of her neck. She could feel the heat of his breath against her skin as he struggled to control his breathing.

She couldn't have controlled hers even if she'd tried. He was still buried deep inside her, and she held him close, savoring the feel of their bodies joined together.

Finally she lifted her head and looked into his clear, gorgeous light brown eyes, and that's when she knew.

He was it for her.

No matter what happened, no matter what he said now, that fact remained.

"I've made some pretty spectacular mistakes in my life," he said quietly. "The latest was when I let you think I'd given up on us."

She tried to climb off him but he held her tight, pulling her down to him, pressing his lips to her temple. "Stay. Stay with me."

"I understood why you might have given up," she said. "I'd lied to you."

"Yeah." He nodded. "Which just proves that I'm not the only one who can make a spectacular mistake." He smiled at her. "That's good to know."

She couldn't smile back. Her heart was in her throat. She'd learned a lot about herself lately, mostly that it was hard to ask for forgiveness, and harder still to give it. To let go and trust. But worth it. Oh, God, so worth it. "I'm so sorry," she whispered.

"I know," he said. "And I'm sorry, too. So damn sorry that I hurt you. But I swear to you, Amy, if you give me another chance, I'll never hurt you again. Not for anything. You can trust me." His gaze held hers prisoner, and it was too much.

Way too much. She felt too open and...naked. She dropped her head to his chest. "I do trust you," she whispered. "I just don't know what I'm doing."

He stroked his good hand down her back. "You'll figure it out. I have faith in you."

Lifting her head, she stared at him, then laughed. "You're not going to be the hero and offer to solve all my problems?"

"I'm not here to solve your problems. I'm here to support you in your own decisions. I'm not going to walk away, Amy. Not now, not when the going gets tough, not ever. I'm right here at your back."

"For how long?"

"For as long as you'll have me. I love you, Amy."

Staggered, she stared at him. "But you don't do love."

"I never said that. I said love hasn't worked out for me. But all it takes is the right one. You're the right one."

No one had ever said such a thing to her before, and it made her heart swell hard against her ribcage. "I love you, Matt. So much."

He smiled like she'd just given him the best gift he'd ever had. She settled against his good side, and they stared up at the star-laden sky. "I knew I'd find something on this journey," she said. "I wasn't sure what, but I knew it'd be something special."

They pulled into the North District office at nine a.m., one full hour late, and Matt knew that hour was going to cost him, in a big way.

He didn't regret being late. Couldn't. He'd meant what he'd said to Amy, that he was no longer putting his job ahead of his life. That had been habit, a self-preservation technique.

And it was chicken shit.

He'd learned something about himself here in Lucky Harbor.

The town trusted him. His friends trusted him. Amy trusted him. And he could trust himself and let happiness in.

Amy was his happiness.

The ranger station parking lot wasn't usually a hotbed of activity, but this morning the entire lot was jam-packed with cars.

"What's going on?" Amy asked.

Matt was staring at the lot. "I have no idea."

They got out looking like a ragtag team from *The Amazing Race*. Matt was still shirtless, the sling in place. Amy's clothes were torn from her breathless, in-the-dark climb down to where Matt had fallen. She was disheveled and glowing.

Not from the climb.

Just looking at her warmed Matt from the inside out.

"Mallory's car is here," Amy said, pointing it out. "And Grace's. And isn't that Josh's car? And Ty's truck? And Sawyer's cop car? What—Why is everyone here? Do you think they're all here supporting you?"

Yeah, that's exactly what he thought.

Proving it, the station door opened, and people filed out, his coworkers, and then Jan, Lucille, Lucille's entire posse…half the town.

"What the hell?" Matt said.

Sawyer reached him first. "Got Riley's assailant in custody. The idiot showed up at the diner last night with a knife, threatening everyone in sight if they didn't produce Riley, and Jan beaned him with a frying pan. She's pressing charges, and Riley will do the same." Sawyer looked at Amy. "Jan told Riley that they were even now. The slate was cleared, and Riley could rent out that little hole-in-the-wall studio apartment above the diner if she wanted."

Ty and Josh reached them. Josh's attention narrowed in on Matt's makeshift splint. "Ah, hell," he said, sliding the torn shirt aside, examining the shoulder until Matt hissed in a breath. "You did it again, didn't you?"

Lucille pushed her way between the two big men, barely coming up past their elbows. "Well?" she demanded of Matt. "I came out here and missed my morning talk shows. The least you can do is give me an exclusive quote on the situation."

Matt shook his head. "I don't know the situation."

Lucille went brows up, looking as if she'd just swallowed the canary. "So if I told you that we all came here to see your sexy tush fired, you'd believe me?"

Matt slid a look to Josh and Ty, both of whom were wearing dark sunglasses and matching solemn expressions, giving nothing away. Some help.

Lucille smiled and patted him on the chest like he was a sad puppy. "Aw, you're too cute to tease. We all came this morning to plead your case. Ty and Josh here told your boss that you couldn't be here because you were busy saving a woman who'd gone into the forest alone." She turned to Amy. "Did you need saving again, honey?"

"Actually," Matt said, holding her tight to his good side. "She saved *me*."

"Sweet," Lucille said. "I saved you, too, don't forget." She elbowed Ty. "See, Facebook isn't *completely* evil." She beamed with pride. "Oh, and you're cleared of any inquiries or blights on your record," she said to Matt casually. "Those Facebook pics were pretty damning." She turned to Amy. "I was thinking an exclusive show."

"Show?"

"Your art. You came to Lucky Harbor to follow your grandma's decades-old adventure, hoping for the same life-changing experiences, right? Do you have any idea what a great story that makes to go with the art? It's fantastic. I can't even make that stuff up. You're going to sell like hotcakes. We're going to make buckets of money."

"How did you know all that?" Amy asked. "About my grandma and everything?"

"Honey, I know all. The question is, did you get your life-changing experience?"

Amy looked at Matt and smiled. "I did."

Matt's entire heart turned over in his chest. "Damn," he said, pulling her in. "Damn, I love you."

"Watch the arm!" Josh warned.

"He's not watching that arm," Ty said as Matt kissed Amy again.

"Christ," Josh said.

Matt ignored them all and kept kissing Amy. A surge of emotion rocked him to his core when she responded with everything she had, and the kiss got even a little more heated. He was vaguely aware of everyone cheering and hooting and hollering, but he didn't give a shit. He had everything he ever wanted, at last.

Raising his head, he looked down at the woman whose smile made it seem as if she were lit up from within. She was filthy, exhausted, probably half starved, and a complete mess. But she took his breath and owned his heart, and he'd never seen anything more beautiful. "Be mine, Amy."

"I already am."

The Chocoholics' Brownies-to-Die-For

4 large eggs
1 cup of sugar
1 cup of brown sugar
½ tsp of salt
2 tsp of vanilla
1 cup of butter (2 sticks)
1½ cups of sifted cocoa powder
½ cup of sifted flour

Preheat the oven to 300° F.

Use a mixer to beat the eggs on medium speed until they turn light yellow. Add both sugars and salt. Mix well. Then gradually add the rest of the ingredients: vanilla, butter, cocoa powder, and flour. Keep mixing until it is all combined but the batter is still lumpy.

Pour into an 8" x 8" greased, nonstick pan and place it in the oven at 300 degrees. After 45 minutes, use a toothpick to check the brownies. Check every five minutes for a total cooking time of up to 60 minutes. When the toothpick comes out clean, remove brownies and let them cool before you cut them.

Voila! Your chocolate fix.

Forever and a Day

Chapter 1

Chocolate makes the world go around.

Tired, edgy, and scared that she was never going to get her life on the happy track, Grace Brooks dropped into the back booth of the diner and sagged against the red vinyl seat. "I could really use a drink."

Mallory, in wrinkled scrubs, just coming off an all-night shift at the ER, snorted as she crawled into the booth as well. "It's eight in the morning."

"Hey, it's happy hour somewhere." This from their third musketeer, Amy, who was wearing a black tee, a black denim skirt with lots of zippers, and kickass boots. The tough-girl ensemble was softened by the bright pink EAT ME apron she was forced to wear while waitressing. "Pick your poison."

"Actually, I was thinking hot chocolate," Grace said, fighting a yawn. She'd slept poorly, worrying about money. And paying bills. And keeping a roof over her head...

"Hot chocolate works too," Amy said. "Be right back."

Good as her word, she soon reappeared with a tray of steaming hot chocolate and big, fluffy chocolate pancakes. "Chocoholics unite."

Four months ago, Grace had come west from New York for a

Seattle banking job, until she'd discovered that putting out for the boss was part of the deal. Leaving the offer on the table, she'd gotten into her car and driven as far as the tank of gas could take her, ending up in the little Washington State beach town of Lucky Harbor. That same night, she'd gotten stuck in this very diner during a freak snowstorm with two strangers.

Mallory and Amy.

With no electricity and a downed tree blocking their escape, the three of them had spent a few scary hours soothing their nerves by eating their way through a very large chocolate cake. Since then, meeting over chocolate cake had become habit—until they'd accidentally destroyed the inside of the diner in a certain candle incident that wasn't to be discussed. Jan, the owner of Eat Me, had refused to let them meet over cake anymore, so the Chocoholics had switched to brownies. Grace was thinking of making a motion for chocolate cupcakes next. It was important to have the right food for those meetings, as dissecting their lives—specifically their lack of love lives—was hard work. Except these days, Amy and Mallory actually *had* love lives.

Grace did not.

Amy disappeared again and came back with butter and syrup. She untied and tossed aside her apron and sat, pushing the syrup toward Grace.

"I love you," Grace said with great feeling as she took her first bite of delicious goodness.

Not one to waste her break, Amy toasted her with a pancake-loaded fork dripping with syrup and dug in.

Mallory was still carefully spreading butter on her pancakes. "You going to tell us what's wrong, Grace?"

Grace stilled for a beat, surprised that Mallory had been able to read her. "I didn't say anything was wrong."

"You're mainlining a stack of six pancakes as if your life depends on it."

"Because they're amazing." And nothing was wrong exactly. Except...everything.

All her life she'd worked her ass off, running on the hamster wheel, heading toward her elusive future. Being adopted at birth by a rocket scientist and a well-respected research biologist had set the standards, and she knew her role. Achieve, and achieve high. "I've applied at every bank, investment company, and accounting firm between Seattle and San Francisco. There's not much out there."

"No nibbles?" Mallory asked sympathetically, reaching for the syrup, her engagement ring catching the light.

Amy shielded her eyes. "Jeez, Mallory, stop waving that thing around—you're going to blind us. Couldn't Ty have found one smaller than a third world country? Or less sparkly?"

Mallory beamed at the rock on her finger but otherwise ignored Amy's comment, unwilling to be deterred. "Back to the nibbles," she said to Grace.

"Nothing to write home about. Just a couple of possible interviews for next week, one in Seattle, one in Portland." Neither job was exactly what Grace wanted, but available jobs at her level in banking had become nearly extinct. So here she was, two thousand miles from home, drowning beneath the debt load of her education and CPA because her parents had always been of the "build character and pave your own road" variety. She was still mad at herself for following that job offer to Seattle, but she'd wanted a good, solid position in the firm—just not one that she could find in the *Kama Sutra*.

Now late spring had turned to late summer, and she was *still* in Lucky Harbor, living off temp jobs. She was down to her last couple of hundred bucks, and her parents thought she'd taken that job in Seattle counting other people's money for a living. Grace had strived to live up to the standards of being a Brooks, but there was no doubt she fell short. In her heart, she knew she belonged, but her brain—the part of her that got that she was only a Brooks on *paper*—knew she'd never really pulled it off.

"I don't want you to leave Lucky Harbor," Mallory said. "But one of these interviews will work out for you. I know it."

Grace didn't necessarily want to leave Lucky Harbor either. She'd found the small, quirky town to be more welcoming than anywhere else she'd ever been, but staying wasn't really an option. She was never going to build her big career here. "I hope so." She stabbed another pancake from the tray and dropped it on her plate. "I hate fibbing to my parents so they won't worry. And I'm whittling away at my meager savings. Plus, being in limbo sucks."

"Yeah, none of those things are your real problem," Amy said.

"No?" Grace asked. "What's my real problem?"

"You're not getting any."

Grace sagged at the pathetic truthfulness of this statement, a situation made all the worse by the fact that both Amy and Mallory *were* getting some.

Lots.

"Remember the storm?" Mallory asked. "When we almost died in this very place?"

"Right," Amy said dryly, "from overdosing on chocolate cake, maybe."

Mallory ignored this and pointed her fork at Grace. "We made a pinky promise. I said I'd learn to be a little bad for a change. And Amy here was going to live her life instead of letting it live her. And you, Miss Grace, you were going to find more than a new job, remember? You were going to stop chasing your own tail and go after some happy and some fun. It's time, babe."

"I *am* having fun here." At least, more than she'd ever let herself have before. "And what it's time for right now is work." With a longing look at the last stack of pancakes, Grace stood up and brushed the crumbs off her sundress.

"What's today's job?" Amy asked.

When Grace had first realized she needed to get a temporary job or stop eating, she'd purposely gone for something new. Something that didn't require wearing stuffy pencil skirts or closed-toe heels or sitting in front of a computer for fifteen hours a day. Because if she had to be off-track and a little lost, then she *was* going to have fun while she was at it, dammit. "I'm delivering birthday flowers to Mrs. Burland for her eightieth birthday. Then modeling at Lucille's art gallery for a drawing class."

"Modeling for an art class?" Mallory asked. "Like... nude?"

"Today they're drawing hands." Nude was *tomorrow's* class, and Grace was really hoping something happened before then, like maybe she'd win the lottery. Or get beamed to another planet.

"If I had your body," Amy said, "I'd totally model nude. And charge a lot for it."

"Sounds like you're talking about something different than modeling," Mallory said dryly.

Grace rolled her eyes at the both of them and stood. She dropped the last of her pocket money onto the table and left to make the floral deliveries. When she'd worked at the bank, she'd gotten up before the crack of dawn, rode a train for two hours, put in twelve more at her desk, then got home in time to crawl into bed.

Things were majorly different here.

For one thing, she saw daylight.

So maybe she could no longer afford Starbucks, but at least she wasn't still having the recurring nightmare where she was suffocating under a sea of pennies that she'd been trying to count one by one.

Two hours later, Grace was just finishing the last of the deliveries when her cell phone buzzed. She didn't recognize the incoming number, so she played mental roulette and answered. "Grace Brooks," she said in her most professional tone, as if she were still sitting on top of her world. Sure, she'd given up designer wear, but she hadn't lost her pride. Not yet anyway.

"I'm calling about your flyer," a man said. "I need a dog walker. Someone who's on time, responsible, and not a flake."

Her flyer? "A dog walker?" she repeated.

"Yes, and I'd need you to start today."

"Today...as in *today*?" she asked.

"Yes."

The man, whoever he was, had a hell of a voice, low and a little raspy, with a hint of impatience. Clearly he'd misdialed. And just as clearly, there was someone else in Lucky Harbor trying to drum up work for themselves.

Grace considered herself a good person. She sponsored a child in Africa, and she dropped her spare change into the charity jars at the supermarket. Someone in town had put up flyers looking to get work, and that someone deserved this phone call. But dog walking...Grace could totally do dog walking. Offering a silent apology for stealing the job, she said, "I could start today."

"Your flyer lists your qualifications, but not how long you've been doing this."

That was too bad because she'd sure like to know that herself. She'd never actually had a dog. Turns out, rocket scientists and renowned biologists don't have a lot of time in their lives for incidentals such as dogs.

Or kids...

In fact, come to think of it, Grace had never had so much as a goldfish, but really, how hard could it be? Put the thing on a leash and walk, right? "I'm a little new at the dog walking thing," she admitted.

"A little new?" he asked. "Or a lot new?"

"A lot."

There was a pause, as if he was considering hanging up. Grace rushed to fill the silence. "But I'm very diligent!" she said quickly. "I never leave a job unfinished." *Unless she was asked how she felt about giving blow jobs during lunch breaks*... "And I'm completely reliable."

"The dog is actually a puppy," he said. "And new to our household. Not yet fully trained."

"No problem," she said, and crossed her fingers, hoping that was true. She loved puppies. Or at least she loved the *idea* of puppies.

"I left for work early this morning and won't be home until late tonight. I'd need you to walk the dog by lunchtime."

Yeah, he really had a hell of a voice. Low and authoritative, it made her want to snap to attention and salute him, but it was also...sexy. Wondering if the rest of him matched his voice, she made arrangements to go to his house in a couple of hours, where there'd be someone waiting to let her inside. Her payment of forty bucks cash would be left on the dining room table.

Forty bucks cash for walking a puppy...

Score.

Grace didn't ask why the person opening the door for her couldn't walk the puppy. She didn't want to talk her new employer out of hiring her because, hello, *forty bucks*. She could eat all week off that if she was careful.

At the appropriate time, she pulled up to the address she'd been given and sucked in a big breath. She hadn't caught the man's name, but he lived in a very expensive area, on the northernmost part of town where the rocky beach stretched for endless miles like a gorgeous postcard for the Pacific Northwest. The dark green bluffs and rock formations were piled like gifts from heaven for as far as the eye could see. Well, as far as *her* eye could see, which wasn't all that far since she needed glasses.

She was waiting on a great job with benefits to come along first.

The house sat across the street from the beach. Built in sprawling stone and glass, it was beautiful, though she found it odd that it was all one level, when the surrounding homes were two and three stories high. Even more curious, next to the front steps was a ramp. A wheelchair ramp. Grace knocked on the door, then caught sight of the Post-it note stuck on the glass panel.

Dear Dogsitter,

I've left door unlocked for you. Please let yourself in. Oh, and if you could throw away this note and not let my brother know I left his house unlocked, that'd be great, thanks. Also, don't steal anything.

Anna

Grace stood there chewing her bottom lip in rare indecision. She hadn't given this enough thought. Hell, let's be honest. She'd given it *no* thought at all past Easy Job. She reminded herself that she was smart in a crisis and could get through anything.

But walking into a perfect stranger's home seemed problematic, if not downright dangerous. What if a curious neighbor saw her and called the cops? She looked herself over. Enjoying her current freedom from business wear, she was in a sundress with her cute Payless-special ankle boots and lace socks. Not looking much like a banking specialist, and hopefully not looking like a B&E expert either…

Regardless, what if this was a setup? What if a bad guy lived here, one who lured hungry, slightly desperate, act-now-think-later women inside to do heinous things to them?

Okay, so maybe she'd been watching too many late-night marathons of *Criminal Minds*, but it could totally happen.

Then, from inside the depths of the house came a happy, high-pitched bark. And then another, which seemed to say, "*Hurry up, lady. I have to pee!*"

Ah, hell. In for a penny…Grace opened the front door and peered inside.

The living room was as stunning as the outside of the house. Wide-open spaces, done in dark masculine wood and neutral colors. The furniture was oversized and sparse on the beautiful, scarred hardwood floors. An entire wall of windows faced the late summer sky and Pacific Ocean.

As Grace stepped inside, the barking increased in volume, intermingled now with hopeful whining. She followed the sounds to a huge, state-of-the-art kitchen that made her wish she knew how to cook beyond the basics of soup and grilled-cheese sandwiches. Just past the kitchen was a laundry room, the doorway blocked by a toddler gate.

On the other side of the gate was a baby pig.

A baby pig that barked.

Okay, not a pig at all, but one of those dogs whose faces looked smashed in. The tiny body was mostly tan, the face black with crazy bugged-out eyes and a tongue that lolled out the side of its mouth. It looked like an animated cartoon as it twirled in excited circles, dancing for her, trying to impress and charm its way out of lockup.

"Hi," she said to him. *Her?* Hard to tell since its parts were so low as to scrape the ground along with its belly.

The thing snorted and huffed in joyous delirium, rolling over and over like a hotdog, then jumping up and down like a Mexican jelly bean.

"Oh, there's no need for all that," Grace said, and opened the gate.

Mistake number one.

The dog/pig/alien streaked past her with astounding speed and promptly raced out of the kitchen and out of sight.

"Hey," she called. "Slow down."

But it didn't, and wow, those stumpy legs could really move. It snorted with sheer delight as it made its mad getaway, and Grace was forced to rethink the pig theory. Also, the sex mystery was solved. From behind, she'd caught a glimpse of dangly bits.

It—*he*—ran circles around the couch, barking with merry enthusiasm. She gave chase, wondering how it was that she had multiple advanced degrees, and yet she hadn't thought to ask the name of the damn dog. "Hey," she said. "Hey you. We're going outside to walk."

The puppy dashed past her like lightning.

Dammit. Breathless, she changed direction and followed him back into the kitchen where he was chasing some imaginary threat around the gorgeous dark wood kitchen table that indeed had two twenty-dollar bills lying on the smooth surface.

She was beginning to see why the job paid so much.

She retraced her steps to the laundry room and found a leash and collar hanging on the doorknob above the gate. Perfect. The collar was a manly blue and the tag said TANK.

Grace laughed out loud, then searched for Tank. Turned out, Tank had worn off the excess energy and was up against the front door, panting.

"Good boy," Grace cooed, and came at him with his collar. "What a good boy."

He smiled at her.

Aw. See? she told herself. *Compared to account analysis and posing nude, this job is going to be a piece of cake.* She was still mentally patting herself on the back for accepting this job when right there on the foyer floor, Tank squatted, hunched, and—

"No!" she cried. "Oh no, not inside!" She fumbled with the front door, which scared Tank into stopping mid-poo. He ran a few feet away from the front door and hunched again. He was quicker this time. Grace was still standing there, mouth open in shock and horror as little Tank took a dainty step away from his *second* masterpiece, pawed his short back legs on the wood like a matador, and then, with his oversized head held up high, trotted right out the front door like royalty.

Grace staggered after him, eyes watering from the unholy smell. "Tank! Tank, wait!"

Tank didn't wait. Apparently feeling ten pounds lighter, he raced across the front yard and the street. He hit the beach, his little legs pumping with the speed of a gazelle as he practically flew across the sand, heading straight for the water.

"Oh, God," she cried. "No, Tank, *no*!"

But Tank dived into the first wave and vanished.

Grace dropped the purse off her shoulder and let it fall to the sand. "*Tank!*"

She dashed closer to the water. A wave hit her at hip level, knocking her back a step as she frantically searched for a bobbing head.

Nothing. The little guy had completely vanished, having committed suicide right before her eyes.

The next wave hit her at chest height. Again she staggered back, gasping at the shock of the water as she searched frantically for a little black head.

Wave number three washed right over the top of her. She came up sputtering, shook her head to clear it, then dived beneath the surface, desperate to find the puppy.

Nothing.

Finally, she was forced to crawl out of the water and admit defeat. She pulled her phone from her purse and swore because it'd turned itself off. Probably because she kept dropping it.

Or tossing it to the rocky beach to look for drowning puppies.

She powered the phone on, gnawed on her lower lip, then called the man who'd trusted her to "be on time, be responsible, and not be a flake." Heart pounding, throat tight, she waited until he picked up.

"Dr. Scott," came the low, deep male voice.

Dr. Scott. *Dr. Scott?*

"Hello?" he said. "Anyone there?"

Oh, God. This was bad. Very bad. Because she knew him.

Well, okay, not really. She'd seen him around because he was good friends with Mallory's and Amy's boyfriends. Dr. Joshua Scott was thirty-four—which she knew because Mallory had given him thirty-four chocolate cupcakes on his birthday last month, a joke because he was a health nut. He was a big guy, built for football more than the ER, but he'd chosen the latter. Even in his wrinkled scrubs after a long day at work, his dark hair tousled and his darker eyes lined with exhaustion, he was drop-dead sexy. The few times that their gazes had locked, the air had snapped, crackled, and popped with a tension she hadn't felt with a man in far too long.

And she'd just killed his puppy.

"Um, hi," she said. "This is Grace Brooks. Your…dog walker." She choked down a horrified sob and forced herself to continue, to give him the rest. "I might have just lost your puppy."

There was a single beat of stunned silence.

"I'm so sorry," she whispered.

More silence.

She dropped to her wobbly knees in the sand and shoved her wet hair out of her face with shaking fingers. "Dr. Scott? Did you hear me?"

"Yes."

She waited for the rest of his response, desperately gripping the phone.

"You *might* have lost Tank," he repeated.

"Yes," she said softly, hating herself.

"You're sure."

Grace looked around the beach. The empty beach. "Yes."

"Well, then, I owe you a big, fat kiss."

Grace pulled her phone from her ear and stared at it, then brought it back. "No," she said, shaking her head as if he could see her. "I don't think you understand. I *lost* Tank. In the water."

He muttered something that she'd have sworn sounded like "I should be so lucky."

"What?" she asked.

"Nothing. I'm two minutes away. I got a break in the ER and was coming home to make sure you showed."

"Well, of course I showed—"

But he'd disconnected.

"Why wouldn't I show?" she asked no one. She dropped her phone back into her purse and got up. Two minutes. She had two minutes to find Tank.

Chapter 2

Okay, so maybe chocolate doesn't make the world go around, but it sure makes the trip worthwhile.

Josh's day had started at five that morning in the gym. Matt and Ty, his workout partners, spent the hour sparring in the ring, beating the shit out of each other while Josh lifted weights. The three of them worked hard while retaining enough breath to sling ongoing insults and taunts. It was what friends were for.

By six-thirty, he was in the ER, patching up a guy who'd gotten in a bar fight in Seattle hours before but had been too drunk to realize he was bleeding profusely as he drove down the highway. From there, Josh had moved on to a heart attack victim and then to a two-year-old who'd swallowed a few pennies and was having understandable trouble passing them.

By noon, Josh wasn't even halfway through his day, and he'd already been overloaded and overworked and was quite possibly teetering on the edge of burnout. He could feel it creeping in on him in unguarded moments, like now when he was parking his car between his house and the beach to deal with Grace Brooks.

He knew who she was. He'd seen her around. Blue eyes, a quick smile, long, shiny blond hair, and a willowy yet curvy body that could drive a man right out of his mind if he gave it too much thought.

As he walked across the sand toward the water, doing his best not to give it *any* thought, he caught sight of her in the water. She was facing the waves, her hands on her head in a distraught pose. With a frown, he picked up the pace, just as something dashed toward him in his peripheral vision.

Something small.

Something evil.

Something named Tank. Josh scooped up the sand-covered puppy and held him away from him. The pug wriggled intently, running in the air, trying to get closer to Josh. Finally giving up, Tank refocused his attention on the woman in the ocean.

"Oh, I see her," Josh said. "And what the hell have you done now?"

Grace was panicked. It was one thing to lose a job. It was another thing entirely to lose *the* job. Damn. Her parents had always told her "keep your head down and work hard" and she'd done her best. She really had.

But she'd still screwed up. And it wasn't like she could call them for advice on this. Neither of them could possibly understand the thought process that had led her to a dog walking job, much less why she'd placed fun as her newest, highest priority. "Tank!" she yelled at the waves. "*Tank?*" Wading back in up to her waist, she turned in a full circle to rescan the beach, then went utterly still.

Standing on the sand was a man. His tall, broad stature implied strength and control, and he was rocking a pair of navy blue scrubs and dark wraparound Ray-Bans.

Holding her archnemesis.

Tank.

The puppy was panting happily away, and Grace could have

sworn he was *smiling.* Forget the pig or alien theory—Tank was a rat. Relief at seeing the thing alive nearly brought her to her knees, but she'd have drowned, so she locked them—just as the next wave hit her from behind.

She was very busy fighting a full-facial, saltwater cavity wash when two big hands gripped her arms and hauled her upright.

Dr. Scott, of course.

She coughed and choked some more—very attractive, she was quite certain. Then she realized that she was up against her rescuer, held there firmly as the water swirled around their calves. "I'm okay," she gasped.

"Sure?"

"Yes," she said, but he didn't let her go. "Really," she promised. "I'm good."

He nodded and continued to hold her against him.

Except…he wasn't holding her at all. *She* was clinging to *him*, soaking up the warmth and strength of him radiating through his now-wet scrubs. Well, crap. Forcing herself to loosen her grip on him, she stepped back, working on searching for a different grip entirely—the one on her fast-failing dignity. Hiking her dress up to her thighs, she frog-marched out of the water as fast as she could so as to avoid being flattened by the next wave. By the time she hit dry sand, she was feeling a little bit like a drowned kitten. One glance down assured her that she didn't look like a drowned kitten. She looked like she was trying out for a wet T-shirt contest.

Yikes.

She decided not to look at herself again and made the mistake of looking instead at her rescuer. He was close, close enough to force her to tilt her head up to see his face, close enough to ascertain that he clearly hadn't shaved that morning.

The dark stubble on his jaw was incredibly disconcerting. And sexy.

"*Arf!*" Tank said from his perch, which was her purse, still lying on the sand. The little shit was standing on it like he owned it, wet, sandy paws and all. "*Arf, arf!*"

Nice. Grace gave herself a big mental thumbs-up for the "fun" that this job had been so far.

Josh nudged Tank off Grace's purse, then attempted to brush the wet sand from the leather. Tank gave a pretend ferocious growl and began a tug-of-war with the strap.

Heathen.

Josh gave him another nudge and rescued the purse. He was doing his damnedest to concentrate on the situation at hand, but that was proving difficult given the sight of Grace, her clothes plastered to her like a second skin. Half of her hair was in a topsy-turvy knot on top of her head, with the rest plastered to her face. The tip of her nose had gotten sunburned, and her mascara was smudged around her drown-in-me blue eyes.

And then there was her mouth.

She had a full lower lip, one that warmed him up considerably and made him think about sex. Actually, everything about her—the oh-shit expression on her face, the way she waved her hands like she was trying to explain herself without words, the delicate clinking of the myriad of thin silver bracelets she wore on her wrist—brought to mind sex.

Sex and chaos.

Pure, unadulterated, trouble-filled chaos. The thing was, he'd been there before, in another time and place, and was no longer interested in such things. No matter how hot the packaging was.

And the packaging was *very* hot. Grace was wearing one of those flimsy little summer dresses that had a way of messing with a guy's brain. The tiny straps had been designed with the sole purpose of making him want to tug them down—with his teeth.

Or maybe that was just him, and the fact that he hadn't had sex in so long he'd nearly forgotten how it felt.

Nearly.

The pulse at the base of Grace's slender neck was beating a little harder and faster than it should be. As a doctor, he knew these things. Plus, his own pulse was going too. Mostly because that hot little sundress was as sheer as tissue paper when wet, and she was most definitely wet.

And cold.

Her underwear was white lace. God bless white lace. And Jesus, he really needed five minutes of shut-eye. And possibly a lobotomy. Or maybe he just needed to get laid.

Like *that* was going to happen when he was working 24/7.

Blowing out a breath, Josh scooped up the puppy that his sister had adopted with the sole purpose of sending Josh over the edge—which was working—and grabbed his shivering dog walker's hand. He led her to his car and directed her to the passenger seat and put Tank into the back.

"W-where are we g-going?"

"Nowhere." Josh cranked the engine and heater, then twisted around to extract his sweatshirt from the backseat.

"N-no, that's okay," she said, shaking her head. "I'll g-get it all wet and sandy."

"Put it on before your teeth chatter out of your head."

Grace complied, then wrapped her arms around herself and huddled into the heater vents. "I'm sorry I lost Tank."

The puppy perked up at his name and took a flying leap into the front seat, landing in Josh's lap. Four paws hit the family jewels with precision. Sucking in a breath, Josh scooped Tank up and was promptly licked for his efforts.

"It's so great that you found him," Grace said.

"Yeah." Josh sighed in grim resignation, swiping the puppy drool off his chin. "*So* great."

* * *

Grace watched Josh set Tank onto the backseat. Again. Tank cried and leaped forward. Josh caught him in midair and dangled him in front of his face so that man and puppy were eye to eye. Tank panted happily, looking thrilled.

Not so the good doctor, though it was hard to tell what he was thinking behind his sunglasses. "You warmed up now?" he asked.

"Arf."

Grace smiled in relief. The puppy was okay. "I guess that means yes."

"I meant you," Josh said.

"Oh!" She laughed. "Yes, thank you."

He just looked at her, and she realized he was waiting for her to get out. Right. He had to get back to work. She opened the door, and he did the same, getting out with Tank tucked under his arm like a football.

"Want me to put him away for you?" she asked, thinking it was the least she could do.

"I've got him."

Grace watched him head toward his house. He was a big guy. Bull-in-a-china-shop big. But he had a way of moving with surprising grace. He was very fit, and *very* easy on the eyes. She wasn't often steered astray by bouts of lust, but she felt it stir within her now. No doubt he would be a very interesting item to add to her list of Fun Things to Do, but he was a doctor. Most would be attracted by that, but not Grace. She knew his world, knew the crazy hours, the life that wasn't really his own, knew what it was like to compete for even a smidgeon of attention. Fair or not, the initials MD after his name would keep him off her list. "You said you'd kiss me if I lost Tank."

The words popped out of her unbidden, and she covered her mouth. Too late. Turning back, Josh shoved the sunglasses to the top of his head and leveled her with a long, assessing look from dark brown eyes.

He looked exhausted. As if maybe he'd been working around the clock without sleep. "Ignore that," she said. "Sometimes I have Tourette's."

Some of the tension went out of his shoulders, and for a beat, his features softened into what might have been amusement. "You want me to kiss you?"

Oh boy. "You were happy I'd lost your puppy?"

He was looking like he was still thinking about smiling as he glanced down at Tank, tucked under his arm. "No. That would make me an asshole."

Right...

"And he's not *my* puppy," he said. "He belongs to my son, given to him by my evil sister, who I'm pretty sure bought him from the devil."

They both looked at Tank, who soaked up the attention as his due. He managed to roll in Josh's arms, over to his back, showing off his good parts with pride.

Such a guy. "If you don't want him, couldn't you just give him back?"

Josh laughed softly. "You don't have any kids, I take it."

Or dogs. "No."

"Trust me," Josh said. "I'm stuck with him."

"Arf," Tank said.

Josh shook his head, then started toward the house again, his wet scrubs clinging to those broad shoulders and very nice butt as his long legs churned up the distance with ease.

Apparently they were done here. "Uh, Dr. Scott?"

"Josh," he corrected.

"Josh, then." Since he hadn't slowed or looked back, she cupped her hands around her mouth. "Should I come by your house at around the same time tomorrow, then?"

His laugh was either amused or horrified. Hard to tell. “No,” he said.

Grace paused, but really, there was no way to mistake the single-syllable word. No was…well, *no*.

Which meant she was fired. Again. One would think she’d be good at that by now, but nope, she didn’t feel good at it.

She felt like crap.

Chapter 3

Happiness is sharing a candy bar. Even better is not having to share.

This is all your fault," Josh told the wriggling puppy as he walked toward his house.

Tank didn't give a shit. He'd caught sight of a butterfly and was growling ferociously, struggling maniacally to get free so he could attack.

Tank was the Antichrist.

"Look, we all know you think you're a badass, but that butterfly could kick your ass with one wing tied behind its back," Josh told him, tightening his grip as he used his other hand to reach into his pocket for his phone.

His *wet* phone, which—perfect—was fried. Seemed about right, given his day so far. "You could have kept running for the hills," he said. "Or at least stayed 'lost' long enough to get me that kiss."

Tank stretched his nonexistent neck and oversized pug head so he could lick Josh's chin again.

"Yeah, yeah." It didn't matter. Grace Brooks was a beautiful woman, but he didn't have time to sleep, much less time to give to a woman.

Although, the way she'd hiked her dress up her bare, toned legs had definitely been worth the price of admission...He let himself into his house, trailing sea water and sand with him. No doubt he'd get a dire text from Nina, his pissy housekeeper, but his phone was dead.

Silver lining.

Toby had started kindergarten this week, so the house was void of the insanity of Zhu Zhu hamster pets and the *whoosh, vrrmm-whoosh* of Toby's ever-present Jedi saber. Anna should be in class—*should* being the operative word. His sister had yet to consider junior college any more seriously than her choice of fingernail polish.

Moving toward the kitchen to dump Tank, Josh stopped short in surprise.

Shit.

Literally.

Grinding his teeth into powder, Josh lifted his shoe, studied the bottom of it, then dangled Tank at eye level. "Have you ever heard of mince meat?"

Tank tried to lick his nose.

"*Not* cool, dog." Josh dealt with the mess. If he left it for Nina, she'd quit for sure since she'd already made it clear that nothing puppy related was on her plate. And that was *all* Josh needed, for yet another person to quit on him. It took a village to run his life, and his village was in mutiny.

He caught sight of the forty bucks still on the kitchen table. Hell. Grace hadn't taken the money. And she needed it, too, which he knew because this was Lucky Harbor. You could drop a pot of gold on the pier and a perfect stranger would hand it back to you, but you couldn't keep a secret to save your life.

Josh stripped out of his wet scrubs in the laundry room and slid Tank a long look. Unconcerned, Tank was snuffling around in his bed, turning his fat, little puppy body in three tight circles before plopping down with a snort and closing his eyes. Apparently he was satisfied with the destruction he'd left in his wake.

Definitely the Antichrist.

The house phone was ringing, probably because his cell was no longer working. Josh grabbed a set of fresh scrubs from the freshly delivered stack that he kept in the basket on the dryer and headed for the door. Later. He'd deal with it all later.

This is how he survived the daily insanity of his life, using his unique ability to prioritize and organize according to importance. Taking care of his family—important. Incoming phone call to inform him he was late—redundant, and therefore not critical.

Josh worked two shifts a week in the ER and four shifts at his dad's practice. His dad had been gone five years and Josh still didn't think of the practice as his own, but it was, complete with all the responsibilities of running it. When he could, Josh also donated a shift to the local Health Services Center. All the work made for a great stock portfolio, but it was hell on his home life.

Hell on Toby.

Something had to give, and soon. Probably Josh's own sanity, but for now, he headed back to the hospital only to be called into a board meeting.

He wasn't surprised by the topic at hand. The board wanted him to sell the practice, incorporating it into the hospital as many of the other local medical practitioners had done. The deal was they'd buy Josh out, pay him to stay on board, and also hire on another doctor to help him with the workload. Plus they'd guarantee the practice the hospital's internal referrals.

It was a dangling carrot.

Except Josh hated carrots.

This wasn't the first time the board had made the offer. They'd been after him all year to sell, each offer getting progressively more aggressive. But Josh didn't like being strong-armed, and he didn't like thinking about how his dad would feel if Josh let his hard-earned practice slip out of his control.

It was eight-thirty by the time he got home that night—half an hour past Toby's bedtime. Last night, the five-year-old had been in bed at this time, asleep on his belly, legs curled under him, butt in the air, his chubby baby face smashed into his pillow. He'd clearly gone to bed directly from the bath because his dark hair had been sticking up in tufts, the same way Josh's always did when he didn't comb it.

Toby's pj's had been—big surprise—Star Wars, and Josh had kneeled by the kid's bed to stroke back the perpetually unruly hair. Toby had stirred, and then…

Barked.

He'd been barking ever since Anna had brought Tank home. It was a passing phase.

Or so Josh desperately hoped.

Toby was the spitting image of Josh, but he had his mother's imagination and her temperament to boot. Josh could read that temperament in every line of his son's carefree body as he slept with wild abandonment. He wondered if Ally would be able to see it. But of course she wouldn't, because to see it, she'd have to actually see Toby, something she hadn't attempted in years.

Hoping the Bean was still up and using actual words tonight, Josh walked in the front door and stopped in his tracks.

Devon Weller, Anna's latest and hopefully soon-to-be-ex-boyfriend, was sitting on the half wall between the dining room and living room, eyeballing his cell phone.

Anna came into sight, arms whipping as she sped her wheelchair around the corner on two wheels. Hard to believe someone so tiny could move so fast, but Josh knew better than to underestimate his twenty-one-year-old sister.

She'd created a figure-eight racecourse between the two couches and the dining room table and was getting some serious speed.

In her lap, squealing with sheer joy and possibly also terror, was Josh's mini-me—not asleep, nowhere close. With his eyes lit with excitement, cheeks ruddy from exertion, Toby was smiling from ear to ear.

Tank was right on their heels—or wheels in this case—barking with wild abandoned delight, following as fast as his short little legs would take him.

For a brief second, Josh stood there rooted to the spot by a deep, undefined ache in his chest, which vanished in an instant as Anna took a corner far too tight, wobbled, and tipped over, sending her and Toby flying.

"Damn," Devon said, and clicked something on his phone with his thumb.

The idiot had been timing the event.

Josh rushed past him to the crumpled heap of limbs. "Don't move," he ordered Anna, pulling Toby off her. He turned Toby in his arms and took in the face that was so like his own, except free of the exhaustion and cynicism that dogged Josh's every breath.

Toby grinned and threw his arms around Josh's neck in greeting. The kid's moods were pure and mercurial, but he loved with a fierceness that always grabbed Josh by the throat. He hugged Toby back hard, and Toby barked.

Letting out a breath, Josh set him aside to lean over Anna, who hadn't moved. He didn't fool himself; he had no delusions of being able to control his sister. She hadn't stayed still simply because he'd ordered her to. "Anna." Gently he pushed the damp hair from her sweaty brow. "Talk to me."

She opened her eyes and laughed outright. "That was *sweet*," she said.

Toby tipped his head back and barked at the ceiling, his voice filled with glee.

Josh sat back on his heels and scrubbed a hand over his face. "Toby should be in bed, Anna. And you could have hurt yourself."

She started to crawl to her chair. "Been there, done that, bought the T-shirt."

Josh scooped her up while Devon sauntered over. Though how he could walk at all with his homeboy jeans at half past his ass was a mystery. Devon righted Anna's wheelchair, and Josh set her into it.

"Oh, relax," she muttered after Josh stood over her, hands on hips. She tugged on Toby's ear. "Hey, handsome. Go get ready for bed, 'k?"

"Arf-arf," Toby said, and turned to the hallway.

Josh caught him by the back of his Star Wars sweatshirt. "You use soap and water today?"

Toby scrunched up his nose and scratched his head.

Josh took that as a no. "Use both now. And toothpaste."

"Arf," Toby said slowly, all hurt puppy face.

But Josh had learned—never cave. "Go on. I'll be right there."

Toby went from sad to excited in a single heartbeat, because if Josh was coming, too, it meant a story. And for a moment, Toby looked young, so fucking painfully young, that Josh's chest hurt again.

Getting home in time to fall into bed exhausted was one thing. Getting home in time to crawl into bed with his son and spend a few minutes before they both crashed was even better. "Pick out a book," he said.

"*Arf!*"

Josh gave Devon a look, and the guy made himself scarce. Devon might be a complete loser but he was a smart loser.

Anna ignored Josh and pushed back her dark hair. She was tiny, always had been, but not frail. Never frail. She had the haunting beauty of Snow White.

And the temperament of Cruella de Vil.

Five years ago, a car accident had left her a highly functioning paraplegic. She was damn lucky to be alive, though it'd been hard to convince a sixteen-year-old to see it that way. "If you can't get him to bed on time," Josh began, "just tell me. I'll come home and do it myself."

"Oh good," Anna said with an impressive eye roll. "You still have the stick up your ass." She headed into the foyer, grabbing her purse off the bench.

"You're still mad about me nixing your Europe trip," he guessed.

"Give the man an A-plus." She snatched her jacket off the low hooks against the foyer wall. "Always knew you were smart. Everyone says so. They say, '*Oh, that Dr. Scott's so brilliant, so sharp.*'" She turned away. "Shame it doesn't run in the family."

"No one says *that*," he said.

"They think it."

Josh's fingers curled helplessly as she struggled into her jacket, but if he offered to help, she'd bite his head off. He wasn't the only Scott family member who hated needing help. "So prove them wrong," he said.

She shrugged. "Too much work."

"Anna, you can't just traipse around Europe with Devon for the rest of the year."

"Why? Because my life is so busy? Because I've even got a life?"

"You've got a life," he said, frustrated. "You're taking classes at the junior college—"

"Yes, Cooking 101 and Creative Writing. Oh, and my creative writing teacher told me I should definitely *not* quit my day job."

He sighed. "You can do anything you want to do. Pick a major. You *are* smart. You're—"

"*Paralyzed*," she said flatly. "And bored. I want to go to Europe with Devon."

God knew what Anna saw in the guy who claimed to be going to a Seattle tech school at night while working on a roofing crew by day. Josh had never so much as seen Devon crack a book, and he sure as hell seemed to have a lot of days off. "How does Devon have the money for Europe?"

"He doesn't. My settlement money from the accident comes in two weeks."

Oh hell no. "*No*."

"I'm going out," she said, both ignoring what he'd said and changing the subject since it didn't suit her.

"Where?" he asked.

"*Out*."

Jesus. Like pulling teeth. "Fine. Be back by midnight."

"You're not Mom and Dad, Josh. And I'm not sixteen anymore. Don't wait up."

"Devon have gas this time?" Last week he'd run out of gas in his truck at two in the morning, with Anna riding shotgun up on Summit Creek.

In answer to the gas question, Anna shrugged. She didn't know and didn't care.

Great. "*Midnight*, Anna."

"Yeah, yeah."

"Wake me up when you're home."

She rolled her eyes again and yelled for Devon, who appeared from the kitchen eating a sandwich. He slid Josh a stoner-lazy smirk, then pushed Anna's chair out the front door and into the night.

Nice. Josh shut the door and ground his teeth. He was all too aware that he *wasn't* Mom and Dad. They'd been gone for five years, killed in the same accident that had nearly taken Anna as well. Josh had been twenty-eight, a brand-new father from his first and only one-night stand, and a single year out of residency when it'd happened. Overnight he'd lost his parents and had suddenly become responsible for a badly injured, headstrong, angry teenager along with his infant son. He'd held it together, barely, but it'd all been a hell of an adjustment, and there'd been more than a few times Josh hadn't been sure he was going to make it.

Sometimes he still wasn't sure.

He locked up, flipped off the kitchen and living room lights, and found Toby jumping on his bed with his Jedi saber, the iridescent green light slicing through the air.

Whoosh, vrrmm-whoosh.

Josh caught him in midleap and swung him upside down, to Toby's screams of delight. Then Josh tossed him onto the bed and crawled in after him.

Toby had a few books on his pillow. He was into superheroes, cars, trains... anything with noise, really. Being read to calmed him, and he snuggled up close and set his head on Josh's shoulder, pointing to the top book. The Berenstain Bears. The cover showed the entire family, but Toby stroked his finger over the mama bear.

He wanted *his* mama bear.

Like a knife to the heart. "Toby."

Toby tucked his face into Josh's armpit but Josh gently palmed the boy's head and pulled him back enough to see his face. "You remember what I told you, right? About your mom? That she had something really important to do, but that she'd be here with you if she could?"

Toby stared at him with those huge, melting chocolate–brown eyes and nodded.

And not for the first time in the past five years, Josh wanted to strangle Ally for walking out on them. For walking out and never so much as looking back. Leaning in, he pressed a kiss to Toby's forehead and then sighed. "You forgot the soap."

"Arf."

Josh woke somewhere near dawn, dreaming about being smothered. When he opened his eyes, he realized he'd fallen asleep in Toby's bed. The Bean had one half, Tank the other, both blissfully sleeping, limbs and paws akimbo.

Josh, bigger than both of them put together times four, had a tiny little corner of the bed. And he meant tiny. His feet were numb from hanging off, and the *Berenstain Bears* book was stuck to his face. Wincing at his sore bones, he shifted, and at the movement, Tank snuffled and stretched.

And farted.

The bedroom was instantly stink-bombed. "Jesus Christ, dog, you smell like a barn."

Tank just gave him a pug grin.

Josh shook his head and eased out of the bed, pulling the covers up over Toby, who was sleeping like he did everything in life—with 100 percent total abandonment.

Envying him that, Josh showered and went downstairs.

Nina was cleaning the kitchen and making Toby's lunch.

"I need you to walk Tank today," he said. "Twice. Once mid-morning and once in the afternoon. He sure as hell better learn to hold it that long if he wants to live."

Nina carefully closed Toby's Star Wars lunch box. "No," she said.

"Okay, okay, I'm only kidding. I'm not going to actually kill him." *Probably.*

"No, I won't walk that dog." Nina was four and a half feet tall, Italian, complete with accent and snapping black eyes that could slay one alive. The housekeeper also possessed the baffling ability to organize Josh's place so that it looked like humans lived there instead of a pack of wild animals. She didn't cook, though. And she didn't mother. The sole reason she made Toby's lunch was because Toby was the only one in the house she actually liked. "I do not care for *that* dog," she said. "He licks me."

"He's a puppy," Josh said. "That's what puppies do."

"He's a nightmare."

Well, she had him there.

Chapter 4

The 12-Step Chocoholics Program: Never be more than 12 steps away from chocolate!

Half an hour later, Josh had gotten Toby onto the school bus, then driven to the office, still having no idea what he was going to do about the damn dog. He would have thumbed through his contact list, except he hadn't replaced his phone yet.

He could rehire Grace. She needed the money but hiring her again would involve being sucked into her sexy vortex. Hell. He left his car, and instead of heading inside the building, he crossed the small side street to the hospital, then walked around to the old west wing, which was now the Health Services Center, run by Mallory Quinn.

She smiled when he entered. "Hey, Doc. Tell me you're here to give me a shift."

"No. Don't you have Dr. Wells today?"

"He ended up with an emergency in Seattle and can't show."

Shit. Josh eyed the filled waiting room. "Martin didn't get you a replacement?"

Mallory shook her head. They both knew Martin Wells thought he was too good to give his time to the HSC, that he felt the ER was lucky to get him once a week on contract from Seattle. "I don't know what I have waiting for me in the office," Josh said. "But I'll try to get back over here."

"Thanks," she said gratefully. "But if you're not here to work, what can I do for you?"

"I need to locate Grace."

Mallory arched a brow. "Grace?"

"I need her dog walking services again."

"But you fired her yesterday."

He grimaced. He'd been sort of hoping she wouldn't know that. Mallory was an amazing nurse, the fiancée of one of his closest friends, and she was as fierce as a mother about the people she cared about—Grace being one of those people. "Yeah, I might have been hasty on that," he said.

Mallory studied him. "She's something, isn't she?"

Yes. Yes, Grace was something all right. "So, do you have her number? My phone died in the ocean."

"Yes, I have her number."

He waited but she didn't give it to him. He looked at his watch. "Mallory."

"You have to promise to apologize for hurting her feelings yesterday."

"I didn't hurt her feelings."

Mallory just gave him a long look. Jesus, he didn't have time for this. Neither of them did. "Fine," he said. "I'll apologize for hurting her feelings. Just tell me where to find her."

"I'm sorry, I can't. It's against the code."

"The code?"

"Yeah, the code. Listen, if one of your friends had gotten hurt by a girl, and then that girl wanted his phone number from you, would you give it out?"

"Mal, you're sleeping with one of my friends every night. Why would I give some girl Ty's number?"

She sighed. "None of this matters right now anyway. Grace isn't going to answer her phone. She's working."

"Walking more dogs into the ocean?"

"Okay, that was your crazy puppy's fault, and no, it's Wednesday morning, so she's at Lucille's art class at the gallery."

"Thanks." Josh moved to the door, then turned back. "Can you call my office and tell them I'm running half an hour behind, and see if someone picked me up a replacement phone yet?"

"It'll cost you."

"Let me guess," Josh said. "Chocolate cake?"

She smiled sweetly. "From the B and B, please."

Tara, the chef at the local B&B, made the best chocolate cake on the planet. "Noted." Josh left HSC and drove through Lucky Harbor, past the pier to Lucille's art gallery. The place was an old Victorian, possessing 150 years of charm and character, sitting comfortably on its foundation in its old age. When he stepped inside, a bell above his head chimed, and Lucille poked her head out of a room down the hall.

She was somewhere near eighty. She favored pink polyester tracksuits and matching lipstick and was the heart and soul of Lucky Harbor—not to mention the Central Station for all things gossip. "Dr. Scott!" she said, beaming in delight at the sight of him, patting her bun as if to make sure it was still stacked on top of her head. "Are you here to join our drawing class?"

"No, I need to speak to one of your students."

"Uh-oh. Do you think Mrs. Tyler's having another heart attack?"

Christ, he hoped not. "Not Mrs. Tyler."

"Whew. Don't tell me Mrs. B's got hemorrhoids again. I keep suggesting that she eat more prunes, but she doesn't listen. You need to tell her."

Mrs. Burland was one of Josh's patients. In fact, she refused to see any doctor other than Josh—but she didn't listen to him any more than she did Lucille. "Not Mrs. B," he said. "I'm looking for Grace Brooks."

Lucille blinked in surprise. "Well, honey, why didn't you say so? Sure, you can speak to her, but she's not one of my students. She's our model."

"Your model?"

"Yes, today we're drawing the nude form."

Not much surprised Josh. Actually, nothing surprised Josh. But this did. "Grace is the nude model?"

"Learning to sketch the nude human form is standard practice for a beginning drawing class," she said. "We always hire a nude model. Last season I did it myself."

While he was adjusting to the horror of that, Lucille went on. "The female form is the most beautiful form on earth. Very natural." She pushed the studio door open, revealing Grace on a pedestal, a robe pooled at her feet, her body twisted into some ballerina pose. Her blond hair was loose, wavy to her shoulders, shining like silk, her limbs bare and toned.

She wasn't nude. At least not completely. She was wearing one of those long gimmick T-shirts so common in beach shops, with the form of a very curvaceous woman on it in a skimpy string bikini.

Lucille grinned at him. "She was feeling a little shy."

Holding her pose, Grace narrowed her eyes on Josh. "What are you doing here?"

"He came to see you," Lucille said.

Grace's eyes narrowed a little bit more. "You draw?"

"Not even a little bit," Josh said. She should have looked ridiculous. She had a knockout body, but it was completely covered up, from chin to shin, in that oversized shirt. Her feet were bare, her toenails painted a bright pink.

She didn't look ridiculous at all. She looked the opposite of ridiculous. In fact, she looked good enough to gobble up with a spoon. Without a spoon. He was thinking his tongue would work...

"Why are you here?" she asked.

"My dog needs a dog walker today."

Not saying a word or moving a single muscle, she managed to say no. It was all in the eyes.

She had amazing eyes.

"You're a dog walker?" Lucille asked Grace in surprise.

"No," she said.

This was news to Josh. "Your flyer said you were an 'experienced dog walker.'"

Grace winced at this, then bit her lower lip as she looked away.

"Hold still, dear," one of the budding artists said.

"Sorry." Grace cleared her expression and got back into her pose. "The flyer wasn't mine," she admitted to Josh. "You called the wrong number."

"I called the wrong number." He absorbed this a minute. "And yet you were willing to go work for a perfect stranger who needed his dog walked?"

"Hey, don't blame me. You were the one willing to hire a perfect stranger."

Unbelievable. "You had references on that flyer!"

"Did you actually call any of them?" she asked.

Suddenly, he needed Advil. "So you'd go work for anyone who called?" He hated that she needed work that badly. "Jesus, Grace, I could have been a psycho."

"Or *mean*," she pointed out.

"I wasn't mean."

Her expression said she thought otherwise. And then there was another thing. The T-shirt. It was hard to get past the huge cartoon breasts, stuffed into that cartoon itty-bitty bikini. And he couldn't help but wonder.

What was she wearing beneath the T-shirt?

"Honey, you're looking a little tense," Lucille said to Grace. "We haven't studied tense yet. Can you go back to serene?"

Grace did just that, and Josh dipped his head and studied his shoes for a long moment, until the desire to strangle Lucille had passed. "Fine," he said, looking up at Grace again. "I'm sorry I didn't keep you on as my dog walker."

"And yet you're not sorry for being mean."

It wasn't often that he didn't know what to do. But he honest to God had no idea what to do with her.

"Look," she said, still holding her pose. "I nearly lost your dog. You had to come into the ocean to save me, and I got you all wet. I was a mess and a terrible dog walker. I get it."

"You weren't *that* terrible."

"Are you just saying that so I'll come back?"

Well, yes. But even he knew that was a trick question. With a minefield all around it. "Please," he said.

Everyone in the room was following this conversation like they were at Wimbledon in the final match, but all eyes had landed on Grace now, waiting breathlessly for her answer.

"You weren't exactly friendly," she finally said, noncommittal.

In unison, the heads swiveled back to Josh, eyes narrowed in censure.

He drew a breath, remembering what Mallory had told him, that he'd hurt Grace's feelings. He hadn't meant to, of course, but even he knew enough about women to understand that didn't mean shit. Once feelings were hurt, it took an act of congress to reinstate status quo. Since he wasn't used to apologizing for his actions, he kept it simple. "You're right. I wasn't friendly. I was overworked, stressed, and in a hurry. I'm sorry."

"Sorry, or desperate?"

Desperate? Hell no. *She* was the desperate one. But if he said so, he'd lose the tentative ground he'd just made. So he pulled out his ace in the hole. "I'll double the pay."

This got her attention enough to make her break the pose. Hell, it got *everyone's* attention.

Even Lucille set down her pencil. "What do you think, ladies?" she asked the room. "Should Grace give Dr. Scott another shot?"

They whispered among themselves like jurors debating his sentence. Josh slid Grace a look. She was looking at him right back, eyes lit with amusement, not looking particularly desperate for the job at all.

"Six to two," Lucille announced, "in favor of Grace giving Dr. Scott another shot."

Grace didn't react, and Josh had the feeling the vote was actually more like six to *three*. "*Triple* the pay," he said. No more messing around. He was already late, and he was sinking fast. The board didn't need another excuse to get on his ass about being unable to handle the workload.

Grace smiled, and it was a really great smile. So great that he felt something twinge inside him, something he'd thought dead. "What's so funny?" he asked.

"*Triple* the pay?" She was still smiling but there was something in her voice that warned him he was on thin ice, but hell if he knew what he'd done now.

"Yeah. Problem?"

Several of the women behind him snorted, the rest nodded in agreement, all of it adding up to him being an idiot.

"I'd have done it for that kiss you promised me," Grace said.

Well, *now* was a fine time to tell him that.

"*Aw.*" Lucille clapped her hands together in utter delight. "Break time, ladies! Let's give these two a moment." She slid a sly look in Josh's direction. "Go ahead, then," she whispered. "Pay her."

Josh shook his head. "My wallet's in the car—"

"Not money, Dr. Scott. The girl said she'd do it for a kiss."

Josh let out a laugh. "Lucille, she was just kidding."

Lucille studied Grace, then slowly shook her head. "No, I don't think she was kidding. Does anyone here think Grace was only kidding?"

Everyone in the room shook their heads in unison. A room full of damn geriatric bobblehead dolls.

Grace stepped down off the pedestal. "It's okay, Lucille," she said, still looking at Josh, her mouth curving slow and sensuous. "We're scaring him. Of course Dr. Scott doesn't have to kiss me to get me to walk his dog." She shrugged at him, like *Hey, this isn't my doing.*

Bullshit it wasn't her doing. But she had such pretty eyes, he thought insanely. Real pretty. And, hell, they were scaring him. Pride stinging just a little bit, feeling like he had something to prove—though he wasn't quite sure what—he stepped close to Grace and bent his head low, his gaze searching hers for a sign that she was being pushed into this.

Her smile broadened.

"You could put a stop to this," he said softly, and unbelievably, she made the sound of a chicken. He straightened and narrowed his eyes. "What does *that* mean?"

"You know what it means."

She was crazy, he decided. A crazy cutie. He had way too much on his plate for this. Too many people to take care of, and she had "take care of me" written all over her. And yet she thought that *he* was a chicken. Interesting.

Infuriating.

And a little bit of a turn-on. But fuck it, he was done thinking. The woman wanted a kiss, and hell if he'd try to talk her out of it. So he leaned in and brushed his mouth over hers. Peach. Her lip gloss was peach, and it was more delicious than anything he could remember.

So was the kiss, chaste as it was, which rocked his socks right off.

Chapter 5

Chocolate is good for three things. Two of them can't be mentioned in polite company.

Grace closed her eyes to enjoy the feel of a man's mouth on hers. Yep, just as heavenly as she remembered. Maybe even more so. She definitely felt a spark.

Actually, she felt a full fireworks display.

When Josh pulled back, she opened her eyes to his dark brown ones and caught his own flash of surprise before he masked it.

"We have a deal, then," he said. "For today."

He hadn't worded it as a question, of course, which was just like a man. But he looked even more exhausted today than he had yesterday, and that both intrigued and worried her. She was extremely aware of his proximity, that his big, bad self wasn't in wet, sandy ER scrubs today. He wore cargo pants and a fisherman's sweater, both in black, both casual but expensive-looking, like he'd walked right out of an ad.

But she was even more aware that the entire art class was watching them.

Avidly.

Her phone buzzed. The incoming text was from Lucille: *Honey, I don't mean to rush you but it's rumored that the good doc has got the best hands in all of Lucky Harbor. Go for it.*

Grace lifted her head and sent Lucille a look.

Lucille smiled innocently.

Grace rolled her eyes and nodded to Josh. "Fine. We have a deal."

He handed her a key to his house and left.

Grace watched him go, thinking that his hands weren't even his best part. "Excuse me a minute," she said to the class, before running to catch up with Josh in the hall.

He turned to face her, and she shook her head, her body still humming from his kiss. "What was that?" she finally managed. "Back there."

"You know what it was."

Yeah. Yeah, she did. Chemistry. Holy Toledo, some damn *hot* chemistry. "But it shouldn't be like this, not between us." They were night and day. Oil and water. He might not know it, but she did. "It was a fluke." That was all she could think, that it was a complete fluke. But his eyes darkened, and in response, her nipples got hard. "Okay, so maybe not," she muttered, and crossed her arms over herself and her fake triple Ds.

He stepped closer, his voice low. "I'd prove it to you, but I'm not into kissing by committee."

She looked over her shoulder and found Lucille and the entire art class leaning out the classroom door, unabashedly eavesdropping. She gave them the "shoo" signal, and they vanished.

"Impressive," he said. "Be sure to use that level of authority on Tank today and try to avoid another swim."

"I really thought he was in the water."

"He likes to play hide-and-seek."

"Good to know." And she still had to take that crazy puppy out for another walk…

"Interesting T-shirt," he said.

She looked down at herself, eternally grateful that she hadn't gone the full Monty route after all. "It's not as good as the real thing, but as it turns out, I'm pretty selective about who sees the real thing."

His smile softened. His eyes crinkled in the corners, and the laugh lines on either side of his mouth deepened, stealing her breath. "Good to know," he mirrored back at her.

It was a genuine smile from a man who didn't appear to do it too often, and it left her a little dazed. Or maybe it was the crazy amount of testosterone coming off him in waves.

"Let me know if you have any trouble today," he said.

"For what you're paying me, there'll be no trouble." And if there was, he'd be the *last* man she'd call, amazing kisser or not, because they had a connection, and she knew the power of it now.

Grace wasn't in Lucky Harbor to make a connection with a man she knew wasn't her type. She was looking for *fun*, that was it, and in spite of Josh being sex-on-a-stick, she wasn't sure he had a lot of fun in him. Steering clear was her smartest option here. And no matter how good he was with his hands, she was going to be smart, if it killed her.

A few hours later, Grace headed to Josh's house. As she parked, she noticed she had an unread text from Mallory.

Hey, head's up. The hottest doctor in town just came by and coerced me into telling him where you were. I folded like a cheap suitcase. Sorry, but he's hard to say no to. Don't be mad. I owe you a cupcake.

Yeah, an entire batch. Grace shook her head and let herself into Josh's house without incident. This time, she carefully leashed Tank *before* she opened his baby gate, and then as a double precaution, she just as carefully picked him up and carried him outside.

She might not be a blood-born Brooks genius, but she was quick on the learning curve.

She avoided the beach entirely, instead setting Tank down to walk alongside the quiet street. Tank sniffed every single rock, every last tree, and then finally chose a spot to hunch and do his business.

"Hey!" A man stuck his head out of a window of the house. "Don't think I don't see that you're not carrying a doodie bag! You come back with a doodie bag and clean that up!"

A doodie bag? Grace had seen a stack of plastic baggies by Tank's leash. Guess she knew what they were for now. She scooped Tank back up. "I hope you're done."

Tank snorted and licked her chin.

"I mean it!" the man yelled at her. "Make sure you take care of that mess or I'll call the cops on you."

Grace took Tank back to the house, securing him in the laundry room. Then she reluctantly grabbed a bag to go do her "doodie" duty. As she turned to the door, she nearly tripped over a young woman in a wheelchair. She was twentyish, petite, dark-haired, her eyes as dark and alluring as the man she had to be related to.

"Anna," she said, introducing herself. "The crazy sister. And you must be the nude girl he kissed."

Grace choked. "*What?*"

"Yeah, you haven't seen?" Anna pulled her phone from a pocket and thumbed a few buttons, then turned the screen for Grace.

It was Lucky Harbor's Facebook page, and a picture of Grace in the bikini T-shirt that was going to haunt her for the rest of her damn life. And her lips were indeed connected to Josh's. The kiss had lasted only a heartbeat, but one would never know it by the picture, which had been captured at just the right nanosecond, showing Grace leaning into Josh with her entire body, both hands on his chest.

She hadn't realized she'd touched him so intimately, but now she could remember the heat radiating through his shirt, the easy strength of him beneath. And he'd smelled delicious.

But God, had she really looked at him so adoringly?

Josh hadn't been so innocent either. He had one big hand cupping her jaw, his thumb clearly stroking her skin in a way that seemed both tender and yet somehow outrageously sexy.

"Cozy," Anna said dryly.

"It's not what it looks like," Grace said, giving her back the phone.

"No?" Anna asked, looking down at the screen again. "Because it looks like you're kissing. You're not kissing?"

"Okay, so we're kissing, but that's only because the day before he'd said he'd kiss me if I lost the dog and then..." Grace trailed off, unable to remember exactly how it was that she'd ended up with Josh's mouth on hers.

On the Internet.

Anna arched a brow.

Grace sighed. "Well, this is embarrassing. We're not... I mean, he and I aren't—"

"Oh, no worries," Anna said. "I know you're not his girl toy. He wouldn't have hired you if you were."

"Girl toy?"

"Yeah, Josh doesn't bring his women home."

Well ouch. "Okay, good." *Great.* Because, hey, she'd already decided that the two of them weren't going to do this. This being anything. So yeah, this was really great.

"Hang on," Anna said. "I just want to share the link with everyone I know..." She hit a few keys, then smiled. "There. God, how I love it when he does something stupid. It's so rare, you know? And then when he finally does it, he really does it right." She unlocked the baby gate, freeing Tank just as a young boy came tearing into the kitchen. He was waving a lightsaber and making some sort of war cry as he ran circles around the kitchen table.

Tank took off right on his heels, barking so hard his back legs kept coming off the floor. Quite the feat, given that his belly swung so low.

The kid was wearing a Star Wars T-shirt. His jeans were streaked with dirt and low enough on his narrow little hips to reveal his underwear waistband, which was also Star Wars. His battered athletic shoes lit up with each step he made, and the right one was untied. He was maybe five, with dark hair that definitely hadn't seen a brush that morning, and his melting, dark chocolate eyes matched Dr. Josh Scott's. He stopped short at the sight of Grace, and Tank plowed into the back of his feet, then fell to his butt and gave out a little startled yelp.

"Toby," Anna said. "You're going to stay here with Grace. I'll be back in an hour."

"Wait…what?" Grace shook her head. "No, I'm just the dog babysitter."

"Yeah?" Anna asked. "Are you babysitting the dog right now?"

"Well, yeah, but—" She broke off at Anna's amused look and whirled around to find the puppy chewing on the kitchen table leg. *Crap.* "Hey," she said. "No chewing on that."

Tank kept chewing. Grace went over there and pried him loose but she was too late. He'd left deep gouges in the beautiful wood.

Anna tugged affectionately on a lock of Toby's hair. "The dogsitter will make you an after-school snack. Don't do anything I wouldn't do, Slugger."

Grace was still shaking her head. A dog was one thing. But a kid? There was no counting the number of ways she could screw this one up. "Wait a minute."

But Anna wasn't waiting. She was actually at the door. "No worries, he's easy. The regular nanny, Katy, ditched Toby today, so we picked him up from school, but I've got things to do, so…"

"We?"

A horn sounded from out front. Grace looked out the window and saw a rusty pickup truck.

"Gotta go," Anna said, and wheeled out.

"But..." But nothing. Anna was gone, gone, gone. And Grace had just been promoted to a job for which she had absolutely no qualifications. She looked at Toby.

Toby looked at her right back, solemn-faced, his dark eyes giving nothing away.

"Hi," Grace said.

"Arf," he said.

"Arf," Tank said, dragging a running shoe that was bigger than himself. He'd already chewed a hole in the toe. Eyes bulging, tongue lolling out the side of his smashed-in face, Tank sat and panted proudly at the prize he offered her.

It was going to be a long hour. She liberated the shoe and searched her brain for some way to relate to a five-year-old kid holding a toy lightsaber. Who barked. "So are you a Jedi warrior?"

Toby swung the lightsaber wide. It lit up and went *whoosh, vrrmm-whoosh.*

Tank promptly went nuts, so naturally Toby swung again.

Whoosh, vrrmm-whoosh.

Toby hit a home run with a cup of juice that had been on the kitchen table, sending it flying through the air. Luckily the cup was plastic. Not so luckily, the juice was grape, and purple sticky liquid splattered like rain on the table, the floor, the counters, Grace, and both Tank and Toby. Even the ceiling took a hit.

Toby dropped the lightsaber as if it were a hot potato.

Tank scooped it up by the handle in his sharp puppy teeth and began running circles around the table again, both belly and lightsaber dragging on the ground, still lighting up, still making *whooshing* noises.

"It's okay," Grace said to a stricken-looking Toby, grabbing a roll of paper towels from the counter, swiping at the kid first. But the sticky clothes didn't appear to bother him any because he stepped free and headed toward the fridge.

Tank dropped the lightsaber, redirecting his reign of terror to licking the floor.

"Toby?" Grace asked. "Where's the trash?"

The boy made a vague gesture over his shoulder toward the back door and stuck his head into the fridge.

Grace went to wipe down the table and instead stared at the stack of twenties, underneath a grape-splotched sticky note that had *Grace* scrawled across it in bold print. She picked up the money and started counting. Twenty, forty, sixty, eighty...*One hundred and sixty bucks.* It took her a minute to figure it out—forty for yesterday, triple that for today.

It was ridiculous, of course, and yet...the things she could do with a hundred and sixty bucks. Staring at it longingly, she thought of her overloaded credit card, her student loans, and the weekly rent she had coming due at the B&B where she'd been living.

Not to mention the cleaning bill for getting grape juice out of today's sundress. Shaking her head, she pocketed forty. Nothing for yesterday since she'd screwed up, and forty for today. Because she wouldn't screw today up. Leaving the rest, she stepped out the back door with the sticky paper towels, which she dumped into the trash can. Now that she had a moment of privacy, she pulled out her cell phone and hit Josh's number to fill him in.

He picked up, sounding harried. "Dr. Scott."

Her brain stuttered at the sound of his low voice, the same low voice that had prompted her into a moment of insanity earlier. That kiss... "One hundred and sixty bucks?" she said in disbelief. "What exactly are you expecting for this hundred and sixty bucks?"

There was a beat of silence. She figured he was probably wondering who the crazy lady was, so she decided to clarify. "It's Grace," she said, trying for calm efficiency. She was used to calm efficiency, after all. Used to order. Used to things balancing.

Or she *had* been used to those things, back when she'd been gainfully employed, making something of herself, something very big and very important. Back way before she'd come to Lucky Harbor and taken on the first job she'd ever had that was completely over her head.

"You needed the money," Josh said. "Right?"

"Well, yes," she admitted reluctantly. "But a hundred and sixty dollars?"

"It's what we agreed on, triple yesterday's pay."

"I didn't mean to accept that. The kiss was my payment." The crazy, wild kiss. The crazy, wild, *wonderful* kiss. She turned back to the door, which had shut behind her.

It was locked. *Uh-oh.*

"What?" he asked.

Had she said that out loud? "Nothing." She peered into the window, thankful that the shades on it were open, but didn't see Toby in the kitchen. "Well, nothing except your sister brought Toby home, and I'm watching him for her for an hour or so."

There was another beat of silence while Josh processed this. Though he was a guy, and therefore a master at hiding his emotions, his thoughts weren't all that hard to decode. Surprise and shock that somehow the same person who'd lost his dog yesterday was now in charge of his kid, and irritation at his sister. "Anna left you in charge of Toby?"

"I guess your nanny got sick, and Anna's boyfriend picked Toby up from school."

Nothing about that sentence seemed to bring him comfort. And it wasn't even the worst bit of news she had to tell him. That honor belonged to the Facebook photo, which she decided he didn't need to know about right now. Or ever. "It's only for an hour," she said, trying to make the best of the situation. "How much can happen in an hour?" She tried the door again. Still locked. She knocked.

Tank came tearing back into the kitchen, running more circles around the table with the lightsaber. But still no sign of Toby. She knocked again.

Tank stopped running in circles and panted at her. Then he turned his attention to the cabinet under the sink, where he started nosing around with what appeared to be a small trash container.

The container wobbled but didn't tip.

Tank then sank his teeth into the plastic liner and tugged until the thing fell over, spilling trash across the kitchen floor. *Crap*. Grace looked around her. She was in the side yard, with two gates at either end—both locked. "I have to go," she said.

"Don't even think about it. What's wrong?"

Oh, so many, *many* things. Tank was going to town on the trash, inhaling whatever he could get at. Toby was still nowhere in sight. That couldn't be good. She knocked again, harder this time.

The puppy looked up from his mission of destroying the world and growled at her.

Grace whirled around, searching for a doormat. Everyone hid a key beneath a doormat. But there was no mat. Most likely because it was safer for Anna in her chair that way. So where would they hide a key?

"*Grace*."

She gave up. "Okay, where is it?" she asked him. "Where do you hide the key for the stupid people who get locked out?"

"You got locked out?"

"No, I'm just asking for the stupid people."

"Where's Toby?"

She took another peek in the window, and oh thank God, there he was, standing on the other side of the door, staring up at her with those big eyes. She pointed to the door.

Toby just looked at her.

Grace sighed. "He's in the kitchen."

"Go to the second planter from the porch," Josh instructed. "Reach into the sprinkler valve box."

Holding the phone in the crook of her neck, Grace smiled at

Toby in what she hoped was a reassuring manner and again pointed to the door handle, gesturing for him to let her in.

Instead, he turned and walked out of the kitchen for parts unknown, his shoelace trailing on the floor, his little Star Wars undies sticking out of his jeans in a way that he'd probably spend the next fifteen years purposely trying to mimic.

"Toby!" she called. "Toby, don't leave the kitchen. *Toby?*"

"Hurry, Grace," Josh said in her ear.

She rushed to the second planter and at the sight there, she dropped her phone. There was a very large spiderweb guarding the valve box. Heart pounding, she scrambled to pick up her phone. "Sorry. You there?"

Nothing. She smacked her phone on her thigh and tried again. "Josh?"

"Yeah. Do you see the key? It's in the metal hide-a-key."

Yeah, she saw the metal hide-a-key. She also saw the spiderweb. The *massive* spiderweb. She toed it and a big, fat, hairy brown spider crawled with badass authority into her line of sight, giving her the evil eye. He was ready to rumble. *Gulp.* Not much truly terrified Grace. Well, aside from clowns and glass elevators. But spiders? Spiders topped her list, and the hairs on the back of her neck stood up.

"Grace?"

"Yeah?" she whispered. Was it her imagination or was the spider giving her a "bring it" gesture with two of its spindly legs?

"There's a pool out back," Josh said. "You can't get to it from the side yard where you are. Toby can swim, but..."

Oh, God. The image of Toby running outside and into the pool on his own was too awful to bear. She closed her eyes, plunged her hand into the sprinkler box while silently chanting "pleasedon'tbitemepleasedon'tbiteme," and pulled out the hide-a-key.

Without getting bitten.

She ran to the back door and let herself in, racing through the kitchen, skidding to a halt in the living room, where Toby was standing on the couch, lightsaber once again in hand, whipping it around.

Whoosh, vrrmm-whoosh.

Grace nearly collapsed with relief. She'd handled millions of dollars of other people's money without breaking a sweat, and yet at this, just one little boy and a puppy, she needed a nap. "Well, that was a fun fire drill."

"Toby?" Josh asked in her ear.

"All in one piece." She sank to the couch and put her head between her knees. "Your house is a little crazy, Dr. Scott."

"You must feel right at home, then."

She heard herself let out a weak laugh. "Hey, *you're* the crazy one." She fingered the money in her pocket. "You can't go around paying people so much money for menial work. They'll take advantage of you."

"I'm not easy to take advantage of."

Okay, so that was undoubtedly true, she thought. "But—"

"Did you lose Tank?"

Only for a minute… "No."

"Did he shit in the house?"

"No."

"Then you're worth every penny," Josh assured her. "Listen, I'm sorry about Anna. I'll get there as soon as I can."

"But—"

But nothing. He was gone. She lifted her head and found Toby standing there, a lock of dark hair falling across his forehead, lightsaber still in one hand, a squirming Tank in the other.

He really was pretty damn cute, she thought. This would be okay. She could totally do this for an hour. It'd be like the time she had to babysit the guys in payroll.

Toby wrinkled his nose like something was stinky, then hastily set Tank down.

The puppy was panting, and his stomach looked uncomfortably full. *Uh-oh.* "Tank," she said, trying to get him outside.

Too late. Tank hunched over and horked up all the trash he'd eaten.

On her feet.

"Arf," Tank said, looking like he felt all better.

"Arf," Toby said.

Chapter 6

There are four basic food groups: plain chocolate, milk chocolate, dark chocolate, and white chocolate.

One painfully long hour later, Grace was exhausted. This was *nothing* like babysitting the guys in payroll. First of all, Tank never stopped moving.

Or barking.

He'd found a forgotten stethoscope from somewhere and had dragged it around and around the living room. Around the couch, up and over the coffee table, until he'd inadvertently trapped the end on a chair leg and been caught up short. A sound like air leaking out of a balloon had come from his throat, and he'd fallen over, legs straight up in the air.

Grace had thought he'd killed himself and had gone running toward him, but before she'd gotten to him, he'd rebounded.

Good as new, he'd been chewing on her sandals five minutes later.

And five minutes after that, the wooden kitchen chairs.

And the wooden banister poles.

And someone's forgotten hat...

She was considering giving him an electrical cord to chew on next when she heard the front door open. Josh stepped inside wearing a white doctor's coat over his sexy office clothes, a stethoscope around his neck like a tie. He picked up Toby and flung him over his shoulder in a fireman's hold, making the kid squeal with abandon.

Josh gave a tired smile at the sound and turned to Grace, Toby still hanging upside down behind him. "Anna?"

"Present," Anna said, rolling in the front door. The driver of the pickup was with her. Twentysomething, with an insolent smile, he slouched against the doorjamb.

Josh nudged the guy back a step until Slacker Dude stood on the other side of the jamb. Josh then shut the door in his face.

"Josh!" Anna was horrified and pissed. "You can't do that to Devon!"

"Just did."

"You—"

"*Later*," he said curtly.

Anna whirled in her chair and sped off down the hallway. Two seconds later, her bedroom door slammed hard enough to shake the windows.

Josh ignored this. "Thanks," he said to Grace, who felt as rattled as the windows. Five-year-old boys, as it turned out, were aliens. They owned battery-operated hamster pets called Zhu Zhus that chirped and whistled and skittered randomly, terrifying pug puppies and temp babysitters alike.

Josh reached into his pocket and pulled out some cash.

"Oh no," she said, backing away. "You don't have to..."

"We didn't negotiate for babysitting fees."

"It's okay."

He gave her a speculative gaze. "Is this one of those 'I would have done it for a kiss' deals?"

She laughed, even as her tummy quivered. "I just meant that this one's on me."

"No," he said softly. "I owe you."

The air between them did that snap-crackle-pop thing again, like static electricity on steroids, and Grace's breath caught. "Okay," she said, just as softly. "You owe me."

Two days later, Grace entered the diner, still thinking about kisses, deals, and sexy doctors named Josh.

And oddly enough, her résumé. She supposed she could add dog walker to it. She'd done it four days in a row now with no mishaps, at least no major ones. She didn't count Tank biting the mailman's pant leg yesterday, because Tank didn't actually break skin. Nor did she count Toby dumping his bottle of bubbles into the pool because, hey, she'd always wanted to see what would happen too. And the pool guy had come right out and fixed everything, so all was okay.

In fact, she could probably now add babysitter to her new and constantly changing résumé as well, since it went nicely with dogsitter, model, and floral delivery person.

Not that any of that went with being a banking investment specialist.

She did finally get calls for interviews. She had a Seattle appointment tomorrow morning. The Portland interview was the following day, early, and would be conducted by Skype. This worked out in her favor because this way she wouldn't miss modeling for Lucille's class. The budding artists were drawing feet this week, so Grace had no wardrobe worries, at least from her feet up.

She tried to imagine her mother or father modeling their bare feet, but couldn't. Because they took life much more seriously than that. They were the real deal.

And Grace was a poser.

It wasn't that she didn't love Lucky Harbor. She did. It was just that what she could find here in the way of a career wasn't…big enough. Important enough. She plopped into the back booth next to a waiting Mallory. Amy showed up two minutes later and dropped a shoe box onto the table. She untied her pink apron, tossed it aside, and sank into the booth, propping her feet up by Grace's hip. "Off duty, thank God."

"What's with the shoe box?" Grace asked, nudging it curiously. "New boots or something?"

"Or something," Amy said. "Somehow, I'm selling like crazy." She was a sketch artist, and she'd found a niche for herself creating color pencil renditions of the local landscape. Lucille's gallery was selling out of everything Amy created nearly as fast as she brought it in. "I can't keep up."

"Keep up?" Grace asked.

"Yeah. At first, I just took people's cash or checks and shoved the receipts into my purse or pockets or wherever."

She was talking about her accounting, Grace realized with horror. She might not be a bean counter anymore, but she still had a healthy respect for the process. "You said at first. What are you doing now?"

"Well, I decided I was being irresponsible," Amy said, "so I started a file."

"That's not a file," Grace said. "That's a box."

"Yeah, whatever. A box worked better." Amy pushed it toward her. "For you."

Grace opened the box. It was full of…everything. There were napkins with numbers and dates scrawled on them, little pieces of paper with more numbers and dates, bigger pieces of paper, receipts, some folded, some crumpled, some not. Grace lifted a round cotton pad with a number scratched onto it in what looked like eyeliner and stared at Amy in disbelief.

Amy shrugged. "So bookkeeping isn't my thing. It's yours, right?"

"Well, yeah, I suppose."

"And?" Amy looked at her expectantly.

"And...?"

"You going to help me or what?"

"How?" Grace asked in disbelief. "By getting you a bigger box?"

"No, by keeping track of my shit." Amy waved her hand. "You know, create a system so I don't look like just another idiot with a box come tax time."

Grace looked at Mallory, who laughed. "Better do it," she told Grace. "Before the IRS takes her away."

Grace pulled the box near her and sighed. "Fine. I'll do the damn books. But it's going to cost you."

"Big bucks?"

"Chocolate cupcakes. *Tara's* cupcakes." Tara was Grace's landlord at the B&B, and there was little that compared to the exquisiteness of Tara's baking. Not that Grace could afford her.

"Done," Amy said. "But I'm going to pay you as well, so be sure to bill me."

"On what, a napkin?"

"Funny."

Over chocolate cupcakes—not Tara's, unfortunately—they discussed the latest and newest. Amy was moving in with her sexy forest ranger, Matt Bowers. Mallory was planning to elope with Ty, a local flight paramedic, to a beach somewhere in the South Pacific—though she wanted a big reception here in Lucky Harbor when they got back. And Grace told them about dog walking for Josh, laughing a little because dog walking hardly compared to relationships. "I didn't realize it would be an ongoing thing," she said. "But the good doctor has this odd ability to get his way."

"Yeah, you know who else is like that?" Amy asked. "*All* men. Is his pug's name really Tank?"

"His sister brought the puppy home for the kid," Mallory said, knowing much more about Josh than any of them since she and Josh worked together at the hospital. "Without asking, I should add. It's Anna's life mission to drive Josh insane."

"Why?" Grace asked.

"I don't know. I think she's trying to make him pay for her being in a wheelchair, which of course isn't his fault. Between her, Toby, and the hospital board all up Josh's ass about selling them the controlling percentage of his practice, he's got to be close to losing it completely."

Actually, every time Grace had seen Josh, he seemed perfectly calm, perfectly in control, and perfectly... yum.

If not entirely too exhausted. "Why would he sell the controlling percentage of his practice?" Grace asked.

"People don't realize how much work a sole practice is," Mallory said. "If something happens to a patient, it's his fault. If a billing error's made and a procedure's wrongly claimed, that's fraud—also his fault. The list is endless, and he's responsible for all of it. That doesn't even count the med school loans, the license requirements, insurance bills, office costs, support systems..." She shrugged. "People think doctors have it easy, but they don't. Josh inherited the practice from his late father, but his first love is the ER. If he sold, he could spend more time there. Or with Toby."

"Then he *should* sell," Grace said.

"Not that easy," Mallory said. "His father was very popular around here, and he built that practice out of love. People come from all over to go see Dr. Weston Scott's son, out of loyalty and affection. It's a huge obligation on Josh's shoulders."

Grace nodded. Oh boy, did she understand family obligation. Hers was to become *Someone Important*. Instead she was walking dogs and delivering flowers and kissing sexy doctors named Josh... She realized conversation had lagged and that Amy and Mallory were staring at her. "What?"

"You tell us what," Mallory said. "Miss Staring-Dreamily-Off-into-Space."

"I wasn't," Grace said. "It's nothing."

"It's something," Amy said.

"Oh, it's something all right," Lucille said helpfully, getting out of the booth to their right. "She left out the kiss." She pulled out her cell phone. "Here."

Oh boy, Grace thought. *Déjà vu.*

And indeed, Lucille produced the infamous Facebook pic.

Mallory's and Amy's eyes cut straight to Grace, and she grimaced. "Okay, so I maybe left a teensy little part out," she admitted.

Amy took Lucille's phone and cocked her head sideways. "What are you wearing? That's one hell of a tiny frigging bikini. I had no idea pink polka dots were your thing."

"Oh, for God's sake." Grace snatched the phone and handed it back to Lucille. "It was you. *You* posted this thing."

"Well of course I did. It's been a slow week. Nothing exciting—until you kissed the town's favorite bachelor." Lucille winked, snagged a cupcake, and went on her way.

Intending to do the same, Grace slid her purse on her shoulder and picked up Amy's box of receipts. "It's getting late." She made a move to slide out of the booth but Amy blocked her exit with one very wicked-looking kickass boot.

"*Fine.*" Grace sagged back. "We kissed, okay? No big deal. And I didn't tell you guys because I didn't want you to make a bigger deal out of it than it is."

"You kissed the hottest doctor in town," Mallory said in disbelief. "Maybe the hottest doctor *ever*, and you don't think it's a big deal?"

"He kissed *me*," Grace corrected, grabbing another cupcake since her exit was blocked. "And are you sure he's the hottest doctor ever? I mean, you've seen *Grey's Anatomy*, right?"

"*Ever*," Mallory maintained, and shrugged helplessly when both Amy and Grace stared at her. "So sue me, I have a thing for late-bloomer nerds."

Grace choked on her cupcake and it almost came out her nose.

"Late-bloomer nerd? Are you kidding me?" Josh was six foot four and solidly built. He had melted dark chocolate eyes and a smile that did more for her than the cupcake she was eating, and a way of moving his big, gorgeous self that always made her clothes want to fall right off. "Nothing about him says nerd." *Nothing.*

"Well, I went to school with him," Mallory said, carefully peeling her cupcake out of its baking paper. "He hit high school at like five-five and was the scrawniest thing you've ever seen. He wore glasses and *still* couldn't see worth shit. Oh, and he was head of the science club and got beat up by the football players unless he did their homework."

"Damn," Amy said, sounding impressed. "He sure turned things around for himself. I bet he enjoys his reunions, being a big-shot doctor and everything. Not to mention he looks like he could kick some serious ass if he wanted."

"He kicks serious ass every single day," Mallory said. "By saving lives. He raised his sister. He's raising his son."

"Speaking of which," Grace said, "what happened to Toby's mom?"

Mallory did a palms-up. "She wasn't from around here and she didn't stick. That's all anyone really knows. Josh doesn't talk about it." She'd finished her cupcake and licked some chocolate off her thumb before concentrating on Grace. "I know you planned to just blow through Lucky Harbor and ended up staying longer than you meant to. And we're glad about that, so very glad." She said this with fierce affection, reaching for Grace's hand. "Because the three of us, we give each other something."

"A hard time?" Grace asked.

"*Hope*," Mallory said. "And courage. You wanted the courage to add some badly needed fun to your life. The kiss with Josh sounds like a good start to me. That's all I'm saying. So don't sweep it under the rug as a fluke or try to forget about it. Enjoy it."

Grace blew out a breath. "Well, sure, cloud the issue with logic."

Mallory smiled. "We made a pact to change our lives, and that's what we're doing. All of us. No man left behind."

Grace was incredibly touched by the "we." She'd never had siblings. Her parents had given her everything they had but they weren't warm and fuzzy by nature. She'd had girlfriends, but they were always schoolmates or coworkers. Her relationships had always been born of circumstance.

Like her.

This wasn't the case with Amy and Mallory. They were the real deal, and better than any sisters she might have spent her childhood wishing for.

Mallory pointed at her. "I mean it!"

Grace ignored her suddenly thick throat. "It's hard to take you seriously when you have a chocolate mustache."

Mallory swiped it off with her forearm. "And it's not like I saw this life of mine coming down the pike, you know. Opening up a Health Services Center, falling in love…I mean, I am so not sitting in a European sidewalk café right now, rearranging my desperately alluring miniskirt and thinking about whether it's too early to ring up U2 or go shopping." She grinned. "That was my secret high school fantasy. But I wouldn't trade this for the world." She looked at Amy. "And you changed your life too. Tell her."

"She knows."

"*Tell* her," Mallory insisted.

"I changed my life," Amy intoned.

Mallory rolled her eyes and gave Amy a shove.

"Fine," Amy said. "I changed things up, opened myself to new experiences. Like…*camping*."

Mallory sighed. "Killing me."

"And love." Amy gave Mallory a little shove back. "See, I can say it. I found someone to love me. *Me*," she repeated, clearly still boggled by that fact.

Grace understood the sentiment. She'd had boyfriends—some

had lasted a night; some that had lasted much longer. She'd even fallen in love and gotten her heart broken. She'd learned a lot—such as how to keep her heart out of the equation.

"The truth is," Amy said, "I came to Lucky Harbor searching for myself. Even though deep down, I was afraid that whatever I found wouldn't be enough. But actually, my real self kicks ass."

"Yeah, it does," Mallory said softly, smiling at her.

Grace stared at the two of them. "You're a pair of saps."

"Look, forget us," Mallory said. "We're not the point. The point is that you're not living up to what you said you'd do. You're not having fun."

"I don't know," Amy said slowly, studying Grace. "Posing in the nude, walking McSexy's dog...Sounds like fun to me."

"I didn't pose nude," Grace said. "*Sheesh!*"

"Well maybe you should," Mallory told her. "And maybe you should have fun with the sexy doctor while you're at it. He's just about perfect."

Grace understood the logic, convoluted as it was. But there was a flaw, a fatal one. Having grown up trying to live up to being damn near perfect, she refused to date it.

The diner door opened, and a man strode in wearing paramedic gear with FLIGHT CARE in white across his chest.

Ty Garrison.

Mallory took one look at the man she was going to marry and grinned dopily. She brushed her hands off and headed straight for him, meeting him in the middle of the nearly empty diner. In her scrubs and sneakers, she seemed tiny compared to the tall, leanly muscled flight medic as she leaned into him. Tiny and cute.

Ty must have thought so, too, because he bent and kissed her with lots of heat, easily boosting her into his arms, the muscles in his shoulders and back rippling as Mallory wrapped herself around him like a pretzel.

"Aw," Grace said in spite of herself.

"Get a room," Amy said.

Behind Ty's back, Mallory flipped Amy the bird and kept kissing her fiancé. They were holding on to each other, and even from the length of the diner, Grace could see how much Ty loved Mallory. It was in every touch, every look. She sighed and pulled out her phone, which was ringing. "Crap," she said, looking at the caller ID.

"Bill collector?" Amy asked.

"Worse. It's my mother."

"The rocket scientist?"

The one and only. Grace sucked in a breath and looked down at what she was wearing before she got a hold of herself and remembered that her mother couldn't actually *see* her. "Mom," she said into the phone. "Hi, what's wrong?"

"What, a mother can't call her only daughter?"

Grace smiled at the imperious tone and could picture her mother in her lab, working in Dior and a white doctor's coat to protect the elegance and sophistication that she couldn't quite hide behind all the degrees and doctorates.

Grace didn't have elegance and sophistication emanating from her every pore because of one simple truth—she hadn't been born into it. She'd done her damnedest to absorb what she could and fake what she couldn't. "It's not the first weekend of the month," Grace said.

"True, but I just finished up that three-week seminar on the design for NASA's new deep-space exploration system, and I realized I missed our monthly check-in. How are you doing, darling?"

This wasn't a "tell me about the weather" sort of question. This was a request for a full, detailed report, and guilt flooded Grace. She quickly scanned through her options. She could tell her mom what she'd been up to—which was that she'd been using her fancy college education not at all—or continue to slightly mislead in order to keep her happy.

Mallory disconnected her lips from Ty and led him back to the Chocoholics' table. He took a cupcake, kissed Mallory, and left.

"And how's Seattle?" Grace's mom asked. "How's your new banking job? You the CEO yet?"

Grace grimaced. "Actually, I've sort of moved on to something else."

"Oh?"

Grace looked down at Amy's shoe box full of receipts. "Something more accounting based." Vague, and hopefully impressive. But there was no denying it truly was a total and complete lie, which meant she was going to hell, doubly so for telling the lie to her own mother.

"A lateral move, at least?"

A beep sounded in Grace's ear, her call-waiting. *Saved by the beep.* "Hold on, Mom." She clicked over. "Hello?"

Nothing. Damn phone. She'd dropped it one too many times. She slapped the phone against her thigh and clicked again. "*Hello?*"

"Grace. You available for tomorrow?"

Josh and his deep voice, the one that continuously did something quite pornographic to every womanly part in Grace's entire body. *Was she available?* Unfortunately, yes. "Hang on a sec." She clicked back to her mom and decided that since she was going to hell, she might as well make her well-meaning mom happy before she did. "I've made a lateral move from my usual banking specialist schtick. Nothing quite as exciting as being a rocket scientist or a biologist, but I am working for a doctor."

"Sounds fascinating," Josh said wryly. "Do I know this doctor?"

Grace froze. *Crap.* "Just a minute," she managed. She smacked herself in the forehead with her phone; then, ignoring both Amy and Mallory gaping at her, she clicked over again. "Mom?"

"Yes, of course, dear. Who else?"

Who else indeed. Grace swiped her damp forehead.

Mallory and Amy, both clearly fascinated by the Grace Show, were hanging on her every word.

Grace twisted in the booth, turning her back on them.

"So tell me about your job," her mom said.

"I'm... working for a doctor," she said again.

"Using your CPA to handle his finances? Or research on that dissertation you never finished?"

She was saved from having to answer when her phone beeped again. "Hold on." She clicked over. "Josh, I can't talk right now."

Nothing.

Good Lord. She really needed a new phone. She smacked it again for good measure and clicked back to her mom. "Sorry, Mom. Yes, I'm going to be putting my CPA to use." She looked at Amy's box. "Sort of. I'm trying some new things out. And some... research. But listen, I've really got to—"

"Trying new things," Josh said. "I like the sound of that."

"Oh for God's sake—*I have to go*." She clicked again and drew in a deep breath. "Mom?"

"Yes. Darling, you sound quite frazzled. You're working hard?"

"*Very*," Grace managed, rubbing the spot between her eyes.

"What? Hello? Grace, I can't hear you—"

Silence.

Grace swore and hit the phone again. "Mom? Sorry, bad reception. But yes, I'm working hard, very hard. Hey, I'm a Brooks, right? That's what we do."

"This conversation just gets more and more interesting," Josh said.

"Oh my God! I thought I told you I had to go!" Grace disconnected him and fanned herself. "Damn, is it hot in here?"

Mallory and Amy were wide-eyed. Mallory opened her mouth to speak, but Grace pointed at her, then grimaced as she spoke into the phone. "Mother?"

"Yes. Grace, what are—"

"Going into a tunnel, Mom. We're going to lose reception—" Grace disconnected, closed her eyes, and took her medicine like a big girl. "I suppose you're still there," she said into the phone.

"Yep," Josh said. "So the dog walking. Overqualified much?"

"I don't want to talk about it."

"I bet."

"I'm going into a tunnel," she said desperately.

"There are no tunnels in Lucky Harbor, Grace."

"Then I'm throwing myself under a bus."

"You can run," he said, clearly vastly amused, "but you can't hide."

And that's where he was wrong. She'd been hiding all her life, right in plain sight. Pretending to be a Brooks, when the truth was, she wasn't pedigreed. She was mutt. She disconnected, tossed her phone to the booth seat, and thunked her head onto the table.

"Wow," Amy said approvingly. "When you embarrass yourself, you go all the way, don't you?"

"I'm going to go to hell for that."

"Nah," Amy said, pushing the tray of cupcakes closer to Grace. "I don't think people go to hell for making an unbelievable ass of themselves. My grandma used to say you go to hell for abusing yourself."

Grace thought about how she'd abused herself in the shower just that very morning and sighed.

Chapter 7

If not for chocolate, there would be no need for control-top hose. An entire garment industry would be devastated.

Thanks to a crazy ER shift, Josh didn't get home until 3:00 a.m. He crawled into bed and immediately crashed, dreaming about a certain beautiful, willowy banking-specialist-slash-model-slash-dog-walker in a wet sundress that clung to her curves and made his heart pound.

And thanks to his own stupidity, he could also dream about kissing said beautiful, willowy blonde.

He got one glorious hour of sleep before he was woken by a puking Anna. Not the flu, but a hangover. Good times.

When he finally got to his office, he found he'd been double booked, but that was nothing new either. First up was Mrs. Dawson, who was experiencing hot flashes and other signs of perimenopause. She'd been coming in once a week or so for months, bringing him casseroles along with her list of gripes and symptoms. At the end of each appointment, she asked him out. Each time, he politely turned her down, saying he never mixed business with pleasure. Today when he gave her the standard line, she pulled out her phone and showed him the Facebook pic of him and Grace kissing.

"Looks like a pretty definite mixing of church and state," she said.

Josh stared at the picture, a little surprised to find that his and Grace's crazy chemistry had absolutely translated to the screen for the world to see. "She's not my patient."

"She's an employee. You pay her to walk your dog."

There was no use in getting annoyed that she knew Grace was his dog walker. Everyone knew it. This was Lucky Harbor, after all. He rose, pulled off his gloves, and tossed them into the trash bin. "See you next week, Mrs. Dawson."

"Humph," Mrs. Dawson said.

Josh walked to the next patient room and pulled the chart from the door holder. Mr. Saunders was dealing with kidney stones. Josh entered the room and pulled on yet another set of gloves. He'd once wondered how many hours a year he spent pulling on and tearing off gloves and figured he didn't really want to know. "How are you doing today, Mr. Saunders?"

"Dying."

"Actually, you're not," Josh said. "It's kidney stones. Once you pass them, you'll feel better."

"You sure?" Mr. Saunders asked.

"Yes."

"Sure sure?" Mr. Saunders asked. "Because it doesn't feel like kidney stones. Last night, I felt like I was having the most painful orgasm of my life. I guess I was probably just passing one of the stones, huh?"

Josh had to keep his head buried in the file as he nodded because how the hell do you confuse passing a kidney stone and an orgasm?

And so his day went, leaving him to wonder if everyone was crazy or if it was just him. By noon, his head was going to blow right off his shoulders, and he knew he couldn't go on like this. He either had to start turning patients away or give up the ER shifts.

"It's a no-brainer," Matt said. He'd brought five-inch-thick deli club sandwiches for lunch. They were spread out in Josh's office as the men watched ESPN highlights on the computer. "Sell the practice to the hospital. Let them bring in another doc, and all your problems go away. You work the hours you want. Simple."

Nothing was ever that simple, but the appeal was growing, and Josh had been thinking about little else for months. It meant giving up his dad's dream, which he hated, but the truth was that Josh couldn't do the dream justice. He'd tried.

When Matt had gone back to work, Josh brought up the contract offer, which he'd read a hundred times. A thousand. He'd had his attorney go over it with a fine-tooth comb. All he had to do was accept the offer with an electronic signature and hit SEND.

His finger hovered over the ENTER key, but then he set his head down on his desk to think about it for a minute. The next thing he knew, Dee, his nurse-practitioner, was calling his name.

"Hey," she grumbled from the doorway, "if you get to nap, so do I." She was in her fifties and resembled Lucy from the Peanuts comic strip. She was that perfect mix of no-nonsense and sweet empathy with his patients, though she rarely felt the need to impart any of that sweet empathy on him.

"Need you to get your cute ass out here," she said. "You've got Nancy Kessler in room one with a bladder infection that she wants cleared up before she goes to Vegas this weekend with her new boyfriend. Randy Lyons is in room two. He nail-gunned his thumb to the roof again. And Mrs. Munson's in three, saying the high pollen count is going to kill her dead."

"You take the allergies," he said. "I'll get the other two."

"Three. You've got thirteen-year-old Ben Seaver in four. He stuck his ding-dong into the Jacuzzi vent."

"Christ," Josh muttered. "*Again?*"

"Here." Dee handed him her coffee. "You probably need it more than I do."

"Thanks." It had far too much sugar and milk in it, but she was right. He needed it bad.

"Your father was never this busy," Dee said.

"Because we've doubled his practice."

"*You* doubled his practice," she said, and gave him a rare pat on the arm. "He'd be proud, but he wouldn't want this for you. Just sign the damn contract, Doctor. Before you burn out."

"I'm not going to burn out."

"Okay, then sign the damn contract before *I* burn out." With that, Dee nabbed back her coffee and left.

Josh's other office staff members consisted of two front office clerks, Michelle and Stacy, and an LPN named Cece. An hour later, Michelle poked her head into the exam room. "Mrs. Porter on line two. Needs to see you today. Says she's dying."

Mrs. Porter wasn't dying; she was lonely. Her kids lived on the East Coast, so she came in at least once a week for attention. Last week she'd had an eye twitch and had self-diagnosed a brain cancer. "Tell her we can get her in tomorrow," he said to Michelle.

"She says she'll be dead tomorrow."

"All right, fine. Squeeze her in today, then."

An hour later, the waiting room was still full. Dee gave Josh the stink eye when he slipped into his office to take an incoming call. It was Toby's school.

Toby hadn't been picked up by Katy, his nanny.

Josh immediately headed for the door, giving a pissed-off Dee an apologetic wave. He got into his car while dialing Katy. She was the sister of one of the nurses at the hospital and had come highly recommended. Problem was, she was only a temporary fix because, soon as her husband's transfer came through, they were moving to Atlanta.

Before Katy, they'd had Trina, who'd quit because of complications. Those complications being Anna. And Suzie, the nanny before Trina, had also left unexpectedly.

Josh was sensing a pattern, and he didn't have time for it.

Katy picked up and immediately said, "Don't hate me but I'm getting on a plane."

Josh let out a breath. "No notice?"

"I couldn't get a hold of you yesterday. I talked to Anna."

Josh considered thunking his head against his steering wheel. "A *day's* notice, then?"

"I'm sorry, Josh," she said with real regret. "But I think my replacement should be *two* nannies. And maybe an enforcer."

Josh called Anna next. She didn't pick up. Shock. He pictured Toby waiting at school with no one there and his stomach cramped. He sped up while mentally thumbing through the contacts on his phone, slowing at Grace's name.

Stopping.

Moving on.

Backing up.

Don't do it, man. She was smart as hell but she was also a really, *really* bad dog walker. No way should he burden her with his kid too. Except she'd already handled Toby yesterday for an hour, and everyone had lived to tell the tale.

She'd come through for him, twice now. Which really begged the question—*exactly who was helping whom here?*

The truth was, she'd already proven more reliable than half the people in his life. And damn if there wasn't something in her eyes that pulled him in like the tide, something extremely unforgettable. He knew she was a little lost, searching for something. He had no idea what but he wanted to help. Which was a very bad idea. He needed another person on his plate like he needed a hole in his head, but he couldn't turn back now. He was drawn to her.

She answered on the third and a half ring with a question in her "hello," as if maybe she'd been playing chicken with her voice mail.

"So," he said. "Daughter of a rocket scientist?"

"I don't want to talk about it."

He laughed. "You busy?"

"Not anymore. Just got back from an interview in Seattle."

This drained his amusement real quick, and his gut tightened—both in relief for her and regret for how he'd feel when she left Lucky Harbor. "How did it go?"

"Good. I think. I just got back and already walked Tank for you. And there were no accidents and no near drownings. No incidents at all, actually. Oh, and whatever your neighbor says about me isn't true. Mostly."

"Mostly?"

"Well... Tank sort of defiled Mrs. Perry's petunias. Twice."

Mrs. Perry was dead serious about her petunias. A few months back, when Josh had been teaching Toby to ride his bike, Toby had ridden through the flower bed.

Mrs. Perry had called the police, claiming vandalism.

Sheriff Sawyer Thompson had shown up on Josh's doorstep doing his damnedest to hide his smile, suggesting that Josh might want to think about teaching Toby to ride in a deserted parking lot instead of making potpourri out of Mrs. Perry's petunias.

The following week, Anna had brought the Antichrist home, and Toby had given up riding his bike, preferring instead to run with the puppy.

And bark.

"Forget Mrs. Perry," Josh said. "I've another job for you."

"Doing?"

He hesitated, not wanting her to say no. "It's a one-time temp position."

"My specialty," she said. "Do I get a hint?"

"I need a babysitter for Toby. Just for an hour or two."

She fell quiet, and Josh didn't want to rush her, but he had patients waiting, a sister to strangle later, and Toby, who was hopefully not waiting alone at the curb at the school that Josh was still five blocks from.

"Was I your last choice?" she finally asked.

"You were my *only* choice."

"Aw," she said. "We're both such accomplished liars."

He laughed softly, and there was another beat of that crazy chemistry, right through the phone.

"I'll do it," she said. "I'll watch Toby for you."

He let out a breath of relief. "Meet us at the house. And, Grace?" He paused. "Thanks."

"Yeah, you probably shouldn't thank me yet."

Josh disconnected and pulled up to the school. Toby stood on the curb, one hand in his teacher aide's, the other clutching a Kung Zhu Ninja warrior to his chest.

Josh got out of the car and crouched in front of him. "Hey, Little Man. Sorry Katy wasn't here to get you. She's moving a little sooner than expected."

Toby nodded and studied the tops of his battered Star Wars sneakers. He had newer pairs but he refused to wear them.

Josh met the teacher aide's eyes. She sent him a censuring look that said, *Epic Fail, Dad.*

Message received, thank you annoying, condescending teacher aide. "Appreciate you waiting with him."

"It's my job," she said. "And you should know, Toby pulled another vanishing act on us today."

"I didn't get a call."

"Because we found him," she said. "Thirty feet up the big oak tree in the playground."

Little black dots floated in Josh's visual field. As an ER doctor, he'd seen exactly what a thirty-foot fall could do to a body. He'd seen everything. "What were you doing up there?" he asked Toby.

Toby had another silent consult with his athletic shoes, so the aide answered for him. "He had a tree frog clenched in one fist."

"Toby doesn't have a frog."

"No," she agreed. "But we do. It was liberated from its terrarium in the kindergarten classroom."

Ah. Now it made sense. Josh looked at Toby. "You saved the frog, huh?"

Toby nodded.

"Oh, and he spoke today," the aide added.

"Yeah?" This was great news. "What did you say?" he asked Toby. "Wait. Let me guess. You solved world hunger. Or…created peace on earth. No, I know, you asked a girl out."

Toby wrinkled his nose like, *Ewwww, a girl?*

Josh grinned at him, and Toby giggled, the sound music to Josh's ears.

"He wanted to know if I'd be his new mommy," the aide said.

Uh-oh. That one had Anna written all over it. Josh sucked in a breath and slid another glance at Toby. "Your aunt teach you that?"

Toby shrugged.

Oh, yeah. *Anna.*

"He also asked the lunch aide and vice principal. And the janitor."

Josh kept his expression calm as he rose and took Toby's hand. Toby used his other to pull up his sagging jeans, and because his Star Wars T-shirt was only half tucked in, there was a strip of pale skin revealed.

His son was going commando.

Josh had no idea why, and hell if he'd ask in front of Judgmental Teacher Aide, so he filed the question away for later. "Ready to go home, Little Man?"

Finally a spark of life. "*Arf.*"

Chapter 8

If chocolate is the answer, the question is irrelevant.

Grace had been at the grocery store when Josh had called and was checking out when she got stopped by Jeanine Terrance, who owned a pottery shop.

"I hear you're an accountant," Jeanine said. "*And* that you're fixing Amy up with a bookkeeping system. I could *really* use a better bookkeeping system."

"Oh," Grace said. "Well, I'm not—"

"Amy swears by you," Jeanine said. "I'd do it myself but the left side of my brain is resistant to numbers. I'd pay you, of course, and not just in pottery either. I'm doing really well this quarter. Or so I think. I'll know better when you fix up my books."

"Yes, but I didn't really plan to start bookkeeping…" Grace broke off at Jeanine's hopeful expression. Hell. One small pottery shop. How much work could it really be? "I guess I could come take a look at what you've got."

"Oh, that's so wonderful!" Jeanine hugged her, then spared a guilty smile. "Um, you should probably know that I'm not quite as organized as Amy."

Since Amy's entire financial portfolio had been shoved into a shoe box, this was cause for some alarm, but Grace had already said yes. She promised to go by later, and drove to Josh's.

Certain parts of her—her naughty parts—were doing the happy dance at getting to see him again. Her other parts—her *smarter* parts—were more reserved. After the humiliating Phone Call Incident where he'd heard way too much about her through her conversation with her mom, she'd sort of hoped to keep some healthy distance between her and Josh for a while.

Like forever.

But he'd dangled this job, and she couldn't really afford to turn it down. She'd told him the truth about the Seattle interview going well, but she didn't have an offer yet. Next up was the Portland interview. And then all she had to do was wait.

She hated waiting.

When she knocked on the front door, wild barking came from inside. Josh answered, looking pretty damn fine in black pants and an azure blue button-down, the ever-present stethoscope around his neck. Grace's morning had been spent in a meeting with several men just as well dressed, just as handsome, but not a single one of them had affected her breathing.

Why did he affect her breathing?

His gaze tracked right to her lips, and a shot of hot, wet desire went straight through her, heading south.

Oh no. No, no, no, she told herself sternly. No matter how good-looking he was, or how he made her knees wobble with just one glance, he wasn't for her. Not even close. He was the kind of man she'd spent her entire life trying to live up to, driven, focused, workaholic...Ain't happening. Not here, not now, not ever. She repeated that to herself a few times, but her body didn't buy into the hype. Her body wanted him.

The barking seemed to have increased in decibels. "Don't tell me it multiplied," she said.

"Okay, I won't tell you."

Hmm. He was also extremely cool and calm under pressure. Something she'd never managed on her best day. And sexy as that was—so damn sexy—she'd discovered that men who had the cool, calm thing down were cool and calm *everywhere*, including their relationships.

She didn't want cool and calm in a relationship. She wanted passion. The big bang.

Fun.

"Arf, arf!" Toby yelled, coming running around the corner.

Josh swung him up and around so that he carried the boy piggyback style. Now there were two faces looking at Grace, both so similar as to be eerie, though Toby's was minus the fine stress lines outside the eyes and the world of knowledge in them.

"Toby's going to try real hard to be good," Josh said.

Toby nodded. Tank was at their feet, running in circles, chasing his own tail. With Toby still on board, Josh bent and scooped up the puppy too. "I can't promise the same for Tank."

Tank panted proudly. "Arf!"

Grace gave the pug a steely-eyed look that said, *Eat my shoes today and die*, which didn't cow him at all. But she had a genuine smile for Toby. "Hey there."

"Arf!"

"Are you and Tank brothers?" she asked him.

Toby smiled and started to speak, but Josh adjusted his hold on Tank and reached back, covering Toby's mouth.

"Wait," Grace said. "I think he was going to actually use words."

"Yeah, but trust me, you don't want to hear them."

Toby pulled Josh's hand away. "Are you my new mommy?"

Grace's mouth fell open in shock, and Toby giggled at the sight.

"Okay, Tiger," Josh said. "You know I love the sound of your laugh, probably more than any sound in the world, but I will squash you like a grape if you say that to one more woman today."

Toby pointed to Anna, who rolled into the living room behind them.

"Yeah, I know," Josh said mildly, sending his sister a glance. "I'm going to squash Anna like a grape too."

Grace was horrified he'd say such a thing to a sweet little boy, much less to his handicapped sister, but Toby just grinned.

Anna did, too, and without a word, continued rolling through the house, ignoring all of them.

Josh set Toby down. "How about you go find something to do that won't get you in trouble," he said.

When the kid was gone, Josh looked at Grace. "I called Mallory."

"You did? For what?"

"I realize that this is a favor, *my* favor," he said. "But I had to make sure you're everything you seem, even with the multiple degrees and what sounds like an...interesting family. And just out of curiosity, what kind of research are you doing for me, by the way?"

She groaned and covered her face. "I told you, I don't want to talk about it."

He laughed softly. "So we're okay?"

"Maybe. What did Mallory say?"

"That I'd be lucky to have you as Toby's nanny. And that she'd hurt me if I hurt you."

"What would you have done if she'd said something bad about me?"

"I'd have brought Toby with me to work. I've done that before."

She couldn't be sure, but it seemed like the big, bad, tough doctor shuddered at the memory. "You won't have to do that today," she said.

He gave her a smile that conveyed gratitude, and also a good amount of something else, something that wobbled her knees as he gestured her inside. Every other time she'd been here, the place had been very neat, but not today. Today it looked like a bomb had gone off, especially the kitchen. There were dishes in the sink and ingredients and utensils all over the counters.

"It's my housekeeper's day off," Josh said, and scooped Toby up, eliciting a squeal of delight. This got even louder when Josh hung Toby upside down before finally setting the kid into a chair in front of a loaded plate.

"After-school snack was Toby's choice today," Josh explained. "Luckily this coincided with a lunch break for me, and I made what we like to call 'guilt pancakes.'"

From the ingredients and stuff scattered on the counter, Grace could tell they were wheat pancakes with blueberries, accompanied by turkey bacon. Her own father wouldn't know a spatula, much less how to turn on the stovetop, so this was impressive.

Josh poured a little dollop of syrup onto Toby's plate, then ruffled the boy's hair, his expression soft with something Grace had never seen from him before.

Affection.

"Be right back, Short Stack," Josh said. "Eat up."

Toby held up his lightsaber with one hand, which was, of course, driving Tank nuts. The little pug was doing his circle-the-table thing, growling ferociously at every *whoosh*, *vrrmm-whoosh*, posturing like he was a Jedi as well.

"Napoleon complex," Josh said to Grace. "He thinks he's bigger than he is."

Toby grabbed a pancake in his free hand. Flattening it on the table, he rolled it up before dipping it into the syrup and then into his mouth.

"Utensils," Josh said.

Toby sighed and dropped his lightsaber to reach for a fork.

Tank's growl came to an abrupt stop when the lightsaber hit the floor, and with a startled snort, he ran off with his tail between his legs.

Toby, holding a fork in one hand, used his other to stuff a huge bite into his mouth.

Josh tapped the unused fork in Toby's hand, then turned to Grace, gesturing that he wanted a word in private. He led her out the back door, shutting it behind them.

She turned to look inside to see if Toby was using the fork or his fingers, but today the blinds on the window were closed.

"Okay, so here's the deal," Josh said. "I lied about it being for an hour or two."

That had Grace turning back to face Josh. "So I'm not the only one going to hell?"

Josh shoved his fingers through his hair, making it stand up on end. He was so broad that he blocked the sun, and with his arms up and bent, he was really testing the seams of his dress shirt in a way that worked for her, big-time.

Suddenly he dropped his arms back to his sides as if they weighed far too much. "Look," he said. "The truth is that I'm late. I'm overbooked. My sister's going to give me a heart attack. I need someone to watch the Bean for me today, and you need money. Plus, he's a good kid, really good, even if he refuses to use utensils or speak English. He will, however, bark at will, and he's excellent at catching spiders."

This stopped her cold. "You have more spiders?"

"No," he said without missing a beat. "No spiders."

"You said spiders," she said. "And I saw a big one in the side yard, in the sprinkler well."

"That spider went south for the winter."

"It's summer."

"He wanted to be the first to get out of town."

"Look at you, with all the lies." But she had to admit, "the Bean" *was* pretty damn cute. And the Bean's father was even cuter—though she was sure he'd object to such an innocuous word as *cute*.

Josh had spoken in a calm, quiet manner, but everything about him said exhausted tension. Not to mention how much he appeared to hate having to ask something of her.

She understood pride. God, how she understood pride. But seriously? Was she really thinking of doing this simply because he was in a bind?

No, a little voice inside her head said. *It's because he's hot*… "How long?"

Josh didn't move, didn't give away any sign of relief, but his eyes warmed. "Eight o'clock, at the latest."

Five hours from now. Grace had no idea what to do with a kid for five hours.

"Offer to kiss her again."

They both whirled around to find the back door cracked and an eyeball peering at them through that crack—at hip height.

Anna, in her wheelchair.

"Sorry," Grace told her. "That ship sailed."

Anna snorted.

Josh pushed the door shut and held it closed with one hand, the other resting on the wood next to her head. "Sorry about that." He leaned into her, forcing her into a door-and-Josh sandwich.

Not a bad place to be when it came right down to it. "So," she said, annoyingly breathless, "eight o'clock, then?"

"Yes, and there's a but."

If it was *his* butt, she was in.

"It's not just for today," he said.

This was the proverbial bucket of ice water. "What?"

"I need help for the rest of the week," he said. "From two until eight…ish."

"Oh my God, Josh." *All week*… "I don't know."

"I'm hiring a replacement nanny. I've already got feelers out. You and Toby can do the preinterviews and save some time if you want. I'd ask Anna to watch him, but she does the early mornings and late nights already. Plus, she's not been all that reliable, and Toby's been through enough."

"Josh..."

"A thousand bucks," he said.

"*Oh my God.*"

"Yes or no, Grace."

He was all hard, unforgiving lines of tough sinew, wrapped in a double dose of testosterone, but it was hard to concentrate on his yummy goodness at the moment, as unbelievable as that was. "A thousand dollars?" she said, dazed. "For half a week? You can't be serious."

"It also comes with free room and board. There's a guesthouse behind my pool. That's where a couple of our nannies have stayed, though not our last one; she was married. It's only seven hundred and fifty square feet, but it's furnished."

Grace shook her head, but the truth was, he'd had her at *free.* She'd been staying at the local B&B, and loving it. The three sisters who ran the place, Tara, Maddie, and Chloe, had been lovely, but the B&B wasn't exactly bank-account friendly. "I'll have more job interviews this week." *Hopefully.*

"We can work that out," he said.

She nodded, but she was thinking that he smelled amazing, even better than chocolate. So much so that she wanted to bite him.

And was he suddenly closer? She leaned her head back on the door to look up at him, into those warm, mocha eyes. Yeah, he was closer. She *could* actually bite him if she wanted. But she was going to be good. "There's no family to help you?" She knew his dad had passed away, but that was all she knew. "What about your mom, or maybe other siblings? Or... Toby's mom?"

"Both my parents are gone," he said. "And I have no other siblings. As for Toby's mom, she's not available."

His face was an impassive mask. Impossible to read. Not too hard to guess his thoughts, though—the guy was in a rough spot with no support system in place. Maybe she was nothing but a sucker, but there was something so appealing about a guy supporting his kid, his sister, and an entire medical practice all on his own, doing everything he could to make it all work. "Okay," she said softly. "I'm in. I'm not sure about the guesthouse; I'll let you know. But I'll take care of Toby for the rest of the week." She expected him to back up and let her go, but he didn't. Her entire visage was the sheer expanse of his chest.

"There's one last thing," he said.

She wondered if he looked as good without his clothes. "What?"

"*That ship sailed?*" he asked, repeating her earlier words to Anna.

Again she tilted her head up. "I just meant we've been there, done that. We already kissed, remember?"

His gaze heated. Yeah, he remembered.

"And it was... fine."

He'd probably shaved that morning but he had a shadow coming in. And his eyes. Fathomless dark pools, as always, giving nothing away of himself or his secrets. "The kiss was... *fine*," he repeated, eyes narrowed.

"Well, yeah." *Fine plus amazing times infinity.*

He just looked at her.

"Okay," she admitted, sagging back against the door. "So it was a little better than fine. But I'm not looking for this. For a guy like you."

"Like me," he said slowly, as if the words didn't quite compute any more easily than "fine" had.

And probably they didn't. Look at him. He could have chemistry with a brick wall. "It's just that I'm not going to be in Lucky Harbor much longer, so while I'm here, I'm aiming for... fun."

"Fun."

"Yeah. It's a new thing I'm trying."

"And you think I'm not," he said with a hint of disbelief, "fun."

"It's nothing personal."

"Hmm." He took a step toward her, and since there was already no place to go, she found herself once again sandwiched between the door and his deliciously hard body. His hands went to her hips, where they squeezed lightly and then slid up her sides, past her ribs, to her arms and her shoulders. By the time he got to her throat and cupped her face, her bones had gone AWOL.

"What are you doing?" she managed.

"Showing you how much fun I can be."

Oh boy. Just his husky whisper sent a shiver down her spine, the sort of shiver a woman wasn't supposed to get for a man she didn't want to be attracted to. And then her body strained a little closer to him.

Bad body!

Josh's eyes met hers and held. He was purposely building the anticipation, along with the heat working her from the inside out.

"Still think I'm not fun?" he asked softly.

"You're not." She swallowed hard. "You're..."

He quirked a brow.

Hot and sexy, and damn. *Fun.* Which meant that she was in big trouble here, going-down-for-the-count kind of trouble. Time to wave the white flag, she decided. And she would. In just a minute...

"Say it, Grace."

"Okay, so maybe you're a *little* fun," she admitted. "But—"

He nibbled her lower lip, soothing it with his tongue, then stroked and teased her with his mouth until she let out a helpless murmur of arousal and fisted her hands in his shirt.

His eyes were heavy-lidded and sexy when he pulled back. "Bullshit, a *little* fun." His mouth curved as he looked down.

Following his gaze, she realized she was still gripping his shirt. She forced herself to smooth her fingers over the wrinkles she'd left. "Fine. You're a barrel of fun. Happy now?"

"Getting there." His eyes were dark with lust and focused on hers, his hands on her back, fingers stroking her through the thin material of her dress. When he lowered his head, he did it slowly, giving her plenty of time to turn away.

She didn't.

Their eyes held until his lips touched hers, and then her lashes swept down involuntarily. She couldn't help it; his lips were warm, firm, and oh how just right…

With a deep, masculine groan, he threaded his hands through her hair and tilted her head to better suit him, parting her lips with his, kissing her lightly at first, then not so lightly. And then everything felt insistent and urgent, and all her bones melted.

By the time he broke the kiss, Grace was unsteady on her feet, and her breathing was more in line with a marathon run. "I'm not sure what that proved exactly," she managed. Except he was the best kisser on the planet…

His eyes were heavy-lidded. His shirt was half untucked—her doing. He stood there looking dangerously alluring and hotter than sin.

He slowly shook his head. Obviously he didn't know what that proved any more than she did. "I'm not looking for a relationship with you either," he said quietly. "I'm not looking for a relationship period. You've seen my life, Grace. Hell, you're living it. You know I'd be crazy to bring a woman into this mess."

"So we're on the same page," she said with relief. Except not really. She *should* feel relief, but didn't, which made no sense. Neither of them wanted this. Where was her relief?

His gaze dropped to her mouth. "Thanks for agreeing to watch Toby for me this week."

"Any time," she whispered, then went up on tiptoes so that when she repeated the two words softly, her mouth brushed his with each syllable.

He groaned, and the sound of it was so innately male, so sensually dominating, that she tingled all over. She leaned into him, and when he groaned again, it rumbled from his chest to hers. “Grace.”

“I know.” She lifted her hands from him and backed away, right into the door, of course.

His hand, low on her back, slid up until he cupped her head in his palm. “Careful.”

They stared at each other some more. Then her hands made their way up his chest, around his neck, her fingers gliding into his hair.

He made another sound low in his throat and pulled her back to him. She wasn’t sure which of them made the next move after that, but then they were kissing again, and damn, she’d been right. The man could kiss, *really* kiss—

The knock on the other side of the door caused her to nearly jump out of her skin.

Josh didn’t jump or let go of her. He pressed a kiss to the soft spot just beneath her ear. “You’re lethal,” he whispered before pulling her clear so he could open the door to Anna.

Toby was in her lap eating a Popsicle, his mouth rimmed in purple.

Anna was smirking. “Whatcha doing?” she asked.

Josh just sent her a long look, one that would have had Grace quivering in her boots if it’d been directed at her.

But Anna wasn’t cowed in the slightest. “Oh, I know,” she said. “You were checking each other’s tonsils.”

“Anna,” Josh said, his tone mild but laced with a clear warning.

She just smiled. “Toby wanted to remind you that you have open house night at school later. And you’re supposed to bring cupcakes for something or another tomorrow.”

Still sucking on the Popsicle, Toby nodded his agreement on this.

“Neither of those things are on the schedule,” Josh said.

“Oops,” Anna said. “They must have gotten erased. Like my Europe trip.”

A muscle twitched in Josh's jaw, but he softened his expression for a solemn Toby, ruffling the boy's hair in reassurance.

Tank was at their feet, squealing and snuffling, trying to coax someone into picking him up. "Arf," he said.

"Arf," Toby said.

Grace's uterus contracted, which she couldn't have explained to save her life. "I can handle the cupcakes," she heard herself say.

Josh looked at her with the expression of someone who was drowning but hadn't expected a rope tossed to him. "Yeah?"

"Yeah." She smiled at Toby. "I'm something of a cupcake expert. Especially *chocolate* cupcakes."

Josh's phone buzzed from the depths of his pocket. He pulled it out and looked at the screen, mouth grim. "Gotta go." He kissed the top of Toby's head. "Be good." He sent Anna a long warning look, then went on the move, towing Grace along with him, his hand on her wrist, forcing her to practically run to keep up with him. They strode through the house and out the front. Josh shut the door firmly, then pressed her back against it, dipping down a little to look into her face.

"We have got to stop meeting like this," she said.

He didn't smile. "We still on the same page?"

"The no-relationship page in spite of the fact that we tend to burn up all the oxygen in a room when we're in it together?" she asked. "Hell yes, we're on the same page. Who needs all that crazy chemistry." She forced a laugh. "Not me…"

"Grace." He wasn't smiling. "If this is too much—"

"No, of course not. We have a deal. I'll watch Toby. Another reason to minimize the whole kissing thing, right? Because I don't kiss my bosses. In fact, my last job didn't work out because I wouldn't…" She grimaced. Damn big mouth of hers. "You know."

Josh's expression was suddenly even *more* serious. "No," he said quietly. "I don't know. Tell me."

Well hell. How did they get here? She rolled her shoulders and looked at the ocean across the street, uncomfortable with the subject *and* the memory she didn't want to tell him about. "It's no big deal. He wanted…things. I didn't want to give him things. The end."

Josh studied her for a moment. "But first you sued the pants off him, or at least smacked him around a little, kicked him where it hurts, right?"

She let out a low laugh. "No." Nothing nearly so satisfactory. She'd simply left Seattle, not willing to fight for the job that she'd realized she'd never be comfortable in. Unnerved about what had happened, scared about her future, she'd gotten in her car and headed out. She'd been thinking only about putting some distance between her and what would have been a bad decision, and then she'd ended up here in Lucky Harbor.

A complete accident that had turned out to be the best accident of her life. A glorious break from the fast track of her life.

"Grace," he said, and waited for her to look at him. "I'm not that guy."

"I know." And she did. "Which is how"—she waved her hand between them and let out a low laugh—"it got a little out of hand just now. My fault, I know, but I just don't want you to think—"

"I don't," he said. "I wouldn't. And you weren't alone in letting it get out of hand." He shook his head. "Not even close. I acted inappropriately. I'm sorry, Grace."

In her world, blame was assigned and cast upon the closest target. In her world, people did not take responsibility for their own mistakes. She met his gaze and gave him the utter, terrifying truth. "It didn't feel inappropriate," she admitted. "It felt…"

"Fun?" His tone was lighter now. Teasing. And she knew they were truly going to be okay. He didn't want this; he didn't have time for this. That made two of them. She'd be leaving soon, going back to her "real life." Soon as she found it. "Anything critical I need to know to ensure Toby's well-being?"

"He's shy and won't tell you if he's hungry or thirsty. He eats dinner at five-thirty, and there's stuff in the freezer with directions included. Be careful not to deviate—he has food allergies. There's a card on the counter listing all the no-nos. And don't let him feed Tank any of his Zhu Zhus. Tank is the Antichrist himself, but even the Antichrist can't digest metal and plastic. That painful lesson cost me six hundred bucks last week."

"Ouch," she said, grateful not to have a pug puppy. Or a Zhu Zhu. "So feed and water the kid, and keep Tank away from the Zhu Zhus. Got it."

"And Anna..."

"I'm thinking she can tell me when she's hungry and thirsty. And she probably knows not to try to inhale any Zhu Zhus, right?"

Josh let out a breath. "Yeah. But she's not your responsibility. Don't let her drive you off."

"She won't need any help?"

"No. Trust me on this, no. And I should probably apologize ahead of time for her."

"We'll be fine, Dr. Scott."

He let out a half laugh. "Back to that, are we?"

"Don't you like it when people call you doctor?"

"Only if they're sitting on my exam table."

She looked into his eyes for a sign that he was being falsely modest, but he wasn't. There was nothing but a mild impatience in his gaze.

And a lingering heat that stoked hers back into flames. "You gotta go."

"Yeah." He leaned in and brushed his mouth over hers, then kissed her with some serious intent before pulling back. "Shit."

She wobbled unsteadily and had to laugh at the both of them, shaken by a kiss. "It's still there."

"Yeah. It's still there."

Chapter 9

There's no Chocoholic's Anonymous because no one wants to quit.

Josh went back to the office, and as he worked through his patients, all he had to do was look at a door and he'd think about the full-body press he'd given Grace.

Twice.

He wanted her, which was just about as crazy as it got, since she was a woman with nothing more than fun on her mind. But he'd been there, done that, and had had his life changed forever. It was how he'd gotten Toby, which he wouldn't change for the world.

But he wasn't about to do it again.

So it made no sense to him, his crazy attraction to Grace. She wasn't his type. Okay, so he didn't have a type. His requirements were warm and sweet—except in bed, where he preferred decidedly not warm and sweet.

But Grace wasn't going to end up in his bed. They'd both said so. They'd agreed to be on the same page in this matter—the no-relationship page. Very grown up.

Christ, he hated being grown up.

"Room one," Dee said as they passed each other in the hallway.

Mrs. Carson was waiting on him. She'd accidentally mixed up her blood pressure meds with her husband's Viagra. Unfortunate that she was also hard of hearing. "Mrs. Carson, you need to get the pill dispenser that we talked about to prevent this from happening."

"What is that, dear?" she yelled, an arthritic hand curled around her ear. "I'm going to grow taller and harder?" She grinned at her own joke, slapping her knee, completely unconcerned that everyone in the building could also hear her. "Not that I wouldn't mind being able to take care of myself in that manner, mind you," she went on. "Paul's a good man, but he's not built for much downstairs, if you know what I'm saying."

Josh did. He just wished he didn't.

"Aw. Your father would have laughed. You're not much fun."

Gee, where had he heard that before?

Josh's next patient was Kenny Liotta, a truck driver who came in every six weeks without fail with a new STD. "You ever think about getting smart?" Josh asked.

Kenny grinned. "Your dad used to ask me the same thing. Problem is, my dick's in charge. And my dick's not the one with the IQ."

Josh shook his head and wrote a script. "Your dick needs to read *Dicks for Dummies*, or it's going to fall off before your next birthday."

Kenny laughed. "But what a way to go, right?"

"No," Josh said. "It's not a good way to go. Go with a hot tub full of blondes in some seedy hotel, from a heart attack of pleasure. Not from an STD."

Kenny nodded. "Yeah, I see your point. You're a good man, Doc. You're not going to sell the practice, are you? Like all the others around here have?"

It was common knowledge that the hospital had been slowly but surely procuring other county medical facilities, from labs to pediatricians to specialists of all kinds. By absorbing them all under one umbrella, it gave the medical center a huge boost in popularity and reputation. This translated to big bucks, of course. Just about every doctor Josh worked with in the area was a part of the hospital in some way.

He was one of the lone holdouts. "I'm thinking about it."

"It's like some socialist takeover. What did they threaten you with, broken kneecaps?"

This made Josh laugh. "You're watching too much TV. If I sell, the world will go on spinning the same way. The level of care here will remain the same as well."

"You sure about that?"

"Yes," Josh said firmly. But if he truly believed it, why hadn't he signed already?

The board didn't understand either. Neither did Matt when he called to see if Josh was ever going to go rock climbing with him again.

"I can't get away," Josh said.

"Jesus. Sign already."

"I'm still thinking."

"Are you still going to be thinking when you're too old to hang off a cliff without worrying that you'll drop your dentures?"

Josh sighed. "Call Ty. He'll rock climb."

"He'll rock climb never. The guy who jumps out of helicopters to rescue people for a living doesn't like heights."

This was true. "Take Amy."

"No go," Matt said. "She told me if I tried to wake her up before dawn again, she'd kill me with my own gun."

This was undoubtedly also true. Amy Michaels was beautiful, sharp, and tough as hell.

"You need some more hours in your day," Matt said. "You're not any fun. Anyone ever tell you that?"

Okay, now this was starting to piss him off. "I'm plenty of fun," Josh said.

"Yeah? When?"

When his tongue had been in Grace's mouth. That had been pretty fucking fun.

"*Sell*," Matt said, and disconnected.

"I'm fun," Josh repeated to no one. He slid his phone away and thought about Grace some more. That was fun all in itself, actually. Too much fun. She was a complete time sink, not to mention a threat to his peace of mind. She made him want things. She made him want to step outside of the box of his life, something he absolutely couldn't do.

No matter how tempting.

He got home at eight-thirty, half an hour late. Toby was bathed and ready for bed, a Zhu Zhu warrior hamster in one fist, his Jedi lightsaber in the other, Tank compliant at his feet. Two perfect angels.

When Grace had arrived at his house earlier, she'd looked soft and willowy in a sundress, cropped sweater, and sandals, her wavy blond hair falling silkily to her shoulders, facial expression dialed to easy, curious intelligence. During their moment against his back door, her hair had gotten mussed—his doing—and her expression hadn't been nearly so calm. Her eyes had been dilated, her mouth wet from his, her nipples hard.

He'd liked that look, a lot.

Now her hair had been put up in some sort of knot, held there by a LEGO piece, with long silky strands escaping wildly, making her look a little bit like a mad scientist. Her sweater was gone, she had something streaked and stained down the front of her sundress, and her expression wasn't serene or aroused.

She was laughing. She and Toby were in the kitchen, counting the cupcakes on the tray at the table, cracking up. Just looking at them had the tension draining from his shoulders. "Sorry I'm late," he said.

"You have an emergency?" she asked, turning a concerned face his way.

"A sixteen-year-old girl pierced her own tongue, and it abscessed. She didn't tell her parents for three days, not until it swelled, blocking her breathing passage."

"Oh my God."

"She's okay. Grounded for life, but okay."

She just stared at him. "Wow. That makes my day seem like a piece of cake. Or as it turns out, a cupcake." She gestured to the tray. "We had to make two batches. We don't want to talk about batch number one."

Toby giggled and shook his head.

"You *made* them?" Josh asked, impressed.

"Yeah. At the expense of your kitchen."

The kitchen was a complete disaster, like a bomb had gone off. Dishes piled high in the sink, chocolate everywhere. "Hey, at least everyone's still alive," he said.

"Well, if that's your only requirement."

He smiled. "You smell like a chocolate cupcake."

Anna wheeled into the kitchen, her attention riveted to the open book in her lap. "Found it, Josh's freshman pic," she said. "He's the one with the thick glasses, braces, and black eye. The black eye happened when he let himself get stuffed into his own locker. He was a lot smaller back then. He was a total loser."

Josh eyed the book. "Is that my yearbook?"

"Relax," Anna said. "It's not like I showed her a pic of your tattoo."

Josh rubbed his forehead. "Has she been dishing out my dirty little secrets all day?" he asked Grace.

"Like candy."

Perfect.

"And tattoo?" Grace asked, her gaze running over his body. "Where?"

"His ass," Anna said helpfully.

Josh covered Toby's ears. "*Hey.*"

"Sorry," Anna said. "His butt."

Grace raised a brow at Josh, clearly trying not to laugh, though whether it was in horror or genuine amusement, he had no idea.

"What is it?" Grace asked.

"I lost a bet," Josh said in his own defense. "And I'm not telling."

Now she *did* laugh. "I thought you were a late-bloomer nerd, not a reformed bad boy."

Anna snorted. "Yes to the nerd. No to the bad boy."

"*I lost a bet,*" he repeated in his defense. *Jesus.* "It's all Matt's fault."

"You could get it removed," Grace said, "if you're embarrassed."

"I'm not embarrassed." Much. "And besides, nobody ever sees it because nobody's ever behind me when I'm..." He tightened his grip on Toby's ears. "Bare-assed."

At this, Grace burst out laughing, and the sound made him smile in spite of himself. She moved to the sink and began washing dishes. Anna, apparently allergic to cleaning up anything, ever, suddenly remembered she had to get online for something. Toby climbed onto a chair to help Grace. Josh shook his head. "You know the rule about standing on chairs, Tobes." Which had been put into place six months ago after an incident involving three stitches above Toby's eyebrow.

"Oh, he's okay," Grace said. "The back of the chair's turned out to keep him from stepping off."

Which is exactly how it'd happened the first time. "It's also that drying sharp knives is a bad idea."

Grace turned to Toby, who was drying a wooden spoon. She arched a brow at Josh. *Overprotective much?*

Josh shook his head, rolled up his sleeves, and joined them.

When they were finished, Grace helped Toby down and squatted in front him, her eyes soft and warm. "Sleep tight," she said, hugging him. "Don't let the bed bugs bite."

Toby hugged her back. "'Night."

Josh's jaw dropped. A *word*, not a bark.

Grace smiled. Toby smiled back, and the sight of it grabbed Josh by the throat so that he couldn't breathe for a second.

Grace rose and grabbed her purse, and Josh walked her out. At her car, she tried to open the driver's door but it stuck.

"Dammit," she muttered.

"Here, let me—"

"No," she said. "It always sticks. I've got it." She yanked hard, and it opened so fast she nearly fell to her ass but he caught her.

He turned her to face him. "You got him to use words."

"I told him that I didn't understand puppy talk." She smiled. "You've got a great kid, Josh."

"I know. And thanks," he said. "For today. For everything. Have you thought about the guesthouse?"

The moonlight slanted over her features. "Some."

He didn't push, not in all that much of a hurry himself to have her sleeping so close. "Tell me how it went today."

She looked at him for a long moment. "He needs more of you."

He drew in a slow, deep breath. "I know."

"And you're right on Tank being the Antichrist, by the way. Although he's possibly the cutest Antichrist I've ever seen."

"And?" Because he was pretty sure there was one.

"And your sister. She..." Grace shook her head, at a loss for words.

"Yeah," he said on a low laugh. "She has that effect on people."

"I think it'd help if you loosened the reins on her a little."

He shook his head. "That's the opposite of what she needs."

"What she needs is to be challenged," she said. "She's bored. And *any* bored twenty-one-year-old is trouble. Plus, I don't know how to tell you this, but she's not nearly as handicapped as she likes people to believe."

Josh was impressed. "It usually takes people weeks to get her number."

"Hmm." She tilted her face up to his. "Would you still be amused if I told you she said that while you're a great doctor, you're also a control freak, only a so-so dad, a totally crappy brother, and an even more totally crappy significant other?"

"No, since it's all mostly true."

She studied him a long moment. "You want to expand on any of that?"

"You've seen my life, Grace. It's…busy." His mouth quirked when she snorted at this newsflash. "My schedule's insane, and I *have* to be somewhat of a control freak to keep it all managed."

"Which is what makes you a great doctor."

"And only a so-so dad," he said, and Christ how he hated *that* admission. "I'd argue the crappy brother part, but she's pretty much dead on about the rest."

"The significant other?" she asked.

"I don't have one, but if I did, yeah, I'd be crappy at that too."

Something crossed her face. Disappointment? That couldn't be. She'd been the first one to say that they weren't going there.

"Toby's got a project at school," she said carefully.

Josh felt a fishing expedition coming.

"A family tree," she said.

Yeah, definitely a fishing expedition.

"He said he couldn't fill in the mom because he didn't have any pictures."

"Toby has a picture of his mom," Josh said. "It's just an older one." He paused. "We split when he was a few months old. He doesn't remember her."

"You have full custody."

"Yes."

She waited, clearly hoping for more. But he didn't have more, and he was too tired to even try.

"He hasn't seen his mom since he was a few months old?" she asked.

"She isn't from this area."

"Aw. That's rough." She softened, clearly feeling sorry for him.

He hated that, both for Toby and himself. They'd done just fine on their own. Well, mostly. He rubbed at the beginning of a headache right between his eyes.

"You're tired," she said softly. "Try to get some sleep." And then she patted him on the arm like he was a pathetic loser.

He stared down at her, torn between showing her just how *not* tired he was and wanting her to leave before he did exactly that.

She patted him again, and he caught her hand.

She stared at his fingers on hers, sighed, then dropped her forehead to his chest. "Do you have to smell good?" she asked, voice muffled. "Like, *always*?"

"I—"

"No, don't answer that." She lifted her head and kissed him on the cheek. Her breath was warm, and she still had that cupcake scent going, and damn if her lips didn't linger. Not one to need an engraved invite, he turned his head and look at that, his mouth lined right up with hers.

Oh yeah. *This* was what he'd needed. All damn day long. His tongue teased the corner of her lip. When she opened for him, hunger took over, setting him on fire. Hauling her up against him, he took control of the kiss, deepening it. She rewarded him with a soft moan that said she was right there with him, and he felt a whole hell of a lot better.

Finally, Grace stepped back, smacking up against her car. Laughing at herself, and him, too, he suspected, she got into her car.

Josh watched her drive away, turning only when he heard Anna's wheels hit the porch behind him.

"Where are you going?" he asked her.

A truck pulled up to the curb and honked, answering his question.

"He should come to the door for you," Josh said.

"God, you're old," she said. "And *he* has a name."

They all had names. Josh had discovered it was easier to just think of each of them as the Boy. Still, Devon had staying power. Not surprising, since Anna was coming into her settlement. He snagged a quickly escaping Anna by the back of her chair. "First, tell me about today."

"There were no casualties, and your girlfriend managed to stay the whole day without quitting on you."

Josh knew better than to let her engage him in a semantics war, so he let the "girlfriend" comment slide. "You were on your best behavior, then."

Anna smiled.

Hmmm…

"Like I said, she stuck it out," Anna said.

"Maybe tomorrow you can resist doing your best to make me look like an ass," he said.

"Maybe tomorrow you could not be one."

"Anna—"

Devon honked again.

Josh slid Anna a look and she shrugged. "He'd come in, but you scare him."

"Bullshit."

"Okay, you don't," she agreed. "But he's got authority issues. Anyway, he did some research and came up with a European itinerary. I e-mailed it to you."

"What about school?"

"School's dumb," she said.

"No. Dumb is quitting school."

"You don't understand."

The family therapist had told Josh not to pretend to understand. That he was never going to know what it was like to be a hormonal teenage girl who'd lost her parents at a critical age, not to mention the use of her legs.

What he *did* understand was that, as usual, *he* was the bad guy.

Anna pushed off toward the truck, and when she was gone, Josh went inside. "Just you and me," he said to Toby. "Ready for bed?"

"*Arf.*"

Chapter 10

Einstein was eating chocolate when he came upon the theory of relativity. Coincidence? I think not.

Grace went back to her room at the B&B that night and sat on the bed watching TV while she eyeballed the balance of her checking account on her laptop. Five hundred dollars cash. That's all she had left to her name, unless she broke into her saved-for-a-rainy-day investments. But it wasn't raining, not quite yet. She'd gotten a call for a second interview on the Seattle banking position, and tomorrow morning was the Skype interview with Portland. An offer from either of them would change everything.

Until then, she could stay here in the B&B and watch her balance dwindle further away or she could go to Josh's guesthouse.

It was no contest, really. Besides, by this time next week, she'd probably, hopefully, have one of the jobs.

And a direction.

There was a knock at the door, and she opened it to one of the B&B owners. Chloe was wearing little hip-hugging army cargoes, a snug, bright red henley, and matching high-tops. Her glossy dark red hair cascaded down her back in an artful disarray that Grace might have hated her for if it hadn't been for Chloe's friendly smile and the plate of chocolate chip cookies in her hands.

"Tara had extra," Chloe said. "I tried to steal 'em but Tara said I had to give them to our guest."

Grace tried to take the plate and laughed when Chloe didn't let go of it. "Want to come in and share?"

"Hell, yeah." Chloe stepped inside. "For a minute there, I was afraid you weren't going to ask me."

They ate cookies and watched a dog training class on TV. The instructor was saying that there were no bad dogs, just bad dog owners.

"Huh," Grace said, thinking of Tank.

And Tank's big, bad, gorgeous hunk of an owner.

"You think an alpha guy can be trained as easily as a dog?" Chloe asked.

Chloe was engaged to Sheriff Sawyer Thompson, definitely an alpha guy, and Grace laughed. "Good luck."

After Chloe left, Grace spent a couple of hours on Amy's shoe box, enjoying the task more than she thought she would. She knew accounting was dry to most, but somehow the numbers soothed her. By the time she went to bed, she had Amy shockingly organized.

The next morning, Grace showered, dressed, and paid up for her stay at the B&B. She'd be sorry to leave the very lovely inn, even more so since they gave her an extra plate of chocolate chip cookies as a going-away gift.

She drove to Josh's place. It was early but she had that interview, and she wanted to make sure she was set up somewhere with Internet.

The front door opened before she knocked. Josh was dressed in a T-shirt and basketball shorts, a messenger bag slung over one shoulder and a duffel bag over the other. To the gym and then to work, she figured. He was also carrying the cupcakes on a tray and had Toby, with his Star Wars backpack, by the hand.

Both man and boy looked at her from twin chocolate gazes, and her heart did a little somersault in her chest. She smiled at Toby. "Enjoy the cupcakes."

Josh eyed her own big duffel bag. "You're going to stay in the guesthouse."

"If that's still okay."

"Very. Give me a minute." He walked with Toby to the end of the block just as a yellow school bus pulled up. They both disappeared onto the bus, and then after a few minutes, Josh reappeared without the cupcake tray.

"The bus driver's a friend," he said to Grace when he'd walked back to the house. "She'll make sure Toby gets into school without getting mobbed on the bus for the cupcakes." He took in Grace's interview suit. "You have an interview today."

"Yes, in an hour."

"I e-mailed you the file of nanny applicants so far."

She nodded. "I'll get on that today and hopefully help you find someone perfect for Toby."

"Thanks." He dropped his bags and took hers. "I'll show you the guesthouse. Whatever you do, don't let me come in with you."

"Why not?"

His gaze ran over her body, tingling and heating every inch it touched, and it touched a lot. "It would be a bad idea," he said in a voice that scraped over her erogenous zones. "For both of us."

She checked her clothes to make sure they hadn't gone up in flames. He was right. It would be a very bad idea.

But at the moment, *very bad* was sounding *really great*. Because once again, he smelled amazing. His T-shirt strained over his biceps and pecs but was loose over his flat, hard abs. When he turned to lead her through the house, the material stretched tight over his athletic-looking back. And then there was his butt in those basketball shorts. Edible. That's how it looked, and she wanted to sink her teeth into—

He turned to say something and caught her staring. She quickly pretended to be watching her own feet. Look at that, her heels were looking a little worn. "Pretty hardwood floors," she said.

"You weren't looking at the floor. You were looking at my ass."

Giving up, she sighed. "Okay, yes," she said as primly as she could. "But it's impolite of you to point it out."

He laughed.

She walked past him so that *she* was in the lead, thinking at least now he couldn't see her face.

"Grace?" he said from behind her.

"Yeah?"

"Your ass is ogle-worthy too."

She bit her lower lip to try to keep her smile in and kept walking. "We're being inappropriate again."

"You started it."

Going out the back door, he led her around the pool to the small guesthouse. There he pushed open the door, dropped her bags inside, and very purposely remained in the entryway.

He was right—the place was tiny. But cute. The living room, kitchen, and bedroom were all open to each other, done in soft blues and neutral colors.

"The bed's behind that screen," Josh said, pointing. "The kitchen's minimally supplied. You've got wireless, but the electrical is crap. Can't run the toaster and the heater at the same time. I'll work on that this weekend."

Grace turned to him in surprise. In her experience, men were either cerebral or good with their hands. And never the two shall meet. She'd pegged this "late-bloomer nerd" as the cerebral type. Not too much of a stretch, given that he was an MD. "You do electrical?"

He gestured to himself. "Not just a pretty face."

This made her laugh. "I just meant because you're a doctor. Doctors usually can't do anything other than...well, doctor."

"Hey, don't judge us all by our pedigree."

She met his gaze, knowing she'd just done exactly that. And she of all people knew better. "Are you really not coming in?"

His eyes darkened, and her body reacted with feminine predictability. "If I come in, you're going to miss your interview."

Her heart skipped a beat. "Oh."

His mouth curved very slightly. "Not in our best interests," he said softly, giving her another of those searing looks that made her knees wobble. "Lock the door behind me, Grace."

When he was gone, she let out a shaky breath and locked the door. She looked over her new place and felt...right at home. She'd had a lovely childhood home back East but she hadn't lived there in years. She'd gone to college, then on to her own places, none of which she'd stayed in too long. She'd attributed that to restlessness, the need to climb the ladder of success. But it'd never mattered what size her place had been or how much it cost; she'd never really found home.

Obviously, this wasn't it either, but the fact that she wanted to unpack and nest reminded her that it had been a damn long time since she'd felt at home like this.

Too long.

"A week," she said out loud to remind herself what she'd told Josh. "This is only for a part of a week."

She did her Skype interview and scored a request to come to the Portland offices for an in-person interview in a few days. Then she texted her parents with the news. She wasn't a complete loser! After that, she left for her modeling job, dropping Anna in town at the girl's request.

To Grace's surprise, Anna was waiting by her car when she came back out of the gallery an hour later. "Aw," she said to the frowning Anna, "you missed me. How sweet."

Anna snorted and got into Grace's car, then sat there like a queen while Grace wrestled with getting the wheelchair folded and into the trunk. "You know," Grace finally said, swiping her brow with her arm, "if you learned how to do that yourself, you could have your own vehicle. One of those adapted vehicles that you could drive yourself."

"Oh, actually I do usually handle it by myself."

Grace gave her a long look, and Anna lifted her hands. "Sorry! But people like to help me, you know? Makes them feel better about being with me." She smiled sweetly.

Grace shook her head. "Don't give me that crap. You were totally amusing yourself by watching me fumble ineptly with your chair."

"Or that." Anna grinned. "You and Josh are the only ones to call me on this stuff, you know that?"

"What else does Josh call you on?"

Anna shrugged. "He says I'm not good at toeing the line. And that he'd get me a special van to drive but that I'm too angry to be on the road."

"So get unangry. Learn to toe the line. I could teach you. Once upon a time, I was most excellent at toeing the line. At least the pretense of it."

"He treats me like a child."

"Then stop acting like one," Grace said. "And while we're on the subject, he cares about you very much. You know that, right?"

Anna shrugged.

"I figured you didn't know, seeing as you treat him the way you do."

"And how do I treat him?" Anna asked.

"How do you think?"

Another shrug.

"I bet if you treated him nicer, he'd loosen up a bit with the reins," Grace said.

"He's not the boss of me."

"So you can do whatever you want."

"Exactly," Anna said.

"And what is it that you want?"

Anna didn't answer for so long that Grace figured she wasn't going to get one. But then Anna finally spoke. "I want my mom and dad back."

Grace kept her eyes on the road but her throat went tight as she nodded. "I can only imagine. But it makes me doubly glad you have other family. Toby, for instance."

"Yeah, the rug rat's pretty cute."

"And Josh," Grace said.

Anna turned away and looked out the window. "Anyone ever tell you that you drive like a girl?"

"I am a girl. Don't you have class today?"

"Missed the bus."

"I'll drive you."

"Missed class already."

Grace looked at her. "Call me crazy, but I'm getting the feeling you don't like your cooking and writing classes."

"Gee, ya think?"

"So why don't you go for something more challenging?"

"Like?"

"Like a degree," Grace said.

"In what? I'm in a wheelchair."

"Are your eyes and brain paralyzed?"

Anna rolled her unparalyzed eyes.

"What interests you?" Grace asked.

"Getting home to see if Devon's there."

"Is he a good guy? Good to you?"

A shrug. "Yeah."

"What do you like about him?"

"He's hot."

"Boys are like drugs," Grace said. "You're supposed to just say no."

This earned her another eye roll. "He doesn't care that I'm..." Anna waved at her legs. "He thinks I'm pretty. And... sexy."

There was something about the way Anna said it that made Grace take another look at her. "You are pretty. You're *beautiful*. But a guy that age thinks *everyone's* sexy."

There it was again, the odd look flickering in Anna's eyes. Uncertainty. "Anna. He's not pushing you for anything you're not ready for, is he?"

"I'm ready for anything."

"Sex. Is he pushing you for sex?"

"I'm paralyzed, not stupid. I'm not a pushover, for anyone."

"Good," Grace said, not feeling better, because Anna's posture didn't match her words.

"Yeah. Good," Anna said.

Grace sighed and took her home. In the driveway, Anna didn't make a move to get out, just faced the side window as she spoke. "So how old were you when you first..."

Grace did the math. Anna had been paralyzed and lost her mom at age sixteen, most likely before she'd had her first anything, leaving her without an influential female in her life. And Grace sincerely doubted Anna would go to Josh about these things. "Forty-five."

Anna snorted.

"Look," Grace said. "There's no right age. Just as long as the guy is right. Are you telling me that Devon is right?"

"He's into me."

"That's not enough. You have to be into him. And not just because he's hot either. You're so smart, Anna. You need a guy to be into you *and* be just as smart."

Another shrug.

"Just promise me you won't let him rush you."

Anna went noncommittal on that, rolling inside the house.

Grace went to the guesthouse and opened her laptop, where she began to weed through the interested applicants for the nanny position. First up was a patient of Josh's, and all she wanted to know was if Josh was still single. Delete. The next applicant was sixty-five and had asked if there was a retirement plan.

Also deleted.

Feeling somewhat discouraged and desperate, Grace finally found two semi-promising applicants and set up interviews for Josh. Then she got Toby from the bus.

"Arf," he said in greeting.

"Arf," she said back. "But I was sort of hoping we could speak in English today too. 'Cause we're going to make pizza for dinner, and dogs don't eat pizza."

"I like pizza!"

She smiled, took his hand, and walked him the half block home. They worked on his handwriting and made pizza, and after that, worked on their Jedi lightsaber skills, dueling in the living room.

"Gotta be the bestest Jedi warrior in all the universe," Toby told her, swinging his lightsaber.

"Awesome," Grace said. "Why?"

"'Cause if I'm the bestest, then my mom'll come."

Grace hunkered before him and stroked a lock of hair from his face. "Actually, I think you already *are* the bestest Jedi in the universe."

He beamed at her for the compliment but went back to practicing. *Swoosh, vrrmm-swoosh.*

Josh got home at eight, looking hot as hell in wrinkled dark blue scrubs and athletic shoes, his hair rumpled, his eyes tired and unguarded. Toby and Tank jumped him on the spot, and the three of them wrestled on the floor like a pack of wolves until suddenly Toby sat straight up, looking green.

"Uh-oh," he said, and threw up on Josh's shoes.

Josh grimaced but handled the situation with calm efficiency, scooping up a distraught Toby, cleaning the mess, and corralling the crazy pug that was running worried circles around a sniffling Toby. Finally, Josh sat the now-shirtless Toby on the kitchen counter and handed him a glass of water. "What did you have for dinner?"

"Pizza," Grace said.

Josh slid Grace a look.

"No pepperoni," she said quickly. "It was on his list of no-nos. Just sausage."

"He's allergic to pork."

Oh, shit. *Double shit.* "It didn't say that on the list. It just said salami and pepperoni."

"Because he doesn't like sausage."

Grace looked at Toby, who was clutching his lightsaber and staring at his bare feet. And she got it. He'd wanted to please her.

Triple shit. She was such an idiot. "I'm so sorry. Do we need to do anything?"

"I think his body took care of it," Josh said dryly. "And where was Anna? She should have known better."

"She went out with friends."

"She was supposed to stay home tonight."

"She said she'd be back before she turned into a pumpkin," Grace told him. "An exact quote."

Josh's mouth was grim but he kept his thoughts on the matter to himself. Grace busied herself picking up the disaster that the house had somehow become over the past few hours. In the living room, in the middle of the chaos, Tank lay on the couch. He was on his back, feet straight up in the air like he was dead, snoring away.

"You don't have to clean up," Josh said, coming into the room behind her, stopping her from picking up by taking her hand in his and pulling her around to face him.

She stared up at him as time stuttered to a stop for a second. Yearning. Aching…

He looked into her eyes, then broke the spell with clear reluctance, stepping back from her as he noticed the puppy, looking like road kill. "How the hell did he learn how to get up on the couch?"

Toby had spent the better part of an hour teaching the pug how to jump that high. Grace nudged the sleepy Tank down, earning a reproachful look and a soft snort. "Sorry about Anna," she said to Josh. "But maybe if you let up on her just a little—"

"You're Toby's babysitter. Not mine."

Right. Gee, she'd almost forgotten there for a moment. Well, clearly she'd done enough here for the night. She grabbed her purse and headed for the door.

"Grace—"

"It's late," she said. She'd had a lifetime to learn how to read the people around her, down to the slightest nuances. Her parents' moods had been quiet, subtle. So she knew exactly when she'd overstayed her welcome. And that was now. "'Night, Josh."

Chapter 11

In heaven, chocolate has no calories and is served as the main course.

The next night when Josh got home, Toby was just getting out of the tub. Grace made a quiet escape to the pool house, which Josh knew was to give him some alone time with his son.

Or she wasn't all that interested to be in his company.

His fault, of course. He'd been an ass the night before. "Tobes," he said, "get into your pj's. I'll be right back." He paused, watching Toby pull on his pj bottoms, sans underwear. "What's with the commando thing?"

Toby shrugged. "Feels best."

Hard to argue with that. "Pick out a book. Give me five minutes." He jogged through the house and caught up with Grace at the back door. "Hey."

"Hey yourself." She smiled, and it was sweet, if not quite reaching her eyes.

Also his fault. He searched for a way to make it right and came up with nothing. Which really, he figured, was for the best.

"Well," she said, a little too brightly, "see you tomorrow—"

Suddenly unable to let her go until he'd at least *tried* to fix this, he caught her hand in his.

She went still, even dug her heels in a little as he turned her to face him.

"I was an ass last night," Josh said.

Grace met his gaze and felt his struggle. She told herself not to care, but she couldn't help herself. "You were tired."

"Okay, so I was a tired ass. I'm still sorry."

This time when she smiled at him, it was a real one. She had no idea what it was about a guy who could say he was sorry…

"Everything go okay today?" he asked.

"You have two interviews for babysitters on Friday."

He nodded. "Good. Thanks. You want to sit in?"

"I'll be in Portland on an interview myself."

Something came and went in his eyes—regret?—but he nodded. "Your Skype interview went well, then."

"Very." She'd gotten the call today that they'd liked her and wanted another interview.

"That's great," he said.

"Yeah." She was trying to work up some enthusiasm. It was, after all, her future, and she wanted a good one. But she also wanted to stop thinking about it. It wasn't hard to distract herself with the view.

She could tell by Josh's dress clothes that he'd worked in his office today. He wore dark trousers that fit his butt perfectly—which she knew because she'd checked it out when he'd bent to pick up Toby earlier. His button-down was dark chocolate brown and shoved up to the elbows. No stethoscope or tie today, but his five o'clock shadow had a five o'clock shadow, and his eyes…His eyes gave her a lot, telling her how much he'd seen, done, been through. When he looked like this, a little rumpled, a lot tired, it softened his features, allowing her to see more of him than he'd probably like. He didn't feel quite so impenetrable to her tonight. He felt… human. Just a regular man, a man who'd most likely saved someone today, probably more than one someone. He did more every day than she could possibly imagine, and she admired him for it, greatly.

She also wanted to hug him. Instead, she reached up to push a lock of hair off his forehead, then caught herself. But before she could pull back, he wrapped his fingers around her wrist and slowly reeled her in.

"Thanks for today," he said quietly, his other hand going to her waist.

She stared at his chest, trying not to notice how her pulse had leaped. "You don't have to keep thanking me. You're paying me."

"I'll do both. And speaking of paying you…"

"Uh-oh," she said, tilting her head up to his.

"I think I need another week to find the right nanny," he said. "You up for that?"

Was she up for a second week of being overpaid and having another excuse to put off her life? "Sure."

"Arf, arf, arf!" came Tank's bark.

"Arf, arf, arf!" came another bark.

Toby's.

Josh dropped his forehead to Grace's shoulder and sighed.

"He spoke English all day," she said. "Until you came home."

He lifted his head and looked at her. "So it's me. He's barking because of me."

Grace hesitated, knowing she had to tell him but hating to add to his full plate of things to worry about. "You know he wants to be a Jedi warrior, right?"

"*Everyone* in Lucky Harbor knows he wants to be a Jedi warrior."

"Yes, but did you know he wants to be the best Jedi warrior ever so that his mom will come home?"

Josh stared at her for a blink, then closed his eyes. "Shit."

The barking increased in intensity, and he pulled free. "I have to go."

"I know." And she did know. A guy like Josh would always have to go: to work, to his family...to everyone but the woman in his life he didn't have time for, or want.

She knew this. She'd been okay with this. So when exactly had that begun to change?

The next morning, Grace woke up early to work on Jeanine's books for her pottery shop. It was icy cold, so she cranked on the heat and then went to the kitchen, where she'd stowed the few groceries she'd bought yesterday. Trying to decide between yogurt and a bagel, she thumbed through her texts, stopping at one from her father.

Hi Pumpkin, your mother tells me how well you're doing. Expect to hear great things from you! Keep it up. Love, Dad

Still staring at the text, she popped a bagel into the toaster. Something sizzled, and then the lights went out. And then Josh's words came back to her, a little too late.

Can't use the heater and the toaster at the same time.

"*Crap.*" There wasn't much to see by, just the predawn light filtering in through the windows. No flames. That was good. But what if she'd started an electrical fire in the walls? Worried, she threw on a robe and ran for the big house. The back slider was locked, but she could see through the living room to the kitchen table. Toby was sitting on it, Indian-style, with Tank in his lap. The two of them were eating cereal out of a huge plastic container. The *same* huge plastic container.

Not a surprise. Tank loved anything edible. Especially if Toby was eating it.

Grace waved. Tank leaped off the table and came barreling at her. Losing traction, he slid on the tile floor and crashed face-first into the slider door. Bouncing back on his butt, he sat there a moment, dazed, before shaking his oversized head, barking at her.

Grace, who'd been working with him on commands since she'd seen that doggie training show, pointed at him. "Tank, *quiet*."

Tank sat.

He did not, however, stop barking. Grace sighed and caught Toby's eye, gesturing to the locked door.

This went no better than it had the last time she'd been locked out. Apparently thinking she was waving, Toby waved back, then arced his lightsaber through the air. "Toby. Come open the door."

He finished *whooshing* first, then having apparently satisfied himself that he'd thoroughly impressed her, opened the door.

Tank was still barking.

"Tank, *quiet*! Toby, where's your dad?"

Toby pointed in the vague direction of the hall. Grace headed that way. The first door—Toby's—was open, revealing a bedroom that looked like a disaster zone of epic proportions.

Anna's door was shut.

Josh's bedroom was at the end, partially open, allowing Grace to peek in. And oh, goodness, there he was, sprawled out flat on his back in the middle of the bed. He was shirtless, and the sheets rode low enough on his hips to reveal a mouth-watering chest, abs to die for, and a happy trail that vanished beneath the sheet and made her want to do the same.

Probably he was naked, and just the thought gave her a hot flash. "Josh?"

He didn't move, so she stepped into the room. She set a hand on his shoulder, but before she could say his name again, he'd grabbed her and tugged hard, rolling her beneath him.

Yep, he was naked.

Very, very naked.

"Mmm," he rumbled. "Like the robe. It's soft." Dipping his head, he nipped at her throat. "I'm over the no-kissing thing, Grace. I want a new deal."

She let out a breathless laugh, her hands wandering over his shoulders and back because, hello, she was only human. He was warm and solid and felt so good nuzzling her neck. Not at all sure he wasn't still in dreamland, she nudged him. "You awake?"

"Shit." He sighed. "Yeah. And Toby's probably up."

Josh was "up," too, and the thought gave her a shiver of arousal. "Toby *is* up. He's eating an entire box of cereal out of the same bowl as Tank."

"Perfect." Josh rolled off her and then stood—still very naked, impressively so. And utterly unconcerned about it in the way that only a man could possibly be.

"Um," she said, losing her train of thought, riveted to the part of him that was the *most* awake, telling herself to close her eyes and preserve his modesty.

But she didn't close her eyes.

He grabbed a pair of jeans off a chair and pulled them on, adjusting himself and giving her another hot flash.

Think, Grace. You came here for a reason. "I've got a problem."

"What now? Anna?"

"No."

He finished buttoning his fly. He stood there, hair tousled, no shirt, no socks, nothing but those loose, low-riding jeans, and it was damn hard to think. "I turned on the heater and—"

He lifted his head. "Not the toaster."

"And the toaster," she admitted.

"Shit, Grace." He headed out the door.

"Sorry!" Feeling like an idiot, she flopped back onto his bed, staring at the ceiling. *Such an idiot.* And since she was, she rolled over and pressed her face into Josh's still-warm pillow, inhaling him.

"What are you doing?"

She squeaked in horrified surprise at Josh's voice and leaped off the bed to find him in the doorway.

"Were you going back to sleep in my bed?" he asked, looking amused.

And since that was far less embarrassing than the truth, she lifted a shoulder. Noncommittal.

Not fooled, he shook his head and tugged her up to go with him to check on the guesthouse. Toby tagged along as well, wanting to see the "big fire!"

Luckily there was no big fire. There was no fire at all. She'd only tripped an electrical breaker, but she'd learned her lesson. And that lesson was, don't go to Josh's bedroom or she'd see things that she wanted but couldn't have.

"I wanted to put out the big flames with my lightsaber," Toby said, disappointed. "That'd make me the bestest warrior ever." He paused. "After you, Daddy. 'Cause you're the first bestest."

Grace's heart cracked in two, and she looked at Josh. He crouched before Toby, hands on his skinny little hips. Toby stared down at his battered Star Wars athletic shoes.

Josh put a finger beneath Toby's chin and gently tilted up his face. "You're already the best warrior there is, Little Man. The very best."

"I'm too small to be the bestest. I want to be as big as you."

"It's not about size."

"It's 'cause I don't have a mommy. Sam and Tommy and Aiden and Kyle, they all have mommies. Kyle's mommy told Tommy's mommy that I don't have one because you wouldn't share me."

Josh didn't say anything for a moment. When he spoke, his voice was a little hoarse, but it was filled with conviction. "This might be hard for you to understand, but once in a very great while, sharing isn't the best thing to do."

"But *everyone* has a mommy," Toby said. "How can I be the bestest Jedi without one?"

"I don't have a mom," Josh told him. "Does that make me less of a Jedi?"

Toby shook his head adamantly. "No, you're still the bestest, Daddy."

"Then how about we be tied?"

Toby thought about that, then nodded solemnly. When Josh opened his arms, Toby walked right into them, curling tightly into Josh's chest.

Grace didn't drop to her knees and crawl into Josh's arms too.

But she wanted to.

Josh watched his son run back to the big house ahead of him and Grace, not surprised when Grace stopped him with a question in her eyes.

"Tommy's mom knew Toby's mom," he said quietly. "But she has only one side of the story."

"What's the other side?"

That Josh had grown up the nerd, the bookworm, the kid who got frisked for his lunch money and stuffed into the lockers. By the time he'd gone to college, he'd finally grown and learned how to fight back. But even as recently as five years ago, a gorgeous woman blowing through town for a wedding and picking him for one hot night together had been more than a little shocking.

And flattering.

He'd fallen for the charming words and amazing body, hook, line, and sinker. And then gotten his heart broken, just the same as Toby. "The other side of the story isn't relevant," he finally said.

"I hear ya," Grace said softly, making him wonder what kind of a story *she* had.

But it was none of his business, even if she was staring up at him with those gorgeous, heart-baring eyes. Open. Sweet.

Welcoming.

He could drown in her if he let himself. The trick was not to let himself.

On Friday, Josh got up at 4:00 a.m. to squeeze in a rock climb with Matt. It'd been weeks since he'd gone, and he needed the icy predawn air, the Olympic Mountains...Plus Matt had said he'd kick Josh's ass if he didn't show.

Not too worried about that ridiculous threat, Josh got ready. He'd seen Ty yesterday when their paths had crossed in the hospital, and Ty had claimed that Matt had been seen muttering something about diamond rings.

Josh had to hear this for himself. He checked on a sleeping Toby, then made sure Anna was in her room. He left her a note reminding her that she'd promised to get Toby dressed, fed, and to the bus stop on time.

As he quietly exited the house, he was surprised to see Grace heading toward her car as well. "What's up?" he asked.

"Heading to Portland," she said. "It's an early interview, and it's a long drive."

Three hours. She was wearing another suit that was all business, softened by high-heeled sandals that had a bow on her ankles. Her hair was in a sophisticated twist, made cute by a few loose strands brushing her temples. It was quite a different appearance than the bathrobe look she'd rocked a few days before, which he'd loved. But he loved this too. She looked like a million bucks, which wasn't why he ached at the sight of her. He didn't care what she wore. There was just something about her that made him feel like a kid on Christmas morning. Like he couldn't wait to see beyond the packaging, couldn't wait to touch. And not just physically, which was what really disconcerted him.

He wanted to touch her from the inside out, which made no fucking sense at all. "Good luck today," he said. "I hope you get what you want."

"It's not what I want. It's what I *require*," she said, and when he arched a brow, she sighed. "Never mind. It's just one of those things my parents always say. Requirements need to be met before needs."

He gave her a longer look, beyond the pretty packaging now, and realized she was taut with tension. "You don't talk much about yourself or your past," he said.

"Nothing really to talk about."

"Everyone has something in their past to talk about."

She lifted a shoulder. "I had a boring childhood."

She was even better than he was at protecting herself. Interesting. "Doesn't sound boring, what with the rocket scientist and all…"

Another shrug. And though he hated when people pushed him for answers he didn't want to give, he couldn't help but push her. "What about *after* your childhood?"

Her gaze slid to his. "You mean like college? Jobs? Boyfriends? Which?"

"Yes."

She let out a short laugh. "I went to college in New York. Interned at a big financial institution and got my CPA. Then got a banking job complete with a nice place to live, a few boyfriends, yada yada. My parents were proud. The end. That answer all your questions?"

Not even close. She was suddenly as defensive as hell, and he was good at reading the symptoms and coming up with conclusions. She hadn't been as happy as she'd wanted to be. "Parental expectations suck."

This forced another laugh out of her. "A little bit, yeah. But they just want the best for me. They always have."

Josh knew the value of silence, and he was rewarded when she sighed. "I'm adopted," she said. "So this whole being an overachieving genius isn't exactly natural for me."

He absorbed what she said, and all she didn't—that she clearly didn't feel she was equipped with the right genes to be on the same level as her adoptive family. Just the thought of her feeling that way gave him a physical ache in his chest. "I hope that they took into account what your hopes and dreams for yourself were, not just theirs."

"What they took into account was that my IQ was high enough to do well for myself."

"They had your IQ tested?" he asked.

"When I was in middle school, to help determine my career path."

"When you were in middle school," he repeated. In middle school, Josh's dad had played football with him, not had his brain tested.

"There's no time to waste when you have high achieving to do," she said.

"In *middle* school?"

"Hey, they love me," she said. "In their own way."

"By making you try to be like them?"

"Not *exactly* like them," she said. "I never did quite get the hang of science, which was a huge disappointment. And anyway, I *wanted* to be like them."

No doubt this was a big part of why she worked so hard at finding the right job now. To please them. To show she deserved the Brooks name.

He didn't give a shit how smart her family was; he wanted to wrap his hands around their necks and rattle the teeth out of their heads for seeing that the baby they'd adopted had grown into an amazing woman.

"What about you?" she asked. "Did your parents expect a lot from you?"

"They expected me to be happy."

"Aw." Her mouth curved into a soft smile. "That's just about the loveliest thing I've ever heard. So are you? Happy?"

Well if that wasn't the million-dollar question and far too complicated to answer at this hour. Instead, he took the computer case from her and set it on her backseat before opening her driver's door. The door didn't stick for him, and she rolled her eyes. "I shouldn't be surprised that you're good with your hands," she said.

His smile heated, and she put her hands to her hot cheeks. "I didn't mean that the way it sounded."

"It's okay. It's true. I'm very good with my hands."

She gave him a laughing shove. "It doesn't matter how good you are," she said. "Since we're not going there."

Yeah. Damn.

Grace looked away, then back into his eyes. "I'll be back in time to get Toby from the bus stop."

"Thanks. I got a bunch more calls on the nanny position."

"Want me to weed out the crazies?" she asked.

"More than I want my next breath."

She laughed again, and the sound of it made him want to smile. "Let me know if you need anything," he said.

"What about if *you* need something?" she asked.

"What?"

"What if *you* need anything, Dr. Scott? You're always the one doing all the caregiving—in your job, here at your house, everywhere. I realize I'm not exactly the best nanny/dog walker, but I'd be happy to help. If you need anything…"

Something actually fluttered in his chest. "You are the perfect nanny/dog walker," he said. "But I'm not all that great with accepting help."

Her mouth quirked. "Tell me something I don't know." She patted him on the chest, got into her car, and in her sexy suit and heels, drove off.

Chapter 12

And on the Eighth day, God created chocolate.

On Monday morning, Grace got up early for a few hours of floral deliveries, and then an hour with Anderson, the local hardware store owner. His bookkeeping system had crashed, and he needed her help. When she asked why he'd called her, he'd said, "because everyone knows you're the go-to accountant in town."

She wasn't sure how she felt about that.

She'd just gotten back to Josh's place and was slipping out of her wedge sandals when she heard the knock at the door. She looked out the glass into the dawn's purple glow and felt her heart leap.

It was Josh, dressed for his office in dark pants, a dark slate button-down, and a dark edgy expression.

She opened the door, and because they were chronic idiots, they stared at each other before she stepped back to let him in.

He shook his head.

Right. He wasn't coming in. Because it was a *bad idea*. Disappointed, she bent to pick up her computer bag, and when she straightened, she collided with Josh.

Who'd apparently changed his mind about coming in. Her hands went to his chest to keep her balance, and the warm strength of him radiated through his shirt. Maybe her hands slid over him, just a little.

Or a lot.

She couldn't help herself. He had a great chest. Great abs too. He had a six-pack— No, she corrected, her fingers wandering…An *eight*-pack. And then there were those side muscles, the obliques, the ones that made even smart women stupid.

"Grace." His voice sounded husky and just a little tight as he grabbed her hands, making her realize they'd been headed south.

"I'm sorry." She tried to snatch them free, but he held on. "I guess I'm feeling a little conflicted about what I want here," she murmured.

"So the mixed signals," he said. "You're doing that on purpose?"

"No." She paused. "Maybe." She grimaced. "*I don't know.*"

"It's okay, take your time." He backed her up against the doorjamb. "You just let me know when you decide."

At the connection of his body to hers from chest to thighs and everything in between, she heard herself whimper in pleasure, the sound shocking in its need and hunger. "Maybe I was hasty about the not-going-there thing," she whispered. "Maybe the not-going-there thing needs to be temporarily revisited."

His eyes were still dark. Still edgy. "You have my undivided attention."

Actually, she didn't. His hands were gliding down her legs and back up again, beneath the hem of her skirt now.

"Josh?"

"Still here."

No kidding. His fingers. Lord, his fingers. "Kiss me," she managed. "That'll help me figure this out—"

She hadn't even finished the sentence before he'd lowered his head and covered her mouth with his. Gentle. Then not so gentle, and when she kissed him back, she felt the growl reverberate deep inside his chest, a soulful, hungry sound that made her go damp.

"Decide anything yet?" he asked, his voice thrillingly rough when he pulled back.

"Another minute." She tugged him back to her.

Apparently that worked for him because he kissed her, his mouth open on hers, igniting flames along her every nerve ending. Her purse clunked to the floor, and her arms wound up around his neck, her hands gliding into his soft, silky hair.

His hands were just as possessive, going straight to her bottom, squeezing, then lifting her up.

The only barrier between them being his pants and her sundress, which was hiked high enough now that it was really only her panties. "Toby? Where's Toby?"

"Already on the bus." His mouth was busy at her ear, his movements masculine and carnal, arousing her almost beyond bearing.

"Anna—" she gasped.

"In her cave, probably still sleeping. Or stirring her cauldron." He slapped his hand to the lock on the door.

The click of it sliding home hung in the air along with their heavy breathing as they stared at each other.

"So we're doing this?" she asked. "We're—" She broke off on a startled gasp when the halter top of her dress gave.

He'd untied her.

"Okay," she breathed on a shaky laugh. "So we are. We're doing this." She let the material slip away from her, baring her breasts.

With a rough groan, he dipped his head and kissed her collarbone. Then lower. When he licked a nipple as if she were a decadent dessert, she heard herself sigh in sheer pleasure.

He pulled back just enough to blow lightly on her wet skin, eliciting a bone-deep shiver. "You're going to be late for work," she murmured, unbuttoning his shirt. In her impatience, she tore off two buttons.

His mouth was on her, gliding from one nipple to the other, then gently nibbling, and he didn't respond.

Quivering from head to toe, she arched back against the wall, giving him more access. "*Josh*."

"You're right," he said silkily, giving her a teasing nip as he moved between her thighs, rocking against her. "I'm going to be late."

She let out an unintelligible sound, and Josh lifted his head. "Tell me you want this, Grace. Because I do. At this moment, I'm right where I want to be." He kissed his way to the outer shell of her ear, his breath hot, chasing a shiver down her spine.

At the moment...

She understood the words, understood the meaning behind them. "I want this," she said, pressing against him. "I want you." She tugged off his shirt, running her fingers over his abs, which quivered at her touch. Her dress was pretty much a belt around her waist by now. No deterrent for Josh, who dipped his head, taking in her bright red thong with a U.S. flag front and center.

"God bless America," he said.

She laughed. He had one hand on her ass, the other on her breast, which was still wet from his mouth. She was halfway to orgasm, and she was laughing.

So was he.

Then their eyes met. The laughter faded, replaced by a driving need to do this. Turning, he gently pushed her to the couch. He followed her down, covering her body with his own as he kissed her, his warm hands shoving her dress up a little more, his fingers sliding to the edge of her panties.

And then beneath.

"I love your sundresses," he said against her mouth. "You always look so cool and calm, except for your eyes. Your eyes show it all."

"My panic?"

"Your passion," he breathed. "For everything."

"I—" She gasped when he slid a finger into her. Then again when it left her, but before she could make a protest, he was back with two fingers, his thumb stroking right over the center of her gravity. "Oh my God."

"Good?"

She bit his shoulder rather than cry out with exactly how good it was.

"So wet," he said hoarsely, his fingers working magic, stroking her just right so that the pressure built shockingly fast.

"Josh—"

He kissed her deep, his tongue mimicking his fingers, moving in the same unhurried motion as she writhed beneath him, lost, completely gone. When she came, it shocked her into crying out his name as she rode the wave.

He stayed with her to the end, patient enough to let her come down at her own speed. When she blinked him into view, she didn't know whether to be embarrassed or thank him. "Has it really been a whole year for you since you did this?" she managed.

"And two months."

"You don't seem out of practice."

"Like getting back on a bike..." He slid down her body. Before, he'd simply scraped her panties aside for quick access, but now he hooked his fingers in the material low on her hips and slowly pulled them down her legs.

"I—" she started, with no idea where she was going with that sentence because he put a big palm on each leg and spread them for his viewing pleasure. Leaning in, he kissed first one inner thigh, then the other.

And then in between.

"Um—" Again, she broke off, unable to remember what the hell she'd wanted to say. She couldn't even remember her own name. She was rocking up into his mouth, biting her lip to keep herself quiet. This wasn't quite effective; she was still making noises, horrifyingly needy noises and little hurry-up whispers and pants as she burst again.

Two orgasms.

Always she'd had to strain for even one, and he'd just given her *two* with shockingly little effort. "Oh my God."

He crawled up her body and kissed her. "Oh my God good?"

"*Amazing.*"

"Amazing works. Grace..."

She met his gaze and saw the seriousness in it. "What?"

"I don't have any condoms."

She stared at him. "*What?*"

His laugh was low and a little wry. "You heard the part about a year and two months, right?"

She let out a very disappointed breath, body still humming, mind whirling. "I'm just off my period. It's been a long time for me, too, and I'm clean. We could—"

"No," he said softly but with utter steel laced beneath. "I'm clean, too, but no. No taking chances."

She figured this had something to do with how he'd gotten Toby, so she nodded and blew out another breath. It didn't help. She wanted him, bad.

"It's okay." His smile was tight as he shifted, making her extremely aware that he was still wound up tight, and hard. *Very* hard. Sitting up, she pushed him back and straddled him.

"Grace—"

"Shhh," she said, kissing her way down his incredible chest, paying special homage to every muscle she came across, and there were many. "Since you're already late..." When she scraped her teeth over one of his flat nipples, he sucked in a breath. His head thunked back to the couch as he let out a heartfelt groan, his hands going straight to her ass.

Clearly, it was his favorite part of her anatomy.

As for *his* anatomy, she couldn't possibly pick one favorite part.

His entire body was an erotic playground. She spent a moment on his abs, licking him like a lollipop, then slid farther to her knees on the hardwood floor. He was straining the front of his pants, a situation easily remedied. She unbuttoned, unzipped, and slid her hands inside, wrapping them around a most impressive erection. This elicited another rough sound from Josh. Leaning over him, she began to kiss her way up his length, prompting him to slide his hands in her hair and—

His phone went off.

"Ignore it," he said hoarsely.

She nodded and readjusted her grip, starting again at the base with her tongue. His fingers tightened in her hair, more a show of need than domination, as he didn't try to direct her. He groaned, and then…his phone buzzed again.

"Fuck." He let go of her to fish through his pocket, pulling out his phone, glaring at it. "*Fuck.*" He sagged back and stared up at the ceiling.

She rose up on her knees and looked at him. "Problem?"

"I have to go." But he didn't move.

"Josh?"

"Yeah." He let out a slow breath and straightened, pulling her off the floor and into his lap. He held her close for a minute, kissed her shoulder, then her neck while he straightened out her dress for her. When he was done with that, he kissed her mouth. He sighed again, then set her on the couch next to him and got to his feet. He stuffed himself back into his pants, which appeared to be *very* uncomfortable. Shaking his head, he made an adjustment, then grabbed his shirt from the floor. He put it on inside out, swore, yanked it off, then righted it and tried again.

"You going to work like that?" she asked.

He looked down at his hard-on. "That bad?"

"Boy Scouts could camp in there."

He snorted, and Grace found herself laughing again. She was

trying to remember that they weren't well suited, that he was the opposite of everything she'd ever wanted, but it wasn't working.

Not even close.

She wanted to tug down his pants and finish what she started.

"Christ, Grace," Josh said on a groan. "Don't look at me like that." He closed his eyes. "I'm standing here trying to mentally recite chemical elements to calm down, and you're looking at me like you want to eat me for breakfast."

She slapped a hand over her eyes. "Oh my God. I was not."

"Yeah, you were."

Okay, she had been doing exactly that. "Sorry!" She paused, lowering her hands. "And you can recite the chemical elements?"

His hands gripped her arms and hauled her up against him. He kissed her and said, very quietly, very seriously, "We okay?"

"Well." She gave him an embarrassed smile. "*I* am…"

Letting out a laugh, Josh let her go and turned for the door. His cell phone was vibrating from the depth of his pocket again. He was already on it before the door shut behind him.

Grace took a moment to fix herself, even though the truth was she needed a lot more than a moment. Her hair was a complete wreck, her body still quivering, but she couldn't seem to get rid of the grin that came from two pretty great orgasms. She did the best she could to look presentable and entered the big house, nearly tripping over Anna. "Sorry!"

Anna studied her for a beat. "You just missed Josh."

Grace worked on looking innocent as they went into the kitchen. "Oh?"

Anna shook her head. "Amateur."

Grace sagged, giving up the pretense. Tank was jumping up and down in hopeful entreaty behind his baby gate, snuffling and snorting. Grace released him from his doggie prison. The puppy immediately caught sight of the lightsaber lying on one of the chairs and began posturing, growling fiercely at it.

"You drive him crazy," Anna said. "You know that, right?"

"It's the lightsaber."

Anna rolled her eyes. "My brother. You drive my brother crazy."

"Actually, I'm pretty sure that's you." Grace gave Tank the signal to sit.

He didn't. Instead, he barked.

Grace took a doggie cookie out of a container on the counter. "*Sit.*"

Tank rolled over. Twice.

"Tank, *sit.*"

Tank offered her a paw to shake, and Grace gave up.

"So," Anna said, "are you going to fall for Josh like the other nannies? Because I don't recommend it. Falling for him is the fastest route to getting fired. Or dumped."

"What are you talking about?"

Tank whirled in circles, then rolled again, clearly going through his entire repertoire of tricks for another cookie.

"Didn't you interview your employer before you took the job?" Anna asked Grace.

"Well, I..." Not this time, she hadn't. "This job sort of happened in a hurry."

Plus she hadn't wanted to probe. Which was entirely different from not wanting to know. Because she did want to know.

Bad.

"You never wondered why none of your predecessors are still around?" Anna asked. "Or why such a great guy with such a great family"—she stopped here to flash a grin so similar to Josh's that Grace blinked—"can't keep a nanny? Or a girlfriend? It's because they all fall hard for him. And he doesn't have a heart, so he doesn't fall back."

"Wow," Grace said.

"I know. You really need to get it together."

"No, I mean you're pretty mean. Anyone ever tell you that?"

Anna didn't seem to take this personally at all. "Mean as a snake," she agreed. "I'm majoring in it at college."

"No, you're not. You're majoring in not-going-to-class."

Anna sighed. "Is this going to turn into another lecture?"

"You're taking cooking and a creative writing class," Grace said. "A *saint* would be bored. I'm telling you, try something more challenging."

Anna shrugged.

"But why not?" Grace asked. "I don't get it. If you're smart enough to be as mean as a snake, then you're smart enough to do something with yourself."

"Like?"

"Like whatever you want," Grace said. "It's wide open. Hell, you could play softball if you wanted."

"Hello, I'm in a wheelchair."

"No, I saw it on the Washington University website," Grace said. "They've got a whole handicapped athletic program, including softball and soccer and self-defense classes."

Anna blinked twice.

"Run out of excuses?" Grace asked her.

Anna snorted. "Didn't anyone ever tell you that you're supposed to be nice to the poor handicapped girl?"

"You have to earn nice."

Anna narrowed her eyes, and Grace shrugged. "It's true. You don't get an ass-pass just because you're handicapped, no matter what you think. And to be honest, you don't seem all that handicapped."

Anna sputtered at this. "Are you blind?"

"No. Are you?"

Anna just stared at her. "I'm *paralyzed*."

"I know. You keep telling me."

"I'm paralyzed from a car accident that killed my parents," Anna said with great emphasis. Clearly she had this routine down, and just as clearly, it usually worked for her. "You're supposed to feel sorry for me. Everyone feels sorry for me. It's what they do."

"Listen," Grace said softly. "I *hate* that you went through that. It must have been hell. *No one* should ever have that happen to them." In fact, just thinking about it brought a punch of emotion that blocked Grace's windpipe, for Anna, for Josh. She physically ached for him and what he'd faced, and she had no idea how he'd managed to keep it all together. "But you lived," she reminded Anna softly.

"So? I still can't play soccer."

"Could you before?"

"Yes! I was *great* before."

"Then you're still great," Grace said. "Play wheelchair soccer."

"That's stupid. And pathetic."

"No, stupid and pathetic is not doing anything at all but bitching about not going to Europe, when really, if you wanted to go, you'd just go. I mean, as you keep saying, you're a grown-up."

Anna let out a low, disbelieving laugh. "I take it back. I don't like you better than the last few babysitters at all."

Grace smiled sympathetically. "They babied you, huh?"

This got some spark. "I don't need babying."

"No kidding!"

That got a very small smile out of Anna, but a genuine one. Then her attention turned to the guy coming down the hall from her bedroom in nothing but boxers, yawning.

"He's gone, right?" Devon asked, his voice sleepy and thick. "Your brother?"

"Yep," Anna said.

"You fell asleep on me last night," Devon said.

Anna let out a laugh that was so completely fake that Grace's eyes flew to her, and then to Devon. But Devon either missed that fact entirely or didn't care. He scratched his head, then his chest. If he scratched his ass next, Grace was going to throw up in her mouth a little bit.

"What do you want to do today?" Anna asked him, so clearly wanting him to get dressed and out of the house that Grace nearly shoved him out the door herself. She wanted to tell Anna to grow a set and kick his ass. But when Grace had been Anna's age, she'd have highly resented anyone telling her what to do. In fact, it would have made her do the opposite, so she bit her tongue, hard.

"Thought we'd go to Seattle and hit some stores," Devon said. "The new snowboards are in."

"Don't you have physical therapy?" Grace asked Anna, trying to toss her a life preserver.

But Anna didn't want one. "Seattle sounds great," she said.

"Cool," Devon said. "But I don't have my wallet."

Anna shrugged. "No problem."

Okay, that was it. "You," Grace said, pointing at Devon. "Out."

"What?"

Grace opened the front door and gestured with a jerk of her chin.

"Dude," he said. "I'm not dressed."

"*Dude*, I don't care. Come back when you can pay your own way."

Devon stalked stiffly out, and Grace shut the door on him. Actually, she slammed it.

Anna's eyes narrowed. "Is this your idea of helping me toe the line? Because it sucks."

"There's the line, and there's common sense. You figure out the difference, and we'll talk."

Anna glared at her for a minute, then shrugged. "I'll need a ride to PT in an hour."

"I'll be here." Grace watched Anna vanish down the hallway, then turned to the little pug demon puppy. "So how do you feel about chocolate pancakes?"

"Arf!"

Chapter 13

Beware of chocolate squares; they make you round.

For several days, Josh was up to his eyeballs in patients with the flu and strep throat. Throat cultures and breathing treatments became his favorite words. By the end of the third day, he was practically swaying on his feet in exhaustion. "We done?" he asked Dee, knowing he still had to face the mountain of paperwork on his desk. "Anyone left to see?"

"No." She knocked on wood. "Don't jinx it or someone'll come knocking. Run while you can."

"What about Mrs. Porter? Didn't I see her on the schedule earlier?"

"She was here, but she got tired of waiting. Said you were cute, but not *that* cute, and she'd see you another day."

"What brought her in?" he asked.

"Headache. She said it was probably because she'd lost her glasses and would just get another pair from Walmart later instead of bothering you."

Josh spent twenty minutes at his desk facing the torturous pile of files before he was paged into the ER. One of the on-contract doctors couldn't show up for the first half of their nightshift, and they needed Josh. He called Anna, who informed him she couldn't babysit the rug rat because she had a date. So Josh called Grace. "I hate to ask," he said, "but—"

"I've got him right here. I heard your call with Anna. We're just getting back."

"Back?"

"I took Anna and Toby to see a soccer game."

This surprised him. Anna had been a big soccer player before the accident. Ever since, it was as if she'd erased soccer from her vocabulary. "Really?"

"Wheelchair soccer."

It wasn't often he was rendered speechless. "She went willingly, or did you have to kidnap her at gunpoint?"

"She went willingly," Grace said, sounding amused. "And said she could have done better than half the girls on the field."

An odd emotion blossomed in Josh's chest. "I owe you," he said softly.

"Actually, at the moment, I owe *you*."

Surrounded by hell, his life completely not his own, he found himself smiling for the first time in days. "I'm open to a deal."

"Sounds promising, Dr. Scott. Talk to you later."

Josh was still smiling when he headed into the ER. The shift was a little crazy, but that was the nature of the beast in any hospital. There was a purpose to all of it, to every orchestrated movement, and unlike everywhere else, here he thrived on chaos.

You thrive on the chaos that is Grace Brooks as well...

Grace might think she was winging life at the moment, but everything she did, everyone she helped along the way, everything she said or felt, came from the bottom of her heart.

He loved that.

It was 1:00 a.m. before he left the ER. He had a few hours to get home and sleep before the madness started again.

He was halfway to his car when he got the call.

Mrs. Porter had just come in, DOA.

Josh ran back into the hospital, but of course, there was no rush. Not for the dead. He grabbed the chart. There'd be no official cause of death until the autopsy, but all signs pointed to an aneurysm.

Josh stared down at Mrs. Porter's body in disbelief. The possibility of an aneurysm had never been on his radar. It was a silent killer. So of course he hadn't seen any signs of any impending illness, and it certainly hadn't been in her patient history, which he knew by heart. Over the years, he'd probably spent a total of *months* talking to her. He knew she liked her margaritas frozen, her music soft and jazzy, and was a secret office supply ho. She didn't have much family or any pets, she'd always said she was allergic to both, and she'd never missed a single episode of *Amazing Race*. She'd planned on someday being the oldest winner.

Soon as she could get over her fear of flying.

And now she was dead.

It wasn't his fault. Logically, he knew this, but he felt guilty as hell, and sick. *Sick* that he hadn't moved his patients along faster earlier in the day so that she'd have waited for him. Because if he'd seen her, maybe there'd have been signs, maybe he'd have somehow known that today was different, that she'd really needed medical care and not just a little TLC.

"I'm sorry," he said, touching her hand, tucking it under the blanket alongside her body. "So damned sorry."

Only utter silence greeted him. Devastated him. Still in his scrubs, he drove home in a fog and found Grace asleep on his living room couch. She sat up, sleepy, rumpled, an apologetic smile on her face. "Didn't mean to fall asleep," she said.

He helped her to her feet, then pulled his hands back from her warm body and shoved them into his pockets, not trusting himself to touch her right now. He felt her curiosity but managed to walk her to the guesthouse without a word.

"Josh?" Standing at her door, bathed in the moonlight, she touched his face. "Bad night?"

Her eyes were fathomless, and as always, he knew that if he looked into them for too long, he'd drown.

But he was already drowning.

She shifted closer and brushed her willowy body against his. Soft. Warm. He could bury himself in her right now and find some desperately needed oblivion.

But taking his grief out on her would be an asshole thing to do. "I'm fine." Still numb, he waited until she went inside to go back to the house.

Not to bed, though. No, that wasn't the kind of oblivion he planned to settle for. He went to the cabinet above the fridge for the Scotch, and then to the couch where Grace had fallen asleep waiting for him. It was still warm beneath the blanket from her body heat. And it smelled like her.

He inhaled deep and poured himself a few fingers.

He'd lost track of the number of shots he'd drunk by the time someone knocked softly on the glass slider. When he didn't move, Grace let herself in.

Josh wasn't drunk but he was close as he eyed her approach. She was wearing a camisole and cropped leggings. No shoes. Her hair was down. No makeup. He wanted to tear off her clothes, toss her down to the couch, and bury himself so deep that he couldn't think.

Couldn't feel.

He watched her cross the room, and some of his thoughts must have been obvious because she stopped just short of his reach and gave him a long, assessing look.

"Saw that the lights were on," she said. "You can't sleep."

He shrugged and tossed back another shot.

"I'm sorry about Mrs. Porter."

He went still, swiveling only his gaze in her direction.

"Since you were doing your impression of the typical tall, dark, and annoyingly silent male," she said, "I went to the source. Facebook." She paused. "Mrs. Porter was very sweet. And I know she adored you. You're a good man, Josh. A good doctor. Don't blame yourself for her death."

Too late.

"It wasn't your fault."

Maybe not. But plenty of other shit *was* his fault. Anna, still floundering in her new life. Toby thinking he had to be a Jedi warrior to warrant his mother's return. His dad's practice getting too big for its britches and losing the personal attention each patient deserved...

And Grace—the last lethal shot to his mental stability that had come out of nowhere.

She stood there, his own personal, gorgeous goddess, running his world in her own way along with her huge heart. She looked so soft and beautiful in the ambient light. So... his. His heart revved at just the sight of her, so he closed his eyes and let his head fall back to the couch. "You need to go."

"Can't."

He didn't ask why not, but she told him anyway. "I think maybe that's the problem," she said softly, and he could feel her leg brush his now.

She was getting braver.

"People go away in your life, don't they, Josh?" she asked. "You get left, abandoned, whether by choice or through no fault of anyone."

He heard more movement; then she tugged off one of his shoes. She was kneeling at his side, a position that brought dark erotic thoughts to mind. "I don't want to talk about it," he said.

"I know." Having gotten his shoes off, she rose up on her knees. "But you aren't okay. And I'm not leaving you."

He stared at her, ashamed to feel his throat tighten. "Grace. Just go."

"No." She lay her head down on his thigh and stroked his other with a gentle hand. "Tell me what to do to help you."

She could start by moving her mouth about two inches to the right.

She didn't. What she *did* do was take the shot glass dangling from his fingers and set it on the coffee table. Then she stood and pulled him up with her, hugging him.

His throat tightened beyond use as he buried his face in her hair and held on to her hard.

"You're going to be okay," she whispered.

No. No, he wasn't. But rather than admit that, he took a deep breath. He didn't want her concern.

She pulled back, and keeping a hold of his hand, led him down the hall to his bedroom.

Bad idea.

The worst sort of bad idea.

Stop her…

He had her by a good foot and at least seventy pounds. It wouldn't be difficult to free himself, but instead he followed along after her like a lost little puppy.

She turned off the lights, and darkness settled over them. Over him. *In* him. He was just about as on edge as it got.

And he wanted her.

Needed her.

But he'd never been very good at asking. Not that she was making him ask…

She pulled him into his bedroom, nudging the door shut with her foot. "Come here."

"You're shaking," he said, wrapping his arms around her trembling body.

Her hands glided up his chest to cup his face. "Not me," she said very gently, eyes shadowed. "You. *You're* shaking."

Well, hell. He tried to pull back, but she gripped him tight and refused to budge. "Josh—"

"I need to go—"

"Honey, this is *your* place." Her fingers slid into his hair, gentle and soothing. Tender. So were her eyes when she tilted his face down to hers to see it in the dim light. "No one's going anywhere," she said. "You're already right where you need to be." Then she locked the door and gave him a push that had him falling onto his bed.

Shit, he was pretty fucking far gone if she could catch him off guard like that. He came up on his elbows, and there she stood in that shimmery top and leggings, looking like everything sweet and warm and caring. *Too* caring. He didn't want that. He wanted her naked and sweaty and screaming his name. "I want to be alone," he said.

"You don't need to be alone tonight."

"You don't know what I need."

She stared down at the hard-on he was sporting, the one straining the front of his scrubs. "I think I have a pretty good idea." She let the straps of her camisole slip to her elbows, and the whole thing fell to her waist. She urged it past her hips with a little wriggle, and it hit the floor. "You sure you don't want to talk about it?"

Sitting up, he settled his hands on her rib cage, fingers spread wide.

"It might help if you did," she said.

He took in her pretty pink bra. It was one of those half-cup things that gave him tantalizing peek-a-boo hints of nipples, which were already hard. They puckered up even tighter, and his mouth watered.

"Josh?"

"Sorry. I haven't heard a word since you took off your top." He closed his eyes. "You shouldn't be here."

"Give me one good reason why not."

He didn't have any logic skills in that moment. None. He searched for words. "I'm temporarily unavailable."

"Incapacitated, maybe." With a hand to the center of his chest, she pushed.

He fell flat to the bed and stared up at the ceiling, which was twirling. And there was something else. He badly wanted to roll her beneath him and take her. Take her hard and fast and dirty. "You need to go, Grace."

"Yeah? And why's that?" she asked. "You might actually let your control slip? Or worse yet, an emotion?" She shook her head, a small smile curving her lips. "You've seen *me* reveal lots of emotions. Fear, sadness, anger...You've seen me totally out of my element and freaked out. You've seen me *everything*. So I think I can handle whatever you've got, big guy."

He blinked. "Big guy?"

She crawled onto the bed and then over him, letting her stomach brush over his erection. "Feels big to me."

Through his haze, Josh felt her hands stroke his thighs. And then higher as her fingers deftly untied and tugged enough to free him. "I'm not feeling gentle," he warned.

"I don't need gentle." She smiled at him. "Remind me sometime to show you my sexual fantasy list. It's quite comprehensive. In fact, you in your scrubs are on it. Being *not* gentle."

He groaned.

"We play doctor. And in a variation, *I* get to be the doctor."

Jesus. "Grace—"

"Shhh," she murmured, her warm breath brushing over him as she wriggled some more, right out of her leggings. At the feel of her bare legs entangled with his, he groaned again.

"I have your attention?" she asked.

"You *always* have my attention."

"Good to know." As light and teasing as her words were, she made a little movement that rubbed her thighs together, and it occurred to him that she was as turned on as he was. He felt himself twitch at the thought. "Grace—"

"No." She covered his mouth with a finger. "You just sit there and look pretty."

His low laugh turned into a husky groan when she grasped him with her hands and let her lips slowly descend over him.

"Oh, Christ." He had to close his eyes after that, his hands fisted tightly in the bedding instead of in her hair, because she was right—he wasn't at all sure he could control himself. Two minutes in, he was drowning in pleasure and hot, desperate need. "Grace—" he gasped, trying to warn her.

She merely let out a hungry little murmur and tightened her grip, humming her approval, and blowing his mind right along with his favorite body part.

He came fast and hard, and he figured he should be mortified—tomorrow. For now, all he could muster was a blissed-out exhaustion…

When he woke several hours later to the alarm, he was all alone, leaving him to wonder—real or Memorex?

The next day came too early, and Grace cursed her alarm. It'd been two when she'd left Josh sprawled out spread-eagle on his bed, eyes rolled back in his head. She'd been pretty sure he'd still been breathing.

He must have been, because his car was already gone.

She drove into Seattle for an interview at a second firm that had called late yesterday, and it went well. On her way back to Lucky Harbor, she got a phone call from Anna.

"Toby's school called. He fell into a mud puddle, and he needs a change of clothes."

"Okay," Grace said. "I'll be there in twenty." When she got to the house, she went through Toby's dresser and pulled out a pair of pants.

"Don't forget socks," Anna said from the doorway.

"Socks." She grabbed those too.

"And shoes. And a shirt. And a coat..."

Grace looked at Anna.

"Apparently, he's quite the mess."

Grace drove the change of clothes to the elementary school, and Anna had been right. Toby was a mess, but a happy one.

"I didn't need new clothes," he said, not quite so happy now that he had to change. Apparently little boys like to wear their mud like badges of honor.

Grace handed him the clothes and gave his hair a tousle. Or tried. Her fingers caught on the mud in his hair. "What, did you bathe in the stuff?"

He grinned, and she shook her head. "See you at the bus stop in a little while, handsome."

She left the school and met Amy and Mallory for a late lunch at Eat Me. Lunch was chocolate cupcakes, of course.

"So sad about Mrs. Porter," Mallory said. "We're all taking it hard at the hospital. Especially Josh." Her eyes cut to Grace. "You hear from him?"

Not since she'd left him boneless and panting on his bed. She shook her head and peeled her cupcake from its wrapper.

"He might need some TLC," Mallory said.

"Whatever you do, don't call it TLC," Amy said. "That'll scare an alpha into next week. Just do him. That's all the TLC he'll need."

Grace, who'd just taken an unfortunate bite of her cupcake, inhaled it up her nose. By the time she'd stopped coughing and swiped at her streaming eyes, both Mallory and Amy were waiting, brows up.

"Stop," Grace managed. "You guys read far too much into everything. Must be all that *TLC* you're both having. It's making you think everyone else is having it too."

"So you're saying that there's nothing going on with you and the doc?" Amy asked.

Well, hell. She couldn't exactly say that. "I'm saying that this was supposed to be just fun. Not anything real. I'm interviewing for jobs that I'm actually trained to do, and—"

"That your *family* wants you to do," Mallory reminded her. "Because if you ask me, life here in Lucky Harbor suits you pretty nicely."

"My parents mean well," Grace said. "They want me to succeed."

"Well of course," Mallory said. "They love you. But I'm thinking success and happiness don't get along. Sometimes you have to sacrifice one for the other."

Grace had strived hard for success all her life, wanting to live up to being a Brooks. It meant a lot to her, but it'd also cost her. Until now she'd not managed to have any real relationships in her life, at least not long-lasting ones. They'd not been important. But now she couldn't imagine her life without Mallory and Amy in it.

"Happiness should always win," Mallory said quietly.

Grace sighed. They ate in companionable silence for a few minutes.

"So on a scale of one to Taylor Lautner," Amy said to Grace, "how good is he?"

Grace thought about hers and Josh's two extremely memorable…moments. "It's not what you think." She paused. "But Josh is ten-point-five Taylor Lautners. No, make that eleven."

This caused a moment of silent appreciation.

"He makes you happy," Mallory said softly.

Grace looked into her friend's warm eyes. Mallory wanted the best for her. She also wanted the best for Josh. It was natural that her romantic heart would want the best for *them*, together. "I've always been a little short on the happy," Grace admitted. "So it's hard to say. But it's what I said I wanted. Fun."

Mallory's gaze never left Grace's as she squeezed her hand, and Grace knew what she was thinking. What they were all thinking.

Yes, Grace had said she wanted only fun. But somehow, when she hadn't been looking, she'd begun to yearn for more.

Far more.

That she'd already set the parameters with Josh was her own fault, so fun it would be. And no more.

"You could do this the easy way and just tell him," Mallory said.

"Tell him what?" Amy wanted to know.

"That she's falling for him," Mallory said.

Grace shook her head. She wasn't falling. She couldn't be falling. Because Josh had a very full life, and there wasn't room for her in it. And she was quite over trying to squeeze herself in where there wasn't room. She'd done that with her parents all her life. And every failed relationship.

No more. Her heart wasn't strong enough to take it.

Amy looked at Mallory. "She's going down the same path I did, poor baby. The path of most resistance."

"I'm not taking *any* path," Grace said, feeling grumpy now as she reached for another cupcake. Her grumpiness hit a new level when both Amy and Mallory merely laughed at her.

"Is watching Toby as hard as you thought it would be?" Mallory asked when she'd controlled herself.

Trick question. Grace had honestly believed that taking care of Toby would be easier than watching after Tank. It hadn't been at all, but she couldn't remember ever enjoying a job more. Not sure what *that* meant. She lifted a shoulder. "Little boys aren't all that different from big boys."

Amy grinned. "Now *there's* a lesson that should be taught to every female in kindergarten to save years of frustration and heartache."

"You really don't think you're falling for him?" Mallory asked Grace.

She shook her head. Her life had always been about the bottom line, about numbers, about getting to the top. It'd never been about emotions, about heart and soul. About falling in love...She knew better than that. "Josh isn't looking for that."

Mallory looked amused. "I meant Toby."

Oh. Right.

"But good to know where you're at," Mallory said.

Yeah. Good to know. Grace's phone rang. A number she didn't recognize.

"Grace Brooks?" came an unfamiliar voice in her ear.

"Yes."

"This is Serena, the nurse at Lucky Harbor Elementary. Toby's not sick or hurt or anything."

"Okay..."

"But he fell in a mud puddle again..."

Since there was only a half hour left of school, Grace just took Toby home with her. She buckled him into his booster seat and slid him a look in the rearview mirror. "Do I want to know?"

"Camel flaunting," he said very solemnly. "Me and Tommy needed to camel flaunt."

This baffled her for a beat; then she had to laugh. "Camouflage?"

"Yes," he said.

"For a battle."

"Yes!"

Grace had never really pictured herself with kids. She didn't know why, exactly. Maybe because she'd never been around them, or because she figured she'd be married to her career as her parents were. But in that moment, sharing a grin in the mirror with Toby, something deep inside her squeezed hard in yearning.

They'd just walked in the front door and let Tank loose when Grace got a call from Anna.

"Need a ride," was all Anna said.

Grace could hear something in the girl's voice. *Tears?* Whatever it was, Grace's stomach dropped. She knew that Anna was supposed to be at physical therapy, but she also knew that Devon was a weasel, and once Anna was in his car, she was pretty much at his mercy.

Grace had tried talking to Anna about it twice since the other day, but Anna was good about avoiding talking.

A definite Scott thing.

Still, Grace couldn't get past the gut feeling that Devon was pushing for things Anna didn't want to give him. "Where are you?" she asked.

Anna rattled off an address that was just outside of Lucky Harbor. It was an area that Grace knew from delivering flowers, and it was not an especially good neighborhood. She looked at Toby, who was swooshing his Jedi lightsaber and making Tank nuts. "On my way." She disconnected. "We're going for a ride, Tobes."

"Tank and I are in the middle of a battle."

"You can finish when we get back."

"A good Jedi never stops in the middle of a battle."

She hunkered down and looked him in the eye. "We have another battle to fight."

He looked excited. "Yeah?"

"Yeah. Picking up your aunt."

His face fell. "Aw, that's no fun. And you promised we'd go to the park."

"Yes, but sometimes things happen."

"Not to Jedis. Bad things like not going to the park never happen to Jedis." Still holding his saber, he took off, his little feet pounding down the hallway. The next noise was the slam of his door.

Okay, so *someone* needed a nap. Though technically, that could apply to Grace as well. She followed him to his room and opened the door. She saw a little boy tush and a little pug tush, both adorable, sticking out from behind Toby's large beanbag chair. The classic "if I can't see you, you can't see me" pose. "Toby? Tank?"

"Don't answer," came a little boy whisper, and then a muffled snort.

A *pug* snort.

"Gee," she said. "Wherever could the Jedi warriors have gone?"

Another pug snort.

And then a giggle. "What a shame I'm all alone," she said. "'Cause I'm really in need of a couple of Jedi warriors, the very best of the best. There's an epic battle ahead. We have to save Aunt Anna."

The two tushes wriggled free, complete with warrior yells and lots of barking. Grace was just leading Toby outside when Josh pulled up.

He got out of his car looking like the day had already been too long. "Need my laptop," he said, eyes shadowed, face drawn. He made time to stop and crouch down to hug Toby before straightening and meeting Grace's eyes.

She wanted to ask him if he was okay. She wanted to give him a hug like he'd given Toby. She wanted to give him a chocolate cupcake and warm milk. She wanted to have him beneath her again, shuddering, her name on his lips as he came.

But mostly she wanted to ask him if there was any chance that he was feeling like this thing might be getting uncomfortably close to being a lot more than just fun. "Hey," she said, and then rolled her eyes at how breathless she sounded.

He'd been pretty far gone last night, both in alcohol and exhaustion, and she suddenly realized he might not even *remember* what had happened.

His dark gaze searched hers for a long beat, but he gave nothing away. Something else he was extremely good at. "Where are you guys going?" he asked.

"Anna needs me to pick her up."

"Devon flake on her again?"

"I don't know. This is where she is." She showed him the address she'd scrawled onto a piece of paper.

He frowned. "That's nowhere close to her PT." He looked at his watch. "My car. Let's go."

They drove in silence. Well, except for the noises Toby and his Zhu Zhu warriors were making in the backseat. Josh turned onto a run-down street, and they all eyeballed the apartment building. Weeds in the asphalt cracks, dead lawn, peeling paint, and bars on the windows of the lower floors. Nice.

Anna was in her chair waiting on the front walk. At the sight of Josh's car, she scowled, and then again when he got out to help her.

"I called Grace," she said unhappily. "Not you."

"Hello to you too." He crouched in front of her, gaze narrowed. "You okay?" He reached out to touch her cheek where her mascara had run as if she'd been crying.

She slapped his hand away. "I'm fine. Just get me out of here."

The drive home was tense, with Josh keeping an eye on a silent Anna, who was huddled in the backseat. Back at home, she rolled into her room, slammed the door, and all went quiet.

Toby picked up his lightsaber. "Can we go to the park?"

"Not right now," Josh said.

"Swimming?"

"Not right now."

Toby tossed up his hands. "You don't let me do anything." And then he walked down the hall and slammed his bedroom door.

In a perfect imitation of Anna.

Josh looked like maybe he wanted to tear out his hair. He moved down the hall and knocked on Anna's door.

"Go away!" she yelled.

Josh strode back into the living room, looking as if he needed a long vacay.

"You okay?" Grace asked him.

"I don't know." He lifted his head and pinned her with his gaze. "Tell me about last night."

"What about it?" she asked carefully, not wanting to fess up to anything he couldn't remember.

He looked at her for another long moment, during which she did her best to look innocent.

"You could start by showing me the rest of that sexual fantasy list," he said.

Okay, she thought with a blush, so he *did* remember.

Gaze dark, he stepped toward her, but his phone went off. Josh swore, grabbed his laptop, then strode to the door.

Grace let out a breath, then sucked it in again when he turned back and lifted her up so that they were nose to nose.

"Now *I* owe *you*," he said softly, then set her down, brushed a kiss over her mouth, and vanished.

Chapter 14

I would give up chocolate, but I'm not a quitter.

It was a long day. At the office, every patient Josh saw wanted to talk about Mrs. Porter. They were devastated. His staff was devastated. By the time he got home, he was more done in than he'd been last night, and that was saying something.

He'd called ahead. Toby was asleep. Anna was heading out as soon as he got home. He could have done whatever he wanted with the evening.

But there was only one thing he wanted to do.

Grace.

The lights in the guesthouse were blazing. Through the windows, he could see Grace sitting on the couch, but she wasn't alone. She was with Mallory and Amy, talking and laughing. In front of them on the coffee table was an opened file box, and papers were scattered across the entire table, bookended by an open laptop and an adding machine.

It was a visceral reminder that Grace had a whole other life outside of his.

She'd taken on two more clients, which he'd heard from Dee, who'd heard it from Lucille, who'd heard it from Anderson at the hardwood store, since he was one of those clients. The other new client was the ice-cream shop on the pier and the two brothers who ran it. Lance and Tucker probably had no bookkeeping system at all, so Grace had her work cut out for her—not that it would be a problem. She seemed to have a way of getting to it all, making everything all work out. He admired that. She was just a sweet, smart, hard-working woman doing her best to find herself. No complaining, no feeling sorry for herself, doing what she had to do to get by.

She had her hair pulled up in a ponytail, but a few pale silk strands had escaped, framing her face, brushing her throat and shoulders.

Just looking at her had his body humming. And though she couldn't possibly see him standing in the dark night, she went still, then turned her head, and peered outside.

Unerringly looking right at him.

She said something to Mallory and Amy, then rose in one fluid motion and stepped outside, shutting the door behind her.

They met in the shadows near the shallow end of the pool.

"Hey," she said, looking like a vision in a loose white top that fell off one shoulder and white shorts showing a mile or two of sexy leg.

"Hey yourself," he said. "How did your day go?"

"Well, I didn't kill Tank, Toby continues to master the English language, and Anna didn't run off today. Progress."

"Great, but I meant you. How are *you*?" She looked surprised, which he didn't like. "You think I don't want to hear about you too?" he asked.

She nibbled on her lower lip.

"Grace?"

"This thing between us... it's still just fun, right?"

He studied her a moment. "How does that translate into me not caring about you?"

She blew out a breath and looked away. "I'm sorry. I guess I'm not very good at this. I don't mix well with a guy like you."

"A guy like me," he said, trying to figure out what that meant.

"Look, it's all me, okay? I knew going into this thing that it couldn't possibly work, but I just kept…" She broke off and looked away. "I'm sorry."

"A guy like me," he repeated again. "Grace, I'm trying like hell to follow you but…"

She looked at him and blinked, as if she didn't understand how he wasn't catching the obvious. "We're so different," she said. "You've got your life in gear, all planned out. I don't know what I'm doing. I'm trying to know but…" She trailed off and looked at him again, as if expecting him to nod in agreement.

But he was still clueless. "If you think my life is working on some *plan* that I've set out," he said, "you haven't been paying attention. *Nothing* is how I planned it. And as for mixing well, I think we mix pretty fucking well."

"Yes, but isn't that just sex?"

"Not yet," he said with grim amusement. "But not for lack of chemistry. And there's no 'just sex' about it."

She stared up at him, apparently speechless. There weren't crickets out tonight, but if there had been, they'd be chirping Beethoven about now. That's when it came to him like a smack upside the back of the head. "Who was the guy?" he asked.

"Guy?"

"The one who screwed you over, the one with some big, grand plan, I'm guessing. A plan that didn't work out in your favor. Was he a doctor?"

Grace drew an audible breath to speak and then shook her head. "That obvious?"

"No," he said. "Or I'd have caught on a lot sooner. And you'd think I would have since I was once burned by a big, grand plan too."

She sighed. "Bryce Howard the third."

"Sounds like a dick already."

She choked out a laugh that spoke more of remembered misery than humor. "He's a friend of the family. His parents are well-known and respected biomedical engineers, on the pioneer front of cardiovascular research."

"Never heard of them."

"We always knew we'd end up together," she said. "It was sort of expected, actually."

"Expected? Didn't anyone realize it's the twenty-first century?"

"It wasn't like that," she said quietly. "I liked Bryce."

And then Josh *really* got it. Christ, he was slow on the uptake. "You loved him."

"Yes." She let out a shaky breath. "I did. I loved him until the day after our engagement, when he came home and told me to pack because we were moving to England for his job, which was a six-year study grant. It was a great opportunity, but..."

"You didn't like being told what your life would look like for the next six years," he guessed.

She nodded her head. "And you know what the really sad thing was? If he'd so much as asked, or even gave a thought to me and my job, I'd have junked it all to go with him."

"So what happened?"

"He left the next day," she said. "And shortly after, my job vanished when the economy dived."

"You could have looked him up," he said. "Gone to him then."

"Thought about it," she admitted. "But by then I was seeing someone else."

"Another PhD?"

"Yes, but a bank guy this time," she said. "Stone Cameron. He lost his job the same day I lost mine, only he'd invested in property instead of stocks. He had a house in Australia. He went there to go surf out the economy problems."

"He ask you to go with?"

"Nope." She shook her head. "This time, I wasn't in the plans at all."

Josh was starting to get the whole picture now, and he didn't like it much. "So your parents had big life plans for you. Bryce had big life plans for you. Stone just had big plans. And no one ever asked you *your* plans."

"No," she said softly. "And I realize I didn't actually have my own plans, but I'd have liked to be asked."

He nodded. He could understand that.

"So I'm just saying, you don't have to feel a responsibility to me just because we…sort of had sex." She let out a low laugh that was far more natural now. "Twice. I'm still okay with this being…"

"Fun."

Her gaze met his, clear and utterly unfathomable. "Yes."

"You think I'd feel a responsibility to you because of good sex," he said slowly.

"Well, it was better than good," she said. "But yes. I think you're exactly the type to feel a responsibility for those who cross your path. You're a rescuer."

Okay, so now on top of assuming he only wanted her out of some sense of responsibility, she'd also lumped him into the same category with all the other mistakes she felt she'd made. And hell if that didn't piss him off. She didn't want him to care. He got that, loud and clear. He didn't want to care either.

But he did. "Look, Grace, no matter what you call this thing between us—fun, a pain in the ass, nothing at all—it doesn't matter. Just don't judge me by the assholes in your past. I deserve more than that, but more importantly, *you* deserve more than that."

She stared up at him, then slowly nodded. "You're right. I'm sorry." She turned back to the guesthouse, and he grimaced.

"Grace—"

"Toby lost a tooth tonight," she said quietly over her shoulder.

"He was excited and tried to wait up for the Tooth Fairy, but he didn't make it. She arrived the minute after he'd conked out."

He slid his hand into his pocket. "Thanks. How much—"

"You're paying me a thousand bucks a week." She faced him again. "I think I can cover it. I can cover a lot of stuff, actually. Except at the end of the day, I'm still just the babysitter. And he's still just an adorable, motherless five-year-old. Who also deserves better." With that last zinger, she let herself into the guesthouse and shut the door quietly.

He stood there for a moment, then nodded. Point for each, which meant it was a draw. Which didn't explain why he felt she'd lanced him alive.

Inside he found Toby deeply asleep, wrapped around both Tank and the lightsaber. The Berenstain Bears book was there, too, with the mama bear front and prominent.

Josh ignored the pain in his chest, the one that said he was *still* failing the people in his life, and gently pulled the lightsaber from Toby's slack grip. Next, he eyed the dog.

Tank opened one eye and gave a look that said, *Don't even try, pal.*

Josh gave up and covered them both.

Tank licked his hand.

Josh bent over Toby and kissed his temple. His son smelled like peanut butter and soap, which he took as a good sign. So was the way the kid smiled in his sleep. A smile with a gaping hole in the front.

"Love you," Josh whispered, the words a heavy weight on his chest.

Toby rolled away, pulling Tank under one arm and the Berenstain Bears book under the other, sighing softly in his sleep. "Arf," he whispered.

The next morning, Grace climbed back onto the modeling pedestal in Lucille's gallery. Today she was artfully draped in a sheet, supposedly like a Grecian goddess, though she suspected she looked more like she was going to a toga party.

"I wouldn't mind being twenty years younger, like you, Grace," Mrs. Gregory said conversationally. "Back to when my boobs were as good as yours."

"You mean *fifty* years," Lucille murmured.

"It's just that I'm tired of hoisting my boobs into a bra every morning." Mrs. Gregory pointed to Grace's breasts. "You don't have to hoist anything. Those babies are standing up on their own."

"That's because it's cold in here," Grace said in her own defense. She was counting down the last twenty minutes of class as she held her pose. After this, she was picking up Anna from PT, and then she had a few more calls to return to applying nannies. She was determined to find the best possible person for Toby. And Tank. And Anna, even though the twenty-one-year-old would deny needing anything from anyone.

And Josh…

Grace could admit that she also wanted the best possible person to take care of Josh. Which was silly. Very silly. Obviously, the man was more than capable of taking care of himself, not to mention everyone around him. He'd proven that managing more than the average human should ever have to between his practice, the ER, Toby, Anna…the loss of his parents.

Sure, he was very used to taking care of people, and it was an extremely appealing part of the man. But maybe he just needed to know it was okay to be on the other side of the fence occasionally.

"Time," Lucille called out to her students, and Grace relaxed. She jumped down off the pedestal and dropped the sheet, revealing the short, strapless sundress she wore beneath. Grabbing her cardigan and purse, she headed to the door. "Gotta go."

"Hold on, dear," Lucille said, and handed her a check and a bottle of wine.

"Oh," Grace said. "Thank you, but I'm not much of a drinker—"

"Check out the label."

It was a color pencil sketch of the Lucky Harbor pier at night, lit up with strings of white lights that glowed out over the water beneath a full moon. Grace had seen the original. The Chocoholics had celebrated Amy's sale of the drawing to the winery a month ago. When she recognized it, pride filled her. "It's beautiful," she said.

"Keep it," Lucille told her. "Maybe you'll have use for it on a date over a nice romantic dinner with the doctor."

"We're not dating—" She broke off at Lucille's smile and shook her head. "Listen, I know you're like the gossip guru in town, but there's no gossip here."

Lucille smiled. "Are you sure?"

"Very," Grace said firmly, ignoring the little ping inside her. Maybe if she'd stop giving Josh reasons *not* to fall for her... "I'm just watching Toby and Tank. Helping Josh out, is all."

"*Josh*, is it now?"

"Yes, that's his name."

"Actually, honey," Lucille said, "we all call him Dr. Scott. Well, unless he's not within hearing distance, and then we call him Dr. McHottie. And none of *us* get to live with him."

"I'm just the babysitter," Grace said. "I stay there because of the crazy hours he keeps. It makes things easier on him. And I'm in the *guesthouse*, not the main house, and only until we find him a replacement. There's no dating going on."

Everyone's ears perked up at this.

"I could take on one more kid," Jenna Burnett said. "For Dr. McHottie, I'd take on quadruplets."

Jenna was a single mom in her midforties, running a day care out of her home. Her three children were teenagers and helped when they got home from school. Jenna was sweet and kind, and probably a viable option for Toby.

"Ask him," Jenna said, seeing that Grace was actually thinking about it. "Tell him I'll give him a great deal." She smiled warmly, but damn, there was definitely something just a little bit hungry behind it.

"Hey, I want to throw my name into the hat too." This from Sierra Hennessy. Sierra owned an upscale clothing shop in Seattle that she paid someone else to manage. The designs were Sierra's own, and because she had four ex-husbands, each more wealthy than the last, she didn't care that she sold only a few dresses a season. She also didn't care that she was considered a man shark. "What's Dr. Scott's stance on marriage?"

Grace managed a smile. "I'll let him know about both your offers. We'll be in touch about interviews." Then she hightailed it out of there. She got to Anna's PT office just in time to see the girl roar off in Devon's truck, flashing a peace sign at Grace.

Grace gritted her teeth and drove to the house, where she waited for the bus. When Toby hopped off it, he was bouncing up and down with excitement. It was Back-to-School night, and later Josh would get to see Toby receive the Student of the Week award. Afterward, Josh had promised him an ice-cream sundae, and then Toby was having his first sleepover at a friend's.

He was so excited he could hardly contain himself. He and Grace walked the half block home, where from hard-earned knowledge, Grace let Tank and Toby run wild laps around the yard until they expelled enough energy in tandem that Toby could sit and do his homework. While he did that, Grace worked on Tank's so-called obedience. This was more an exercise in patience for Grace than anything else, but she was determined.

They had mac and cheese and turkey hot dogs for an early dinner—no deviating from the planned menu—and then waited for Josh to show up to take Toby to Back to School night.

Except he didn't show.

Grace called Josh but got no answer. She called Anna. No answer there either. Finally, she drove Toby to his elementary school herself, pretty much steamed at everyone with the last name of Scott except for Toby.

Toby's teacher was thrilled to see him. "Sadie had her kittens, Toby. Want to go look?"

When Toby whooped and raced off, Grace looked at the teacher. "How much time before the awards?"

"At least half an hour."

"Can I leave him here while I go get his father?" Grace asked.

"Dr. Scott?"

"Yes. I'm sure he just got hung up at the office..."

One of the moms sidled close. A tall, perfectly-put-together, gorgeous brunette. "I'm sorry, but I couldn't help overhearing. Angela Barrison," she said, introducing herself. "I'll be happy to keep an eye on Toby while you go get Dr. Scott." She smiled a sort of tiger smile. "And if you could let him know that *I'm* the one watching Toby for you, that'd be great. I'd like to apply for the position."

"The nanny position?" Grace asked.

"*Any* position."

Grace shook her head all the way to her car.

Josh's office was in the building directly adjacent to the hospital. She tore into the lot, stomped up to his suite, and yanked open the door. Righteous anger was blooming within her, propelling her forward, ready to tear him a new one for missing something so important to Toby.

And something else was blooming too.

Worry.

This was unlike him, very much so. He never blew off anything that anyone needed, but especially Toby. His son came first with him. Family always came first. So this bothered her.

She hadn't expected to feel worry for the man who appeared to have it all. Hell, she hadn't meant to feel anything for him at all, but she did.

Far too much.

The waiting room was empty, the front office lit but also empty. And her worry amped up a notch. "Josh?" she called, walking down the hallway.

She came to a large office decorated in masculine dark wood, the huge mahogany desk loaded with paperwork and files. The lamp was lit. There was a mug of something on the corner and an open laptop in the middle.

Behind the desk was a large executive chair. In it was one Dr. Josh Scott, leaning back, feet up.

Fast asleep.

Chapter 15

Forget roses, send chocolate.

Josh hated falling asleep in his office chair. It never failed to give him a kink in his neck and make him grumpy as hell. So when he leaned back and let his eyes drift shut, he told himself he was merely resting his eyelids.

"Josh?"

Her voice, Grace's voice, came to him on a breath of air, and he relaxed into the leather chair.

"I have a case for you, Dr. Scott." Grace stood in his office doorway in a nurse's uniform, but not any uniform that Dee might wear. Nope, this one had come right out of the Victoria's Secret catalog, complete with stilettos.

Looking holy-shit-hot, she sauntered into his office and slid between his legs, leaning over him in the chair, blocking him in with her body. His hands went to her hips to pull her in even closer, needing her so badly he was shaking but he refused to rush. If this was all they were going to have, this erotic dream, then he wanted it to last. He kissed her neck, then traced his tongue over the spot, eliciting the sweetest, most sensuous sigh he'd ever heard. This fueled a bone-deep desire to mark her as his, and he sucked the patch of skin into his mouth.

"Josh..."

No. No talking, or he'd wake up. He kissed the spot, slipping his hands beneath the short hem of her uniform, and groaned. No panties. God, he was a goner...

"Josh."

He grabbed her wrist and tugged so that she fell into his lap with a gasp that had him opening his eyes.

No nurse's uniform. Damn. It really was just a dream...

"Sorry," Grace said, wriggling, trying to free herself. "I didn't mean to startle you awake. You were really out."

Med school and residency had taught Josh how to sleep light and come awake fast, but apparently he'd forgotten the art of both. Then again, certain parts of him were *very* awake, getting more so by the second thanks to the squirming Grace was doing.

She wore another of her sundresses, this one sky blue, the color of her eyes. It'd risen high on her thighs, and he decided to help it along, sliding a hand up her leg, pushing the material as he went.

"What are you doing?" she asked, nice and breathless.

"Seeing if I should salute the flag on your panties," he said. "I'm patriotic, Grace."

"These don't have a flag on them."

Aw, now see, that was just a challenge, and he'd never been able to resist a challenge. His fingers tangled with hers, trying to work the hem while she rocked around some more.

That had enough of a noticeable effect on him that her eyes widened at the feel of him hard beneath her. "Um..."

He met her gaze.

"You're..."

"Yeah," he said thickly. "I've been like this all week."

Okay, so not really. It was hard to maintain a boner while treating the flu or putting in stitches, but he'd given it the old college try.

And it *had* been a hell of a week. "I was dreaming about you. You were modeling for me."

"In the bikini T-shirt?" she asked.

"Try again."

She met his gaze and blushed gorgeously at whatever she saw on his face. "I…"

"Go ahead, guess," he said. "It's from your sexual fantasy list."

The air crackled around them.

"And not that I'm *not* completely enjoying this lap dance of yours," he said, "but what are you doing here and where's Toby?"

She looked at him as if maybe he wasn't as awake as he'd thought. "You're late for Back to School night. You weren't answering your cell. I came to check on you."

"Ah, shit." He stood up and let her slide down his body, but not before he caught a quick flash of peach silk. He *loved* peach silk.

But Toby was waiting, and Josh had indeed known about tonight. Damn, he couldn't believe he'd fallen asleep like that. Or maybe after eighty hours at the job this week so far, he could believe it. He shut his laptop, grabbed his keys and his phone, and keeping his fingers wrapped around Grace's wrist, began to tug her to the door. But then he stopped and looked down into her concerned face. She'd come to get him because she cared about Toby.

And because she cared about him too?

He thought maybe she was getting there. More than she planned to, and that did something to him.

People had cared about him before, of course. Toby loved him, unconditionally. His patients liked him. Ty, Matt…his staff. Hell, even his sister, though he wouldn't bet against the house on that one. But how often could he say that any of those people had put him first?

"Josh?" Grace murmured. "You okay?"

"I will be." Letting go of her, he moved back to his desk, opening his laptop again. He didn't have to bring up the hospital's contract offer; it'd been up for weeks. Months. His dad no longer needed him, but Toby did. Anna did. And Josh needed to do what was right for him too. He'd loved his dad, loved the memory of his dad right here in this office, helping people.

But it was no longer as relevant as making his own life work. Josh scrolled to the end, electronically signed on the bottom line, and hit SEND.

Done. Carrot bitten. Hell, carrot *swallowed*.

Just like that—though there were no trumpets, no fat ladies singing—Josh's life was irrevocably changed. He moved back to Grace at the door.

She was staring at him very solemnly. "What did I just miss?" she asked.

Josh didn't really have words. He felt a little off his center of gravity, like he was standing at the edge of a cliff with one foot in the air already. It was a new feeling for him. "Nothing yet," he said, and because she was standing so close, looking so cute and yet utterly, effortlessly sexy, he backed her to the door.

"Josh," she said. Just that, just his name as her hands went to his chest.

Not to push him away, he noticed with some satisfaction. Though she wasn't exactly sold on this, on them, not yet. Not even close. But the way her pulse beat at the base of her throat told him the move had excited her.

"You feel warm," she said, and gave him a worried frown.

He pressed into her a little. Yeah, he *was* feeling warm. He was starting to feel a bunch of things. "Don't worry, it's not contagious."

Her brow creased more tightly in that adorable expression of concern. "You're sick?"

"Probably." He slid a hand down her back to her very nice ass and rocked her into him. "Definitely."

She blinked, then caught onto his light, teasing tone. She relaxed, letting out a little sigh that went straight through him. "You poor man. All work and no play."

Yeah. But that was going to change.

Or so he hoped.

Too bad that by the time it did, she'd probably be long gone, having taken a job and a life that suited her far more than *his*. Leaning in, he kissed her, soft and light, then pulled back. "Let's go get Toby."

They made it to the school in time to see Toby get his Student of the Week award. Grace watched Toby beam with happiness at his father's presence and felt her heart clutch. Josh's expression was much more subdued but no less genuine, and Grace's heart kicked again.

After, she left to give them some alone time, heading to the diner to meet Amy and Mallory. Jan, the diner's owner, stopped her at the door. Jan was short and round and appeared to cut her dark hair by putting a bowl over her head to use as a guideline. She wasn't big on customer service, rarely speaking to her customers unless it was to yell at them to pipe down because *American Idol* was on the TV. "Got something for you," she said.

This took Grace by surprise. In all the time she'd known Jan, the woman had never spoken directly to her.

Jan held out a memory stick.

"What's this?" Grace asked.

"My laptop died. This is my backup bookkeeping. I need you to get on it ASAP. I'm a little behind."

"Okay..."

Jan was looking impatient to be back in front of her TV. "You're a number cruncher, yes?"

"Well, actually," Grace said, "I'm in banking—"

"You're doing Amy's books," Jan said.

"Yes, because she's my friend."

"And Lance's and Tucker's. And Anderson's. And Jeanine's."

Yeah, okay, so she'd gotten shystered into doing a lot of bookkeeping. She was good at it. And as it turned out, she also liked it.

She liked the way numbers balanced at the end of the day, how she didn't have to take her work home with her to stress about at night. "These are all one-time things," she said to Jan. "Really. I'm just sort of setting them up."

"I'll pay you," Jan said. "And also give you free food. As much as you can eat."

Grace had her mouth open to refuse but she closed it, inexcusably drawn in by this. "As much as I want?"

"As much as your skinny ass can take," Jan said, waving the memory stick enticingly.

Grace sighed and took it. Skinny? Not even close. "How long ago did your laptop die?"

"A month."

Great...

She made her way to the back booth. "Sucker," a waiting Mallory said.

Amy came out from the kitchen, making a big deal about setting the tray of cupcakes down just right, twisting the tray and nearly blinding Grace and Mallory with...

"*Oh my God*," Mallory said, and screamed.

Grace put her fingers in her ears but grinned wide.

Amy was wearing a rock on her ring finger.

Mallory jumped up and down and screamed some more, and then wore herself out and sank into the booth for a cupcake.

"I actually don't even need chocolate," Amy said, staring at her ring in dazed marvel. "Never thought I'd say that."

Mallory laughed and took a second cupcake. "I'll eat it for you."

"I'm getting married," Amy said softly. She looked up at the two of them, her eyes shiny. "Can you believe it?"

Grace knew that Amy hadn't had much luck in love before coming to Lucky Harbor. But Matt Bowers, a very sexy forest ranger and all-around great guy, had changed that for her.

Mallory's life was changing too.

Everyone's life was changing.

Except for Grace's.

Mallory squeezed her hand, making her realize she'd gone quiet. "You okay?"

"Oh, I'm good, and *very* happy for both of you." And she meant that, from the bottom of her heart. "I love how you've both figured out what was missing in your lives and went out and got it for yourselves."

"You know that what was missing wasn't a man, right?" Amy asked. "Because I didn't need a man to make me whole. I just needed to open myself up to new experiences. The man part sort of fell in my lap."

Mallory grinned. "Ditto."

"Well, thankfully, I don't need a man to make me whole," Grace said. "Because there's a definite man shortage in my life."

"Liar," Amy said.

"Hey," Grace said. "I'm just his dog walker and part-time nanny. It's temporary. Very temporary."

Amy turned to Mallory. "Time for the big guns."

Mallory pulled out her phone, thumbed to Lucky Harbor's Facebook page, and showed it to Grace. The latest entry read:

Ladies, our favorite doc, Josh Scott, is actively seeking a new nanny. Many have applied, and all have been turned down by his interim nanny, Grace Brooks.

Is she just being extraordinarily careful?

Or is she saving the position for herself?

A picture is worth a thousand words...

Accompanying this was indeed a picture, taken from inside the elementary school's kindergarten classroom. Toby was up on the makeshift stage, accepting his award.

The class was full of proud, smiling parents.

And in the back of the room stood Grace, beaming at the stage, a flush on her cheeks.

That wasn't the most damning part. Nope, that honor went to Josh, standing just behind her, his arms around her, his shoulders much broader than hers, his jaw pressed to her temple as he also looked toward the stage. There was something about the stance, the body language, the way the air practically shimmered between them. Not that there was any air between them. He was so tight to her that a sheet of paper wouldn't have fit.

"Well that's just..." Grace trailed off. Sexy.

Hot.

In fact, she was getting a hot flash right now.

"Standing a little close, aren't you, for nanny and the professor?" Amy asked dryly.

"Doctor," Grace said absently. "He's a doctor."

"So is that why he's close enough to take your body temperature without a thermometer?"

Grace shook her head. "This picture couldn't have been taken even an hour ago." And that wasn't all. She looked happy in that picture.

"The good stuff travels fast in Lucky Harbor," Amy said. "You know that."

"And that's not the only fast thing," Mallory said. "You guys have moved pretty fast."

"Says the woman who slept with her fiancé on the first night she met him," Amy said dryly.

"*Second* night," Mallory said primly.

"This picture was taken out of context," Grace complained. "*Completely.*"

"Of course," Mallory agreed, nodding. Then she shook her head. "Um, so how do you take a picture out of context?"

Amy snorted.

"The classroom was packed," Grace said. "Standing room only. We were forced to be so squished."

"Interesting how his arms look quite comfortable around her," Mallory noted to Amy.

"And notice the postcoital look about her," Amy offered back.

Grace bit her lower lip and stared at the picture. She did seem to have a certain orgasmic glow. Jeez, how long did such a thing last anyway?

Josh didn't have the glow. Even though technically he'd been the last one to, um, *have* an orgasm, he was looking a little edgy, a little rough and tumble. Like maybe he needed another reason to glow. Grace bit her lip harder at the thought. "We haven't been together. Not exactly."

"*Not exactly?*" Amy asked, brows up. "Is that what you kids call it these days?"

Mallory cracked up at this, and Grace sighed. "It's more like coitus interruptus. Twice. Once because he was called in to work and another because he fell asleep."

Amy grinned. "Anyone ever tell you you're supposed to keep them awake for the good stuff?"

Mallory was smiling but her question was serious. "So are you two going to be a real thing, then, not just a fun thing?"

Something clenched deep inside Grace at the thought, but she couldn't decide if it was a good clench or a bad one. *Liar, liar...* "I've run the numbers," she said. "It wouldn't work. First of all, he's a doctor. He gets a lot of points taken off for that."

"People usually add points for doctors," Mallory said.

"Not me," Grace said. "I was raised by a few of them, remember? Trust me, they don't make good relationship material."

Mallory squeezed her hand. "Honey, Josh isn't like your family. He's warm and loving."

"Not to mention hot as hell," Amy added.

Grace shook her head. "Sorry, the points are already deducted.

And taking into account his schedule, and then the standard deviation from the *average* man's schedule, I figure ninety percent of his time would go elsewhere. I'd never get uninterrupted coitus."

"Penis math," Amy said. "Impressive." She looked at Mallory. "See, this is why a guy shouldn't date an accountant."

"I'm not an accountant," Grace corrected. "I'm a floral-delivery-girl-slash-model-slash-babysitter."

"Slash doctor's sort-of girlfriend?" Amy asked.

Both she and Mallory cracked up.

Grace grabbed a cupcake, stood, and headed to the door.

"Aw," Amy called after her. "At least grab a second one for Josh. Chocolate is the next best thing to sex..."

Chapter 16

If at first you don't succeed,
have chocolate and try again.

Much later that night, Grace was lying in the bed of the guesthouse. The sheets were soft, and she could tell they'd been washed in the same detergent as Josh's because her nipples got hard at the scent. When she found herself pressing her face to them instead of sleeping, she got out of bed and strode to the windows.

The night was hot. Muggy. The lights in the big house had been off when she'd gotten back from the diner. She knew Toby had gone to a friend's house to sleep for the night. She had no idea where Josh was; either he was out or he was sleeping.

Anna could be anywhere.

Just in front of her, the pool gleamed, the water looking dark and inviting. Grace stripped out of her camisole and panties and pulled on a bathing suit. She'd just go cool off, and maybe then she could sleep. To help with that, she grabbed the bottle of wine Lucille had given her the other day. She found a corkscrew in the kitchen but couldn't locate a wineglass. No problem. She simply took the entire bottle with her and headed outside, where she sat on the edge of the pool and let her feet dangle in the water.

Heaven.

She watched the moon and stars and sipped wine for a while, wondering if this counted as fun. It felt decadent and different. But fun?

Maybe if she wasn't alone.

Maybe if Josh was with her...

That was a disconcerting thought, so she took another sip of the wine, set the bottle at her hip, and slipped into the pool with hardly a ripple.

It felt so good that she dived deep. The deliciously cool water rushed over her body, instantly bringing down her body temp. She swam a few laps, then lazily floated to the far side of the pool. She leaned on the edge, kicking gently, looking out at the rising moon, sipping more wine. Eventually she realized that some time had gone by and that there was now a light on in the big house. Her dreamy haze was interrupted by a disturbance in the water at the other end of the pool, and suddenly Josh was there, emerging at her side.

Her heart stopped, then started again when he leaned close, the heat of his body instantly enveloping her even as the chlorine-scented water rushed off his face and shoulders. He could stand up here where she couldn't, the water hitting him midchest.

Their eyes met. His lashes were wet and spiky, his eyes dark and deep and intense. He didn't speak, and neither did she. Reaching out, he stroked the wet hair at her temple, drawing his finger slowly down her cheek to the corner of her mouth, his gaze following the movement.

Suddenly the cool water felt as heated as the air around them, and she shivered. "Josh—"

He put a finger over her lips, then paused for a beat before lowering his face to hers. Replacing his finger with his mouth, his tongue traced the line of her lower lip.

She heard a moan. Hers, of course, low and throaty as Josh's hands slid up her back. Using the water's momentum to curl her into his chest, she fell into him willingly. He nuzzled her neck, his lips warm against her now-chilled skin, and she sucked in a breath.

Lifting his head, he met her gaze. His fingers cradled her head so he could run his lips along her jawline to the soft skin of her neck. Oh, God. His tongue there, right there on the vulnerable spot beneath her ear, and just like that, he had her.

Whatever he wanted... anything. Because she wanted it too.

He kissed her, slow and hungry and powerful, and the night, the moon, the stars, everything spun all around her. He deepened the kiss, turning it into a second one and then a third, and then so many more she lost count, his warm hands brushing her breasts and then her bare nipples.

He'd untied and removed her bikini top.

He raised his head, and she arched in the moonlight, wanting him to touch her some more, wanting his mouth on her.

But he just looked at her, and she couldn't tell what he was thinking. Needing some more liquid courage, she reached for the wine bottle, but he took it gently from her fingers. Watching her intently, he took a sip from the bottle, and then another, drinking more deeply. Catching up.

She couldn't take her eyes off him.

He set the bottle down and kissed her. His mouth was chilled from the wine, but fiery desire flamed through her, through him, too, if the groan that rumbled up from his chest meant anything. He offered her another sip from the bottle, then drank again himself. Lifting her up, he put his lips to her nipple, his fingers dancing down her spine, making her shiver. Everything he did felt so sensual, so slow and dreamlike.

Erotic.

She nearly went over the edge right then and there. With one more touch she might have, but his eyes met hers. They were dark, showing nothing but a reflection of the moon.

Nothing of the man.

She slid her hands up his delicious abs and up to his chest, humming in pleasure at the feel of all the firm muscle at her disposal. It wasn't enough. She needed more. "Josh—"

He kissed her throat, her collarbone, her shoulders as his fingers trailed down her belly, caressing her through the fabric of her bikini bottom. It didn't deter him. He merely slid the material aside and then his fingers touched her, knowingly caressing, then dipping inside her as he kissed her deeply, his tongue mirroring his hand's motion.

Grace pressed tight to him, loving the feel of his hard, wet body against hers, and he *was* hard. Everywhere. She palmed him gently, using her thumb to tease him, and his hips jerked into her touch. Fisting a hand in her hair, he kissed her harder, his mouth searing and very serious. "Out of the pool," he finally said, his voice low and commanding. And then he lent his hands to the cause, vaulting himself out in one easy economical movement that had all his muscles bunching. Reaching back for her, he pulled her out with no effort at all. "Come on."

She had no idea where to, and she didn't care. She willingly followed.

Josh pulled her wet bod in close. Her skin was deliciously chilled against his and her breath warm against his throat. They ground against each other, and he wasn't sure what she was thinking, but he was sure of one thing.

They were finally doing this.

He kissed her again, swift and rough, and she moaned and clutched at him eagerly.

"Now, Josh," she whispered. "Please now."

Hell yeah. He pulled back and eyed their surroundings. There was the patio table, but one of the legs was faulty. He had two plush lounge chairs only a few feet away, just beneath the terrace, protected by the bushes he'd yet to prune back for the year.

Perfect.

He pulled Grace over to one, nudged her onto it, and followed her down. Her mouth caught his attention first, and he kissed it long and hard, leaving it swollen and wet as he shifted down toward her breasts. He laved at one gorgeously pebbled nipple, loving how that made her gasp. She was making little panting whimpering sounds that were fueling his lust and need to the point of no return. He should stop this and get them inside, but he didn't want to move. The cool air, her hot body squirming beneath his, her hands running over him everywhere she could reach, it all felt so good. He slid a hand to the small of her back, then to her ass, tilting her so that her sweet spot caught his thigh as she rocked her hips. They were still learning about each other, but he was starting to know her body now, and what she needed. Mouth on hers, he set a rhythm, and her legs tightened on him like a vise.

"*Josh*."

"I know."

Her nails dug into his biceps as she squirmed some more, her breathing gone heavy. Close, he thought, so close, and then she tore her mouth from his. "Oh, God. I'm going to—"

"Come. Do it."

She burst into wild shudders in his arms. Absorbing her cry, Josh held her to him and watched as she rode out the waves of pleasure.

She was the sexiest thing he'd ever seen.

When she finally sagged back onto the lounge, she tugged him down over the top of her. "Tell me you have a condom. You'd better have a condom!"

"In my pocket."

This caused some trouble since his shorts were still drenched from the pool, but she managed to get her fingers on the packet when he sat up a little. Slapping his hands away, she insisted on doing the honors herself, which meant that by the time she'd painstakingly rolled the condom down his length, he was quivering, vibrating with need.

"Now," she said, and guided him home.

Nothing had ever felt so good. Then she arched her hips and he saw fireworks. "Grace," he whispered hoarsely, nipping at her jaw. "We've got to slow down."

"Later."

She was completely out of control, he thought. And she wasn't alone. Already breathing crazily, he set his forehead to hers with a little groan as she continued to rock up against him as he moved within her, trying to get him to speed up.

"Please," she whispered sweetly, her fingers in his hair, her body straining and moving with his in a way that took him straight to the edge. He could feel everything tightening within him as he barreled like a freight train to the end of the line. "Grace, Christ. Don't move."

But of course she kept moving. His fingers dug into her hips, but there was no hope of reining her in. He didn't even know why he'd tried. She drew him deeper into her body, and, he suspected, into her heart and soul.

There was no holding back, not then, and not when she cupped his face and looked up at him, letting him see everything as she burst again. Her eyes went opaque, his name torn from her lips as her muscles contracted, clenching him so tightly it was his undoing. He came right along with her, thrusting hard into her body before finally falling over her in a boneless heap. He tried to pull back but she wouldn't let him, keeping her arms and legs wrapped tight around him. Finally she allowed him to shift his hands from her ass to the lounge, to support his own weight again.

They remained like that for a few long moments, his head resting beside hers on the cushion, breathing the same air, their damp limbs entangled.

It was the most perfect moment he could remember, and he planned to rewind and repeat the entire experience. Just as soon as he could move.

Grace lay there wrapped up in a big, warm, sated Josh, thinking she'd never felt so amazing when she heard the slider open.

"Hey, Josh?"

Anna.

Grace's head shot up and bashed Josh in the chin hard enough to cause stars to dance in her vision.

"Josh," Anna yelled. "I've been calling you for ten damn minutes!" Oblivious, she rolled outside, staring down at the cell phone in her hand, grabbing up Josh's cell as she passed the patio table where it lay discarded.

"Oh my God," Grace whispered, staring up at Josh in horror, shoving at him, trying to get the big lug off of her.

Josh, of course, didn't budge. There was no budging him unless he wanted to be budged. With his still sleepy, heavy-lidded gaze locked on hers, he spoke over his shoulder to his sister. "Give us a minute."

Anna finally looked up. She had no way of seeing much. The night was dark, only a sliver of a moon. They were in the shadows, and Josh still had his shorts on, preserving most of his modesty. He was completely covering Grace, not that *that* helped any.

Anna narrowed her eyes as if trying to see through the dark, then slapped a hand over her eyes. "*Eww!* Are you *kidding* me?"

"A minute," Josh repeated in his no-nonsense, calm but steely voice.

"Fine. But call your son, who's been demon-dialing you for half an hour." With that, Anna whirled, then wheeled back to the house, dropping Josh's phone onto the table without further word.

Josh dived into the pool's depths to find Grace's bikini top. Once he'd retrieved it, he tied the straps at her back and neck while she adjusted her bottoms. He helped her make sure everything was back in place because she was pretty much a bowl of jelly. Then he strode directly to his phone and called Toby.

"Well?" Grace asked worriedly when he'd hung up.

"He's fine. He just wants to come home." His gaze met hers. "Grace—"

"If you're going to say you're sorry, please don't. Or if you regret it, or if it was just plain awful and—"

He shut her up with a kiss. A really great kiss, with lots of heat and tongue. When they ran out of air, he pressed his forehead to hers. "I was going to thank you. I needed you tonight. You were there for me."

It took her a moment to understand he didn't mean the sex on the lounge, but when she'd come to his office. What didn't take a moment was the realization that he'd said he needed her. Not someone. Or anyone.

Her.

That this big, strong, proud man who never needed anyone had said such a thing moved her far more than she'd expected. Reaching up, she cupped his jaw. "You were having a bad day?"

"A bad year." He hesitated, then covered her hand with his. "I sold my practice to the hospital tonight."

She controlled her instinctive gasp. "You did?"

"Yeah."

She was blown away. "Are you okay?"

He brought her hand to his mouth and kissed her palm. "At the moment, I don't have much blood in my brain to be anything but very okay."

She smiled.

He smiled back, then kissed her. "'Night, Grace."

"'Night."

Chapter 17

Chocolate is nature's way of making up for Mondays.

Josh went through several straight days of craziness at work. He never second-guessed his decision to sell, but there was no immediate magic opening of his schedule. After the smoke cleared, there were a hell of a lot of people who wanted to talk to him. His staff was safe; that had been a nonnegotiable condition of the contract. Everyone still had jobs, status quo.

But even though he'd discussed it ahead of time with everyone in his office, now that it had been done, they all needed reassurance. Josh understood that, but it didn't help with the insanity, which also included more hospital board meetings. The board had been ecstatic about his decision, and as planned, they brought in another doctor to lighten the load.

Dr. Tessa McGinley. Josh knew her. They'd gone through residency together. Though they were the same age, Tessa had a warm, almost grandmotherly appeal to her that made her seem twice his age. She wasn't made for ER work, but that was a benefit as far as Josh was concerned, since he coveted the ER. The bottom line was that Tessa had been tailor-made for a practice like his, where patient care was the number-one priority.

Best yet, starting tomorrow, she'd be splitting Josh's days at the office, giving him room to add more ER shifts. More time for Toby.

A life.

He thought about that as he dealt with four flu sufferers, three routine physicals, two cases of strep, and a partridge in a pear tree. He thought about a lot of things, such as Grace. He hadn't seen her since the night they'd christened his lounge chair. He had no idea what her plans were, but his were leaning toward Operation: Get Her Alone in the Pool Again.

But he was gritty-eyed with exhaustion. He thought maybe he could lie down on his bed and sleep for the rest of his life.

Going to get better now, Josh told himself. Starting tomorrow. Tomorrow he wouldn't be too tired to give something more to the people in his life.

For now, he left work and headed to the pier. It was the night of the Summer Festival, an annual event featuring music, food, and booths from the local merchants. He'd promised Mallory that he'd put in an hour at the Health Services Center booth, making nice and taking blood pressure readings for the passersby.

In exchange, and since Grace had gone for another interview in Portland—something he didn't want to think about too much—Mallory had arranged for a babysitter for Toby. Thanks to the teen center that she ran as a part of the HSC, she had lots of money-hungry teenagers at her disposal, and tonight she'd lined him up with Riley. Riley wasn't a local girl but a teen Amy had rescued from the streets not too long ago.

Toby loved her.

So with Toby taken care of, Josh arrived at the pier. The hot, muggy day had turned into a hot, sultry night, and he rolled up his sleeves as he walked through the salty ocean air. He spent an hour in the booth, taking the blood pressure of every senior citizen in

Lucky Harbor. When it was Lucille's turn, she merely winked at him when he suggested her blood pressure was a little too high and that she needed to slow down some.

"I'll slow down when I'm dead," she said, and waved in her entire blue-haired posse for their turn. Mrs. Tyler asked how Josh felt about cougars, and he really hoped she meant the kind in the wild.

Mrs. Munson grabbed his ass.

Mrs. Dawson asked him for a breast exam.

Josh was thinking about moving to the South Pacific and living on a deserted island beach when Dr. Tessa McGinley showed up to relieve him.

"Careful," he warned her. "They bite."

She was just over five feet, adorably round, and had one of those contagious smiles. "Want me to defend your honor?" she asked, laughing at him.

"You think I'm joking. I'm telling you, stay on your toes."

She didn't look perturbed in the slightest. "I think I can handle anything that comes up."

Josh was thinking *good luck* when Matt and Ty rescued him. The sun was sinking on the water, and the festival was kicking into high gear as the three of them sat on the pier near the dance floor.

"Hey," Ty said, toasting Josh with his beer. "Heard you got lucky."

Josh scowled. "How the fuck did you hear that?"

Ty went still for a beat and then laughed. "I meant regarding getting Dr. McGinley as a partner. But let's talk about what you thought I meant."

Josh slouched in his chair. "Let's not."

Ty and Matt were grinning at him, the assholes. "Shut up," he said without any real heat, and watched the dancers. Amy and Grace were dancing together in the center of the rambunctious crowd.

Matt was watching Amy. "Amy's worried that Grace'll take the first decent job to come along simply because it's what she's been told she should do," he said. "Rather than follow what makes her happy."

Josh had worried about the same thing. But it wasn't his deal to decide for Grace what made her happy. "And?"

"And so, if something or someone is making her happier than a fancy job but is being a pussy about saying so, he should step up."

Josh shook his head. "You don't know what you're talking about."

Matt laughed. "I'm currently 'getting lucky' every single day because I stepped up. I think I know what I'm talking about."

"I'm not you," Josh said. "And Grace isn't looking for that kind of relationship. Being here is a diversion for her, nothing more."

"Bullshit," Matt said. "Women don't work that way."

"Okay," Josh said. "So maybe I'm not looking for that kind of relationship either."

"More bullshit," Matt said, shaking his head at Ty like, *Can you believe this idiot?*

Ty pointed his beer at Josh. "Want to know what I think?"

"No," Josh said.

"I think you have a case of being a little girl. Maybe you should prescribe yourself a heavy dose of man-the-fuck-up."

Josh rolled his eyes as the two of them laughed their asses off over how clever they were. He turned to the dance floor again, watching Grace move with an easy rhythm.

Last night, she'd arranged for two babysitter interviews for him, vanishing instead of taking part in the interview process. He hadn't understood until he'd talked with Jenna Burnett and Sierra Hennessy. Jenna had wanted to know how much downtime they would get to spend together without "the kid," and Sierra had wanted to discuss his stance on prenups.

Not a big surprise that neither were going to work out.

He had two more interviews for tomorrow, and he wasn't sure he had any faith that either of them would be any more right for them than Jenna or Sierra had been. He knew he needed to step up and get more involved in the interview process because the clock was ticking down. Any day now, Grace was going to find a job, and she'd stop playing Mary Poppins.

He'd deal with it. He'd pick up the pieces and go on. But for now, watching her move so gorgeously and easily to the music, he wished time would stop. She wore a lacy camisole top, one of those sheer numbers, with another camisole beneath it, showing off lean, toned arms. Her skirt was short and made of a lightweight gauzy material that flirted with her thighs and blew his brain cells right and left. Her strappy sandals had heels, making her bare legs look long and sleek. The need to start at her toes and lick his way up those legs to the promised land was strong.

"You might be too much of a pussy to claim *your* woman," Matt said, rising to his feet, "but I'm not." He headed for Amy, moving in close to her, reaching out to tuck a stray strand of hair behind her ear.

Josh watched Grace smile at the couple as she moved aside, leaving room for Matt to wrap his arms hard around Amy.

Josh pushed to his feet and met Grace on the edge of the dance floor.

She smiled. "You dance?"

He gave her a boogie move that had gotten him laid once or twice in college and made her laugh. "I didn't know," she said.

"There's a lot you don't know about me."

"Like the time you and the sheriff got drunk and went streaking on the pier?" she asked sweetly.

He sighed. "Why do you listen to Anna?"

She was grinning wide. "Did you really?"

"Yeah." He grimaced, making her laugh again.

"Honesty," she said. "I like that. Is lying against the doctor's oath or something?"

"Hell, no. I lie all the time. Just tonight, on the walk from my car to the pier, I told Mrs. Lyons that she was looking good."

"Is she the one wearing the chartreuse green spandex shorts?"

"Yes," he said. "And for the record, we were stupid punk-ass seventeen-year-olds who thought we had something to show off to the world."

"Oh, you *do* have something to show off, Dr. Scott."

Shaking his head, he reached for her, pulling her into him as the music slowed. She fit against his body like the last pieces of a puzzle, and he felt himself relax for the first time in days.

"So what are some of your other lies?" she asked.

"Hmm..." He thought about it. He'd just lied to Ty and Matt about this being nothing more than a diversion. Not that he planned on saying *that*. Which probably counted as yet another lie. "This morning I told Toby that Santa Claus was alive and well and making toys as we speak."

"Aw. That's sweet, Josh."

His jaw was pressed to hers. He could feel her thighs and breasts pressing against him. She had one arm wound up around his neck, her fingers playing in his hair, making him want to purr like a big cat. "Sweet," he repeated.

"Yeah." She nudged closer. "*Sweet.*"

"I'm not feeling sweet, Grace."

She very purposely rocked against the zipper of his pants. A zipper that was slightly strained. "Mmm. I suppose not," she murmured. "Just as well, really. Sweet's overrated."

Then she rocked again, laughing softly when he tightened his grip on her. He had a hand low on her back, itching to go lower, to run up her bare leg and beneath her skirt. He'd been thinking about doing that, or some version of it, all damn day. For two damn days really, ever since the pool, when he'd had her bare, wet body in his hands.

Scratch that. He'd been thinking about getting his hands on her since he'd accidentally hired her to walk Tank and gotten the call that she'd lost the dog. He could still see her, standing on the beach, her sundress plastered to her like a second skin, completely see-through.

She'd looked like a sun-kissed goddess.

Another couple bumped into them. Lucille and Mr. Wykowski. Mr. Wykowski was eighty, but he had all his own teeth and still had a driver's license, so every female senior citizen in Lucky Harbor was constantly chasing him. He winked at Josh. "It's a night for getting lucky, eh, boy?"

Josh met Grace's gaze as the other couple danced off. "It's a night for something," he said.

The music was shifting again, gearing up for a faster-paced song. Night was upon them, the sun a mere memory on the horizon. All around them people danced, laughed, talked, drank. No one was paying them any attention, so Josh took Grace's hand and led her off the dance floor.

The bar was run by an old friend, Ford Walker.

"How's it going?" Ford asked. "Hear the little guy is doing great."

"Student of the week," Josh said proudly. He looked at Grace. "A drink?"

"A beer, please."

Ford served them up two longnecks. "So now that you're going to have all this free time, I can finally get you on our basketball team, right? Three on three. It's been just me and Jax ever since Sawyer pussied out. Pulled his Achilles. We need your height."

"Count me in," Josh said, and took Grace down the pier, lit by strings of white holiday lights that twinkled in the dark. Instead of walking to the end, where they'd be highlighted as if they were in a fishbowl, he directed her to the wood stairs that led down to the beach.

The sand was damp and giving, the water pounding the shore

hard enough to drown out most of the sounds of the festival as they walked and sipped their beers. It'd been a long week, a big week. A week of irrevocable change. Josh had made a lot of mistakes in his life, and he'd tried to learn from all of them. He definitely tried to not repeat them.

Hiring Grace had been his favorite mistake so far. That he'd gotten to this place where he'd sold the practice and was going to live his life in a way far more suited to him was because of her. Even knowing she was going to leave, he still felt that way. "Have you heard back from any of the jobs you've interviewed for?" he asked, trying to sound neutral.

"I think Seattle and Portland are both going to offer. They're both good, strong opportunities in my field."

He wasn't the only one who sounded carefully neutral. She had her face averted. He tilted her head up and searched her eyes. "Is that what you want?" he asked.

"I'm working on figuring that out." Her gaze was unguarded, letting him see her hopes and dreams and doubts and fears. It was the last that got him.

She was at the proverbial fork in the road, and he'd been there, right there, wanting to do the best thing, the *right* thing. "I gave up my dad's expectations for me when I sold the practice," he said quietly. "I let it all go, knowing, or at least hoping, he'd understand." He paused. "Maybe you need to give up your parents' expectations and do what's right for you."

She drew in a deep breath and nodded. "I know. But I've been living for their expectations so long, it's taking me some time to figure out what mine are."

Around them, the ocean continued to batter the shore. The silence was comfortable as he took in the fact that oddly enough, their problems weren't all that different from one another.

"How about you?" she asked after a few minutes. "What do you want for yourself?"

What did he want? For things to be different. For this to be what *she* wanted. "I want to have time to breathe."

"You think that will happen now?"

"Christ, I hope so," he said. "I haven't seen enough of Toby."

"I helped him with his homework earlier," she said. "It was that family tree thing." She paused. "You and his mom weren't married?"

"No. Technically, we weren't even dating."

"A one-night stand?" she asked.

"Sort of."

She gave him an expectant look, and he blew out a breath. Was he really going to do this? He *never* did this. "You don't know this about me," he said. "But I wasn't exactly the cool kid on the block growing up."

"I do know. You were the late-bloomer nerd."

He sighed, and she smiled. "People like to talk about you," she said.

Yeah, and how he loved that. "Well, nothing much changed for me between being that kid who'd get stripped and tied to the flagpole and graduating high school."

"What?" She straightened, eyes flashing fury for the kid he'd been. "Who did that to you?"

"Easy, Tiger. I'm just saying, you grow up getting picked on, you aren't exactly prepared when the summer before college you suddenly grow a foot and women start paying attention to you. Then add a few years and the initials M. and D. after your name, and it gets even worse."

She blinked. "So women started throwing themselves at you? That must have eased your pain quite a bit."

Yeah. A lot, actually. But it didn't mean he'd instantly known what he was doing. "I met Toby's mom at a friend's wedding. She was from Dallas, and just in town for the weekend." It'd been the day from hell. He'd lost his first patient that day, a teenager who'd coded out on the table from an overdose before Josh could help him. Josh had gone to the wedding in a fucked-up frame of mind. Aided by a few beers, a beautiful stranger, and apparently one faulty-as-hell condom, he'd done his best to forget the day.

Which had turned out to be impossible. "Ally had been working as a waitress to earn enough money to go to Nashville and have a singing career," he said. Wildly enthusiastic about everything, she'd sucked him in like a crazy breath of fresh air from the only life he'd been living at the time—the hospital. She'd done everything big—live, laugh, love. And God, that had been his undoing, her abundant passion. He'd fallen for her, hook, line, and sinker. "When she found out she was pregnant, things changed."

"Did she stay in Lucky Harbor to be with you?"

"For a little while." Josh had thought Ally would come to love him, too, but love hadn't been the draw for her. She'd liked the idea of being a doctor's wife and had figured it'd pay off better than being a singer. "She was going to have a perfect life," he said, "but she figured out pretty quickly that I was about as far from perfect as one could get. Not to mention already married—to my job."

Grace's eyes flashed with fire again, but when she finally spoke, her voice was gentle. "So what happened?"

"Toby was born. I caught him, actually, held him in my hands and cut the cord." His heart still caught at the memory, every single time. One minute he'd been living the selfish life that came with his job, the life he'd always wanted. And the next, he'd been holding this gloppy, squirming, pissed-off little rug rat. He'd held Toby in his hands, stared down into his own dark eyes, and had felt something open wide deep inside him.

Then Toby had yawned and gone to sleep on him. "He changed my entire life." Ally's too, but in a different way. She hated the 24/7 care the baby demanded. She hated the changes in her body. She hated that Josh was gone so much working. "One day I came home after a brutal double shift, and Ally handed me Toby. Said he was changed and fed. Then she grabbed her keys and her purse and walked out the door."

She hadn't looked back, not once in the past five years.

Grace looked horrified. "So she left you alone with Toby? She just walked away from you?"

"I really was a pretty crappy partner," he said. "I was at work all the time. And she wasn't cut out for the domesticated sort of home life a baby required."

"But to just leave you and Toby. That must have been awful for you."

"I didn't have much time to dwell. A month later, a drunk driver hit my dad's car head-on and killed both him and my mom. And then Anna came to live with me too."

"Oh my God, Josh."

He shrugged. Yeah, those first two years with Toby and Anna and his work had been a deep, dark hell. He didn't like to remember the terror of having a baby, of dealing with Anna's injuries, not to mention her mental state—which hadn't been anything close to the downright sunny nature she displayed now in comparison.

Grace was quiet a moment. "Did you know I've never even so much as had a dog?"

He smiled, rubbing his jaw against her hair, loving that she wasn't going to shower him with sympathy that he didn't want. "That fact wasn't on your dog flyer."

She let out a low laugh. "My parents were too busy trying to save the world to have pets. I'm surprised they made time to adopt me. I have this recurring nightmare where I've turned into a rocket scientist and my ass has gone flat."

He laughed, and the hand he had low on her spine slid down a little, giving her a quick squeeze. "It's perfect."

She smiled up at him.

"What?"

"I like your laugh," she said.

"Maybe it's the hand on your ass that you like."

"Why, Dr. Scott, are you flirting with me?"

"Desperately," he said. "Is it working?"

She laughed. "Depends on the end goal. And also, if it matches my end goal."

"Maybe you should spell yours out for me. Slowly and in great detail."

She smiled, a demure little smile that belied the heat in her eyes, and hell if the woman didn't turn him completely upside down and sideways.

And turn him on…

Then she went up on her very tiptoes and leaned in, her lips brushing his earlobe as she did what he'd suggested, telling him in detail *exactly* what her end goal was.

He nodded solemnly, memorizing everything, every last little detail, before taking her hand and heading up the stairs.

Chapter 18

Chocolate is better than sex. It can't make you pregnant, and it's always good.

Grace had to take three steps for every one of Josh's much longer strides, but she was laughing as she did. "Gee, Dr. Scott, in a hurry?"

He didn't bother to answer her, just continued to steer them across the sand with the single-minded purpose of a man on a mission. She laughed again, and he tossed a look over his shoulder at her that had her swallowing the amusement and shivering in anticipation.

All her life she'd done what was expected, taken the "right" path. But Lucky Harbor, and her time in it, was supposed to be different.

She'd made it different. She'd made it hers. She'd never forget it.

Or him. "Where are we going?" she asked.

"Somewhere more secluded than this."

"And the hurry?" she asked.

"I want to get you alone before you forget any of your end game or we're interrupted again."

"No worries," she said. "I was very serious about my end game."

Their eyes caught. "Thought you don't do serious," he said. "You do fun."

"Is that what you're looking for tonight?"

His gaze was fathomless. "It's a start."

She quivered. "I need to tell Mallory and Amy I'm leaving. Give me a minute?"

"I'll get the car."

Grace found Amy and Matt sitting at a booth sharing a pitcher of beer and trying to swallow each other's tongues. Since Mallory and Ty were still on the dance floor doing the same thing, Grace texted them both without disturbing them. This had the additional benefit of not having to explain that she intended to go do the same thing that they were doing.

Heading toward the lot, she walked past a bunch of tables, all filled with people enjoying the night. Something niggled at her, and she turned back, realizing that one of the people was Devon.

With a girl who wasn't Anna.

Grace stared at him in shock. "What are you doing?"

Devon turned away, pulling the girl with him into the shadows, and in another heartbeat they were gone, vanishing into the night.

Grace wondered if Anna was here as well, but she hadn't seen her all night. It'd probably be impossible to maneuver around the crowded pier and the beach in her chair. Not only was the girl missing out on the festival, but also her boyfriend was a rat-fink bastard. Grace turned to walk away and plowed into a brick wall.

A brick wall that was Josh's chest.

"Hey," he said, catching her. "I got held up." He took a second look at her. "What's wrong?"

She couldn't tell him, not here. He and Anna rarely saw eye to eye on anything, *especially* Devon, which was mostly due to his fiercely protective instincts, not to mention the fact that Devon was a complete ass. If Grace gave Josh proof of that right now, she wasn't sure exactly what he'd do, but he'd do *something.*

And then there was how Anna would feel to not be the first to hear about Devon's indiscretions. "Nothing's wrong," she said.

Josh didn't buy it, but he didn't push either. He obviously had other things on his mind at the moment. Such as getting her alone.

On the way to the car, they were stopped multiple times by people wanting to tell Josh their ailments. Everyone wanted to talk to him, to let him know that their throat hurt, or that they were feeling better, or that they planned on calling his office for an appointment next week.

"How do you do it?" she marveled. "How do you keep track of everyone's various ailments and quirks and needs?"

"I don't know. I guess I've always had a good memory. My brain retains everything, even really stupid, useless stuff."

"Yeah?" she asked. "Everything?"

"Just about."

"What was I wearing that day you hired me?"

"White lace panties."

She laughed. "What?"

"You were all wet from the water. Your dress was sheer."

"That's not your brain's memory," she said. "That's your *penis's.*"

He grinned and leaned in to nip at her bottom lip. "I love it when you say *penis* in that prim schoolteacher tone, like you're saying a forbidden word in public."

She felt herself blush. "What would you rather I call it?"

His eyes darkened. "We'll go over our body parts, and what they like to be called, in great detail tonight. But we have to get out of here first. The key is lack of eye contact. Don't look at anyone. I don't care if it's God himself, just keep moving, got it?"

"Yes, sir."

"I like that. More of that," he said.

"Um, excuse me, Grace?" It was Mindy, who owned the florist shop that Grace delivered for. She sent both Josh and Grace a shy smile. "I hope I'm not interrupting..."

The look on Josh's face was resigned, but to his credit he did make respectful eye contact. "It's okay," he said.

Mindy relaxed slightly. "It's just that I haven't been sleeping."

Josh let out a breath. "I have office hours tomorrow," he said. "From eight to—"

"Actually"—she turned to Grace—"it's you I need to talk to. I need some bookkeeping help. I heard you're the one in town to go to for this sort of thing. You helped Lucille, Anderson, and Amy, right?"

"Yes, but—"

"I'll pay," Mindy said. "Whatever they're paying."

Since Amy was paying in cupcakes, and Grace needed more cupcakes like she needed another sexually frustrated alpha male standing impatiently at her side, she started to shake her head, but Mindy grabbed her hands.

"It would mean so much to me," she said urgently, "to have someone trustworthy handling my books. My ex, he"—she drew in a shaky breath—"he screwed things up for me financially. Like I said, I really need your help."

Grace felt her stomach clench in sympathy and understanding and nodded. "Okay."

"Oh, thank you. Thank you so much! Now?"

"No," Josh said. "Not now." He took Grace's hand in a firm, inexorable grip. "Tomorrow. She'll help you tomorrow." And he pulled her away, through the crowd, across the lot, once again moving so that she was practically running to keep up with his long legs and relentless stride.

"That was rude," she said breathlessly.

He didn't bother to respond.

"People are going to think we're in a hurry to..."

He slid her a look that said, *We* are *in a hurry to…*

There were people milling around in the lot. One or two called out to Josh, but the man was on a mission and didn't veer from his path.

"Josh," Grace said on a breathless laugh. "Slow down."

He didn't, not even a little. And when several ladies from the drawing class she'd modeled for tried to wave her over, he tightened his grip on her. "No eye contact," he reminded her, and beeped his car unlocked, practically shoving her into the passenger seat. She might have objected to the way he was manhandling her except his big, warm hands were sliding over her body, making themselves at home, and she couldn't quite catch her breath. He shut the door and was in the driver's seat before she could so much as blink.

"What if those ladies needed to talk to me?" she asked.

"*I* need to talk to you."

She laughed. "You want to talk? Really? Because you're looking a little bit like the big bad wolf over there. But if you want to talk, hey, I'm game." She leaned back in the guise of settling in comfortably. "How was your day?"

Josh reached across the console and pulled her into his lap.

"So it was a good day, then?" she teased.

"Fantastic. Tell me it's about to get even better."

She rocked a little, feeling his arousal beneath her, hard and quite insistent. "Mmm. Maybe…"

"Don't tease me. I'm beyond that."

"Aw. Poor baby."

"I mean it," he said in a low, very serious voice. "If we're interrupted again…"

She laughed. "At least we made it to the end last time."

"That wasn't the end. That was just the beginning." His dark eyes met hers. "A year, Grace. I went without sex for a whole year. I have some moves stored up."

"Yeah?" she asked, breathless at the thought. "Show me."

He covered her mouth with his, sliding a hand into her hair to angle her head the way he wanted it. She was getting to know him, and she knew that he was a man who rarely acted without thinking. His moves were always rational, calm.

Controlled.

But there was nothing controlled about him now as his hands wandered madly from her face to her waist to her hips, ending up back in her hair while he kissed her hard, his tongue tangling with hers.

And suddenly a Josh-induced orgasm right here, right now, seemed like the best idea she'd had all night.

Needing to touch him, Grace wrapped her arms around him and pushed her hands beneath his shirt, encountering sleek, smooth sinew.

His groan rumbled in her ear, and she pressed even closer. He was breathing unevenly, a fact she liked, very much. His hands were busy, the heat of them seeming to scald her skin as they dug into her hips. He was huge and hard and pressed up against her core, which worked for her. He'd completely forgotten their surroundings, which she liked even more. Then his hands slid beneath the hem of her dress, and she forgot their surroundings, too, beginning to pant before he'd even touched anything vital. He moved his lips to her neck, kissing and tracing his magic tongue down her throat as his wandering fingers stroked the wet silk of her panties.

The knock on the window startled them.

It was Lucille, one hand covering her eyes. "Sorry!" she yelled through the glass.

"I know I took an oath to save lives," Josh muttered, "but I'm going to kill her."

Grace scooted back into the passenger seat, desperately righting her clothing as she did. Josh checked her progress, then rolled the window down an inch.

"I'm sorry!" Lucille told him again, eyes still covered. "But a couple of the guys were messing around on the pier, and Anderson fell in. He hasn't surfaced. They're looking for him but—"

Josh was already out of the car. "Call nine-one-one," he called back to Grace, and took off running toward the pier.

Grace called 911, then took Josh's keys and locked up his car, moving quickly with Lucille to the water, anxious to know if Anderson had been found. An almost hushed crowd was gathered down on the beach, and they headed that way, taking the stairs as fast as Lucille could move.

There was a huddle in the water, three people making their way toward shore, a figure being carefully supported between them. One of the men was bent over the still one. It was too dark to see what he was doing or even who he was—but Grace knew.

Josh.

He and the others staggered ashore. Josh dropped to his knees, situating the overly still man between them, careful with his neck and spine.

"Oh thank God, they found him," Lucille breathed, and put her hands to her mouth. "I just hope they were in time."

The other men crouched on the opposite side of Anderson, water streaming off all of them. Grace recognized one of them as Sheriff Sawyer Thompson. The other was Ty, Mallory's fiancé. Sawyer borrowed a phone from someone on the beach and was on it, probably to dispatch, while Josh checked for a pulse. He must have gotten one because he nodded to Ty before beginning compressions, his movements quick and efficient.

"Oh no," Lucille whispered, and clutched at Grace. "He's not breathing."

"Josh'll fix it." Grace gripped Lucille's icy fingers and prayed that was true. In her heart, she knew that if Anderson could be saved, Josh was the man to do it.

But Anderson was awfully still, and there was blood on his face and head. He could have broken bones too; she couldn't tell from here but knew Josh was worried about the same thing given the extremely cautious way he'd handled Anderson's body. Just as he stopped to once again check for a heartbeat and pulse, sirens whooped, and red-and-blue flashing lights lit up the night as the ambulance pulled into the lot above.

And then, an even more welcome sound—Anderson choking up seawater, convulsing with the violence of it, his muscles spasming.

Sawyer and Ty let out audible breaths of relief. Sawyer stood up and pushed the crowd back. Ty accepted several jackets from people standing near, using them to cover Anderson.

Josh had deftly turned Anderson on his side to more effectively cough up what looked like gallons of water. As the EMS team ran down the pier stairs and hit the beach, Anderson tried to push himself up but Josh held him down, talking to him quietly.

"Dammit," Lucille said, her eyes glistening, tears of relief on her cheeks. "I can't hear what they're saying."

Grace didn't need to hear to know that Josh was working to keep Anderson calm and still. She was riveted to the sight. All of the men were drenched, but none of them appeared to even notice, worried only about Anderson.

Josh gave out orders to the EMS, and working together they got Anderson on the gurney, covered him in blankets, and then loaded him into the ambulance. Josh hopped into the back alongside his patient, and the doors closed. A minute later, the ambulance pulled out of the lot, lights going, sirens silent.

"Everyone in town is here," Lucille said to Grace. "They won't have any traffic on the road."

Grace nodded a little numbly, struck by the sudden feeling of fragility. Life was fragile.

Short.

Too short. Fingering Josh's keys, she left the pier and drove home. Well, not home exactly, she reminded herself.

Josh's home. Which he'd managed to make for himself and his

family in spite of believing that he'd not given them much. It was a good home, too, warm and safe. But for now, tonight, it was silent and dark. Lifeless without Josh in it.

She found Anna by the pool, staring into the moonlit water. "Hey." Grace plopped down on a lounge chair near her. "You missed the action tonight."

"I can't maneuver the pier by myself."

"I'd have helped you."

This had Anna looking at her. "Why?"

"Why? Well, why not?"

"Because I've been a bitch to you."

"Yeah," Grace said. "But you're a bitch to everyone, so I never take it personally."

Anna laughed. It sounded a little rusty. And unhappy. Grace knew that what she had to tell her wasn't going to help. "I think I saw Devon there," she said carefully.

Anna shook her head. "He's in Seattle. At a family thing."

Grace grimaced. "Okay, let me rephrase. I *definitely* saw him at the festival. With a girl."

Anna went still. "Just when I thought I could learn not to hate you."

"If I were you, I'd want to know," Grace said, not hurt by Anna's words. She understood. She might not know firsthand the tragedy of losing her parents and becoming paralyzed, but she knew boy pain.

"You don't know anything about our relationship," Anna said.

"I know you like him." Grace wished Anna would open up to her so she could try to help—although she knew how everyone in the Scott family felt about accepting help. Stubborn to the end, the entire lot of them. "And I know that the way you feel about him means that you don't want him feeling it for someone else."

Anna shook her head but didn't speak as she turned away so Grace couldn't see her face.

Grace's heart squeezed tight. She knew damn well that Devon

had been pushing Anna for sex. It didn't take a rocket scientist to figure out that if Anna wasn't ready, then Devon had gone after it somewhere else. "I'm proud of you for not caving to the pressure."

"You don't know what you're talking about," Anna shot back.

"So explain it to me."

"I *want* to cave to the pressure. I want to..."

"Have sex?"

Anna didn't answer, and Grace sighed. "Honey, if you can't even say the word, you're so not ready."

"I am," Anna said unconvincingly, and began wheeling toward the house.

Grace sighed. "If you need anything—"

"I won't."

"If your brother needs anything—"

Anna let out another rusty-sounding laugh, this one with a hint of tears in it, but she stopped at the door, her back still to Grace. "He won't."

"He had a rough evening," Grace said quietly.

"Yeah, because he called me earlier to check in and told me I needed to stop seeing Devon. I read him the riot act."

"Actually, I didn't know that," Grace said. "I meant that Anderson nearly drowned tonight at the festival, and Josh had to perform CPR to save him."

Anna turned to her, eyes hooded. "That's what Josh does. He saves people."

Grace paused, wondering at the bitterness in Anna's voice. "You say that like it's a bad thing."

Anna was quiet a moment. "Do you think everyone should be saved?" she finally asked.

Okay, they were definitely not talking about Anderson. Grace moved closer. "Anna—"

"I'm fine. We're Scotts. We're always fine. Haven't you learned that yet?"

When Anna had rolled into the house, Grace pulled out her cell phone and called the hospital, inquiring after Anderson. She was told that no information could be given out about a patient, so she went to the next best source.

Facebook.

Luckily, Lucille was already on the case:

Thanks to the swift, heroic measures of Dr. Josh Scott, one of our very own was saved tonight.

Anderson, manager of Anderson Hardware Store, fell off the pier, hitting the water and his head. He'd have drowned if not for the three men who dived into the dark ocean after him: Sheriff Sawyer Thompson, flight care paramedic Ty Garrison, and Dr. Josh Scott.

And, oh my, can I just say how incredibly handsome these three hunks looked all wet and sweaty from their efforts?

Anderson's at General, suffering a mild concussion, broken ankle, and probably a few sore ribs.

Thanks, Dr. Scott. You are one Hunkalicious Doctor.

Anderson, get well. And stay off the pier!

Grace logged off, crawled into bed, and hoped that wherever he was, Josh had at least gotten some dry clothes.

She had no idea how long she'd been out when she awoke suddenly, heart pounding in the dark. She peered at her cell phone on the nightstand.

Midnight.

She sat up just as a soft knock sounded on her door. Padding barefoot across the room, she peered out the peephole.

Dark, disheveled hair. Dark and shadowed eyes. Scrubs. Grace's heart kicked hard as she opened the door to one clearly exhausted Dr. Josh Scott.

Chapter 19

A chocolate in the mouth is worth two on the plate.

Josh had told himself he was going straight to bed. He needed the sleep. But his body got its wires crossed, and he ended up at the guesthouse instead.

Grace answered his knock with a sleep-flushed face and crazy hair, wearing a little tank top and boxers—emphasis on *little.*

Cute.

Hot.

"Anderson?" she asked, brow furrowed, eyes concerned.

He didn't want to talk about Anderson. He wanted Grace naked and screaming his name. But if there was a way to say that without sounding like a complete asshole, he didn't have the brain capacity to find the words. "He's got a hell of a headache and sore ribs, but he's going to be okay."

"That's what Facebook said too," she said. "Are you okay? You must be dead on your feet. Come on, come in and take a load off. My bed's warm."

He raised his head and looked into her sweet baby blues. "Anyone here?"

"No."

"Anyone *due* to be here?"

"No."

"Are you planning on starting a fire with the heater and toaster? Is anyone going to call you and need you to count their money?"

"No." She bit her lower lip to hold back a smile, the sexy witch. "Why? Do you have nefarious intentions?" she asked with a soft hopefulness that had lust and amusement warring for space within him.

He took a step and bumped into her, crowding into her space. "Yes. I have nefarious intentions. Lots of them. You should be running for the hills, Grace."

She held her ground, sliding a hand up his chest, hooking it around his neck, not speaking.

Josh didn't remember moving, but then he had her up against the wall, his arms tight around her, her legs around his waist. "The whole fucking place can come down," he said against her mouth. "We're not stopping."

"Show me," she said.

Grace hadn't meant the words as a dare but Josh appeared to take them that way. He lifted his head and held her gaze, one hand on her ass, the other reaching out to hit the lock on the door. "Phone?"

"On the counter."

Still holding her, he walked over to her phone and shoved it inside the fridge.

"Yours?" she asked.

"DOA from the ocean. Again."

"What if someone needs you?"

"Fuck the rest of the world," he said, his voice thrillingly rough.

She cupped his face and offered him a slow smile. "How about just me?"

His eyes darkened as he backed her to the bed and nudged her onto the mattress. "Tell me you still have condoms."

She rolled to her hands and knees and crawled to the nightstand. He groaned, making her realize the sight she'd just presented. Deciding to own it, she wriggled her hips and was rewarded with another rough sound from him, inherently male, as she yanked open the drawer to reveal a full box of condoms.

"That's a good start," he said, setting a knee on the bed. He moved so fast she didn't have time to react before his warm hand wrapped around her ankle and tugged.

She fell flat, facedown on the bed, laughing when he yanked her toward him, giving her a world-class wedgie. Then he flipped her over to face him. Her cami had risen up a little, and his gaze swept over her body, heating every inch it touched. His deep, rumbling groan was low and possessive, and everything within her quivered.

"Your shirt," she said. She needed it gone, yesterday.

He impatiently tore it off and tossed it behind him.

Oh, that was better, she thought, taking in his broad, sculpted chest, feeling herself go damp at the sight of all those muscles bunching as he moved. *Much* better.

As if reading her mind, his lips curved, sending more heat through her because she knew exactly what those lips could do to her, the places he could take her. He had a way of making her feel sexy, beautiful. Like she was special. He had a way of sending all her doubts scattering, of reinstating her confidence.

Her parents had educated her and made sure that her horizons were broad. But Josh had given her something new.

He made her *feel*.

The soft material of her cami gave him no resistance when he lifted it over her head and sent it sailing somewhere in the direction of his discarded shirt. "Mmm," he said, bending to kiss a breast as he hooked his fingers into the silk boxers low on her hips. They hit the floor next. "Christ, you're beautiful," he said as he stroked a hand up her leg, settling it low on her belly. "And wet." His thumb glided over her, spreading her a little on each pass, making her moan and shift impatiently. But he simply continued to tease and torment, that knowing finger nearly driving her right over the edge. "Please..." she finally gasped.

"After you come."

"But—"

"Shhh." Then he dropped to his knees beside the bed, pulled her to the edge, and put his mouth on her. The first stroke of his tongue shot her heart rate to the moon. "Did you just...*shush* me?" she barely managed to ask.

He pulled back just enough to blow a breath over her, making her shiver and moan and pant. "There's a code," he said. "A guy code."

Her only response was a throaty moan because his tongue was back. And good Lord, she could no more ignore that tongue than she could have stopped breathing.

"The guy code says you get yours first," he said.

She opened her mouth to say something to that, she had no idea what, but all that came out was a low, desperate cry as he very gently nibbled at her.

And then not so gently.

And in less time than it would take to make toast and screw up the electricity, she nearly burst out of her skin. "*How* do you always do that?" she gasped.

"I know your body." He climbed onto the bed, caressing his way up her thighs, wrapping her legs around his hips. "I love your body."

And she loved his. "I hope the guy code says it's time."

He smiled as he cupped her butt in one hand. Leaning over her, his other hand slid up her back and into her hair as he whispered, "Yeah, it's time." He pressed a kiss at her damp temple, her cheek, her mouth, while she lay still trembling in little aftershocks from the orgasm. Lacing their fingers together, he slid their hands up over her head, and then executed a slow grind against her that had her eyes closing from the pleasure of the friction.

"Grace," he said softly, nipping at her lower lip until she looked at him. When she did, he kissed her deeper, harder. She could feel the burn low in her belly as she began to rise to peak again. Wrapping her arms around him, she had the sudden, irrational wish that she'd never have to let go. Not exactly in keeping with this being just fun. But then he slid into her in one thrust, and she could no longer think at all. She whimpered for more, and he gave it, slow and steady, until she adjusted to him, then hard and fast as they climbed together. She clutched at him, panting his name, giving herself over to him fully, wondering if he could possibly feel what she was feeling. Which was entirely too much.

His head was thrown back, his big body taut as a bow. Pressing her harder into the bed, he tightened his grip on her and plunged deep. Moving together in just the right rhythm, her toes curled, and he shuddered against her as they rode each other to a mind-blowing completion.

When he finally sank down over her, muscles quivering, hands still possessively gripping her butt as he fought to catch his breath, she smiled. "Feel better?"

He rolled to his back so that she was straddling him. "Getting there."

A long time later, they were a tangle of damp sheets and exhausted limbs in the warm night. Grace couldn't have moved to save her life.

Josh pulled her in close, wrapped his arms around her, and let out a long, slow breath. Relaxed to the bone, she thought. It gave her a surge of feminine satisfaction that she'd gotten him there and it put a big grin on her face.

"Hmm," he said in a voice so low on the register she could barely hear it. "I'd swipe that smile off your face, but my body isn't working."

"Later," she promised him, hearing the exhaustion in his voice, snuggling in closer, stroking a hand down his back. "Josh?"

"Yeah?"

"Watching you tonight, working so hard to save Anderson..." She shook her head, moved again at the memory. "It was amazing." She snuggled in close and kissed one corner of his mouth, then the other. "I was so proud of you," she whispered.

The words seemed to rejuvenate him. He tugged the sheet from her, an urgent energy behind his movements that resonated within her as well. In a blink of an eye, he was pressing her back into the mattress, the sure and solid weight of his body as comforting as it was arousing.

It felt more right than anything she'd ever felt. *He* felt right.

He came up on his forearms, his eyes locked on hers as he slowly pushed inside her. Unable to keep still, she arched up with a soft gasp, wrapping her legs around his waist.

"So good," he murmured, then lowered himself again, his hands sliding up her back, pulling her in close. "Always so fucking good with you." He brushed his lips over hers, his eyes never leaving her face as he began to move inside her, slowly at first. She met him thrust for thrust, trying to urge him on by biting his lower lip. He hissed in a breath and gripped her hard, holding her still, forcing her to take the slow, tortuous climb, making her feel every single inch of him.

And she did feel him, she felt everything, and when the pure emotion overtook her, she felt her throat tighten, her eyes sting. She sobbed when she burst, feeling his release hit him too. Afterward, he pulled her in tight and held her close. Lulled by the feel of his warm strength, the comforting scent of him surrounding her, she drifted off, with him still buried deep.

Josh knew he needed to get up, but lying here with Grace wrapped around him like he was her own personal body pillow was really doing it for him.

He'd shown up here tonight and pretty much taken what he'd needed from her without a thought to the after. This wasn't supposed to keep happening, and yet it did. And each time, feelings got deeper.

At least for him.

He had no idea what that meant for them now and wasn't all that eager to find out if things had changed between them. Of course they'd changed, because in his experience, right about now was when things tended to go to shit.

"Hey," Grace murmured, her head on his chest, fingers gliding back and forth from pec to pec. "You okay?"

"That was going to be my question to you."

She lifted her head and looked into his eyes. "Nice deflection, Dr. Scott."

He blew out a breath and lay back, staring up at the ceiling. He felt unsure, and that was an extremely new and uncomfortable sensation.

"Are you... feeling claustrophobic?" she asked. "Maybe contemplating a trip to Australia to go surfing?"

He shook his head at her polite tone. "Not all men are dicks like your exes, Grace."

"Touché. And right back at you."

He tilted his head down and met her gaze. "I haven't dated anyone with a dick."

"You know what I mean."

"Actually, I don't."

"It means," she said, coming up on an elbow to lean over him, eyes flashing, "that I might have called this 'just fun' but that doesn't mean I'd walk away if the going got tough."

God, she was gorgeous when riled up. "So that wasn't some sort of pity fuck?"

She pulled back to stare at him, then laughed, dropping her head to his chest.

"Just what a man loves. Being laughed at in bed."

"I don't do pity fucks," she said, still grinning, pissing him off a little. "And I especially don't do pity fucks with doctors. Doctors don't need pity fucks."

Some of his annoyance drained away. "What *do* doctors need?"

She climbed on top of him, effectively taking care of the rest of his annoyance. "I'll show you," she said.

It was 3:00 a.m. before Josh could move again, and his blanket—a warm, sated, boneless Grace—murmured in soft protest. He stroked a soothing hand down her back.

She let out a sexy little purr and fell back into a deep sleep. He managed to untangle himself and rolled out of the bed without her stirring.

As he moved around the room searching out the scrubs he'd carelessly discarded earlier, his gaze kept wandering back to the bed. To the woman in it.

Dead to the world.

When he was dressed, he bent over her and brushed a kiss over her mouth. "'Night," he whispered.

She let out a barely there snore that made him smile as he left the guesthouse, carefully locking the door behind him. He entered his house and moved down the hall. Toby's door was open but he wasn't there; he was still at his friend Conner's. Anna's door was also open, and he found his sister sitting in her chair at her bedroom window, staring out into the dark night.

"Hey," he said, startled to see her. She did her best to avoid him these days. Something else he was going to have to fix in all his new spare time that he didn't yet have. "No adventure tonight?" he asked carefully. Something was obviously wrong. Not that she'd tell him.

"Hard to have an adventure on wheels."

His chest ached, and he drew a slow, painful breath. "What adventure would you like to have?"

She sighed, then wheeled to face him. "Don't you ever get tired of trying to make my life work for me?"

"No."

She stared at him and then shook her head. "Well I do. I hate being a pathetic burden."

"Anna, you are smart, attitude-ridden, and scary as hell. You're a lot of other things, too, but you are not, nor have you ever been, a pathetic burden."

She shrugged.

"What if it was me?" he asked her quietly. "Me hurt in the accident. Me in a chair. Would you think of me as a burden?"

"Would I have to wipe your drool?"

He sighed. Her teen years had been hell on wheels. Literally. Once in a while he thought he saw glimpses of the gentler, kinder version of Anna that she'd been as a young girl, but right now wasn't one of those times.

"Fine," she said, caving. "I'd kick your ass every day until you no longer felt sorry for yourself."

"So consider your ass kicked," he said.

"I'm still going to Europe."

He'd done a lot of thinking about this, and the idea of Anna alone in Europe gave him the cold sweats. But she was twenty-one, and the truth was, he couldn't stop her. And he did understand her need to go, to prove her independence. He really did. He just was terrified for her. "You can get adventure closer to home and closer to your support system."

"My support system works twenty-four-seven and doesn't have time for his own life, much less mine."

Guilt sliced him. "That's going to change. You know I sold the practice."

"I'm still doing this."

Since there was nothing to say to that, he turned to go.

"Josh?"

He looked back, wondering what she was going to fling at him now. "Yeah?"

"Thanks."

He was so surprised she could have knocked him over with one little push. "For?" he asked warily.

"For not seeing me as pathetic."

Chapter 20

Coffee makes it possible to get out of bed but chocolate makes it worthwhile.

Josh walked into his office the next day and found his office staff and Tessa huddled over the scheduling computer. They looked up in unison, paused, and then—still in unison—grinned.

"Nice," Dee said to him.

"What?" He looked behind him; he was the only one there.

"You got some," Dee said.

Michelle and Tessa smiled and nodded.

Josh worked at not reacting. He had a good staff, but they were a pack of vultures. If they sensed a weakness, they'd attack.

"'Bout time, if you ask me," Michelle said. "So it's a good day to ask for a raise?"

"I'm thinking you don't have enough work to do," Josh said in his boss voice.

They all scattered, except for Tessa. "I'm beginning to see why you signed on the dotted line," she said. "Having a life looks good on you."

The morning went so smoothly that Josh got an actual lunch

break. He met Ty and Matt at the Love Shack, Lucky Harbor's bar and grill. They'd beaten him there and were seated at a table hunched over *Cosmo* magazine.

"It was on the table when I got here," Matt said in his defense.

Josh eyed the open magazine. "You don't already know how to satisfy your boyfriends in bed?"

Matt ignored this. "Did either of you know there's ninety-nine ways to give a blow job? That's *ninety-nine* nights of blow jobs."

"Look at you with the math skills," Josh said.

Matt flipped him off while Ty flipped the page. "'*How to Give Your Hoo-Ha a Spa Day*.' Huh," he said. "I didn't know a woman's hoo-ha needed a spa day."

Ford came out from behind the bar to take their order. "Saw you on FB," he said to Josh.

"Ty was a part of the rescue too."

"I meant with the pretty babysitter at your son's Back-to-School night." Ford laughed. "Caught by Lucille, huh? Gotta be stealth, man. Geriatric stealth."

Josh didn't bother to sigh. "Like you didn't get on Facebook all last year when you started seeing Tara."

At this, Ford let out an unabashed grin, because they all knew it was true. While dating Tara, he'd found himself in the middle of an all-out whose-dick-is-bigger contest with her ex, which had been splashed across the entire town like it'd been first-line news. Ford was a world-class sailing pro and had a gold medal and buckets of money, but to this day, he was most famous for that abs contest, which had been legendary. As had the fallout, which had involved Ford breaking his leg climbing an apple tree to impress the girl.

"At least I didn't end up in my ER getting my leg set in a cast," Josh said.

Ford laughed good-naturedly and took their order. When he was gone, Matt looked at Josh. "So how's it going with your Grace anyway? Still having fun playing house?"

He'd been working at not replaying every detail of last night in his head over and over again. Working, and failing. Last night had been…incredible. "Says the guy who just put a rock on his girlfriend's finger."

Matt shrugged. "Turns out I like commitment. Who knew?"

"Yeah? And what's your excuse?" Josh asked Ty.

Ty's lips curved. "I took a page from your book."

"Mine?"

"I like the idea of the whole family thing, like you have with Toby and Anna. I want that. I want that with Mallory."

Their food came, and while Josh ate his chicken sandwich, he thought of his "whole family thing." He had his sister, who missed their mom and dad like she missed her own legs and was dating a first-class asshole. His son, who had spent far too many nights going to bed without any parent at all. The family unit everyone thought he had wasn't what it was supposed to be, and that killed him.

He'd made the first step—selling the practice. He only hoped he'd done it in time to repair his relationships. It wasn't something he could write a prescription for. He couldn't order a scan and diagnose a solution. "I've fucked it up."

"Yeah?" Ty asked. "With the hot nanny?"

"No." *Yes*. "Never mind."

"That's the first sign of losing it," Ty said. "Disagreeing with yourself. And trust me, I should know."

Josh managed a brief smile at the memory of Ty coming apart at the seams not so long ago but Matt kept his eyes on Josh. Concerned.

"Stop," Josh said to him. "I'm not losing it."

"Maybe you should."

"Huh?"

"You're wrapped pretty tight," Matt said. "You should get in the ring with one of us. Release some tension."

"I've seen you two in the ring," Josh said. "It's like Extreme

Cagefighting. On steroids. I like being able to walk out of the gym after a workout."

"One time," Ty said. "I only needed help one time. And it's because he sucker punched me."

Matt smiled smugly. "That's what happens when you stop to take a call from your fiancée when you're still in the ring."

"I'm not getting in the ring," Josh said, and stood. He dropped cash on the table. "I've got to get back."

His waiting room was calm and quiet. The front desk was calm and quiet. Everything was calm and quiet.

"There's no one waiting for me?" he asked Michelle.

"Tessa's got it moving along pretty good."

He eyed the schedule. "What about Mrs. B?"

"Oh, she's already been seen. She had some arthritic flare-up."

Josh was stunned. Mrs. B. had never been willing to see anyone else before. "And Lisa Boyles? She was bringing in her three kids for sports physicals."

"Tessa finished early and offered to see them, and Lisa took her up on it. That's who she's with right now."

"Okay..." He felt a little off center. "I'll go get some charting done."

"Sure."

But when he got to his office and sat down, the charting didn't appeal. Where was a fast-paced ER emergency when he needed one? Anderson couldn't fall off the pier now?

He saw patients that afternoon but it remained quiet and sedate. Not at all what he was used to.

But what you wanted...

Except suddenly he wasn't keeping the world going around. It was going around without him, all on its own.

And he didn't know if he liked it.

* * *

That night for the first time in months, Josh got home in time for dinner. He walked into his house and blinked. His living room had been turned into a fort. Blankets and sheets had been stretched across the couches, tucked into the entertainment center, into shelves, anywhere and everywhere. He crouched down, and yep, it was filled with what appeared to be every single toy Toby owned.

He entered the kitchen to find Toby and Grace sitting on the counter, eating chocolate cupcakes. Josh met Grace's gaze, and the air did that unique crackle thing while her slow smile brought back memories of the night before.

Slow hands. Deep, wet, unending kisses. Bodies hot and damp and meshed together. Heady, erotic pleasures…

"Daddy, *cupcakes*!" Toby said.

"I'm sorry." Josh pretended to scrub out his ear. "Was that *English*?"

Toby grinned.

Josh pulled him up for a hug and came away a little sticky. "You're supposed to eat the dessert, not bathe in it."

This earned him another grin. "Try it!" Toby demanded, holding out his cupcake.

Josh took a bite, and he had to admit that the soft, spongy chocolate cupcake was pretty damn amazing. He took another bite, pretending to go for Toby's fingers, earning him a belly laugh.

Best sound ever. He started laughing as well when he turned and found Grace watching them with a smile. "Hope you don't mind," she said. "It's a backward dinner."

"We *love* backward dinners!" Toby said.

They'd never had a backward dinner.

Tank was sitting on the floor at Toby's feet. He let out a loud "arf!" followed by a pathetically sad whine.

"He's sad 'cause Grace said he can't have chocolate," Toby said. "Chocolate's bad for dogs. They go like this…" He mimed choking on his own tongue, complete with bugging-out eyes and the sound effects to go with it, before dramatically falling off the stool to the floor. There he kicked once, twice, and then "died."

"Nice," Josh said.

Toby smiled proudly and sat back up as Tank climbed into his lap, licking his face.

"We don't feel sorry for Tank," Grace told Josh. "He got his dessert."

"He ate a bag of powdered sugar," Toby said.

Josh looked at the tiny Tank. "When you say bag of powdered sugar..."

"The *entire* bag, including the paper." Grace shook her head. "He has an eating disorder."

They all looked at Tank, who snorted, then burped, emitting a little puff of white.

"You gonna eat with us, Daddy?" Toby asked. "We're having mac and cheese!"

"My favorite," Josh said dryly.

Toby grinned. "No, it's *my* favorite."

Josh thought about the nutritional content of the unopened box of mac and cheese on the counter, which probably was about as healthy as eating the actual box, and grimaced. "Where's Nina?"

"On a date!" Toby said.

Now that Toby had regained his mastery of the English language, apparently he felt the need to speak in exclamation points.

"You should join us," Grace said, her voice sounding a little husky now, reminding him of how she sounded the night before, when he'd been buried deep. *Oh, please, Josh*, she'd said in that same voice. Pretty sure he *had* pleased, he cleared his throat and looked at the box again.

"Afraid?" she asked.

"Yes. For my arteries."

She pointed to the counter and the half-empty bag of baby carrots there. "We're combating it with veggies."

"Toby doesn't eat carrots."

"I do so!" Toby claimed, and shocked Josh to the core by picking up a carrot. Of course he dipped it in a bowl of what looked like salad dressing until there was no carrot to be seen before jamming it into his mouth, dripping dressing everywhere.

Josh let out a breath.

Grace was looking at him, amused. "It's nonfat vanilla yogurt."

Josh shuddered at that combination but had to admit he couldn't object. "Where's Anna?"

Grace's smile faded some. "Out. Not sure where. How was work?"

In the past, the answer to this question would have been "*crazy.*" But that didn't apply today. "Manageable."

"You sound surprised. Dr. McGinley not doing a good job?"

"She's doing a great job." So great that Josh still felt discombobulated at how easily his world had gone on without him. He looked at the box of mac and cheese and decided he just couldn't do it. He went to the freezer and pulled out a couple of steaks. While he defrosted them in the microwave, he headed out the back door and started the barbeque. The thing was brand spanking new and huge. He'd bought it two years ago and had never used it, not once, but it started right up with a big, satisfactory *whoomph*, not so unlike Toby's lightsaber.

Grace was standing in the open door watching him. "Feeling manly?"

He took in her pretty little sundress as she stepped outside. It had spaghetti straps and tiny buttons down the front and came to midthigh. "I'm feeling something."

She smiled. "What is it with men and big toys that turns them into Neanderthals?"

"It's not the toys. It's the 'big.' We like everything big."

"Well you have no worries there."

He wasn't touching that one with a ten-foot pole. Or a nine-inch one… "Are we playing?"

She looked him over from head to toe and back again. It wasn't the first time Josh had been undressed by a woman's eyes, but it was the first time it'd given him a hard-on. And he knew she liked what she saw because the pulse at the base of her throat kicked into gear.

Liking that, he took a step toward her, planning on showing her more of his "Neanderthal" side.

"Arf, arf!" Tank came barreling out the back door, chased by Toby with his lightsaber, both heading right for Grace full speed ahead.

Josh stepped in front of her to bear the brunt of the inevitable impact, bending low to grab for Tank just as Toby swung the lightsaber—

And accidentally collided with Josh's head. Josh staggered back and tripped over Tank. The puppy yelped, and Josh shifted his weight, but the damn dog wound his way between Josh's legs. To avoid killing him, Josh shifted again, and this time lost his balance. He fell, hitting with teeth-jarring impact, smacking his head on the concrete. Stars burst behind his eyeballs, and then...

Nothing.

Chapter 21

Always have chocolate on the To Do list to make sure you get at least one thing done.

Josh?"

He heard the voice coming at him from far away. It sounded urgent, and old habit had him responding to that urgency. He blinked his eyes open, then immediately wished he hadn't as pain sliced through his head, making him want to toss his cookies.

Or in this case, cupcakes.

"Josh, oh my God. Can you hear me?"

"Shhh." He closed his eyes again. Shit, that chocolate had been a very bad idea. "Toby—"

Grace was on her knees at his side. "He's fine. The dog's fine. I'm fine, thanks to you. We're all fine. Now please open your eyes again and talk to me."

Hell, no. If he did that, he'd *definitely* toss his cupcakes.

"Arf! Arf, arf, arf!"

Oh, Jesus, the Antichrist's barking was going to split open his head.

"Quiet, Tank," Grace said. "Toby, baby, grab him and put him in the laundry room, please. Anna, good, you're back. Get a phone in case we need to call nine-one-one."

"Got it," Anna said, sounding so unusually shaken that Josh did open his eyes. Look at that, Antichrist number two was worried about him. Nice change. "No nine-one-one."

"You need a doctor," Grace told him.

"I *am* a doctor. What the hell did I hit, a Mack truck?"

She held him down when he tried to sit up, and did so with surprising strength. "Stay," she said, like he was Tank.

"I'm fine." Except her fingers looked like...long French fries.

And she had two heads. And as strong and sure of herself as she sounded, all four of her eyes were filled with concern.

So sweet. He was used to doing the worrying. Hell, he was good at it. The best...

But it was nice to have someone else doing it for a change. He concentrated on that for a moment, then let his gaze wander. Four breasts too. Mmm. That was even nicer than having her worry about him. Four perfect handfuls— Wait. He'd need four hands for this. He lifted his hands to his face. One, two, three, four...ah, perfect. "It'd work," he said, and closed his eyes again.

Grace's heart was in her throat as she ran her fingers through Josh's hair, looking for the bump. She found it at the back of his head, a nice goose egg that had panic sliding down her spine. "Time to call nine-one-one," she said to Anna.

"On it," Anna said.

"No." Again Josh stirred, and it was like trying to hold back a stubborn mule. A two-hundred-pound, six-foot-plus stubborn *ass*, she thought grimly, sitting back on her heels. "Josh—"

"Ice," he said, snatching the phone from Anna's hand with surprising reflexes, especially given that a second before he'd been out cold. "I just need a bag of ice."

Anna rolled her eyes at the command but went wheels up to the kitchen.

Josh managed to get to his feet, looking like he felt the world spin on its axis before staggering two steps to sink rather heavily to the porch swing.

"Josh, you need to take it easy for a change."

He was green and getting greener and was covered in a fine sheen of sweat. He looked over at Toby standing there silent, somber, clutching his lightsaber in two little fists. "I'm fine, Squirt, no worries."

"Do you have blood?" Toby asked in a small, wavering voice. "Because when a Jedi warrior bleeds, he dies."

Josh ran his fingers through his hair, then showed his blood-free fingers to Toby, who didn't look convinced.

"I'm okay," Josh promised. "I'm going to live to fight another battle."

At that, Toby smiled a little, revealing the gap in the front where he'd lost his tooth. Adorable, but Grace was over the macho bullshit. "You need to go be checked out, Josh."

"I'm fine."

Did he really think he could fool her the way he fooled Toby? "If you're fine, how many fingers am I holding up?"

He focused in on her with what appeared to be great effort. "Two."

Lucky guess and they both knew it. Unfortunately, he was a man through and through, and therefore had a penis, which meant that there'd be no reasoning with him.

Anna came back with a bag of ice.

Josh placed it on the back of his thick noggin and settled more carefully on the swing, leaning his head against the wall behind him. Eyes closed. "Hey, Little Man," he said to Toby, "didn't you want to watch *Transformers*?"

"You said no 'cause I already watched too much TV this week."

"I counted wrong," Josh said. "Go ahead. Have Anna put it on for you."

Toby swung his lightsaber, *whoosh, vrrmm-whoosh* and ran back into the house, followed by a much slower moving, more reluctant Anna. "If you die," she said, pointing at Josh, "I'll kill you."

When she was gone, Grace moved in. "Nicely done. Now tell me what to do for you."

"How long was I out?"

"A minute."

"A minute, or a few seconds?"

"Seconds," she admitted. "But—"

"I'm good, Grace. I just need to sit here for a bit."

"Josh—"

"Tea," he said. "Can you make tea?"

"Sure." She jumped up and went in the kitchen. There she found Anna, with Devon.

"What are you doing here?" Grace asked him.

"Visiting." He hooked an arm around Anna's neck and pulled her in, making her chair squeak as it slid sideways. He gave her a kiss on the temple.

Tender. Sweet. And full of shit. Grace tried to wordlessly convey to Anna that she was better than this. That she deserved more.

But Anna wasn't having the silent conversation. Or any conversation. "I came home to get a sweatshirt. We're heading back out," she said, only her eyes revealing the concern at leaving Josh right now—which of course she was far too stubborn to actually voice out loud.

Devon took the handles of her chair and turned her, wheeling her out of the kitchen. Just before they got to the door, he looked back over his shoulder at Grace and sent her a fuck-you smile.

Dammit!

Okay, one problem at a time, she thought. Josh first. She made the tea as quickly as she could, checked on Toby—blissfully watching *Transformers* with Tank on the couch—and rushed back out to Josh.

Who hadn't moved, not a single inch as far as she could tell. His big, long body was stretched out in the chair, his head back, cushioned on the ice against the wall.

Far too still.

Heart in her throat, she set the tea down and crouched at his side, laying a hand on his thigh.

He jerked, swore beneath his breath, then sent her a dark look.

"Sorry," she said on a relieved breath. "You were just so still. I thought..." She shook her head. "I brought your tea."

"I don't drink tea."

"Then why did you have me make it?"

"So you'd stop hovering."

She grated her teeth, then sat beside him and—what the hell—drank the tea. "Luckily for you," she said, "I can't hurt someone who's already hurt. Now tell me how you really feel."

"Could use a few aspirin. Or ten."

"Is aspirin okay with a head injury?"

"Grace."

Right. He was a doctor. He knew such things. She stood up, then narrowed her eyes. "Wait a minute. Is this another one of those things where I go running to get you the aspirin and then you don't want it?"

"Actually, it's one of those I'm-going-to-throw-up things, and I want you to be far, far away."

Grace wasn't thrilled that Josh had gone to bed instead of joining them for dinner. She'd cooked the steaks, checking up on him every five minutes until the stubborn lug told her to go away and not come back. She was pretty sure he meant just for a little while, and not for the rest of his life.

She put Toby to bed and sat at the kitchen table working for her bookkeeping clients, still surprised that she'd somewhat accidentally started a business, albeit a small one. Nothing nearly so impressive as working at a big-time investment firm or bank in Seattle, but she was enjoying it anyway. She had no idea what she'd do if she got one of the jobs she'd tried for, and since she'd gotten a call today from Seattle for a final interview the day after tomorrow, that seemed likely.

She was still working when Anna came home a few hours later. Grace stood up to make another drive-by check on Josh.

"Why do you get to act all crazy over a guy and I don't?" Anna asked.

"You have to earn the crazy," Grace said. "You're not old enough yet."

"He doesn't like it when people hover," Anna warned.

"How about when they care?"

"Nope," Anna said. "He's not overly fond of that either."

"Are you sure it's not just him being a stupid guy and not knowing how to deal with someone caring about him?"

This stopped Anna. "I don't know," she finally said after giving that some thought. "He's just always been the one to do the taking care of." She hesitated. "Now that you mention it, I don't know if that's because he's had to, or if he'd actually welcome help."

"Maybe you should find out sometime," Grace suggested. She moved down the hall to Josh's bedroom.

The room was dark, but she'd left the bathroom light on. His bedroom furniture was dark wood, masculine. The bed was huge and dominated the room. Josh lay sprawled on his stomach, face turned away.

She moved into the room and sat on the edge of the bed, gliding her fingers over his forehead, brushing his hair back.

He sighed. "It's been two minutes."

"Twenty. Do you feel nauseous?"

"Grace, I'm fine. Go away."

"What's your name?"

He let out a long breath. "Ticked off and looking for a new nanny."

"Funny. Follow my finger."

He smacked her finger away.

"You are such a big baby," she told him. "If one of your patients acted like this, you'd—"

"Assume they were good to go."

She could see that he'd showered, which freaked her out. He could have fallen, and she had no idea what she'd have done with a two-hundred-pound, wet, unconscious male. She knew what to do with a two-hundred-pound, wet *conscious* one, but that was entirely different.

He'd pulled on a pair of sweatpants, barely. They were so low on his hips as to be indecent, giving her a good look at his broad back that led down to a very sexy pair of twin dimples, and a hint of a tattoo.

Grace grinned wide, unable to help herself as she ran her fingers over the sweats, nudging them down enough to expose…a lightning bolt. She laughed softly, and he muttered a very bad word.

"*Why are you still here?*"

"You have a concussion," she reminded him. "I'm not leaving you alone."

"*Mild* concussion. Jesus. Stop hovering."

"Okay, I'd like to talk to Dr. Scott, not Asshole Josh."

He snorted, then let out a long-suffering breath. It hadn't escaped her that he hadn't moved. And he was looking extremely tense, his muscles rock hard with strain, which was confirmed when she stroked her hand along his back and felt the stress there.

Aw, the poor baby. Leaning over him, using two hands, she began to work the tension from his shoulders and back. She thought about massaging his ass as well, but she didn't want to take advantage of the man when he was down. "Tell me what I can do for you," she said softly as she worked.

He let out a muffled groan into his pillow. "That. Don't stop. Ever."

"I won't." Especially since touching him was pure pleasure. His skin was warm, smooth, and smelled so good she wanted to eat him up with a spoon. "What else do you need? Anything."

He groaned again. "I'm going to hope that promise doesn't have an expiration date."

She went still, then laughed softly. "You can think of sex *now*?"

"I can think of sex always. It's a special, God-given talent. Wake me up later."

"But—"

"*Much* later."

Hmm. "Tell me what to look for, Josh."

She couldn't see his eyes since they were closed, but she sensed them rolling around in his head in annoyance. "Brain damage," he said. "Bleeding, swelling, loss of muscle control. Death."

She gasped. "*What?*"

"But if I'm still in pain, death is fine," he said. "Just leave me dead. DNR."

Do not resuscitate. Doctor humor. "That's not funny, Josh."

"Look, it's not a big thing, okay? As long as my elevator goes to the top floor, let me be."

"*But how will I know?*"

"Grace." His voice held annoyance, frustration, and—his saving grace—affection. "You'll know."

"Okay, but you need to get better soon," she said, just as annoyed, frustrated, and affectionate. "So I can smack you."

Chapter 22

Life without chocolate is like a beach without water.

Josh?"

He had no idea how much later it was when he heard her whisper his name. He thought how odd it was that only the day before the sound of his name on her lips would have made him hard. Now he wanted to strangle her. "*No*," he said.

"I haven't asked you anything yet."

He pried open one eye, noted the clock on his nightstand said midnight, and closed it again. Maybe she'd think he'd died.

"*Josh*."

He sighed and rolled to his back. She wasn't going to give up. Ever. He knew that now. "I'm still breathing."

She sank to the bed at his hip and put her hand on his bare chest. Her fingers stroked him lightly, from one pec to another, her pinkie dragging over his left nipple.

His annoyance abruptly faded, and the age-old question of whether or not an injured man could get aroused was answered.

Yes, he could.

"Are you nauseous?" she asked.

"No. And I know my name, and I'm not hot or cold. I'm just right."

"Can you follow my finger?"

"Grace, I have a finger for you."

She sighed. "Fine. I'll see you in a few hours."

"Eight," he said. "*Eight* hours."

"Uh-huh..."

He knew she was totally humoring him, but her hand was *still* gliding over him, and her touch felt so good that he didn't give a shit. In fact, he fell asleep just like that, sprawled out like a dog begging for his parts to be stroked...

And woke up a few hours later, overheated. It *was* a fever, he thought dazedly. He'd joked about dying, he'd mocked death, and now he really was going to kick the bucket.

Then his blanket moved. And moaned softly.

Not a blanket. It was Grace.

It was two in the morning, dark except for the bathroom light, which slanted over his bed.

Grace was still in her cute, gauzy little sundress. No shoes. He was under the covers, and she was on them, so she must have fallen asleep during one of her million checks. He was flat on his back, and she was curled up into his side, her head on his shoulder, hair in his face, breathing steadily, deeply, doing that almost-but-not-quite snoring thing, which made him smile.

The smile made his head hurt and reminded him why she was here in the first place. But he hurt a lot less than he had several hours ago. So much so that he rolled, tucking her beneath him.

She came instantly awake with a confused, befuddled, "What?"

He stroked the hair from her face. She'd stayed with him. She'd worried about him. She'd not left his side. He tried to remember the last time someone had been there for him instead of the other way around—and couldn't. "You nauseous?" he asked.

She blinked. "Uh..."

"What's your name?"

She blinked again and narrowed her eyes. "You're making fun of me. I've been worried, you know, and—"

"Are you feverish?" He pressed his lips to her temple. "Nope." He stroked a hand down her throat to her chest, spreading his fingers wide as she'd done to him, stroking sideways. He loved her breasts. They were full and soft.

Except the nipples.

Her nipples were always hard for him.

"What are you doing?" she asked.

"Seeing if you're getting a chill."

"By copping a feel?"

"Are you cold, Grace?"

"No."

He smiled and lowered his head, lightly clamping his teeth on her nipple over her thin sundress.

She gasped.

"If you're not cold," he said, "then you're turned on."

"There are other options!"

"Name one." He switched to her other nipple, and she moaned, arching up into his mouth, her fingers gliding into his hair and over his injury.

Which made him hiss in pain.

"Oh God, I'm sorry."

Keeping a hold of her, he rolled to his back so that she straddled him. Then he urged the spaghetti straps to her elbows and tugged her dress to her waist. "Always."

She frowned. "Always what?"

"You always make me feel better," he said, cupping a breast.

She made a sound of pure arousal even as she shook her head. "Josh—"

He tugged her bra cups down and pulled her over him so he could suck her into his mouth.

"Oh. Oh, that feels so good," she said shakily. "But you're not up for this."

Gripping her hips, he ground against her, showing her exactly how "up" he was.

"Josh, seriously. You need to be still, not—"

"I'm going to be very still." He reached out and blindly opened his nightstand drawer, producing a condom.

He knew he had her when she took it. She tugged the sheet from between them, then untied his sweats and pushed them off before rolling the condom down his length. He ran his hands along her sweet thighs, pushing her dress as high as he could. She rose up and took him inside her.

She gasped, then covered her mouth with her hands. Watching her fight to keep in her moans of pleasure drove him right to the very edge. Gripping her tight, he thrust up inside her wet heat, hard, and oh, Christ. Christ, she felt amazing.

Warm hands covered his on her hips. She pulled them from her and lifted them to the headboard above his head, tightening her fingers on his. "Still," she whispered. "You have to stay very still."

He opened his eyes to find her face only inches from his. Deep blue orbs stared down at him, and his breath lodged in his throat.

Apparently satisfied that he was going to relinquish control, she let go of his hands and skimmed hers down his shoulders and chest to his stomach and back up again. And then she began to move on him.

Slow.

Achingly slow.

Grace's hips rocked, and her head fell back as she took her pleasure from his body. Every time he so much as rocked his hips, she stopped. This was her ride, and she had places to go. And it was a hell of a ride. She nipped gently at his lips, nothing guarded or shielded in her gaze, nothing held back. He could see anything and everything in those eyes, and he didn't understand how it could be, but this between them just kept getting better.

She was going easy, clearly not wanting to hurt him, but he needed more. He rocked up, changing the angle, creating a deeper penetration. Inhaling sharply, she bowed over him, entwining her fingers with his as she kissed him, her muscles quivering as the pressure built. Lost in the sight of her, he whispered her name, and then again.

It sent her skittering over the edge, her entire body shuddering in gorgeous relief above him, and he groaned as the wave took him under right along with her.

It was the most erotic experience of his life.

"I should go," she whispered against his jaw.

"A minute." He pulled her into him and stroked a hand down her damp back. "In a minute."

Grace opened her eyes and nearly leaped right out of her skin.

Toby was nose to nose with her.

And so was Tank.

Toby was on a stool leaning over the bed. Tank was actually on the bed.

On her.

At least until she sat up and dislodged him. With a reproachful look, the pug rolled aside like a boneless glob. Grace looked at Josh, who was flat on his stomach, sprawled out, and thankfully covered by the blanket.

Equally thankfully, she was fully dressed—and *not* covered by the blanket. Huh. The doctor was a bed hog.

Toby smiled at her. "Whatcha doing in my daddy's bed?"

Yeah, Grace, whatcha doing in his daddy's bed? She tried not to eyeball Josh's sweatpants on the floor behind Toby as she reached for the book on the nightstand. *The Berenstain Bears Forget Their Manners*. "Reading him a bedtime story," she improvised. Which was better than explaining the middle-of-the-night bootie call.

"It's not bedtime," Toby said.

And to think she'd been excited when he'd started using his words. "Well—"

"Hey, Squirt," Josh said, opening his eyes. "Cereal for breakfast?"

"Yeah!"

"How about you go pour it."

"By myself?" Toby asked.

"Yep."

"Oh boy!"

Toby leaped off the stool and ran for the door.

When he was gone, Grace covered her face. "Oh my God."

"He didn't see anything."

She rolled to her feet. "I was in your bed! We could have scarred him for life!"

"Grace, we weren't doing anything. Well, I wasn't. You were snoring."

"I don't—" She smoothed her dress down and searched out her sandals, shoving her feet into them. She glanced at herself in the mirror over his dresser and groaned. Hair, wild. Lips, swollen. Face, flushed.

Nipples, hard.

"Dammit!" She clapped her hands over them. "It's like they're broken!"

Josh let out a low laugh. "They just like me more than your other parts."

She didn't know about that. Her other parts liked him, too, a lot.

He got up much more slowly than she. Naked, of course. The man didn't have a single ounce of self-consciousness in his entire body. Not that he needed to. "What are you doing?" she hissed. "Put some clothes on!"

"Christ, woman." He appeared to be holding his head onto his shoulders. "Shhh."

She narrowed her eyes. "Your head didn't seem to hurt so badly a little while ago."

"The brain is motivated to avoid pain by seeking pleasure."

"The brain, huh? Because I'm pretty sure the body part that was seeking pleasure sits quite a bit lower than your brain."

He let out a low laugh, but it was weak. Softening, Grace slid her arms around him, trying to guide him back to the bed. Not a hardship, since he was warm and sleek and hard.

Everywhere.

The hardest part of him was poking her in the belly. Seemed her nipples weren't the only things broken.

Looking both amused and pained at the both of them, he extracted himself from her grip and strode butt-ass naked to the sweats on the floor, which he pulled on. "What's up for you today?" he asked.

"The usual variety of jobs. Tomorrow I have another interview."

He froze for a beat. "Seattle?"

"Yeah," she said, more than a little distracted by the way the sweats sat so low on his hips. "You have a few more nanny applicants." It was her turn to pause. "One of them is Sarah Tombs, Mindy's sister, from the florist shop. She's going to an online college and is looking for a way to work part-time. I could check her out if you'd like."

"That'd be great."

She nodded. "The other is Riley."

"Amy's Riley?"

"Yes. She's taking college classes in the mornings," she said. "She needs a job for the afternoons or evenings. She loves kids, she loves Toby, and more importantly, he loves her."

Josh said nothing to this as he pulled on a T-shirt, his muscles bunching and unbunching in a way that made her lose her train of thought again. When he finally spoke, it was a complete subject change. "I heard you picked up a few more clients."

"Yeah, it's getting totally out of hand. Mindy brought me her paperwork. In *grocery store bags*." She shook her head. "What is wrong with people?"

He smiled. "Lots."

The smile made her want to hug him, and maybe love him up some more. Stupid smile. She backed to the door. "I'll be back in time to get Toby."

"We'll be okay today. Do what you have to do."

"You're not going to work?" This had her heart stopping short. "You're not better."

"I'm fine. Just not fine enough to treat people."

She looked him over carefully. He had shadows beneath his eyes. His brow was furrowed. His mouth was tight. He was holding it together—the guy clearly knew no other way—but he was feeling like shit. She shook her head. "I'm going to cancel the floral deliveries—"

"No. Don't."

"You're—"

"*Fine*," he said finally. "I'll pick up Toby from school and take him to the pier. We'll play arcade games and eat crap."

Aw. She pictured it, Toby running around in hog heaven, and Josh trying to find something to eat that wasn't a hot dog. "You're a good dad, Josh."

He didn't have any obvious reaction, but she knew him now and felt his surprise. Had no one ever told him such a thing? The thought made her heart melt. And it wasn't the fleeting kind of melt either. It was the kind that made her want to burrow into him and make him feel good some more. In lots of ways...

Which in turn reminded her that she was *this* close to a job—finally—and he was *this* close to getting a nanny, and then this time with him would be over.

And when it was, there'd be no reason to see him. At least no reason that didn't involve doing what they'd both said they didn't want to do—have a relationship.

Chapter 23

The best drug is chocolate.

The next day, Grace had her Seattle interview and got on the road heading back to Lucky Harbor. Her passenger was a big, shiny, fancy file folder with a formal offer and all the big, shiny, fancy benefits that went with it.

It was a really good offer. It didn't involve shoe boxes filled with receipts, modeling various body parts, or doggie poo. It didn't involve grumpy paraplegics or terrifyingly adorable Jedi warriors. This job would be all checks and balances, spreadsheets, and detailed analysis programs for a midsized bank with growth potential.

No messy emotions.

Now it was just a matter of deciding if she wanted it. This thought was so disconcerting that she had to pull over and stare at herself in the rearview mirror.

Of course she wanted the job. It was a good salary and had full benefits. It was what she'd been aiming for, and it would make her family proud.

But it also meant walking away from all the things and people who'd come to mean so much to her.

The break's over, she told herself firmly. Fun was fun but it was time to follow through on her life plans. *Past* time.

She headed to the pier. She'd called Sarah for a preliminary nanny interview. They were meeting in twenty minutes at the diner. She was halfway through town when she saw Anna on the sidewalk, wheeling furiously along, steam practically coming out of her ears. Grace pulled over and got out of the car. She could tell Anna had been crying, but since she didn't have a death wish, she didn't mention it. "What are you doing?"

"What does it look like?"

"Well, it looks like you're on a mission to kill someone," Grace said. "And since you won't look good in an orange jumpsuit, I thought we could discuss."

"I'd totally rock an orange jumpsuit."

"*No one* rocks orange. Talk to me."

Anna rolled her eyes. "You even sound like him now."

Grace sighed. There was no hurrying a Scott, ever. "You getting in the car or what?"

Anna took a moment to swipe the mascara from beneath her eyes. "Yeah. Sure." Once she got into the front seat, she looked at the folder Grace had set on the dash. "What's that?" she asked, opening the file without waiting for an answer.

"Hey, that's private," Grace said.

"Holy shit, they're going to pay you a *buttload*," Anna exclaimed, eyeballing the bottom line on the offer. "What is it you do again? Add up other people's money?"

Grace sighed. "Something like that."

"I want a job that pays this."

"Get a degree."

"There you go, sounding like my brother again." Anna flipped through the papers for a moment, thoughtful. Silent.

"I'm interviewing Sarah at the diner. Want to help?"

"I guess."

Inside Eat Me, Jan brought them iced tea as they met with Sarah and her nice, neat, freshly printed résumé. She was local, and everyone liked her. She had a list of references a mile long, and she could start immediately.

It was a no-brainer.

After Sarah left the table, Grace looked at Anna. "So?"

"So what?"

"What did you think?"

"She's like Mary Poppins," Anna said.

Yeah. Dammit. She was perfect. Far more perfect than Grace. Which was *not* the point, she told herself. She'd never meant for this job to become anything more than a temp position on the way to the Real World.

"You look annoyed," Anna said. "You've been looking for someone to replace you for weeks. Why aren't you doing the happy dance?"

"She's talking about getting married to her fiancé. She'll be too busy with wedding plans to play with Toby."

"She said they're planning on eloping."

"Exactly," Grace said. "Which means she'll just up and go away for two weeks. Toby doesn't need that kind of disruption; he's had enough."

"So hire Riley."

"Yes, but Riley's so...young."

Anna stared at her, then laughed. "Let me get this straight. First you can't find a viable candidate. Now you've got not one but *two*, and you don't want either?"

"I didn't say that."

Anna shook her head. "You really are as nuts as I thought."

"Pot, kettle," Grace said. "Now tell me what the hell you were doing wheeling down the highway like a Formula One driver minus a racetrack."

"You first. Tell me why you're not happy about your job offer, the one any normal person would be celebrating already by now."

They stared at each other, at an impasse.

"You first," Anna bargained with the same talent as her brother. "And then I'll tell you."

"Uh-huh," Grace said. "And I'd totally say yes, except you're a weasel and a non-truth teller—"

"Non-truth teller?"

"Nicer than saying liar," Grace said with a shrug.

"Okay, fine." Anna shifted in her chair. "Today was the day."

"The day..."

"With Devon," Anna said. "The day I agreed to finally...you know. Do the deed."

"Oh." Grace's stomach clenched. "And? Are you okay?"

"Yeah. I really thought I was ready. I'm twenty-freaking-one."

Grace held her breath. *Tell me you didn't go through with it...*

"I got there," Anna said. "To his place. And it was still his same stinky, old bedroom with the huge bong in a corner and the posters of Megan Fox on the walls, and no pillowcases on the pillows..."

Pig.

"I mean, I don't know what I expected," Anna said. "I guess I thought somehow it'd be romantic and special. You know?"

"I do know. And it should be romantic and special. What happened?"

"I changed my mind."

Grace let out the breath she'd been holding. "It's okay. It's okay to change your mind."

Anna lifted a shoulder, then shook her head. "Devon was all pissed off about it."

Tell me I have a reason to call the cops and have his ass arrested. "Did he hurt you?"

"No. Of course not. I wouldn't let a guy hurt me." Anna's voice caught. "But he was a total jerk about it. Wouldn't give me a ride home."

Asshole. "So you took your wheels to the highway?" Grace asked. "Why didn't you call someone, Josh or me?"

"Josh's at work."

"He'd have come anyway," Grace said. "And you know it. And I would have as well."

"Without killing Devon?"

Tough question. "Okay, so Josh might have struggled with that, but you can call me, Anna. *Always.* I'll pick you up no questions asked and take you wherever you need to go. Well, except the one place you actually *want* to go. I don't have enough credit on my Visa to get us to Europe, sorry. But I do have a full tank of gas, which gives us about two hundred miles in any direction."

Anna rolled her eyes, but she also *almost* smiled. "I still want to go to Europe."

"I've heard this song."

"And then after Europe, I figured out what I want to do with my life. Other than driving the people in it crazy."

"Anna." Grace covered Anna's hand with hers. Anna's was calloused and strong from spinning the wheels on her chair. As strong as the woman it belonged to. "There's no need to stop something you're so good at."

Anna snorted.

Grace smiled at her, then let the amusement fade. "You know you can do whatever you want, right? Climb mountains, cure world hunger, rule the universe?"

"I want to work with people like me. Help them, like, adjust. I know," she said quickly. "I know I'm mean and obnoxious, but that's me. That has nothing to do with my legs not working. I think I'm pretty damn well adjusted when it comes to that."

"I agree," Grace said quietly. "So you want to be a counselor? A therapist?"

"Psychologist. Specializing in obnoxious teenagers." She smiled. "Who better, right?"

"Nice," Grace said. "You'd probably have to lose the scowl, maybe turn on your self-editor, but nice. Really nice. Do it."

"It's just that I've said that I'd go to school like a million times over the past three years, and every time Josh got me all admitted and registered and everything, and I've flaked."

"So don't flake," Grace said.

"I can't tell him. He won't believe me. He's lost faith."

"Anna." Grace shook her head. "He's never lost faith in you. Have a little faith in *him*." Because Anna wasn't looking sure, Grace went on. "You're a born fighter. So fight for what you want."

Anna nodded, then smiled.

"What?"

"Your turn. You have to tell me stuff now. About your job offer."

"Well," Grace said. "It's a good one."

"Duh."

"It's everything my parents ever wanted for me. And I thought it was everything I wanted as well."

"But it's not?"

"No, it is." Grace hesitated. She didn't know how to express her feelings on this because they were so new. Her "big job" was going to satisfy her goal to be a successful career woman. But she'd discovered something during her time here in Lucky Harbor—happiness. Shouldn't that be a goal too? "I don't want to leave Lucky Harbor," she admitted. "I like it here. It feels more like home than…well, home."

Anna didn't laugh. She didn't roll her eyes or make a single sarcastic statement. She just nodded. "Well, then, there's really only one thing to do."

"What's that?"

"It's painful," Anna warned. "You're going to have to take your own advice and fight for what you want."

Grace stared at her as the door to the diner opened. Josh strode in like a man on a mission. He wore navy scrubs, his hospital ID hanging around his neck, and a deep scowl on his face.

Jan started toward him, order pad in her hand, before she caught sight of his expression and backed off.

He headed straight toward Anna and Grace, mouth grim as he turned to Anna. "I just got three phone calls that you were wheeling yourself down the highway and sobbing, refusing all rides."

And he'd run out of the ER in the middle of his shift to come find her. Grace's heart melted.

But not, apparently, Anna's. "That's stupid," she said. "Who said I was sobbing? I want to talk to that person!"

Josh was not amused. "What the fuck happened?"

He'd spoken quietly, but he was standing over them, and as big as he was—not to mention incredibly charismatic—people were looking.

"Look," Anna said, pointing out the window. "A puppy."

Josh's eyes narrowed, but he took a deep breath and slid into the booth. "Anna—"

"Grace got the job!"

Josh's eyes cut to Grace. They were laser sharp as always, but for an instant, just the briefest of instants, something not quite identifiable flickered. She wanted to see it again, wanted to reach for it, or better yet, have him give it to her willingly.

"Congratulations," he said quietly. Calmly. As if it mattered not one bit, when they both knew it mattered a whole hell of a lot.

"It's not a done deal," she said.

"They're going to pay her beaucoup bucks," Anna said. "She'd be crazy not to take it."

"You deserve it," Josh said quietly.

"Okay!" Anna said, turning her chair away from the table. "So who's ready to go home?"

Grace stood up and went through her purse for cash to cover

their bill. Josh put a hand on hers and turned and sent a look in Jan's direction.

Jan jerked her chin in acknowledgment. She'd put it on Josh's account.

In the parking lot, Grace hesitated. She figured Anna would go with Josh, but Anna was at Grace's car, struggling with her chair. Grace looked at Josh. "I've got her."

Jaw tight, he stepped forward and helped Anna get into Grace's car before turning to his.

Twenty minutes later, Grace had dropped Anna at home and met Toby at the bus stop. They'd no sooner walked in the door than Josh showed up.

"Hey," Grace said, surprised, "you done with your shift?"

"No. I drove over there but I need to do this. Where's Anna?"

"In her room."

She could hear his phone going crazy in his pocket. Josh ignored it and headed down the hall. Not wanting to be near the impending explosion, Grace took Toby into the kitchen, setting him up with carrots and yogurt dip. But as it turned out, voices could carry.

"Just tell me what the hell you were doing alone on the highway like that," came Josh's voice.

"Coming home from Devon's."

"I told you not to see him anymore."

"That's not your decision to make," Anna said.

"What happened there, Anna?" His voice was low and controlled. Angry.

"You don't want to know," she said.

"I do want to know."

"You *don't*."

Their voices were escalating. Grace shoved more carrots at Toby, then looked around for Tank, thinking the pup could be counted on for a good diversion. Surely he'd be chewing on a piece of furniture or doing something bad. But Tank was sitting at her feet, looking wistful and sad at being left out of the carrot party.

Where was a loud "arf arf" when she needed one?

"Puppies like carrots," Toby said.

"Choking hazard," Grace said.

"Talk to me," Josh said to Anna.

"Fine!" came Anna's raised voice. "I was going to lose my virginity today! Happy now? Are you thrilled I told you?"

"Anna." Josh's voice sounded tight, like he was having trouble getting the words out. "You can tell me anything, you know that. But this...with *him*? Jesus. How stupid can you be?"

Uh-oh, Grace thought. He'd just waved a red cape in front of the bull.

From down the hall, silence thundered, so thick Grace could scarcely breathe through it.

But apparently Anna could. "I can do what I want with my life. I'm a *grown-up*."

"Then act like one." Josh wasn't yelling like Anna, but he was close. "And you're not a grown-up until you can support yourself."

"Daddy's mad," Toby whispered.

Grace again looked at a calm, quiet Tank. "Are you kidding me?" she asked the puppy. "Really, you're going to behave *now*?"

"This is stupid!" Anna yelled at her brother. "It's not like you're a saint! You don't have to follow any rules or listen to anyone! You get to do whatever—and whoever—you want."

"Anna—" He broke off, and Grace imagined him shoving his fingers into his already disheveled hair in frustration. She felt the frustration as her own because she knew that everything he did was for his family. Anna knew that too. Grace waited for him to say so, even as she knew he wouldn't.

"The way I live my life," he said, "the things I do, aren't up for discussion. Period."

"Even the babysitter?"

Grace sucked in a breath. Toby looked at her with a thoughtfulness that belied his five years, while she did her best to look innocent. "More yogurt?" she asked desperately. "Jedis need strong bones. Here, have some milk too."

"Tank's sad," Toby said. "He wants a carrot."

Tank spun in circles before sitting and offering a paw and a hopeful smile.

"See?" Toby said. "He's saying please."

Grace gave up and went to the cabinet for a doggie cookie.

"I just wanted to be normal," Anna flung at her brother, her words booming down the hall. "I wanted to feel like a woman, Josh. And Grace said—"

"Wait a minute. Grace knew?"

Oh, crap.

"She guessed," Anna said. "And it's not like I could tell *you*. You couldn't possibly have understood because you're like a machine. No feelings allowed."

This was followed by another thundering beat of silence, during which Grace hoped Josh wasn't killing his sister. But he'd taken an oath to save lives, so probably he was just grinding his teeth into powder.

"If that's how you feel," he finally said, sounding very tired, "then you should go."

"That's what I'm saying! I want to go to Europe!"

"No, I mean go. Move out. If you can't be happy here, or at college, then you need to go figure your life out and learn to support yourself."

Another silence, this one loaded with utter shock.

Grace grimaced. Perfect—an ultimatum, which, *hello*, never worked, *especially* on angry twenty-one-year-olds. Plus, Anna was so similar to Josh, down to every last stubborn hair on her stubborn head. How could he not see that?

Granted, Grace didn't have a whole hell of a lot of experience with blood ties. Actually, she had zero experience with blood ties. But even she knew that no one could tell Josh what to do. So why would he think it'd work on the sister who was so much like him?

Grace started down the hall with some half-baked idea of trying to butt in and somehow finesse the situation and ran smack into Josh coming out of Anna's room. "Sorry," she said. "I thought maybe I could help..."

"You can't," Anna said from her doorway, eyes flashing. "No one can help because he's an overbearing, uptight, rigid asshole who doesn't listen."

"I *always* listen," Josh said. "You just don't like what I say." He looked at Grace for backup, and she hesitated.

"Jesus," Josh said, and tossed up his hands as Anna wheeled past them both, heading toward the door. "Where are you going?" he asked her.

"What do you care? You told me to move out."

"Oh, for chrissakes, Anna. I didn't—"

The door slammed.

Josh inhaled sharply and turned to Grace.

She tried a weak smile. "Well that went well, huh? Talking it out..." She trailed off when he rolled his eyes. "Okay, so it didn't. But an ultimatum, Josh? Really? You're a doctor. You're supposed to be smarter than that."

"Excuse me?"

God save her from annoying alphas. "Oh, come on," she said. "You lost that fight the minute you tried to tell her what to do instead of discussing it—"

"Discussing it *never* works with her."

"Are you sure you actually gave it a shot?" Grace asked.

Josh's eyes narrowed. "I've tried everything over the past five years. Asking, telling, begging..."

She doubted the last part. She couldn't imagine Josh begging for anything. Well, that wasn't entirely true. The night Mrs. Porter had died and he'd been drunk, he'd begged a little then. *Don't stop, Grace. Oh fuck, please don't ever stop.*

He probably didn't want to be reminded of that right now.

The truth was, his parents' deaths had thrust him into some uncomfortable, unnatural roles—being his sister's parent, the head of household, protector...everything. He'd been wearing all the hats and working an incredibly demanding job on top of it. It'd taken its toll on their relationship.

But Anna wasn't that same sixteen-year-old anymore either. "She's growing up," Grace said. "She's old enough to make her own mistakes."

"And you're an expert on family now?" he asked. "You, the queen of running away from your own family problems?"

"Okay, now that's not really fair," she said slowly, stung. "I didn't exactly run away—"

"No, you just lied rather than tell them your dreams don't match theirs."

She opened her mouth but he wasn't done. "You took Anna's side." He said this in his quiet, calm voice. His professional, detached voice, and that really got to her.

Her parents talked to her in that same voice when she'd disappointed them or had somehow—no matter how inadvertently—stepped off the expected path.

No judgment, never that, but no real emotional attachment either. No feeling.

She processed the unexpected pain of that as well.

Josh mistook her silence for something else. "You took her side," he repeated, "over me."

She found her voice, which was *not* void of emotion, thank you very much. She was getting pissed off. "I didn't realize we were taking sides."

"And then," he went on, "you pulled the passive-aggressive card by going behind my back about Anna—"

"Now wait a minute." She realized he'd been spoiling for a fight since he'd walked in the door, and ding-ding, he'd just gotten one. "You don't know what you're talking about," she said. "And I'm *not* passive aggressive. I just..."

He cocked a brow and waited with a mock patience that had her temper hitting the boiling point. She no longer had things to prove, not to anyone, and certainly not to herself. "You know what?" she said. "*Never mind.* I'm done talking to you when you're like this."

"This?" he repeated.

"You. When you're being all mule-headed and obstinate and—"

"Those are the same things, Grace."

"Smug," she added. "An overeducated, arrogant...*doctor*." After this final insult, she inhaled a deep breath and then let it out again. "Okay, never mind the doctor part. That's my own hang-up showing. I didn't mean that part."

"I thought you were done talking to me."

"Argh!" She grabbed her purse and whirled to the door. She got all the way to it before she remembered she was still on the clock. She executed an about-face. "Are you going back to the hospital?"

"Have to."

"Fine. And you should know, I interviewed Sarah. Assuming you trust my passive-aggressive judgment, she's perfect for you and could start immediately."

"Handy, since you got the job you wanted."

"Actually," she said, "you have no idea what I want."

"Then tell me."

Yeah, Grace, tell him. But he was standing there, so big and sure of himself, shoulders stretched impossibly broad, strong enough to take on the weight of his entire world.

Which he'd done.

And what had *she* done? Exactly as he'd accused her—she'd blindly followed a path set out for her, not spending time second-guessing that path or even standing up for what her own hopes and dreams might be.

That shamed her. Embarrassed her to the bone. She had no idea how to tell him that what she wanted was to throw away the only thing she'd ever been good at and start over. That what she really wanted was to keep this little make-believe world she'd created for herself. So she said nothing at all and went into the kitchen. "How about making more cupcakes?" she asked Toby.

"Oh boy!"

The front door shut, and Grace felt twinges of unidentifiable emotions.

Regret.

Anxiety.

Loss.

And something else, something that left her stomach uneasy, because it felt like heartbreak.

Are you having fun now?

Chapter 24

Chocolate is cheaper than therapy, and you don't even need an appointment.

Fifteen minutes later, Josh was back in the ER, trying to keep his mind on his patients, which wasn't easy. Why had he picked a fight with Grace? Because she'd integrated herself into his life so that he could no longer imagine it without her? Because she'd gotten a job he wasn't even convinced she wanted and would be leaving? It made no sense. He'd always known she'd be leaving. And if she took the Seattle job, she wouldn't be far.

But that wasn't the point. The point was that it wouldn't be the same.

His fault.

All his own fucking fault. He called Riley and asked if she was free to watch Toby so that Grace could leave if she wanted to. Riley promised to head over to his house, no worries.

Josh spent the next five hours working, and at the end of his shift, all he wanted was to crash. Mallory caught up to him in the hallway. She was in pink scrubs, hair up, looking a little frazzled. "Got a minute?" she asked.

The ER had been a mess all day. There'd been a five-car pileup on the highway, the usual heart attacks and hangovers, and a mob of strep throat infections. She'd kept up with him every step of the way. "For you, always."

She smiled. "Aw. Don't make me tell Ty I'm marrying his good friend instead of him."

"Tell him you realized you needed a real man."

She laughed, but he couldn't manage the same. She looked at him for a long beat; then her smile faded. "Oh, Josh. You didn't."

"What?"

"You screwed it up?"

He shook his head. "What makes you think that *I* screwed it up?"

"Because you have a penis."

Josh let out a breath. "Maybe there was nothing to screw up."

"Oh my God. And how does a guy as smart as you get so dumb?"

"*Dumb?*"

"Yes, dumb! You fell for her, Josh, I know it. We *all* know it. It's all over your face. It's all over the way you act with her."

"I don't act any different with her than I do with everyone else," he said.

"Really? So you pay all your babysitters a thousand dollars a day?"

"A *week*," he muttered.

But she wasn't listening. She was ranting on him some more. "I mean, I can't understand how you can't see it. Have you looked at yourself in that pic on Facebook? Or noticed how much more relaxed you are these past weeks?" She smacked him on the chest. "*Relaxed*, Josh. *You!* Hell, you even sold your practice so that you could have a private life. So wake up and smell the damn cupcakes—you're crazy about her. You even let yourself depend on her. You, the King-of-Depending-on-No-One!"

"I *pay* her to be dependable."

"Yes, well, you've paid me on occasion to work in your practice when you were short an RN," she reminded him. "Does that mean we're doing it by your pool like a pair of teenagers?"

"She told you?" he asked in disbelief.

"No, actually. Anna did," she admitted. "And then both Amy and I pounced all over Grace for details—which she wouldn't give, by the way. You know why that is, Josh?"

He wasn't afraid of much, but even he knew to be afraid of Mallory when her eyes were crazy like they were now, so he said nothing.

"It's because you don't give details when you're *falling*." She drew a deep breath and studied him, hands on hips.

He held his ground in case she decided to hit him again, because for a little thing, she hit hard.

"Let me just say this. I love you, but if you hurt Grace in any way, I'm going to—" She huffed a minute. "Well, I don't know what. Depends on what you did."

Again with the assumption it was him.

Because it was, you dumbass... He pinched the bridge of his nose. "Look, it's late. I'm tired. *You're* tired. Did you need a minute to tell me something important or just to yell at me?"

She sighed. "I almost forgot. I wanted to know if you could pick up a shift at HSC this week."

"Depends on when Grace leaves and if I have someone to cover Toby."

"Oh, yeah. Right." Mallory sighed and got quiet, very quiet. "I keep telling myself she's not going to really go, you know?"

He did know. He knew because he'd been doing the same thing. The thought of Grace heading off to Seattle gave him a gut ache.

And a heartache.

Which proved Mallory's point, of course. He *was* crazy about Grace, and he really had absolutely no idea how she felt. In the beginning, he'd mistakenly believed she needed him. That he was the one doing *her* the favor.

He'd been wrong. Very wrong.

Grace didn't need a man to be the center of her universe. She wasn't dependent on anyone. She would never be one more thing on any man's plate to take care of. What had he been thinking to assume that? Especially since the truth was that *she'd* been taking care of him since day one. "I'm going home now," he said. "Unless you want to hit me again."

"Do I need to?" she asked.

"No."

She studied him for a long beat, then surprised him by sighing and stepping in to hug him tight. "It's okay to be stupid in love," she assured him, patting him like he was a little boy instead of a full-grown man who was a head and a half taller than her. "*Once*," she said, this last word spoken in a definite warning tone. Then she stepped back and out the door before he could tell her that he'd already used his allotment of stupid in love.

Just over five years ago.

Except hindsight was always twenty-twenty. And he knew now that what he'd had with Ally hadn't been so much love as lust. As for what he had with Grace, he wasn't sure. It felt more like heartburn than anything else.

On the way home, he called Anna. She still didn't pick up, but two minutes later he got a text from her that said he should leave her the hell alone, that she was with friends, that she was fine, and she'd come talk to him when she was "grown up" enough not to want to kill him.

He figured that might be a while. He drove by Devon's place to make sure she wasn't with him, but it was dark and no one answered the door. Relieved, he headed home.

His house was dark, too, just one small lamp in the living room.

When he walked in, Grace stood up from the couch. "Toby's asleep," she said, and handed him his mail. Actually, she slapped it to his chest. "We had spaghetti. There's leftovers, if you're able to stomach canned sauce." She headed to the door.

"You stayed," he said.

She whipped around to glare at him.

Yeah. Admittedly, it wasn't his finest opening. But he was dizzy with exhaustion and worry, and completely out of his element. Never a good combo. "I meant that I expected Riley—"

"I told her I had Toby," she said. "Because I did. Did you really think I wouldn't? That I'd just walk away?"

Whatever she saw in his face made her come close and stab him in the chest with her finger.

Ouch. Jesus, the women in his life were scary.

"You did," she said in disbelief. "You thought the going had gotten tough, so I'd get going. Well, bite me, Dr. Scott. This job might have started out as a favor—for *you* I might add—but it's not just a simple floral delivery or bookkeeping job." She stabbed at him again. "This isn't about the bottom line, or what balances and what doesn't. It's about a dog, and a kid, and a girl, and a man, all of whom needed me—or so I thought."

"Grace—"

"No, I believe I just told you what you can do. *Bite. Me.*" She headed for the door again, but Josh was done with people yelling at him and/or walking away from him today. Done and over it, and pissed off to boot. He snagged her by the back of her sweater and reeled her in.

She sent daggers at him but he was also done talking. He scooped her up and took her caveman style down the hall to his bedroom. There he set her down, shut and locked the door, and backed her to the wall, caging her in.

She opened her mouth—no doubt to blast him—so he covered that sexy mouth with his own. His hand slid to the nape of her neck to hold her still while he kissed her like he was drowning and she was his only hope.

Because she was his only hope.

Grace knew she should push free and walk out of Josh's room, but there was a problem with that. A big one.

He had her up against the wall, held there by well over six feet of worked-up testosterone. It should have infuriated her. Instead, her brain must have mixed up the signals because she was suddenly hot as hell. She shifted against his body and made herself hotter. "Move," she said, the token protest, made out of a need to not set back feminism by caving to the sheer dominating force of his personality.

He held still, forearms on either side of her head, face close.

"*Move*," she repeated.

He did. He moved backward to his bed, taking her with him. He sat, pulling her into the vee of his spread legs as he did, removing her clothes with shocking speed and letting out a low, rough groan at the sight of her body bared to him.

It did something to her, the sound of his arousal, seeing it in his intense expression, like he was completely lost in her. Screw feminism, she decided weakly, trying to get his clothes off, too, but then he threaded his fingers into her hair and kissed her harder, pulling her onto his lap.

Naked, she straddled him, rocking onto his hard length, feeling him through his scrubs. She'd been mad at him, so very mad, but now that emotion morphed into something else—a desperate need for a Josh-induced orgasm.

"Grace. *Christ.*" He ground his hips upward as he pressed her down onto him, sliding her along with his motions, making her moan in pleasure as the hunger began to build within her. Hell, who was she kidding, the hunger for him was always there.

"I need you." He nipped at her ear. "I've always needed you, Grace."

Her heart swelled against her rib cage. "Then take me."

In the next beat, he had a condom and she'd untied his scrubs, freeing the essentials. And oh God, the essentials were ready, willing, and able. He slid home, and they both gasped at the shocking pleasure. Then Josh claimed her mouth with his, and as he began to move inside her, he claimed her body as well. She cried out his name as he thrust up into her, drawing her tighter with every smooth stroke.

It was exactly what she needed, and exactly not enough. "More," she pleaded, digging her fingers into him.

He ran hot kisses along her jaw to her ear as he changed the pace, driving into her hard and fast, hoarsely whispering how good she felt wrapped around him, how he'd thought about doing this all day, wanting to be inside her like this, just like this, all the time.

It made her come, and as she clenched around him, he threw his head back, eyes shut tight, jaw clenched as he slowed for her to ride out the waves of pleasure. When she had, he took over, tucking her beneath him. Pressing her into the bed, he roughly grasped her ass with both hands, squeezing as he plunged deep and hard, his expression fierce. He'd held back for her, she knew, and now he couldn't appear to hold back at all. Her heart, already taxed, turned over in her chest. It undid her, *he* undid her, and the words tumbled out of her unbidden. "I love you, Josh."

His eyes flew open as he went over the edge, pulsing inside her, shuddering in her arms, breathing heavy. She was breathing heavy, too, but hers was sheer panic. *I love you?*

Josh rolled over to his back, taking her with him. "Grace."

Heart pounding, she pressed her face into his throat. *Be the bed, be the bed...*

He stroked her damp hair and pressed his mouth to her temple.

She didn't move.

She didn't breathe.

"*Grace.*"

She tightened her eyes. She was asleep. She had left the planet. She was on a different time continuum. She—

Someone knocked on the door. Then came the little voice. "Daddy?" This was immediately followed by the knob turning, and right then and there, Grace had heart failure.

Thankfully, the door was locked.

"Hold on, Tobes," Josh called out, eyes on Grace. "We're not done," he said to her softly, then pushed up and off the bed. "I'm coming."

And she was going. Rolling off the bed, she grabbed up her clothes and dashed into Josh's bathroom.

On the other side of the door, she heard Josh greet Toby.

"I want popcorn."

"Little late for that, Little Man."

"I need water."

"That we can do," Josh assured him.

As their voices faded, Grace realized they'd moved down the hall. She shoved herself into her clothes and made her escape, not immune to the irony that she was absolutely proving Josh's "queen of running away" and "passive aggressive" statements.

And he was right, of course. Oh how she hated to admit that, but it was true. She *was* running away. She *was* being passive aggressive, both of which really chapped her ass.

But she was thoroughly unequipped to deal with this situation.

In fact, this situation required the Chocoholics. She texted both Mallory and Amy, and like the BFFs they were, they met her at the diner despite the midnight hour.

Mallory was wearing a pair of sweats that were clearly Ty's, looking like she'd just crawled out of bed. "I hope this is good," she said with a yawn. "I just left the sexiest man on the planet, and I have to be at work at six."

"I told Josh I love him," Grace said.

Mallory immediately softened into a goofy smile. "Awwww!"

"No." Grace pointed at her. "No awwww. You want to know why? Because *I* said it first! Do you know what that means? It means *I said it first*!"

"Well, hell," Amy said with a wince. "That's never a good idea."

"Ya think?" Grace asked, her voice resembling Minnie Mouse. God. It was a nightmare. And it wasn't as if he'd called or texted or come after her to try to discuss.

He'd let her go.

Okay, she knew he couldn't have come after her. He had Toby. But he might have called…

"What did he do when you said it?" Mallory asked.

"Nothing, because Toby woke up and wanted popcorn." Grace leaned over and thunked her head on the table a few times.

"Don't do that—you'll knock something loose," Amy said. "Here, have another cupcake."

"A cupcake isn't going to fix this," Grace said. "I need at least two."

Mallory handed her another. "What were you doing when you said it?"

Grace sighed. "We were…in the moment."

Amy winced again.

"Will you stop doing that?" Grace demanded. "Just tell me how to fix this."

"That's easy," Mallory said calmly. "Tell him when you're *not* in the moment so he knows it's real."

Grace's heart clutched. "You think it's real?"

Mallory took her hand and squeezed it. "Yeah, I do. But it doesn't matter what I think. It's what *you* think."

"Have you seen him frustrated and pissed off?" Amy asked.

Grace thought of how Josh had looked when Anna had fought with him over Devon. And his expression when Grace had told him to "bite me." Yeah, it was safe to say she'd seen him frustrated and pissed off. "Yes."

"Have you seen him upset?"

She remembered how he'd looked talking about the loss of his parents. How he'd been after Mrs. Porter's death. Or when he'd realized Toby wanted to be a good Jedi for his mom. Or when Anna had left. "Yes."

"Did his reactions to those emotions scare you off?" Amy asked.

"No." Grace sighed. "Actually, they made me care about him even more." Which was her answer, she supposed.

"You realize he's a package deal," Mallory said. "Right? He's got Toby and Anna. You'd be an instant family if you take him on, and that's a big deal."

"Of course I realize that. And I love them all." Grace heard the words, then clapped a hand over her mouth. "What *is* that? Why does that word keeping slipping out?"

"It's because love is one of those really bossy bitches," Amy said. "There's no telling it what to do."

Mallory nodded and toasted a cupcake to that. Then she set the cupcake down and got serious as she turned to Grace. "Honey, just promise me something."

"What?"

"That you won't be so driven by your past that you throw away your future. You need to go back. You need to face him and deal with this or he's going to think you didn't mean it."

Go back…When she'd first blurted out her "I love you," she'd been so embarrassed that all she'd thought about was getting out of there. She hadn't thought how Josh would take her vanishing act. But she was thinking now, and she knew the truth. Mallory was right. Her leaving told him that she hadn't meant it and that her running off was her extricating herself from his life. Maybe his parents hadn't left him on purpose, but Ally had. Anna had.

Grace had. She stood up.

"Tell him you meant it," Mallory said. "Tell him—"

Amy stuffed a cupcake into Mallory's mouth. "She'll figure it out, Ace."

Grace wrapped her two cupcakes in a napkin for later. She was hoping things went well but in case they didn't, there was always chocolate. She drove home. And when exactly Josh's house had turned into *home*, she couldn't say. But Josh wasn't there, and neither was Toby. Afraid something had happened to Anna, she texted him: *You okay? Toby? Anna?*

His response came quickly: *Got called into ER. Brought Toby with me. Nothing from Anna.*

Grace turned around and drove to the ER. She found Toby in his Star Wars pj's playing with his Zhu Zhus in the nurse's station. "They have popcorn here," he said happily, clutching a full bag of it.

Grace turned to the nurse's aide watching him. "Is Josh with a patient?"

"Yes. And he's going to be busy for a while."

"Can you ask him if I can take Toby home for him?"

The aide came back with the okay, with absolutely no indication on what Josh thought about Grace showing up. She took Toby home and tucked him back into bed before making herself comfortable on the couch to wait for Josh.

But he never came home.

Chapter 25

Maybe man cannot live on chocolate alone,
but a woman can.

Grace woke up at 6:00 a.m., her face stuck to the couch, someone tugging on her sleeve.

Toby.

He'd liberated Tank from behind the baby gate. The puppy was prancing like a miniature dancing bear. A miniature dancing bear that had to go potty. Scooping him up, Grace ran for the front door, getting him outside just in time for him to race to the closest tree and lift a stumpy leg.

Toby, still in his Star War's pj's, trotted across the yard to join him in anointing the tree.

Grace didn't bother to sigh. When Tank finished, he pawed at the grass with his back feet, head high, proud of his business. Toby loped back to Grace, grinning with his own pride.

Grace gathered both the dog and child back inside and checked her phone.

Nothing.

She was playing Scrabble Junior with Toby when her cell finally buzzed with an incoming call, which she pounced on. But it wasn't Josh.

It was Anna. "Hey," Grace said, "I've been so worried."

Anna didn't say anything. Grace checked the phone to make sure she had reception. "Anna?"

Nothing, but she was there; Grace could feel her in the gaping silence. "Anna," she said softly. "You okay?"

Anna didn't say anything.

"Just tell me where you are," Grace said, heart aching. "I'll come get you. Are you at Devon's?"

Disconnect.

"Road trip," Grace said to Toby.

He immediately hopped up and grabbed Tank and his Jedi saber. Grace was too worried to argue with him. "Get the leash."

"Tank can't be a Jedi on a leash," Toby said.

"He's not big enough to be a Jedi," Grace said.

This caused Toby to beam with pride that *he* was apparently big enough, and he went for the leash.

Grace drove to Devon's building. The place looked dark and still, as if no one was there, but Grace couldn't get rid of her bad feeling. Not in a hurry to get out of the car in this neighborhood, she tried Anna's cell phone again.

It went straight to voice mail this time, so either it was off or it'd run out of juice. While she was still staring down at her phone, unsure of her next move, it buzzed.

Josh.

Oh God. She'd wanted to hear from him, *needed* to hear from him, and now that he was calling, she wanted to fall into a big hole and live in Denial City. The phone vibrated more intently, and she imagined Josh waiting impatiently on the other end of the line. "Hey," she answered, wincing at how breathless she sounded.

"I'm off work," he said. "We have to talk."

Even knowing he was right, she couldn't go there right now. She couldn't do anything until she knew that Anna was okay. "About that..."

"What? Where are you and Toby?"

She didn't want to tell him where she was, not yet. Anna had told him she was with friends. If she turned out to be here at Devon's, Josh wouldn't be happy to know it. "Give me a few. I'll meet you back at the house."

"What's going on, Grace?"

Shit. He was too damn smart for her. "Okay, fine. I'm outside Devon's place. I got two hang-ups from Anna. I think she wants help and she's too stubborn to ask for it. I have *no* idea where she might have gotten that stubbornness, but I have a feeling it has to do with her last name."

"Stay put," he said. "I'm on my way."

"Staying put." Gladly.

"And, Grace? We still have to talk."

Oh boy. She could hardly wait. She disconnected and stared at the dark apartment.

"Is Anna in there?" Toby asked.

"Not sure." A text beeped in and she glanced at it, figuring it would be from Mallory or Amy wondering how it'd gone with Josh.

Which of course, it hadn't gone at all.

But the text wasn't from Amy or Mallory. It was from Anna.

I need you.

Grace called Josh. "I'm going in," she told him. "Anna needs me now."

"Wait for me. The neighborhood is shit, and so is that building. I'm five minutes out."

She wasn't going to wait five minutes, not after Anna's text.

"Grace," Josh said, voice tight.

"Tunnel."

"We don't have any tunnels," he said. "Don't—"

She disconnected and winced. "Whoops." She turned in her seat and eyed Toby, unsure what to do. And Josh was right; they *were* in a crap neighborhood. Leaving Toby in the car wasn't an option, but she didn't want to bring him inside with her either.

In the end, her urgency to get to Anna made her decision for her. "Okay," she said on the sidewalk, hunkering down in front of Toby and Tank. The two of them, boy and dog, stood side by side, facing her like two little warriors, both so adorable and serious that her heart swelled against her rib cage. "Don't let go of my hand," she said to Toby. "No matter what. That's your only job, to hold on to me at all costs, okay?"

Toby, holding his lightsaber, nodded solemnly. "Arf."

Oh God, she couldn't take it. He was upset; that was the only time he barked these days. Giving him a quick but warm hug, while silently sending Josh a *please hurry*, she straightened, and they went inside the building.

Devon opened the door to her knock. He took one look at the whole brigade, and a muscle tightened in his jaw. "Busy," he said, and tried to close the door.

Not thinking beyond *must get inside*, Grace reacted instinctively and stuck her foot in the door to block it open.

Devon slammed it on her, and Grace doubled over from the oh-holy-shit pain in her foot. She'd seen a foot get slammed in a door on TV a hundred times, and not once did anyone scream in pain. But then again, none of them were ever wearing wedge sandals.

Devon opened the door wide with clear intent to slam it again, but then Tank squirmed through the opening. Even through the agony radiating up from Grace's foot, she heard Toby cry out for his dog. She envisioned what the door would do to Toby's lanky little body or Tank's adorable, fat little one, and she threw herself at Devon. He fell backward, taking her down with him. She landed hard, writhing at the new fire in her foot.

"You crazy bitch!" Devon yelled. He rolled them so that he was on top, smacking her head hard on the floor. She saw stars, and then Tank was suddenly there, growling and snarling as he...

Bit Devon on the ass.

"*What the fuck*..." Devon shoved off Grace, hand on his butt, staring in shock at the little dog. "You little piece of—" Going up on his knees, he reached out and snatched Tank up by the throat.

Tank chirped in alarm, his eyes bugging out even more than usual, paws flailing like a cat on linoleum.

Toby, in his Star Wars pj's and wild bed-head hair, cried out, "Let go of my dog!"

Anna appeared in her chair from the hallway. She was out of breath, like maybe she'd just been fighting to get into the chair on her own, but she rolled directly up behind Toby and snatched him up into her lap. "*Hey!*" she yelled at Devon. "What are you doing? Put the dog down!"

Devon staggered to his feet, Tank still dangling. "It bit me on the ass!"

"That's *my* dog," Toby yelled from his perch on Anna's lap. He dropped his lightsaber and wrapped his arms around his aunt's neck.

Tank gave a sharp cry, signaling that Devon's grip had tightened, and Grace reacted without thinking. From the floor, she grabbed up the lightsaber and whacked Devon in the back of his knees. They buckled, and he collapsed to the floor.

Tank got loose and ran for Toby and Anna.

"That's assault," Devon snarled at Grace. "*Twice!* Not to mention trespassing. I didn't invite you in here. I'm calling the cops."

"Call them," Anna said. "I'll tell them it was self-defense. Grace came in to protect me."

"I didn't do anything to you!"

"You got me into your bed. You moved my chair out of my reach so that I couldn't get to it. You—"

This was the last word Anna got out because Josh had appeared in the open front door. He picked Devon up by the front of his shirt and slammed him into the wall.

Devon, feet hanging off the ground by a good six inches, gave the same sort of desperate squeak that Tank had given only a moment before.

"Grace," Josh said, not taking his eyes off Devon. "Call nine-one-one."

It was his tone that made her react. The utterly calm tone that said everything was going to be okay now that he was here. She slapped her hands on her pockets but couldn't find her phone. She sat up, moved her foot wrong, and cried out before she could bite it back.

"I wasn't doing anything to her, man," Devon said. "Nothing she didn't want done! Tell him, Anna, Jesus!"

"It's true, Josh," Anna said. "I thought I wanted to...but I found his ex's panties in the bed and I changed my mind."

"For the *second* time!" Devon said.

Anna shook her head, like she couldn't believe she'd ever liked him. "He didn't hurt me," she said to Josh. "He's just a scum bucket."

Josh let go of Devon and pointed at him to stay put. Devon slid down the wall to the floor and wisely sat. Josh strode to Grace and crouched at her side, implacable, coolheaded, every inch of him the ER doctor now. Sharp, assessing eyes roamed over her as he gently cupped the back of her head, feeling the bump there. His jaw clenched, the only sign he gave of what he was feeling. He shifted his attention to her foot, his long, knowing fingers probing in exactly the place to make her suck in a breath.

His gaze slid up to hers. "Where else are you hurt?"

"Nowhere."

"He touch you?"

"*She* attacked me!" Devon said.

Josh slid him a look that would have had Grace peeing in her pants. Devon zipped his mouth.

"I'm so sorry I brought Toby in here," Grace rushed to tell him on a shaky breath, feeling so guilty she could hardly draw more air. "I didn't know what to do. Anna needed me and—"

"I know." Josh squeezed her hip gently. "Don't move." On his knees at Grace's side, he scooped up Toby, hugging both him and Anna close.

"Won the battle, Daddy," Toby said, and wrapped an arm around Josh's neck. Anna set her head down on Josh's shoulder, fisting both hands in his shirt, holding on, eyes closed tight. He murmured something softly to her that had her nodding but not letting go of him. Stroking a hand up her back, he palmed her head and let her cling. Grace watched, throat burning, heart warm.

The police came. An ambulance came. The fire department came, which turned out to be because someone in a neighboring apartment had seen the flash of the lightsaber and thought there was an electrical fire.

It took about two hours for everything to wind down, and when it did, Grace was taken for X-rays. She was sitting on one of Josh's ER beds when he came in, X-ray in hand.

Her heart immediately kicked into gear.

He didn't say anything at first. He simply hung the X-ray on the wall, flipped on the light to read it, and turned to her. His eyes were serious, so serious she felt the breath catch in her throat. "Grace, I—"

"Knock-knock." The curtain swung back to reveal Sheriff Sawyer Thompson. "Heard there was a party in here." He nodded to Grace's foot. "Is it broken?"

"No," Grace said.

"Actually, yes," Josh said, eyes narrowed at Sawyer. "And don't even think about it."

"Think about what?" Grace asked.

Sawyer sighed. "It's just for questioning, Josh."

"What's just for questioning?" Grace asked.

Sawyer turned to her. "I need to bring you into the station."

Chapter 26

Save Earth. It's the only planet with chocolate.

Josh was pacing the front room of the sheriff's station. Grace's broken foot had been set in a cast. Devon had been questioned and was being held. Anna had been questioned and let go. She was sitting quietly in her chair next to the bench on which Toby was perched, the two of them playing games on her phone.

Grace was still in the back with Sawyer.

Josh had no idea what was taking so long. Sawyer was definitely one of the good guys, but this was pissing him off.

Mallory came rushing through the front door. "Just heard from Lucille that Grace was arrested. *What the hell?*"

Josh didn't even bother to ask how Lucille knew that Grace had been taken in. "It's not an arrest. It's just formalities. She clocked Devon with the lightsaber, and he's claiming assault."

"Well fuck formalities."

Yeah, they were on the same page on that.

"They okay?" Mallory asked quietly, gesturing to Anna and Toby.

"Toby is. I don't know about Anna yet. She's playing it close to the vest."

"She's strong, Josh."

"Stronger than me," he said, and looked up to find Anna's eyes on him. There was something in her gaze that he hadn't seen in years.

Warmth.

Affection.

Regret.

He shook his head at the last and moved toward her and Toby, hunkering down before them. He pulled Toby in for a hug. "You did good today, Little Man."

"Better than any other Jedi?"

"Better than *every* other Jedi." He ruffled Toby's hair and turned to Anna. "Proud of you."

Her eyes filled. Swearing beneath his breath, he set Toby down and pulled her tight. Dropping her head to his shoulder, she did what she so rarely did. She completely lost it, sobbing like her heart had just broken.

Toby stepped up behind her and very gently patted her on the back.

"I'm s-sorry," she hiccupped. "I didn't mean to get Grace h-hurt or arrested—"

"She's not arrested," Josh assured her. "And you didn't get her hurt. That was Devon." He tightened his grip on her even as he pulled back enough to see her face. "You promise he didn't hurt you?"

"I promise. And we didn't— God, Josh." She covered her face. "I don't want to talk to you about this."

"It's me or someone else, Anna-Banana," he said gently. "We're done with this angry shit."

She sniffed and nodded.

"Promise me."

"I don't feel quite so angry anymore," she whispered, then sniffed again and wiped her nose on the hem of his shirt, laughing soggily when he grimaced. "Watching Grace go ape-shit on Devon's ass was kind of empowering," she said. "I could do that, with some self-defense classes."

"Anna—"

"For paraplegics like me. They have classes like that, you know. Grace found them for me at Washington University."

He looked into her eyes. "Yeah?"

"And there's soccer too. I want to go there and live in the dorms, like a normal college student. And next year I want to go on their abroad program. I'm going to see the world, Josh. My way, not yours."

"Can you do it without a douche-bag boyfriend?"

"Yeah."

"Good." Josh leaned back on the bench, exhausted, and more than a little worried about Grace. But beyond that, there was something new blooming in his chest.

Or rather, the lack of something old. He'd felt like a family tonight with Toby and Anna. A real family.

That was all Grace. It was *still* Grace, and she wasn't even in the room. He'd actually believed that he didn't have anything at stake with her, that it would cost him nothing to enjoy the fun while it lasted. To enjoy her.

But he'd been wrong. He'd had his family at stake, his heart. Everything.

And she loved him. It'd been a shock to hear her say it. After she had, all he'd wanted to do was hear it again, but he quickly realized during her vanishing act that it'd been a mistake on her part. She hadn't meant to say it at all.

She loved him, but she didn't *want* to love him.

He'd found someone he'd never in a million years expected—someone who'd put it all on the line for him, someone to love *him*—not for being a doctor or a dad, but just for being Josh.

And he'd blown it.

The front door of the station opened and more people arrived. Amy. Matt. Ty. Lucille and her entire posse.

Hell, half the town.

Lucille and her gang were carrying posters that said things like FREE GRACE. One of the sheriffs confiscated the posters when an eighty-five-year-old Mrs. Burland hit one of them over the head. He said he'd arrest her for police brutality, but he was afraid of starting a riot.

Finally, Sawyer came out of the back, leading Grace, on crutches, and everyone started yelling at Sawyer at once.

"She was only protecting Anna!"

"You can't arrest her!"

"We won't let you take her!"

Sawyer held up a hand, and the din stopped on a dime. "You people are crazy, you know that?"

The yelling renewed, but again Sawyer stopped them. "She's not arrested! We just had some questions that needed answers. Seriously, you all need a life. Grace is free to go."

Grace was standing in the middle of the crowd looking a little bowled over at the support. And also a little unstable on her feet, especially when everyone began to move in too close. Josh waded in, parted the seas, and drew her up against him, crutches and all.

Grace hadn't seen him coming, but the minute Josh's warm, strong arms surrounded her, she sighed. "Hey," she said, breathless. The crutches were a bitch, and all the people were a little disconcerting, but that wasn't what had stolen the air from her lungs.

Nope, that was all Josh, and the way he'd somehow pushed through the crowd to get to her. It was how he'd pulled her in tight, as if she were the most precious thing to him, as if he couldn't wait another second to touch her.

She liked that, a lot.

Everyone around them seemed a little crazy, but she realized that they were here for her.

Her.

In her world, she'd always had to earn acceptance, approval, even love. But from the very beginning, it'd been different here. She had Amy and Mallory, who had accepted her as is, and the rest of Lucky Harbor had eventually done the same, no questions asked. She'd never experienced anything like it. It was humbling.

It was amazing.

And then there were Toby and Anna.

And Josh…

Behind them, Sawyer was shoving people toward the door. "Out. Everyone out." He eyed Lucille's FREE GRACE sign and shook his head at her.

Unrepentant, she grinned, then turned to Grace. "You did good, hon, protecting the tot. If Dr. Scott doesn't realize what a catch he has, we'll all make sure to hit him with our signs when he comes out of the station."

"Hell," Josh said. "I'm right here."

"He ought to make an honest woman out of you," Mr. Saunders said, ignoring Josh. "If he doesn't, *I* will."

"No, *I* will," Mr. Wykowski said, waving his cane.

"Easy, boys." Lucille looped an arm into each of theirs. "There are plenty of honest women to go around."

Sawyer pointed to the door. He wasn't the kind of guy people messed with. If he wanted the place empty, the place got empty, in a hurry. In less than two minutes, it was just Josh and Grace. Even Anna and Toby had gone outside to wait.

In the ensuing silence, Sawyer shook his head, muttered something to himself that sounded like "fucking Mayberry," and gave Josh and Grace a nod. "I'll be in the back."

Then they were alone. Nerves danced in Grace's belly.

"You okay?" Josh tilted her face up to his, searching her features as if he couldn't get his fill.

She gave herself permission to do the same. She had no idea what her future held exactly, but for the first time in her life, that was okay. She'd found herself. Here, in this town.

With this man.

And that was enough. She'd found her own way, not because of what her job title was or how much money she pushed around, but because of who she was. On the inside. Which, as it turned out, had nothing to do with numbers at all. "I'm okay. Devon's not pressing charges."

Josh let out a breath and pushed the hair from her face, tracing a finger along her temple, tucking a strand behind her ear. "I missed you last night."

Out of all the things that she'd expected him to say, that was just about last on the list. She pulled back to meet his gaze. "But after I left, you didn't even call."

"I thought you needed some space. My mistake," he said quietly.

"No, it's mine," Grace said in a rush, the words needing to get out. "I'm sorry about what I said. It was too soon. I shouldn't have—"

Josh cut her off with a kiss that made her toes curl. "Don't be sorry," he said when they broke apart. "I love you, Grace. I think I have since day one when you jumped into my life with both feet, giving me all you had just to help me out."

She stared up at him, feeling the anxiety in her chest break free, giving way to hope and love. "You should know that it wasn't all from the goodness of my heart. It was also for the goodness of my very sad bank account."

His mouth curved. "Liar. You'd do just about anything to help anyone, even people who only a few months ago were perfect strangers." And though he kept his eyes on hers, he gestured outside with a jerk of his chin, where everyone in town was straining their eardrums trying to catch their conversation.

"They're trying to see if you're making an honest woman out of me," she said.

"Working on it," he said. "It'd help if you threw yourself at me in front of them."

She laughed and did just that, flinging down her crutches and hitting him midchest. Her cast weighed her down a bit but he seemed to have no problem catching her. She wrapped herself around him like a monkey and buried her face against his throat, breathing him in. "You haven't asked me if I'm taking the job."

"It doesn't matter."

She lifted her head. "No...?"

"Either way, we'll make it work."

Her breath caught as her heart filled with so much love and hope she didn't know if she could contain it all. "Yeah?"

"Yeah."

Nope. Nope, she couldn't contain it all, some of it spilled out in the form of a dopey smile. "You really wouldn't mind dating a woman who lived far away?"

His gaze roamed her features hungrily. "Hell, Grace. I'd go to Australia to visit you. I don't care about the job, or where you lay your head down at night, as long as your heart's mine."

Her heart melted. "I'm not taking the Seattle job, Josh."

He closed his eyes. "So the offer was from Portland, then. All right, so we'll get intimately familiar with frequent-flyer miles."

She slid her fingers into his hair and waited until he opened his eyes and looked at her. "I didn't take that job either."

His eyes narrowed slightly. He was catching on. "Give me a hint," he said.

"It involves shoe boxes." She drew in a deep breath and said it out loud for the first time. "I've lived in quite a few places in my life, and none of them ever felt like home. Until Lucky Harbor. For the first time, I feel like I belong somewhere. Here. I'm going to stay and open a small bookkeeping firm. I might have to supplement the income at first with other jobs, but as it turns out, I like mixing it up. What do you think?"

His smile was a thousand watts. "I think it's perfect. *You're* perfect. You know how much I love you, right? You, just the way you are."

"Really?"

He pulled her in tighter and buried his face in her hair, inhaling her in. "Forever," he said, and as he lowered his head to kiss her, a wild cheer went up from the crowd outside the window.

Epilogue

One year later

Grace woke from a Maui sun-soaked snooze when a shadow blocked her rays. She opened her eyes and took in the sight of Josh in nothing but loose board shorts, slung so low on his hips as to be indecent. His big, built body was tanned and wet from his ocean swim. *Very* wet, and he had a wicked gleam in his gaze. "Don't," she warned him. "Don't you dare—"

With a badass grin, he scooped her out of the oversized lounge chair on the private beach of their honeymoon house and up against his drenched body.

"—get me wet," she finished weakly.

"Oh, I'm going to get you wet, Mrs. Scott. *Very* wet." He nuzzled her for a moment, then dropped down onto the lounge, with her now on top of him. He made himself comfortable, his hands roaming freely over her body as he did. "Mmm. You smell like a coconut. You know I love coconuts."

She did. She knew this firsthand…It'd been a lovely few days, and they had a few more left. They'd gotten married six months ago, but this had been their first opportunity for a getaway. Anna had come home on college break to watch Toby and Tank for them.

They'd made the most of their alone time, and Grace lay there on top of Josh in sated, contented quiet. Working their way down her sexual fantasy list had proven exhausting business, and they had yet to start on Josh's, although sitting on him as she was, she could tell he was ready to get going.

Josh entwined his fingers with hers and drew them up to his mouth, kissing her palm, regarding her with a serious look on his face. "Promise me something."

"Anything."

His free hand slid to her still-flat belly. At only three months pregnant, she wasn't yet showing at all. "We skip the Star Wars DVDs with this one."

The Chocoholics' Cupcakes-Worth-the-Fat-Grams

Cupcakes

1 7-ounce milk chocolate bar
¼ cup butter
1⅔ cups boiling water
2⅓ cups unsifted flour
2 cups light brown sugar
2 teaspoons baking soda
1 teaspoon salt
2 eggs
½ cup sour cream
1 teaspoon vanilla

Preheat oven to 350°F.

Combine chocolate, butter, and boiling water in medium bowl. Stir until smooth. In large bowl, combine flour, sugar, baking soda, and salt. Gradually add chocolate mixture to dry ingredients, beating well. Blend in eggs, sour cream, and vanilla. Beat till smooth, about 1 minute.

Pour into cupcake tins (approximately 24 cupcakes) and bake at 350 degrees for 35 to 40 minutes.

Frosting

2½ tablespoons cocoa
1 cup sugar
1 stick butter
¼ cup milk
½ teaspoon vanilla

Sift cocoa and sugar in a saucepan. Add butter and milk and bring to a rolling boil for 60 seconds. Add vanilla. Pour into a small mixing bowl and beat until cooler and spreadable.

Frost cooled cupcakes and enjoy the scrumptiousness!

Becca Thorne is looking
for inspiration in Lucky Harbor.
Sam Brody might be just what she needs…

Please see the next page for a preview of

It's in His Kiss.

Chapter 1

Oh, yeah," Becca Webber murmured with a sigh of pleasure as she wriggled her toes in the wet sand. The sensation was better than warm chocolate-chip cookies. Better than finding the perfect dress on sale. Better than...well, she'd say orgasms, but it'd been awhile and she couldn't remember for sure.

"You're perfect," she said to the Pacific Ocean. "So perfect that I'd marry you and have your babies, if I hadn't already promised myself to my ereader."

"Not even going to ask."

At the deep male voice behind her, Becca squeaked and whipped around.

She'd thought she was alone on the rocky beach lined with stacks of moss-lined sandstone towers. Alone with her thoughts, her hopes, her fears, and all her worldly possessions stuffed into her car parked in the pier lot about three hundred yards back.

But she wasn't alone at all. Not ten feet away, between her and a long Ferris Wheel-lined pier, stood a man. He wore a skintight rash guard t-shirt and loose board shorts, both dripping wet and clinging to his very hot bod. He had a surfboard tucked under a mouth-watering bicep like it weighed nothing.

Maybe it was the damp, sun-kissed, unruly light brown hair, the longish strands more than a little wild and blowing in his face. Maybe it was the face itself, which was striking for the features carved in granite and a set of matching ice-blue eyes. Maybe it was that he carried himself like he knew he was at the top of the food chain. But the wary city girl in her didn't trust anyone, not even a sexy-looking surfer dude, and she took a few steps backward, thinking about the Swiss Army knife she'd tucked into her pocket since The Incident.

The man didn't react, didn't seem bothered by her retreat at all, other than the slightest tilt of the corners of his mouth. "You stranded?" he asked, voice low but thankfully not aggressive.

Was she stranded? Only of her own making. "I'm good," she said, and didn't add "thanks" as she would have in the old days. The "old days" being before, when she was still a people pleaser. In any case, her being "good" was more than a bit of an exaggeration, but what she happened to be was none of his business.

Sexy Surfer gave her a quick nod and left her alone to continue his retreat from the water. Becca watched him stride up the pier steps and then vanish from sight before she turned her attention back to the ocean.

Whitecaps flashed from the last of the day's sun and a salty breeze blew over her as the waves crashed onto the shore. Big waves. Had the guy really been out in that? She had to admit the thought made him seem even sexier.

Shaking that off, she let out a long, purposeful breath, and with it a lot of her tension.

But not all...

She wriggled her toes some more, waiting for the next wave. There were a million things running through her mind, most of them floating like dust motes through an open, sun-filled window, never quite landing. Still, a few managed to hit with surprising emphasis—such as the realization that she'd done it. She'd packed up and left home.

Her destination had been the Pacific Ocean. She'd always wanted to see it, and she could now say it met her expectations. The knowledge that she'd fulfilled one of her dreams felt glorious, and she was nearly as light as a feather.

Nearly.

Because, of course, there were worries. The mess she'd left behind, for one. Staying out of the rut she'd just climbed out of, for another. And a life. She wanted—needed—a life. And employment would be good, something temporary, a filler of sorts, mostly because she'd become fond of eating.

But standing in this cozy, quirky little Washington state town she'd yet to explore, those worries all receded a little bit. She would get through this, she always did. After all, the name of this place nearly guaranteed it.

Lucky Harbor.

She liked the lucky part, because she was determined to chase some *good* luck for a change.

After a while, the sun finally gently touched down on the water, sending a chill through the early June evening. Becca turned to go back to her car. Sliding behind the wheel, she pulled out her phone and accessed the ad she'd found on Craigslist.

Cheap waterfront warehouse converted into three separate living spaces. Cheap. Furnished, sort of. Cheap. Month to month. Cheap.

It worked for Becca on all levels, especially the cheap part. She had the first month's rent check in her pocket, and she was meeting the landlord at the building. All she had to do was locate it. Her GPS led her away from the pier, to the other end of the harbor, down a narrow street lined with maybe ten warehouse buildings.

Problem.

None of them had numbers indicating their address. After cruising up and down the street three times, she admitted defeat and parked. She called the landlord, but she only had his office phone, and it went right to voice mail.

She was going to have to ask someone for help, which wasn't exactly her strong suit.

It wasn't even a suit of hers at all.

She looked around. The only person in sight was a kid on a bike, coming straight at her on the narrow sidewalk.

"Watch it, lady!" he yelled.

A city girl through and through, Becca held her ground. "You watch it," she said. "And which building is two-oh-three?"

The kid narrowly missed her and kept going, yelling over his shoulder, "Ask Sam. Sam knows everything."

Okay, perfect. She cupped her hands around her mouth to yell back, "Where's Sam?"

"That one!" The kid jerked his chin toward the building off to her right.

It was a warehouse like the others, industrial, old, the siding battered by the elements and the salty air. It was built like an A-frame barn, with both of the huge front and back sliding doors opened.

The last of the sunlight slanted through, highlighting everything in gilded gold, both the wood hull of a boat in the center of the space, and the guy using some sort of planer along the wood. The air itself was throbbing with the beat of the loud indie rock blaring out from some unseen speakers.

From the outside, the warehouse hadn't looked like much but, as she stepped into the vast doorway, she realized the inside was a wide open space with floor-to-rafters windows nearly three stories high. It was clean as a store, and the boat hull looked like a piece of art.

Just like the guy working on it. His shirt was damp and clinging to his every muscle as it bunched and flexed with his movements. It was all so beautiful and intriguing—the boat, the music, the man himself right down to the corded veins on his forearms—that it was like a movie, the montage of scenes that always played with a sound track.

Then she realized she recognized the board shorts slipping low on the guy's lean hips.

Sexy Surfer.

Though he couldn't have possibly heard her over the hum of his power tool and the loud music, he turned to face her, straightening. And as she already knew, the view of him from the front was just as heart-stopping as it was from the back.

"Me again," she said with a little wave. "You Sam, by any chance?"

Giving her no indication he recognized her from the beach, he didn't move a single muscle other than one flick of his thumb, which turned off the planer. His other hand went into his pocket and extracted a remote. With another flick, the music stopped.

"There's a no trespassing sign on the door," he said.

And just like that, the pretty montage sound track playing in her head came to a screeching halt. She backed up a step and glanced at the outside wall, where there was indeed a sign that read: *No Trespassing.* Damn. "You're right," she said, "sorry."

He gave a barely there curt nod, and with another flick of his thumb, the tool came back to life. And then the music. Apparently done with her, he once again bent over his work.

Hmm. A real people person then.

From somewhere within the warehouse, a phone rang, accompanied by a flashing red light clearly designed in case the phone couldn't be heard over the tools. One ring, then two. Three. The guy didn't make a move toward it.

On the fourth ring, the call went to a machine, where a preprogrammed male voice intoned, "Lucky Harbor Charters. We're cranking into high gear for the summer season. Coastal tours, deep sea fishing, scuba, name your pleasure. Leave a message at the tone, or find us at the harbor, northside."

A click indicated the caller hung up, but then the phone immediately rang again.

Sexy Surfer still made no move toward it.

Becca glanced around for someone else, anyone else, but there was no one in sight.

Of course there was no one is sight, because God forbid anything ever come easy. Her first instinct was to run out of there with her tail between her legs. Instead, she lifted her chin, stepped farther inside, and raised her voice to carry over the sound of his planer, the music, and the phone, which was now ringing for a third time. "Um, hi," she said. She might have decided to live life instead of letting it live her but she could still be polite while doing it. "Excuse me?"

Nothing.

Looked around, she followed the cord of his planer to an electric outlet in the floor. She walked to it and pulled out the cord.

The planer stopped.

So did her heart when Sexy Surfer turned his head. He took her in, the fact that she was still there and that she was holding the cord to his planer, and a single brow arched in disbelief.

"Sam," she said, moving closer to him so he could hear her over his music. "Do you know him?"

"Who's asking?"

"Me." She flashed a smile. Having come from a family of entertainers, most of them innate charmers to boot, she knew how to make the most of what she'd been given. "I'm Becca Webber. I'm new to town. And actually, I'm a bit lost. I'm looking for 203 Harbor Street. I think I'm on Harbor Street, but the buildings don't have numbers on them. Some kid on a bike told me to ask Sam, because apparently Sam knows everything. So are you Sam or not?"

Grumpy Sexy Surfer didn't return her smile. Nor did he look particularly charmed, as clearly she'd dare to step into his Man Cave and interrupt his work, which he apparently took incredibly seriously.

"You're looking for the building directly to the north," he finally said.

She nodded and then shook her head with a laugh. "And north would be which way exactly?"

He held her gaze for another beat, then let the plane dangling in his big hand slowly slide to the floor by its cord before striding toward her.

He was beautiful, as rugged and tough as the boat he was working on but only the man was exuding a bunch of testosterone. She didn't have any really great experience with an overabundance of testosterone, so she found herself taking several steps back, to the doorway.

He didn't stop until he was in that doorway with her, and he was taking up a lot of space. *All* of the space, actually. He was six feet plus of lean, hard muscle, with a lot of sawdust clinging to him. For some reason, this made her get a hot flash as he lifted an arm and pointed to the right.

"You have to go around the corner to get to the front door of the building."

"Around the corner," she repeated, inhaling the scent of fresh wood, something citrusy, and a lot of heated male skin. The combination was pretty damn heady. Too bad he didn't have much of a personality to go with it. "Thanks," she said. "I'm the new tenant there. Or one of them anyway. I think there's three apartments in total."

He nodded and then walked back inside without another word, proving her point about the personality. He headed directly for the electrical outlet, where he plugged his planer back in.

"Nice talking to you," she said, unable to resist.

He glanced back at her, and though his eyes were narrowed, there was a very slightly amused quirk of his lips that told her he was indeed in on the joke.

So at least he knew that he was an abrupt ass.

"I take it you haven't seen it yet," he said.

"The loft? No."

The amusement made it to his eyes then and changed his features from hard and ungiving to—wow—open, and almost friendly.

Almost.

It was nearly enough to distract her from what he was implying about the building she'd rented. Nearly but not quite. "Why?" she asked. "Is it bad?"

But he'd gone back to work, flicking the planer on again, and the music too, bending over the hull of the boat as if he'd already forgotten about her.

Nice. But she'd certainly been invisible before. In fact, she was real good at that. And if that thought caused a little pang of loneliness inside her still-hurting heart, she shoved it deep and ignored it because she knew better.

Leaving the warehouse, she turned right. To her new place. To a new beginning.